THE HIGHEST PRAISE FOR JEAN M. AUEL AND *THE PLAINS OF PASSAGE*

"AUEL BRINGS ALIVE A WORLD THAT HAS BEEN IRRETRIEVABLY LOST TO US." —*Chicago Sun-Times*

"THRILLING. . . . This magical book is rich in details of all kinds . . . but it is the depth of the characters' emotional lives . . . that gives the novel such a stranglehold."
—*Cosmopolitan*

"PURE ENTERTAINMENT AT ITS SUBLIME, WHOLLY EXHILARATING, BEST. . . . Auel, a superb raconteur, has crafted a consistently engaging adventure story with a solid historical underpinning." —*Los Angeles Times*

"A GRIPPING STORY . . . A major book that truly has something for everyone and can only enhance her high reputation as a writer, storyteller and historian."
—*Boston Sunday Herald*

"AN ADMIRABLE JOB . . . EXHILARATING, EXCITING AND BELIEVABLE." —*Miami Herald*

"AS WELCOME AS LETTERS FROM A LONG-LOST FRIEND. . . . Impeccably researched . . . as warm and inviting as its campfire milieu." —*Publishers Weekly*

"HAS AN ENDING SO GOOD I WILL BE STANDING IN LINE WHEN BOOK FIVE GETS HERE."
—Barbara Liss, *Houston Chronicle*

EARTH'S CHILDREN

The Plains
of Passage

Jean M. Auel

BANTAM BOOKS

NEW YORK · TORONTO · LONDON · SYDNEY · AUCKLAND

This edition contains the complete text
of the original hardcover edition.
NOT ONE WORD HAS BEEN OMITTED.

THE PLAINS OF PASSAGE
A Bantam Book / published by arrangement with the author

PRINTING HISTORY
Crown edition published 1990
Bantam Export edition / October 1991
Bantam edition / November 1991

Earth's Children is a trademark of Jean M. Auel

ISBN 0-553-28941-1

Published simultaneously in the United States and Canada

Bantam Books are published by Bantam Books, a division of Bantam Doubleday
Dell Publishing Group, Inc. Its trademark, consisting of the words "Bantam
Books" and the portrayal of a rooster, is Registered in U.S. Patent and Trademark
Office and in other countries. Marca Registrada. Bantam Books, 666 Fifth Avenue,
New York, New York 10103.

PRINTED IN THE UNITED STATES OF AMERICA

OPM   0 9 8 7 6 5 4 3 2 1

For LENORE,
   the last to come home,
   whose namesake appears in these pages,
and for MICHAEL,
   who looks forward with her,
and for DUSTIN JOYCE and WENDY,
   with love.

STYLIZED FEMALE FORM. Engraving on a mammoth's tusk.
Height 6 1/8 in. / 15.5 cm. Předmost, Moravia, Czechoslovakia.

PIERCED STAFF
with Abstract Decorations.
Found at Laugerie Haute.
Musée Les Eyzies, Dordogne, France.

N

Zelandonii

Lanzadonii

Clan Encounter

Losadunai

GREAT MOTHER R.

MILES
0   400
0   KM   400

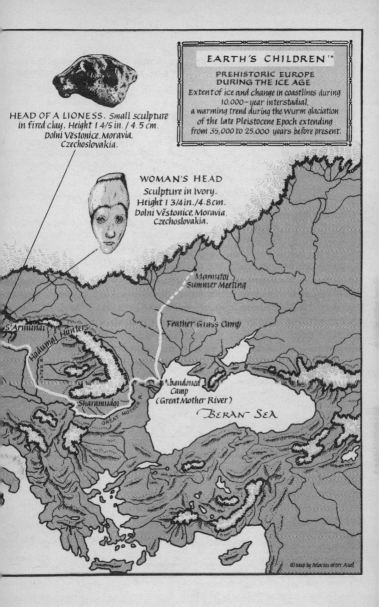

HEAD OF A LIONESS. Small sculpture
in fired clay. Height 1 4/5 in. / 4.5 cm.
Dolní Věstonice, Moravia,
Czechoslovakia.

EARTH'S CHILDREN™

PREHISTORIC EUROPE
DURING THE ICE AGE
Extent of ice and change in coastlines during
10,000-year interstadial,
a warming trend during the Würm glaciation
of the late Pleistocene Epoch extending
from 35,000 to 25,000 years before present.

WOMAN'S HEAD
Sculpture in ivory.
Height 1 3/4 in./4.8 cm.
Dolní Věstonice, Moravia,
Czechoslovakia.

Mamutoi
Summer Meeting

Feather Grass Camp

S'Armunai
Hadumai Hunters

Abandoned
Camp
(Great Mother River)

BERAN SEA

Sharamudoi

GREAT MOTHER

© Map by Palacios after Auel

1

The woman caught a glimpse of movement through the dusty haze ahead and wondered if it was the wolf she had seen loping in front of them earlier.

She glanced at her companion with a worried frown, then looked for the wolf again, straining to see through the blowing dust.

"Jondalar! Look!" she said, pointing ahead.

Toward her left, the vague outlines of several conical tents could just be seen through the dry, gritty wind.

The wolf was stalking some two-legged creatures that had begun to materialize out of the dusty air, carrying spears aimed directly at them.

"I think we've reached the river, but I don't think we're the only ones who wanted to camp there, Ayla," the man said, pulling on the lead rein to halt his horse.

The woman signaled her horse to a stop by tightening a thigh muscle, exerting a subtle pressure that was so reflexive she didn't even think of it as controlling the animal.

Ayla heard a menacing growl from deep in the wolf's

throat and saw that his posture had shifted from a defensive
stance to an aggressive one. He was ready to attack! She
whistled, a sharp, distinctive sound that resembled a bird call,
though not from a bird anyone had ever heard. The wolf gave
up his stealthy pursuit and bounded toward the woman astride
the horse.

"Wolf, stay close!" she said, signaling with her hand at
the same time. The wolf trotted beside the dun yellow mare
as the woman and man on horseback slowly approached the
people standing between them and the tents.

A gusty, fitful wind, holding the fine loess soil in suspension, swirled around them, obscuring their view of the spear
holders. Ayla lifted her leg over and slid down from the
horse's back. She knelt beside the wolf, put one arm over his
back and the other across his chest, to calm him and hold him
back if necessary. She could feel the snarl rumbling in his
throat and the eager tautness of muscles ready to spring. She
looked up at Jondalar. A light film of powdery dirt coated the
shoulders and long flaxen hair of the tall man and turned the
coat of his dark brown mount to the more common dun color
of the sturdy breed. She and Whinney looked the same.
Though it was still early in the summer, the strong winds off
the massive glacier to the north were already desiccating the
steppes in a wide band south of the ice.

She felt the wolf tense and strain against her arm, then
saw someone new appear from behind the spear holders,
dressed as Mamut might have dressed for an important ceremony, in a mask with aurochs's horns and in clothes painted
and decorated with enigmatic symbols.

The mamut shook a staff at them vigorously and shouted,
"Go away, evil spirits! Leave this place!"

Ayla thought it was a woman's voice shouting through
the mask, but she wasn't sure; the words had been spoken in
Mamutoi, though. The mamut dashed toward them shaking
the staff again, while Ayla held back the wolf. Then the
costumed figure began chanting and dancing, shaking the
staff and high-stepping toward them quickly, then back again,
as though trying to scare them off or drive them away, and
succeeding, at least, in frightening the horses.

She was surprised that Wolf was so ready to attack,
wolves seldom threatened people. But, remembering behavior
she had observed, she thought she understood. Ayla had often
watched wolves when she was teaching herself to hunt, and

she knew they were affectionate and loyal to their own pack. But they were quick to drive strangers away from their territory, and they had been known to kill other wolves to protect what they felt was theirs.

To the tiny wolf pup she had found and brought back to the Mamutoi earthlodge, the Lion Camp was his pack; other people would be like strange wolves to him. He had growled at unknown humans who had come to visit when he was barely half-grown. Now, in unfamiliar territory, perhaps the territory of another pack, it would be natural for him to feel defensive when he first became aware of strangers, especially hostile strangers with spears. Why had the people of this Camp drawn spears?

Ayla thought there was something familiar about the chant; then she realized what it was. The words were in the sacred archaic language that was understood only by the mamuti. Ayla didn't understand all of it, Mamut had just begun to teach her the language before she left, but she did gather that the meaning of the loud chant was essentially the same as the words that had been shouted earlier, though cast in somewhat more cajoling terms. It was an exhortation to the strange wolf and horse-people spirits to go away and leave them alone, to go back to the spirit world where they belonged.

Speaking in Zelandonii so the people from the Camp wouldn't understand, Ayla told Jondalar what the mamut was saying.

"They think we're spirits? Of course!" he said. "I should have known. They're afraid of us. That's why they're threatening us with spears. Ayla, we may have this problem every time we meet people along the way. We are used to the animals now, but most people have never thought of horses or wolves as anything but food or pelts," he said.

"The Mamutoi at the Summer Meeting were upset in the beginning. It took them a while to get used to the idea of having the horses and Wolf around, but they got over it," Ayla said.

"When I opened my eyes that first time in the cave in your valley and saw you helping Whinney give birth to Racer, I thought the lion had killed me and I had awakened in the spirit world," Jondalar said. "Maybe I should get down, too, and show them I am a man and not attached to Racer like some kind of man-horse spirit."

Jondalar dismounted, but he held on to the rope attached to the halter he had made. Racer was tossing his head and trying to back away from the advancing mamut, who was still shaking the staff and chanting loudly. Whinney was behind the kneeling woman, with her head down, touching her. Ayla used neither ropes nor halters to guide her horse. She directed the horse entirely with the pressures of her legs and the movements of her body.

Catching a few sounds of the strange language the spirits spoke, and seeing Jondalar dismount, the shaman chanted louder, pleading with the spirits to go away, promising them ceremonies, trying to placate them with offers of gifts.

"I think you should tell them who we are," Ayla said. "That mamut is getting very upset."

Jondalar held the rope close to the stallion's head. Racer was alarmed and trying to rear, and the mamut with her staff and shouting didn't help. Even Whinney looked ready to spook, and she was usually much more even-tempered than her excitable offspring.

"We are not spirits," Jondalar called out when the mamut paused for a breath. "I am a visitor, a traveler on a Journey, and she"—he pointed toward Ayla—"is Mamutoi, of the Mammoth Hearth."

The people glanced at each other with questioning looks, and the mamut stopped shouting and dancing, but still shook the staff now and then while studying them. Maybe they were spirits who were playing tricks, but at least they had been made to speak in a language everyone could understand. Finally the mamut spoke.

"Why should we believe you? How do we know you are not trying to trick us? You say she is of the Mammoth Hearth, but where is her mark? She has no tattoo on her face."

Ayla spoke up. "He didn't say I was a mamut. He said I was of the Mammoth Hearth. The old Mamut of the Lion Camp was teaching me before I left, but I am not fully trained."

The mamut conferred with a man and a woman, then turned back. "This one," she said, nodding toward Jondalar, "he is as he says, a visitor. Though he speaks well enough, it is with the tones of a foreign tongue. You say you are Mamutoi, yet something about the way you speak is not Mamutoi."

Jondalar caught his breath and waited. Ayla did have an

unusual quality to her speech. There were certain sounds she could not quite make, and the way she said them was curiously unique. It was perfectly clear what she meant, and not unpleasant—he rather liked it—but it was noticeable. It wasn't quite like the accent of another language; it was more than that, and different. Yet it was just that: an accent, but of a language most people had not heard and would not even recognize as speech. Ayla spoke with the accent of the difficult, guttural, vocally limited language of the people who had taken in the young orphan girl and raised her.

"I was not born to the Mamutoi," Ayla said, still holding Wolf back, though his growl had ceased. "I was adopted by the Mammoth Hearth, by Mamut, himself."

There was a flurry of conversation among the people, and another private consultation between the mamut and the woman and man.

"If you are not of the spirit world, how do you control that wolf and make horses take you on their backs?" the mamut asked, deciding to come right out with it.

"It's not hard to do if you find them when they are young," Ayla said.

"You make it sound so simple. There must be more to it than that." The woman couldn't fool a mamut, who was also of the Mammoth Hearth.

"I was there when she brought the wolf pup to the lodge," Jondalar tried to explain. "He was so young that he was still nursing, and I was sure he would die. But she fed him cut-up meat and broth, waking up in the middle of the night as you do with a baby. When he lived, and started to grow, everyone was surprised, but that was only the beginning. Later, she taught him to do what she wished—not to pass water or make messes inside the lodge, not to snap at the children even when they hurt him. If I hadn't been there, I would not have believed a wolf could be taught so much or would understand so much. It's true, you must do more than find them young. She cared for him like a child. She is a mother to that animal, that's why he does what she wants."

"What about the horses?" the man who was standing beside the shaman asked. He'd been eying the spirited stallion, and the tall man who was controlling him.

"It is the same with the horses. You can teach them if you find them young and take care of them. It takes time and patience, but they will learn."

The people had lowered their spears and were listening with great interest. Spirits weren't known to speak in ordinary language, although all the talk of mothering animals was just the kind of strange talk that spirits were known for—words that were not quite what they seemed.

Then the woman of the Camp spoke. "I don't know about being a mother to animals, but I do know that the Mammoth Hearth doesn't adopt strangers and make them Mamutoi. It's not an ordinary hearth. It is dedicated to Those Who Serve the Mother. People choose the Mammoth Hearth, or are chosen. I have kin in the Lion Camp. Mamut is very old, perhaps the oldest man living. Why would he want to adopt anyone? And I don't think Lutie would have allowed it. What you say is very difficult to believe, and I don't know why we should."

Ayla sensed something ambiguous in the way the woman spoke, or rather in the subtle mannerisms that accompanied her words: the stiffness of her back, the tension in the set of her shoulders, the anxious frown. She seemed to be anticipating something unpleasant. Then Ayla realized that it wasn't a slip of the tongue; the woman had purposely put a lie in her statement, a subtle trick in her question. But because of her unique background, the trick was blatantly transparent.

The people who had raised Ayla, known as flatheads, but who called themselves Clan, communicated with depth and precision, though not primarily with words. Few people understood they had a language at all. Their ability to articulate was limited and they were often reviled as less than human, animals that could not talk. They used a language of gestures and signs, but it was no less complex.

The relatively few words the Clan spoke—which Jondalar could hardly reproduce, just as she was not quite able to pronounce certain sounds in Zelandonii or Mamutoi—were made with a peculiar kind of vocalization, and they were usually used for emphasis, or for names of people or things. Nuances and fine shades of meaning were indicated by bearing, posture, and facial aspects, which added depth and variety to the language, just as tones and inflections did in verbal language. But with such an overt means of communication, it was almost impossible to express an untruth without signaling the fact; they could not lie.

Ayla had learned to perceive and understand the subtle signals of body movement and facial expression as she was learning to speak with signs; it was necessary for complete comprehension. When she was relearning to speak verbally from Jondalar, and becoming fluent in Mamutoi, Ayla discovered that she was perceiving the inadvertent signals that were contained in the slight movements of face and posture even of people who spoke with words, though such gestures were not intentionally meant to be a part of their language.

She discovered that she was understanding more than words, though it caused her some confusion and distress at first, because the words that were spoken did not always match the signals that were given, and she did not know about lies. The closest she could come to untruth was to refrain from speaking.

Eventually she learned that certain small lies were often meant as courtesies. But it was when she gained an understanding of humor—which usually depended on saying one thing but meaning another—that she suddenly grasped the nature of spoken language, and the people who used it. Then her ability to interpret unconscious signals added an unexpected dimension to her developing language skills: an almost uncanny perception of what people really meant. It gave her an unusual advantage. Though she wasn't able to lie herself, except by omission, she usually knew when someone else was not telling the truth.

"There was no one named Lutie in the Lion Camp when I was there." Ayla decided to be direct. "Tulie is the headwoman, and her brother Talut is the headman."

The woman nodded imperceptibly as Ayla went on.

"I know that a person is usually dedicated to the Mammoth Hearth, not adopted. Talut and Nezzie were the ones who asked me, Talut even enlarged the earthlodge to make a special winter shelter for the horses, but the old Mamut surprised everyone. During the ceremony, he adopted me. He said that I belonged to the Mammoth Hearth, that I was born to it."

"If you brought those horses with you to Lion Camp, I can understand why old Mamut might say that," the man said.

The woman looked at him with annoyance and said a few words under her breath. Then the three people spoke together again. The man had decided the strangers were probably people and not spirits playing a trick—or if they were, not harmful ones—but he did not believe they were exactly who they claimed to be. The tall man's explanation for the strange behavior of the animals was too simple, but he was interested. The horses and wolf intrigued him. The woman felt they spoke too easily, volunteered too much, were too forthcoming, and she was sure there was more to it than either of them said. She didn't trust them and she wanted nothing to do with them.

The mamut's acceptance of them as human came only after apprehending another thought that would, to one who understood such things, account for the extraordinary behavior of the animals much more plausibly. She was sure the blond woman was a powerful Caller, and the old Mamut must have known she was born with an uncanny control over animals. Perhaps the man was, too. Later, when their Camp arrived at the Summer Meeting, it would be interesting to talk to the Lion Camp, and the mamuti would be sure to have some thoughts about these two. It was easier to believe in magic than the preposterous notion that animals could be domesticated.

During their consultation, there was a disagreement. The woman was uncomfortable, the strangers disturbed her. If she had thought about it, she might have admitted she was afraid. She didn't like being around such an overt demonstration of occult power, but she was overruled. The man spoke.

"This place where the rivers join is a good place to camp. We have had good hunting, and a herd of giant deer are coming this way. They should be here in a few days. We will not mind if you choose to camp nearby and join us in the hunt."

"We appreciate your offer," Jondalar said. "We may camp nearby for the night, but we must be on our way in the morning."

It was a guarded offer, not quite the welcoming that he had often received from strangers when he and his brother had traveled together on foot. The formal greeting, given in the name of the Mother, offered more than hospitality. It was considered an invitation to join them, to stay with them and live among them for a time. The man's more limited invitation showed their uncertainty, but at least they weren't being threatened with spears anymore.

"Then, in the name of Mut, at least share an evening meal with us, and eat with us in the morning, too." That much welcome the headman could offer, and Jondalar sensed he would have liked to offer more.

"In the name of the Great Earth Mother, we would be happy to eat with you tonight, after we have set up our camp," Jondalar agreed, "but we must leave early."

"Where are you going in such a hurry?"

The directness that was typical of the Mamutoi still caught Jondalar by surprise, even after all the time he'd lived with them, especially when it came from a stranger. The headman's question would have been thought somewhat impolite among Jondalar's people; not a major indiscretion, just a sign of immaturity, or lack of appreciation for the more subtle and indirect speech of knowing adults.

But, Jondalar had learned, candor and directness were considered proper among the Mamutoi, and lack of openness was suspect, though their ways were not as completely open as they seemed. Subtleties existed. It was a matter of how one expressed directness, how it was received, and what was not said. But the forthright curiosity of the headman of this Camp was, among the Mamutoi, entirely appropriate.

"I am going home," Jondalar said, "and I'm bringing this woman back with me."

"Why should a day or two make any difference?"

"My home is far to the west. I've been gone . . ." Jondalar stopped to consider, "four years, and it will take another year to get back, if we are lucky. There are some dangerous crossings—rivers and ice—along the way, and I don't want to reach them at the wrong season."

"West? It looks like you're traveling south."

"Yes. We are heading for Beran Sea and the Great Mother River. We will follow her upstream."

"My cousin went west on a trading mission, some years back. He said some people there live near a river they also call the Great Mother," the man said. "He thought it was the same one. They traveled west from here. Depends how far upstream you want to go, but there is a passage south of the Great Ice, but north of the mountains to the west. You might make your Journey much shorter by going that way."

"Talut told me of the northern route, but no one seems to be sure that it is the same river. If it's not, it could take longer trying to find the right one. I came the southern way, and I know that route. Besides, I have kin among the River People. My brother was mated to a Sharamudoi woman, and I lived with them. I'd like to see them once more. It's not likely that I will ever see them again."

"We trade with the River People . . . seems to me I did
hear about some strangers, a year or two ago, living with
that group that a Mamutoi woman joined. It was two brothers,
now that I think about it. The Sharamudoi have different
mating customs, but as I recall, she and her mate were going
to be joining with another couple—some kind of an adoption,
I suppose. They sent word inviting any Mamutoi relations
who wanted to come. Several went, and one or two have
gone back since."

"That was my brother, Thonolan," Jondalar said, pleased
that the account tended to verify his story, although he still
could not say his brother's name without feeling pain. "It
was his Matrimonial. He joined with Jetamio, and they
became cross-mates with Markeno and Tholie. Tholie was
the one who first taught me to speak Mamutoi."

"Tholie is a distant cousin of mine, and you are the
brother of one of her mates?" The man turned to his sister.
"Thurie, this man is kin. I think we must welcome them."
Without waiting for an answer, he said, "I am Rutan, headman of Falcon Camp. In the name of Mut, the Great Mother,
you are welcome."

The woman had no choice. She would not embarrass her
brother by refusing to extend a welcome along with him,
though she thought of a few choice things to say to him
privately. "I am Thurie, headwoman of Falcon Camp. In the
name of the Mother, you are welcome here. In summer, we
are Feather Grass Camp."

It was not the warmest welcome he had ever received.
Jondalar detected a definite reservation and restriction. She
was welcoming him "here," to this place specifically, but
this was a temporary location. He knew Feather Grass Camp
referred to any summer hunting camp site. The Mamutoi were
sedentary in the winter, and this group, like the rest, lived
in a permanent encampment or community of one or two
large or several smaller semisubterranean earthlodges, which
they called Falcon Camp. She had not welcomed him there.

"I am Jondalar of the Zelandonii, I greet you in the name
of the Great Earth Mother, whom we call Doni."

"We do have extra sleeping places in the mamut's tent,"
Thurie continued, "but I don't know about the . . . animals."

"If you would not mind," Jondalar said, if only for the
sake of courtesy, "it would be easier for us to set up our
own camp nearby, rather than stay within your Camp. We

appreciate your hospitality, but the horses need to graze, and they know our tent and will return to it. They might be uneasy coming into your Camp.''

"Of course," Thurie said, relieved. They would make her uneasy, too.

Ayla realized she needed to exchange welcomes, too. Wolf seemed less defensive, and Ayla tentatively relaxed her hold on him. I can't sit here holding Wolf all the time, she thought. When she stood up, he started to jump up on her, but she motioned him down.

Without extending his hands or offering to come any closer, Rutan welcomed her to his Camp. She returned the greeting, in kind. "I am Ayla of the Mamutoi," she said, then added, "of the Mammoth Hearth. I greet you in the name of Mut.''

Thurie added her welcome, hedging to restrict it to only this place, as she had done with Jondalar. Ayla responded formally. She wished more friendliness had been shown, but she supposed she couldn't blame them. The concept of animals traveling willingly with people could be frightening. Not everyone would be as accepting as Talut had been of the strange innovation, Ayla realized, and with a pang, she felt the loss of the people she loved from Lion Camp.

Ayla turned to Jondalar. "Wolf is not feeling so protective now. I think he will mind me, but I should have something to restrain him while he's around this Camp, and for later, to hold him back in case we meet other people,'' she said in Zelandonii, not feeling able to speak freely around this Camp of Mamutoi, though wishing she could. "Maybe something like that rope guider you made for Racer, Jondalar. There's a lot of spare rope and thongs in the bottom of one of my pack baskets. I am going to have to teach him not to go after strangers like that; he has to learn to stay where I want him to.''

Wolf must have understood that raising their spears was a threatening gesture. She could hardly blame him for springing to the defense of the people and horses that made up his strange pack. From his point of view, it was perfectly understandable, but that didn't mean it was acceptable. He could not approach all the people they might meet on their Journey as though they were strange wolves. She would have to teach him to modify his behavior, to meet unknown people with more restraint. Even as the thought came to her, she

wondered if there were other people who understood that a
wolf would respond to the wishes of a woman, or that a horse
would let a human ride on his back.

"You stay there with him. I'll get the rope," Jondalar
said. Still holding on to Racer's lead, though the young stallion had calmed down, he looked for the rope in Whinney's
pack baskets. The hostility of the Camp had abated somewhat, the people seemed hardly more guarded than they
would be toward any strangers. From the way they were
watching, their fear seemed to have been replaced by
curiosity.

Whinney had settled down, too. Jondalar scratched and
patted her and spoke affectionately while he rummaged
through the pack baskets. He was more than fond of the
sturdy mare, and though he loved Racer's high spirits, he
admired Whinney's serene patience. She had a calming effect
on the young stallion. He tied Racer's lead rope to the thong
that held the pack baskets on his dam. Jondalar often wished
he could control Racer the way Ayla controlled Whinney,
with no halter or lead rope. But as he rode the animal, he
was discovering the amazing sensitivity of a horse's skin,
developing a good seat, and beginning to guide Racer with
pressure and posture.

Ayla moved to the other side of the mare with Wolf.
When Jondalar gave her the rope, he spoke to her quietly.
"We don't have to stay here, Ayla. It's still early. We can
find another place, on this river or another."

"I think it's a good idea for Wolf to get used to people,
especially strangers, and even if they're not too friendly, I
wouldn't mind visiting. They are Mamutoi, Jondalar, my
people. These may be the last Mamutoi I will ever see. I
wonder if they are going to the Summer Meeting? Maybe we
can send a message to Lion Camp with them."

Ayla and Jondalar set up their own camp a short distance
away from Feather Grass Camp, upstream along the large
tributary. They unpacked the horses and let them free to
graze. Ayla felt a moment of concern watching them disappear into the dusty blowing haze, as they wandered away
from their camp.

The woman and man had been traveling along the right
bank of a large river, but some distance from it. Though

flowing generally south, the river meandered across the landscape, twisting and turning as it gouged a deep trench out of
the flat plains. By keeping to the steppes above the river
valley, the travelers could take a more direct route, but one
that was exposed to the unremitting wind and the harsher
effects of sun and rain on open terrain.

"Is this the river Talut talked about?" Ayla asked, unroll-
ing her sleeping furs.

The man reached into one of a pair of pack baskets for
a rather large, flat piece of mammoth tusk with markings
incised on it. He looked up toward the section of the dingy
sky that glowed with an unbearably bright but diffused light,
then at the obscured landscape. It was late afternoon, that
much he could tell, but not much more.

"There's no way to know, Ayla," Jondalar said, putting
the map back. "I can't see any landmarks, and I'm used to
judging the distance traveled by my own legs. Racer moves
at a different pace."

"Will it really take a whole year to reach your home?"
the woman asked.

"It's hard to say for sure. Depends on what we find along
the way, how many problems we have, how often we stop.
If we make it back to the Zelandonii by this time next year,
we can count ourselves lucky. We haven't even reached
Beran Sea, where the Great Mother River ends, and we will
have to follow her all the way to the glacier at her source,
and then beyond," Jondalar said. His eyes, an intense and
unusually vivid shade of blue, looked worried, and his forehead wrinkled in a familiar furrow of concern.

"We'll have some large rivers to cross, but it's that glacier that worries me most, Ayla. We have to cross over it
when the ice is frozen solid, which means we have to reach
it before spring, and that's always unpredictable. A strong
south wind blows in that region that can warm the deepest
cold to melting in one day. Then the snow and ice on top
melt, and break up like rotten wood. Wide cracks open and
the snow bridges over them collapse; streams, even rivers of
meltwater flow across the ice, sometimes disappearing into
deep holes. It's very dangerous then, and it can happen very
suddenly. It's summer now, and though winter may seem a
long way off, we have much farther to travel than you might
think."

The woman nodded. There was no point in even thinking

about how long the Journey would take, or what would happen when they arrived. Better to think of each day as it came, and plan only for the next day or two. Better not to worry about Jondalar's people, and whether they would accept her as one of them the way the Mamutoi had.

"I wish it would stop blowing," she commented.

"I am tired of eating grit, too," Jondalar said. "Why don't we go visit our neighbors, and see if we can get something better to eat."

They took Wolf with them when they returned to Feather Grass Camp, but Ayla kept him close. They joined a group that had gathered near a fire over which a large rump was spitted. Conversation was slow to start, but it wasn't long before curiosity became warm interest and fearful reserve gave way to animated talk. The few people who inhabited those periglacial steppes had little opportunity to meet anyone new, and the excitement of this chance encounter would fuel discussions and fill the stories of Falcon Camp for a long time to come. Ayla became friendly with several of the people, particularly a young woman with a baby daughter just at the age of sitting unassisted and laughing out loud, who charmed them all, but mostly Wolf.

The young mother was very nervous at first when the animal singled out her child for his solicitous attention, but when his eager licks made her giggle with delight, and he showed gentle restraint, even when she grabbed handfuls of fur and pulled, everyone was surprised.

The other children were eager to touch him, and before long Wolf was playing with them. Ayla explained that the wolf had grown up with the children of Lion Camp, and probably missed them. He had always been especially gentle with the very young, or the weak, and he seemed to know the difference between the unintentional overzealous squeeze from a toddler and the purposeful pull of a tail or ear by an older child. He allowed the former with patient forebearance, and he repaid the latter with a warning growl, or a gentle nip that did not break skin but showed that he could.

Jondalar mentioned that they had recently left the Summer Meeting, and Rutan told them that necessary repairs to their earthlodge had delayed their departure or they would have been there. He asked Jondalar about his travels and about Racer, with many people listening. They seemed more reluctant to question Ayla, and she didn't volunteer much, though the mamut would have liked to have taken her aside for private discussions of more esoteric subjects, but she preferred to stay with the Camp. Even the headwoman was more relaxed and friendly by the time they headed back to their own camp, and Ayla asked her to pass on her love and remembrances to Lion Camp when they finally reached the Summer Meeting.

That night, Ayla lay awake thinking. She was glad she had not let natural hesitation about joining the Camp that had been less than welcoming stop her. Given the opportunity to overcome their fear of the strange or unknown, they had been interested and willing to learn. She had learned, too, that traveling with such unusual companions was likely to inspire strong reactions from anyone they might happen to meet along the way. She had no idea what to expect, but there could be little doubt that this Journey was going to be far more challenging than she had imagined.

2

Jondalar was eager to be off early the next morning, but Ayla wanted to go back and see the acquaintances she had made at Feather Grass Camp before they left, and while Jondalar grew impatient, Ayla spent some time making her farewells. When they finally left, it was near noon.

The open grassland of gently rolling hills and far-seeing distances, through which they had been traveling since they left the Summer Meeting, was gaining elevation. The fast-moving current of the tributary river, originating on higher ground, surged with more vigor than the meandering main stream, and it cut a deep channel with steep banks through the wind-sifted loess soil. Though Jondalar wanted to go south, they were forced to travel west, then northwest, while they looked for a convenient place to cross.

The farther they traveled out of their way, the more irritable and impatient Jondalar felt. In his mind, he was questioning his decision to take the longer southern route, rather than the northwestern one that had been suggested—more than once—and in which direction the river seemed determined to take them. True, he wasn't familiar with it, but if it was so much shorter, perhaps they should go that way. If he could just be certain that they would reach the plateau glacier farther to the west, at the source of the Great Mother River, before spring, he would do it, he told himself.

It would mean giving up his last opportunity to see the Sharamudoi, but was that so important? He had to admit that he did want to see them. He had been looking forward to it. Jondalar wasn't sure if his decision to go south really came from his desire to take the familiar, and therefore, safer way to get Ayla and himself back, or his desire to see people who were family to him. He worried about the consequences of making the wrong choice.

Ayla broke into his introspection. "Jondalar, I think we can cross here," she said. "The bank on the other side looks easy to get up."

They were at a bend in the river, and they stopped to study the situation. As the turbulent, swiftly flowing stream swept around the curve, it cut deeply into the outside edge, where they were standing, making a high, steep bank. But the inner side of the turn, on the opposite bank, rose gradually out of the water, forming a narrow shore of hard-packed gray-brown soil backed by brush.

"Do you think the horses can get down this bank?"

"I think so. The deepest part of the river must be near this side, where it cuts into the bank. It's hard to tell how deep it is, or whether the horses will have to swim. It might be better if we would dismount and swim, too," Ayla said, then noticed that Jondalar seemed displeased, "but if it's not too deep, we can ride them across. I hate to get my clothes wet, but I don't feel like taking them off to swim across, either."

They urged the horses over the precipitous edge. Hooves slipped and slid down the fine-grained soil of the bank and into the water with a splash as they were dunked in the fast current and carried downstream. It was deeper than Ayla had thought. The horses had a moment of panic before they got accustomed to their new element and started swimming against the current toward the sloping opposite shore. As they started up the gradual slope on the inner curve of the bend, Ayla looked for Wolf. Turning around, she saw him still on the high bank, whining and yelping, running back and forth.

"He's afraid to jump in," Jondalar said.

"Come, Wolf! Come on," Ayla called. "You can swim." But the young wolf whined plaintively and tucked his tail between his legs.

"What's wrong with him? He's crossed rivers before," Jondalar said, annoyed at another delay. He had hoped to travel a good distance that day, but everything seemed to be conspiring to stall them.

They had gotten off to a late start, then had been forced to double back toward the north and west, a direction he didn't want to go, and now Wolf wouldn't cross the river. He was also aware that they should stop and check the contents of the pack baskets, after their dunking, even if they were closely woven and essentially watertight. To add to his irritation, he was wet, and it was getting late. He could feel the wind cooling, and he knew they ought to change clothes and let the ones they were wearing dry. The summer days were warm enough, but the soughing night winds still brought the chill breath of the ice. The effects of the massive glacier that crushed the northern lands under sheets of ice as high as mountains could be felt everywhere on earth, but nowhere as much as on the cold steppes near its edge.

If it were earlier, they could travel in wet clothes; the wind and sun would dry them while they rode. He was tempted to start south anyway, just to get some distance behind them . . . if they could only get moving.

"This river is faster than he's used to, and he can't walk up to it. He has to jump in, and he's never done that before," Ayla said.

"What are you going to do?"

"If I can't encourage him to jump, I'll have to go get him," she replied.

"Ayla, I'm sure if we just rode off, he'd jump in and follow you. If we're going to travel any distance at all today, we have to go."

The withering look of disbelief and anger that appeared on her face made Jondalar wish he could take back his words. "Would you like to be left behind because you were afraid? He doesn't want to jump into the river because he hasn't done anything like it before. What can you expect?"

"I just meant . . . he's only a wolf, Ayla. Wolves cross rivers all the time. He just needs some reason to jump in. If he didn't catch up with us, we'd come back for him. I didn't mean that we should leave him here."

"You won't have to worry about coming back for him. I'll get him now," Ayla said, turning her back on the man and urging Whinney into the water.

The young wolf was still whining, sniffing the broken ground left by the horses' hooves, and looking at the people and the horses across the watery trench. Ayla called out to him again as the horse entered the current. About halfway across, Whinney felt the ground beneath her giving way. She whinnied with alarm, trying to find firmer footing.

"Wolf! Come here, Wolf! It's only water. Come on, Wolf! Jump in!" Ayla called out, trying to coax the apprehensive young animal into the swirling river. She slid off Whinney's back, deciding she would swim across to the steep bank. Wolf finally got up his courage and jumped in. He landed with a splash and started swimming toward her. "That's it! That's good, Wolf!"

Whinney was backing around, struggling with her footing, and Ayla, with her arm around the wolf, was trying to reach her. Jondalar was already there, up to his chest in water, steadying the mare and starting toward Ayla. They all reached the other side together.

"We'd better hurry if we're going to travel any distance today," Ayla said, eyes still flashing anger as she started to remount the mare.

"No," Jondalar said, holding her back. "We're not leaving until you change out of those wet clothes. And I think we should rub down the horses to dry them off, and maybe that wolf, too. We've traveled far enough today. We can camp here tonight. It took me four years to get here. I don't care if it takes four years to get back, just so I get you there safely, Ayla."

As she looked up at him, the look of concern and love in his rich blue eyes melted her last vestiges of anger. She reached for him as he bent his head to her, and she felt the same unbelievable wonder that she had felt the first time he put his lips on hers and showed her what a kiss was, and an inexpressible joy in knowing that she was actually traveling with him, going home with him. She loved him more than she knew how to express, even more now after the long winter when she had thought he didn't love her and would leave without her.

He had feared for her when she went back into the river and now he pressed her to him, holding her. He loved her more than he ever believed it was possible for him to love anyone. Until Ayla, he didn't know he could love so much. He nearly lost her once. He had been sure she was going to stay with the dark man with the laughing eyes, and he couldn't bear the thought that he might lose her again.

With two horses and a wolf for companions, in a world that had never before known they could be tamed, a man stood alone with the woman he loved in the middle of a vast, cold grassland, filled with a great abundance and diversity of animals, but few humans, and contemplated a Journey that would stretch across a continent. Yet there were times when the mere thought that any harm might come to her could overwhelm him with such fear, he almost couldn't breathe. At those moments, he wished he could hold her forever.

Jondalar felt the warmth of her body and her willing mouth on his, and he felt his need for her rise. But that would wait. She was cold and wet; she needed dry clothes and a fire. The edge of this river was as good a place as any to camp, and if it was a little too early to stop, well, it would give them time to dry out the clothes they were wearing, and they could start early tomorrow.

"Wolf! Put that down!" Ayla shouted, rushing to get the leather-wrapped package from the young animal. "I thought you had learned to stay away from leather." When she tried to take it away, he playfully hung on with his teeth, shaking his head back and forth and growling. She let go, stopping the game. "Put it down!" she said sharply. She brought her hand down as though she meant to strike his nose but stopped short. At the signal and command, Wolf tucked his tail between his legs, abjectly scooted toward her, and dropped the package at her feet, whining in appeasement.

"That's the second time he's gotten into these things," Ayla said, picking up the package and some others he had been chewing on. "He knows better, but he just can't seem to stay away from leather."

Jondalar came to help her. "I don't know what to say. He drops it when you tell him, but you can't tell him if you're not there, and you can't watch him all the time . . . What's this? I don't remember seeing this before," he said, looking quizzically at a bundle that was carefully wrapped in a soft skin and securely tied.

Flushing slightly, Ayla quickly took the package from him. "It's . . . just something I brought with me . . . something . . . from Lion Camp," she said, and she put it on the bottom of one of her pack baskets.

Her actions puzzled Jondalar. They had both limited their possessions and traveling gear to the minimum, taking little that was not essential. The package wasn't large, but it wasn't small either. She could probably have added another outfit in the space it took. What could she be taking with her?

"Wolf! Stop that!"

Jondalar watched Ayla going after the young wolf again and had to smile. He wasn't sure, but it almost seemed that Wolf was purposely misbehaving, teasing Ayla to make her come after him, playing with her. He had found a camp shoe of hers, a soft moccasin-type of foot-covering that she sometimes wore after they made camp, particularly if the ground was frozen or damp and cold and she wanted to air out or dry her regular, sturdier footwear.

"I don't know what I'm going to do with him!" Ayla said, exasperated, as she came toward the man. She was holding the object of his latest escapade, and she looked sternly at the miscreant. Wolf was creeping toward her, seemingly contrite, whining in abject misery at her disapproval; but a hint of mischief lurked beneath his distress. He knew she loved him, and the moment she relented, he would be wriggling and yelping with delight and ready to play again.

Though he was adult size, except for some filling out, Wolf was hardly more than a puppy. He had been born in the winter, out of season, to a lone wolf whose mate had died. Wolf's coat was the usual gray-buff shade—the result of bands of white, red, brown, and black that colored each outer hair, creating the indistinct pattern that allowed wolves to fade invisibly into the natural wilderness landscape of brush, grass, earth, rock, and snow—but his mother had been black.

Her unusual coloring had incited the primary and other females of the pack into badgering her unmercifully, giving her the lowest status and eventually driving her away. She roamed alone, learning to survive in between pack territories for a season, until she finally found another loner, an old male who had left his pack because he couldn't keep up any more. They fared well together for a while. She was the stronger hunter, but he was experienced and they had even begun to define and defend a small piece of territory of their own. It might have been the better diet that two of them working together were able to secure, or the companionship and nearness of a friendly male, or her own genetic predisposition that brought her into heat out of season, but her elderly companion was not unhappy and, without competition, was both willing and able to respond.

Sadly, his stiff old bones were not able to resist the ravages of another harsh winter on the periglacial steppes. He did not last long into the cold season. It was a devastating loss for the black female, who was left to give birth alone—in winter. The natural environment does not tolerate very well animals with much deviation from the norm, and seasonal cycles enforce themselves. A black hunter in a landscape of tawny grass, dun earth, and windblown or drifted snow is too easily seen by canny and winter-scarce prey. With no mate or friendly aunts, uncles, cousins, and older siblings to help feed and care for the nursing mother and the new pups, the black female weakened, and one after another her babies succumbed until there was only one left.

Ayla knew wolves. She had observed and studied them from the time she first started hunting, but she had no way of knowing the black wolf who tried to steal the ermine she had killed with her sling was a starving, lactating female; it was the wrong season for pups. When she tried to retrieve her pelt and the wolf uncharacteristically attacked, she killed it in self-defense. Then she saw the animal's condition and realized she must have been a loner. Feeling a strange kinship with a wolf she knew had been driven from its pack, Ayla was determined to find the motherless pups, who would have no family to adopt them. Following the wolf's trail back, she found the den, crawled in, and found the last pup, unweaned, eyes barely open. She took it with her to Lion Camp.

It had been a surprise to everyone when Ayla showed them the tiny wolf pup, but she had arrived with horses who answered to her. They had grown used to them and the woman who had an affinity for animals, and they were curious about the wolf and what she would do with it. That she was able to raise it and train it was a wonder to many. Jondalar was still surprised at the intelligence the animal displayed; intelligence that seemed almost human.

"I think he's playing with you, Ayla," the man said.

She looked at Wolf and couldn't resist a smile, which

brought his head up and caused his tail to start thumping the ground in anticipation. "I think you're right, but that isn't going to help me keep him from chewing on everything," she said, looking at the shredded camp shoe. "I might as well let him have this. He's ruined it already, and maybe he won't be so interested in the rest of our things for a while." She threw it at him, and he leaped up and caught it in the air with, Jondalar was almost sure, a wolfish grin.

"We'd better get packed up," he said, recalling that they hadn't traveled very far south the day before.

Ayla looked around, screening her eyes from the bright sun just beginning to climb the sky toward the east. Seeing Whinney and Racer in the grassy meadow beyond the brushy wooded lobe of land that the river curved around, she whistled a distinctive call, similar to the whistle she used to signal Wolf, but not the same. The dark yellow mare raised her head, whinnied, then galloped toward the woman. The young stallion followed her.

They broke camp, packed the horses, and were nearly ready to start out when Jondalar decided to rearrange the tent poles in one basket and his spears in another to balance out his load. Ayla was leaning against Whinney while she waited. It was a comfortable and familiar posture for both of them, a way of touching that had developed when the young filly was her only companion in the rich but lonely valley.

She had killed Whinney's mother, too. By then she had been hunting for years, but only with her sling. Ayla had taught herself to use the easily concealed hunting weapon, and she rationalized her breaking of Clan taboos by hunting primarily predators, who competed for the same food and sometimes stole meat from them. But the horse was the first large, meat-providing animal she had killed, and the first time she had used a spear to accomplish the deed.

In the Clan, it would have been counted as her first kill, if she had been a boy and allowed to hunt with a spear; as a female, if she used a spear, she would not have been allowed to live. But killing the horse had been necessary for her survival, though she did not select a nursing dam to be the one to fall into her pit-trap. When she first noticed the foal, she felt sorry for it, knowing it would die without its mother, yet the thought of raising it herself didn't occur to her. There was no reason why it should; no one had done it before.

But when hyenas went after the frightened baby horse, she remembered the hyena that had tried to drag off Oga's baby son. Ayla hated hyenas, perhaps because of the ordeal she'd had to face when she killed that one and exposed her secret. They were no worse than any other natural predator and scavenger, but to Ayla they had come to represent everything that was cruel, vicious, or wrong. Her reaction then was just as spontaneous as it had been the other time, and the swift stones hurled with a sling were just as effective. She killed one, drove the others off, and rescued the helpless young animal, but this time, instead of an ordeal, she found company to relieve her loneliness, and joy in the extraordinary relationship that developed.

Ayla loved the young wolf as she would a bright and delightful child, but her feeling for the horse was of a different nature. Whinney had shared her isolation; they had grown as close as any two such dissimilar creatures could. They knew each other, understood each other, trusted each other. The yellow mare was not merely a helpful animal companion, or a pet, or even a well-loved child. Whinney had been her only companion for several years and was her friend.

But it had been a spontaneous, even irrational, act the first time Ayla climbed on her back and rode like the wind. The sheer excitement of it brought her back. In the beginning she did not purposely try to direct the horse, but they were so close that their understanding of each other grew with each ride.

While she waited for Jondalar to finish, Ayla watched Wolf playfully chewing on her camp shoe and wished she could think of a way to control his destructive habit. Her eye casually noted the vegetation on the spit of land where they had camped. Caught between the high banks on the other side of the river as it curved around the sharp bend, the low land on this side flooded every year, leaving fertile loam to nourish a rich variety of brush, herbs, even small trees, and the rich pasture beyond. She always noticed the plants in her vicinity. It was second nature for her to be aware of everything that grew and, with a knowledge that was so ingrained it was almost instinctive, to catalogue and interpret it.

She saw a bearberry shrub, a dwarf evergreen heath plant with small, dark green, leathery leaves, and an abundance of small, round, pink-tinged white flowers that promised a rich crop of red berries. Though sour and rather astringent, they tasted fine when they were cooked with other food, but more than food, Ayla knew the juice of the berry was good for relieving the burning sensation that could occur when passing water, especially if it was pinkish with blood.

Nearby was a horseradish plant with small white flowers clustered in a bunch on stems with small narrow leaves, and lower down, long, pointed, shiny dark green leaves, growing up from the ground. The root would be stout and rather long with a pungent aroma and a burning hot taste. In very small quantities, it was an interesting flavor with meats, but Ayla was more intrigued with its medicinal use as a stimulant for the stomach, and for passing water, and as an application to sore and swollen joints. She wondered if she should stop to collect some, and then decided that she probably shouldn't take the time.

But she reached for her pointed digging stick with no hesitation when she saw the antelope sage plant. The root was one of the ingredients of her special morning tea, one she drank during her moon time when she bled. At other times she used different plants in her tea, particularly the golden thread that always grew on other plants and often killed them. Long ago Iza had told her about the magic plants that would make the spirit of her totem strong enough to defeat the spirit of any man's totem, so no baby would start growing inside her. Iza had always warned her not to tell anyone, particularly a man.

Ayla wasn't sure if it was spirits that caused babies. She thought a man had more to do with it, but the secret plants worked anyway. No new life had started in her when she drank the special teas, whether she was near a man or not. Not that she would have minded, if they were settled in one place. But Jondalar had made it clear to her that with such a long Journey ahead of them, it would be a risk to get pregnant along the way.

As she pulled out the root of the antelope sage and shook the dirt off, she saw the heart-shaped leaves and long yellow tubular flowers of snakeroot, good for preventing miscarriage. With a twinge of sorrow, she remembered when Iza had gone to get that plant for her. When she stood up and went to put the fresh roots she had collected into a special basket that was attached near the top of one of the pack baskets, she saw Whinney selectively biting off the tops of wild oats. She liked the seeds, too, she thought, when they were cooked,

and her mind, continuing its automatic medicinal cataloguing,
added the information that the flowers and stalks aided
digestion.

The horse had dropped dung, and she noticed flies buzzing around it. In certain seasons insects could be terrible, she
thought, and decided she would watch for insect repellent
plants. Who knew what kind of territory they would have to
travel through?

In her offhand perusal of the local vegetation she noted
a spiny bush that she knew was the variety of wormwood
with the bitter taste and strong camphor smell, not an insect
repellent, she thought, but it had its uses. Nearby were
cranesbills, wild geraniums with leaves of many teeth and
five-petaled reddish-pink flowers, that grew into fruits that
resembled the bills of cranes. The dried and powdered leaves
helped stop bleeding and heal wounds; made into a tea it
healed mouth sores and rashes; and the roots were good for
runny stools and other stomach problems. It tasted bitter and
sharp, but was gentle enough for children and old people.

Glancing around toward Jondalar, she noticed Wolf again,
still chewing on her shoe. Suddenly she stopped her mental
ruminations and focused again on the last plants she had
noted. Why had they caught her attention? Something about
them seemed important. Then it came to her. She quickly
reached for her digging stick and started breaking up the
ground around the bitter-tasting wormwood with the strong
smell of camphor, and then the sharp, astringent, but relatively harmless geranium.

Jondalar had mounted and was ready to go when he turned
to her. "Ayla, why are you collecting plants? We should be
leaving. Do you really need those now?"

"Yes," she said, "I won't be long," going next after the
long, thick horseradish root with the burning hot taste. "I
think I know a way to keep him away from our things,"
Ayla said, pointing at the young canine playfully gnawing on
what was left of her leather camp shoe. "I'm going to make
'Wolf repellent.' "

They headed southeast from their camping place to get
back to the river they had been following. The windswept
dust had settled overnight, and in the stark, clear air the

boundless sky revealed the distant reach of the horizon that had been obscured before. As they rode across country their entire view, from one edge of the earth to the other, north to south, east to west, undulating, billowing, constantly in motion, was grass; one vast, encompassing grassland. The few trees that existed near waterways only accentuated the dominant vegetation. But the magnitude of the grassy plains was more extensive than they knew.

Massive sheets of ice, two, three, up to five miles thick, smothered the ends of the earth and sprawled over the northern lands, crushing the stony crust of the continent and depressing the bedrock itself with its inconceivable weight. South of the ice were the steppes—cold, dry grassland as wide as the continent, marching from western ocean to eastern sea. All the land bordering the ice was an immense grassy plain. Everywhere, sweeping across the land, from lowland valley to windblown hill, there was grass. Mountains, rivers, lakes, and seas that provided enough moisture for trees were the only intrusions into the essential grassy character of the northern lands during the Ice Age.

Ayla and Jondalar felt the level ground begin sloping downhill toward the valley of the larger river, though they were still some distance from the water. Before long they found themselves surrounded by tall grass. Stretching to see over the eight-foot growth, even from Whinney's back, Ayla could see little more than Jondalar's head and shoulders between the feathery tops and the nodding stems of minuscule florets, turning gold with a faintly reddish tinge, atop the thin, blue-green stalks. She glimpsed his dark brown mount now and then, but recognized Racer only because she knew he was there. She was glad for the advantage of height the horses gave them. Had they been walking, she realized, it would have been like traveling through a dense forest of tall green grass waving in the wind.

The high grass was no barrier, parting easily in front of them as they rode, but they could see only a short distance past the nearest stalks, and behind them the grass sprang back, leaving little trace of the way they had come. Their view was limited to the area immediately around them, as though they took with them a pocket of their own space as they moved. With only the brilliant incandescence tracing its familiar path through the clear deep blue above, and the bend-

ing stalks to show the direction of the prevailing wind, it
would have been more difficult to find their way, and very
easy to become separated.

As she rode, she heard the soughing wind and the high
whine of mosquitoes zinging by her ear. It was hot and close
in the middle of the dense growth. Though she could see the
tallgrass swaying, she barely felt a breath of wind. The buzz
of flies and a whiff of fresh dung told her that Racer had
recently dropped scat. Even if he hadn't been just a few paces
ahead, she would have known it was the young stallion who
had passed that way. His scent was as distinctively familiar
to her as that of the horse she was riding—and her own. All
around was the rich humus odor of the soil, and the green
smell of burgeoning vegetation. She did not classify smells
as bad or good; she used her nose as she did her eyes and
ears, with knowledgeable discrimination to help her investigate and analyze the perceptible world.

After a time, the sameness of the scenery, of long green
stalk after long green stalk, the rhythmic gait of the horse,
and the hot sun almost directly above, made Ayla lethargic;
awake, but not fully aware. The repetitive tall, thin, jointed
grass stems became a blur she no longer saw. Instead, she
began to notice all the other vegetation. Much more than
grass grew there, and as usual, she took mental note of it,
without consciously thinking about it. It was simply the way
she saw her environment.

There, Ayla thought, in that open space—some animal
must have made that by rolling in it—those are goosefoots,
what Nezzie called goosefoots, like the pigweed near the
clan's cave. I should pick some, she mused, but made no
effort to do so. That plant, with the yellow flowers and leaves
wrapped around the stem, that's wild cabbage. That would
be good to have tonight, too. She passed it by as well. Those
purple-blue flowers, with the small leaves, that's milk vetch,
and it has a lot of pods. I wonder if they're ready? Probably
not. Up ahead, that wide white flower, sort of rounded, pink
in the middle, it's wild carrot. It looks like Racer stepped on
some of the leaves. I should get my digging stick, but there's
more over there. Seems to be a lot of it. I can wait, and it's
so hot. She tried to swat away a pair of flies that buzzed
around her sweat-damp hair. I haven't seen Wolf for a while.
I wonder where he is?

She turned to look for the wolf and saw him following

close behind the mare, sniffing the ground. He stopped, lifting his head to catch another scent, then disappeared into the grass on her left. She saw a large blue dragonfly with spotted wings, disturbed by the wolf's passage through the dense living screen, hovering near the place he had been, as though marking it. A short time later, a squawk and a whir of wings preceded the sudden appearance of a great bustard taking to the air. Ayla reached for her sling, wrapped around her head across her forehead. It was a handy place to keep it to get it quickly, and it kept her hair out of the way besides.

But the huge bustard—at twenty-five pounds the heaviest bird on the steppes—was a speedy flier for its size, and it was out of range before she got a stone out of her pouch. She watched the mottled bird with dark-tipped white wings building up speed, its head stretched forward, its legs backward, as it flew away, wishing she had known what Wolf had scented. The bustard would have made a wonderful meal for all three of them, with plenty left over.

"Too bad we weren't faster," Jondalar said.

Ayla noticed he was putting a light spear and his spear-thrower back in his pack basket. She nodded as she wrapped her leather sling back around her head. "I wish I had learned to use Brecie's throwing stick. It's so much faster. When we stopped by that marsh where all the birds were nesting on the way to hunt mammoths, it was hard to believe how quick she was with it. And she could get more than one bird at a time."

"She was good. But she probably practiced as long with that throwing stick as you did with your sling. I don't think that kind of skill is something to be gained in one season."

"But if this grass wasn't so tall, I might have been able to see what Wolf was going after in time to get my sling and some stones out. I thought it was probably a vole."

"We should keep our eyes open for anything else that Wolf might scare up," Jondalar said.

"I had my eyes open. I just can't see anything!" Ayla said. She looked at the sky to check the position of the sun, and she stretched up to try to see over the grass. "But you're right. It wouldn't hurt to think about getting fresh meat for tonight. I've seen all kinds of plants that are good to eat. I was going to stop and gather some, but they seem to be all over, and I'd rather do it later and have them fresh, not after they've wilted in this hot sun. We still have some of the

bison roast left that we got from Feather Grass Camp, but it
will only last one more meal, and there's no reason to use the
dried traveling meat at this time of year, when there is plenty
of fresh food around. How much longer before we stop?''

"I don't think we're far from the river—it's getting
cooler, and this high grass usually grows in lowlands around
water. Once we reach it, we can start looking for a place to
camp as we go downriver," Jondalar said, starting out again.

The stand of high grass extended all the way to the river's
edge, though it was intermixed with trees near the damp
bank. They stopped to let the horses drink, and they dismounted to quench their own thirst, using a small, tightly
woven basket as a dipper and cup. Wolf soon darted out of
the grass, noisily lapped up his own drink, then plopped down
and watched Ayla, with his tongue hanging out, panting
heavily.

Ayla smiled. "Wolf is hot, too. I think he has been
exploring," she said. "I'd like to know all the things he's
found out. He sees a lot more than we do in this high grass.''

"I'd like to get beyond it before we make camp. I'm
used to seeing farther and this makes me feel closed in. I
don't know what's out there, and I like knowing what's
around me," Jondalar said, as he reached for his mount.
Holding on to Racer's back just below his stiff, stand-up
mane, with a strong jump the man threw a leg over and,
bracing himself with his arms, landed lightly astride the
sturdy stallion. He guided the horse away from the softened
riverbank to firmer ground, before heading downriver.

The great steppes were by no means a single, huge, undif-
ferentiated landscape of gracefully swaying stalks. Tallgrass
grew in selected areas of ample moisture, which also contained a great diversity of other plants. Dominated by grasses
more than five feet tall but ranging up to twelve feet in
height—big bulbous bluestem, feather grasses, and tufted fescues—the colorful forb meadows added a variety of flowering
and broad-leaved herbs: aster and coltsfoot; yellow, many-
petaled elecampane and the big white horns of datura;
groundnuts and wild carrots, turnips and cabbages; horseradish, mustard, and small onions; irises, lilies, and buttercups;
currants and strawberries; red raspberries and black.

In the semiarid regions of little rainfall, shortgrasses, less
than a foot and a half tall, had evolved. They stayed close
to the ground with most of the growth underneath, and vigor-

ously sent out new shoots, especially in times of drought. They shared the land with brush, particularly artemisias like wormwood and sage.

Between those two extremes were the midgrasses, filling niches too cold for shortgrass or too dry for tallgrass. Those meadows of moderate moisture could be colorful, too, with many flowering plants intermixed with the grassy ground cover of wild oats, foxtail barley, and, particularly on slopes and uplands, little bluestems. Cordgrass grew where the land was wetter, needlegrass in cooler areas with poor, gravelly soils. There were many sedges, too stalks were solid in sedges, jointed where leaves grew out of the stems of grasses—including cotton grass, primarily in tundra and wetter ground. Marshes abounded with tall phragmite reeds, cattails, and bulrushes.

It was cooler near the river, and as afternoon wore into evening, Ayla was feeling pulled two ways. She wanted to hurry and see an end to the stifling tallgrass, but she also wanted to stop and collect some of the vegetables she was seeing along the way for their evening meal. A rhythm began to develop to her tension; yes she would stop, no she would not, sounded over and over in her mind.

Soon the rhythm itself overcame any meaning in the words, and a silent throbbing that felt as though it should have been loud filled her with apprehension. It was disturbing, this sense of deep, loud sound she could not quite hear. Her discomfort was emphasized by the tallgrass crowding in close all around her, which allowed her to see, but not quite far enough. She was more used to seeing long distances, far vistas, to seeing, at least, beyond the immediate screen of grass stems. As they continued, the feeling became more acute, as though it was coming closer, or they were drawing nearer to the source of the silent sound.

Ayla noticed that the ground seemed freshly disturbed in several places, and she wrinkled her nose as she sniffed a strong, pungent, musky smell, trying to place it. Then she heard a low growl issue from Wolf's throat.

"Jondalar!" she called out, and she saw that he had stopped and was holding his hand up, signaling her to stop. There was definitely something ahead. Suddenly, the air was split by a great, loud, blasting scream.

3

"olf! Stay here!" Ayla com-
W manded the young animal,
who was inching forward with curiosity. She slid off Whinney's back and moved to catch up with Jondalar, who had
dismounted as well, and was cautiously moving through the
thinning grass ahead toward the shrill screams and loud rumbles. She reached his side as he stopped, and they both parted
the last tall stalks to see. Ayla bent down on one knee to
hold Wolf as she looked, but she could not move her eyes
away from the scene in the clearing.

An agitated herd of woolly mammoths was milling
about—it had been their feeding that had created the clearing
near the edge of the tallgrass region; a large mammoth
required over six hundred pounds of feed every day, and a
herd could strip a considerable area of vegetation quickly.
The animals were all ages and sizes, including some that
could not have been more than a few weeks old. That meant
it was a herd of, primarily, related females: mothers, daughters, sisters, aunts, and their offspring; an extended family

led by a wise and canny old matriarch, who was noticeably larger.

At a quick glance, the overall color of the woolly mammoths was a reddish brown, but a closer look revealed many variations of the basic shade. Some were more red, some more brown, some tended toward yellow or gold, and a few looked almost black from a distance. The thick, double-layered coats covered them entirely, from their broad trunks and exceptionally small ears, to their stubby tails ending in dark tufts, and their stumpy legs and broad feet. The two layers of fur contributed to the differences in color.

Though much of the warm, dense, amazingly silky-soft underwool had been shed earlier in the summer, the next year's growth had already started, and was lighter in color than the fluffy, though coarser, wind-breaking overlayer, and gave it depth and highlights. The darker outer hairs, of varying lengths, some up to forty inches long, hung down like a skirt along the flanks, and quite thickly from the abdomen and dewlap—the loose skin of the neck and chest—creating a padding underneath them when they lay down on frozen ground.

Ayla was entranced by a pair of young twins with beautiful reddish-golden fur accented by spiky black guard hairs, who peeked out from behind the huge legs and long ochre skirt of their hovering mother. The dark brown hair of the old matriarch was shot with gray. She noticed, as well, the white birds that were constant companions of the mammoths, tolerated or ignored whether they sat on the top of a shaggy head, or adroitly avoided a massive foot, while they feasted on the insects that the great beasts disturbed.

Wolf whined his eagerness to investigate the interesting animals more closely, but Ayla held him back, while Jondalar got the restraining rope from Whinney's basket. The grizzled matriarch turned to look in their direction for a long moment—they noticed that one of her long tusks was broken off—then she turned her attention back to more important activity.

Only very young males stayed with the females, they usually left the natal herd sometime after they reached puberty at about twelve, but several young bachelors, and even a few older ones were included in this group. They had been drawn by a female with a deep chestnut-colored coat. She was in

heat, and that was the cause of the commotion Ayla and
Jondalar had heard. A female in heat, estrus, the reproductive
period when females were able to conceive, was sexually
attractive to all males, sometimes more than she liked.

The chestnut female had just rejoined her family group
after outdistancing three young males in their twenties, who
had been chasing her. The males, who had given up, but
only temporarily, were standing away from the close-packed
herd resting, while she sought respite from her exertions
within the midst of the excited females. A two-year-old calf
rushed up to the object of the male's attention, was greeted
by a gentle touch of a trunk, found one of the two breasts
between her front legs and began to suckle, while the female
reached for a trunkful of grass. She had been chased and
harassed by the males all day, and had had little opportunity
to feed her calf, or even to eat or drink herself. She was not
to have much chance then.

A medium-size bull approached the herd and began touching the other females with his trunk, well down from the tail
between their hind legs, smelling and tasting, to test their
readiness. Since mammoths continued to grow all their lives,
his size indicated he was older than the three who had been
chasing the beleaguered female before, probably in his thir-
ties. As he neared the chestnut-furred mammoth, she moved
away at a fast walk. He immediately abandoned the others
and started after her. Ayla gasped when he released his huge
organ from its sheath and it started to swell into a long curving S-shape.

The young man beside her heard the sudden intake of
breath and glanced at her. She turned to look at him, and
their eyes, equally astonished and full of wonder, held for a
moment. Although they had both hunted mammoths, neither
of them had observed the great woolly beasts very often from
so near, and neither had ever seen them mate. Jondalar felt
a quickening in his own loins as he watched Ayla. She was
excited, flushed, her mouth slightly open, taking quick
breaths, and her eyes, opened wide, held a sparkle of curiosity. Fascinated by the awesome spectacle of the two massive
creatures about to show honor to the Great Earth Mother, as
She required of all Her children, they quickly turned back.

But the female ran in a large arc, keeping ahead of the
larger bull, until she made it back to her family herd again,
though it made little difference. In a short time she was being

chased again. One male caught up to her and managed to mount, but she was uncooperative and got out from under him, though he sprayed her hind legs. Sometimes her calf tried to follow the chestnut as she sped away from the bachelors several more times, before it finally decided to stay with the other females. Jondalar wondered why she was trying so hard to avoid the interested males. Didn't the Mother expect female mammoths to honor Her, too?

As though they had mutually decided to stop and eat, it was quiet for a while, with all the mammoths moving slowly south through the tallgrass tearing out trunkful after trunkful in a steady rhythm. In the rare moment of relief from the harassment of the males, the chestnut mammoth stood with her head low, looking very tired as she tried to feed.

Mammoths spent most of the day, and night, eating. Though it could be of the roughest, poorest quality—they could even eat shreds of bark torn off with tusks, though that was more often winter feed—mammoths needed huge quantities of the fibrous fare to sustain them. Included in the several hundred pounds of roughage consumed every day, which they passed through their bodies within twelve hours, was a small, though necessary, addition of succulent, broad-leaved, more nutritious plants, or occasionally a few choice leaves of willow, birch, or alder trees, higher in food value than the coarse tallgrass and sedge, but toxic to mammoths in large quantities.

When the great woolly beasts had moved some distance away, Ayla tied the restraining rope on the young wolf, who was if anything even more interested than they were. He kept wanting to get closer, but she didn't want him to disturb the herd or annoy them. Ayla felt the matriarch had given them leave to stay, but only if they kept their distance. Leading the horses, who were exhibiting some nervousness and excitement as well, they circled around through the tallgrass and followed the herd. Though they had been watching for some time, neither Ayla nor Jondalar was inclined to leave yet. There was still a sense of anticipation lingering around the mammoths. Something was coming. Perhaps it was just that the mating they felt privileged, almost invited, to observe, was still incomplete, but it seemed more than that.

As they slowly followed after the herd, they both studied the huge animals closely, but each from a separate perspective. Ayla had been a hunter from an early age, and had

observed animals often, but her prey was ordinarily much
smaller. Mammoths weren't usually hunted by individuals;
they were hunted by large, organized, and coordinated
groups. She had actually been closer to the great beasts
before, when she had gone to hunt them with the Mamutoi.
But while hunting there was little time to watch and learn,
and she didn't know when she would ever have the opportunity to get such a good look at them, both female and male,
again.

Though she was aware of their distinctive shape in profile,
this time she took particular note of it. The head of a mammoth was massive and high-domed—with large sinus cavities
that helped to warm the searing cold winter air as it was
breathed—accentuated by a hump of fat and a conspicuous
topknot of stiff, dark hair. Just below the high head was the
deep indentation of the nape of its short neck, leading to a
second hump of fat high on the withers above the shoulders.
From there, the back sloped steeply to the small pelvis and
almost dainty hips. She knew from the experience of butchering and eating mammoth meat that the fat of the second
hump had a different quality from that of the three-inch-thick
layer of blubber that lay under the tough inch-thick skin. It
was more delicate, tastier.

Woolly mammoths had relatively short legs for their size,
making it somewhat easier for them to acquire their food,
since they fed primarily on grass, not the high green leaves
of trees as did their browsing warm-climate relatives; there
were few trees on the steppes. But like them, the mammoth's
head was high up off the ground, and too big and heavy,
especially with enormous tusks, to be supported by a long
neck so that it could reach food or drink directly the way
horses or deer did. The evolution of the trunk had solved the
problem of bringing food and water to the mouth.

The furry, sinuous snout of the woolly mammoth was
strong enough to tear out a tree, or to pick up a heavy chunk
of ice and send it crashing down to break into smaller, more
usable pieces for water in winter, and dexterous enough to
select and pluck a single leaf. It was also marvelously adapted
to pulling grass. It had two projections on the end of it. A
fingerlike appendage on the upper part, which it could deli-
cately control, and a broader, flattened, very flexible structure
on the lower part, almost like a hand, but without bones or
separate fingers.

Jondalar was amazed at the dexterity and strength of the trunk as he watched a mammoth wrap the muscular lower projection around a bunch of closely growing tallgrass, then hold it together while the upper digit fingered more stems that were growing nearby into its clutch, until it had accumulated a good sheaf. Getting a grip by closing the upper finger around the bunch like an opposing thumb, the furry trunk yanked the grass out of the ground, roots and all. After shaking off some of the dirt, the mammoth stuffed it all in its mouth, and while it was chewing, reached for more.

The devastation that a herd left behind them as they made their long migrations across the steppes was considerable, or so it seemed. But for all the grass ripped out by its roots, and bark stripped from trees, their disturbance was beneficial to the steppes, and to other animals. By clearing away the woody-stemmed tallgrass and small trees, a place was made for richer forbs and new grass to grow, food that was essential to several of the other inhabitants of the steppes.

Ayla suddenly shivered and felt a strange sensation deep in her bones. Then she noticed the mammoths had stopped eating. Several raised their heads and faced the south with their furry ears extended, moving their heads back and forth. Jondalar noticed a change in the dark red female, who had been chased by all the males. Her tired look was gone; she seemed, instead, to be anticipating. Suddenly she roared a deep, vibrating rumble. Ayla sensed a head-filling resonance, then felt the chill of gooseflesh as an answer, like the low growl of distant thunder, came from the southwest.

"Jondalar," Ayla said. "Look over there!"

He looked where she had pointed. Rushing toward them, amidst a cloud of dust rising as if flung up by a whirlwind, only his domed head and shoulders visible above the tallgrass, was a huge, pale russet mammoth with fantastic and immense, upward-curving tusks. Where they started, side by side in the upper jaw, they were huge. They flared out as they grew downward, then they curved upward and spiraled inward, slowly tapering to worn tips. Eventually, if he didn't break them, they would form a great circle with their tapered ends crossing in front.

The thick-furred Ice Age elephants were rather compact, seldom exceeding eleven feet at the shoulder, but their tusks grew to enormous size, the most spectacular of any of their kind. By the time a prime male mammoth reached the end of his seventy years, his great curved shafts of ivory could be a full sixteen feet in length, weighing two hundred sixty pounds each.

A strong, acrid, musky odor arrived long before the russet bull did, sending a wave of frenzied excitement through the females. When he reached the clearing, they ran toward him, giving him their scent with great splashes of urine, squealing, trumpeting, and rumbling their greetings. They surrounded him, turning and backing up to him, or trying to touch him with their trunks. They were attracted, but also overwhelmed. The males, however, retreated to the edge of the group.

When he was close enough for Ayla and Jondalar to get a good look at him, they, too, were awed. He held his great domed head high, displaying his proud coils of ivory to best advantage. Far exceeding in length and diameter the smaller and straighter tusks of the females, his impressive tusks made even the more than respectable ivory of the large bulls seem puny. His small, thickly furred ears that were extended, his dark, stiff, erect topknot, and his light reddish-brown coat, long hairs loose and flying in the wind, added fullness to his already massive size. Towering nearly two feet above the largest bulls, and twice the weight of the females, he was by far the most gigantic animal either of them had ever seen. After surviving through hard times and good for more than forty-five years, he was in peak condition, a dominant bull mammoth in his prime, and he was magnificent.

But it was more than the natural dominance of his size that had made the other males back off. Ayla noticed that his temples were greatly swollen and from midway between his eyes and ears, the rich russet fur of his cheeks was stained with black streaks by a musky, viscous fluid that was constantly draining. He was also continuously dribbling and occasionally gushing an acrid, strong-smelling urine, which coated the fur on his legs and the sheath of his organ with a greenish scum. She wondered if he was sick.

But the swollen temporal glands and other symptoms were not a sickness. Among woolly mammoths, not only did females come into heat, estrus, each year fully adult males went into lust, a period of heightened sexual readiness, called musth. Although a male mammoth reached puberty around twelve, he did not begin musth until he was close to thirty, and then only for a week or so. But, by the time he reached his late forties, and was in his prime, if he was in top condition, he could be in musth for three or four months each year. Though any male past puberty could mate with a receptive estrus female, bulls were far more successful when they were in musth.

The big russet bull was not only dominant, he was in full rut and he had come, in answer to her call, to mate with the female in heat.

At close range, male mammoths knew when females were ready to conceive by their scent, just as most four-legged male animals did. But mammoths ranged over such large territories that they had evolved an additional way to communicate that they were ready for mating. When a female was in estrus, or a male was in musth, the pitch of their voices lowered. Very low-pitched sounds do not die out across long distances the way higher tones do, and the deep rumbling calls that were made only then, carried for miles across the vast plains.

Jondalar and Ayla could hear the low rumbles of the estrus female clearly enough, but the male in musth had such quiet-seeming deep tones that they barely heard him. Even in ordinary circumstances, mammoths often communicated across distances with deep rumbles and calls that most people were not aware of. Yet the bull mammoth's musth calls were actually extremely loud, deep-voiced roars; the female estrus call was even louder. Though a few people could detect the sonic vibrations of the deep tones, most elements of the sounds were so low-pitched that they were below the range of human hearing.

The chestnut female had been holding off the bevy of younger bachelors, who had also been drawn by her attractive odors and by the sonorous rumbling of her low-pitched calls, which could be heard at a great distance by other mammoths, if not people. But she wanted an older, dominant male to sire her potential young, one whose years of living had already proved his health and survival instincts, and one she knew was virile enough to be a sire; in other words, one in musth. She didn't think about it in quite that way, but her body knew.

Now that he was here, she was ready. Her long fringe of hair swaying with each step, the chestnut female ran toward the great bull, bellowing her sonorous rumbles and waving her furry little ears. She passed her water in a great splash, then, stretching her trunk toward his long, S-shaped organ, she sniffed and tasted his urine. Groaning thunderously, she pivoted around and backed into him, her head high.

The huge bull laid his trunk across her back, caressing and calming her; his huge organ nearly touched the ground. Then he reared up and mounted, placing his two front legs far forward on her back. He was nearly twice her size, so much larger that it seemed he would crush her, but most of his weight was carried on his hind legs. With the hooked end of his double-curved, marvelously mobile organ, he found her low-slung opening, then lifted up and penetrated deeply. He opened his mouth to bellow a roar.

The deep rumble that Jondalar heard sounded muted and far away, though he felt a throbbing sensation. Ayla heard the roar only slightly louder, but she shuddered violently as a shivering vibration tore through her. The chestnut mammoth and the russet bull held the position for a long moment. The long reddish strands of his full coat of hair shimmied over his whole body with the intensity and strain, though the movement was slight. Then he dismounted, gushing as he withdrew. She moved forward and uttered a low-toned and prolonged, pulsating bellow, which sent a powerful chill down Ayla's spine and raised gooseflesh.

The whole herd ran to the dark red female, trumpeting and rumbling, touching her mouth and her wet opening with their trunks, defecating and splashing their water in an outburst of excitement. The russet bull seemed unaware of the joyful pandemonium as he stood resting with his head down. Finally they calmed down and began wandering away to feed. Only her calf stayed nearby. The chestnut female rumbled deeply again, then rubbed her head against a russet shoulder.

None of the other males approached the herd with the big bull nearby, though the chestnut was no less tempting. Besides lending male mammoths irresistible charm, to females, musth also conferred dominance over males, making them very aggressive even toward those who were larger, unless they were also in that excited state. The other bulls shied away, knowing the russet would be easily irritated. Only another musth bull would try to face him, and only if he was close to the same size. Then, if they were both attracted by the same female, and found themselves in the vicinity of each other, they would invariably fight, with severe injury or death a possible result.

Almost as though they knew the consequences, they took

great pains to avoid each other and thus avoid fights. The deep-toned calls and the pungent urine trails of the musth male did more than announce his presence to eager females, they also announced his location to other males. Only three or four other bulls were in musth at the same time, during the six- or seven-month period that females might come into estrus, but it was unlikely that any of those who were also in lust would challenge the big russet for the female who was in heat. He was the dominant bull of the population, whether in musth or not, and they knew where he was.

As they continued to watch, Ayla noticed that even when the dark red female and lighter-colored male began to feed, they stayed close together. At one point the female strayed a few feet away, reaching for a particularly succulent trunkful of herbs. One young bull, hardly more than an adolescent, tried to inch toward her, but as she ran back to her consort, the russet bull lunged at him, voicing his rumbling growl. The sharp, pungent scent and distinctive deep roar made their impression on the young male. He quickly ran away, then lowered his head in deference and kept his distance. Finally, as long as she stayed near the musth bull, the chestnut female could rest and feed without being chased.

The woman and man could not quite bring themselves to leave immediately, though they knew it was over, and Jondalar was again beginning to feel the pressure of getting on their way. They felt awed, and honored, to have been included in witnessing the mating of the mammoths. More than merely having been allowed to observe, they felt a part of it, as though they had joined in on a moving and important ceremony. Ayla wished she could run up and touch them, too, to express her appreciation and share their joy.

Before they left, Ayla noticed that many of the plant foods she had seen all along the way were growing nearby, and she decided to gather some, using her digging stick for roots and a special knife, rather thick but strong, to cut stems and leaves. Jondalar got down beside her to help, though he had to ask her to point out exactly what she wanted.

It still surprised her. During the time they lived with the Lion Camp, she had learned the customs and patterns of work of the Mamutoi, which were different from the ways of the Clan. But even there, she often worked with Deegie or Nezzie, or many people worked together, and she had forgotten his willingness to do work that the men of the Clan would have considered the job of women. Yet, since the early days in her valley, Jondalar had never hesitated to do anything that she did, and he was surprised that she didn't expect him to share in the work that needed to be done. With just the two of them, she became aware of that side of him again.

When they finally did leave, they rode in silence for some time. Ayla kept thinking about the mammoths; could not get them out of her mind. She thought, too, about the Mamutoi, who had given her a home and a place to belong when she had no one. They called themselves the Mammoth Hunters, though they hunted many other kinds of animals, and gave the huge woolly beasts a unique place of honor, even while hunting them. Besides providing them with so much of what was necessary for existence—meat, fat, hides, wool for fibers and cordage, ivory for tools and carvings, bones for dwellings and even fuel—mammoth hunts had deep spiritual meaning to them.

She felt even more Mamutoi now, though she was leaving. It was not by chance, she felt, that they had come upon the herd when they did. She was sure there was a reason for it, and wondered if Mut, the Earth Mother, or maybe her totem, was trying to tell her something. She had found herself thinking often, lately, about the Great Cave Lion spirit that was the totem Creb had given her, wondering if he still protected her though she was no longer Clan, and where a Clan totem spirit would fit into her new life with Jondalar.

The tallgrass finally began thinning out, and they moved closer to the river looking for a place to camp. Jondalar glanced toward the sun descending in the west and decided it was too late to try to hunt that evening. He wasn't sorry they had stayed to watch the mammoths, but he had hoped to hunt for meat, not only for their meal that night, but to last for the next few days. He didn't want to have to use the dried traveling food they had with them unless they really needed it. Now they'd have to take the time in the morning.

The valley with its luxuriant bottomland near the river had been changing, and the vegetation altered with it. As the banks of the swift waterway were rising in elevation, the character of the grass changed and, to Jondalar's relief, became shorter. It barely reached the bellies of the horses. He preferred being able to see where they were going. Where the ground began to level out near the top of a slope, the landscape took on a familiar feel. It wasn't that they had ever been in that particular locality before, but that it was similar to the region around the Lion Camp, with high banks and eroded gullies leading to the river.

They climbed a slight rise and Jondalar noticed that the course of the river was veering to the left, toward the east. It was time to leave this watery vein of life-supporting liquid meandering slowly toward the south and angle westward across country. He stopped to consult the map Talut had carved on the slab of ivory for him. When he looked up, he noticed Ayla had dismounted and was standing on the edge of the bank looking across the river. Something about the way she stood made him think she was upset or unhappy.

He shifted his leg over, got down from his mount, and joined her on the bank. Across the river he saw what had drawn her to the edge. Tucked into the slope on a terrace halfway up the opposite side was a large, long mound with tufts of grass growing up the sides. It seemed to be a part of the riverbank itself, but the arched entrance closed by a heavy mammoth-hide drape revealed its actual nature. It was an earthlodge like the one the Lion Camp called home, where they had lived during the previous winter.

As Ayla stared at the familiar-looking structure, she remembered vividly the inside of the Lion Camp's earthlodge. The roomy semisubterranean dwelling was strong and built to last many years. The floor had been carved out of the fine loess soil of the riverbank and was below ground level. Its walls and rounded roof of sod covered with river clay were firmly supported by a structure of more than a ton of large mammoth bones, with deer antlers entwined and lashed together at the ceiling, and a thick thatch of grass and reeds between the bone and the sod. Benches of earth along the sides were made into warm beds, and storage areas were dug down to the cold permafrost level. The archway was two large curved mammoth tusks, with the butt ends in the ground and the tips facing each other and joined. It was by no means a temporary construction, but a permanent settlement under one roof, large enough to support several large families. She was sure the makers of this earthlodge had every intention of returning, just as the Lion Camp did every winter.

"They must be at the Summer Meeting," Ayla said. "I wonder which Camp's home that is?"

"Maybe it belongs to Feather Grass Camp," Jondalar suggested.

"Maybe," Ayla said, then stared in silence across the rushing stream. "It looks so empty," she added after a while. "I didn't think when we left that I would never see Lion Camp again. I remember when I was sorting through things to take to the Meeting, I left some behind. If I'd known I wasn't going back, I might have taken them with me."

"Are you sorry you left, Ayla?" Jondalar's concern showed, as always, in the worry wrinkles on his forehead. "I told you I would stay and become a Mamutoi, too, if you wanted me to. I know you found a home with them and were happy. It's not too late. We can still turn back."

"No, I'm sad to be leaving, but I'm not sorry. I want to be with you. That's what I've wanted from the beginning. And I know you want to go home, Jondalar. You have wanted to go back ever since I've known you. You might get used to living here, but you would never really be happy. You would always miss your people, your family, the ones you were born to. It's not as important to me. I will never know who I was born to. The Clan were my people."

Ayla's thoughts turned inward, and Jondalar watched a gentle smile soften her face. "Iza would have been so happy for me if she could have known I was going with you. She would have liked you. She told me long before I left that I wasn't Clan, though I couldn't remember anyone or anything except living with them. Iza was my mother, the only one I knew, but she wanted me to leave the Clan. She was afraid for me. Before she died, she told me, 'Find your own people, find your own mate.' Not a man of the Clan, a man like me; someone I could love, who would care for me. But I was alone so long in the valley, I didn't think I ever would find anyone. And then you came. Iza was right. As hard as it was to leave, I needed to find my own people. Except for Durc, I could almost thank Broud for forcing me to go. I would never have found a man to love me, if I hadn't left the Clan, or one that I cared about so much."

"We aren't so different, Ayla. I didn't think I'd ever find anyone to love, either, even though I knew many women among the Zelandonii, and we met many more on our Journey. Thonolan made friends easily, even among strangers, and he made it easy for me." He closed his eyes for an anguished moment, flinching from the memory, as a deep sorrow touched his face. The pain was still sharp. Ayla could see it whenever he talked about his brother.

She looked at Jondalar, at his exceptionally tall, muscular body, at his long, straight, yellow hair tied back with a thong at the nape of his neck, at his fine, well-made features. After watching him at the Summer Meeting, she doubted that he needed his brother's help to make friends, especially with women, and she knew why. Even more than his build or his handsome face, it was his eyes, his startlingly vibrant and expressive eyes, which seemed to reveal the inner core of this very private man, that gave him a magnetic appeal and a presence so compelling that he was nearly irresistible.

Just the way he was looking at her that moment, his eyes filled with warmth and desire. She could feel her body respond to the mere touch of his eyes. She thought of the chestnut mammoth, who kept refusing all the other males, waiting for the big russet bull to come, and then not wanting to wait anymore, but there was pleasure in prolonging the anticipation, too.

She loved looking at him, filling herself with him. She thought he was beautiful the first time she saw him, though she had no one to compare him with. She had since learned that other women loved looking at him, too; considered him remarkably, even overwhelmingly attractive; and that it embarrassed him to be told about it. His outstanding good looks had brought him at least as much pain as pleasure, and to stand out for qualities that he had nothing to do with, did not bring him the satisfaction of accomplishment. They were gifts of the Mother, not the result of his own efforts.

But the Great Earth Mother had not stopped with mere outward appearances. She had endowed him with a rich and lively intelligence, that tended more toward a sensitivity and understanding of the physical aspects of his world, and a natural dexterity. Abetted by training from the man to whom his mother had been mated when he was born, who was acknowledged as the best in his field, Jondalar was a skilled maker of stone tools who had honed his craft on his Journey by learning the techniques of other flint knappers.

For Ayla, though, he was beautiful not merely because he was exceptionally attractive by the standards of his people, but because he was the first person she could remember seeing who resembled her. He was a man of the Others, not of the Clan. When he first came to her valley, she had studied his face minutely, if not obviously, even in his sleep. It was such a wonder to see a face with the familiar look of her own after so many years of being the only one who was different, who did not have heavy brow ridges and a sloped-back forehead, or a large, high-bridged, sharp nose, in a face that jutted out, and a jaw with no chin.

Like hers, Jondalar's forehead rose up steeply and smoothly, without heavy brow ridges. His nose, and even his teeth, were small by comparison, and he had a bony protuberance below his mouth, a chin, just as she did. After seeing him, she could understand why the Clan thought of her as having a flat face and bulging forehead. She had seen her own reflection in still water, and she believed what they had told her. In spite of the fact that Jondalar towered over her as much as she had towered over them, and that she had since been told by more than one man that she was beautiful, deep inside she still thought of herself as big and ugly.

But because Jondalar was male, with stronger features and angles more pronounced, to Ayla, he resembled the Clan more than she did. They were the people she grew up with, they were her standard of measure, and unlike the rest of her kind, she thought they were quite handsome. Jondalar, with a face that was like hers, and yet more like a Clan face than hers, was beautiful.

Jondalar's high forehead smoothed as he smiled. "I'm glad you think she would have approved of me. I wish I could have met your Iza," he said, "and the rest of your Clan. But I had to meet you first or I would never have understood that they were people, and that I *could* meet them. The way you talk about the Clan, they must be good people. I'd like to meet one some time."

"Many people are good people. The Clan took me in after the earthquake, when I was little. After Broud drove me away from the Clan, I had no one. I was Ayla of No People until the Lion Camp accepted me, gave me a place to belong, made me Ayla of the Mamutoi."

"The Mamutoi and the Zelandonii are not so different. I think you will like my people, and they will like you."

"You haven't always been so sure of that," Ayla said. "I remember when you were afraid they would not want me, because I grew up with the Clan, and because of Durc."

Jondalar felt a flush of embarrassment.

"They would call my son an abomination, a child born

of mixed spirits, half-animal—you called him that, once—
and because I birthed him, they would think even worse of
me.''

"Ayla, before we left the Summer Meeting, you made
me promise to tell you the truth, and not to keep things to
myself. The truth is that I was worried in the beginning. I
wanted you to come with me, but I didn't want you to tell
people about yourself. I wanted you to hide your childhood,
lie about it, even though I hate lies—and you never learned
how. I was afraid they would reject you. I know how it feels,
and I didn't want you to be hurt that way. But I was afraid
for myself, too. I was afraid they would reject me for bringing you, and I didn't want to go through that kind of thing
again. Yet I couldn't bear to think of living without you. I
didn't know what to do.''

Ayla remembered only too well her confusion and despair
over his agony of indecision. As happy as she had been with
the Mamutoi, she had also been miserably unhappy because
of Jondalar.

"Now I know, though it took almost losing you before I
realized it," Jondalar continued. "No one is more important
to me than you, Ayla. I want you to be yourself, to say or
do whatever you think you should, because that's what I love
about you, and I believe, now, that most people will welcome
you. I've seen it happen. I learned something important from
the Lion Camp and the Mamutoi. Not all people think alike
and opinions can be changed. Some people will stand by you,
sometimes those you least expect to, and some people have
enough compassion to love and raise a child whom others
call abomination.''

"I didn't like the way they treated Rydag at the Summer
Meeting," Ayla said. "Some of them didn't even want to
give him a proper burial." Jondalar heard the anger in her
voice, but he could see tears threatening behind the anger.

"I didn't like it either. Some people won't change. They
won't open their eyes and look at what is plain to see. It
took me a long time. I can't promise you that the Zelandonii
will accept you, Ayla, but if they don't we'll find some other
place. Yes, I want to return. I want to go back to my people,
I want to see my family, my friends. I want to tell my mother
about Thonolan, and ask Zelandoni to look for his spirit in
case he hasn't found his way to the next world yet. I hope
we will find a place there. But if not, it's not so important

to me anymore. That's the other thing I learned. That's why I told you I would be willing to stay here with you, if you wanted me to. I meant it."

He was holding her with both his hands clasping her shoulders, looking into her eyes with fierce determination, wanting to be sure she understood him. She saw his conviction, and his love, but now she wondered if they should have left.

"If your people don't want us, where will we go?"

He smiled at her. "We'll find another place, Ayla, if we have to, but I don't think we will. I told you, the Zelandonii are not so different from the Mamutoi. They will love you, just as I do. I'm not even worried about it anymore. I'm not sure why I ever was."

Ayla smiled at him, pleased that he was so sure of his people's acceptance of her. She only wished she could share his confidence. He might have forgotten, or perhaps not realized, what a strong and lasting impression his first reaction to learning about her son and her background had made on her. He had jerked away and looked upon her with such disgust that she would never forget it. It was just as though she were some dirty, filthy hyena.

As they got under way again, Ayla kept thinking about what might await her at the end of her Journey. It was true, people could change. Jondalar had changed completely. She knew there was not the least bit of that feeling of aversion left in him, but what about the people he had learned it from? If his response was so immediate, and so strong, his people must have taught it to him as he was growing up. Why should they react any differently to her than he had? As much as she wanted to be with Jondalar, and as glad as she was that he wanted to take her home with him, she was not altogether looking forward to meeting the Zelandonii.

4

They stayed close to the river as they continued on their way. Jondalar felt almost certain that the course of the stream was making a turn toward the east, but he worried that it might only be a wide swing in its general meandering. If the waterway was changing direction, this would be the place they would leave it—and the security of following an easily defined route—to strike out across country, and he wanted to make sure they were in the right place.

There were several places they could have stopped for the night but, consulting the map often, Jondalar was looking for a campsite that Talut had indicated. It was the landmark he needed to verify their location. The place was regularly used and he hoped he was right in thinking it was nearby, but the map showed only general directions and landmarks and was imprecise, at best. It had been quickly scratched onto the slab of ivory as an aid to the verbal explanations he had been given, and a reminder of them, and it was not meant to be an accurate representation of the route.

When the bank continued to rise and pull back, they kept

to the high ground for the wider view it offered, though it
was drawing away somewhat from the river. Below, closer
to the flowing water, an oxbow lake was drying into a marsh.
It had begun as a side loop of the river that swayed back and
forth, as all flowing water did when traversing open land.
The loop eventually closed back on itself, and then filled in
with water to form a small lake, which became isolated when
the river changed course. With no source of water, it began
to dry out. The sheltered lowland was now a wet meadow
where marsh reeds and cattails thrived, with water-loving bog
plants filling its deep end. Over time, the green swale would
become a grassy meadow enriched by this wetland stage.

Jondalar almost reached for a spear when he saw a moose
break out of the wooded cover near the edge and walk out
into the water, but the large deer was out of range, even with
his spear-thrower, and it would be difficult for them to
retrieve it from the bog. Ayla watched the ungainly-seeming
animal with the overhanging nose and large palmate antlers,
still in velvet, walking into the marsh. He lifted his long legs
high, plopping his broad feet, which kept him from sinking
into the mucky bottom, until the water reached his flanks.
Then he submerged his head and came up with a mouthful
of dripping duckweed and water bistort. Nearby waterfowl,
nesting in the reeds, ignored his presence.

Beyond the marsh, well-drained slopes with gullies and
cut banks offered protected crannies for forbs such as goosefoot, nettles, and mats of hairy-leaved, mouse-eared chick-
weed with small white flowers. Ayla loosened her sling and
took a few round stones from a pouch in readiness. At the
far end of her valley there had been a similar location, where
she had often observed and hunted the exceptionally large
ground squirrels of the steppes. One or two could make a
satisfying meal.

With the rugged terrain leading to open fields of grass, it
was their favored habitat. The rich seeds from the nearby
grasslands, stored safely in caches while the squirrels hiber-
nated, sustained them in spring to breed so that at just the
time new plants appeared, they would bear their young. The
protein-rich forbs were essential for the young to reach maturity before winter. But no ground squirrels chose to show
themselves while the people were passing, and Wolf seemed
unable, or unwilling, to flush them.

As they continued south, the great granite platform

beneath the broad plain that stretched far to the east warped upward into rolling hills. Once, in ages long past, the land they were traveling over had been mountains that had long since worn down. Their stumps were a stubborn shield of rock that resisted the immense pressures that buckled land into new mountains, and the fiery inner forces that could shake and rend a less stable earth. Newer rock had formed on the ancient massif, but outcrops of the original mountains still pierced the sedimentary crust.

In the time when mammoths grazed the steppes, the grasses and herbs, like the animals of that ancient land, flourished not only in great abundance, but with a surprising range and diversity, and in unexpected associations. Unlike later grasslands, these steppes were not arranged in wide belts of certain limited kinds of vegetation, determined by temperature and climate. They were, instead, a complex mosaic with a richer diversity of plants, which included many varieties of grasses and prolific herbs and shrubs.

A well-watered valley, a highland meadow, a hilltop, or a slight dip in elevation, each invited its own community of plant life, which grew close beside complexes of unrelated vegetation. A slope facing south might harbor warm-climate growth, surprisingly different from the cold-adapted boreal vegetation on the north face of the same hill.

The soil of the rugged upland Ayla and Jondalar were traversing was poor, and the grass cover thin and short. The wind had eroded deeper gullies, and in the upper valley of an old spring-flood tributary, the riverbed had gone dry and, lacking vegetation, had drifted into sand dunes.

Though later found only in high mountain reaches, in this rough terrain not far from lowland rivers, singing voles and pikas were busily cutting grass, to be dried and stored. Instead of hibernating in winter, they built tunnels and nests under the snowdrifts that accumulated in dips and hollows and on the lee side of rocks, and fed on their stored hay. Wolf spied the small rodents and took out after them, but Ayla didn't bother with her sling. They were too small to make a meal for people, except in large numbers.

Arctic herbs, which did well in the wetter northern land of bogs and fens, benefited in spring from the additional moisture of the melting drifts and grew, in an unusual association, alongside small hardy alpine shrubs on exposed outcrops and windswept hills. Arctic cinquefoil, with small

yellow flowers, found protection from the wind in the same
sheltered pockets and niches preferred by pikas, while on
exposed surfaces, cushions of moss campion with purple or
pink blossoms formed their own protective hummocks of
leafy stems in the cold drying winds. Beside them, mountain
avens clung to the rocky outcrops and hills of this rugged
lower land, just as it did on mountainsides, its low evergreen
branches of tiny leaves and solitary yellow flowers spreading
out, over many years, into dense mats.

Ayla noticed the fragrant scent of pink catchfly, just
beginning to open their blooms. It made her realize that it
was getting late, and she glanced toward the sun lowering in
the western sky to verify the hint her nose had detected. The
sticky flowers opened at night, offering a haven to insects—
moths and flies—in return for spreading pollen. They had
little medicinal or food value, but the pleasant-smelling
flowers pleased her, and she had a fleeting notion to pick
some. But it was already late in the day and she didn't want
to stop. They ought to be making camp soon, she was thinking, particularly if she was going to make the meal she had
been thinking about before it got dark.

She saw blue-purple pasqueflowers, erect and beautiful,
each rising from expanding leaves covered with fine hairs
and, unbidden, the medical associations came into her
mind—the dried plant was helpful for headaches and wom-
en's cramps—but she enjoyed it as much for its beauty as
for its usefulness. When her eye was caught by alpine asters
with long thin petals of yellow and violet growing from
rosettes of silky, hairy leaves, her fleeting notion became a
conscious temptation to gather a few, along with some of the
other flowers, for no reason except to enjoy them. But where
would she put them? They would only wilt, anyway, she
thought.

Jondalar was beginning to wonder if they had missed the
marked campsite, or if they were farther away from it than
he had thought. He was reluctantly coming to the conclusion
that they were going to have to make camp soon and look
for the landmark campsite tomorrow. With that, and the need
to hunt, they would probably lose another day, and he didn't
think they could afford to lose so many days. He was deep
in thought, still worrying about whether he had made the
right decision in continuing south, and imagining the dire
consequences, and was not paying close attention to a com-

motion on a hill to their right, except for noticing that it seemed to be a pack of hyenas that had made a kill.

Though they often scavenged, and when hungry were satisfied with the most noxious of rotten carcasses, the large hyenas with their powerful, bone-cracking jaws were also effective hunters. They had pulled down a yearling bison calf, nearly full-grown, but not fully developed. His lack of experience with the ways of predators had been his undoing. A few other bison were standing around, apparently safe now that one had succumbed, and one was watching the hyenas, bawling uneasily at the smell of fresh blood.

Unlike mammoths, and steppe horses, which were not exceptionally large for their species, the bison were giants. The one nearby stood nearly seven feet at the withers and was heavily built in the chest and shoulders, though his flanks were almost graceful. His hooves were small, adapted to running very fast over firm dry soils, and he avoided bogs in which he would become mired. His large head was protected by massive long black horns, six feet across, that curved out and then up. His dark brown, hairy coat was heavy, especially in the chest and shoulders. Bison tended to face into the frigid winds and were better protected in front, where the hair fell in a fringe that was up to thirty inches long, but even his short tail was covered with hair.

Although they were all grass eaters, the various grazers did not eat precisely the same food. They had different digestive systems or different habits and made subtly different adaptations. The highly fibrous stems that sustained horses and mammoths were not sufficient for bison and other ruminants. They needed grass sheaths and leaves that were higher in protein, and bison preferred the low-growing, more nutritious shortgrass of the drier regions. They only ventured into the midgrass and tallgrass regions of the steppes in search of new growth, usually in spring when all the lands were rich with fresh grass and herbs—which was also the only time of the year when their bones and horns grew. The long, wet, green spring of the periglacial grassland, gave bison, and several other animals, a long season for growing, which resulted in their heroic proportions.

In his dark and introspective mood, it took a few moments for the possibilities of the scene on the hill to make an impact on Jondalar. By the time he was reaching for his spearthrower and a spear with the idea of also bringing down a bison, as the hyenas had, Ayla had already assessed the situation, but had decided on a somewhat different course of action.

"Hai! Hai! Get away from there! Go on, you filthy beasts! Get out of here!" she shouted, galloping Whinney toward them, as she hurtled stones with her sling. Wolf was beside her, looking pleased with himself, as he growled and puppy-barked at the retreating pack.

A few yelps of pain made it clear that Ayla's stones had reached their mark, though she had held the force of her weapon in check and aimed for nonvital parts. If she had wished, her stones could have been fatal; it wouldn't have been the first time that she had killed a hyena, but that had not been her intention.

"What are you doing, Ayla?" Jondalar asked, riding toward her as she was returning to the bison the hyenas had killed.

"I'm chasing those filthy, dirty hyenas away," she said, though it certainly must have been obvious.

"But why?"

"Because they are going to share that bison kill with us," she replied.

"I was just going after one of those that are standing around," Jondalar said.

"We don't need a whole bison, unless we're going to dry the meat, and this one is young and tender. The ones that are standing around are mostly tough old bulls," she said as she slid off Whinney to chase Wolf away from the downed animal.

Jondalar looked more closely at the gigantic bulls, who had also retreated from Ayla's hazing, and then at the young one on the ground. "You're right. This is a male herd, and that one probably left his mother's herd recently and just joined this male group. He still had a lot to learn."

"It's a fresh kill," Ayla announced, after she examined it. "They've only torn out the throat, and the gut, so far, and a little of the flank. We can take what we want, and leave the rest for them. Then we won't need to take the time to hunt down one of those others. They can run fast, and they might get away. I think I saw a place down by the river that may have been a camp. If it's the one we're looking for, there's still time for me to make something nice tonight with all the food we gathered and this meat."

She was already cutting through the skin up from the stomach to the flank before Jondalar really grasped all that she had said. It had happened so fast, but suddenly all his concerns about losing an extra day because of having to hunt and look for the camp were gone.

"Ayla, you're wonderful!" he said, smiling as he dismounted from the young stallion. He pulled a sharp flint knife, that was hafted to a handle of ivory, out of a stiff rawhide sheath attached to his waist thong, and went to help butcher out the parts they wanted. "That's what I love about you. You're always full of surprises that turn out to be good ideas. Let's get the tongue, too. Too bad they already got to the liver, but after all, it is their kill."

"I don't care if it is theirs," Ayla said, "so long as it's a fresh kill. They've taken enough from me. I don't mind taking something back from those nasty animals. I hate hyenas!"

"You really do, don't you? I never hear you talk that way about other animals, not even wolverines, and they scavenge rotten meat sometimes and are more vicious and smell worse."

The hyena pack had been edging back toward the bison they had expected to feast on, snarling their displeasure. Ayla flung a few more stones to drive them back again. One of them whooped, then several cackled a loud laugh that made her skin crawl. By the time the hyenas decided to chance her sling once more, Ayla and Jondalar had gotten what they wanted.

They rode off, heading down a gully toward the river, with Ayla leading the way, leaving the rest of the carcass behind with the snarling beasts, who had immediately returned and begun to tear it apart again.

The signs she had seen were not of the camp itself, but a marker cairn pointing the way. Inside the heaped-up pile of stones were some dry emergency rations, a few tools and other implements, a fire drill and platform with some dry tinder, and a rather stiff fur with patches of hair falling out. It would still offer some protection from the cold, but it needed to be replaced. Near the top of the cairn, firmly anchored by heavy stones, was the broken-off end of a mammoth tusk with its tip aiming toward a large boulder partly submerged in the middle of the river. On it a horizontal diamond shape was painted in red, with the V-shaped angle at the right end repeated twice, forming a chevron pattern pointing downstream.

After putting everything back exactly as they found it, they followed the river until they came to a second cairn with a small tusk pointing inland toward a pleasant glade set back from the river, surrounded by birch and alder trees, with a few pines. They could see a third cairn, and when they reached it, they found beside it a small spring of fresh, pure sparkling water. There were also emergency rations and implements inside this pile of stones, and a large leather tarp, also stiff, but which could be made into a tent or a lean-to. Behind the cairn, near a circle of stones that outlined a shallow pit black with charcoal, was a pile of deadfall and driftwood that had been gathered.

"This is a good place to know about," Jondalar said. "I'm glad we don't have to use any of the supplies, but if I lived in this region and had to use it, I'd be relieved to know this is here."

"It is a good idea," Ayla said, marveling at the foresight of those who had planned and set up the campsite.

They quickly removed the pack baskets and halters from the horses, coiling the thongs and heavy cords that held them on, and set the animals loose to graze and relax. Smiling, they watched as Racer immediately got down on the grass and rolled on his back, as though he had an itch he couldn't wait to scratch.

"I'm feeling hot and itchy, too," Ayla said, untying the thongs around the soft tops of her footwear and kicking them off. She loosened her belt, which held a knife sheath and pouches, took off a necklace of ivory beads with a decorated pouch attached, and pulled off her tunic and leggings, then raced for the water with Wolf bounding beside her. "Are you coming?"

"Later," Jondalar said. "I'd rather wait until after I get the wood, so I don't take dirt and bark dust to bed with me."

Ayla returned soon, changed into a different tunic and leggings that she wore in the evenings, but put her belt and necklace back on. Jondalar had unpacked, and she joined him in setting up their camp. They had already developed a pattern of working together that needed little decision making. They both put up the tent, spreading out an oval ground cloth, then anchoring slender wooden shafts in the earth to support a shaped leather tarp made of several hides sewn together.

The conical tent had rounded sides and an opening at the top to let smoke out if they needed to make a fire inside, though they seldom did, and an extra flap sewn on the inside with which to close the smoke hole against the weather, if they wished.

Cords were fastened around the bottom of the tent to tie it down to pegs pounded in the ground. In case of strong winds, the ground cloth could be tied to the cover tarp with additional ropes, and the entrance flap could be fastened down securely. They carried a second tarp with them to make a better-insulated double-walled tent, though they'd as yet had little occasion to use it.

They spread open their sleeping furs, laying them out the long way of the oval, which left just enough room to fit their pack baskets and other belongings along the sides, and Wolf at their feet if the weather was bad. They had begun with two separate sleeping rolls, but they had quickly managed to combine them so they could sleep together. Once the tent was up, Jondalar went to gather more firewood, to replace whatever they would use, while Ayla began to prepare food.

Though she knew how to start a fire with the fire-making kit in the cairn, by twirling the long stick between her palms against the flat platform of wood to make a coal that could be blown into a flame, Ayla's fire-making kit was unique. While living alone in her valley, she had made a discovery. She had accidentally picked up a piece of iron pyrite from the litter of stones beside the stream, instead of the hammerstone she was using to make new tools for herself from flint. But she had made fires often, and she understood the implications quickly when striking the iron pyrite and flint together created a long-lived spark that burned her leg.

It took several trials at first, but she had long since worked out the best way to use the firestone. Now she could make fire more quickly than anyone with a fire-drill and hearth, and hard concentrated effort, could even imagine. The first time Jondalar had seen it, he couldn't believe it, and the sheer wonder of it had contributed to her being accepted by the Lion Camp when Talut wanted them to adopt her. They thought she had done it with magic.

Ayla thought it was magic, too, but she believed the magic was in the firestone, not in her. Before they left her valley for the last time, she and Jondalar had collected as many of the grayish-yellow metallic stones as they could, not

knowing if they would ever find them in any other place.
They had given some to the Lion Camp and other Mamutoi,
but still had many left. Jondalar wanted to share them with
his people. The ability to make a fire quickly could be
extremely useful, for many purposes.

Inside the ring of stones, the young woman made a small
pile of very dry bark shavings and the fuzz from fireweed as
tinder, and laid beside it another pile of twigs and smallwood
for kindling. Nearby was some of the dry deadfall from the
woodpile. Getting down very close to the tinder, Ayla held
a piece of iron pyrite at an angle that she knew from experience would work best, then struck the magical yellowish
stone, down the middle of a groove that was forming from
use, with a piece of flint. A large, bright, long-lived spark
flew from the stone and landed on the tinder, sending a wisp
of smoke into the air. Quickly she put her hand around it
and blew gently. A small coal glowed with a red light and a
shower of tiny sun-yellow sparks. A second breath produced
a small flame. She added twigs, and smallwood, and when
it was going well, a stick of deadfall.

By the time Jondalar returned, Ayla had several roundish
stones, collected from a dry wash near the river, heating in
the fire for cooking, and a nice chunk of bison spitted over
the flames, the outer layer of fat sizzling. She had washed
and was cutting up cattail roots, and another white starchy
root with dark brown skin called groundnuts, preparing to put
them in a tightly woven waterproof basket half-full of water,
in which the fat-rich tongue was waiting. Beside it was a
small pile of whole wild carrots. The tall man put down his
load of wood.

"It smells good already!" he said. "What are you
making?"

"I'm roasting the bison, but that's mostly for traveling.
It's easy to eat cold roast along the way. For tonight, and
tomorrow morning, I'm making soup with the tongue and
vegetables, and the little bit we have left from Feather Grass
Camp," she said.

With a stick, she fished a hot stone from the fire and
brushed the ashes off with a leafy twig. Then, picking up a
second stick and using them as tongs, she lifted the stone
and dropped it in the basket with the water and the tongue.
It sizzled and steamed as it transferred its heat to the water.

Quickly she dropped several more stones in the basket pot, added some leaves she had cut up, and put on a lid.

"What are you putting in the soup?"

Ayla smiled to herself. He always like to know the details of her cooking, even the herbs that she used for making tea. It was another of his little traits that had surprised her because no man of the Clan would ever dream of showing so much interest, even if he might have been curious, in anything that was in the memories of the women.

"Besides these roots, I'm going to add the green tops of the cattails, the bulbs, leaves, and flowers of these green onions, slices of peeled thistle stalks, the peas from milk vetch pods, and I just put in some sage and thyme leaves, for flavor. And maybe I'll put some coltsfoot in it because it has a kind of salty taste. If we're going near Beran Sea, maybe we can get some more salt. We had it all the time when I lived with the Clan," she mentioned. "I think I'll mash up some of that horseradish I found this morning, for the roast. I just learned about that at the Summer Meeting. It's hot, and you don't need much, but it gives the meat an interesting taste. You might like it."

"What are those leaves for?" he asked, indicating a bunch she had picked but not mentioned. He liked to know what she used and how she thought about food. He enjoyed her cooking, but it was unusual. There were some tastes and flavors that were unique to her methods, and not like the tastes of foods he had grown up with.

"This is goosefoot, to wrap the roast in when I put it away. They are good together when they're cold." She paused, looking thoughtful. "Maybe I'll sprinkle some wood ashes on the roast; they taste a little salty, too. And I might add some of the roast to the soup after it browns, for color, and taste. With the tongue and the roast, it should be a good rich broth, and for tomorrow morning, it will be nice to cook up some of the grain we brought with us. There will be tongue left, too, but I'll wrap it in dried grass and put it in my meat-keeper for later. There's room, even with the rest of our raw meat, including the piece we took for Wolf. As long as it stays cold at night, it should all keep for a while."

"It sounds delicious. I can hardly wait," Jondalar said, smiling with anticipation, and something more, Ayla thought. "By the way, do you have an extra basket I can use?"

"Yes, but why?"

"I'll tell you when I get back," he said, grinning with his secret.

Ayla turned the roast, then removed the stones and added more hot ones to the soup. While the food was cooking, she sorted through the herbs she had gathered for "Wolf repellent," putting aside the plant she had gathered for her own uses. She mashed up some of the horseradish root in a bit of broth for their meal, then began mashing the rest of the hot root and bruising the other harsh, sharp, strong-smelling herbs she had gathered that morning, trying to develop the most noxious combination of the plants that she could imagine. She thought the hot horseradish would be the most effective, but the strong camphor smell of the artemisia could be very helpful, too.

But the plant she had put aside occupied her thoughts. I'm glad I found it, she was thinking. I know I don't have enough of the herbs I need for my morning tea to last for the whole Journey. I'm going to have to find more along the way to make sure I don't have a baby, especially being with Jondalar so much. She smiled at the thought.

I'm sure that's how babies get started, no matter what people say about spirits. I think that's why men want to put their organs in that place where babies come from, and why women want them to. And why the Mother made that Her Gift of Pleasure. The Gift of Life is from Her, too, and She wants Her children to enjoy making new life, especially since giving birth is not easy. Women might not want to give birth if the Mother hadn't made the starting of them Her Gift of Pleasure. Babies are wonderful, but you don't know how wonderful until you have one. Ayla had been privately developing her unorthodox ideas about the conception of life during the winter as she had been learning about Mut, the Great Earth Mother, from Mamut, the old teacher of the Lion Camp, though the original idea had occurred long before.

But Broud wasn't a pleasure for me, she recalled. I hated it when he forced me, but now I'm sure that's how Durc got started. No one believed I would ever have a baby. They thought my Cave Lion totem was too strong for any man's totem spirit to overcome. It surprised everyone. But it only happened after Broud began forcing me, and I could see his look in my baby. He had to be the one that started Durc growing inside me. My totem knew how much I wanted a baby of my own—maybe the Mother did, too. Maybe that was the only way. Mamut said the way we know Pleasures are a Gift from the Mother is that they are so powerful. It's very hard to resist them. He said it is even harder for men than for women.

That's the way it was with that dark red mammoth. All the males wanted her, but she didn't want them. She wanted to wait for her big bull. Is that why Broud wouldn't let me alone? Even though he hated me, the Mother's Gift of Pleasure was more powerful than his hatred?

Maybe, but I don't think he was doing it only for the Pleasures. He could get that from his own mate, or any woman he wanted. I think he knew how much I hated it and that made his Pleasure more. Broud may have started a baby in me—or maybe my Cave Lion let himself be defeated because he knew how much I wanted one—but Broud could only give me his organ. He couldn't give me the Mother's Gift of Pleasures. Only Jondalar did that.

There must be more to Her Gift than just the Pleasures. If She just wanted to give Her children a Gift of Pleasure, why would She put it in that place, where children are born from? A place of Pleasures could be anywhere. Mine aren't exactly where Jondalar's are. His Pleasure comes when he is inside me, but mine is at that other place. When he gives me Pleasure there, everything feels wonderful, inside and all over. Then I want to feel him inside me. I would not want to have my place of Pleasure inside. When I'm very sensitive, Jondalar has to be very gentle, or it can hurt, and giving birth is not gentle. If a woman's place of Pleasure was inside, it would make giving birth much harder, and it's difficult enough as it is.

How does Jondalar always know just what to do? He knew how to give me Pleasures before I knew what they were. I think that big mammoth knew how to give that pretty red one Pleasures, too. I think she made that loud deep sound because he made her feel them, and that's why all her family was so happy for her. Ayla's thoughts were causing tingling sensations and a warming glow. She glanced toward the wooded area where Jondalar had gone, wondering when he'd be back.

But a baby doesn't start every time Pleasures are shared. Maybe spirits are necessary, too. Whether it's the totem spirits of the Clan men, or the essence of a man's spirit that the

Mother takes and gives to a woman, it still starts when a man puts his organ inside and leaves his essence there. That's how She gives a child to a woman, not with spirits, with Her Gift of Pleasure. But She decides which man's essence will start the new life, and when the life will begin.

If the Mother decides, why does Iza's medicine keep a woman from getting pregnant? Perhaps it won't let a man's essence, or his spirit, mix with a woman's. Iza didn't know why it worked, but it does seem to, most of the time.

I would like to let a baby start when Jondalar shares Pleasures with me. I want to have a baby so much, one that's a part of him. His essence or his spirit. But he's right. We should wait. It was so hard for me to have Durc. If Iza hadn't been there, what would I have done? I'd want to be sure there were people around who would know how to help.

I will keep drinking Iza's tea every morning, and I won't say anything. She was right. I shouldn't talk too much about babies starting from a man's organ, either. It made Jondalar so worried when I mentioned it, he thought we'd have to stop having Pleasures. If I can't have a baby yet, at least, I want to have Pleasures with him.

Like those mammoths were having. Is that what that big mammoth was doing? Making a baby start in that dark red one. That was so wonderful, sharing their Pleasures with the herd. I'm so glad we stayed. I kept wondering why she was running away from all those others, but she wasn't interested in them. She wanted to choose her own mate, not go with anyone who wanted her. She was waiting for that big light brown bull, and as soon as he came, she knew he was the one. She couldn't wait, she ran right to him. She had waited long enough. I know how she feels.

Wolf loped into the clearing, proudly holding up an old rotting bone for her to see. He dropped it at her feet and looked up expectantly. "Whew! That smells rotten! Where did you get that, Wolf? You must have found where someone's leavings were buried. I know you love rotten. Maybe this is a good time to see how you like hot and strong," she said. She picked up the bone and spread some of the mixture she had been making on Wolf's prize. Then she threw it into the middle of the clearing.

The young animal eagerly dashed after it, but he sniffed it warily before he picked it up. It still had the wonderful rotten odor he adored, but he wasn't sure about that other strange smell. Finally he snatched it with his mouth. But very quickly he dropped it and began snorting and snuffling and shaking his head. Ayla couldn't help it. His antics were so funny that she laughed out loud. Wolf sniffed the bone again, then backed off and snorted, looking very displeased, and ran toward the spring.

"You don't like that, do you, Wolf? Good! You're not supposed to like it," she said, feeling the laughter bubbling up inside her as she watched. Lapping water didn't seem to help much. He lifted a paw and rubbed it down the side of his face, trying to wipe his muzzle, as though he thought that would get rid of the taste. He was still snorting and huffing and shaking his head as he ran into the woods.

Jondalar crossed his path, and when he reached the glade he found Ayla laughing so hard there were tears in her eyes. "What is so funny?" he asked.

"You should have seen him," she said, still chortling. "Poor Wolf, he was so proud of that rotten old bone he found. He didn't know what happened to it, and he tried everything to get the taste out of his mouth. If you think you can stand the smell of horseradish and camphor, Jondalar, I think I've found a way to keep Wolf away from our things." She held out the wooden bowl she had been using to mix the ingredients. "Here it is. 'Wolf repellent!' "

"I'm glad it works," Jondalar said. He was smiling, too, but the glee that filled his eyes wasn't caused by Wolf. Ayla finally noticed that his hands were behind his back.

"What have you got behind your back?" she asked, suddenly curious.

"Well, it just happens that when I was out looking for wood I found something else. And if you promise to be good, I just might give you some."

"Some what?"

He brought the filled basket in front of him. "Big, juicy, red raspberries!"

Ayla's eyes lit up. "Oh, I love raspberries."

"Don't you think I know it? What do I get for them?" he asked with a twinkle in his eye.

Ayla looked up at him and, walking toward him, smiled, a big beautiful wide smile that filled her eyes and beamed her love for him, and the warmth she had been feeling, and her delight because he wanted to give her a surprise.

"I think I just got it," he said, letting out the breath he

realized he'd been holding. "Oh, Mother, you are beautiful when you smile. You're beautiful all the time, but especially when you smile."

Suddenly he was consciously aware of her, aware of every feature and detail. Her long, thick, dark blond hair, gleaming with highlights where the sun had lightened it, was held back out of her way with a thong. But it had a natural wave and loose strands that had escaped the leather binding curled around her tanned face; one fell down her forehead in front of her eyes. He restrained an urge to reach out and move it aside.

She was tall, a good match for his own six-foot, six-inch frame, and the lithe, flat, wiry muscles of real physical strength were sharply defined in her long arms and legs. She was one of the strongest women he'd ever met; as physically powerful as many men he knew. The people who had raised her were endowed with an appreciably greater bodily strength than the taller but lighter-weight people she was born to, and though Ayla was not considered particularly strong when she lived with the Clan, she had developed a far greater strength than she normally might have, just to keep up. Coupled with years of observing, tracking, and stalking as a hunter, she used her body with ease and moved with uncommon grace.

The sleeveless leather tunic she wore, belted, over leather leggings fit comfortably, but did not hide her firm, full breasts, which could have seemed heavy but didn't, or her womanly hips that curved back to her well-rounded and firm rear. The laces at the bottom of her leggings were open and she was barefoot. Around her neck was a small, beautifully embroidered and decorated leather pouch, with crane feathers along the bottom, which showed the bumps of the mysterious objects it held.

Hanging from the belt was a knife sheath made of stiff rawhide, the hide of an animal that had been cleaned and scraped but not processed in any way, so that it dried hard in whatever shape it was formed, though a good, thorough wetting could soften it again. She had tucked her sling into the right side of her belt, next to a pouch that held several stones. On the left side was a rather strange, pouchlike object. Though old and worn, it was obvious that it had been made from a whole otter skin, cured with the feet, tail, and head left on. The throat had been cut and the insides removed through the neck, then a cord was strung through slits and pulled tight to close. The flattened head became the flap. It was her medicine bag, the one she had brought with her from the Clan, the one Iza had given her.

She does not have the face of a Zelandonii woman, Jondalar was thinking; they would notice a foreign look, but her beauty was unmistakable. Her large eyes were gray-blue—the color of fine flint, he thought—and wide-spaced, outlined with lashes a shade or two darker than her hair; her eyebrows were somewhat lighter, between the two in color. Her face was heart-shaped, rather wide with high cheekbones, a well-defined jaw, and a narrow chin. Her nose was straight and finely made, and her full lips, curving up at the corners, were opened and pulled back, showing her teeth in a smile that lit up her eyes and announced her sheer pleasure in the very act of smiling.

Though her smiles and laughter had once singled her out as different, and caused her to restrain them, Jondalar loved it when she smiled, and her delight in his laughter, joking, and playfulness magically transformed the already pleasing arrangement of her features; she *was* even more beautiful when she smiled. He suddenly felt overwhelmed by the sight of her and his love for her, and silently thanked the Mother again for giving her back to him.

"What do you want me to give you for the raspberries?" Ayla said. "Tell me, and it's yours."

"I want you, Ayla," he said, his voice suddenly ragged with feeling. He put the basket down, and in an instant he had her in his arms, kissing her with fierce emotion. "I love you. I don't ever want to lose you," he said in a hoarse whisper, kissing her again.

A heady warmth rushed through her and she responded with a feeling as strong. "I love you, too," she said, "and I want you, but can I push the meat away from the fire first? I don't want it to burn while we're . . . busy."

Jondalar looked at her for a moment as though he hadn't understood her words; then he relaxed, gave her a hug, and backed off a step, smiling ruefully. "I didn't mean to be so insistent. It's just that I love you so much, sometimes it's hard to hold. We can wait until later."

She was still feeling her warm, tingling response to his ardor and wasn't sure she was ready to stop, now. She regretted, a little, her comment that had interrupted the moment. "I don't have to put the meat away," she said.

Jondalar laughed. "Ayla, you are an unbelievable woman," he said, shaking his head and smiling. "Do you have any idea how remarkable you are? You're always ready for me, any time I want you. You always have been. Not just willing to go along, whether you feel like it or not, but right there, ready to interrupt anything, if that's what I want."

"But, I want you, whenever you want me."

"You don't know how unusual that is. Most women want some coaxing, and if they're in the middle of doing something, most are not willing to be interrupted."

"The women I grew up with were always ready whenever a man gave her the signal. You gave me your signal, you kissed me and let me know you wanted me."

"Maybe I'll be sorry I said this, but you can refuse, you know." His forehead wrinkled with the effort of trying to explain. "I hope you don't think you have to be ready every time I am. You aren't living with the Clan anymore."

"You don't understand," Ayla said, shaking her head, trying just as hard to make him understand. "I don't think I have to be ready. When you give me your signal, I am ready. Maybe it's because that's how women of the Clan always behaved. Maybe it's because you were the one who taught me how wonderful it is to share Pleasures. Maybe it's because I love you so much, but when you give me your signal, I don't think about it, I feel it inside. Your signal, your kiss that tells me you want me, makes me want you."

He was smiling again, with relief and pleasure. "You make me ready, too. Just looking at you." He bent his head to her, and she reached up to him, molding herself against him as he pressed her tight.

He restrained the impetuous eagerness he felt, though an extraneous feeling of pleasure that he could still feel so eager for her crossed his mind. Some women he'd tired of after a single experience, but with Ayla it always seemed new. He could feel her firm strong body against his, and her arms around his neck. He slid his hands forward and held the sides of her breasts as he bent farther to kiss the curve of her neck.

Ayla removed her arms from around his neck and began to untie her belt, dropping it and all the implements attached to it to the ground. Jondalar reached under her tunic, lifting it as he found the round shapes with the hard, upright nipples.

He lifted the tunic farther, exposing a dark pink areola surrounding the raised and sensitive node. Feeling the warm fullness in his hand, he touched the nipple with his tongue, then took it in his mouth and pulled in.

Tingling strings of fire raced to the place deep within as a small moan of pleasure escaped her lips. She could hardly believe how ready she was. Like the dark red mammoth, she felt as though she had been waiting all day and could hardly wait another moment. A fleeting picture of the big russet bull, with his long, curved organ, flashed through her mind. Jondalar let go, and she took hold of the neck opening of her tunic and pulled it over her head in one smooth motion.

He caught his breath at seeing her, caressed her smooth skin, and reached for both full breasts. He fondled one hard nipple, squeezing and rubbing, while he suckled and pulled and nibbled on the other. Ayla felt delightful shocks of excitement, and she closed her eyes as she gave herself up to them. When he stopped the delicious caressing and nuzzling, she kept her eyes closed, and soon she felt herself being kissed. She opened her mouth to admit a gently exploring tongue. When she put her arms around his neck, she could feel the wrinkles of his leather tunic against her still sensitive nipples.

He moved his hands over the smooth skin of her back and felt the movement of her firm muscles. Her immediate response had added to his own ardor, and his hard, erect manhood strained against his clothing.

"Oh, woman!" he breathed. "How I want you."

"I am ready for you."

"Just let me get these off," he said. He unfastened his belt, then pulled his tunic up his back and over his head. Ayla saw the straining bulge, caressed it, and then began untying his drawstring, while he loosened hers. They both stepped out of their leggings and reached for each other, standing close in a long, slow, sensuous kiss. Jondalar quickly scanned the clearing, looking for a place, but Ayla dropped down to her hands and knees, then looked back up at him with a playful smile.

"Your fur may be yellow, and not light brown, but you are the one I choose," she said.

He smiled back and dropped down behind her. "And your hair isn't deep red, it's the color of ripe hay, but it holds something that is, something like a red flower with many petals. But I don't have a furry trunk to reach you. I'll have to use something else," he said.

He pushed her forward slightly, separated her cheeks to expose her moist, female opening, then bent down to taste her warm salt. He reached his tongue forward and found her hard nodule buried deep in her folds. She gasped and moved to give him easier access, while he prodded and nuzzled, then dipped deep into her inviting opening to taste and explore. He always loved to taste of her.

Ayla was moving on a wave of sensations, hardly aware of anything except the hot pulses of feeling coursing through her. She was more than usually sensitive, and every place he touched or kissed burned its way through her to the ultimate spot deep within that tingled with fire and yearning. She didn't hear her own breath coming faster, or the cries of pleasure she made, but Jondalar did.

He straightened up behind her, moved in closer, and found her deep well with his eager straining manhood. As he started penetrating, she rocked back, pushing herself on him until she took all of him in. He cried out at her unbelievably warm welcome, then, holding her hips, pulled back a ways. He reached around with his hand and found her small hard node of pleasure and stroked it as she pushed back in. His sensation nearly found its peak. He pulled back once more and, sensing her readiness, stroked faster and harder, as he penetrated fully. She cried out her release, and his own voice cried out with hers.

Ayla was lying stretched out, face down in the grass, the pleasant weight of Jondalar on top of her, and felt his breath on the left side of her back. She opened her eyes and, without any desire to move, watched an ant crawling on the ground around a single stem. She felt the man stir and then roll over, keeping his arm around her waist.

"Jondalar, you are an unbelievable man. Do you have any idea how remarkable you are?" Ayla said.

"Haven't I heard those words before? Seems to me I said them to you," he said.

"But they're true for you. How do you know me so well? I get lost inside my own self, just feeling what you do to me."

"I think you were ready."

"That's true. It's always wonderful, but this time, I don't

know. Maybe it was the mammoths. I've been thinking about that pretty red mammoth, and her wonderful big bull—and you—all day.''

"Well, maybe we'll have to play at being mammoths again," he said, with a big smile, as he rolled over on his back.

Ayla sat up. "All right, but right now I'm going to go play in the river before it gets dark"—she bent down and kissed him and tasted herself on him—"after I check on the food."

She ran to the fireplace, turned the bison roast again, took out the cooking stones and added a couple more from the dying fire that were still hot, put a few pieces of wood in the flames, and ran toward the river. It was cold when she splashed in, but she didn't mind. She was used to cold water. Jondalar soon joined her, carrying a large, soft buckskin hide. He put it down and entered more carefully, finally taking a deep breath and plunging in. He came up pushing his hair out of his eyes.

"That's cold!" he said.

She came up beside him and, with a mischievous smile, splashed him. He splashed her back, and a noisy water fight ensued. With one last splash, Ayla bounded out of the water, grabbed the soft hide, and began to dry herself. She handed it to Jondalar when he emerged from the river, then hurried back to the campsite and quickly dressed. She was ladling the soup into their personal bowls as Jondalar walked up from the river.

5

The last rays of the summer sun gleamed through the branches of the trees as it dropped over the edge of the high ground to the west. Smiling at Jondalar with contentment, Ayla reached into her bowl for the last ripe raspberry and popped it in her mouth. Then she got up to clean up and arrange things for a quick and easy departure in the morning.

She gave Wolf the leftovers from their bowls and put cracked and parched grains—the wild wheat, barley, and goosefoot seeds that Nezzie had given her when they left—into the warm soup and left it at the edge of the firepit. The cooked bison roast and tongue from their meal were put into a rawhide parfleche in which she stored food. She folded the large envelope of stiff leather together, tied it with sturdy cords, and suspended it from the center of a tripod of long poles, to keep it out of the reach of night prowlers.

The tapering poles were made from whole trees, tall, thin, straight ones with the branches and bark stripped off, and Ayla carried them in special holders sticking up from the back of Whinney's two pack baskets, just as Jondalar carried the shorter tent poles. The lengthy poles were also used on occasion to make a travois that could be dragged behind the horses to transport heavy or bulky loads. They took the long wooden poles along with them because trees that would make suitable replacements were so rare on the open steppes. Even near rivers there was often little more than tangled brush.

As the twilight deepened, Jondalar added more wood to the fire, then got the slab of ivory with the map scratched on it and brought it back to study it by the firelight. When Ayla finished and sat beside him, he seemed distracted and had that look of anxious concern that she'd often noticed the past few days. She watched him for a while, then put some stones in the fire to boil water for the evening tea it was her custom to make, but instead of the flavorful but innocuous herbs she generally used, she took some packets out of her otter-skin medicine bag. Something calming might be helpful, maybe feverfew or columbine root, in a woodruff tea, she thought, though she wished she knew what the problem was. She wanted to ask him but wasn't sure if she should. Finally she made a decision.

"Jondalar, do you remember last winter when you weren't sure how I felt, and I wasn't sure how you felt?" she said.

He had been so deeply immersed in his thoughts that it took a few moments before he comprehended her question. "Of course I remember. You don't have any doubts how much I love you, do you? I don't have any doubts about your feelings for me."

"No, I don't have any doubts about that, but misunderstandings can be about many things, not just if you love me, or if I love you, and I don't want to let anything like last winter ever happen again. I don't think I could stand to have any more problems just because we didn't talk about it. Before we left the Summer Meeting, you promised to tell me if anything was bothering you. Jondalar, something is bothering you, and I wish you would tell me what it is."

"It's nothing, Ayla. Nothing you have to worry about."

"But it's something you have to worry about? If something is worrying you, don't you think I should know about it?" she said. She took two small tea holders, each woven out of split reeds into a fine mesh, out of a wicker container in which she kept various bowls and utensils. She paused for a moment, considering, then selected the dried leaves of feverfew and woodruff, added to chamomile for Jondalar, and just the chamomile for herself, and filled the tea holders. "If it concerns you, it must concern me, too. Aren't we traveling together?"

"Well, yes, but I'm the one who made the decision, and I don't want to upset you unnecessarily," Jondalar said, getting up for the waterbag, which was hanging from a pole near the entrance to the tent that was set back a few paces from the fireplace. He poured a quantity of liquid into a small cooking bowl and added the hot stones.

"I don't know if it's necessary or not, but you are already upsetting me. Why not tell me the reason?" She put the tea holders into their individual wooden cups, poured steaming water over them, and put them aside to steep.

Jondalar picked up the marked piece of mammoth tusk and looked at it, wishing it would tell him what lay ahead and whether he was making the right decision. When it was just his brother and him, it didn't matter too much. They were on a Journey, an adventure, and whatever came along was part of it. He wasn't sure, then, if they would ever return; he wasn't even sure if he wanted to. The woman he was forbidden to love had chosen a path that led even farther away, and the one he was expected to mate was . . . just not the one he wanted. But this Journey was different. This time, he was with a woman he loved more than life itself. He not only wanted to get back home, but he wanted to get her there, and safely. The more he thought about the possible dangers they might encounter along the way, the more he imagined even greater ones, but his vague worries were not something he could easily explain.

"I'm just worried about how long this Journey will take. We need to reach that glacier before the end of winter," he said.

"You told me that before," she said. "But why? What will happen if we don't reach it by then?" she asked.

"The ice starts to melt in spring and it becomes too dangerous to attempt a crossing."

"Well, if it's too dangerous, then we won't attempt it. But if we can't cross it, what do we do then?" she asked, pushing him to think about alternatives he had avoided thinking about. "Is there any other way to go?"

"I'm not sure. The ice we have to cross is just a small plateau glacier that's on a highland north of the great mountains. There is land to the north of it, but no one ever goes that way. It would take us even more out of our way, and it's cold. They say the northern ice is closer there, it dips south in that region. The land between the high mountains of the south and the great ice of the north is the coldest anywhere. It never gets warm, not even in summer," Jondalar said.

"But isn't it cold on that glacier you want to cross?"

"Of course, it's cold on the glacier, too, but it's a shorter way, and on the other side it's only a few days to Dalanar's Cave." Jondalar put down the map to take the cup of hot tea Ayla was handing him, and he stared into the steaming contents for a while. "I suppose we could try a northern route around the highland glacier, if we had to, but I would not want to. That's flathead country, anyway," Jondalar tried to explain.

"You mean people of the Clan live north of that glacier we're supposed to cross?" Ayla asked, stopping just as she was taking the tea holder out of her cup. She was feeling a strange mixture of dread and excitement.

"I'm sorry. I guess I should call them Clan people, but they are not the same as the ones you knew. They live very far from here, you would not believe how far. They are not the same at all."

"But they are, Jondalar," Ayla said, then took a sip of the hot, flavorful liquid. "Maybe their everyday language and ways might be a little different, but all Clan people have the same memories, at least the older memories. Even at the Clan Gathering, everyone knew the ancient sign language that is used to address the spirit world, and spoke to each other with it," Ayla said.

"But they don't want us in their territory," Jondalar said. "They already let us know that when Thonolan and I happened to be on the wrong side of the river."

"I'm sure that's true. People of the Clan don't like to be around the Others. So, if we can't cross the glacier when we get there, and we can't go around it, then what do we do?" Ayla asked, going back to the original problem. "Can't we wait until the glacier is safe to cross again?"

"Yes. I suppose we'd have to, but it might be almost a year until the next winter."

"But if we waited a year, then we could make it? Is there a place we could wait?"

"Well, yes, there are people we could stay with. The Losadunai have always been friendly. But I want to get home, Ayla," he said, with a tone of such anguish that it made her realize just how important it was to him. "I want us to get settled."

"I want to get settled, too, Jondalar, and I think we should do everything we can to try to get there while it's still safe to cross the glacier. But if it's too late, it doesn't mean we won't get back to your home. It only means a longer wait. And we would still be together."

"That's true," Jondalar said, acquiescing but not happy. "I guess it wouldn't be so bad if we did get there late, but I don't want to wait around for a whole year," he said, and then his frown tightened. "And maybe if we went the other way, we would get there in time. It's still not too late."

"There is another way to go?"

"Yes, Talut told me we could go around the north end of the mountain range we'll be coming to. And Rutan of Feather Grass Camp said the route was northwest of here. I've been thinking that maybe we should go that way, but I had hoped to see the Sharamudoi once more. If I don't see them now, I'm afraid I never will, and they live around the south end of the mountains, along the Great Mother River," Jondalar explained.

Ayla nodded, thinking, Now I understand. "The Sharamudoi are the people you lived with for a while; your brother mated a woman of those people, right?"

"Yes, they are like family to me."

"Then of course we must go south so you can visit them one last time. They are people you love. If it means we may not get to the glacier in time, then we'll wait until the next season for crossing. Even if it means waiting another year before we reach your home, don't you think it would be worth it to see your other family again? If part of the reason you want to go home is to tell your mother about your brother, don't you think the Sharamudoi would like to know what happened to him? They were his family, too."

Jondalar frowned, then brightened. "You're right, Ayla. They would want to know about Thonolan. I've been so worried about whether I made the right decision, I just didn't think it through." He smiled his relief.

Jondalar watched the flames dancing over the blackened sticks of wood, leaping and cavorting in their short-lived joy as they beat back the encroaching dark. He sipped his tea, still thinking about the long Journey ahead of them, but he didn't feel quite as anxious about it. He looked over at Ayla. "It was a good idea to talk it over. I guess I'm still not used to having someone around that I can talk to about . . . things. And I think we can make it in time or I wouldn't have decided to go this way in the first place. It will make a longer trip, but at least I know this route. I don't know the northern way."

"I think you made the right decision, Jondalar. If I could, if I hadn't been cursed with death, I would visit Brun's clan," Ayla said, then added, so low that he could hardly hear her, "If I could, if I only could, I would go to see Durc one last time." The forlorn, empty sound of her voice made him aware that she was feeling her loss acutely just then.

"Do you want to try to find him, Ayla?"

"Yes, of course I want to, but I can't. It would only cause everyone distress. I was cursed. If they saw me they would think I was an evil spirit. I am dead to them, and there isn't anything I could do or say that would convince them that I am alive." Ayla's eyes seemed to be looking far away, but they were seeing an inner vision, a memory.

"Besides, Durc isn't the baby I left behind. He is getting close to manhood, though I was late in reaching womanhood, for a woman of the Clan. He is my son, and he may lag behind the other boys, too. But soon Ura will be coming to live with Brun's clan—no, it's Broud's clan now," Ayla said, frowning. "This is the summer of the Clan Gathering, so this fall Ura will leave her clan and go to live with Brun and Ebra, and when they are both old enough, she will be Durc's mate." She paused, then added, "I wish I could be there to welcome her, but I would only scare her, and maybe make her think Durc is unlucky, if the spirit of his strange mother won't stay where she belongs in the other world."

"Are you sure, Ayla? I mean it, we'll take the time to look for them, if you want," Jondalar said.

"Even if I wanted to find him," she said, "I wouldn't know where to look. I don't know where their new cave is, and I don't know where the Clan Gathering is. It is not meant for me to see Durc. He is not my son anymore. I gave him to Uba. He is Uba's son now." Ayla looked up at Jondalar. He noticed that tears were threatening. "I knew when Rydag died I would never see Durc again. I buried Rydag in Durc's

carrying cloak, the one I took with me when I left the Clan,
and in my heart, I buried Durc at the same time. I know I
will never see Durc again. I am dead to him, and it's best if
he is dead to me."

The tears were wetting her cheeks, though she seemed
oblivious to them, as though she didn't know they had begun.
"I'm really lucky, you know. Think of Nezzie. Rydag was
a son to her, she nursed him even if she didn't give birth to
him, and she knew she would lose him. She even knew that
no matter how long he lived, he would never have a normal
life. Other mothers who lose their sons can only imagine
them in another world, living with spirits, but I can imagine
Durc here, always safe, always lucky, always happy. I can
think of him living with Ura, having children at his hearth
. . . even if I will never see them." The sob in her voice
finally opened the way to let her grief out.

Jondalar took her in his arms and held her. Thinking of
Rydag made him sad, too. There was nothing anyone could
have done for him, though everyone knew Ayla had tried.
He was a weak child. Nezzie said he always had been. But
Ayla had given him something no one else could. After she
came and started teaching him, and the rest of the Lion
Camp, to talk the way the Clan did, with hand signs, he was
happier than he had ever been. It was the first time in all his
young life that he had been able to communicate with the
people he loved. He could let his needs and wishes be known,
and he could let people know how he felt, especially Nezzie,
who had taken care of him since his real mother died, at his
birth. He could finally tell her that he loved her.

It had been a surprise to the members of the Lion Camp,
but once they realized that he wasn't just a rather clever
animal, without the ability to speak, but instead, a different
kind of person, with a different kind of language, they began
to understand that he was intelligent, and to accept him as a
person. It had been no less a surprise to Jondalar, even though
she had tried to tell him, after he began to teach her to speak
with words again. He had learned the signs along with the
others, and he had come to appreciate the gentle humor and
the depth of understanding in the young boy from the ancient
race.

Jondalar held the woman he loved as she heaved great
sobs in the release of her sorrow. He knew Ayla had held

back her grief over the death of the half-Clan child that Nezzie had adopted, who had reminded her so much of her own son, and understood she was grieving for that son as well.

But it was more than Rydag or Durc. Ayla was grieving for all her losses: for the ones from long ago, her loved ones from the Clan, and for the loss of the Clan itself. Brun's clan had been her family, Iza and Creb had raised her, cared for her, and in spite of her difference, there was a time when she thought of herself as Clan. Though she had chosen to leave with Jondalar because she loved him and wanted to be with him, their talk had made her realize how far away he lived; it would take a year, maybe two years just to travel there. The full understanding of what that meant had finally come to her; she would never return.

She was not only giving up her new life with the Mamutoi, who had offered her a place among them, she was giving up any faint hope she might have had of seeing the people of her clan again, or the son she had left with them. She had lived with her old sorrows long enough so that they had eased a little, but Rydag had died not long before they left the Summer Meeting, and his death was still too fresh, the grief still too raw. The pain of it had brought back the pain of her other losses, and the realization of the distance she would be putting between them had brought the knowledge that the hope of recovering that part of her past would have to die, too.

Ayla had already lost her early life, she had no idea who her real mother was, or who her people were, the ones she had been born to. Except for faint recollections—feelings more than anything—she could not remember anything before the time of the earthquake, or any people before the Clan. But the Clan had banished her; Broud had put the curse of death upon her. To them she was dead and now she came to the full understanding that she had lost that part of her life when they turned her out. From this time on, she would never know where she came from, she would never meet a childhood friend, she would never know anyone, not even Jondalar, who would comprehend the background that made her who she was.

Ayla accepted the loss of her past, except that which lived in her mind and in her heart, but she grieved for it, and she wondered what lay ahead when she reached the end of her

Journey. Whatever awaited her, whatever his people were like, she would have nothing else; only her memories . . . and the future.

Within the wooded glade it was completely black. Not the faintest hint of a silhouette or darker shadow could be discerned against the surrounding background, except for a faint redness from the lingering coals in the fireplace, and the blazing epiphany of stars. With only a slight breeze penetrating the protected grove, they had moved their sleeping furs outside the tent. Ayla lay awake under the starlit sky, staring up at the patterns of constellations and listening to the night sounds: the wind sifting through the trees, the soft liquid running of the river, the *chirk* of crickets, the harsh *harumph* of a bullfrog. She heard a loud plunk and splashing, then the eerie *who-whoing* of an owl, and in the distance, the deep roar of a lion and the loud trumpet of a mammoth.

Earlier Wolf had quivered with excitement at the sound of wolf howls and then run off. Not long afterward she heard wolf song again, and an answering howl much closer. The woman was waiting for the animal to return. When she heard his panting breath—he must have been running, she thought—and felt him snuggle up to her feet, she relaxed.

She had just dozed off when she suddenly found herself wide awake. Alert and tense, she lay still, trying to discover what woke her. First she felt the rumbling, almost silent growl vibrating through her coverings from the warm spot at her feet. Then she heard faint snufflings. Something was in camp with them.

"Jondalar?" she said softly.

"I think the meat is drawing something. It could be a bear, but I think it's more likely to be a wolverine or a hyena," Jondalar replied, his whisper barely audible.

"What should we do? I don't want anything to get our meat."

"Nothing, yet. Whatever it is may not be able to reach it. Let's wait."

But Wolf knew exactly what was nosing around and had no intention of waiting. Wherever they set up camp, he defined it as his territory and took it upon himself to defend it. Ayla felt him leave, and an instant later heard him snarl menacingly. The growling response had an entirely different

tone and seemed to come from higher up. Ayla sat up and
reached for her sling, but Jondalar was already on his feet
with the long shaft of a spear resting on his spear-thrower in
readiness.

"It's a bear!" he said. "I think he's up on his hind legs,
but I can't see a thing."

They heard movement, shuffling sounds from somewhere
between the fireplace and the poles from which the meat was
suspended, then the growling warnings of the animals facing
off. Suddenly, from the other side, Whinney neighed, then,
even louder, Racer voiced his nervousness. There were more
sounds of movement in the dark, and then Ayla heard the
particular excited deep snarling rumble that signaled Wolf's
intention to attack.

"Wolf!" Ayla called out, trying to prevent the dangerous
encounter.

Suddenly, amid vicious snarls, a sonorous bellow rang
out, then a stumbling into the fireplace. Ayla heard the whistle of an object moving rapidly through the air nearby. A
solid *thunk* was followed by a howl, and then the noise of
something crashing through the trees, moving away fast. Ayla
whistled the call she used for Wolf. She did not want him to
follow.

She knelt down to hug the young wolf with relief when
he came to her, while Jondalar built up the fire again. In the
firelight, he saw a trail of blood left behind by the retreating
animal.

"I was sure my spear had found that bear," the man said,
"but I couldn't see where it hit. I'd better track it in the
morning. A wounded bear can be dangerous, and we don't
know who will be using this campsite next."

Ayla came to examine the trail. "I think it's losing a lot
of blood. It may not go far," she said, "but I was worried
about Wolf. That was a big animal. It could have hurt him."

"I'm not sure if Wolf should have attacked like that. He
could have caused that bear to go after someone else, but it
was a brave thing to do, and I'm glad to know he's so quick
to protect you. I wonder what he'd do if anyone ever really
tried to hurt you," Jondalar said.

"I don't know, but Whinney and Racer were anxious
about that bear. I think I'll see how they are."

Jondalar wanted to check on them, too. They found the
horses had moved in close to the fire. Whinney had learned

long ago that the fire made by people usually meant security, and Racer was learning from his own experience, as well as from his dam. They seemed to relax after the comforting words and touches of the people they trusted, but Ayla felt uneasy and knew she'd have trouble going back to sleep. She decided to make herself some calming tea and went into the tent to get her otter-skin medicine bag.

While the cooking stones were heating, she stroked the fur of the worn bag, remembering when Iza gave it to her and recalling her life with the Clan, especially the last day. Why did Creb have to go back into the cave? she thought. He might still be alive, even though he was getting old and weak. But he wasn't weak during that last ceremony the night before, when he made Goov the new Mog-ur. He was strong again, The Mog-ur, just like before. Goov will never be as powerful as Creb was.

Jondalar noticed her pensive mood. He thought she was still thinking about the child who had died and the son she would never see again, and he didn't quite know what to say. He wanted to help but didn't want to intrude. They were sitting together close to the fire, sipping the tea, when Ayla happened to look up at the sky. She caught her breath.

"Look, Jondalar," she said. "In the sky. It's red, like a fire, but high up and far away. What is it?"

"Ice Fire!" he said. "That's what we call it when it's red like that, or sometimes Fires of the North."

They watched the luminous display for a while as the northern lights arced across the sky like gossamer drapes blowing in a cosmic wind. "It has white bands in it," Ayla said, "and it's moving, like streaks of smoke, or white chalky water rippling through it. And other colors, too."

"Star Smoke," Jondalar said. "That's what some people call it, or Star Clouds when it's white. It has different names. Most people know what you mean when you use any name like that."

"Why haven't I seen this light in the sky before, I wonder?" Ayla said, feeling awe, and a touch of fear.

"Maybe you lived too far south. That's why it is also called Fires of the North. I haven't seen it very often and never this strong, or this red, but people who have made northern Journeys claim the farther north you go, the more you see it."

"But you can only go as far north as the wall of ice."

"You can travel north beyond the ice, if you go by water. West of the place where I was born, several days' distance, depending on the season, the land comes to an end at the edge of the Great Waters. It is very salty, and it never freezes, although large chunks of ice are sometimes seen. They say some people have traveled beyond the wall of ice in boats, when they are hunting animals that live in the water," Jondalar said.

"You mean like the bowl boats the Mamutoi used to cross rivers?"

"Like them, I think, but bigger and stronger. I never saw them, and I wasn't sure if I believed the stories until I met the Sharamudoi and saw the boats they make. Many trees grow along the Mother River, near their Camp, big trees. They make boats out of them. Wait until you meet them. You won't believe it, Ayla. They don't just cross the river, they travel on it, both upstream and downstream in those boats."

Ayla noticed his enthusiasm. He was really looking forward to seeing them again, now that he had resolved his dilemma. But she was not thinking about meeting Jondalar's other people. The strange light in the sky worried her. She wasn't sure why, exactly. It was unnerving and she wished she understood what it meant, but it didn't fill her with fear the way earthly disturbances did. She was terrified of any movements of the earth, especially earthquakes, not just because the shaking of what should be solid earth was frightening in itself, but because they had always signaled drastic, wrenching change in her life.

An earthquake had torn her away from her own people and given her a childhood that was alien to everything she had known, and an earthquake had led to her ostracism from the Clan, or at least given Broud an excuse for it. Even the volcanic eruption far to the southeast that had showered them with fine, powdered ash seemed to have presaged her leaving the Mamutoi, though the choice had been hers and not forced on her. But she didn't know what signs from the sky meant, or even if this was a sign.

"Creb would think a sky like this was a sign of something, I'm sure," Ayla said. "He was the most powerful mog-ur of all the clans, and something like this would make him want to meditate until he understood what it meant. I think Mamut would think it was a sign, too. What do you think, Jondalar? Is it a sign of something? Maybe of something . . . not good?''

"I . . . I don't know, Ayla." He was hesitant to tell her the beliefs of his people that when the northern lights were red, it was often considered a warning, but not always. Sometimes it just presaged something important. "I'm not One Who Serves the Mother. It could be a sign of something good.''

"But this Ice Fire is a powerful sign of something, isn't it?''

"Usually. At least most people think so.''

Ayla mixed a little columbine root and wormwood into her chamomile tea, making a somewhat more than mildly calming drink for herself, but she was uneasy after the bear in their camp and the strange glow in the sky. Even with the sedative, Ayla felt as though sleep was resisting her. She tried every position to fall asleep, first on her side, then her back, then the other side, even her stomach, and she was sure her tossing and turning was bothering Jondalar. When she finally did drop off, her sleep was disturbed by vivid dreams.

An angry roar shattered the silence, and the watching people jumped back with fear. The huge cave bear pushed at the gate to the cage and sent it crashing to the ground. The maddened bear was loose! Broud was standing on his shoulders; two other men were clinging to his fur. Suddenly one was in the monstrous animal's grip, but his agonized scream was cut short when a powerful bear hug snapped his spine. The mog-urs picked up the body and, with solemn dignity, carried it into a cave. Creb, in his bearskin cloak, hobbled in the lead.

Ayla stared at a white liquid sloshing in a cracked wooden bowl. The liquid turned bloodred, and thickened, as white, luminous bands moved in slow ripples through it. She felt an anxious worry, she had done something wrong. There wasn't supposed to be any liquid left in the bowl. She held it to her lips and drained it.

Her perspective changed, the white light was inside her, and she seemed to be growing larger and looking down from high above at stars blazing a path. The stars changed to small flickering lights leading through a long endless cave.

Then a red light at the end grew large, filling her vision, and with a sinking, sickening feeling, she saw the mog-urs sitting in a circle, half-hidden by stalagmite pillars.

She was sinking deeper into a black abyss, petrified with fear. Suddenly Creb was there with the glowing light inside her, helping her, supporting her, easing her fears. He guided her on a strange trip back to their mutual beginnings, through salt water and painful gulps of air, loamy earth and high trees. Then they were on the ground, walking upright on two legs, walking a great distance, going west toward a great salty sea. They came to a steep wall that faced a river and a flat plain, with a deep recess under a large overhanging section; it was the cave of an ancient ancestor of his. But as they approached the cave, Creb began fading, leaving her.

The scene grew hazy, Creb was fading faster, was nearly gone, and she felt panicky. "Creb! Don't go, please don't go!" she called out. She scanned the landscape, searching desperately for him. Then she saw him at the top of the cliff, above his ancestor's cave, near a large boulder, a long, slightly flattened column of rock that tilted over the edge, as though frozen in place as it was about to fall. She called out again, but he had faded into the rock. Ayla felt desolate; Creb was gone and she was alone, aching with sorrow, wishing she had something of his to remember, something to touch, to hold, but all she had was an overwhelming sorrow. Suddenly she was running, running as fast as she could; she had to get away, she had to get away.

"Ayla! Ayla! Wake up!" Jondalar said, shaking her.

"Jondalar," she said, sitting up. Then, still feeling the desolation, she clung to him, as tears fell. "He's gone . . . Oh, Jondalar."

"It's all right," he said, holding her. "It must have been a terrible dream. You were shouting and crying. Do you think it would help if you told me?"

"It was Creb. I dreamt about Creb, and that time at the Clan Gathering when I went into the cave and those strange things happened. For a long time afterward, he was very upset with me. Then, just as we were finally getting back together, he died, before we could even talk very much. He told me Durc was the son of the Clan. I never was sure what he meant. There was so much I wish we could have talked about, so much I wish I could ask him now. Some people just thought of him as the powerful Mog-ur, and his missing eye and arm made him seem ugly and more frightening. But they didn't know him. Creb was wise and kind. He understood the spirit world, but he understood people, too. I wanted to talk to him in my dream, and I think he was trying to talk to me."

"Maybe he was. I never could understand dreams," Jondalar said. "Are you feeling better?"

"I'm all right now," Ayla said, "but I wish I knew more about dreams."

"I don't think you should go looking for that bear alone," Ayla said after breakfast. "You're the one who said a wounded bear could be dangerous."

"I'll be watchful."

"If I go with you, both of us can be watchful, and staying at the campsite won't be any safer. The bear could come back while you're gone."

"That's true. All right, come along."

They started into the woods, following the bear's trail. Wolf decided to track the bear and plunged ahead through the underbrush, heading upstream. They had traveled less than a mile when they heard a commotion ahead, snarls and growls. Hurrying ahead, they found Wolf, his bristles raised, a low growl deep in his throat, but holding his head low and his tail between his legs, staying well back from a small pack of wolves who were standing guard over the dark brown carcass of the bear.

"At least we don't have to worry about a dangerous wounded bear," Ayla said, holding her spear and thrower ready.

"Just a pack of dangerous wolves." He was also standing braced to hurl his spear. "Did you want some bear meat?"

"No, we have enough meat. I don't have room for more. Let's leave that bear to them."

"I don't care about the meat, but I wouldn't mind having the claws and the big teeth," Jondalar said.

"Why don't you take them? They are yours by right. You killed the bear. I can chase the wolves away with my sling long enough for you to get them."

Jondalar didn't think it was something he would have

tried by himself. The idea of driving a pack of wolves away from meat they had claimed as theirs seemed a dangerous thing to do, but he remembered her actions of the day before, chasing away the hyenas. "Go ahead," he said, taking out his sharp knife.

Wolf became very excited when Ayla started to throw stones and chase the wolf pack, and he stood guard over the bear carcass as Jondalar quickly cut away the claws. The teeth were somewhat harder to dig out of the jaws, but the man soon had his trophies. Ayla was watching Wolf, smiling. As soon as his "pack" had chased away the wild pack, his entire manner and posture changed. He was holding his head up, his tail straight back, in the stance of a dominant wolf, and his snarl was more aggressive. The pack's leader was watching him closely and seemed close to challenging him.

After they relinquished the bear carcass to the pack again and were walking away, the pack leader threw back his head and howled. It was deep-voiced and powerful. Wolf lifted his head and howled in return, but his song lacked the resonance. He was younger, hardly even full grown, and it showed in his tone.

"Come on, Wolf. That one's bigger than you, not to mention older and wiser. He'd have you on your back in a heartbeat or two," Ayla said, but Wolf howled again, not in challenge, but because he was in a community of his kind.

The other wolves of the pack joined in until Jondalar felt surrounded by a chorus of yips and howls. Then, just because she felt like it, Ayla lifted her head and howled. It sent a shiver down the man's back and raised gooseflesh. To his ear, it was a perfect imitation of the wolves. Even Wolf cocked his head toward her, then voiced another long wail of more confident tones. The other wolves answered in kind and soon the woods were again filled with the spine-tingling, beautiful wolf song.

When they got back to camp, Jondalar cleaned up the bear claws and canine teeth, while Ayla packed Whinney, and he was still packing, not quite ready to go when she was done. She was leaning against the mare, absently scratching her and feeling the comfort of her presence, when she noticed that Wolf had found another rotten old bone. This time he kept to the far edge of the glade, growling playfully with his rank prize, keeping an eye on the woman, but making no attempt to bring it to her.

"Wolf! Come here, Wolf!" she called. He dropped his bone and came to her. "I think it's time to begin teaching you something new," she said.

She wanted him to learn to stay in one place when she told him to, even if she went away. It was a command that she felt would be important for him to learn, though she feared he would be a long time in the learning. Judging from the reception they had received thus far from people they had met, and Wolf's reaction, she worried about him going after strangers from another "pack" of humans. Ayla had once promised Talut that she would kill the wolf herself if he ever hurt anyone at Lion Camp, and she still felt it was her responsibility to make sure that the carnivorous animal she had brought into close contact with people would not harm anyone. Beyond that, she worried about his safety. His threatening approach immediately caused a defensive reaction, and she feared that some frightened hunter might try to kill the strange wolf that seemed to be threatening his Camp, before she could prevent it.

She decided to begin by tying him to a tree and telling him to stay there while she walked away, but the rope around his neck was too loose, and he slipped his head out of it. She tied it tighter the next time, but worried that it would choke him if it was too tight. As she had suspected, he whined and howled and jumped up trying to follow her when she backed away. From the distance of several yards, she kept telling him to stay there, signaling a stop motion with her hand.

When he finally settled down, she came back and praised him. After a few more attempts, she saw that Jondalar was ready, and she let Wolf go. It was enough practicing for that day, but after struggling to untie the knots Wolf had stretched tighter with his straining against them, she wasn't pleased with the rope around his neck. First she'd had to adjust it exactly right, neither too tight nor too loose, and then she found it was difficult to untie the knots. She was going to have to think about that.

"Do you really think you'll be able to teach him not to threaten strangers?" Jondalar asked, after watching the first seemingly unsuccessful attempts. "Didn't you tell me that it's natural for wolves to be mistrustful of others? How can you hope to teach him something that is against his natural inclinations?'' He mounted Racer while she put the rope away, and then she climbed on Whinney's back.

''Is it a natural inclination for that horse to let you ride on his back?'' she asked.

''I don't think that's the same, Ayla,'' Jondalar said as they started out from the camp riding the horses side by side. ''Horses eat grass, they don't eat meat, and I think they are by nature more inclined to avoid trouble. When they see strangers, or something that seems threatening, they want to run away. A stallion may fight another stallion sometimes, or something directly threatening, but Racer and Whinney want to get away from a strange situation. Wolf gets defensive. He's much more ready to fight.''

''He would run away, too, Jondalar, if we'd run with him. He gets defensive because he's protecting us. And, yes, he's a meat eater, and he could kill a man, but he doesn't. I don't think he would unless he thought one of us was threatened. Animals can learn, just like people can. It's not his natural inclination to think of people and horses as his 'pack.' Even Whinney has learned things that she would not have if she lived with other horses. How natural is it for a horse to think of a wolf as a friend? She even had a cave lion for a friend. Is that a natural inclination?''

''Maybe not,'' Jondalar said, ''but I can't tell you how worried I was when Baby showed up at the Summer Meeting and you rode straight up to him on Whinney. How did you know he'd remember you? Or Whinney? Or that Whinney would remember him?''

''They grew up together. Baby . . . I mean Baby . . .''

The word she used meant ''baby'' but it had an odd sound and inflection, unlike any language she and Jondalar usually spoke, a rough, guttural quality, as though spoken from the throat. Jondalar could not reproduce it, could hardly even approximate the sound; it was one of the relatively few spoken words from the language of the Clan. Though she had said it often enough that he recognized it, Ayla had formed the habit of immediately translating any Clan word she happened to use to make it easier. When Jondalar referred to the lion Ayla had raised from a cub, he used the translated form of the name she had given him, but it always struck him as incongruous that a gigantic male cave lion should have the name ''Baby.''

". . . Baby was . . . a cub when I found him, a baby. He hadn't even been weaned. He'd been kicked in the head, by a running deer, I think, and was almost dead. That's why his mother left him. He was like a baby to Whinney, too. She helped me take care of him—it was so funny when they started playing with each other, especially when Baby would sneak up and try to get Whinney's tail. I know there were times when she waved it at him on purpose. Or they'd each grab an end of a hide and try to pull it away from each other. I lost so many hides that year, but they made me laugh."

Ayla's expression turned pensive. "I never really learned to laugh until then. The people of the Clan didn't laugh out loud. They didn't like unnecessary noises, and loud sounds were usually meant for warnings. And that look you like, with teeth showing, that we call a smile? They made it to mean they were nervous, or feeling protective and defensive, or with a certain hand sign as implying a threatening gesture. It wasn't a happy look to them. They didn't like it when I was little if I smiled or laughed, so I learned not to do it very much."

They rode along the river's edge for a distance, on a flat, wide stretch of gravel. "Many people smile when they're nervous, and when they meet strangers," Jondalar said. "It's not meant to be defensive or threatening, though. I think a smile is meant to show that you're not afraid."

Going ahead in single file, Ayla leaned to the side to guide her horse around some brush growing beside a streamlet that was making its way to the river. After Jondalar had developed the halter device that he used to guide Racer, Ayla also started using one to help lead Whinney occasionally, or to tie her to something to keep her in one location, but even when the horse was wearing it, Ayla never used it when she was riding. She had never intended to train the animal when she first got on the mare's back, and the mutual learning process had been gradual and, in the beginning, unconscious. Though once she realized what was happening, the woman did purposely train the horse to do certain things, it was always within the framework of the deep understanding that had grown between them.

"But if a smile is meant to show that you are not afraid, doesn't that mean you think you have nothing to be afraid of? That you feel strong and have nothing to fear?" Ayla said, when they rode abreast again.

"I never really thought about it before. Thonolan always smiled and seemed so confident when he met new people, but he wasn't always as sure as he seemed. He tried to make people think that he wasn't afraid, so I suppose you could say it was a defensive gesture, a way of saying I'm so strong I have nothing to fear from you."

"And isn't showing your strength a way of threatening? When Wolf shows his teeth to strangers, isn't he showing them his strength?" Ayla pressed.

"There may be something about them that is the same, but there is a big difference between a smile of greeting and Wolf baring his teeth and growling."

"Yes, that's true," Ayla conceded. "A smile makes you feel happy."

"Or at least relieved. If you've met a stranger and he smiles back at you, that usually means you've been welcomed, so you know where you stand. Not all smiles are necessarily meant to make you happy."

"Maybe feeling relieved is the beginning of feeling happy," Ayla said. They rode together in silence for a while; then the woman continued. "I think there is something similar about a person smiling in greeting when he is feeling nervous around strangers, and people of the Clan having a gesture in their language of showing their teeth that means they're nervous or implying a threat. And when Wolf shows his teeth to strangers, he's threatening them because he's feeling nervous and protective."

"Then when he shows his teeth to us, to his own pack, it's his smile," Jondalar said. "There are times when I'm convinced he's smiling, and I know he teases you. I'm sure he loves you, too, but the trouble is, it's natural for him to show his teeth and threaten people he doesn't know. If he's protecting you, how are you going to train him to stay where you tell him, if you're not there? How can you teach him not to attack strangers if he decides he wants to?" Jondalar's concern was serious. He wasn't sure that taking the animal with them was such a good idea. Wolf could create a lot of problems. "Remember, wolves attack to get their food; that's the way the Mother made them. Wolf is a hunter. You can teach him many things, but how can you teach a hunter not to be a hunter? Not to attack strangers?"

"You were a stranger when you came to my valley, Jondalar. Do you remember when Baby came back to visit me

and found you there?'' Ayla asked, as they again separated
into single file to start up a gully leading away from the river
toward the highland.

Jondalar felt a flush of heat, not exactly embarrassment,
but a recollection of the strong emotions of that encounter.
He had never been so scared in his life; he had been sure he
was going to die.

It took some time to pick their way up the shallow ravine,
around rocks that washed down during spring floods, and
black-stemmed artemisia brush that burst into life when the
rains came and retreated into dry stalks that appeared dead
when they stopped. He thought about the time Baby came
back to the place where Ayla had raised him and found a
stranger on the broad ledge in front of her small cave.

None of them were small, but Baby was the biggest cave
lion he'd ever seen, nearly as tall as Whinney, and more
massive. Jondalar was still recovering from the mauling that
same lion, or his mate, had given him earlier when he and
his brother had foolishly broached their den. It was the last
thing Thonolan was ever to do. Jondalar was sure he was
seeing his last moments when the cave lion roared and gathered himself to spring. Suddenly Ayla was between them,
holding up her hand in a motion to stop, and the lion stopped!
It would have been comical the way that huge beast pulled
himself up short and twisted around to avoid her, if he hadn't
been so petrified. The next thing he knew, she was scratching
the gigantic cat and playing with him.

"Yes, I remember," he said, when they reached the highland and again rode side by side. "I still don't know how
you made him stop in the middle of that attack on me."

"When Baby was just a cub, he made a game of attacking
me, but when he started to grow, he got too big for me to
play that kind of game with him. He was too rough. I had
to teach him to stop," Ayla explained. "Now I have to teach
Wolf not to attack strangers, and to stay behind if I want him
to. Not only so he won't hurt people, but so they won't hurt
him."

"If anyone can teach him, Ayla, you can," Jondalar said.
She had made her point, and if she could, it would make
Wolf easier to travel with, but he still wondered how much
trouble the wolf might cause them. He had delayed their
crossing the river and chewed up their things, though Ayla
had apparently worked out that problem, too. It wasn't that he

didn't like the animal. He did. It was fascinating to observe a wolf so closely, and it surprised him how friendly and affectionate Wolf was, but he did require extra time, attention, and provisions. The horses took some extra care, but Racer was so responsive to him, and they were a real help. The trip back was going to be difficult enough; they didn't need the added burden of an animal that was almost as worrisome as a child.

A child, that would be a problem, Jondalar thought as he rode. I only hope the Great Earth Mother doesn't give Ayla a child before we get back. If we were already there and settled, it would be different. Then we could think about children. Not that we can do anything about it, anyway, except ask the Mother. I wonder what it would be like to have a small one around?

What if Ayla is right? What if children are started by Pleasures? But we've been together for some time, and there are no signs of children yet. It has to be Doni who puts the baby inside a woman, but what if the Mother decides not to give Ayla a child? She did have one, even if it was mixed. Once Doni gives one, She usually gives more. Maybe it's me. I wonder, can Ayla have a baby that would come from my spirit? Can any woman?

I've shared Pleasures and honored Doni with many. Did any of them ever have a baby that I started? How does a man know? Ranec knew. His coloring was so strong, and his features so unusual, you could see his essence in some of the children at the Summer Meeting. I don't have such strong coloring or features . . . or do I?

What about that time the Hadumai hunters stopped us on the way here? That old Haduma wanted Noria to have a baby with blue eyes like mine, and after her First Rites, Noria told me she would have a son of my spirit, with my blue eyes. Haduma had told her. I wonder if she ever had that baby?

Serenio thought she might have been pregnant when I left. I wonder if she had a child with blue eyes the color of mine. Serenio had one son, but she never had any others after that, and Darvo was almost a young man. I wonder what she'll think of Ayla, or what Ayla will think of her?

Maybe she wasn't pregnant. Maybe the Mother still hasn't forgotten what I did, and it's Her way of telling me I don't deserve a child at my hearth. But She gave Ayla back to me. Zelandoni always told me Doni would never refuse me anything I asked Her, but she warned me to be careful what I asked for, because I would get it, she said. That's why she made me promise not to ask the Mother for her, when she was still Zolena.

Why would anyone ask for something if he didn't want it? I never really understand those who speak to the spirit world. They always have a shadow on their tongue. They used to say Thonolan was a favorite of Doni, when they talked about his flair for getting along with people. But then they say beware of the Mother's favors. If She favors too much, She doesn't want you to be away from Her for too long. Is that why Thonolan died? Did the Great Earth Mother take him back? What does it really mean when they say Doni favors someone?

I don't know if She favors me or not. But now I know Zolena made the right choice when she decided to embrace the zelandonia. It was right for me, too. What I did was wrong, but I would never have made the Journey with Thonolan if she hadn't become Zelandoni, and I would never have found Ayla. Maybe She does favor me, a little, but I don't want to take advantage of Doni's goodness to me. I have already asked Her to get us back safely; I can't ask Her to give Ayla a child of my spirit, especially not now. But I wonder, will she ever have one?

6

Ayla and Jondalar turned away from the river they had been following, veering toward the west in their general southerly route, and traveled across country. They came upon the valley of another large watercourse that was flowing east on its way to joining, somewhat downstream, the one they had left behind. The valley was broad, with a gentle grassy slope leading to a swift river that was racing through the middle of a level floodplain, strewn with stones of various sizes, ranging from large boulders to fine sandy gravel. Except for a few tufts of grass and an occasional flowering herb, the rocky course was bare, scoured of vegetation by the spring deluge.

A few logs, whole trees stripped of leaves and bark, sprawled across the rubbled clearing, while tangled alder brush and shrubs with grayish hairy leaves hovered near the edge. A small herd of giant deer, whose extravagant palmate antlers made the large rack of the moose seem small, were feeding along the outer fringe of woolly willows clustered in the damp lowland near the water.

Wolf was full of high spirits and had been darting under

and around the legs of the horses, particularly Racer. Whinney seemed able to ignore his exuberance, but the stallion was more excitable. Ayla thought the young horse would have responded to Wolf's playfulness in kind if he had been allowed to, but with Jondalar guiding his movement, the wolf's antics only distracted him. The man was not pleased, since it required him to keep a closer control over the horse. His irritation was building up, and he was considering whether he should ask Ayla if she couldn't keep the wolf away from Racer.

Suddenly, much to Jondalar's relief, Wolf dashed away. He had caught the scent of the deer and gone to investigate. The first sight of the long legs of a giant deer was irresistible; Wolf decided it was another tall, four-legged animal for him to play with. But when the stag he approached lowered his head to fend off the charging animal, Wolf halted. The magnificent spreading antlers of the powerful deer were each twelve feet long! The great beast nibbled on the broad-leaf grass at his feet, not unmindful of the carnivore, but indifferent to him, as though he knew he had little to fear from a lone wolf.

Ayla, watching, smiled. "Look at him, Jondalar. Wolf thought that megaceros was another horse he could pester."

Jondalar smiled, too. "He does look surprised. Those antlers are a little more than he expected."

They rode slowly toward the water, understanding without saying so that neither of them wanted to startle the massive deer. They both felt a sense of awe as they neared the enormous creatures that towered over them, even on horseback. With a stately gracefulness, the herd edged away as the people and horses approached, not frightened, but cautious, browsing on the woolly willow leaves as they went.

"They are a little more than I expected, too," Ayla said. "I've never been this close before."

Though only slightly larger than moose in actual physical size, the giant deer, with their magnificent, elaborate antlers, spreading out and up from the tops of their heads, seemed enormous. Each year the fantastic horns were shed and the new pair that grew in to replace them extended to greater lengths and more complexity, eventually reaching twelve feet or more on some old males in a single season. But even when their heads were bare, that greatest member of the deer tribe was huge in comparison with any other of its kind. The

shaggy fur and massive shoulder and neck muscles, which
had developed to support the weight of the immense horns,
contributed to their formidable aspect. Giant deer were animals of the plains. The prodigious antlers were an encumbrance in woodland, and they avoided any trees taller than
brush; some had been known to starve to death, trapped by
their own glorious rack caught in the branches of a tree.

When they reached the river, Ayla and Jondalar stopped
and studied the waterway and the surrounding area to deter-
mine the best place to cross. The river was deep and the
current swift, and large jagged boulders created rapids in
places. They checked the conditions both upstream and downstream, but the nature of the river seemed consistent for some
distance. Finally they decided to try to cross at a place that
seemed relatively free of rocks.

They both dismounted, tied the side pack baskets to the
backs of their horses, and placed inside the foot-coverings
and the warm outerwear they had donned in the chill of the
morning. Jondalar removed his sleeveless shirt, and Ayla
considered stripping entirely so she wouldn't have to worry
about drying her clothes, but a check of the water temperature
with her foot changed her mind. She was used to cold water,
but this fast-moving stream felt as icy as the water she had
left out the night before and found in the morning with a thin
frozen film on top. Even wet, the soft buckskin-leather tunic
and leggings would provide some warmth.

Both the horses were agitated, moving back from the wet
edge with prancing steps, whickering, neighing, and tossing
their heads. Ayla put the halter with the lead rope on Whinney to help guide the horse across the water. Then, sensing
the mare's growing unease, the young woman hugged the
shaggy neck and talked to her with the comforting private
language she had invented when they were together in the
valley.

She had developed it unconsciously, building on the complex signs, but primarily on the few words that were part of
the language of the Clan, and she had added the repetitive
nonsense sounds she and her son had begun to use, to which
she had assigned meaning. It also included horse sounds,
which she had gained a sense of and learned to mimic, an
occasional lion grunt, and even a few bird whistles.

Jondalar turned to listen. Though he was accustomed to
her speaking to the horse that way, he had no idea what she

was saying. She had an uncanny ability to reproduce the
sounds the animals made—she had learned their language
when she lived alone, before he had taught her to speak
verbally again—and he thought the language had a strange,
otherworldly quality.

Racer shifted his feet and tossed his head, squealing anxiously. Jondalar spoke to him in soft tones while he stroked
and scratched him. Ayla watched, noticing how the tall man's
wonderfully sensitive hands had an almost instant calming
effect on the skittish young horse. It pleased her to see the
closeness that had developed between them. Then her
thoughts turned for a moment to the way his hands could
make her feel, and she flushed slightly. He didn't calm her.

The horses were not the only nervous animals. Wolf knew
what was coming and was not anticipating the cold swim.
Whining and pacing up and down the bank, he finally sat
down and pointed his nose up, voicing his complaint in a
mournful howl.

"Come here, Wolf," Ayla said, stooping down to hug
the young animal. "Are you a little frightened, too?"

"Is he going to give us problems again, crossing this
river?" Jondalar said, still feeling annoyed at the wolf for
bothering him and Racer earlier.

"It's not a problem for me. He's just a little nervous, like
the horses are," Ayla said, wondering why Wolf's perfectly
understandable fears seemed to annoy Jondalar, especially
when he was so understanding of the young stallion.

The river was cold, but the horses were strong swimmers,
and once they were coaxed in, they had no problem reaching
the opposite shore, leading the humans as much as being led
by them. Even Wolf was no trouble. He danced and whined
on the bank, advancing on the cold water and retreating a
few times, then finally he plunged in. With his nose held
high, he struck out after the horses that were piled high with
packs and bundles, and the humans swimming alongside.

Once they gained the other side, they stopped to change
and dry off the animals, then continued on their way. Ayla
remembered previous river crossings she had made when she
had traveled alone after leaving the Clan, and she was grateful
for the sturdy horses. Getting from one side to the other of
a river was never easy. At the least, when traveling on foot,
it usually involved getting wet. But with the horses, they

could cross many smaller watercourses with little more than a splash or two, and even big rivers posed far less difficulty.

As they continued traveling southwest, the terrain changed. The hills of the uplands, that were graduating into higher foothills as they approached the mountains to the west, were crossed with the deeply cut narrow valleys of rivers they had to cross. Some days Jondalar felt that they spent so much time going up and down, they made little progress forward, but the valleys offered sheltered campsites out of the wind, and the rivers supplied the necessary water in a land that was otherwise dry.

They stopped at the top of a high hill within the central area of the hilly upland plains that ran parallel to the rivers. A vast panorama commanded their view in all directions. Except for the faint gray shapes of mountains far to the west, the expansive vista was uninterrupted.

Though the windy, arid land could not have been more different, the steppes, spread out before the two riders in a monotone of endless waving grass flowing over low rolling hills, evoked the sea with its featureless regularity. The analogy went deeper. For all the monotonous uniformity, the ancient grassland rippling in the wind was deceptively rich and varied, and like the sea, supported a profuse and exotic array of life. Outlandish creatures, displaying a flourish of biologically costly social adornments in the form of luxurious horns and antlers, shags, ruffs, and humps, shared the great steppes with other animals grown to magnificent size.

The woolly giants, mammoths and rhinoceroses, resplendent in dense double furs—long flowing hair trailing over warm downy underlayers—with thick layers of sustaining fat, flaunted extravagant tusks and exaggerated nose horns. Giant deer, bedecked with stately racks of immense palmate antlers, grazed alongside aurochs, the splendid wild forerunners of herds of placid domestic cattle, which were nearly as huge as the massive bison that sported such enormous horns. Even small animals displayed the size that was the result of the richness of the steppes; there were great jerboas, giant hamsters, and ground squirrels that were among the largest found anywhere.

The extensive grasslands also supported a bounty of other

animals, many with remarkable proportions. Horses, asses, and onagers partitioned space and food on the lowlands; wild sheep, chamois, and ibex divided higher ground. Saiga antelopes raced across the flatlands. Gallery forests along river valleys, or near ponds and lakes, and the occasional wooded steppes and tundra played host to deer of all varieties, from sported fallow and gentle roe deer to elk, red deer, and reindeer—called moose, elk, and caribou when they migrated to other lands. Hares and rabbits, mice and voles, marmots, susliks, and lemmings abounded in huge numbers; toads, frogs, snakes, and lizards had their place. Birds of every shape and size, from large cranes to tiny pipets, added their voice and color. Even insects had a role to play.

The tremendous herds of grazers, as well as the browsers and seed eaters, were culled and kept in check by the ones who ate meat. Carnivores, who were more adaptable in their range of environment and could live wherever their prey lived, also reached tremendous size because of the abundance and quality of their food supply. Gigantic cave lions, up to twice the size of their later southern descendants, hunted the young and old of even the largest grazers, though a woolly mammoth in its prime had little to fear. The usual choice of the great cats were the huge bison, aurochs, and deer, while packs of oversize hyenas, wolves, and dholes selected from more middle-size game. They divided the plentiful prey with lynxes, leopards, and small wildcats.

Monstrous cave bears, essentially vegetarian and only limited hunters, were twice the weight of the smaller brown or black bears, which also preferred an omnivorous diet that often included grass, though the white bear of the icy coasts subsisted on meat from the sea. Vicious wolverines and steppe polecats took their toll of smaller animals, including the vast number and variety of rodents, as did the sinuous sables, weasels, otters, ferrets, martens, minks, and stoats that became ermines in snow. Some foxes also turned white, or the rich gray called blue, to match the winter scenery and hunt in stealth. Tawny and golden eagles, falcons, hawks, crows, and owls snatched unsuspecting, or unlucky, small prey on the wing, while vultures and black kites cleaned up the leavings of others on the ground.

The great diversity and size of the animals that lived on those ancient steppes, and their bonus of exaggerated and richly enhanced appendages and supplementary growths, could only be sustained by an environment of exceptional quality. Yet it was a frigid, sere, demanding land surrounded by mountain-high barriers of ice and bleak oceans of frozen water. It seemed a contradiction that such a harsh environment could provide the richness that was necessary for the lavish growth of the animals but, in fact, the environment was entirely right for it. The cold, dry climate fostered the growth of grass and inhibited the growth of trees.

Trees, such as oaks or spruces, are luxuriant growths, but they take a long time and ample moisture to mature. Woodlands may feed and support a range of other plants and animals, but trees need resources to maintain themselves, and they do not encourage the development of multitudes of large animals. A few animals may eat nuts or fruits and others may browse leaves, or even twig tips from a tree, but bark and wood are largely inedible, and grow back slowly once destroyed. The same energy and soil nutrients put into an equal weight of grass will feed many, many more, and the grass will constantly renew itself. A forest may be the quintessential example of rich, productive vegetable life, but it was grass that gave rise to the extraordinary and abundant animal life, and it was the complex grassland that supported and maintained it.

Ayla was feeling uncomfortable, but she wasn't sure why. It was nothing specific, just a strange, edgy feeling. Before they started down the high hill, they had watched storm clouds gathering over the mountains to the west, seen flashes of sheet lightning, and heard distant rolling thunder. The sky above, however, was a clear, deep blue, with the sun still high, though past the zenith. It was unlikely to rain nearby, but she didn't like thunder. The deep rolling roar always reminded her of earthquakes.

Maybe it's just that my moon time should start in a day or two, Ayla thought, trying to dismiss the feeling. I had better keep my leather straps handy, and the mouflon wool Nezzie gave me. She told me it was the best padding to use when traveling, and she was right. The blood washes right out in cold water.

Ayla had not seen onagers before, and with her thoughts turned inward, she wasn't paying attention as they proceeded down the slope. She thought the animals she saw in the distance were horses. But when they got closer, she began to notice differences. They were slightly smaller, their ears were longer, and their tails were not a flowing tress of many hair strands, but a shorter, thin shaft covered with the same kind of hair that was on their bodies, with a darker tuft at the end. Both kinds of animals had erect manes, but the onagers' were more uneven. The coats of the animals in the small herd were a light reddish brown on their backs and sides, and a much paler, almost white coloring underneath, even on their legs and muzzles, but they had a dark stripe along their backbones, plus another across their shoulders, and several bands of the darker shade on their legs.

The young woman compared them with the general coloring of the horses. Though her dun coat was a shade lighter than average, with a rich golden yellow tone, most steppe horses were a similar neutral grayish-brown shade and generally resembled Whinney. Racer's deep brown color was unusual for his breed. The mare's stiff thick mane was a dark gray, and the color extended down the middle of her back to her long, loose tail. Her lower legs were dark, too, almost black, and above that, only the bare suggestion of stripes showed on her upper legs. The bay stallion's color was too dark to show the black feral stripe that ran down his backbone very well, but his black mane, tail, and legs followed the typical pattern.

To someone who was knowledgeable about horses, the body conformation of the animals ahead was somewhat different, as well, yet they did seem to be horses. Ayla noticed that even Whinney showed more interest than she usually did at the sight of other animals, and the herd had stopped grazing and was watching them. Wolf was interested, too, and had assumed a stalking posture, ready to take out after them, but Ayla signaled him to stay. She wanted to observe them. One of the onagers suddenly voiced a sound and the woman noticed another difference. It wasn't a neigh, or a whinny, but rather a more strident braying sound.

Racer tossed his head and neighed an answer, then gingerly stretched his head forward to sniff at a large pile of fresh dung. It looked and smelled like horse dung to Ayla, when she rode up alongside Jondalar. Whinney nickered and sniffed the pile, too, and as the odor wafted up to her a while longer, Ayla thought she detected a faint undercurrent of something else, perhaps from somewhat different food preferences.

"Are those horses?" she asked.

"Not exactly. They're like horses, the way elk are like reindeer, or moose are like megaceroses. They're called onagers," Jondalar explained.

"I wonder why I haven't seen them before."

"I don't know, but they do seem to like this kind of country," he said, inclining his head in a gesture that indicated the rocky hills and sparse vegetation of the arid, semidesert upland plains they were riding through. Onagers were not a cross between horses and asses, though they appeared to be, but rather a unique and viable species, with some characteristics of both, and extremely hardy. They could subsist on even coarser food than horses, including bark, leaves, and roots.

When they got closer to the herd, Ayla noticed a pair of young ones and couldn't help smiling. They reminded her of Whinney when she was young. Just then the wolf yelped to get her attention.

"All right, Wolf. If you want to chase those . . . onagers"—she said the unfamiliar word slowly, getting used to the sound—"go ahead." She was pleased with the progress she was making in training him, but he didn't like staying in one place for long. He was still too full of puppyish enthusiasm and curiosity. Wolf yelped and bounded after the herd. With a startled burst, they raced away with a sustained speed that soon left the young, would-be hunter behind. He caught up with Ayla and Jondalar as they were approaching a broad valley.

Though the valleys of rivers carrying the silt of slowly eroding mountains still cut across their path, the land was falling off gradually toward the basin of the Great Mother River delta and Beran Sea. As they were traveling south, the summer was deepening, and warm winds caused by the passage of atmospheric depressions across the sea added to the increasing temperatures of the season, and to weather disturbances.

The two travelers no longer wore outer clothes, not even when they first got up. Ayla thought the cool, crisp air of early morning was the best time of the day. But the late afternoon was hot, hotter than usual, she thought, wishing for a nice cool stream to swim in. She glanced at the man riding a few paces ahead. He was bare to the waist, and barelegged, wearing only a loincloth. His long blond hair, pulled back into a thong at the nape of his neck, had lighter streaks from the sun, and was darker where the sweat had made it wet.

She caught glimpses of his clean-shaven face and liked being able to see his strong jaw and well-defined chin, though she still had a residual feeling that it was odd to see a grown man without a beard. He had explained to her once that he liked to let his beard grow in winter, to warm his face, but he always cut it off in summer, because it was cooler. He used a special sharp flint blade, one that he knapped himself and replaced when needed, to shave himself every morning.

Ayla, too, had stripped down to a short garment, patterned after Jondalar's loincloth. Both were basically a length of soft leather, worn between the legs, and held on with a cord around the waist. His garment was worn with the loose end at the back tucked inside, and the one in front left out in a short flap. Hers was also held on with a cord around the waist, but she started with a longer piece, and she wore both loose ends out, pulled together at the sides, to hang down in a sort of apron in front and back. The effect was of a short skirt open at the sides. With the soft porous leather to sit on, riding for long periods on the back of a sweaty horse was more comfortable, though the buckskin across the animal's back helped, too.

Jondalar had used the high hill to check their location. He was pleased with their progress, which made him feel easier about the Journey. Ayla noticed that he seemed more relaxed. Part of it, she knew, was his increasing skill in managing the young stallion. Though he had ridden the animal frequently before, traveling on horseback gave him the constant association that developed an understanding of Racer's character, preferences, and habits, and allowed the horse to learn his. Even his muscles had learned to adjust to the animal's motion and his seat was more comfortable, both for him and the stallion.

But Ayla thought his easy, relaxed riding indicated more than greater facility on horseback. There was less tension in his movements, and she sensed that his concern had diminished. Though she couldn't see his face, she guessed that his frown of worry would be gone, and that he might be in a

mood for smiling. She loved it when he smiled and felt playful. She watched the way his muscles moved beneath his
tanned skin as he matched Racer's gait with a gentle up-and-
down motion, and she felt a glow of warmth that was not
from the temperature . . . and smiled to herself. She loved
watching him.

Toward the west, they could still see the mountains rising
up purple in the distance, capped by glistening white that
pierced the dark clouds hanging below. They seldom saw the
icy peaks, and Jondalar was enjoying the rare pleasure. Most
often they were hidden by low misty clouds that clung like
soft white furs cloaking a sparkling secret, opening just
enough to reveal tempting glimpses and make them more
desirable.

He was feeling warm, too, and wished they were closer
to those snow-tipped mountaintops, at least as close as the
Sharamudoi lodges. But when he noticed the glint of water
in the valley below and glanced at the sky to check the position of the sun, though it was earlier than usual, he decided
they might as well stop and make camp. They were making
good time, traveling faster than he had estimated, and he
didn't know how long it would take to reach the next source
of water.

The slope supported a rich growth of grass, primarily
feather grasses, fescues, and herbs mixed with varieties of
quick-seeding annual grasses. The thick loess subsoil, which
supported a black fertile loam that was high in the humus of
decaying plantlife, even encouraged trees, which, except for
the occasional scrub pine struggling for subsoil water, were
unusual for the steppes in this vicinity. An open mixed woods
of birch and larch, conifers that dropped their needles in winter, marched downhill with them, with alder and willow filling in lower down. At the bottom of the slope, where the land
leveled out some distance from the gurgling stream, Ayla was
surprised to see an occasional dwarfed oak, beech, or linden
in some of the open places. She had not seen many large-
leaf trees since she left the cave of Brun's clan, on the well-
watered southern end of the peninsula that jutted into Beran
Sea.

The small river weaved its way around brush as it meandered across the level valley floor, but one loop edged close
to some tall, thin willows that were an extension of the more
thickly forested slope of the other side. They usually liked to

cross a river before making camp, so they wouldn't have to get wet when they started in the morning, and they decided to camp near the willows. They rode downstream, looking for a place to cross, and found a wide, stony, fordable crossing, then rode back.

While they were setting up the tent, Jondalar found himself watching Ayla, conscious of her warm, tanned body, and thinking how lucky he was. Not only was she beautiful—her strength, her supple grace, the assurance of her movements, all pleased him—but she was a good traveling companion, contributing equally to their well-being. Though he felt responsible for her safety and wanted to protect her from harm, there was comfort in knowing he could rely on her. In some ways, traveling with Ayla was like traveling with his brother. He had felt protective toward Thonolan, too. It was his nature to be concerned for those he cared about.

But only in some ways. When the young woman lifted her arms to shake out the ground cover, he became aware that the skin was lighter on the underside of her rounded breasts, and he had an urge to compare the tone with her browned arm. He didn't think that he might be staring, but he did notice when she stopped working and turned toward him. When he caught her eye, Ayla smiled slowly.

Suddenly he felt an urge to do more than compare skin tones. It pleased him to know that if he wanted to share Pleasures with her right then, she would be willing. There was comfort in that, too. It wasn't as necessary to seize every opportunity. The feeling was as strong, but the urgency was less, and sometimes waiting a bit made it better. He could think about it and enjoy the anticipation. Jondalar smiled back.

After they set up camp, Ayla wanted to explore the valley. It was unusual to find such a thickly wooded area in the middle of the steppes, and she was curious. She hadn't seen such vegetation for years.

Jondalar wanted to explore, too. After their experience with the bear at the campsite near the grove of trees, he wanted to check for tracks or other indications of the animals that might be in the vicinity. With Ayla taking along her sling and collecting basket, and Jondalar his spear-thrower with a couple of spears, they headed into the willows. They left the horses to graze, but Wolf was eager to accompany them. The woods were an unusual place for him, too, full of fascinating scents.

Back from the water, the willow trees gave way to alder, then birch mixed with larch became common, and there were some good-size pines. Ayla eagerly picked a few cones when she saw they were stone pines, for the large, delicious pine nuts they contained. But more unusual to her were the occasional large-leafed trees. In one area, still on the level valley plain but near the bottom of the slope that led to the open grassland above, was a pure stand of beech trees.

Ayla looked them over carefully, comparing them with her memory of similar trees that grew near the cave where she had lived as a child. The bark was smooth and gray, and the leaves were oval narrowing to a point at the end with shallow sharp teeth around the edge, and silky white underneath. The small brown nuts, encased in their bristly husk, were not yet ripe, but the mast of nuts and shells on the ground from last season showed the plentiful yield. She recalled that beechnuts were hard to crack. The trees were not as large as the ones she remembered, but respectable. Then she noticed the unusual plants growing under the trees and knelt down to take a closer look.

"Are you going to collect those?" Jondalar asked. "They look dead. There're no leaves on them."

"They aren't dead. That's how they grow. Here, feel how fresh it is," Ayla said, breaking off the upper few inches of the foot-high, smooth, leafless stem with slender branches the whole length of it. The entire plant was a dull reddish color, including the flower buds, without a hint of green.

"They grow from the roots of other plants," Ayla said, "like the one Iza used to put on my eyes when I cried, except those were white, and kind of shiny. Some people were afraid of them because they thought their color looked like the skin of a dead person. They were even named . . ."—she thought for a moment—"something like dead man's plant, or corpse plant."

She stared into space as she remembered. "Iza thought my eyes were weak because they watered, and it bothered her." Ayla smiled at the thought. "She'd get a fresh one of those white corpse plants and squeeze the juice right out of the stem into my eyes. If they were sore from crying too much, it always made them feel better." She was silent for a time, then shook her head slightly. "I'm not sure if these are good for eyes. Iza used them for little cuts and bruises, and for certain growths."

"What are they called?"

"I think her name for them would be . . . what is your name for this tree, Jondalar?"

"I'm not sure. I don't think they grow near my home, but the Sharamudoi name is 'beech.' "

"Then I think these would be called 'beechdrops,' " she said, getting up and brushing her hands together to dust them off.

Suddenly Wolf froze, his nose pointed toward the deep woods. Jondalar noticed his stalking posture and, remembering how Wolf had scented the bear, reached for a spear. He laid it on top of the groove in his spear-thrower, a shaped piece of wood about half the length of a spear, which was held in a horizontal position with his right hand. He fitted the hollow at the butt of the spear into the notch at the back of the thrower. Then he put his fingers through the two loops near the front of the throwing weapon, which reached a place just short of the middle of the spear, to hold the shaft in place as it rested on top of his spear-thrower. It was done quickly with a smooth motion, and he stood with knees slightly flexed, ready to cast. Ayla had reached for stones and was ready with her sling, wishing she had brought her spear-thrower, too.

Moving through the sparse undergrowth, Wolf made a dash toward a tree. There was a scurry of movement in the beechnut mast, then a small animal raced straight up the smooth trunk. Standing up on his hind legs, as though he was trying to climb the tree as well, Wolf yelped after the furry creature.

Suddenly a commotion up in the branches of the tree attracted their attention. They caught sight of the rich sable-brown coat and long sinuous shape of a beech marten chasing after the loudly chittering squirrel, who thought it had just escaped up the tree. Wolf wasn't the only one who thought the squirrel was worthy of interest, but the large weasellike animal, a foot and a half in length with a bushy tail that added another twelve inches to its dimensions, had a much better chance of success. Racing through the high branches, it was as nimble and fleet as its intended prey.

"I think that squirrel jumped out of the cooking skin into the coals," Jondalar said, watching the drama unfold.

"Maybe he'll get away," Ayla said.

"It's doubtful. I wouldn't wager a broken blade on it."

The squirrel was chittering loudly. An excited jay squawking a raucous caw added to the disturbance, then a willow tit stridently announced its presence. Wolf couldn't stand it, he had to join in. Stretching his head back, he voiced a long howl. The small squirrel climbed out to the end of a limb; then, to the surprise of the two watching people, it leaped into the air. Spreading its legs, it stretched out the broad skin flap that extended along the sides of its body, joining the front and back legs, and soared through the air.

Ayla caught her breath as she watched the flying squirrel avoiding branches and trees. The bushy tail acted as a rudder, and by changing the position of its legs and tail, which changed the tension on the gliding membrane, the squirrel could steer clear of objects in its flight path as it descended in a long, smooth curve. It was aiming for a tree some distance away and, when it drew near, it turned both its tail and body up, and landed low on the trunk, then quickly scurried up. When it reached some high branches, the furry little animal turned around and climbed down again, headfirst, its outstretched hind claws stuck into the bark to anchor it. It looked around, then disappeared into a small hole. The dramatic leap and soaring glide had prevented its capture, though not even that amazing feat was always successful.

Wolf was still up on his hind legs against the tree looking for the squirrel that had so easily eluded him. He dropped down, began sniffing through the underbrush, then suddenly dashed away, chasing something else.

"Jondalar! I didn't know squirrels could fly," Ayla said, with a smile of surprised wonder.

"I should have made that wager, but I've never seen them before, though I have heard of them. I don't think I really believed it. People always talked of seeing the squirrels flying at night, and I thought it was probably a bat that someone mistook for a squirrel. But that was definitely not a bat." With a wry smile he added, "Now I'll be one of those that no one quite believes when he talks about seeing a flying squirrel."

"I'm glad it was just a squirrel," Ayla said, suddenly feeling a chill. She glanced up and noticed that a cloud was blocking the sun. She felt a shiver across her shoulders and down her back, though it wasn't really cold. "I didn't know what Wolf was after this time."

Feeling a bit foolish for reacting so strongly to a threat he only imagined, Jondalar relaxed his grip on his spear and thrower, but still held on. "I thought it might have been a bear," he said. "Especially with these thick woods."

"Some trees always grow near rivers, but I haven't seen trees like these since I left the Clan. Isn't this a strange place for them to be?"

"It is unusual. This place reminds me of the land of the Sharamudoi, but that's south of here, even south of those mountains we see to the west, and near Donau, the Great Mother River."

Suddenly Ayla stopped where she was. Nudging Jondalar, she silently pointed. At first he didn't see what had caught her attention, then he noticed a slight movement of a foxy-red coat, and saw the three-pronged antlers of a roe deer. The commotion and the smell of wolf had caused the small wary deer to freeze. It had stood without moving, hidden in the brush, waiting to see if there was anything to fear from the predator. With the four-legged hunter gone, it had cautiously begun to move away. Jondalar's spear and spear-thrower were still in his right hand. He raised it slowly, and taking aim, hurled the spear at the throat of the animal. The danger it feared had come from an unexpected direction. The hard-flung spear landed true. Even as it hit, the roe deer attempted to leap away, took a few bounding steps, then crashed to the ground.

The flight of the squirrel and the unsuccessful sable were quickly forgotten. Jondalar crossed the distance to the roe deer in a few steps, with Ayla beside him. While Ayla turned the head, he knelt down beside the still struggling animal and slit its throat with his sharp blade to finish it off quickly and let it bleed. Then he stood up.

"Roe Deer, when your spirit returns to the Great Earth Mother, thank Her for giving us one of your kind, that we may eat," Jondalar said quietly.

Ayla, standing beside the man, nodded, then prepared to help him skin and butcher their dinner.

7

"I hate to leave the hide. Roe deer makes such soft leather," Ayla said as she put the last piece of meat in her parfleche, "and did you see the fur on that sable?"

"But we don't have time to make leather, and we can't take much more with us than we already have," Jondalar said. He was erecting the tripod of poles from which the parfleche full of meat would be suspended.

"I know, but I still hate to leave it."

They hung the parfleche; then Ayla glanced toward the fireplace, thinking about the food she had just put on to cook, though nothing was apparent. It was cooking in a ground oven, a hole in the ground lined with hot rocks into which she had put the deer meat seasoned with herbs, along with mushrooms, bracken fern fiddleheads, and cattail roots she had gathered, all wrapped in coltsfoot leaves. She then added more hot rocks on top and a layer of dirt. It would be a while before it was done, but she was glad they had stopped early enough—and had been lucky enough to get fresh meat soon enough—to cook it that way. It was a favorite method since it made food both flavorful and tender.

"I'm hot and the air feels heavy and humid. I'm going to go and cool off," she said. "I'm even going to wash my hair. I saw some soaproot growing downstream. Are you going to come for a swim?"

"Yes, I think I will. I may even wash my hair, if you can find enough of that soaproot for me," Jondalar said, his blue eyes crinkling with a smile as he held up a lank strand of greasy blond hair that had fallen across his forehead.

They walked side by side along the broad sandy bank of the river. Wolf bounded after them, running in and out of brush, exploring new scents. Then he dashed ahead and disappeared around a bend.

Jondalar noticed the trail of horse hooves and wolf track they had made earlier. "I wonder what someone would make of spoor like this," he said, grinning at the thought.

"What would you make of it?" Ayla asked.

"If Wolf's track was clear, I'd think a wolf was trailing two horses, but in some places it's obvious that the horse prints are on top of the wolf prints, so he can't have been following. He was walking with them. That would confuse a tracker," he said.

"Even if Wolf's prints were clear, I'd wonder why a wolf was following these two horses. The tracks show they are both strong and healthy, but look at the impression, how deep it is, and the set of the hooves. You can tell they're carrying weight," Ayla said.

"That would confuse a tracker, too."

"Oh, there they are," Ayla said, seeing the rather tall, somewhat straggling plants with light pink flowers and leaves shaped like spear points, that she had noticed earlier. With her digging stick she quickly loosened several roots and pulled them out.

On their way back, she searched for a flat, hard stone or piece of wood, and a rounded stone to crush the soaproot and release the saponin, which would foam into a light cleansing lather in the water. At a bend, upstream but not too far from their campsite, the small river had scoured out a waist-deep pool. The water was cool and refreshing, and after washing, they explored the rocky river, swimming and wading farther upstream until they were stopped by a churning waterfall and swift rapids where the sloping sides of the valley narrowed and became steeper.

It reminded Ayla of the small river in her valley, with its fuming, churning waterfall blocking her way upstream, though the rest of the area made her think more of the mountain slopes around the cave where she grew up. There was a waterfall there that she remembered, a gentler, mossy one that had led her to a small cave she had claimed as her own, and that had more than once offered her a haven.

They let the current carry them back, splashing each other and laughing along the way. Ayla loved the sound of Jondalar's laughter. Though he smiled, he didn't laugh often, tending instead to exhibit a more serious demeanor, but when he did, it was such a big, hearty, exuberant laugh, it came as a surprise.

When they got out and dried off, it was still warm. The dark cloud Ayla had noticed earlier was gone from the sky above them, but the sun was lowering toward a black and brooding mass languishing in the west, whose ponderous movement was emphasized by a ragged layer streaming swiftly beneath it in the other direction. Once the fireball dropped behind the somber clouds and banked above the western ridge, it would cool off fast. Ayla looked for the horses and saw them in an open meadow on the slope, some distance from camp, but within range of a whistle. Wolf was not in sight; still exploring downstream, she assumed.

She got out the long-toothed ivory comb and a brush made of stiff mammoth-hair bristles that Deegie had given her, then pulled their sleeping roll out of the tent and spread it out to sit on while she combed her hair. Jondalar sat beside her and began to comb his own hair with a three-pronged comb, struggling with some tangles.

"Let me do that for you, Jondalar," she said, getting up on her knees behind him. She combed loose the knots in his long, straight yellow hair, a lighter shade than hers, admiring the color. When she was younger, her hair had been almost white, but it had become somewhat darker and resembled Whinney's coat with its ashy golden hue.

Jondalar closed his eyes while Ayla worked on his hair, but he was aware of her warm presence behind him as her bare skin brushed against his now and then, and by the time she was through, he was feeling a warmth from more than the sun.

"Now it's my turn to comb your hair," he said, getting up to move behind her. For a moment, she thought about objecting. It wasn't necessary. He didn't have to comb her hair just because she had combed his, but when he lifted her thick hair off her neck and pulled it through his fingers, like à caress, she acquiesced.

Her hair had a tendency to curl, and it tangled easily, but he worked carefully, freeing each snarl with very little pulling. Then he brushed her hair until it was smooth and nearly dry. She closed her eyes, feeling a strange, shivery delight. Iza had combed her hair for her when she was a little girl, gently pulling out the tangles with a long, smooth, pointed stick, but no man ever had. Jondalar's combing of her hair gave her an intense feeling of being cared for and loved.

And he discovered that he enjoyed combing and brushing her hair. The dark gold color reminded him of ripe grass, but with sun-bleached highlights that were nearly white. It was beautiful, and so thick and soft, handling it was a sensuous pleasure that made him want more. When he finished, he put the brush down, then lifted up the slightly damp tresses, and, moving them aside, bent down to kiss her shoulders and the back of her neck.

Ayla kept her eyes closed, feeling the tingles caused by his warm breath and soft lips as he brushed them lightly over her skin. He nibbled at her neck and caressed both her arms, then reached around to hold both breasts, lifting them and feeling their pleasant substantial weight, and the firm, upright nipples in his palms.

When he reached around to kiss her throat, Ayla lifted her head and turned slightly, then felt his hot rigid organ against her back. She turned around and took it in her hands, enjoying the softness of the skin that covered the warm hard shaft. She put one hand above the other, and moved them firmly up and down, and Jondalar felt a surge of sensation, but the feeling magnified beyond measure when he felt the warm wetness of her mouth enclose him.

Letting out an explosive sigh, he closed his eyes as the sensations coursed through him. Then he opened his eyes a crack to watch, and could not help but reach for the soft beautiful hair that filled his lap. When she drew him in farther, he thought for a moment he could not hold back and would give it up at that instant. But he wanted to wait, wanted the exquisite pleasure it gave him to Pleasure her. He loved to do it, loved knowing he could. He would almost be willing to give up his own Pleasure to Pleasure her . . . almost.

Hardly knowing how she got there, Ayla found herself on her back on top of their sleeping roll, with Jondalar stretched out beside her. He kissed her. She opened her mouth a little, just enough to allow his tongue entrance, and put her arms around him. She loved the way it felt when his lips were firmly on hers, with his tongue gently exploring. Then he pulled away and looked down at her.

"Woman, do you have any idea how much I love you?"

She knew it was true. She could see it in his eyes, his brilliant, vivid, unbelievable blue eyes that caressed with their look, and even from a distance, could send shivers through her. His eyes expressed the emotions he tried so hard to keep under control. "I know how much I love you," Ayla said.

"I still can hardly believe it, that you are here with me, and not back at the Summer Meeting mated to Ranec." At the thought of how close he came to losing her to the charming, dark-skinned carver of ivory, he suddenly clutched her to him tightly with fierce need.

She held him, too, grateful that their long winter of misunderstanding had finally ended. She had sincerely loved Ranec—he was a good man and would have made a good mate—but he wasn't Jondalar, and her love for the tall man who was holding her in his arms was beyond anything she could explain.

His powerful dread of losing her eased, replaced, as he felt her warm body beside him, by a desire for her that was as strong. Suddenly he was kissing her neck and her shoulders and her breasts, as though he couldn't get enough of her.

Then he stopped and took a deep breath. He wanted to make it last, and he wanted to use his skill to give her the best he could—and he was skilled. He had been taught by one who knew, and with more love than she should have felt. He had wanted to please and had been more than willing to learn. He had learned so well that among his people there was a joke about him that had often been made: it was said he was an expert in two crafts; he was also an excellent knapper of flint tools.

Jondalar looked down at her, watching her breathe, loving the sight of her full, womanly form, and delighting in the mere fact of her existence. His shadow fell across her, blocking the heat of the sun. Ayla opened her eyes and looked up. The brilliant sun behind him gleaming through his fair hair surrounded his shadowed face with a golden aura. She wanted him, was ready for him, but when he smiled and bent down to kiss her navel, she closed her eyes again and gave herself up to him, knowing what he wanted, and the Pleasures he could make her feel.

He held her breasts, then slowly ran his hand along her side, to the curving in of her waist and lush swelling of her hip, then down her thigh. She tingled at the touch. He brought his hand back up her inner thigh, feeling the special softness there, and over the springy golden curls of her mound. He caressed her stomach, then bent to kiss her navel before he reached for her breasts again, and kissed both nipples. His hands were like gentle fire, feeling warm and wonderful, and left her burning with excitement. He caressed her again, and her skin remembered every place he touched.

He kissed her on the mouth and gently, slowly, kissed her eyes and her cheeks, her chin and her jaw, then breathed into her ear. His tongue found the hollow of her throat and continued down between her breasts. He took each one in his hands and held them together, delighting in their fullness, the slight salty taste of her, and the feel of her skin, as his own desire was mounting. His tongue tickled one nipple, and then the other, and then she felt the deep throbbing surge as he pulled it in his mouth. He explored her nipple with his tongue, pressing, pulling, nibbling lightly, then reached for the other with his hand.

She pressed up to him, losing herself in the sensations coursing through her body, and centered on the seat of pleasure she felt deep within. With his warm tongue, he found her navel again, and as a light wind blew cool on her skin, he circled and then dropped lower, to the soft curly fur of her mound, then for a quick moment to her warm slit and hard node of her Pleasure. She raised her hips to him, and cried out.

He nestled between her legs, and with his hands, opened her to look at her warm rosy flower of petals and folds. He dipped down to taste—he knew her taste and loved it—then held back no longer, and reveled in exploring her. His tongue found the familiar folds, reached into her deep well, and then reached up higher for the small, hard node.

As he worked his tongue over it, suckling and nibbling,

she cried out again and again, her breath coming faster, and the surge inside building. All feeling was turned inward, there was no wind, no sun, only the rising intensity of her senses. He knew it was coming, and though he could hardly hold back himself, he slowed and backed off, hoping to draw it out, but she reached for him unable to wait. As it came closer, building, growing, tightening with anticipation, he could hear her moans of pleasure.

Suddenly it was there, the powerful shuddering waves seizing her, then with a convulsive cry, crashing over her. She burst with the spasm of release, and with it came the indescribable desire to feel his manhood inside her. She reached for him, trying to bring him to her.

He felt her spurt of wetness and, sensing her need for him, raised up, clasping his eager shaft to guide it into her deep and welcoming well. She felt him enter and raised up to meet him as he plunged in. The embrace of her warm folds encircled him, and he penetrated deeply, feeling no fear that his size was more than she could hold. That was part of the wonder of her, that she matched him.

He pulled out, feeling the exquisite pleasure of the movement, and with complete abandon, plunged in again, deeply, while she raised up tight against him. He almost reached his peak, but the intensity backed down, and he pulled out again, then pushed in again, and again, and again, with each stroke building higher. Pulsing with the sensations of his movement, she felt the fullness of him, then his drawing back and filling her again, and was beyond feeling anything else.

She heard his strong breathing, and her own, as their cries mingled. Then he cried out her name, she rose to meet him, and, with a great overflowing burst, they felt a release that matched the fiery sun in its glowing flame as it shot its last bright rays into the valley, and dropped behind the dark and rolling clouds, outlined in burnished gold.

After a few more strokes, he relaxed on top of her, feeling her rounded curves beneath him. She always loved that moment with him, the feeling of his weight on her. He never felt heavy; it was just a comfortable pressure and a closeness that warmed her while they rested.

Suddenly a warm tongue was licking her face, and a cold nose was exploring their closeness. "Go away, Wolf," she said, shoving the animal away. "Go on, get out of here."

"Wolf, go away!" Jondalar said harshly, adding his com-

mand, and pushing the cold wet nose away, but the mood
was broken. As he lifted off Ayla and rolled to his side, he
felt a trifle annoyed, but he couldn't really be angry; he felt
too wonderful for that.

Getting up on one elbow, Jondalar looked at the animal
that had backed off a few paces and was sitting on his
haunches watching them with his tongue hanging out, panting. He could have sworn the animal was grinning at them,
and he smiled wryly at the woman he loved. "You've been
getting him to stay. Do you think you'll be able to teach him
to go when you want him to?"

"I think I'm going to try."

"It's a lot of work, having a wolf around," Jondalar said.

"Well, yes, it takes a little effort, especially since he's
so young. So do the horses, but it's worth it. I like having
them around. They are like very special friends."

At least, the man thought, the horses gave something
back. Whinney and Racer carried them, and their gear;
because of them, their Journey might not take as long. But
except for flushing out an animal once in a while, Wolf didn't
seem to contribute much. Jondalar decided, though, not to
mention his thoughts.

With the sun behind the angry rolling black clouds, dis-
coloring to a livid red and purple as though battered and
bruised by the churning, it cooled off quickly in the wooded
valley. Ayla got up and splashed into the river once more.
Jondalar followed in after her. Long before, when she was
growing up, Iza, the Clan medicine woman, had taught her
the purification rituals of womanhood, even though she
doubted that her strange and—even she admitted—ugly
adopted daughter, would ever have need for some of them.
Nonetheless, she felt it was her duty, and she explained,
among other things, how to take care of herself after being
with a man. She stressed that, whenever possible, purification
with water was especially important to a woman's totem
spirit. Washing, no matter how cold the water, was a ritual
that Ayla always remembered.

They dried off again and dressed, put the sleeping furs
back in the tent, and rekindled the fire. Ayla removed the
dirt and the stones from the ground oven and, with her
wooden tongs, retrieved their meal. Afterward, while Jondalar rearranged his packs, she made her preparations for an
easy departure, including their usual morning meal of food

from the evening before, eaten cold except for the hot herbal tea. Then she put cooking stones to heat for boiling water; she made tea often, varying the ingredients for taste or need.

The horses wandered back as the last streaks of the departing sun colored the sky. Usually they fed during part of the night, since they traveled so much during the day and needed large quantities of the rough grass of the steppes to sustain them. But the meadow grass had been especially rich and green, and they liked to stay near the fire at night.

While Ayla was waiting for the stones to heat, she contemplated the valley in the last glow of twilight, adding to her observations the knowledge gained during the day: the steeply sloping sides that abruptly joined the broad flat valley floor with its little river winding down the middle. It was a rich valley, reminding her of her childhood with the Clan, but she didn't like the place. Something about it made her uneasy, and the feeling worsened with the coming of night. She was also feeling some fullness and a little backache, and she attributed her disquiet to the slight discomforts she occasionally experienced when her moon time was coming on. She wished she could go for a walk, activity usually helped, but it was already too dark.

She listened to the wind moaning as it sighed through the swaying willow trees, silhouetted against silvery clouds. The glowing full moon, encircled by a distinct halo, took turns hiding behind, then brilliantly illuminating the softly textured sky. Ayla decided some willowbark tea might relieve her discomfort and quickly got up to cut some fresh. While she was at it, she decided to gather some flexible willow withes.

By the time their evening tea was ready and Jondalar joined her, the night air was damp and cold, cold enough for outer clothes. They sat close to the fire, glad to be sipping the hot tea. Wolf had hovered close to Ayla all evening, following her every step, but he seemed content to curl up by her feet when she sat near the warm flames, as though he'd done enough exploring that day. She picked up the thin, long willow twigs and began weaving with them.

"What are you making?" Jondalar asked.

"A head covering, to make a shade from the sun. It is getting very hot in the middle of the day," Ayla explained. She paused for a moment, then added, "I thought you might find use for one."

"You are making that for me?" he said with a smile.

"How did you know I was wishing I had something to shade the sun today?"

"A woman of the Clan learns to anticipate the needs of her mate." She smiled. "And you are my mate, aren't you?"

He smiled back. "Without doubt, my woman of the Clan. And we'll announce it to all the Zelandonii at the Matrimonial of the first Summer Meeting we join. But how can you anticipate needs? And why must Clan women learn that?"

"It's not difficult. You just think about someone. It was hot today, and I thought about making a head covering . . . making a sun hat . . . for myself, so I knew it must be hot for you, too," she said, picking up another willow withe to add to the broadly conical hat that was beginning to take shape. "Men of the Clan don't like to ask for anything, especially for their own comfort. It is not considered manly behavior for them to think about comfort, so a woman must anticipate a man's needs. He protects her from danger; it's her way of protecting him, to make sure he has the right clothing and eats well. She doesn't want anything to happen to him. Who would protect her and her children then?"

"Is that what you are doing? Protecting me so I will protect you?" he asked, grinning. "And your children?" In the firelight, his blue eyes were a deep violet, and they sparkled with fun.

"Well, not exactly," she said, looking down at her hands. "I think it's really the way a Clan woman tells her mate how much she cares for him, whether she has children or not." She watched her rapidly moving hands, though Jondalar had the feeling that she didn't need to see what she was doing. She could have made the hat in the dark. She picked up another long twig, then looked directly at him. "But I do want to have another child before I get too old."

"You have a long way to go for that," he said, putting another piece of wood on the fire. "You're still young."

"No, I'm getting to be an old woman. I am already . . ." She closed her eyes to concentrate as she pressed her fingers against her leg, saying the number words he had taught her, to verify to herself the right word for the number of years she had lived. ". . . Eighteen years."

"That old!" Jondalar laughed. "I have seen twenty-two years. I'm the one who is old."

"If it takes us a year to travel, I will be nineteen years

when we reach your home. In the Clan, that would be almost too old for childbearing.''

"Many Zelandonii women have children at that age. Maybe not their first, but their second or third. You are strong and healthy. I don't think you're too old to have children, Ayla. But I will tell you this. There are times when your eyes seem ancient, as though you've lived many lifetimes in your eighteen years.''

It was an unusual thing for him to say, and she stopped her work to look at him. The feeling she evoked in him was almost frightening. She was so beautiful in the light of the fire, and he loved her so much, he didn't know what he would do if anything ever happened to her. Overcome, he looked away. Then, to ease the moment, he tried to introduce a lighter subject.

"I'm the one who should worry about age. I'd be willing to wager that I will be the oldest man at the Matrimonial,'' he said, then laughed. "Twenty-three is old for a man to be mated for the first time. Most men my age have several children at their hearths.''

He looked at her, and she saw again that look of overwhelming love and fear in his eyes. "Ayla, I want you to have a child, too, but not while we're traveling. Not until we're safely back. Not yet.''

"No, not yet,'' she said.

She worked quietly for a while, thinking about the son she had left behind with Uba, and about Rydag, who had been like her son in many ways. Both of them lost to her. Even Baby, who was, in a strange way, like a son—at least, he was the first male animal she found and cared for—had left her. She would never see him again. She looked at Wolf, suddenly worried that she might lose him, too. I wonder, she thought, why is my totem taking all my sons away from me? I must be unlucky with sons.

"Jondalar, do your people have any special customs about wanting children?'' Ayla asked. "Women of the Clan are always supposed to want sons.''

"No, not really. I think men want a woman to bring sons to his hearth, but I think women like to have daughters first.''

"What would you like to have? Someday?''

He turned to study her in the light of the fire. Something

seemed to be bothering her. "Ayla, it doesn't matter to me. Whatever you want, or whatever the Mother gives you."

Now it was her turn to study him. She wanted to be sure he really meant it. "Then I think I'm going to wish for a daughter. I don't want to lose any more children."

Jondalar didn't quite know what she meant and didn't know how to respond. "I don't want you to lose any more children, either."

They sat quietly while Ayla worked on the sun hats. Suddenly, he asked, "Ayla, what if you are right? What if children are not given by Doni? What if they are started by sharing Pleasures? You could have a baby starting inside you right now, and not even know it."

"No, Jondalar. I don't think so. I think my moon time is coming on," she said, "and you know that means no babies have started."

She didn't usually like to talk about such personal matters with a man, but Jondalar had always been comfortable around her then, not like the Clan men. A woman of the Clan had to be especially careful not to look directly at a man when she was going through her woman's curse. But even if she wanted to, she couldn't exactly go into seclusion or avoid Jondalar while they were traveling, and she sensed that he needed reassurance. She considered, for a moment, telling him about Iza's secret medicine that she had been taking to fight off any impregnating essences, but she couldn't do it. Ayla could no more tell a lie than Iza could, but, short of a direct question, she could refrain from mentioning it. If she didn't bring it up, it wasn't likely that a man would think to ask if she was doing something to prevent pregnancy. Most people wouldn't think it was possible that such powerful magic could exist.

"Are you sure?" he asked.

"Yes, I'm sure," she said. "I am not pregnant. No baby has started growing inside me." He relaxed then.

As Ayla was finishing up the sun hats, she felt a soft sprinkling of rain. She hurried to finish. They brought everything inside the tent with them, except the parfleche hanging from the poles, and even the damp Wolf seemed happy to curl up at Ayla's feet. She left the lower part of the entrance flap open for him, in case he needed to go out, but they closed the smoke-hole flap when the rain began coming down harder. They cuddled together when they first lay down, then rolled over, but they both had trouble sleeping.

Ayla was feeling anxious, and achy, but she tried not to toss and turn too much so she wouldn't disturb Jondalar. She listened to the pattering of rain on the tent, but it didn't lull her to sleep the way it usually did, and after a long while she wished it were morning so she could just get up and leave.

Jondalar, after all his worry, and being reassured that Ayla had not been blessed by Doni, began to wonder, again, if there was something wrong with him. He lay awake thinking, wondering if his spirit, or whatever essence it was that Doni took from him, was strong enough, or if the Mother had forgiven him his youthful indiscretions and would allow it.

Maybe it was her. Ayla said she wanted a child. But, with all the time they spent together, if she wasn't pregnant, it could be that she couldn't have children. Serenio never had any more . . . unless she was expecting when he left. . . . As he stared into the darkness of the inside of the tent, listening to the rain, he wondered if any of the women he had known had ever given birth, and if any babies had been born with his blue eyes.

Ayla was climbing, climbing, a steep rocky wall, like the steep path up to her cave in the valley, but it was much longer, and she had to hurry. She looked down at the small river swirling around the bend, but it wasn't a river. It was a waterfall, cascading in a wide spray over jutting rocks softened by lush green moss.

She looked up, and there was Creb! He was beckoning to her and making the sign to hurry. He turned around and started climbing, too, leaning heavily on his staff, leading her up a steep but climbable grade beside the waterfall, toward a small cave in a rocky wall hidden by hazelnut bushes. Above the cave, at the top of a cliff, was a large, flattened boulder tilting over the edge, ready to fall.

Suddenly she was deep in the cave, following a long, narrow passage. There was a light! A torch with its beckoning flame, and then another, and then the sickening roar of an earthquake. A wolf howled. She felt a whirling, spin-

ning vertigo, and then Creb was inside her mind. "Get out!"
he commanded. "Hurry! Get out now!"

She sat up with a start, throwing her sleeping furs off,
and bolted for the tent opening.

"Ayla! What is it!" Jondalar said, grabbing her.

Suddenly a brilliant flash of light could be seen through
the skin of the tent, and in a bright outline around the seams
of the smoke-hole flap, and the crack around the entrance left
open for Wolf. It was followed almost instantly by a loud,
sharp boom. Ayla screamed, and Wolf howled outside the
tent.

"Ayla, Ayla. It's all right," the man said, holding her
in his arms. "It's just lightning and thunder."

"We have to get out! He said to hurry. Get out now!"
she said, fumbling into her clothes.

"Who said? We can't go out there. It dark, and it's
raining."

"Creb. In my dream. I had that dream again, with Creb.
He said. Come on, Jondalar! We have to hurry."

"Ayla, calm down. It was just a dream, and probably the
storm. Listen to it. It sounds like a waterfall out there. You
don't want to go out in that rain. Let's wait until morning."

"Jondalar! I have to go. Creb told me to, and I can't
stand this place," she said. "Please, Jondalar. Hurry." Tears
were streaming down her face, though she was oblivious to
them, as she piled things into pack baskets.

He decided he might as well. It was obvious she wasn't
going to wait until morning, and he'd never get back to sleep
now. He reached for his clothes while Ayla opened the
entrance flap. The rain poured in as though someone had
spilled it from a waterbag. She went outside and whistled,
loud and long. It was followed by another wolf howl. After
a wait, Ayla whistled again, then began tearing the tent stakes
out of the ground.

She heard the hoofbeats of the horses and cried with relief
to see them, though the salt of her tears was lost in the
pouring deluge. She reached out to Whinney, her friend who
had come to help her, and hugged the soaking-wet mare
around the sturdy neck and felt the frightened horse shivering.
She swished her tail and circled nervously with small prancing steps; at the same time she turned her head and flicked

her ears back and forth, trying to find and identify the source of her apprehension. The horse's fears helped the woman bring her own under control. Whinney needed her. She spoke to the animal in gentling tones, stroking and trying to calm her, and then felt Racer leaning on them, if anything more frightened than his dam.

She tried to settle him, but he soon backed away in prancing little steps. She left them together while she hurried to the tent for the harnesses and pack baskets. Jondalar had rolled up sleeping furs and piled them in his pack before he heard the sound of hooves, and he had gotten harnesses and Racer's halter ready.

"The horses are very frightened, Jondalar," Ayla said when she came into the tent. "I think Racer's ready to bolt. Whinney is calming him a little, but she's scared, too, and he's making her more nervous."

He picked up the halter and went out. The wind and the pouring rain washed over him in sheets, almost knocking him down. It was raining so hard that he felt as though he were standing in a waterfall. It was much worse than he thought. Before long the tent would have been awash, and the rain would soon have soaked the ground cover and their sleeping furs. He was glad Ayla had insisted they get up and leave. In another flash of light, he saw her struggling to tie pack baskets on Whinney. The bay stallion was beside them.

"Racer! Racer, come here. Come on, Racer," he called. A great roaring boom tore through the air, sounding as though the very skies were breaking apart. The young stallion reared and neighed, then pranced and pivoted in erratic circles. His eyes were rolling, showing whites, his nostrils were flaring, his tail was lashing violently, and his ears were flicking in all directions, trying to focus on the source of his fears, but they were inexplicable and all around him, and that was terrifying.

The tall man reached up for the horse, trying to put his arms around the neck to bring him down, talking to the animal to steady him. There was a strong bond of trust between them, and the familiar hands and voice were settling. Jondalar managed to get the halter device on, and, picking up the harness straps, he hoped the next nerve-shattering bolt of lightning and blast of thunder would hold off.

Ayla came to get the last of their things from inside the tent. The wolf was behind her, though she hadn't noticed the animal before. When she backed out of the conical skin shelter, Wolf yelped, started running toward the willow woods, then ran back and yelped at her again.

"We're going, Wolf," she said, and then to Jondalar, "It's empty. Hurry!" She ran toward Whinney and dumped the armload she carried into a pack basket.

Ayla had communicated her distress, and Jondalar was afraid Racer wouldn't stand still much longer. He didn't worry about dismantling the tent. He yanked the support poles out through the smoke hole, tearing off the flap, dropped them in a pack basket, then bunched up the heavy waterlogged skins and stuffed them in after. The skittish horse rolled his eyes and backed away as Jondalar reached for the mane as a hold to leap on. Though his jump was a bit awkward, he managed to gain his seat, and then he was nearly pitched off when Racer reared. But he threw his arms around the stallion's neck and held on.

Ayla heard a long wolf howl and a strange deep roar as she climbed on Whinney's back, and she turned to see Jondalar holding on to the rearing stallion. As soon as Racer settled back down, she leaned forward urging Whinney to go. The mare sprang ahead in a fast gallop, as though something were chasing her, as though, like Ayla, she couldn't wait to get away from there. Wolf bounded ahead, racing through brush, and as Racer and Jondalar followed close on her heels, the menacing roar grew louder.

Whinney tore through the woods of the level valley floor, dodging around trees, jumping over obstacles. Keeping her head low, with her arms around the horse's neck, Ayla let the mare find her own way. She couldn't see anything in the darkness and the rain, but she sensed they were heading toward the slope leading to the steppes above. Suddenly another burst of lightning flashed, filling the valley with instant brilliance. They were in the beech woods and the slope was not far. She glanced back at Jondalar and gasped.

The trees behind him were moving! Before the light died, several tall pines leaned precariously, then it went dark. She hadn't noticed the rumble growing louder until she waited to hear the trees fall and became aware that the sound was drowned out by the overpowering noise. Even the crack of thunder seemed to dissolve into the booming roar.

They were on the slope. She knew from the change in Whinney's pace that they were climbing up, though she still couldn't see. She could only trust to the mare's instincts. She felt the animal slip, then recover her footing. Then they broke out of the woods and were in a clearing. She could even see the rolling clouds through the rain. They must be in that meadow on the slope where the horses had grazed, she thought. Racer and Jondalar pulled up alongside. He, too, was hunched over his horse's neck, though it was too dark to see more than the shape of their silhouette, a black-on-black shadow.

Whinney was slowing, and Ayla could feel her labored breathing. The woods on the other side of the meadow were thinner, and Whinney was no longer racing at a frantic pace, dodging trees. Ayla sat up straighter, but still kept her arms around her mare's neck. Racer had pulled ahead in his burst of speed, but soon he slowed to a walk and Whinney caught up. The rain was easing up. The trees gave way to brush, and then grass, and then the slope leveled out as the steppes opened out before them in a darkness softened only slightly by clouds lighted by a hidden moon through a veil of rain.

They stopped, and Ayla dismounted to let Whinney rest. Jondalar joined her and they stood side by side trying to see into the darkness below. Lightning flashed, but it was farther away, and the thunder followed later in a low growl. In a dazed state, they stared out over the black chasm of the valley, knowing that some great destruction was taking place though they could see nothing. They realized they had barely escaped a terrible disaster, but they didn't yet comprehend its dimensions.

Ayla felt a strange prickly sensation on her scalp and heard a faint crackling. Her nose crinkled at the acrid smell of ozone; it was a peculiar burning odor, but not of fire, nothing as earthy as that. Suddenly it occurred to her that it must be the smell of the streaking fire in the sky. Then she opened her eyes in wonder and fear and, in a moment of panic, grabbed for Jondalar. A tall pine, rooted in the slope below, but sheltered from the cutting winds by a rocky outcrop and projecting high above the steppes, glowed with an eerie blue light.

He put his arm around her, wanting to protect her, but he felt the same sensations, and fears, and knew these otherworldly fires were beyond his control. He could only hold her close. Then, in an awesome display, a jagged crackling bolt arced across the glowing clouds, branched out into a network of fiery darts, and in a blinding flash leaped down and speared the tall pine, illuminating the valley and the steppes with the clarity of noon. Ayla started at the sharp crack, so loud it left her ears ringing, and she cringed as the booming roar reverberated across the sky. In that moment of radiance they saw the destruction they had so narrowly escaped.

The green valley was ravaged. The entire level floor was a heavy, swirling maelstrom. Opposite them, on the far slope, a mudslide had piled a jumble of boulders and fallen trees halfway across the wild waters, leaving a raw scar of reddish soil exposed.

The cause of the torrential onslaught was a set of circumstances not unusual. It had begun in the mountains to the west, and with atmospheric depressions over the inland sea; warm, moisture-laden air had swirled upward and condensed into huge billowing clouds with white windblown tops that hung stalled and motionless over the rocky hills. This warm air had been invaded by a cold front, and the turbulence of the resulting combination had created a thunderstorm of uncommon intensity.

The rains had poured from the bloated skies, disgorging into dips and hollows that gushed into creeks, burst over rocks, and surged into streams overfilling with frantic haste. Gathering momentum, the tumultuous water, abetted by the continuing deluge, raged down the steep hills, fountained over barriers, and crashed into sister streams, joining together into walls of rampaging, devastating force.

When the flash flood reached the green dell, it erupted over the waterfall and, with a ravenous roar, engulfed the entire valley, but the lush, verdant depression held a surprise for the churning waters. During the era, extensive movements of the earth were uplifting the land, raising the level of the small inland sea to the south, and opening passageways to an even larger sea farther south. Within recent decades, the uplift had closed off the valley, forming a shallow basin, which had been filled by the river, creating a small lake behind the natural dam. But an outlet had broken through a few years before and drained the small reservoir of water, leaving in its wake moisture enough for a wooded valley in the middle of the dry steppes.

A second mudslide, farther downstream, had dammed the outlet channel again, containing the raging floodwaters within the confines of the valley and causing a backwash. Jondalar thought the scene below must have come from some nightmare. He could hardly believe what he had seen. The entire valley was a wild, turbulent, frenzied slurry of mud and rocks, sloshing back and forth, churning brush and whole trees torn out by their roots, and splintered by the battering.

No living thing could have survived in that place, and he shuddered to think what would have happened if Ayla hadn't wakened and insisted that they leave. He doubted if they would have made it to safety without the horses. He glanced around; they were both standing with heads down, feet apart, looking as exhausted as he thought they must be. Wolf was beside Ayla, and when he saw Jondalar look his way he lifted his head straight up and howled. The man had a fleeting memory of a wolf howl disturbing his sleep, just before Ayla woke up.

Another lightning bolt flashed, and at the sound of the thunder, he felt Ayla shiver violently in his arms. They were not out of danger yet. They were wet and cold, everything was soaked, and, in the middle of the open plain in a thunderstorm, he had no idea where to find shelter.

8

The tall pine that had been struck by lightning was burning, but the hot pitch that fed the fire had to contend with the dousing rain, and the sputtering flames shed little light. It was enough, though, to highlight the general contours of the nearby landscape. There was not much in the way of shelter on the open plains, except some low brush growing beside a nearly overflowing runoff ditch that was dry most of the year.

Ayla was staring down into the darkness of the valley, as if spellbound by the scene they had seen below. While she stood there, the rain began coming down harder again, sluicing over them, drenching their already soaked clothing, and finally winning out over the struggling fire in the tree.

"Ayla, come on," Jondalar said. "We've got to find some shelter and get out of this rain. You're cold. We're both cold, and wet."

She stared for a moment longer, then shuddered. "We were down there." She looked up at him. "Jondalar, we would have died if we'd been caught in that."

"But we got out in time. Now we need to find shelter.

If we don't find someplace to warm up, it won't matter that we got out of the valley."

He picked up Racer's lead rope and started toward the brush. Ayla signaled Whinney and followed, with Wolf at her side. When they reached the ditch, they noticed that the low bushes led to a thicker stand of higher brush, almost low trees, farther back from the valley on the steppes, and they headed for that.

They pushed their way into the center of the dense growth of sallow. The ground around the slender, many-stemmed bases of the silvery green willow brush was wet, and rain still filtered in through the narrow leaves, but not quite as hard. They cleared woody stems out of a small pocket, then removed the pack baskets from the horses. Jondalar pulled out the heavy bundle of wet tent and shook it out. Ayla grabbed the poles and set them around the inside of the brush pocket, then helped spread the skins of the tent, still tied to the ground cover, over them. It was a haphazard construction, but for now they just wanted shelter from the rain.

They brought their pack baskets and other things into the makeshift shelter, tore leaves off the trees to line the wet ground, and spread out their damp sleeping furs. Then they took off their outer clothes, helped each other wring out the soaked leather, and draped them on branches. Finally, shivering hard, they huddled down and pulled their sleeping furs around them. Wolf came in and shook himself vigorously, spraying water, but everything was so wet that it hardly mattered. The steppe horses, with their thick shaggy coats, much preferred cold, dry winter to the drenching summer storm, but they were used to living outside. They stood close together beside the stand of brushy growth and let the rain pour over them.

Within the damp shelter, too wet to even consider a fire, Ayla and Jondalar, wrapped in heavy furs, cuddled close together. Wolf curled up on top of their sleeping furs, pressing close to them, and finally, their combined body heat warmed them. The woman and man dozed a bit, though neither of them slept much. Near dawn the rain slacked off, and their sleep deepened.

Ayla listened, smiling to herself, before opening her eyes. Within the medley of birdsong that had awakened her, she could distinguish the sharp elaborate call notes of a pipet. Then she heard a melodious warble that seemed to be getting louder, but when she tried to find the source of the trilling song, she had to look carefully to see the drab, brown, inconspicuous little skylark just landing. Ayla rolled on her side to watch him.

The skylark walked along the ground easily and quickly, well balanced by its large hind claws, then bobbed its crested head and came up with a caterpillar in its beak. With quick, jerky steps, it rushed toward a bare scrape in the ground near the stems of a sallow bush, where a camouflaged cluster of newly hatched fluffy chicks suddenly sprang to life, each open mouth begging to be filled with the delectable morsel. Soon a second bird, similar in markings though slightly more drab, and nearly invisible against the dun earth of the steppes, appeared with a winged insect. While she stuffed it into an open mouth, the first bird leaped into the air and climbed in circles until he was almost lost from view. But his presence was not lost. He had disappeared into a spiral of incredibly glorious song.

Ayla softly whistled the musical call, replicating the sounds with such precision that the mother bird stopped pecking at the ground in search of food and turned in her direction. Ayla whistled again, wishing she had some grain to offer, as she had done when she lived in her valley and first began imitating bird calls. After she had gained skill, they came when she called, whether she offered grain or not, and became company for her during those lonely days. The mother skylark approached, looking for the bird that was invading the territory of her nest, but when she found no other skylarks, she went back to feeding her young.

Whistled repetitive phrases, more mellow and ending with a chuckling sound, perked Ayla's interest even more. Sandgrouse were big enough to make a decent meal, and so were those cooing turtledoves, she thought, looking around to see if she could spot the buxom birds that resembled the brown sandgrouse in general size and shape. In the low branches, she saw a simple twig nest with three white eggs in it before she saw the plump pigeon with its small head and bill and short legs. Its soft, dense plumage was a pale brown, almost pinkish, and its strongly patterned back and wings, which somewhat resembled the shell of a turtle, glistened with iridescent patches.

Jondalar rolled over, and Ayla turned to watch the man lying beside her, breathing with the deep rhythms of sleep. Then she became aware of her need to get up and relieve herself. She was afraid that if she moved he would wake up, and she hated to disturb him, but the more she tried to forget about it, the more urgent her need became. Maybe if she moved slowly, she thought, trying to ease out of the warm, slightly damp furs wrapped around them. He snorted and snuffled and rolled over as she extricated herself, but it was when he reached for her and found her missing that he woke up.

"Ayla? Oh, there you are," he mumbled.

"Go back to sleep, Jondalar. You don't have to get up yet," she said as she crawled out of their nest in the brush.

It was a bright, fresh morning, the sky a clear sparkling blue without a hint of a cloud in sight. Wolf was gone, probably hunting or exploring, Ayla thought. The horses had moved off, too; she saw them grazing near the edge of the valley. Though the sun was still low, steam was already rising from the wet ground, and Ayla felt the humidity as she hunkered down to pass her water. Then she noticed the red stains on the inside of her legs. Her moon time, she thought. She'd been expecting it; she'd have to wash herself and her undergarment, but first she needed the mouflon wool.

The runoff ditch was only half-full, but the streamlet flowing through it was clear. She leaned over and rinsed her hands, drank several cupped handfuls of the cool running liquid, and then hurried back to their sleeping place. Jondalar was up, and he smiled when she made her way into their shelter within the sallow brush to get one of her pack baskets. She pulled it out in the open and began rummaging through it. Jondalar brought both of his baskets out with him, then went back for the rest of their things. He wanted to see how much damage had been done by the soaking rains. Wolf came loping back just then and went straight to Ayla.

"You're looking satisfied with yourself," she said, roughing up his neck fur, so thick and full it was almost a mane. When she stopped, he jumped up on her, putting his muddy paws on her chest, nearly at the level of her shoulders. He caught her by surprise, almost knocking her down, but she recovered her balance.

"Wolf! Look at all this mud," she said, as he reached to lick her throat and face, and then, with a low rumbling growl, he opened his mouth and took her jaw in his teeth. But for all his impressive canine armaments, his action was as restrained and gentle as if he'd been handling a new puppy. No tooth broke skin; they hardly made an impression on it. She buried both her hands in his ruff again, pushed his head back, and looked at the devotion in his wolfish eyes with as much affection as he showed her. Then she grabbed his jaw with her teeth, and gave him the same kind of growling, gentle love-bite back.

"Now, get down, Wolf. Look at the mess you've made of me! I'm going to have to wash this, too." She brushed off the loose, sleeveless leather tunic she wore over the short leggings that had been used as undergarments.

"If I didn't know better, Ayla, I could almost be frightened for you when he does that," Jondalar said. "He's gotten so big, and he is a hunter. He could kill someone."

"You don't have to worry about Wolf when he does that. That's the way wolves greet each other and show their love. I think he's glad we woke up in time to get out of the valley, too."

"Have you looked down there?"

"Not yet . . . Wolf, get away from there," she said, pushing him away when he began to sniff between her legs. "It's my moon time." She looked aside and flushed slightly. "I came to get my wool, and I haven't had the chance to look."

While Ayla attended to her personal needs, washing herself and her clothes in the little stream, tying on the straps that held the wool in place, and getting something else to wear, Jondalar walked toward the edge of the valley to pass his water and looked down. There was no sign of a campsite, or of any place there could be one. The natural basin of the valley was partially filled with water, and the logs and trees and other floating debris were bobbing and dipping as the agitated water continued to rise. The small river that fed it was still blocked at the outlet, and still creating backwash, though it was not sloshing with the sweeping back-and-forth movement of the night before.

Ayla quietly moved beside Jondalar, who had been staring intently at the valley and thinking. He looked up when he felt her presence.

"This valley must get narrow downstream, and something must be blocking the river," he said, "probably rocks or a mudslide. It's holding the water in. Maybe that's why it was so green down there, it may have done it before."

"The flash flood alone would have washed us away if it had caught us," Ayla said. "My valley used to flood every spring, and that was bad enough, but this . . ." She could find no words to express her thought, and she unconsciously finished her sentence with the motions of Clan sign language that to her conveyed more strongly and precisely her feelings of dismay and relief.

Jondalar understood. He, too, was at a loss for words and shared her feelings. They both stood silently watching the movement below; then Ayla noticed his forehead knotting with concentration and concern. Finally he spoke.

"If the mudslide, or whatever it is, gives way too quickly, that water washing downstream will be very dangerous. I hope there are no people that way," he said.

"It won't be any more dangerous than it was last night," Ayla said. "Will it?"

"Last night it was raining, so people might expect something like a flood, but if this breaks through, without the warning of a rainstorm, it would catch people by surprise, and that would be devastating," he explained.

Ayla nodded, then said, "But if people are using this river, wouldn't they notice that it had stopped flowing and try to find out why?"

He turned to face her. "But what about us, Ayla? We're traveling, and we wouldn't have any way of knowing that a river had stopped running. We could be downstream of something like this sometime, and we wouldn't have any warning."

Ayla turned back to look at the water in the valley and didn't answer immediately. "You're right, Jondalar," she said then. "We could get caught in another flash flood without warning. Or the lightning could have hit us instead of that tree. Or an earthquake could open up a crack in the ground and take everyone except a little girl, leaving her alone in the world. Or someone could get sick, or be born with a weakness or a deformity. The Mamut said no one can know when the Mother will decide to call one of Her children back to Her. There's nothing to be gained by worrying about things like that. We can't do anything about them. That's for Her to decide."

Jondalar listened, still frowning with worry; then he relaxed and put his arms around her. "I worry too much.

Thonolan used to tell me that. I just started thinking about what would happen if we were downstream of that valley, and remembered last night. And then I thought about losing you, and . . .'' He tightened his arms around her. "Ayla, I don't know what I would do if I ever lost you," he said, with sudden fervor, holding her to him. "I'm not sure I'd want to go on living."

She felt a tinge of worry at his strong reaction. "I hope you would go on living, Jondalar, and find someone else to love. If anything ever happened to you, a piece of me, of my spirit, would be gone with you, because I love you, but I would go on living, and a piece of your spirit would always be living with me."

"It wouldn't be easy to find someone else to love. I didn't think I'd ever find you. I don't know if I'd even want to look," Jondalar said.

They started back, walking together. Ayla was quiet for a while, thinking, then said, "I wonder if that's what happens when you love someone, and that person loves you back? I wonder if you exchange pieces of each other's spirit. Maybe that's why it hurts so much to lose someone you love." She paused, then continued. "It's like the men of the Clan. They are hunting brothers, and they exchange a piece of each other's spirit, particularly when one saves the other's life. It's not easy to go on living when a piece of your spirit is missing, and each hunter knows a piece of himself will go to the next world if the other goes, so he will watch and protect his brother, do almost anything to save his life." She stopped and looked up at him. "Do you think we have exchanged pieces of our spirits, Jondalar? We are hunting partners, aren't we?"

"And you once saved my life, but you are much more than a hunting brother," he said, smiling at the idea. "I love you. I understand now why Thonolan didn't want to go on living when Jetamio died. Sometimes I think he was searching for a way into the next world, so he could find them, Jetamio and the baby who was never born."

"But if anything ever happened to me, I wouldn't want you to follow me to any spirit world. I'd want you to stay right here, and find someone else," Ayla said, with conviction. She didn't like all his talk about next worlds. She wasn't sure what some other world after this one would be like, or even, deep in her heart, if one really existed. What she did know was that to get to any next world, you had to die in this one, and she didn't want to hear about Jondalar dying, either before or after she did.

Thinking about worlds of the spirit led to other random thoughts. "Maybe that's what happens when you get old," she said. "If you exchange pieces of your spirit with people you love, after you've lost a lot of them, so many pieces of your spirit have gone with them to the next world that there's not enough left to keep you alive in this world. It's like a hole inside of you that keeps getting bigger, so you want to go to the next world where most of your spirit and your loved ones are."

"How do you know so much?" Jondalar asked with a little smile. For all her lack of knowledge of the world of the spirits, her ingenuous and spontaneous observations made sense to him in a way, and displayed a genuine and thoughtful intelligence, though he had no way of knowing if there was any merit in the ideas. If Zelandoni were there, he could ask her, he thought. Then suddenly he realized they were going home, and he would be able to ask her, some day soon.

"I lost pieces of my spirit when I was a little girl and the people I was born to were taken by the earthquake. Then Iza took a piece when she died, and Creb, and so did Rydag. Even though he isn't dead, even Durc has a piece of me, of my spirit, that I will never see. Your brother took a piece of you with him, didn't he?"

"Yes," Jondalar said, "he did. I will always miss him, and always hurt about it. Sometimes I still think it was my fault, and I would have done anything to save him."

"I don't think there is anything you could have done, Jondalar. The Mother wanted him, and it is for Her to decide, not for someone to search for a way to the next world."

When they got back to the tall sallow brush where they had spent the night, they began going through their belongings. Almost everything was at least damp, and many things were still very wet. They untied the swollen knots that still tied the ground cover to the upper shaped part of the tent and, each taking an end and twisting in opposite directions, tried to wring the pieces out. But too much twisting put a strain on the stitching. When they decided to erect the tent to begin letting it dry out, they discovered they had lost some of the tent poles.

They spread the ground cover out over the brush, and

then checked their outer clothes, which were also still quite wet. Objects that were in the pack baskets had fared a little better. Many things were damp, but would probably dry soon enough, if they had a warm, dry place to air them out. The open steppes would be fine during the day, but that's when they needed to travel, and it could get damp and cool on the ground at night. They did not look forward to sleeping in a wet tent.

"I think it's time for some hot tea," Ayla said, feeling discouraged. It was already later than usual. She got a fire started and put heating stones in it, thinking about breakfast. That was when she realized they didn't have the food left from their evening meal the night before.

"Oh, Jondalar, we don't have anything to eat this morning," she complained. "It's still down in that valley. I left the grains in my good cooking basket near the hot coals in the fireplace. The cooking basket is gone, too. I have others, but it was a good one. At least I still have my medicine bag," she said with obvious relief when she found it. "And the otter skin still resists water, even as old as it is. Everything inside is dry. At least I can make tea for us, I have some good-tasting herbs in it. I'll get some water," she said, then looked around. "Where's my tea-making basket? Did I lose that, too? I thought I brought it into the tent when it began to rain. It must have dropped when we were hurrying to leave."

"We left something else back there that isn't going to make you very happy," Jondalar said.

"What?" Ayla said, looking upset.

"Your parfleche, and the long poles."

She shut her eyes and shook her head in dismay. "Oh, no. That was a good meat-keeper and it was full of roe deer meat. And those poles. They were just the right size. It's going to be hard to replace them. I'd better see if anything else was lost and make sure the emergency food is all right."

She reached for the pack basket where she kept the few personal things she was taking with her and the clothing and equipment that would be used later. Though all the baskets were wet, and sagging, the spare ropes and cords on the bottom had kept the contents of this one reasonably dry and undamaged. The food they were using along the way was near the top of the basket; below it the emergency traveling-food package was still securely wrapped and essentially dry.

She decided this might be a good time to look over all their supplies just to be certain nothing was spoiled, and to judge how long the food they had with them would last.

She took out all the various kinds of dried preserved food she had brought with them and spread it out on top of their sleeping roll. There were berries—blackberries, raspberries, bilberries, elderberries, blueberries, strawberries, alone or mixed together—that had been mashed and dried into cakes. Other sweet varieties were cooked down, then dried to a leathery texture, sometimes with added pieces of small hard apples, tart but high in pectin. Whole berries and wild apples, along with other fruits such as wild pears and plums, were sliced or left whole, and sweetened a bit as they dried in the sun. Any of them could be eaten as they were, or soaked or cooked with water, and were often used to flavor soups or meats. There also were grains and seeds, some that had been partially cooked and then parched; some shelled and roasted hazelnuts; and the stone-pine cones full of rich nuts she had collected from the valley the day before.

Vegetables were also dried—stems, buds, and particularly starchy roots, such as cattail, thistle, licorish fern, and various lily corms. Some were steam-cooked in ground ovens before being dried, but others were dug, peeled, and strung immediately on cords made of the stringy bark of certain plants or sinew from the backbone or leg tendons of various animals. Mushrooms were also strung, and for flavor were often hung over smoky fires to dry, and certain edible lichens were steamed and dried into dense, nutritious loaves. Their provisions were rounded out by a large selection of dried smoked meat and fish, and in a special packet, put aside for emergencies, was a mixture of ground-up dried meat, clean rendered fat, and dried fruits, molded into small cakes.

The dried food was compact and kept well; some of it was more than a year old and had come from the previous winter's supplies, but the quantities of certain items were quite limited. Nezzie had collected it for them from friends and relatives who had brought it to the Summer Meeting. Ayla had drawn sparingly from their store of food; for the most part they were living off the land. It was the season for it. If they could not survive by harvesting the bounty of the Great Earth Mother when Her offerings were rich, they could never hope to survive traveling across country during leaner times.

Ayla packed everything back up. She had no intention of depending on their dried traveling food for their morning meal, though the steppes had fewer fat birds to feed after they ate. A pair of sandgrouse fell to her sling and were roasted on a spit; some pigeon eggs that would never hatch were lightly cracked and put directly in the fire in their shells. Contributing to a filling breakfast was the fortunate find of a marmot's cache of spring beauty corms. The hole in the ground was under their sleeping furs and filled with the sweet and starchy vegetables, which had been gathered earlier by the small animal when the rootlike corms were at their peak. They were cooked with the rich pine nuts Ayla had gathered the day before, which were released from the pine cones by fire and cracked with a rock. Some fresh ripe dewberries rounded out the meal.

After they left the flooded valley, Ayla and Jondalar continued south, veering slightly toward the west, drawing imperceptibly closer to the mountain range. Though it was not an exceptionally high range, the taller peaks of the mountains were perpetually covered with snow, often shrouded with mists and clouds.

They were in the southern region of the cold continent and the character of the grassland had changed subtly. It was more than simply a profusion of grass and herbs that accounted for the diversity of animals that thrived on the cold plains. The animals themselves had evolved differences in diets and migratory patterns, spatial separations, and seasonal variations, which all contributed to the wealth of life. As in later times on the great equatorial plains far to the south— the only place that came close to matching the profound richness of the Ice Age steppes—the great abundance and variety of animals shared the productive land in complex and mutually sustaining ways.

Some specialized in eating particular plants, some in particular parts of plants; some grazed the same plants at slightly different stages of development; some fed in places that others did not go, or they followed later, or migrated differently. The diversity was maintained because eating and living habits of one species fit in between or around those of another in complementary niches.

Woolly mammoths needed great quantities of fibrous filler, rough grasses, stems, and sedges, and because they tended to bog down in deep snows, marshes or sphagnum meadows, they kept to the firm, windswept ground near the glaciers. They made long migrations along the wall of ice, moving south only in spring and summer.

Steppe horses also required bulk; like mammoths, they digested coarse stems and grasses quickly, but were somewhat more selective, preferring the mid-height varieties of grass. They could dig down through snow to find feed, but this used up more energy than they gained, and it was a struggle for them to travel when snow piled up. They could not subsist for long in deep snow and preferred the hard-surfaced, windy plains.

Unlike mammoths and horses, bison needed the leaves and sheaths of grass for the higher protein content and tended to select shortgrass, utilizing the areas of mid- and tallgrass only for new growth, usually in spring. In summer, however, an important, if inadvertent, cooperation was practiced. Horses used their teeth like clippers to bite through the tough stalks. After the horses had passed by, cutting down the stems, the densely rooted grass was stimulated to send out new leaves of regrowth. The migrations of horses were often followed, after an interval of a few days, by the gigantic bison, who welcomed the new shoots.

In winter, bison moved to southern ranges of variable weather and more snow, which kept low-growing grass leaves moist and fresher than in the dry northern plains. They were skilled at sweeping snow aside with their noses and cheeks to find their preferred close-to-the-ground feed, but the snowy steppes of the south were not without risk.

Though it kept them warm in the relatively dry cold, even of the south where more snow fell, the heavy, shaggy coats of bison and other warmly dressed animals that migrated south in winter could be hazardous or even fatal when the climate turned cold and wet, with frequent shifts between freezing and thawing. If their coats became soaking wet during a thaw, they could be vulnerable to a fatal chill during a subsequent freeze, especially if a cold snap caught them resting on the ground. Then, if their long hair froze fast, they would be unable to get up. Excessively deep snow, or icy crusts on top of snow, could also be fatal, as well as winter blizzards, or falling through the thin ice of oxbow lakes, or flooding river valleys.

Mouflon and saiga antelopes also thrived by selectively foraging on plants adapted to very dry conditions, small herbs and ground-hugging leafy shortgrass, but unlike bison, saiga did poorly on broken terrain or in deep snow, and they were not able to leap well. They were fast long-distance runners that could outdistance their predators only on the firm level surfaces of the windy steppes. Mouflon, the wild sheep, on the other hand, were expert climbers and used steep terrain to escape, but they could not dig through snow that piled up. They preferred the windblown rocky high ground.

The goatlike species related to mouflon, chamois and ibex, divided their range by altitude, or by differences of terrain and landscape, with the wild goat-antelope, ibex, taking the highest ground with the steepest crags, followed at slightly lower elevations by the smaller and very nimble chamois, with the mouflon below them. But they were all found in rough terrain of even the lowest levels of the arid steppes, since they were adapted to cold, so long as it was dry.

Musk-oxen were also goatlike animals, although larger, and their heavy double coats, which resembled the fur of mammoths and woolly rhinoceroses, made them seem bigger and more "oxlike." They nibbled continuously on the low shrubs and sedges, and they were particularly adapted to the coldest regions, preferring the extremely cold, windy, open plains close to the glacier. Though their underwool was shed in summer, musk-oxen became stressed if the weather turned too warm.

Giant deer and reindeer kept to open ground in herds, but most other deer were browsers of tree leaves. The solitary woodland moose were rare. They loved the summer leaves of deciduous trees, and the succulent pondweeds and water plants of marshes and lakes, and with broad hooves and long legs, they could negotiate marshy, boggy bottomlands. In winter they survived on the more indigestible grass, or high willow twigs of trees that grew on the low ground of river valleys, their splay-footed long legs easily carrying them through the windblown snow that drifted and piled up there.

Reindeer were winter-loving animals, feeding on lichens that grew on barren soil and rocks. They could smell the favored plants, even through snow, from a long distance, and their hooves were adapted to digging down through deep snows if they needed to. In summer they ate both grass and leafy shrubs.

Elk and reindeer both preferred alpine meadows or herbaceous highlands during spring and summer, but below the elevation of the ranging sheep, and the elk tended to eat grasses more than shrubs. Asses and onagers invariably preferred the arid higher hills, while bison ranged a bit lower, though they generally climbed higher than horses, which had a broader choice of terrain than mammoths or rhinoceroses.

Those primal plains with their complex and diverse grasslands sustained in great multitudes a fantastic mixture of animals. No single place on a later earth did more than approximate parts of it. The dry, cold environment of high mountains could not compare, though there were similarities. Mountain-dwelling sheep, goats, and antelopes extended their range to the lower ground then, but large herds of plains animals could not exist in the steep, rocky terrain of high mountains when the climate of the lowlands changed.

The soggy and fragile northern bogs were not the same. They were too wet for much grass to grow, and their stinting, acid soils caused plants to develop toxins to avoid being grazed by the great multitudes, which would destroy such delicate slow-growing flora. The varieties were limited and offered poor nutrients for the diversity of large herding animals; there was not sufficient feed. And only those with wide oplaying hooves, like reindeer, could live there. Huge creatures of great weight with large stumpy legs, or fast runners with narrow dainty hooves became mired in the soft, wet land. They needed firm, dry, solid ground.

Later, the grassy plains of warmer, more temperate regions developed distinct bands of more limited vegetation controlled by temperature and climate. They offered too little diversity in summer, and too much snow in winter. Snow also bogged down animals that required firm ground, and it was difficult for many to push aside to reach food. Deer could live in woods where the snow was deep, but only because they browsed leaves and twig tips from trees that grew above the snow; reindeer could dig through snow to reach the lichen on which they fed in winter. Bison and aurochs subsisted, but they were reduced in size, no longer reaching their full potential. Other animals, such as horses, decreased in number as their preferred environment shrunk.

It was the unique combination of all the many elements of the Ice Age steppes that fostered the magnificent multitudes, and each was essential, including the bitter cold, the withering winds, and the ice itself. And when the vast glaciers shrank back to polar regions and disappeared from the lower latitudes, so, too, did the great herds and gigantic animals become dwarfed or disappear entirely from a land that had changed, a land that could no longer sustain them.

While they traveled, the missing parfleche and long poles preyed on Ayla's mind. They were more than useful, they might be necessary during the long trip ahead. She wanted to replace them, but it would take more than an overnight stop, and she knew Jondalar was anxious to keep moving.

Jondalar, however, was not happy about the wet tent, nor the thought of depending on it for shelter. Besides, it wasn't good for wet skins to be folded up and packed together so tight; it could make them rot. They needed to be spread out to dry, and the hides would probably need to be worked as they were drying to keep them pliable, in spite of the smoking they had received when the leather was made. That would take more than a day, he was sure.

In the afternoon they approached the deep trench of another large river, which separated the plain from the mountains. From their vantage point on the plateau of the open steppes, above the broad valley with its wide, swiftly flowing waterway, they could see the terrain on the other side. The foothills across the river were fractured with many dry ravines and gullies, the ravages of flooding, as well as many more running tributaries. It was a major river, channeling a good proportion of the runoff, which drained the eastern face of the mountains into the inland sea.

As they rounded the shoulder of the steppe plateau and rode down the slope, Ayla was reminded of the territory around the Lion Camp, though the more broken landscape across the river was different. But on this side she saw the same kind of deep-cut gullies carved out of the loess soil by rain and melting snow, and high grass drying into standing hay. On the floodplain below, isolated larch and pine trees were scattered among leafy shrubs, and stands of cattails, tall phragmite reeds, and bulrushes marked the river's edge.

When they reached the river, they stopped. This was a major watercourse, wide and deep, and swollen from the recent rains. They were not at all sure how they were going to get across. It was going to take some planning.

"It's too bad we don't have a bowl boat," Ayla said, thinking of the skin-covered round boats the Lion Camp had used to cross the river near their lodge.

"You're right. I think we are going to need some kind of a boat to get across this without getting everything all wet. I'm not sure why, but I don't remember having so much trouble crossing rivers when Thonolan and I were traveling. We just piled our gear on a couple of logs and swam across," Jondalar said. "But I guess we didn't have as much, only a back frame for each of us. That's all we could carry. With the horses, we can take more with us, but then, we have more to worry about."

As they rode downstream, looking over the situation, Ayla noticed a stand of tall, slender birches growing near the water. The place had such a familiar feeling that she half expected to see the long, semisubterranean earthlodge of the Lion Camp tucked into the side of the slope at the back of a river terrace, with grass growing out of the sides, a rounded top, and the perfectly symmetrical arched entrance that had so surprised her when she first saw it. But when she actually saw such an arch, it gave her an eerie, spine-tingling shock.

"Jondalar! Look!"

He looked up the slope where she was pointing. There he saw not just one, but several, perfectly symmetrical arch-ways, each an entrance to a circular, dome-shaped structure. They both dismounted and, finding the path up from the river, climbed to the Camp.

Ayla was surprised at how eager she was to meet the people who lived there, and realized how long it had been since they had seen or spoken to anyone besides each other. But the place was empty, and planted in the ground between the two curved mammoth tusks whose tips were joined together at the top, forming the arched entrance to one of the dwellings, was a small carved ivory figure of a female with ample breasts and hips.

"They must be gone," Jondalar said. "They left a donii to guard each lodge."

"They're probably hunting, or at a Summer Meeting, or visiting," Ayla said, feeling real disappointment that there

were no people. "That's too bad. I was looking forward to
seeing someone." She turned to go.

"Wait, Ayla. Where are you going?"

"Back to the river." She looked puzzled.

"But this is perfect," he said. "We can stay here."

"They left a mutoi—a donii—to guard their lodges. The
spirit of the Mother is protecting them. We can't stay here
and disturb Her spirit. It will bring us bad luck," she said,
knowing full well that he knew it.

"We can stay, if we need to. We just can't take anything
we don't need. That's always understood. Ayla, we need
shelter. Our tent is soaked. We have to give it a chance to
dry out. While we're waiting, we can go hunting. If we get
the right kind of animal, we can use the hide to make a bowl
boat to cross the river."

Ayla's frown slowly changed to an enlightened smile, as
she grasped his meaning and realized the implications. They
did need a few days to recover from their near disaster and
replace some of their losses. "Maybe we can get enough hide
to make a new parfleche, too," she said. "Once it's cleaned
and dehaired, rawhide doesn't take that long to set up, not
any longer than it takes to dry meat. It just has to be stretched
and left to get hard." She glanced down toward the river.
"And look at those birches down there. I think I could make
good poles out of some of those. Jondalar, you're right. We
need to stay here for a few days. The Mother will understand.
And we could leave some dry meat for the people who live
here, to thank them for the use of their Camp . . . if we're
lucky with our hunting. Which lodge should we stay in?"

"The Mammoth Hearth. That's where visitors usually
stay."

"Do you think there is a Mammoth Hearth? I mean, do
you think this is a Mamutoi Camp?" Ayla asked.

"I don't know. It's not one big earthlodge that everyone
lives in like Lion Camp," Jondalar said, looking at the group
of seven round dwellings covered with a smooth layer of
hardened earth and river clay. Rather than a single, large,
multifamily longhouse, like the one they had lived in during
the winter, this place had several smaller dwellings clustered
together, but the purpose was the same. It was a settlement,
a community of more-or-less related families.

"No, it's like Wolf Camp, where the Summer Meeting
was," Ayla said, stopping in front of the entrance of one of

the small dwellings, still a bit reluctant to push the heavy drape aside and enter the home of strangers without being invited, in spite of generally understood customs that had developed out of a mutual necessity for the sake of survival in time of need.

"Some of the younger people at the Summer Meeting thought the big lodges were old-fashioned," Jondalar said. "They liked the idea of an individual lodge for just one or two families."

"You mean they wanted to live by themselves? Just one lodge with one or two families? For a winter Camp?" Ayla asked.

"No," he said. "No one wanted to live alone all winter. You never see just one of these small lodges by itself; there are always at least five or six, sometimes more. That was the idea. The people I talked to thought it was easier to build a smaller lodge for a new family or two, than to crowd into one big lodge until they had to build another. But they wanted to build near their families, and stay with their Camps, and share in the activities and the food that everyone worked together to collect and store for winter."

He pushed aside the heavy skin hanging from the joined tusks that formed the entrance, ducked under it and stepped inside. Ayla stood back, holding up the drape to shed some light.

"What do you think, Ayla? Does it look like a Mamutoi lodge?"

"It could be. It's hard to tell. Remember that Sungaea Camp we stopped at on the way to the Summer Meeting? It wasn't very different from a Mamutoi Camp. Their customs may have been a little different, but they were like the Mammoth Hunters in many ways. Mamut said even the funeral ceremony was very similar. He thought they were once related to Mamutoi. I did notice the patterns of their decorations were not the same, though." She paused, trying to think of other differences. "And some of their clothes—like that beautiful shoulder blanket made out of mammoth and other wools on the girl who had died. But even Mamutoi Camps have different patterns. Nezzie always knew what Camp someone was from just by the small changes in the style and shape of the patterns on their tunics, even when I couldn't see very much difference at all."

With the light coming in from the entrance, the main

supporting construction was plain to see. The lodge was not framed with wood, although a few of the birch poles were strategically placed; it had been built out of mammoth bones. The large sturdy bones of the huge beasts were the most abundant and accessible building material available on the essentially treeless steppes.

Most of the mammoth bones used for building material did not come from animals that had been hunted and killed for that purpose. They were from animals that had died of natural causes, gathered from wherever they happened to fall on the steppes or, most often, from accumulated piles that had been swept up by flooding rivers and deposited at certain bends or barriers in the river, like driftwood. Permanent winter shelters were often built on river terraces near such piles, because mammoth bones and tusks were heavy.

It usually took several individuals to lift a single bone and no one wanted to carry them very far; the total weight of the mammoth bones that were used to construct one small dwelling was two or three thousand pounds or more. Building such shelters was not the activity of a single family, but a community effort, directed by someone with knowledge and experience, and organized by someone with the ability to persuade others to help.

The place they called a Camp was a settled village, and the people who lived there were not nomadic followers of the itinerant game, but essentially sedentary hunters and gatherers. The Camp might be left vacant for a while in the summer, when the inhabitants went to hunt or gather produce, which was brought back and kept in nearby storage pits, or to visit family and friends from other villages to trade gossip and goods, but it was a permanent home site.

"I don't think this one is the Mammoth Hearth, or whatever that hearth is called here," Jondalar said, letting the drape fall behind him. It raised a cloud of dust.

Ayla straightened the small female figure, whose feet were purposely only a suggestion, leaving the legs in a peg-like shape that had been pushed into the ground to stand guard in front of the entrance, then followed Jondalar to the next lodge.

"This one is probably either the leader's lodge or the mamut's, maybe both," Jondalar said.

Ayla noticed that it was slightly larger, and the woman-figure in front was somewhat more elaborate, and she nodded agreement. "A mamut, I think, if they are Mamutoi, or people like them. Both the headwoman and the headman of the Lion Camp had hearths that were smaller than Mamut's, but his was used for visitors, and by everyone for gathering."

They both stood at the entrance, holding up the drape, waiting for their eyes to adjust to the dimmer light within. But two small lights continued to glow. Wolf growled, and Ayla's nose detected a scent that made her nervous.

"Don't go in, Jondalar! Wolf! Stay!" she commanded, making the sign with her hand as well.

"What is it, Ayla?" Jondalar said.

"Can't you smell it? There's an animal in there, something that can make a strong smell, a badger, I think, and if we scare it, it will make a terrible stink that lingers. We won't be able to use this lodge, and the people who live here will have trouble getting rid of the smell. Maybe if you hold the drape back, Jondalar, it will come out by itself. They dig burrows and don't like the light much, even if they do hunt in the day sometimes."

Wolf started a low rumbling growl, and it was obvious he was straining to go in after the fascinating creature. But like most members of the weasel family, the badger could spray an attacker with the powerfully strong and acrid contents of its anal glands. The last thing Ayla wanted was to be around a wolf that stunk of that strong musky odor, and she wasn't sure how long she could hold Wolf back. If the badger didn't come out soon, she might have to use a more drastic way to rid the lodge of the animal.

The badger did not see well with its small and inconspicuous eyes, but they were watching the lighted opening with unwavering attention. When it seemed obvious the badger was not going to leave, she reached up for the sling that was wrapped around her head, and into the pouch hanging from her waist for stones. Ayla put a stone in the bulging pocket of the sling, took aim on the reflecting points of light, and with a quick and expert spin to gain momentum, hurled the stone. She heard a thud, and the two small lights went out.

"I think you got him, Ayla!" Jondalar said, but they waited a while to make sure there was no movement before entering the lodge.

When they did, they were aghast. The rather large animal, three feet from tip of nose to end of tail, was sprawled on the ground with a bloody wound on its head, but it had quite obviously spent some time within the dwelling, destructively exploring everything it could find. The place was a shambles! The hard-packed earthen floor was scratched up and pits had been dug in it, some containing the animal's waste. The woven mats that had covered the floor were torn to shreds, along with various woven containers. Hides and furs on the raised bedplatforms were chewed and ripped apart, and the stuffing of feathers, wools, or grasses of bed padding were strewn over all. Even a portion of the densely compacted wall had been dug out; the badger had made its own entrance.

"Look at this! I would hate to return and find something like this," Ayla said.

"That's always a danger when you leave a place empty. The Mother doesn't protect a lodge from Her other creatures. Her children must appeal to the spirit animal directly and deal with the animals of this world themselves," Jondalar said. "Maybe we can clean this lodge up a little for them, even if we can't repair all the damage."

"I'm going to skin that badger and leave it for them, so they know what caused all this. They should be able to use the hide, anyway," Ayla said, picking the animal up by the tail to take it outside.

In better light, she noted the gray back with its stiff guard hairs, the darker underparts, and the distinctive black-and-white striped face, verifying that it was, indeed, a badger. She slit its throat with a sharp flint knife and left it to bleed out. Then she went back to the earthlodge, pausing for a moment before she went in to look around at the rest of the domed dwellings nearby. She tried to visualize what it would be like with people, and she felt a strong pang of regret that they were gone. It could be very lonely without other people. She suddenly felt very grateful for Jondalar, and for a moment she was almost overwhelmed by the love she felt for him.

She reached for the amulet around her neck, felt the comforting objects inside the decorated leather bag, and thought of her totem. She didn't think of her Cave Lion protecting spirit as much as she once had. It was a Clan spirit, though Mamut had said her totem would always be with her. Jondalar always referred to the Great Earth Mother when he talked about the spirit world, and she thought of the Mother more now, since the training she had been receiving from Mamut, but she always felt it was her Cave Lion who had brought

Jondalar to her, and she felt moved to communicate with her totem spirit.

Using the ancient sacred language of silent hand signs that was used to address the spirit world, and to communicate with other clans whose few spoken everyday words and more common hand signs were different, Ayla closed her eyes and directed her thoughts to her totem.

"Great Spirit of Cave Lion," she gestured, "this woman is grateful to be found worthy; grateful to be chosen by the powerful Cave Lion. The Mog-ur always told this woman that a powerful spirit was difficult to live with, but it was always worth it. The Mog-ur was right. Though the tests and trials have sometimes been difficult, the gifts have matched the difficulty. This woman is most grateful for the gifts inside, the gifts of learning and understanding. This woman is also grateful for the man her great totem Spirit guided to her, who is taking this woman back with him to his home. The man does not know the Clan Spirits, and does not fully understand that he was also chosen by the Spirit of the Great Cave Lion, but this woman is grateful he was also found worthy."

She was about to open her eyes, then had another thought. "Great Cave Lion Spirit," she continued, in her mind and with her silent language, "The Mog-ur told this woman that totem spirits always want a home, a place to return where they are welcome and want to stay. This traveling will end, but the people of the man do not know the spirits of Clan totems. The new home of this woman will not be the same, but the man honors the spirit animal of each, and the people of the man must know and honor the Cave Lion Spirit. This woman would say the Great Spirit of the Cave Lion will always be welcome and will always have a place wherever this woman is welcome."

When Ayla opened her eyes, she saw Jondalar watching her. "You seemed . . . occupied," he said. "I didn't want to disturb you."

"I was . . . thinking about my totem, my Cave Lion," she said, "and your home. I hope he will be . . . comfortable there."

"The spirit animals are all comfortable near Doni. The Great Earth Mother created and gave birth to all of them. The legends tell about it," he said.

"Legends? Stories about the times before?"

"I guess you could say they were stories, but they are told in a certain way."

"There were Clan legends, too. I used to love it when Dorv told them. Mog-ur named my son after one of my favorites, 'The Legend of Durc,' " Ayla said.

Jondalar felt a moment of surprise and a twinge of disbelief at the thought that the people of the Clan, the flatheads, could have legends and stories. It was still difficult for him to overcome certain ingrained ideas he had grown up with, but he had already been made aware that they were much more complex than he would have thought possible; why couldn't they have had legends and stories, too?

"Do you know any Earth Mother legends?" Ayla asked.

"Well, I think I remember part of one. They are told in a way to make them easier to remember, but only special zelandonia know them all." He paused to remember, then began in a chanting singsong:

"Her birth waters gushed, filling rivers and seas,
Then flooded the land and gave rise to the trees.
From each drop that spilled, new grass and leaves grew
Till sprouting green plants filled all the earth's view."

Ayla smiled. "That's wonderful, Jondalar! It tells the story with a nice feeling, and a nice sound, something like the rhythms of the Mamutoi songs. It would be very easy to remember that."

"It is often sung. Different people sometimes make different songs for it, but the words mostly stay the same. Some people can sing the whole story, with all the legends."

"Do you know any more?"

"A little. I've heard it all, and generally know the story, but the verses are long, a lot to remember. The first part is about Doni being lonely and giving birth to the sun, Bali, 'the Mother's great joy, a bright shining boy,' then they tell how She loses him and becomes lonely again. The moon is Her lover, Lumi, but She created him, too. That story is more of a woman's legend; it's about moon times, and becoming a woman. There are other legends about Her giving birth to all the spirit animals, and to the spirit woman and man, to all of Earth's Children."

Wolf barked then, an attention-getting puppy bark that he found did accomplish his aim, encouraging him to keep it beyond the puppy stage. They both looked in his direction and then saw the cause of his excitement. Below, on the sparsely wooded, grassy floodplain of the large river, a small herd of aurochs were straggling by. The wild cattle were huge, with massive horns and shaggy coats, mostly of a solid reddish color so deep it was almost black. But among the herd were a couple of animals that sported large white spots, primarily around the face and forequarters, mild genetic aberrations that showed up occasionally, particularly among aurochs.

At almost the same moment, Ayla and Jondalar looked at each other, gave each other a knowing nod, then called their horses. Quickly removing the pack baskets, which they took inside the dwelling, and taking their spear-throwers and spears, they mounted and headed toward the river. As they neared the grazing herd, Jondalar stopped to study the situation and decide upon the best approach. Ayla halted as well, following his lead. She knew carnivorous animals, particularly the smaller ones, although animals as large as lynx and the massively powerful cave hyena had been among her prey, and a lion had once lived with her, and now a wolf, but she was not as familiar with the grazers and browsers that were normally hunted for food. Though she had found her own ways to hunt them when she lived alone, Jondalar had grown up hunting them and had much more experience.

Perhaps because she had been in a mood to communicate with her totem, and the world of the spirits, Ayla was in a strange state of mind as she watched the herd. It seemed almost too coincidental that, just when they had decided that the Mother would not object if they stayed a few days to replenish their losses and hunt for an animal with a sturdy hide and plenty of meat, suddenly a herd of aurochs should appear. Ayla wondered if it was a sign, from the Mother or, maybe, from her totem, that they had been guided there.

It was not so unusual, however. All through the year, especially during the warmer seasons, various animals, in herds or singly, migrated through the gallery forests and lush grasslands of large river valleys. At any particular site along a major river, it was usual to see some type of animal wander along at least every few days, and in certain seasons whole processions passed by daily. This time it happened to be a herd of wild cattle, exactly the right kind of animal for their needs, though several other species would also have served.

"Ayla, do you see that big cow over there?" Jondalar asked. "The one with the white on its face and across the left shoulder?"

"Yes," she said.

"I think we should try for her," Jondalar said. "She's full grown, but from the size of her horns, she doesn't look too old, and she's off by herself."

Ayla felt a chill of recognition. Now she was convinced it was a sign. Jondalar had chosen the unusual animal! The one with the white spots. Whenever she had been faced with difficult choices in her life, and after much thought had finally reasoned, or rationalized, her way to a decision, her totem had confirmed that it was the correct one by showing her a sign, an unusual object of some sort. When she was a girl, Creb had explained such signs to her and told her to keep them for good luck. Most of the small objects that she carried in the decorated pouch around her neck were signs from her totem. The sudden appearance of the aurochs herd, after they had made their decision to stay, and Jondalar's decision to hunt the unusual one, seemed strangely akin to signs from a totem.

Though their decision to stay at this Camp had not been an agonizingly personal one, it was an important one that had required serious thought. This was the permanent winter home of a group of people who had invoked the power of the Mother to guard it in their absence. While the needs of survival did allow a passing stranger to use it in case of necessity, it had to be with legitimate reason. One did not incur the possible wrath of the Mother lightly.

The earth was richly populated with living creatures. In their travels they had seen uncounted numbers of a great variety of animals, but few people. In a world so empty of human life, there was comfort in the thought that an invisible realm of spirits was aware of their existence, cared about their actions, and perhaps directed their steps. Even a stern or inimical spirit who cared enough to demand certain actions of appeasement was better than the heartless disregard of a harsh and indifferent world, in which their lives were entirely in their own hands, with no one else to turn to in time of need, not even in their thoughts.

Ayla had come to the conclusion that if their hunt was successful, it would mean that it was all right for them to use the Camp, but if they failed, they would have to go.

They had been shown the sign, the unusual animal, and to gain good luck they must keep a part of it. If they could not, if their hunt was unsuccessful, it would mean bad luck, a sign that the Mother did not want them to stay, and that they should leave immediately. The young woman wondered what the outcome would be.

9

Jondalar studied the disposition of the aurochs herd along the river. The cattle were spread out between the bottom of the slope and the edge of the water among various small pastures of rich green grass, which were interspersed with brush and trees. The spotted cow was alone in a small lea, with a dense stand of birch and alder brush at one end separating her from several other members of the herd. The brush continued along the base of the slope, giving way to clumps of sedge and sharp-leaved reeds on wet low ground at the other end, which led into a marshy inlet choked with tall phragmite reeds and cattails.

He turned to Ayla and pointed toward the marsh. "If you ride along the river past those reeds and cattails, and I come up on her through that opening in the alder brush, we'll have her between us and can ride her down."

Ayla looked over the situation and nodded agreement. Then she dismounted. "I want to tie down my spear holder before we start," she said, fastening the long, tube-shaped rawhide container to the straps that held on the riding blanket of soft deerskin. Inside the stiff leather holder were several well-made, graceful spears with slender round bone points, ground and polished to a fine sharpness and split at the base, where they were attached to the long wooden shafts. Each spear was fletched at the back end with two straight feathers and indented with a notch in the butt.

While Ayla was tying down her holder, Jondalar reached for a spear from the spear holder on his back, attached by a strap that went over one shoulder. He had always worn his spear holder when he'd hunted on foot, and he was used to it, though when he'd traveled by walking on his own two legs, and had worn a backframe, spears were kept in a special holder on the side of it. He placed the spear on his spear-thrower to have it in readiness.

Jondalar had invented the spear-thrower during the summer he lived with Ayla in her valley. It was a unique and startling innovation, an inspired creation of sheer genius that had risen out of his natural technical aptitude and an intuitive sense of physical principles that would not be defined and codified for hundreds of centuries. Though the idea was ingenious, the spear-thrower itself was deceptively simple.

Shaped from a single piece of wood, it was about a foot and a half in length and an inch and a half wide, narrowing near the front end. It was held horizontally and had a groove down the center where the spear rested. A simple hook carved into the back of the thrower fit into the notch in the butt of the spear, acting as a backstop and helping to hold the spear in place while it was being thrown, which contributed to the accuracy of the hunting weapon. Near the front of Jondalar's spear-thrower two soft buckskin loops were attached on either side.

To use it, the spear was laid on the spear-thrower with its butt up against the backstop hook. The first and second fingers were put through the leather loops at the front of the spear-thrower, which reached a place somewhat back from the center of the much longer spear, at a good balance point, and loosely held the spear in place. But a more important function came into play when the spear was thrown. Holding the front of the thrower securely as the spear was cast caused the back end to raise up, which, like an extension of the arm, added length. The greater length increased leverage and momentum, which in turn increased the power and distance of the flight of the spear.

Hurling a spear with a spear-thrower was similar to throwing it by hand; the difference was in the results. With it, the long shaft with the sharp point could be propelled more than twice as far as a spear thrown by hand, with many times the force.

Jondalar's invention utilized mechanical advantage to transmit and amplify the force of muscle power, but it wasn't the first implement to use those principles. His people had a tradition of creative invention and had utilized similar ideas in other ways. For example, a sharp piece of flint held in the hand was an effective cutting tool, but attaching a handle to it gave the user an extraordinary increase in force and control. The seemingly simple idea of putting handles on things—knives, axes, adzes, and other carving, cutting, and drilling tools, a longer one on shovels and rakes, and even a form of detachable handle to throw a spear—multiplied their effectiveness many times. It was not just a simple idea, it was an important invention that made work easier and survival more probable.

Though the ones who had come before them had slowly developed and improved various implements and tools, the people like Jondalar and Ayla were the first to imagine and innovate to such an extravagant degree. Their brains could make abstractions easily. They were capable of conceiving of an idea and planning how to implement it. Beginning with simple objects that utilized advanced principles that were intuitively understood, they drew conclusions and applied them in other circumstances. They did more than invent usable tools, they invented science. And from the same wellspring of creativity, utilizing that same power to abstract, they were the first people to see the world around them in symbolic form, to extract its essence and reproduce it; they originated art.

When Ayla finished tying down her holder, she remounted. Then, seeing that Jondalar had a spear in readiness, she also placed a spear on her spear-thrower and, holding them easily but carefully, started in the direction Jondalar had indicated. The wild cattle were moving slowly along the river, grazing as they went, and the cow they had singled out was already in a different location, and not so isolated. A bull calf and another cow were now close by. Ayla followed the river, guiding Whinney with knees, thighs, and body movements. As she closed in on their intended prey, she saw the tall man on his horse across the green lea approaching through the opening in the brush. The three aurochs were between them.

Jondalar raised his arm, which held the spear, hoping Ayla would realize he meant it as a signal to wait. Perhaps he should have gone over the strategy in greater depth before they separated, but it was hard to plan the tactics of a hunt too precisely. So much depended upon the situation they found, and the actions of the prey. The two additional animals that were now grazing near the white-spotted cow added another complication, but there was no need to hurry. The animals did not seem alarmed by their presence, and he wanted to work out a plan before they rushed in.

Suddenly the cows lifted their heads, and their contented indifference became anxious concern. Jondalar looked beyond the animals and felt a surge of annoyance that approached real anger. Wolf had arrived, and he was moving toward the cattle with his tongue lolling out, managing to look both menacing and playful at the same time. Ayla hadn't noticed him yet, and Jondalar had to stifle an urge to shout to her and tell her to call him off. But a shout would only startle the cows and probably set them off at a run. Instead, when a wave of his arm caught her eye, he pointed at the wolf with his spear.

Ayla noticed Wolf then, but she wasn't sure from Jondalar's motions what he wanted, and she tried to signal back to him in Clan gestures, asking him to explain. Though he did have a basic understanding of the language of the Clan, Jondalar wasn't thinking of gestures as language just then and didn't recognize her signs. He was concentrating on how to salvage a deteriorating situation. The cows had begun lowing, and the calf, sensing fear from them, began bawling. They all looked ready to break away. What had started out to be almost perfect conditions for an easy kill was rapidly becoming a losing effort.

Before things got worse, Jondalar urged Racer forward, just as the solid-colored cow bolted, running away from the oncoming horse and man, toward the trees and brush. The bawling calf followed her. Ayla waited only long enough to be sure which animal Jondalar was going after, then she, too, galloped after the spotted one. They were converging on the aurochs that was still standing in the pasture, watching them and lowing nervously, when the animal suddenly broke into a run, heading toward the marsh. They raced after it, but as they closed in, the cow suddenly dodged and doubled back, dashing between both horses toward the trees at the opposite end of the meadow.

Ayla shifted her weight, and Whinney quickly changed direction. The mare was accustomed to quick changes. Ayla had hunted from horseback before, though usually it was for smaller animals that were downed with her sling. Jondalar had more trouble. A guiding rein wasn't as quick a command as a shift in body weight, and the man and his young stallion had far less experience hunting together, but after some initial hesitation they were soon pounding after the white-spotted aurochs as well.

The cow was heading at a dead run for the grove of trees and thick brush ahead. If she made it to cover, it would be difficult to follow her through it, and there was a good chance that she could get away. Ayla on Whinney and, behind them, Jondalar riding Racer were gaining on the aurochs, but all grazing animals depended on speed to escape predators, and wild cattle could be nearly as fleet as horses when pressed.

Jondalar urged Racer on, and the horse responded with an all-out burst of speed. Trying to steady his spear so he could make an attempt to get the fleeing animal, Jondalar pulled up alongside Ayla, then surged ahead, but at a subtle signal from the woman, the mare kept pace. Ayla held her spear ready to hurl as well, but even at a gallop she rode with an easy, effortless grace that was the result of practice, and her initial training of the horse that had been unintentional. She felt that many of her signals to the horse were more an extension of thought than an act of guidance. She had only to think of how and where she wanted the mare to go, and Whinney complied. They had such an intimate understanding of each other, she hardly realized that the subtle movements of her body that accompanied the thought had given a signal to the sensitive and intelligent animal.

As Ayla was taking aim with her spear, suddenly Wolf was racing alongside the fleeing cow. The aurochs was distracted by the more familiar predator, and it veered to the side, slowing its stride. Wolf leaped at the huge aurochs, and the great spotted cow turned to fend off the four-legged predator with large sharp horns. The wolf fell back, then sprang again and, trying to find any vulnerable place, clamped down on the soft, exposed nose with sharp teeth and strong jaws. The huge cow bellowed, raised her head, lifting Wolf off the ground, and shook him, trying to rid herself of the cause of her pain. Dangling like a limp fur bag, the dazed young canine held on.

Jondalar had been quick to see the change of pace, and he was prepared to take advantage of it. He raced toward them at a gallop and hurled his spear with great force from close quarters. The sharp bone point pierced the heaving sides, sliding in deeply between ribs to vital inner organs. Ayla was just behind him and her spear found its mark a moment later, entering at an angle just behind the rib cage on the opposite side, penetrating deep. Wolf hung on to the cow's nose until she dropped to the ground. With the weight of the large wolf pulling her down, she fell heavily on her side, breaking Jondalar's spear.

"But he was a help," Ayla said. "He did stop the cow before she reached the trees." The man and woman strained to roll the huge aurochs over to expose its underside, stepping over the thick blood that had pooled below the deep cut Jondalar had made in its throat.

"If he hadn't started chasing her when he did, that cow probably wouldn't have started running until we were almost on top of her. It would have been an easy kill," Jondalar said. He picked up the shaft of his broken spear, then threw it down again, thinking he might have been able to save it if Wolf hadn't pulled the cow over on it. It took a lot of work to make a good spear.

"You can't be sure of that. That cow was quick to dodge us, and a fast runner, too."

"Those cows weren't bothered by us at all, until Wolf came. I tried to tell you to call him away, but I didn't want to shout and drive them off."

"I didn't know what you wanted. Why didn't you tell me in Clan signs? I kept asking you, but you weren't paying attention," Ayla said.

Clan signs? Jondalar thought. It hadn't occurred to him that she was using Clan language. That would be a good way to signal. Then he shook his head. "I doubt if it would have done any good," he said. "He probably wouldn't have stopped even if you had tried to call him."

"Maybe not, but I think Wolf could learn to be a help. He already helps me flush small game. Baby learned to hunt

with me. He was a good hunting partner. If a cave lion can
learn to hunt with people, Wolf could, too," Ayla said, feeling defensive about him. After all, they had killed the
aurochs, and Wolf did help.

Jondalar thought Ayla's judgment of the skills a wolf was
capable of learning was unrealistic, but there was no point in
arguing with her. She treated the animal like a child, as it
was, and it would only make her defend him more.

"Well, we'd better gut this cow before it starts to swell.
And we'll have to skin it out here and divide it into pieces
so we can pack it up to the Camp," Jondalar said, and then
another problem occurred to him. "But what are we going
to do about that wolf?"

"What about Wolf?" Ayla asked.

"If we cut that aurochs into pieces and carry part of it
up to the Camp, he'll be able to eat the meat left here," the
man said, his irritation rising, "and when we come back here
to get more, he'll be able to get to the meat we brought up
to the Camp. One of us would have to stay here to watch it,
and the other will have to stay there, but then how do we
bring any more back up there? We're going to have to set
up a tent here to dry the meat instead of using the lodge at
the Camp, just because of Wolf!" He was exasperated with
the problems he perceived the wolf to be causing and was
not thinking clearly.

But he made Ayla angry. Maybe Wolf would go after the
meat if she wasn't there, but he wouldn't touch it as long as
she was with him. She would just make sure Wolf stayed
with her. He wasn't that much of a problem. Why was Jondalar picking on him so much? She started to answer him, then
changed her mind and whistled for Whinney. With a smooth
bound, she mounted, then turned back to Jondalar. "Don't
worry about it. I'll get that cow up to the Camp," she said
as she rode away, calling Wolf to her.

She rode hard back to the earthlodge, jumped down and
hurried inside, and came out with a stone axe with a short
handle, one Jondalar had made for her. Then she mounted
again and urged Whinney toward the birch woods.

Jondalar watched her ride up and saw her coming back
down and go into the woods, wondering what she was planning. He had started the belly cut to remove the intestines
and stomach of the cow, but he was having mixed feelings

as he worked. He did think he was justified in his concerns about the young wolf, but he was sorry he had brought them up to Ayla. He knew how she felt about the animal. His complaints were not going to change anything, and he had to admit her training had accomplished much more than he would have thought possible.

When he heard her chopping wood, he suddenly realized what she planned to do, and he headed for the woods, too. He saw Ayla hacking fiercely at a tall, straight birch tree from the center of the grove of closely spaced trees, venting her anger in the process.

Wolf isn't as bad as Jondalar says, she was thinking. Maybe he did almost scare off that aurochs, but then he did help. She paused for a moment, resting, and frowned. What if they hadn't made a kill, wouldn't that have meant they weren't welcome? That the spirit of the Mother didn't want them to stay at the Camp? If Wolf had spoiled their hunting, she wouldn't be thinking of how to move that cow, they would be leaving. But if they were meant to stay, he couldn't have spoiled their hunting, could he? She started chopping again. It was getting too complicated. They had killed the spotted cow, even with Wolf's interference—and his help— so it was all right to use the lodge. Maybe they had been guided to this place, after all, she thought.

Suddenly Jondalar appeared. He tried to take the axe from her. "Why don't you look for another tree and let me finish this one," he said.

Though not as angry, Ayla resisted his assistance. "I told you I'd get that cow up to the Camp. I can do it without your help."

"I know you can, the same way you brought me to your cave in the valley. But with both of us, you'll have your new poles much faster," he said, then added, "And yes, I have to admit, you are right. Wolf did help."

She stopped in midstroke and looked up at him. His brow revealed his earnest concern, but his expressive blue eyes showed mixed feelings. Though she didn't understand his misgivings about Wolf, the powerful love he felt for her showed in his eyes, too. She felt drawn to those eyes, to the sheer male magnetism of his closeness, to the fascination that he didn't fully realize he had or know the strength of, and felt her resistance evaporate.

"But you're right, too," she said, feeling a little contrite.
"He did make them run before we were ready, and he might
have spoiled the hunt."

Jondalar's frown vanished in a relieved smile. "So we're
both right," he said. She smiled back, and the next moment
they were in each other's arms, and his mouth found hers.
They clung together, relieved that their argument was over,
wanting to cancel out the distance that had come between
them with physical closeness.

When they stopped expressing their fervent relief, but still
stood with their arms around each other, Ayla said, "I do
think Wolf could learn to help us hunt. We just have to teach
him."

"I don't know. Maybe. But since he's going to be traveling with us, I think you should teach him as much as he'll
learn. If nothing else, maybe you can train him not to interfere when we're hunting," he said.

"You should help, too, so he'll mind both of us."

"I doubt that he'll pay attention to me," he said. Then
seeing that she was ready to disagree, he added, "But if you
want, I'll try." He took the stone axe from her and decided
to bring up another idea she had raised. "You said something
about using Clan signs when we don't want to shout. That
could be useful." As Ayla went to look for another tree of
the right shape and size, she was smiling.

Jondalar examined the tree she had been working on to
see how much more chopping it would need. It was difficult
to cut down a hard tree with a stone axe. The brittle flint of
the axe head was made rather thick so that it would not break
too easily from the force of the blow, and a strike did not
cut in deeply, but instead chipped a little away. The tree
looked more as if it had been gnawed than cut. Ayla listened
to the rhythmic sound of stone hitting wood as she carefully
examined the trees in the grove. When she found one that
was suitable, she notched the bark then looked for a third.

When the necessary trees were cut down, they dragged
them out to the clearing and, using knives and the axe,
stripped the branches, then lined them up on the ground. Ayla
judged the size and marked them, and they cut them all to
an equal length. While Jondalar removed the internal organs
from the aurochs, she walked back to the lodge for ropes and
a device she had made of leather straps and thongs knotted

and braided together. She brought along one of the torn floor mats as well when she returned, then signaled for Whinney and adjusted the special harness on her.

Using two of the long poles—the third was only necessary for the tripod she used to keep food out of the reach of prowling scavengers—she attached the narrower ends to the harness she had put on the horse, crossing them over above the withers. The heavier ends dragged on the ground, one on either side of the mare. With ropes, they fastened the grass mat across the more widely spread poles of the travois, near the ground, and attached extra ropes to tie down and hold the aurochs.

Looking at the size of the huge cow, Ayla began to wonder if perhaps it would be too much even for the strong steppe horse. The man and woman both strained to get the aurochs on the travois. The mat offered only minimal support, but by tying the animal directly to the poles, it did not drag on the ground. After their efforts, Ayla was even more concerned that the load would be too much for Whinney, and she almost changed her mind. Jondalar had already removed the stomach, intestines, and other organs; perhaps they should skin it out right there and cut it into more manageable pieces. She didn't feel the need to show him that she could bring it to the Camp alone any more, but since it was already loaded on the travois, she decided to have Whinney give it a try.

If Ayla was surprised when the horse began to pull the heavy load over the rough terrain, Jondalar was even more so. The aurochs was bigger and heavier than Whinney, and it was a strain, but with only two points dragging, and most of the weight borne by the poles resting on the ground, the load was manageable. The slope was more difficult, but the sturdy horse of the steppes accomplished even that effort. On the uneven ground of any natural surface, the travois was by far the most efficient conveyance to transport loads.

The device was Ayla's invention, the result of need, opportunity, and an intuitive leap. Living alone with no one to help her, she often found herself with the need to move things that were too heavy for her to carry or drag alone— such as a whole, full-grown animal—and usually had to break them down into smaller pieces, and then had to think of some way to protect what was left behind from scavengers. Her unique opportunity was the mare she had raised, and the chance to utilize the strength of a horse to help her. But her special advantage was a brain that could recognize a possibility and devise the means.

Once they reached the earthlodge, Ayla and Jondalar untied the aurochs, and after words and hugs of thanks and praise, they led the horse back down to get the animal's innards. They, too, were useful. When they reached the clearing, Jondalar picked up his broken spear. The front of the shaft had snapped off; the point was still embedded in the carcass, but the long straight back section was still whole. Perhaps he could find a use for it, he thought, taking it with him.

Back at the Camp they removed Whinney's harness. Wolf was nosing around the inner organs; intestines were a favorite of his. Ayla hesitated a moment. If she'd had need, she could have used them for several purposes, from fat storage to waterproofing, but it wasn't possible to take much more than they already had with them.

Why did it seem, she thought, that just because they had horses and were able to take more with them, they needed more? She recalled that when she left the Clan and was traveling on foot, she carried everything she needed in a pack basket on her back. It was true that their tent was much more comfortable than the low hide shelter she had used then, and they did have changes of clothes, and winter ones that they weren't using, and more food and utensils, and . . . she'd never be able to carry everything in a pack basket now, she realized.

She threw the useful, though presently unnecessary, intestines to Wolf, and she and Jondalar turned to butchering the wild beef. After making several strategic cuts, together they began to pull off the hide, a process that was more efficient than skinning it with a knife. They only used a sharp implement to sever a few points of attachment. With a little effort, the membrane between the skin and the muscle separated cleanly, and they ended up with only the two holes of the spear points marring a perfect hide. They rolled it up to keep it from drying too quickly, and they put the head aside. The tongue and brains were rich and tender, and they planned to eat those delicacies that night. The skull with its large horns, however, they would leave for the Camp. It could have special meaning for someone, and if not, there were many useful parts to it.

Then Ayla took the stomach and bladder to the small stream that supplied water for the Camp to wash them, and Jondalar went down to the river to find brush and slender trees that could be bent to make a round bowl-shaped frame for the small boat. They also searched for deadfall and driftwood. They would need several fires to keep animals and insects away from their meat, as well as a fire inside overnight.

They worked until it was nearly dark, dividing the cow into large segments, then cutting the meat into small tongue-shaped pieces and hanging them to dry over makeshift racks made of brushwood, but they still didn't finish. They brought the racks into the lodge overnight. Their tent was still damp, but they folded it and brought it in, too. They would set it up again the next day when they brought the meat out, to let the wind and the sun finish the drying.

In the morning, after they cut up the last of the meat, Jondalar began to construct the boat. Using both steam and hot rocks heated in the fire, he bent the wood for the boat frame. Ayla was very interested and wanted to know where he learned the process.

"My brother, Thonolan. He was a spearmaker," Jondalar explained, holding down the end of a small straight tree that he had formed into a curve, while she lashed it to a circular section with sinew made of a tendon from the hind legs of the aurochs.

"But what does spearmaking have to do with making a boat?"

"Thonolan could make a spear shaft perfectly straight and true. But to learn how to take the bend out of wood, you first have to learn how to bend wood, and he could do that just as well. He was much better at it than I am. He had a real feel for it. I suppose you could say his craft was not only making spears, but shaping wood. He could make the best snowshoes, and that means taking a straight branch or tree and bending it completely around. Maybe that's why he felt so much at home with the Sharamudoi. They were expert wood shapers. They used hot water and steam to bend out their dugouts to the shape they wanted."

"What is a dugout?" Ayla asked.

"It's a boat carved out of a whole tree. The front end is shaped to a fine edge, the back end, too, and it can glide through the water so easily and smoothly, it's like cutting with a sharp knife. They're beautiful boats. This one we're making is clumsy by comparison, but there are no big trees around here. You'll see dugouts when we reach the Sharamudoi.''

"How much longer before we get there?"

"It's quite a long ways, yet. Beyond those mountains," he said, looking west, toward the high peaks indistinct in the summer haze.

"Oh," she said, feeling disappointed. "I was hoping it wouldn't be so far. It would be nice to see some people. I wish someone had been here at this Camp. Maybe they'll come back before we leave." Jondalar noticed a wistfulness in her tone.

"Are you lonely for people?" he asked. "You spent such a long time alone in your valley, I thought you'd be used to it."

"Maybe that's why. I spent enough time being alone. I don't mind it for a while, sometimes I like it, but we haven't seen any people for so long . . . I just thought it would be fun to talk to someone," she said, then looked at him. "I'm so happy you are with me, Jondalar. It would be so lonely without you."

"I am happy, too, Ayla. Happy I didn't have to make this trip alone, happier than I can say that you came with me. I'm looking forward to seeing people, too. When we reach the Great Mother River, we should meet some. We've been traveling across country. People tend to live near fresh water, rivers or lakes, not out in the open."

Ayla nodded, then held the end of another slender sapling, which had been heating over hot rocks and steam, while Jondalar carefully bent it into a circle, then helped him lash it to the others. Judging from the size of it, she began to see that it would take the entire hide of the aurochs to cover it. There would be no more than a few scraps left over, not enough to make a new rawhide meat-keeper to replace the one she had lost in the flash flood. They needed the boat to cross the river, she would just have to think of something else to use. Maybe a basket would work, she thought, tightly woven, long in shape, and rather flat, with a lid. There were cattails and reeds and willows, plenty of basket-making materials around, but would a basket work?

The problem with carrying freshly killed meat was that blood continued to seep out, and no matter how tightly woven, it would eventually leak through a basket. That was why thick, hard rawhide worked so well. It absorbed the blood, but slowly, and didn't leak, and after a period of use, could be washed and redried. She needed something that would do the same thing. She'd have to think about it.

The problem of replacing her parfleche stayed on her mind, and when the frame was finished, and they left it to wait for the sinew to dry hard and firm, Ayla headed down to the river to collect some basket-making materials. Jondalar went with her but only as far as the birch woods. Since he was all set up for shaping wood, he decided to make some new spears, to replace those that had been lost or broken.

Wymez had given him some good flint before he left, roughed out and preshaped so that new points could be made easily. He had made the bone-pointed spears before they left the Summer Meeting, to show how they were done. They were typical of the kind his people used, but he had learned how to make the flint-tipped Mamutoi spears as well, and because he was a skilled flint knapper, they were faster for him to make than shaping and smoothing bone points.

In the afternoon Ayla started to make a special meat-keeping basket. When she lived in the valley, she had spent many long winter nights easing her loneliness by making baskets and mats, among other things, and she had become very quick and adept at weaving. She could almost make a basket in the dark, and her new carrying container for meat was finished before she went to bed. It was made extremely well, she had thought carefully about the shape and size, materials and tightness of weave, but she wasn't quite satisfied with it.

She went out in the darkening twilight to change her absorbent wool and wash the piece she was wearing in the small stream. She put it near the fire to dry, but out of Jondalar's sight. Then, without quite looking at him, she lay down in their sleeping furs beside him. Women of the Clan were taught to avoid men as much as possible when they bled, and never to look at them directly. It made Clan men very nervous to be around women during that time. It had surprised her that Jondalar had no qualms about it, but she still felt uncomfortable, and she took pains to be discreet in caring for herself.

Jondalar had always been considerate of her during her moon times, sensing her disquiet, but once she was in bed, he leaned over to kiss her. Though she kept her eyes closed,

she responded with warmth, and when he rolled over on his
back again, and they were lying side by side watching the
play of firelight on the walls and ceilings of the comfortable
structure, they talked, though she was careful not to look at
him.

"I'd like to coat that hide after it's mounted on the
frame," he said. "If I boil up the hooves and scraps of hide
and some bones together with water for a long time, it will
make a very thick and sticky kind of broth, that dries hard.
Do we have something that I can use to cook that in?"

"I'm sure we can think of something. Does it have to
cook long?"

"Yes. It does need to cook down, to thicken."

"Then it might be best to cook it directly over the fire,
like a soup . . . maybe a piece of hide. We'll have to watch
it, and keep adding water, but as long as it stays wet, it won't
burn . . . wait. What about the stomach of that aurochs? I've
been keeping water in it, so it wouldn't dry out, and to have
it handy for cooking and washing, but it would make a good
cooking bag," Ayla said.

"I don't think so," Jondalar said. "We don't want to
keep adding water. We want it to get thick."

"Then I suppose a good watertight basket and hot stones
might be best. I can make one in the morning," Ayla said,
but as she lay quietly, her mind wouldn't let her sleep. She
kept thinking that there was a better way to boil down the
mixture Jondalar wanted to make. She just could not quite
think of it. She was nearly asleep when it came to her. "Jondalar! Now I remember."

He, too, was dozing off but was jerked awake. "Huh!
What's wrong?"

"Nothing's wrong. I just remembered how Nezzie rendered out fat, and I think it would be the best way to cook
your thick stuff. You dig a shallow hole in the ground, in
the shape of a bowl, and line it with a piece of hide—there
should be a big enough piece left from the aurochs for that.
Break up some bones and scatter them over the bottom, then
put in the water and the hooves and whatever else you want.
You can boil it for as long as we keep heating stones, and
the little pieces of bone will keep the hot stones from actually
touching the leather, so it won't burn through."

"Good, Ayla. That's what we'll do," Jondalar said, still
half-asleep. He rolled over and was soon snoring.

But there was still something else on Ayla's mind that kept her awake. She had planned to leave the aurochs's stomach for the people of the Camp to use as a waterbag when they left, but it needed to be kept wet. Once it dried out, it got stiff, and would not go back to its original, pliable, nearly waterproof condition. Even if she filled it with water, it would eventually seep out and evaporate away, and she didn't know when the people would return.

Suddenly it came to her. She almost called out again, but muffled it in time. He was sleeping, and she didn't want to wake him. She would let the stomach dry out and use it to line her new meat-keeper, shaping it while it was still wet to fit exactly. As she fell asleep in the darkened lodge, Ayla felt pleased that she had thought of a way to replace the very necessary item that had been lost.

During the next few days, while the meat dried, they were both busy. They finished the bowl boat and coated it with the glue Jondalar made by boiling down the hooves, bone, and hide scraps. While it was drying, Ayla made baskets, for the meat they were leaving as a gift for the people of the Camp, for cooking to replace those she had lost, and for gathering, some of which she planned to leave behind. She gathered vegetable produce and medicinal herbs daily, drying some to take with them.

Jondalar accompanied her one day to look for something to make into paddles for the boat. Shortly after they started out, he was pleased to find the skull of a giant deer that had died before the large palmate antlers were shed, giving him two of equal size. Though it was early, he stayed out with Ayla for the rest of the morning. He was learning to identify certain foods himself, and in the process he was beginning to understand how much Ayla really knew. Her knowledge of plants and her memory for their uses were incredible. When they returned to the Camp, Jondalar trimmed the tines off the broad antlers and attached them to sturdy, rather short poles, making entirely serviceable paddles.

The next day he decided to use the wood-shaping apparatus he had set up to bend the wood for the boat frame, to straighten shafts for new spears. Shaping and smoothing them took most of the next couple of days, even with the special tools he had with him, carried in a roll of leather tied with thongs. But while he was working, every time he passed by the side of the earthlodge where he had thrown it, Jondalar noticed the truncated spear shaft he had brought up from the valley and felt a flush of annoyance. It was a shame that there wasn't a way to salvage that straight shaft, short of making a cropped and unbalanced spear out of it. Any of the spears he was working so hard to make could break just as easily.

When he was satisfied that the spears would fly true, he used yet another tool, a narrow flint blade with a chisellike tip hafted to an antler-tine handle, to hollow out a deep notch in the thicker butt ends of the shafts. Then, from the prepared flint nodules he had with him, Jondalar knapped new blades and attached them to the spear shafts with the thick glue he had made as a coating for the boat, and fresh sinew. The tough tendon shrank as it dried, making a strong, solid bond. He finished by affixing pairs of long feathers, found near the river, from the numerous white-tailed eagles, falcons, and black kites that lived in the region feeding on the abundance of susliks and other small rodents.

They had set up a target, using a thick, grass-stuffed bed pad that the badger had torn up and made worthless. Patched with scraps from the aurochs, it absorbed the force of a throw without damage to the spears. Both Jondalar and Ayla practiced a little every day. Ayla did it to maintain her accuracy, but Jondalar was experimenting with different lengths of shaft and sizes of point to see which would work best with the spear-thrower.

When his new spears were finished and dried, he and Ayla took them to the target area to try them out with the spear-thrower and choose which ones each wanted. Though they were both very adept with the hunting weapon, some of their practice casts inevitably went wide of the mark and missed the cushioned target, usually landing harmlessly on the ground. But when Jondalar cast a newly completed spear with a powerful throw, and not only missed the target, but hit a large mammoth bone that was used as an outdoor seat, he flinched. He heard a crack as it bent and bounced back. The wooden shaft had splintered at a weak spot about a foot back from the point.

When he walked over to examine it, he noticed that the brittle flint tip had also shattered along one edge and spalled off a large chip, leaving a lopsided point that was not worth salvaging. He was furious with himself for wasting a spear that had taken so much time and effort to make, before it could be used for anything worthwhile. In a sudden surge of anger, he cracked the bent spear across his knee and broke it in two, then threw it down.

When he looked up, he noticed Ayla watching him, and he turned away, flushed with embarrassment over his outburst, then stooped down and picked up the broken pieces, wishing he could dispose of them unobtrusively. When he looked up again, Ayla was getting ready to cast another spear as though she hadn't seen anything. He walked over to the earthlodge and dropped the broken spear near the shaft that had broken during the hunt, then stared down at the pieces, feeling foolish. It was ridiculous to get so angry over breaking a spear.

But it is a lot of work to make one, he thought, looking at the long shaft with the end broken off, and the section of the other spear with the broken flint point still attached that happened to be lying just in front. It's too bad those pieces can't be put together to make a whole spear.

As he stared at them, he began to wonder if maybe he could, and he picked up both pieces again, examining the broken ends carefully. He fitted them together and, for a while, the splintered ends stayed attached, then fell apart again. Looking over the entire long shaft, he noted the hollowed-out indentation he had carved at the butt end for the pointed hook of the spear-thrower, then turned it around to look again at the broken end.

If I carved a deeper hold at this end, he thought, and shaved the end of this piece with the broken flint to a tapered point, and put them together, would they stay? Full of excitement, Jondalar went into the lodge and got out his roll of leather and took it outside. He sat down on the ground and unrolled it, displaying the variety of carefully made flint tools, and picked out the chisel tool. Setting it down nearby, he examined the broken shaft and reached for his flint knife from the sheath on his belt and began to cut away the splinters and make a smooth end.

Ayla had stopped practicing with her spear-thrower and put it and her spears in the holder that she had adapted to wear across her back over one shoulder, the way Jondalar did. She was walking back toward the lodge carrying some plants she had dug up when he came striding toward her with a big smile on his face.

"Look, Ayla!" he said, holding up the spear. The piece with the broken point still attached was fitted into the top end of the long spear shaft. "I fixed it. Now I'm going to see if it works!"

She followed him back to the practice target and watched him set the spear on the thrower, pull back and take aim, then hurl the spear with great force. The long missile hit the target, then bounced back. But when Jondalar went to check, he found that the broken point attached to the small tapered shaft was embedded firmly in the target. With the impact, the long shaft had come loose and bounced back, but when he went to inspect it, he found it was undamaged. The two-part spear had worked.

"Ayla! Do you realize what this means?" Jondalar was nearly shouting with excitement.

"I'm not sure," she said.

"See, the point found its mark, then separated from the shaft without breaking. That means, all I have to make next time is a new point and attach it to a short piece like this. I don't have to make a whole new long shaft. I can make two points like this, several, in fact, and will only need a few long shafts. We can carry a lot more short shafts with points than long full spears, and if we lose one, it won't be so hard to replace. Here, you try it," he said, working loose the broken point from the target.

Ayla looked over. "I'm not very good at making a long spear shaft straight, and my points are not as beautiful as yours," she said. "But even I could make one of these, I think." She was as excited as Jondalar.

On the day before they planned to leave, they checked over their repairs of the damage caused by the badger, placed the skin of the animal in a way that they hoped would make it obvious that it was the cause of the mess, and put out their gifts. The basket of dried meat was hung from a mammoth bone rafter to make it difficult for any other prowling animal to find. Ayla displayed other baskets, and hung several bunches of dried medicinal herbs and food plants as well, particularly those that were commonly used by the Mamutoi.

Jondalar left the owner of the lodge an especially well made spear.

They also mounted the partly dried skull of the aurochs cow, with its huge horns, on a pole outside the lodge, so that scavengers could not get to it, either. The horns and other bony parts of the skull were useful, and it was a way of explaining what kind of meat was in the basket.

The young wolf and the horses seemed to sense an impending change. Wolf bounded around them full of excitement and energy, and the horses were restless, with Racer living up to his name, breaking into short, fast-breaking dashes, and Whinney staying closer to the Camp, watching for Ayla and nickering when she saw her.

Before they went to bed, they packed everything except their sleeping rolls and breakfast essentials, including the dry tent, though it was harder to fold and fit into the pack basket. The hides had been smoked before the skins were made into a tent, so that even after a thorough soaking, they would remain reasonably pliable, but the portable shelter was still somewhat stiff. It would become more flexible again with use.

On their last night in the comfort of the lodge, Ayla watched the flickering light of the dying fire playing across the walls of the substantial shelter, feeling her emotions flicker across her mind with a similar play of brightness and shadow. She was eager to be on their way again, but sorry to be leaving a place that, in the short time they had been there, had come to feel like home—except there were no people. In the past few days, she had caught herself looking up at the crest of the slope hoping to see the people who lived at the Camp returning before they had to leave.

Though she still wished they would arrive unexpectedly, she had given up hoping, and she was looking forward to reaching the Great Mother River and perhaps meeting someone along its route. She loved Jondalar, but she was lonely for people, for women and children, and elders, for laughing and talking, and sharing with others of her kind. But she didn't want to think much beyond the next day, or the next Camp of people. She didn't want to think about Jondalar's people, or how long they still had to travel before they reached his home, and she didn't want to think about how they were going to cross that large, fast river with only a small round boat.

Jondalar lay awake as well, worried about their Journey and eager to be moving again, though he did think their stay had been very worthwhile. Their tent was dry, they had replenished their meat and replaced necessary equipment that had been lost or damaged, and he was excited about the development of the two-part spear. He was glad he had the bowl boat, but even with it, he was worried about crossing the river. It was a large waterway, wide and swift. They were probably not very far from the sea, and it was not likely to get smaller. Anything could happen. He would be glad when they reached the other side.

10

Ayla woke often during the night, and her eyes were open as the first morning glow crept in through the smoke hole and sent its faint illuminating fingers into the tenebrious crannies to disperse the dark and bring the hidden shapes out of the concealing shadows. By the time the obscuring night had retreated to a dim half-light, she was wide awake and could not go back to sleep.

Moving quietly away from Jondalar's warmth, she slipped outside. The night chill enveloped her bare skin and, with its cooling hint of the massive layers of ice to the north, clothed her with gooseflesh. Looking out across the misty river valley, she saw the vague formations of the still unlighted land on the opposite side, silhouetted against the glowing sky. She wished they were already over there.

Rough warm fur brushed against her leg. Absently she patted the head and scratched the ruff of the wolf who had appeared beside her. He sniffed the air and, finding something interesting, raced off down the slope. She looked for the horses and made out the yellowish coat of the mare grazing in one of the grassy leas near the water. The dark brown horse was not visible, but she was sure he was nearby.

Shivering, she walked through the damp grass toward the small creek and sensed the rising of the sun in the east. She watched the western sky shade from glowing gray to pastel blue, with a scattering of pink clouds, reflecting the glory of the morning sun hidden behind the crest of the slope.

Ayla was tempted to walk up and see the rising sun, but she was stopped by a glint of dazzling brilliance from the other direction. Though the gully-scarred slopes across the river were still wrapped in a somber gray gloom, the mountains to the west, bathed in the clear light of the new day's sun, stood out in vivid relief, etched with such perfect detail that it seemed she could reach out and touch them. Crowning the low southern range, a glittering tiara sparkled from the icy tips. She watched the slowly changing patterns with wonder, held by the magnificence of the back side of the sunrise.

By the time she reached the little stream of clear water that was racing and skipping down the slope, the morning chill had burned off. She put down the waterbag she had taken from the lodge and, checking her wool, was glad to see that her moon time seemed to be over. She unfastened her straps, took off her amulet, and stepped into a shallow pool to wash. When she was through, she filled the waterbag at the splashing cascade that ran into the slight depression of the pool, then got out and pushed the water off with one hand and then the other. Putting her amulet back on and picking up the washed wool and her straps, she hurried back.

Jondalar was knotting a tie around their rolled-up sleeping furs when she stepped down into the semisubterranean earthlodge. He looked up and smiled. Noticing that she wasn't wearing her leather straps, his smile took on a decidedly suggestive look.

"Maybe I shouldn't have been so quick to roll up the furs this morning," he said.

She flushed when she realized he was aware that she was past her moon time. Then she looked directly into his eyes, which were full of teasing laughter, love, and burgeoning desire, and smiled back. "You can always unroll them again."

"There go my plans for an early start," he said, pulling an end of the thong that released the knot on the sleeping roll. He unrolled it and stood up as she walked to him.

After their morning meal, it took little time for them to finish packing. Gathering all their possessions and the boat, along with their animal traveling companions, they moved down to the river. But deciding the best way to get across was another matter. They stared at the expanse of water rushing past, so wide that details of the bank on the other side were difficult to see. With its fast current sliding over and around itself in subdued ripples and eddies, making small choppy waves, the sound of the deep river was almost more revealing than its look. It spoke its power in a muted, gurgling roar.

While he was making the circular craft, Jondalar had thought often about the river and how to use the boat to get across. He had never made a bowl boat before, and he had only ridden in one a few times. He had become fairly adept at handling the sleek dugout canoes when he lived with the Sharamudoi, but when he tried his hand at propelling the round bowl boats of the Mamutoi, he found them very clumsy. They were buoyant, hard to tip over, but difficult to control.

The two peoples not only had different types of materials at hand to construct their floating craft, they used boats for different purposes. The Mamutoi were primarily hunters of the open steppes; fishing was only an occasional activity. Their boats were used primarily to get themselves and their possessions across waterways, whether small tributaries or the rivers that swept down, continent-wide, from the glaciers of the north to the inland seas of the south.

The Ramudoi, the River People moiety of the Sharamudoi, fished the Great Mother River—though they referred to it as hunting when they went after the thirty-foot sturgeons—while the Shamudoi half hunted chamois and other animals that lived on the high cliffs and mountains that overlooked the river and, near their home, confined it in a great gorge. The Ramudoi lived on the river during the warm seasons, taking full advantage of its resources, including the large durmast oaks that lined its banks, which were used to make their beautifully crafted and maneuverable boats.

"Well, I think we should just put everything in it," Jondalar said, picking up one of his pack baskets. Then he put it down and picked up the other one instead. "It's probably a good idea to put the heaviest things on the bottom, and this one has my flint and tools in it.''

Ayla nodded. She, too, had been thinking about getting them all across the river with their belongings intact, and she had tried to anticipate some of the potential problems, remembering her few excursions in the Lion Camp's bowl boats. ''We should leave a place for each of us on opposite sides, so it stays balanced. I'll leave room for Wolf to be with me.''

Jondalar wondered how the wolf would behave in the fragile floating bowl, though he refrained from saying anything. Ayla saw his frown, but kept her peace. ''We should each have a paddle, too,'' he said, handing one to her.

''With all of this, I hope we'll be able to fit,'' she said, putting the tent in the boat, thinking she might use it for a seat.

Though it was cramped, they managed to get everything into the hide-covered boat, except the poles. ''We may have to leave those behind. There's no room for them,'' Jondalar said. They had just replaced the ones they had lost.

Ayla smiled and held up some cord she had kept out. ''No, we won't. They'll float. I'll just tie them to the boat with this so they won't drift away,'' she said.

Jondalar wasn't sure that was a good idea, and he was framing an objection as he thought about it, but Ayla's next question distracted him.

''What are we going to do about the horses?'' she said.

''What about the horses? They can swim across, can't they?''

''Yes, but you know how nervous they can get, especially about something that they haven't done before. What if they get frightened by something in the water and decide to go back? They won't try again to cross the river by themselves. They won't even know we're on the other side. We would have to come back and lead them across, so why not just lead them to begin with?'' Ayla explained.

She was right. The horses probably would get apprehensive, and could just as easily go back as across, Jondalar thought. ''But how are we going to lead them when we're in the boat?'' he said. This was becoming complicated. Trying to manage a boat could be difficult enough without trying to manage panicked horses, besides. He was feeling more and more worried about crossing this river.

"We put on their halters with lead ropes, and tie the ropes to the boat," Ayla said.

"I don't know . . . That may not be the best way. Maybe we should think about it some more," he said.

"What is there to think about?" she said, as she was wrapping cord around the three poles. Then she measured out a length and fastened it to the boat. "You were the one who wanted to get started," she added, while she put Whinney's halter on, attached a lead rope to it, then fastened it to the boat on the opposite side of the poles. Holding the slack, she stood beside the boat, then turned to Jondalar. "I'm ready to go."

He hesitated, then nodded decisively. "All right," he said, getting Racer's halter from his pack basket and calling the horse to him. The young stallion lifted his head and neighed when the man first tried to slip the halter over his head, but after Jondalar talked to him and stroked his face and neck, Racer calmed down and allowed it. He tied the rope to the boat, then faced Ayla. "Let's go," he said.

Ayla signaled to Wolf to get into the boat. Then, with both of them still holding the lead ropes, to maintain control of the animals, they pushed the boat into the water and scrambled to get in.

From the beginning, there was trouble. The swift current took hold of the small craft and swept it along, but the horses were not quite ready to enter the wide stream. They reared back as the boat was trying to pull away, jerking the boat so violently that it nearly tipped over, making Wolf stumble to regain his footing and eye the situation nervously. But the load was so heavy that the boat righted itself quickly, though it rode very low in the water. The poles had stretched out in front, trying to follow the strong current.

The pull on the horses by the river trying to propel the boat downstream, and the anxious words of encouragement from Ayla and Jondalar, finally convinced the balky animals to enter the water. First Whinney put in a tentative hoof and found bottom, then Racer, and, with the constant tug, they both finally jumped in. The bank fell off sharply, and they were soon swimming. Ayla and Jondalar had no choice but to let the current carry them along downstream until the entire, unlikely combination of three long poles, followed by a round, heavily laden boat carrying a woman, a man, and a very tense wolf, with two horses behind, stabilized. Then they let go of the lead ropes and each took up a paddle and attempted to change their direction so that they were moving across the current.

Ayla, on the side facing the opposite shore, was not at all familiar with using a paddle. It took several tries, with Jondalar giving advice while he was trying to row away from the shore, before she got the hang of it, and managed to use it in cooperation with him to direct the boat. Even then, it was slow going, with the long poles in front and the horses behind, eyes rolling with fear as they were involuntarily pulled along by the current.

They did begin to make progress in crossing the river, though they were traveling much faster downstream. But ahead, the large swift waterway, surging down the gradual decline of the land on its way to the sea, was making a sharp curve toward the east. A back current, eddying off a projecting sand spit of the near shore, caught the poles that were racing along in front of the boat.

The long shafts of birch, free-floating except for the cords that held them, turned back around and hit the hide-covered boat with a hard bump near Jondalar, making him fear that it had caused a hole. It jarred everyone aboard, and gave a spin to the small round bowl boat, which jerked on the lead ropes of the horses. The horses whinnied in panic, swallowing mouthfuls of water, and tried desperately to swim away, but the relentless current pulling the boat to which they were tied inexorably pulled them along.

But their efforts were not without effect. They caused the little boat to be jerked back and twist around, which yanked on the poles, making them bang into the boat again. The turbulent current, and the jerking and bumping of the overloaded craft, made it bob and bounce and ship water, adding more weight. It was threatening to sink.

The frightened wolf had been cowering with his tail between his legs beside Ayla on the folded tent, while she was frantically trying to steady the boat with a paddle she didn't know how to use, with Jondalar shouting instructions she didn't know how to apply. The whinnying of the panicked horses turned her attention to them and, seeing their fear, she suddenly realized she had to cut them free. Dropping her paddle to the bottom of the boat, she took her knife from the sheath at her waist. Knowing that Racer was more excitable,

she worked at his rope first, and with only a little effort the
sharp flint blade cut through.

His release caused more bumping and spinning, which
was just too much for Wolf. He leaped from the boat into
the water. Ayla watched him swimming frantically, quickly
cut through Whinney's rope, and jumped in after him.

"Ayla!" Jondalar screamed, but he was jerked around
again as the suddenly released and lighter-weight boat started
rotating and crashing into the poles. When he looked up,
Ayla was trying to tread water, encouraging the wolf who
was swimming toward her. Whinney, and beyond her, Racer,
were heading for the far shore, and the current was taking
him even faster downstream, away from Ayla.

She glanced back and caught one last glimpse of Jondalar
and the boat as it rounded the bend of the river and felt a
heart-stopping moment of fear that she would never see him
again. The thought flashed through her mind that she should
not have left the boat, but she had little time to worry about
it just then. The wolf was coming to her, struggling against
the current. She took a few strokes toward him, but when she
reached him, he tried to put his paws on her shoulders and lick
her face and in his eagerness he dunked her under the water.
She came up sputtering, hugged him with one arm, and
looked for the horses.

The mare was swimming for the shore, pulling away from
her. She took a deep breath and whistled, loud and long. The
horse pricked up her ears and turned toward the sound. Ayla
whistled again, and the horse altered direction and tried to
swim to her as she reached out toward Whinney with strong
strokes. Ayla was a good swimmer. Going generally with the
current, though at a diagonal across it, it nevertheless took
some effort to reach the wet shaggy animal. When she did,
she almost cried with relief. The wolf reached them soon
after, but he kept on going.

Ayla rested for a moment, holding on to Whinney's neck,
and only then noticed how cold the water was. She saw the
rope trailing in the water, attached to the halter Whinney still
wore, and it occurred to her how dangerous it could be for
the horse if the rope got tangled in some floating debris. The
woman spent a few moments trying to unfasten the knot, but
it was swollen tight, and her fingers were stiff with cold. She
took a deep breath and started swimming again, not wanting

to put an added burden on the horse and hoping the exercise
would help warm her.

When they finally gained the far shore, Ayla stumbled
out of the water, exhausted and shivering, and fell to the
ground. The wolf and the horse were little better. They both
shook themselves, spraying water everywhere, then Wolf
dropped down, breathing hard. Whinney's shaggy coat was
heavy even in summer, though it would be much thicker in
winter when the dense underfur grew in. She stood with her
feet spraddled and her body quivering, her head hanging
down and her ears drooping.

But the summer sun was high, and the day had warmed,
and once she had rested, Ayla stopped shivering. She stood
up, looking for Racer, sure that if they had made it across,
the stallion would have, too. She whistled, her call for Whinney first, since Racer usually came along whenever she whistled for his dam. Then she made Jondalar's call whistle for
him, and she suddenly felt a stab of worry about the man.
Had he made it across the river in that flimsy little boat? And
if he had, where was he? She whistled again, hoping the man
would hear and respond, but she wasn't unhappy when the
dark brown stallion came galloping into view, still wearing
the halter, with a short length of lead rope hanging from it.

"Racer!" she called out. "You did make it. I knew you
would."

Whinney greeted him with a welcoming nicker and Wolf
with enthusiastic puppy barks that worked their way into a
full-throated howl. Racer responded with loud neighs, which
Ayla was sure contained a sound of relief at finding his familiar friends. When he reached them, Racer touched noses with
Wolf, then stood near his dam with his head over her neck,
drawing comfort after the frightening river crossing.

Ayla joined them and gave him a hug, then patted and
stroked him before removing his halter. He was so used to
the device that it didn't seem to bother him, and it did not
interfere with his grazing, but Ayla thought the dangling rope
could create problems, and she knew she wouldn't like to
wear something like that all the time. She then took Whinney's halter off and tucked them both into the waist thong of
her tunic. She thought about removing her wet clothes, but
she felt the need to hurry, and they were drying on her.

"Well, we've found Racer. Now it's time to find Jondalar," she said aloud. The wolf looked at her expectantly, and

she directed her comments at him. "Wolf, let's find Jondalar!" She mounted Whinney and started off downstream.

After many spins, turns, and bumps, the small, round, hide-covered boat, with Jondalar's assistance, was calmly following the current again, this time with the three poles trailing behind. Then, with the single paddle and considerable effort, he began to propel the small craft across the large river. He discovered that the three trailing poles tended to stabilize the floating bowl, keeping it from rotating and making it easier to control.

All the while, as he worked his way toward the land that was slipping past, he was berating himself for not jumping into the river after Ayla. But it had happened so fast. Before he knew it, she was out of the boat and he was being carried away on the swift stream. It was pointless to jump into the river after she was out of sight. He couldn't have swum back to her against the current, and they would lose the boat and everything in it.

He tried to console himself with the knowledge that she was a strong swimmer, but his concern caused him to increase his efforts to get across the river. When he finally reached the opposite shore, far downstream of their starting point, and felt the bottom grate against the rocky beach that jutted out from the inside corner of a bend, he breathed a ragged sigh. Then he climbed out and dragged the heavily loaded small boat up on the shore and sank down, giving in to his exhaustion. After a few moments, though, he stood up and started walking back along the river in search of Ayla.

He stayed close to the water, and when he came to a small tributary stream that was adding its measure to the river, he just waded through it. But some time later, when he reached another river of more than respectable size, he hesitated. This was not a river that could be waded, and if he attempted to swim across so close to the major watercourse, he'd be swept into it. He'd have to walk upstream beside the smaller river until he found a more suitable place to attempt a crossing.

Ayla, riding on Whinney, reached the same river not long after, and she also headed upstream for a distance. But a

decision about where to cross on horseback required different
considerations. She didn't go nearly as far as Jondalar did
before she turned her horse into the water. Racer and Wolf
followed behind, and, with only a short swim across the middle, they were soon across. Ayla started down toward the large
river but, looking back, she saw Wolf heading the other way.

"Come on, Wolf. This way," she called. She whistled
impatiently, then signaled Whinney to continue. The canine
hesitated, started toward her, then went back again before he
finally followed her. When she reached the large river, she
turned downstream and urged the mare to a gallop.

Ayla's heart beat faster when she thought she saw a
round, bowl-shaped object on a rocky beach ahead. "Jondalar! Jondalar!" she shouted, racing toward it at full speed.
She jumped down before her horse came to a full stop and
rushed toward the boat. She looked inside it, and then around
the beach. Everything seemed to be there, including the three
poles, everything except Jondalar.

"Here's the boat, but I can't find Jondalar," she said
aloud. She heard Wolf yip, as if in response. "Why can't I
find Jondalar? Where is he? Did the boat float here by itself?
Didn't he make it across?" Then it struck her. Maybe he
went looking for me, she thought. But if I was coming down
the river, and he was going upstream, how did we miss each
other. . .

"The river!" she almost shouted. Wolf yipped again.
Suddenly she recalled his hesitation after they had crossed
the large tributary. "Wolf!" she called.

The large four-legged animal ran toward her and jumped
up, putting his paws on her shoulders. She grabbed the thick
fur of his neck with both hands, looked at his long muzzle
and intelligent eyes, and remembered the young, weak boy
who had reminded her so much of her son. Rydag had sent
Wolf to look for her once, and he had traveled across a long
distance to find her. She knew he could find Jondalar, if she
could only make him understand what she wanted.

"Wolf, find Jondalar!" she said. He jumped down and
began sniffing around the boat, then started back the way
they had come, upstream.

Jondalar had been waist-high in water, carefully picking
his way across the smaller river, when he thought he heard

a faint bird whistle that sounded somehow familiar—and impatient. He stopped and closed his eyes, trying to place it, then shook his head, not even sure if he'd actually heard it, and continued across. When he reached the other side and started walking toward the major river, he couldn't stop thinking about it. Finally his worry about finding Ayla began to push it out of his mind, though it kept nagging at him.

He'd been walking for quite a while in his wet clothes, knowing that Ayla was wet, too, when it occurred to him that he perhaps should have taken the tent, or at least something for shelter. It was getting late, and anything could have happened to her. She might even be hurt. The thought made him scan the water, the bank, and the vegetation nearby more carefully.

Suddenly he heard the whistle again, this time much louder and closer, followed by a yip, yip, yip, and then a full-blown wolf howl and the sound of hoofbeats. Turning around, he broke into a great welcoming smile as he saw the wolf coming straight for him with Racer close behind, and best of all there was Ayla riding Whinney.

Wolf jumped up on the man, put his huge paws on Jondalar's chest, and reached up to lick his jaw. The tall man grabbed his ruff, as he'd seen Ayla do, and then gave the four-legged beast a hug. Then he pushed the wolf away as Ayla raced up on the horse, jumped down, and ran to him.

"Jondalar! Jondalar!" she said as he took her in his arms.

"Ayla! Oh, my Ayla," he said, crushing her to his chest.

The wolf jumped up and licked both of their faces, and neither one of them pushed him away.

The large river, which the two riders along with the horses and the wolf had crossed, emptied into the brackish inland body of water that the Mamutoi called Beran Sea just north of the huge delta of the Great Mother River. As the travelers neared the many-mouthed culmination of the watercourse that had wound its way across the breadth of the continent for nearly two thousand miles, the downward slope of the land leveled off.

The magnificent grasslands of this flat southern region surprised Ayla and Jondalar. A rich new growth, unusual so late in the season, burgeoned across the open landscape. The violent thunderstorm with its downpour of flooding rains, exceptional in its timing and very widespread, was responsible for the unseasonal greening. It brought a springlike resurgence to the steppes of not only grass, but colorful blooms: dwarf iris in purple and yellow, deep red multipetaled peonies, spotted pink lilies, and vetch in variable colors from yellow and orange to red and purple.

Loud whistling and squawking called Ayla's attention to the vociferous black-and-rose birds that were wheeling and dipping, separating and coming together in large flocks, creating a confusion of ceaseless activity. The heavy concentration of the noisy, gregarious, rose-colored starlings that had gathered nearby made the young woman uneasy. Though they bred in colonies, fed in flocks, and roosted together at night, she didn't recall ever seeing so many of them at one time.

She noticed kestrels and other birds were also congregating. The noise was growing louder, with a strident humming undercurrent of expectation. Then she noticed a large dark cloud, though, strangely, except for that one cloud, the sky was clear. It seemed to be moving closer, riding on the wind. Suddenly the great horde of starlings became even more agitated.

"Jondalar," she called to the man who had ridden ahead of her. "Look at that strange cloud."

The man looked, then stopped as Ayla pulled abreast again. While they watched, the cloud grew visibly larger, or perhaps closer.

"I don't think that's a rain cloud," Jondalar said.

"I don't think it is, either, but what else could it be?" Ayla said. She had an unaccountable desire to seek shelter of some kind. "Do you think we should put up the tent and wait it out?"

"I'd rather keep going. Maybe we can outdistance it, if we hurry," Jondalar said.

They urged the horses to a faster gait across the green field, but both the birds and the strange cloud outpaced them. The strident noise rose in intensity, overpowering even the raucous starlings. Suddenly Ayla felt something hit her arm.

"What was that?" she said, but even before she got the words out, she was hit again, and again. Something landed on Whinney, then bounced away, but more came. When she looked at Jondalar, riding just ahead of her, she saw more of the flying, jumping things. One landed just in front of her, and in the moment before it got away, she slapped her hand on it.

She picked it up carefully to look at it more closely. It was an insect, about the length of her middle finger, thick-bodied with long rear legs. It looked like a large grasshopper, but it wasn't a drab green color that would blend easily into the background, like the ones she had seen jumping through dry grass. This insect was striking for its brightly colored stripes of black, yellow, and orange.

The difference was wrought by the rain. During the season that was normally dry, they were grasshoppers, shy, solitary creatures, who could abide others of their kind only long enough to mate, but a remarkable change took place after the hard rainstorm. With the growth of tender new grass, the females took advantage of the abundance of food by laying many more eggs, and many more larvae survived. As the grasshopper population grew, surprising changes took place. The young grasshoppers developed startling new colors, and they began to seek out each other's company. They were no longer grasshoppers; they had become locusts.

Soon, large bands of brightly colored locusts joined with other bands, and when they exhausted their local food supply, the locusts took to the air in masses. A swarm of five billion was not uncommon, easily covering sixty square miles and eating eighty thousand tons of vegetation in a single night.

As the leading edge of the cloud of locusts began dropping down to feed on the new green grass, Ayla and Jondalar were engulfed by the insects swarming all around them, hitting and bouncing off them and their horses. It wasn't hard to urge Whinney and Racer to a gallop; it would have been all but impossible to restrain them. As they raced at top speed, pelted by the deluge of locusts, Ayla tried to look for Wolf, but the air was thick with flying, bouncing, hopping, leaping insects. She whistled as loud as she could, hoping he would hear above the strident roar.

She almost ran into a rose-colored starling as it swooped down and caught a locust right in front of her face. Then she realized why the birds had gathered in such large numbers. They were drawn to the immense food supply, whose bold colors were easy to see. But the sharp contrasts that attracted the birds also enabled the locusts to locate each other when they needed to fly to new feeding grounds, and even the huge flocks of birds did little to reduce the swarms of locusts as long as the vegetation remained abundant enough to support the new generations. Only when the rains stopped and the grasslands returned to their normal dry condition that could feed only small numbers, would the locusts become well-camouflaged, innocuous grasshoppers again.

The wolf found them shortly after they left the swarm behind. By the time the voracious insects were settled on the ground for the night, Ayla and Jondalar were camped far away. When they started out the next morning, they headed north again and slightly east, toward a high hill to get a view above the flat landscape that might give them some idea of the distance to the Great Mother River. Just beyond the crest of the hill they saw the edge of the area that had been visited by the cloud of locusts, the swarming mass blown by the strong winds toward the sea. They were overwhelmed by the devastation.

The beautiful, springlike countryside full of bright flowers and new grass was gone, stripped clean. As far as they could see the land was denuded. Not a leaf, not a blade of grass, not a single hint of green dressed the bare soil. Every bit of vegetation had been devoured by the ravenous horde. The only signs of life were some starlings searching out the last few locusts that had fallen behind. The earth had been ravaged, laid open, and left indecently exposed. Yet she would recover from this indignity, brought on by creatures of her own making in their natural cycles of life, and from hidden root and windblown seed she would clothe herself in green once again.

When the woman and man looked the other way, they were greeted with an entirely different vista, one that set their pulses racing. Toward the east, a vast expanse of water glinted in the sun; it was Beran Sea.

As she looked, Ayla realized that it was the same sea she had known in her childhood. At the southern end of a peninsula that jutted down from the north into that great body of water was the cave where she had lived with Brun's clan when she was young. Living with the people of the Clan had often been difficult. Still she had many happy memories of her childhood, although thoughts of the son she had been forced to leave behind inevitably saddened her. She knew this was as close as she would get to the son she would never see again.

It was best for him to live with the Clan. With Uba as his mother, and old Brun to train him to hunt with a spear, and a bola, and a sling, and to teach him the ways of the Clan, Durc would be loved and accepted, not reviled and made fun of the way Rydag had been. But she couldn't help wondering about him. Was his clan still living on the peninsula, or had they moved closer to some of the other clans that lived on the mainland or in the high eastern mountains?

"Ayla! Look, down there. That's the delta, and you can see Donau, or at least a small part of it. On the other side of the large island, see that brown muddy water? I think that's the main northern arm. There it is, the end of the Great Mother River!" Jondalar said, excitement filling his voice.

He, too, was overcome with memories that were tinged with sadness. The last time he had seen that river, he had been with his brother, and now Thonolan was gone to the world of the spirits. Suddenly he remembered the stone with the opalescent surface that he had taken from the place where Ayla had buried his brother. She had said it held the essence of Thonolan's spirit, and he planned to give it to his mother and Zelandoni when he returned. It was in his pack basket. Maybe he should get it out and carry it with him, he thought.

"Oh, Jondalar! Over there, by the river, is that smoke? Are people living near that river?" Ayla said, excited at the prospect.

"There could be," Jondalar said.

"Let's hurry, then." She started back down the hill with Jondalar riding beside her. "Who do you think it might be?" she asked. "Someone you know?"

"Maybe. The Sharamudoi sometimes come this far in their boats to trade. That's how Markeno met Tholie. She was with a Mamutoi Camp that had come for salt and shells." He stopped and glanced around, looking more closely at the delta and the island just across a narrow channel; then he studied the land downstream. "In fact, I don't think we are very far from the place where Brecie had Willow Camp set up . . . last summer. Was it just last summer? She took us there after her Camp rescued Thonolan and me from the quicksand. . . ."

Jondalar closed his eyes, but Ayla saw the pain. "They were the last people my brother ever saw . . . except for me.

We traveled together for a while longer. I kept hoping he would get over her, but he didn't want to live without Jeta-mio. He wanted the Mother to take him,'' Jondalar said. Then, looking down, he added, "And then we met Baby.''

Jondalar looked up at Ayla, and she saw his expression change. The pain was still there, and she recognized that special look that showed when his love for her was almost more than he could bear; more than she could bear. But there was something else, too, something that frightened her.

"I could never understand why Thonolan wanted to die . . . then.'' He turned away and, urging Racer to a faster pace, called back, "Come on. You said you wanted to hurry.''

Ayla signaled Whinney to a fast run, trying to be more careful, and she trailed behind the man on the galloping stal-lion who was racing toward the river. But the ride was exhila-rating and had the effect of driving away the strange, sad mood that the place had evoked in both of them. The wolf, excited by the fast pace, ran along with them, and when they finally reached the water's edge and stopped, Wolf lifted his head and voiced a melodious wolf song of long drawn-out howls. Ayla and Jondalar looked at each other and smiled, both thinking it was an appropriate way to announce that they had arrived at the river that would be their companion for the greater part of the rest of their Journey.

"Is this it? Have we reached the Great Mother River?'' Ayla said, her eyes sparkling.

"Yes. This is it,'' Jondalar said, then looked toward the west, upstream. He did not want to dampen Ayla's excite-ment at reaching the river, but he knew how far they had yet to go.

They would have to retrace his steps all the way back across the breadth of the continent to the plateau glacier that covered the highland at the headwaters of the extensive river, and then beyond, almost to the Great Water at the edge of the earth, far to the west. Along its winding, eighteen-hun-dred-mile course, Donau—the river of Doni, the Great Earth Mother of the Zelandonii—swelled with the waters of more than three hundred tributaries, the drainage of two glaciered mountain chains, and acquired a burden of sediment.

Often splitting into many channels as she meandered across the flatter stretches of her length, the great waterway transported the prodigious accumulation of silt suspended

within her voluminous spill. But before reaching the end of
her course, the fine gritty soil settled out into an immense
fan-shaped deposit, a mud-clogged wilderness of low islands
and banks surrounded by shallow lakes and winding streams,
as though the Great Mother of rivers was so exhausted from
her long journey that she dropped her heavy load of silt just
short of her destination, then staggered slowly to the sea.

The broad delta they had reached, twice as long as it was
wide, began many miles from the sea. The river, too full to
be held within a single channel in the flat plain between the
ancient massif of raised bedrock to the east and the gentle
rolling hills that dropped gradually from the mountains to the
west, divided into four main arms, each taking a different
direction. Channels interlaced the diverging arms, creating a
labyrinth of meandering streams that spread out to form
numerous lakes and lagoons. Great expanses of reed beds
surrounded firm land that ranged from bare sandy spits to
large islands complete with forests and steppes, populated by
aurochs and deer, and their predators.

"Where was that smoke coming from?" Ayla asked.
"There must be a Camp nearby."

"I think it might have been from that big island we saw
downstream there, across the channel," Jondalar said, pointing in the general direction.

When Ayla looked, all she saw at first was a wall of tall
phragmite reeds, their feathery purple tops bending in the
light wind, more than twelve feet above the waterlogged
ground from which they grew. Then she noticed the beautiful
silvery-green leaves of sallow extending up beyond them. It
took a moment before she made another observation that puzzled her. Sallow was usually a shrub that grew so close to
water that its roots were often flooded in wet seasons. It
resembled certain willows, but sallows never grew to the
height of trees. Could she be mistaken? Could those be willow trees? She seldom made a mistake like that.

They started downstream, and when they were opposite
the island they headed into the channel. Ayla looked back to
make sure the dragging poles of the travois, with the bowl
boat lashed between them, were not snagged; then she
checked that the crossed ends in front moved freely as the
poles floated up behind the mare. When they were repacking,
getting ready to leave the large river behind, they originally
planned to leave the boat. It had served its purpose in getting

them and their things across, but after all the work it had taken to make it, even though the crossing had not gone exactly as they had planned, they both hated to abandon the small round boat.

Ayla was the one who thought about fastening it to the poles, even though it meant Whinney would have to wear the harness and drag it constantly, but it was Jondalar who realized that it would actually make crossing rivers easier. They could load up the boat with their gear so it wouldn't get wet, but rather than trying to lead the horses across with a rope fastened to a boat, Whinney could swim across at her own pace, pulling an easy, floating load. When they tried it out on the next river they had to cross, they even found it unnecessary to unharness her.

There was a tendency for the current to drag at the boat and poles, which worried Ayla, especially after the way Whinney and Racer had panicked when they were being pulled into a situation on the other river over which they had no control. She decided to redesign the leather straps of the harness so that she could cut it loose in an instant if it seemed to endanger her mare, but the horse compensated for the tug of the stream and accepted the burden with little trouble. Ayla had taken the time to let the horse get familiar with the new idea, and Whinney was used to the travois and trusted the woman.

But the large open bowl was a container that invited filling. They started using it to carry wood, dry dung, and other materials for burning that they picked up along the way for the evening fire, and sometimes they left their pack baskets in the boat after crossing water. There had been several streams of various sizes that had found their way to the inland sea, and Jondalar knew that many tributaries would cut across their path as they continued their Journey, traveling beside the Great Mother River.

As they waded into the clear water of the outside channel of the delta, the stallion shied and whinnied nervously. Racer was uneasy about rivers since his frightening adventure, but Jondalar had been very patient about guiding the sensitive young animal across the smaller waterways they had met, and the horse was overcoming his fear. It pleased the man, since many more rivers would have to be crossed before they reached his home.

The water was slow moving, but so transparent that they

could see fish swimming among the water plants. After making their way through the tall reeds, they gained the long, narrow island. Wolf was the first to reach the tongue of land. He shook himself vigorously, then ran up the sloping shore of hard-packed wet sand mixed with clay, which led to a bordering woods of beautiful silver-green sallows grown to the size of trees.

"I knew it," Ayla said.

"What did you know?" Jondalar said, smiling at her satisfied expression.

"These trees are just like those bushes we slept in that night it rained so hard. I thought they were sallows, but I've never seen any the size of trees before. Sallows are usually bushes, but these could be willows."

They dismounted and led the horses into the cool airy woods. Walking in silence, they noticed the shadows of the leaves, swaying in the light breeze, dappling the rich, grassy, sunlit ground cover, and through the light open woodland they saw aurochs grazing in the distance. They were downwind, and, when the wild cattle caught their scent, the animals moved away rapidly. They've been hunted by people, Jondalar thought.

The horses clipped off mouthfuls of the green fodder with their front teeth as well, while they moved through the delightful wooded land, prompting Ayla to stop and begin untying Whinney's harness.

"Why are you stopping here?" Jondalar asked.

"The horses want to graze. I thought we might stop for a while."

Jondalar looked worried. "I think we should go a little farther. I'm sure there are people on this island, and I'd like to know who they are before we stop."

Ayla smiled. "That's right! You did say this was where the smoke was coming from. It's so beautiful here—I almost forgot."

The terrain had been gradually rising in elevation, and farther inland alders, poplars, and white willows began to appear in the sallow woods, lending variation to the light grayish-green foliage. Later a few firs and an ancient variety of pines, that had existed in that region as long as the mountains themselves, added a background of deeper green to the mosaic, with larch contributing a lighter shade, all highlighted by the greenish-gold tufts of ripening steppe grasses waving in the wind. Ivy climbed up tree trunks while liana hung down from branches of the denser forest canopy, and in the sunlit glens prostrate shrubs of pubescent oak and taller hazel brush played their tone against the living landscape.

The island rose no more than twenty-five feet above the water, then leveled out into a long field that was a steppeland in miniature with fescues and feather grasses turning gold in the sun. They crossed the narrow width of the island and looked down a far more precipitous slope of sand dunes, anchored with beach grass, sea holly, and sea kale. The sandy slopes led to a deeply curved inlet, almost a lagoon, outlined with tall, purple-topped reeds, mixed in with cattails and bulrushes, and many varieties of smaller aquatic plants. On the inlet, the water-lily pads were so thick that the water was hardly visible, and perched on them were uncountable numbers of herons.

Beyond the island was a wide, muddy-brown channel, the northernmost arm of the great river. Close to the end of the island they watched a stream of clear water enter the main channel, and Ayla was amazed to see the two currents, one transparent, one brown with silt, running next to each other, with a distinct division of color. Eventually, though, the brown water dominated as the main channel muddied the clear stream.

"Look at that, Jondalar," Ayla said, pointing to the sharp definition of the parallel running waters.

"That's how you know when you're on the Great Mother River. That arm that will take you directly to the sea," he said. "But look over there."

Beyond a grove of trees, off to the side of the inlet, a thin stream of smoke reached for the sky. Ayla smiled with anticipation, but Jondalar had reservations as they headed for the smoke. If that was smoke from a fireplace, why hadn't they seen anyone? The people must have seen them by now. Why hadn't they come to greet them? Jondalar shortened the rope he was using to lead Racer and patted his neck reassuringly.

When they saw the outline of a conical tent, Ayla knew they had arrived at a Camp, and she wondered what people these were. They could even be Mamutoi, she thought, as she signaled Whinney to follow close. Then she noticed Wolf standing in his defensive posture, and she whistled the signal she had taught him. He retreated to her side as they entered the small encampment.

11

Whinney followed closely behind Ayla as the woman walked into the Camp, to the fireplace that was still sending up a wavering wisp of smoke. There were five shelters arranged in a semicircle, and the firepit, dug slightly into the ground, was in front of the central one. The fire was burning briskly, the Camp had obviously been used recently, but no one announced any claim to the place by coming out to greet them. Ayla looked around, glancing inside the dwellings that were open, but she saw no one. Puzzled, she studied the shelters and the Camp more closely to see if she could learn any more about who the people were, and why they were gone.

The main part of each of the structures was similar to the conical tent used by the Mamutoi for their summer Camps, but there were noticeable differences. Where the Mammoth Hunters often enlarged their living space by attaching semicircular side tents made of hides to the main dwelling unit, often using another pole to help support the side additions, the shelters of this Camp had, instead, additions made of reeds

and marsh grasses. Some were simply sloping roofs mounted
on slender poles, others were completely enclosed, rounded
additions made of thatch and woven mats, attached to the
main dwelling.

Just outside the entrance flap of the nearest one, Ayla saw
a pile of brown cattail roots on a mat of woven reeds. Beside
the mat were two baskets. One was tightly woven and held
slightly muddy water, the other was half-full of shiny white,
freshly peeled roots. Ayla walked over and took a root out
of the basket. It was still wet; it must have been placed there
only a moment before.

As she put it back, she noticed a strange object lying on
the ground. It was made of cattail leaves woven to resemble
a person, with two arms sticking out the sides and two legs,
and a piece of soft leather wrapped around it like a tunic.
Two short lines for eyes had been drawn on the face with
charcoal, and another line shaped into a smile. Tufts of
feather grass had been fastened to the head as hair.

The people Ayla had grown up with did not make images,
except for simple totem signs, such as the marks on her leg.
She had been deeply scratched by a cave lion as a small girl,
leaving her left thigh scarred with four straight lines. A similar mark was used by the Clan to indicate a cave lion totem.
That was why Creb had been so sure that the Cave Lion was
her totem, in spite of the fact that it was considered a male
totem. The Spirit of the Cave Lion had chosen her and
marked her himself, and would therefore protect her.

Other Clan totems were indicated in similar ways, with
simple signs often derived from the movements or gestures
of their sign language. But the first truly representative image
she had ever seen was the rough sketch of an animal Jondalar
had drawn on a piece of leather used for a target, and she
was puzzled at first by the object on the ground. Then, with
a flash of recognition, she knew what it was. She had never
had a doll when she was growing up, but she recalled similar
objects that Mamutoi children played with and realized it was
a child's plaything.

It was suddenly obvious to Ayla that a woman had been
sitting there with her child only moments before. Now she
was gone and she must have left in a great hurry, since she
had abandoned her food and had not even taken her child's
toy with her. Why would she leave in such a hurry?

Ayla turned and saw Jondalar, still holding Racer's lead

rope, bent down on one knee amidst a scattering of flint chips and examining a piece of the stone he had noticed. He looked up.

"Someone ruined a very good point with a badly made final stroke. It should have been just a tap, but it landed off the mark, and too hard . . . as though the knapper was suddenly interrupted. And here's the hammerstone! It was just dropped." The nicks on the hard oval stone indicated its long use, and the experienced flint knapper found it difficult to imagine anyone dropping and leaving a favored tool.

Ayla looked around and saw fish drying on a rack, with whole ones on the ground close by. One had been split open but left on the ground. There was more evidence of interrupted tasks, but no sign of the people.

"Jondalar, there were people here not very long ago, but they left in a big hurry. Even the fire is still burning. Where is everyone?"

"I don't know, but you're right. They left in a hurry. They just dropped everything and . . . ran away. As if they were . . . afraid."

"But why?" Ayla said, looking around. "I don't see anything to be afraid of."

Jondalar started to shake his head, then noticed Wolf sniffing around the abandoned Camp, poking his nose into the entrances of the tents and around the places where things had been left. Then his attention was drawn to the hay-colored mare grazing nearby, dragging an arrangement of poles and bowl boat, strangely unconcerned about both the people and the wolf. The man turned to look at the young dark-brown stallion that followed him so willingly. The animal was arrayed with pack baskets and riding blanket and was standing beside him patiently, held only by a single rope attached to his head with cord and leather.

"I think that may be the problem, Ayla. We don't see it," he said. Wolf suddenly stopped his nosy exploring, gazed intently at the woods, then started into them. "Wolf!" he called. The animal stopped and looked back at the man, wagging his tail. "Ayla, you'd better call him back or he'll find the people of this Camp, and scare them even more."

She whistled, and he ran to her. She fondled his ruff but was frowning at Jondalar. "Are you saying we scare them? That they ran away because they were afraid of us?"

"Remember Feather Grass Camp? The way they acted

when they saw us? Think how we must seem to people when
they first see us, Ayla. We are traveling with two horses and
a wolf. Animals don't travel with people, they usually avoid
them. Even the Mamutoi at the Summer Meeting took a while
to get used to us, and we arrived with Lion Camp. When
you think about it, Talut was very brave to invite us, with
our horses, to his Camp when we first met him," Jondalar
said.

"What should we do?"

"I think we should leave. The people of this Camp are
probably hiding in the woods watching us, thinking we must
come from some place like the spirit world. That's what I
would think if I saw us coming without any warning."

"Oh, Jondalar," Ayla wailed, feeling a rush of disappointment, and loneliness, as she stood in the middle of the
vacated Camp. "I was so looking forward to visiting with
some people." She looked around the Camp once more, then
nodded her head in acquiescence. "You're right. If the people
are gone and didn't want to welcome us, we should leave. I
just wish I could have met the woman with the child who
left that plaything, and talked to her." She started walking
toward Whinney, who was just beyond the Camp. "I don't
want people to be afraid of me," she said, turning to the
man. "Will we be able to talk to anyone on this Journey?"

"I don't know about strangers, but I'm sure we'll be able
to visit with the Sharamudoi. They might be a little wary at
first, but they know me. And you know how people are.
After they get over their initial fright, they get very interested
in the animals."

"I'm sorry we frightened these people. Maybe we could
leave them a gift, even if we didn't share their hospitality,"
Ayla said. She began to look through her pack baskets. "I
think some food would be nice, some meat, I think."

"Yes, that's a good idea. I have some extra points. I
think I'll leave one to replace the one that toolmaker ruined.
There is nothing more disappointing than to spoil a good tool
just when you're about to finish it," Jondalar said.

As he reached into his pack for his leather-wrapped tool
kit, Jondalar recalled that when he and his brother were traveling they met many people along the way, and they were
usually welcomed and often helped. There had even been a
couple of occasions when their lives had been saved by
strangers. But if people were going to be afraid of them

because of their animal companions, what would happen if Ayla and he ever needed help?

They left the Camp and climbed back up the sandy dunes to the level field at the top of the long, narrow island, stopping when they reached the grass. They looked down at the thin column of smoke from the Camp and the brown silty river below, its noticeable current heading for the broad blue expanse of Beran Sea. With unspoken assent, they both mounted and turned east to get a better—and a last look at the great inland sea.

When they reached the eastern tip of the island, though still within the banks of the river they were so close to the choppy waters of the sea that they could watch its waves washing sandbars with briny foam. Ayla looked out across the water and thought she could almost see the outline of a peninsula. The cave of Brun's clan, the place where she had grown up, had been at its southern tip. It was there that she had given birth to her son, and there she had to leave him when she was forced out.

I wonder how big he is? she said to herself. Taller than all the boys his age, I'm sure. Is he strong? Healthy? Is he happy? Does he remember me? I wonder. If only I could just see him one more time, she thought, then realized that if she was ever going to look for him, this would be her last chance. From here, Jondalar planned to turn west. She would never be this close to her clan, or Durc, again. Why couldn't they go east, instead? Just make a short side trip before they went on? If they skirted the northern coast of the sea, they could probably reach the peninsula in a few days. Jondalar did say he would be willing to go with her if she wanted to try to find Durc.

"Ayla, look! I didn't know there were seals in Beran Sea! I haven't seen those animals since I was a youngster and went on a trek with Willomar," Jondalar said, his voice full of excitement and longing. "He took both Thonolan and me to see the Great Waters, and then the people who live near the edge of the earth took us north on a boat. Have you seen them before?"

Ayla looked toward the sea, but closer in, where he was pointing. Several dark, sleek, streamlined creatures, with light gray underbellies, were humping clumsily along a sandbar that had formed behind some nearly submerged rocks. While they watched, most of the seals dived back into the water, chasing a school of fish. They watched heads bobbing up while the last of them, smaller and younger, dove into the sea again. Then they were gone, disappearing as quickly as they had come.

"Only from a distance," Ayla said, "during the cold season. They liked the floating ice offshore. Brun's clan didn't hunt them. No one could reach them, though Brun once told about a time he saw some on the rocks near a sea cave. Some people thought they were winter water spirits, not animals at all, but I saw little ones on the ice once, and I didn't think water spirits had babies. I never knew where they went in the summer. They must have come here."

"When we get home, I'll take you to see the Great Waters, Ayla. You won't believe it. This is a large sea, much bigger than any lakes I've ever seen, and salty I'm told, but it's nothing compared to the Great Waters. That's like the sky. No one has ever reached the other side."

Ayla heard the eagerness in Jondalar's voice, and she sensed his yearning to be home. She knew he wouldn't hesitate to go with her to look for Brun's clan and her son, if she told him that she wanted to. Because he loved her. But she loved him, too, and knew that he would be unhappy about the delay. She looked at the great sweep of water, then closed her eyes trying to hold back tears.

She wouldn't know where to look for the clan, anyway, she thought. And it wasn't Brun's clan anymore. It was Broud's clan now, and she would not be welcome. Broud had cursed her with death; she was dead to them all, a spirit. If she and Jondalar had frightened the Camp on this island because of the animals, and their seemingly supernatural ability to control them, how much more would they scare the clan? Including Uba, and Durc? To them, she would be returning from the spirit world, and the companionable animals would be proof of it. They believed a spirit who came back from the land of the dead came to do them harm.

But once she turned west, it would be final. From this time on, for the rest of her life, Durc would be no more than a memory. There would be no hope of ever seeing him again. That was the choice she had to make. She thought she had made it long ago; she didn't know the pain would be still so sharp. Turning her head so Jondalar would not see the tears that filled her eyes as she stared at the deep blue expanse of water, Ayla said a silent goodbye to her son for the last time. A fresh stab of grief filled her and she knew she would carry the ache in her heart with her forever.

They turned their backs on the sea and started walking through the waist-high steppe grass of the large island, giving the horses a rest and time to graze. The sun was high in the sky, bright and hot. Shimmering heat waves rose up from the dusty ground, bringing the warm aroma of earth and growing things. On the treeless plain atop the long narrow strip of land, they moved within the shade of their grass hats, but the evaporation of the surrounding river channels made the air humid and beads of sweat trickled down their dusty skin. They were grateful for the occasional cool breath from the sea, a fitful breeze filled with the rich scent of the life within its deep waters.

Ayla stopped and unwound her leather sling from her head and tucked it into her waistband, not wanting it to get too damp. She replaced it with a rolled piece of soft leather, similar to the one Jondalar wore, bound across her forehead and tied in the back, to absorb the moisture that dripped from her forehead.

When she continued, she noticed a dull greenish grasshopper spring up, then drop back down and hide in its camouflaged disguise. Then she saw another. More of them chirked sporadically, bringing to mind the swarming locusts. But here they were just one of a variety of insects, like the butterflies flicking their bright colors in a quivery dance across the tops of the fescue, and the harmless drone fly, that resembled a stinging honeybee, hovering over a buttercup.

Though the raised field was much smaller, it had the familiar feeling of the dry steppes, but when they came to the other end of the island and looked out, they were astonished by the vast, strange, wet world of the massive delta. To the north, on their right, was the mainland; beyond a fringe of river brush, a grassland of muted greenish-gold. But to the south and west, spreading all the way to the horizon, and in the distance seeming as solid and substantial as the land, was the marshy outlet of the great river. It was an extensive bed of rich green reeds, swaying in a motion as constant as the sea with the gusty rhythm of the wind, broken only by occasional trees casting shadows across the waving green and the winding paths of open waterways.

As they moved down the slope through the open woods, Ayla became aware of the birds, more varieties than she had ever seen in one place before, some of them unfamiliar. Crows, cuckoos, starlings, and turtledoves each called to their kind in distinctive voices. A swallow, chased by a falcon, swooped and twisted, then dived into the reeds. High-flying black kites and ground-skimming marsh harriers searched for dead or dying fish. Small warblers and flycatchers flitted from thicket to tall tree, while tiny stints, redstarts, and shrikes darted from branch to branch. Gulls floated on air currents, hardly moving a feather, and ponderous pelicans, majestic in flight, sailed overhead flapping wide powerful wings.

Ayla and Jondalar emerged at a different section of the river when they reached water again, near a clump of goat willow bushes that was the site of a mixed colony of marsh birds: night herons, little egrets, purple herons, cormorants, and at this place, mostly glossy ibises all nesting together. In the same tree, the grassy roosting place of one variety was often only a branch away from the nest of an entirely different species, and several held eggs or young birds. The birds seemed to be as indifferent to the people and animals as they were to each other, but the busy place, bustling with incessant activity, was an attraction impossible for the curious young wolf to ignore.

He approached slowly, trying to stalk, but was distracted by the plethora of possibilities. Finally he made a dash toward a particular small tree. With loud squawking and flapping of wings, the nearby birds lifted into the air and were immediately followed by more who noticed the warning. Still others took to wing. The air was filling with marsh birds, clearly the dominant bird life in the delta, until more than ten thousand individuals of several different species from the mixed colony were wheeling and turning in dramatic flight.

Wolf raced back toward the woods, his tail between his legs, howling and yipping in fear over the commotion he had caused. Adding to the tumult, the nervous, frightened horses were rearing and screaming; then they galloped into the water.

The travois acted as a restraining force on the mare, who was more even tempered to begin with. She settled down fairly soon, but Jondalar had a great deal more trouble with the young stallion. He ran into the water after the horse, swimming where it deepened, and was soon out of sight. Ayla managed to get Whinney across the channel and back to the mainland. After she calmed and comforted the horse, she unhitched the dragging poles and removed the harness to let the mare run free and relax in her own way. Then she whistled for Wolf. It took several more whistles before he came, and then it was from a different direction much farther downstream, far away from the site of the nesting birds.

Ayla took off her own wet clothes and changed into dry ones from her pack basket, then gathered wood to make a fire while she waited for Jondalar. He, too, would need to change, and fortunately his pack baskets happened to be in the bowl boat, which kept them dry. It was some time before he found his way back, riding toward Ayla's fire from the west. Racer had gone far upstream before Jondalar caught up with him.

The man was still angry with Wolf, and it was apparent not only to Ayla but to the animal. The wolf waited until Jondalar finally sat down with a cup of hot tea after changing clothes, and then he approached, crouching down on his front legs, wagging his tail like a puppy wanting to play and whining with a pleading tone. When he got close enough, Wolf tried to lick his face. The man pushed him away at first. When he did allow the persistent animal closer, Wolf seemed so pleased that Jondalar had to relent.

"It seems as though he's trying to say he's sorry, but that's hard to believe. How could he? He's an animal. Ayla, could Wolf know that he misbehaved and be sorry for it?" Jondalar asked.

Ayla wasn't surprised. She had seen such actions when she was teaching herself to hunt and observing carnivorous animals, which she had chosen to be her prey. Wolf's actions toward the man were similar to the way a young wolf often behaved toward the male leader of a pack.

"I don't know what he knows, or what he thinks," Ayla said. "I can only judge from his actions. But isn't that how it is with people? You can never know what someone really knows or thinks. You have to judge by actions, don't you?"

Jondalar nodded, still not sure what to believe. Ayla didn't doubt that Wolf was sorry, but she didn't think it would make much difference. Wolf used to behave the same way to her when she was trying to teach him to stay away from the leather footwear of the people of Lion Camp. It took her a long time to train the wolf to leave them alone, and she didn't think he was ready to give up chasing birds just yet.

The sun was skimming the craggy high peaks at the southern end of the long chain of mountains to the west, lending a glittering sparkle to the icy facets. The range dropped from the heights of the southern tors as it marched north, and the sharp angles smoothed out to rounded crests blanketed with shimmering white. Toward the northwest, the mountaintops disappeared behind a curtain of clouds.

Ayla turned into an inviting opening in the wooded fringe of the river delta and pulled to a stop. Jondalar followed behind. The small grassy lea was a somewhat larger space within a pleasant open strip of woodland that led directly to a quiet lagoon.

Though the main arms of the great river were full of muddy silt, the complex network of channels and side streams that weaved through the reeds of the huge delta was clean and drinkable. The channels occasionally widened into large lakes or placid lagoons that were surrounded by an assortment of reeds, rushes, sedges, and other water plants, and were often covered with water lilies. The sturdy lily pads offered resting places for the smaller herons and innumerable frogs.

"This looks like a good place," Jondalar said, lifting his leg over Racer's back and landing lightly. He removed his pack baskets, riding blanket, and halter, and turned the young stallion loose. The horse headed straight for the water, and a moment later Whinney joined him.

The mare entered the river first and began drinking. After a short time she started pawing the water, making big splashes that soaked her chest and the young stallion who was drinking nearby. She bent her head down, sniffing at the water, her ears forward. Then, gathering her legs beneath her, she got down on her forelegs, dropped lower, and rolled over on her side, and finally onto her back. Holding her head up and with legs flailing the air, she squirmed with delight, rubbing her body on the bottom of the lagoon, then flung herself over to her other side. Racer, who had been watching his dam rolling in the cool water, could wait no longer, and in a similar manner lowered himself for a roll in the shallows near the bank.

"You would have thought they'd had enough of water today," Ayla said, moving up beside Jondalar.

He turned, the smile from watching the horses still on his face. "They do love to roll in the water, not to mention the mud or dust. I didn't know horses liked to roll so much."

"You know how much they like to be scratched. I think it's their way of scratching themselves," the woman commented. "Sometimes they scratch each other, and they tell each other where they want to be scratched."

"How can they tell each other that, Ayla? Sometimes I think you imagine that horses are people."

"No, horses are not people. They are themselves, but watch them some time, when they stand head to tail. One will scratch the other with teeth, and then wait to be scratched back at the same place," Ayla said. "Maybe I'll give Whinney a good combing with the dry teasel later. It must get hot and itchy under the leather straps all day. Sometimes I think we should leave the bowl boat behind . . . but it has been useful."

"I'm hot and itchy. I think I'm going to take a swim, too. This time without clothes," Jondalar said.

"I will, too, but first I want to unpack. Those clothes that got wet are still damp. I want to hang them over those bushes so they will dry." She took a damp bundle out of one of her baskets and began draping the clothing across the branches of an alder bush. "I'm not sorry the clothes got wet," Ayla said, arranging a loincloth. "I found some soaproot and washed mine while I was waiting for you."

Jondalar shook out one garment, helping her to hang up the clothes, and discovered it was his tunic. He held it up to show her. "I thought you said you washed your clothes while you were waiting for me," he said.

"I washed yours after you changed. Too much sweat makes the leather rot, and they were getting badly stained," she explained.

He didn't recall worrying too much about sweat or stains when he had traveled with his brother, but he was rather pleased that Ayla did.

By the time they were ready to go into the river, Whinney was coming out. She stood on the bank with her legs spread apart, then started shaking her head. The vigorous shake worked back along her body all the way to her tail. Jondalar held up his arms to ward off the spray. Ayla, laughing, ran into the water and, with both hands, rapidly scooped out more water to splash at the man as he was wading in. As soon as he was knee deep, he returned the favor. Racer, who had finished his bath and was standing nearby, received a share of the dousing and backed away, then he headed for the shore. He liked water, but under conditions of his own choosing.

After they tired of playing and swimming, Ayla began to notice the possibilities for their evening meal. Growing out of the water were spearhead-shaped leaves and white three-petaled flowers that darkened to purple at the center, and she knew the starchy tuber of the plant was filling and good. She dug some out of the muddy bottom with her toes; the stems were fragile and broke off too easily to pull them out. As Ayla waded back to the shore, she also gathered water plantain to cook, and tangy watercress to eat raw. A regular pattern of small wide leaves growing out from a center that was floating on the surface drew her attention.

"Jondalar, be careful not to step on those water chestnuts," she said, pointing out the spiky seeds littering the sandy shore.

He picked one up to look more closely. Its four barbs were arranged in such a way that while one always caught the ground, the others pointed upward. He shook his head, then threw it down. Ayla bent to pick it up again, along with several others.

"These are not so good to step on," she said in answer to his quizzical look, "but they are good to eat."

On the shore, in the shade beside the water, she saw a familiar tall plant with blue-green leaves and looked around for any other plant with fairly large flexible leaves to protect her hands while she picked them. Though she would have to exercise care while they were fresh, the stinging nettle leaves would be delicious when cooked. A water dock, growing at the very edge of the water and standing nearly as tall as the man, had three-foot basal leaves that would work just fine, she decided, and they could be cooked, too. Nearby there was also coltsfoot and several kinds of ferns that had flavorful roots. The delta offered an abundance of foods.

Offshore, Ayla noticed an island of tall grass reeds with

cattails growing along the edges. It was likely that cattails would always be a staple for them. They were widespread and prolific, and so many parts were edible. Both the old roots, pounded to remove the fibers from the starch, which was made into dough or soup thickening, and the new roots, eaten fresh or cooked, along with the base of the flower stalks, not to mention the heavy concentration of pollen, which could also be made into a kind of bread, were all delicious. When young, the flowers, bunched together near the end of the tall stalk, like a piece of a cat's furry tail, were also tasty.

The rest of the plant was useful in other ways: the leaves for weaving into baskets and mats, and the fuzz from the flowers after they went to seed made absorbent padding and excellent tinder. Though with her iron pyrite firestones Ayla didn't need to use them, she knew that the previous year's dry woody stems could be twirled between the palms to make fire, or they could be used as fuel.

"Jondalar, let's take the boat and go out to that island to collect some cattails," Ayla said. "There's a lot of other good things to eat growing out there in the water, too, like the seed pods of those water lilies, and the roots. The root-stalks of those reeds are not bad either. They're under the water, but since we are wet from swimming anyway, we might as well get some. We can put everything in the boat to bring it back."

"You've never been here before. How do you know these plants are good to eat?" Jondalar asked as they unfastened the boat from the travois.

Ayla smiled. "There were marshy places like this near the sea not far from our cave on the peninsula. Not as big as this, but it got warm there in the summer, too, like it is here, and Iza knew the plants and where to find them. Nezzie told me about some others."

"I think you must know every plant there is."

"Many of them, but not every plant, especially around here. I wish there was someone I could ask. The woman on that big island, who left while she was cleaning roots, would probably know. I'm sorry we couldn't visit with them," Ayla said.

Her disappointment was apparent, and Jondalar knew how lonely she was for other people. He missed people, too, and wished they could have visited.

They brought the bowl boat to the edge of the water and scrambled in. The current was slow but more noticeable from the buoyant round craft, and they had to start using the paddles quickly to keep from being carried downstream. Away from shore and the disturbance they had caused with their bathing, the water was so clear that schools of fish could be seen darting over and around submerged plants. Some were of fairly good size and Ayla thought she would catch a few later.

They stopped at a concentration of water lilies that was so dense, they could hardly see the surface of the lagoon. When Ayla slipped out of the boat and into the water, it was not easy for Jondalar by himself to keep the bowl boat in place. The boat had a tendency to spin when he attempted to back-paddle, but when Ayla's feet found the bottom while she was holding on to the side, the small floating bowl steadied. Using the stems of the flowers as a guide, she searched out the roots with her toes and loosened them from the soft soil, collecting them when they floated to the surface in a cloud of silt.

When Ayla hoisted herself back into the boat, she sent it spinning again, but with both of them using the paddles, they got it under control, then aimed for the island that was densely covered with reeds. When they drew near, Ayla noticed that it was the smaller variety of cattail that grew so thickly near the edge, along with bay willow brush, some nearly the size of trees.

They paddled into the heavy growth looking for a bank or sandy shore, forcing their way through the vegetation. But when they pulled the reeds aside, they could not find solid ground, not even a submerged sandbar, and after they pushed through, the passage they made closed rapidly behind them. Ayla felt a sense of foreboding, and Jondalar an eerie feeling of being captured by some unseen presence as the jungle of tall reeds surrounded them. Overhead they saw pelicans flying, but they had a dizzying impression that their straight flight was curving around. When they looked between the large grassy stalks, back the way they had come, the opposite shore seemed to be slowly revolving past them.

"Ayla, we're moving! Turning!" Jondalar said, suddenly realizing that it was not the land opposite but they who were revolving as the winding stream swung the boat and the entire island around.

"Let's get out of this place," she said, reaching for her paddle.

The islands in the delta were impermanent at best, always subject to the whims of the Great Mother of rivers. Even those that supported a rich growth of reeds could wash out from underneath, or the growth that started on a shallow island could become so dense that it would extend a tangle of vegetation out over water.

Whatever the initial cause, the roots of the floating reeds bound together and created a platform for decaying matter—organisms from the water as well as vegetation which fertilized the rapid growth of more reeds. With time, they became floating islands supporting a variety of other plants. Reed mace, narrow-leaved smaller varieties of cattail, rushes, ferns, even the bay willow brush that eventually became trees, grew along the edges, but extremely tall reed grass, reaching twelve feet in height, was the primary vegetation. Some of the quagmires developed into large floating landscapes, treacherously deceptive with their tangled illusion of solidity and permanence.

Using the small paddles, but no small effort, they forced the little round boat back out of the floating island. But by the time they reached the periphery of the unstable quagmire again, they discovered they were not opposite the land. They were facing the open water of a lake, and across it was a sight so spectacular that they caught their breaths. Outlined against the background of dark green was a dense concentration of white pelicans; hundreds upon thousands of them packed together, standing, sitting, lying on tussocky nests of floating reeds. Above, more of the huge colony were flying at many levels, as though the nesting grounds were too full and they were coasting on their great wings waiting for a space.

Primarily white, with a slight wash of pink and wings edged by dark gray flight feathers, the large birds with their long beaks and sagging throat pouches were tending pods of fuzzy pelican chicks. The noisy young birds hissed and grunted, the adults responded with deep, hoarse cries, and in such great numbers that the combination was deafening.

Partially concealed by reeds, Ayla and Jondalar watched the huge breeding colony, fascinated. Hearing a deep grunting cry, they looked up as a low-flying pelican, coming in for a landing, sailed by overhead on wings that spanned ten feet. It reached a spot near the middle of the lake, then folded back its wings and dropped like a rock, hitting the water with a splash in a clumsy, ungainly landing. Not far away, another pelican with wings outstretched was rushing across the open expanse of water, trying to lift itself into flight. Ayla began to understand why they chose to nest on the lake. They needed a great deal of space to raise themselves into the air, though once up, their flight was artfully graceful.

Jondalar tapped her arm and pointed toward the shallow water near the island where several of the large birds were swimming abreast, moving forward slowly. Ayla watched for a while, then smiled at the man. Every few moments the whole row of pelicans simultaneously dipped their heads into the water, and then altogether, as though on command, lifted them out, dripping water from their great long bills. A few, but not all of them had caught some of the fish they were herding. The next time others might feed, but all continued to move and dip, perfectly synchronized with each other.

Single pairs of another variety of pelican with somewhat different markings, and earlier hatched, more mature young, nested at the edges of the large colony. Within and around the compact aggregation other species of water birds were also nesting and breeding: cormorants, grebes, and a variety of ducks, including white-eyed and red-crested pochards and ordinary mallards. The marsh teemed with a profusion of birds, all hunting and eating the countless fish.

The entire vast delta was an extravagant, ostentatious demonstration of natural abundance; a wealth of life flaunted without shame. Unspoiled, undamaged, ruled by her own natural law and subject only to her own will—and the great void whence she sprang—the great Mother Earth took pleasure in creating and sustaining life in all its prolific diversity. But pillaged by a plundering dominion, raped of her resources, despoiled by unchecked pollution, and befouled by excess and corruption, her fecund ability to create and sustain could be undone.

Though rendered sterile by destructive subjugation, her great productive fertility exhausted, the final irony would still be hers. Even barren and stripped, the destitute mother possessed the power to destroy what she had wrought. Dominion cannot be imposed; her riches cannot be taken without seeking her consent, wooing her cooperation, and respecting her needs. Her will to life cannot be suppressed without paying the ultimate penalty. Without her, the presumptuous life she created could not survive.

Though Ayla could have watched the pelicans for much longer, she finally began to pull up some of the cattails and put them into the boat, since that was the reason they had come. Then they started paddling back around the mass of floating reeds. When they came in sight of land again, they were much closer to their camp. As soon as they appeared, they were greeted by a long, drawn-out howl, full of tones of distress. After his hunting foray, Wolf had followed their scent and found their camp with no trouble, but when he had not found them, the young animal became anxious.

The woman whistled in return, to ease his fears. He ran to the edge of the water, then lifted his head and howled again. When he stopped, he sniffed their tracks, ran back and forth on the bank, then plunged in and started swimming toward them. As he neared, he veered away from the boat and headed for the mass of floating reeds, mistaking it for an island.

Wolf tried to reach the nonexistent shore, just as Ayla and Jondalar had done, but splashed and struggled between the reeds, finding no firm land. Finally he swam back to the boat. With difficulty, the man and the woman grabbed the waterlogged coat of the animal and hauled him into the skin-covered bowl. Wolf was so excited and relieved that he jumped up on Ayla and licked her face, and then did the same to Jondalar. When he finally settled down, he stood in the middle of the boat and shook himself, then howled again.

To their surprise, they heard an answering wolf howl, then a few yips, and another reply. They were surrounded by another series of wolf howls, this time sounding very close. Ayla and Jondalar stared at each other with a chill of apprehension as they sat naked in the small boat and listened to the howls of a pack that came not from the shore across the water, but from the insubstantial floating island!

"How can there be wolves there?" Jondalar said. "That is not an island, there is no land, not even a shifting sandbar." Maybe they weren't really wolves at all, Jondalar thought, shuddering. Maybe they were . . . something else . . .

Looking carefully between the reed stalks in the direction of the last wolf call, Ayla caught a glimpse of wolf fur and two yellow eyes watching her. Then a movement above caught her eye. She looked up and, partly hidden by foliage,

she saw a wolf looking down at them from the crotch of a
tree, with his tongue lolling out.

Wolves didn't climb trees! At least no wolf she ever saw
climbed a tree, and she had watched many wolves. She
tapped Jondalar and pointed. He saw the animal and caught
his breath. It looked like a real wolf, but how did it get up
in the tree?

"Jondalar," she whispered, "let's go. I don't like this
island that is not an island, with wolves that can climb trees
and walk on land where there is none."

The man felt just as edgy. They quickly paddled back
across the channel. When they were close to shore, Wolf
jumped out of the boat. They climbed out, quickly dragged
the small craft up on the dry land, then got their spears and
spear-throwers. Both horses were facing the direction of the
floating island, their ears pricked forward, tension communicated in their stance. Normally wolves were shy and did not
bother them, especially since the mixed scents of horses,
humans, and another wolf presented an unfamiliar picture, but
they weren't sure about these wolves. Were they ordinary, real
wolves or something . . . unnatural?

Had not their seemingly supernatural control over animals
frightened away the inhabitants of the large island, they might
have learned from the people who were familiar with the
marshland that the strange wolves were no more unnatural
than they were themselves. The watery land of the great delta
was home to many animals, including reed wolves. They
lived primarily in the woodlands on the islands, but they
had adapted so well to their waterlogged environment over
thousands of years that they could travel through the floating
reed beds easily. They had even learned to climb trees,
which, in a shifting, flooding landscape, gave them a tremendous advantage when they were isolated by floods.

That wolves could thrive in an environment that was
almost aquatic was evidence of their great adaptability. It was
the same adaptability that allowed them to learn to live with
humans so well that over time, though still able to breed with
their wild forebears, they become so fully domesticated that
they almost appeared to be a different species, many of them
hardly resembling wolves at all.

Across the channel on the floating island, several wolves
could now be seen, two of them in trees. Wolf looked expectantly from Ayla to Jondalar, as though waiting for instruc-

tions from the leaders of his pack. One of the reed wolves voiced another howl; then the rest joined in, sending a chill down Ayla's spine. The sound seemed different from the wolf song she was used to hearing, though she could not say precisely how. It may have been that the reverberations from the water changed the tone, but it added to her feelings of uneasiness about the mysterious wolves.

The standoff suddenly ended when the wolves disappeared, leaving as silently as they had come. One moment the man and woman with their spear-throwers, and Wolf, were facing a pack of strange wolves across an open channel of water, the next moment the animals were gone. Ayla and Jondalar, still holding their weapons, found themselves staring intently at harmless reeds and cattails, feeling vaguely foolish and unsettled.

A cool breeze, raising gooseflesh on their bare skin, made them aware that the sun had dropped behind the mountains to the west and night was coming on. They put their weapons down, hurriedly dressed, then quickly built up their fire and finished setting up camp, but their mood was subdued. Ayla found herself often checking the horses, and she was glad they had chosen to graze in the green field where they were camped.

As darkness surrounded the golden glow of their fire, the two people were strangely quiet, listening, as the night sounds of the river delta filled the air. Squawking night herons became active at dusk, then chirping crickets. An owl sounded a series of mournful hoots. Ayla heard snuffling in the woods nearby and thought it was a boar. Piercing the distance, she was startled by the laughing cackle of a cave hyena, then closer, the frustrated scream of a large cat who missed a kill. She wondered if it was a lynx, or perhaps a snow leopard, and she kept anticipating the howl of wolves, but none came.

With velvety darkness filling in every shadow and outline, an accompaniment to the other sounds grew that filled in all the intervals between them. From every channel and riverbank, lake and lily-pad-covered lagoon, a chorus of frogs serenaded their unseen audience. The deep bass voices of marsh and edible frogs developed the tone of the amphibian choir, while fire-bellied toads added their *bonging,* bell-like melody. In counterpoint were the fluty trills of variegated toads, blended with the gentle croon of spadefoot toads, all set to the cadence of the tree frog's sharp *karreck-karreck-karreck*.

By the time Ayla and Jondalar got into their bedroll, the incessant song of the frogs had faded into the background of familiar sounds, but the anticipated wolf howls, when they finally were heard in the distance, still gave Ayla chills. Wolf sat up and answered their call.

"I wonder if he misses a wolf pack?" Jondalar said, putting his arm around Ayla. She cuddled against him, glad for his warmth and closeness.

"I don't know, but I worry, sometimes. Baby left me to find his mate, but male lions always leave their home territories to look for mates from another pride."

"Do you think Racer will want to leave us?" the man asked.

"Whinney did for a while and lived with a herd. I'm not sure how the other mares took to her, but she came back after her stallion died. Not all male horses live with female herds. Each herd only chooses one, and then he has to fight off the other males. The young stallions, and older ones, usually live together in their own herd, but they are all drawn to the mares when it is their season to share Pleasures. I'm sure Racer will be, too, but he would have to fight with the chosen stallion," Ayla explained.

"Maybe I can keep him on a lead rope during that time," Jondalar said.

"I don't think you'll have to worry for a while. It is usually in spring that horses share Pleasures, soon after they drop their foals. I'm more worried about the people we may meet on our Journey. They don't understand that Whinney and Racer are special. Someone may try to hurt them. They don't seem very willing to accept us, either."

As Ayla lay in Jondalar's arms, she wondered what his people would think of her. He noticed that she was quiet and pensive. He kissed her, but she did not seem as responsive as usual. Perhaps she was tired, he thought, it had been a full day. He was tired, himself. He fell asleep listening to the chorus of frogs. He woke up to the thrashing and calling out of the woman in his arms.

"Ayla! Ayla! Wake up! It's all right."

"Jondalar! Oh, Jondalar," Ayla cried, clinging to him. "I was dreaming . . . about the Clan. Creb was trying to tell me something important, but we were deep in a cave and it was dark. I couldn't see what he was saying.''

"You were probably thinking about them today. You talked about them when we were on that large island looking at the sea. I thought you seemed upset. Were you thinking that you were leaving them behind?'' he asked.

She closed her eyes and nodded, not sure if she could voice the words without tears, and she hesitated to mention her concerns about his people, whether they would accept not only her, but the horses, and Wolf. The Clan and her son had been lost to her, she did not want to lose her family of animals, too, if they managed to reach his home safely with them. She only wished she knew what Creb had been trying to tell her in her dream.

Jondalar held her, comforting her with his warmth and love, understanding her sorrow but not knowing what to say. His closeness was enough.

12

The northern arm of the Great Mother River, with its meandering network of channels, was the winding, twisting upper boundary of the extensive delta. Brush and trees hovered close to the outer edge of the river, but beyond the narrow border, away from the immediate source of moisture, the woody vegetation quickly gave way to steppe grasses. Riding almost due west through the dry grassland, close to the wooded strip but avoiding the sinuous turns of the river, Ayla and Jondalar followed the left bank upstream.

They ventured into the marshy wetlands frequently, usually making camp close to the river, and they were often astonished by the diversity they found. The massive river mouth had seemed so uniform in the distance when they had viewed it from the large island, but at close hand it revealed a wide range of landscapes and vegetation, from bare sand to dense forest.

One day they rode past fields upon fields of cattails, with brown flowerheads bunched into the shape of sausages, topped by spikes covered with masses of yellow pollen. The

next, they saw vast beds of tall phragmite reeds, more than
twice Jondalar's height, growing together with the shorter,
more graceful variety; the slender plants grew nearer the
water and were more densely packed together.

The islands formed by the deposition of suspended silt,
usually long, narrow tongues of land made up of sand and
clay, were buffeted by the waters of the surging river and the
conflicting currents of the sea. The result was a variegated
mosaic of reed beds, wetlands, steppes, and forests in many
different stages of development, all subject to rapid change
and full of surprises. The shifting diversity extended even
beyond the boundary. The travelers unexpectedly came upon
oxbow lakes that were completely cut off from the delta,
between banks that had begun as isles of sedimentation in the
river.

Most islands were originally stabilized by beach plants
and giant lyme grass that reached nearly five feet, which the
horses loved—the high salt content attracted many other grazing animals as well. But the landscape could change so rapidly that they sometimes found islands, within the confines
of the immense mouth of the river, with beach plants still
surviving on inland dunes beside fully mature woods, complete with trailing lianas.

As the woman and man traveled beside the great river,
they often had to cross small tributaries, but the running
streams were hardly noticeable as the horses splashed through
them, and the small rivers were not difficult to negotiate. The
wet lowlands of slowly drying channels that had changed
course were another matter. Jondalar usually detoured around
them. He was acutely aware of the danger of swampy fens
and the soft silty soil that often formed in such places,
because of the bad experience he and his brother had had
when they had come that way before. But he didn't know
the dangers that were sometimes hidden by rich greenery.

It had been a long, hot day. Jondalar and Ayla, looking
for a place to camp for the night, had turned toward the river
and saw what appeared to be a likely possibility. They headed
down a slope toward a cool, inviting glen with tall sallows
shading a particularly green lea. Suddenly a large brown hare
bounded into view on the other side of the field. Ayla urged
Whinney on as she reached for the sling at her waist, but as
they started across the green, the horse hesitated when the
solid earth beneath her hooves became spongy.

The woman felt the change of pace almost immediately, and it was fortunate that her first instinctive reaction was to follow the mare's lead, even though her mind was on securing dinner. She pulled up short just as Jondalar and Racer came pounding up. The stallion, too, noticed the softer ground, but his momentum was greater, and it carried him a few steps farther.

The man was almost thrown as Racer's front feet sank into a slurry of thick, silty mud, but he caught himself and jumped down alongside the horse. With a sharp whinny and a wrenching twist, the young stallion, his hind legs still on solid ground, managed to pull one leg out of the sucking morass. Stepping back and finding firmer support, Racer pulled until his other foot was suddenly released from the quicksand with a slurping pop.

The young horse was shaken, and the man paused to lay a calming hand on his arching neck, then he twisted off a branch from a nearby bush and used it to prod the ground ahead. When that was swallowed, he took the third long pole, which was not used for the travois, and explored with it. Though covered with reeds and sedge, the small field turned out to be a deep sinkhole of waterlogged clay and silt. The horses' agile retreat had averted a possible disaster, but they approached the Great Mother River with more caution from then on. Her capricious diversity could hold some unwelcome surprises.

Birds continued to be the dominant wildlife of the delta, particularly several varieties of herons, egrets, and ducks, with large numbers of pelicans, swans, geese, cranes, and some black storks and colorful glossy ibises nesting in trees. Nesting seasons varied with species, but all of them had to reproduce during the warmer times of year. The travelers collected eggs from all the different birds for quick and easy meals—even Wolf discovered the trick of cracking shells—and developed a taste for some of the mildly fishy-flavored varieties.

After a time they became accustomed to the birds of the delta. There were fewer surprises as they began to know what to expect, but one evening, as they were riding close to silvery sallow woods beside the river, they came upon a stunning scene. The trees opened up on a large lagoon, almost a lake, though at first they thought it was a firmer landscape, since large water-lily plants covered it completely. The sight that had arrested their attention was hundreds of the smaller squacco herons, standing—long necks curved into an S and long beaks poised to stab at fish—on nearly every single one of the sturdy lily pads that surrounded each fragrant blooming white flower.

Beguiled, they watched for a while, then decided to leave, afraid that Wolf might come bounding up and frighten the birds off their roosts. They were a short distance beyond the place, setting up their camp, when they saw hundreds of the long-necked herons climbing into the air. Jondalar and Ayla stopped and gazed at the sight as the birds, flapping large wings, became dark silhouettes against the pink clouds of the eastern sky. The wolf came loping into camp then, and Ayla supposed he had routed them. Though he made no real attempt to catch any, he had such fun chasing the flocks of marsh birds that she wondered if he did it because he enjoyed watching them lift into the air. She was certainly awed by the sight.

Ayla woke the next morning feeling hot and sticky. The heat was already gathering force, and she didn't want to get up. She wished they could just relax for a day. It wasn't so much that she was tired, just tired of traveling. Even the horses need a rest, she thought. Jondalar had been pushing to keep going, and she could sense the need that was driving him, but if one day would make that much difference in crossing the glacier he kept talking about, then they were already too late. They would need more than one sure day of the right kind of weather to be certain of safe travel. But when he got up and started packing, she did, too.

As the morning progressed, the heat and humidity, even on the open plain, were becoming oppressive, and when Jondalar suggested that they stop for a swim, Ayla instantly agreed. They turned toward the river and welcomed the sight of a shaded clearing that opened to the water. A seasonal streambed that was still slightly soggy and filled with decaying leaves left only a small patch of grass, but it created a cool, inviting pocket surrounded by pines and willows. It led to a muddy backwater ditch, but a short distance beyond, at a bend in the river, a narrow, pebbly beach jutted into a quiet pool, dappled with sun filtering through overhanging willows.

"This is perfect!" Ayla said with a big smile.

As she started to unhitch the travois, Jondalar asked, "Do you really think that's necessary? We won't be here long."

"The horses need a rest, too, and they might like to have a good roll or a swim," she said, removing the pack baskets and riding blanket from Whinney. "And I'd like to wait for Wolf to catch up with us. I haven't seen him all morning. He must have caught the scent of something wonderful that's giving him a good chase."

"All right," Jondalar said, and he started untying the thongs of Racer's pack baskets. He put them into the bowl boat beside Ayla's and gave the stallion a friendly slap on the rump, to let him know that he was free to follow his dam.

The young woman quickly shed her few garments and waded into the pool, while Jondalar stopped to pass his water. He glanced up at her, then couldn't look away. She was standing in shimmering water up to her knees, in a beam of sunlight coming through an opening in the trees, bathing in brilliance that lighted her hair into a golden halo, and gleamed off the bare tanned skin of her supple body.

Watching her, Jondalar was struck again by her beauty. For a moment, his strong feelings of love for her overpowered him, seeming to catch in his throat. She bent down to lift a double handful of water to splash down on herself, accenting the rounded fullness of her backside and exposing the paler skin of her inner thigh, and sending a flush of heat and wanting through him. He looked down at the member he was still holding in his hand and smiled, beginning to think of more than swimming.

She looked at him as he started into the water, saw his smile, and a familiar, compelling look in his intense blue eyes, then noticed the shape of his manhood changing. She felt a deep stirring in response; then she relaxed and a tension she didn't realize was there, drained away. They were not going to travel any more today, not if she could help it. They both needed a change of pace, a pleasantly exciting diversion.

He had noticed her eyes glance down at him, and at some level noted the welcome response and a slight change in her posture. Without really changing position, her stance became somehow more inviting. His reaction was obvious. He could not have hidden it if he'd wanted to.

"The water is wonderful," she said. "It was a good idea you had, to go swimming. It was getting so hot."

"Yes, I'm feeling a heat," he said, with a wry grin as he waded toward her. "I don't know how you do it, but I have no control around you."

"Why would you want to? I don't have any around you. You just have to look at me that way, and I'm ready for you." She smiled, the big beautiful smile that he loved.

"Oh, woman," he breathed as he took her in his arms. She reached up for him as he bent down to touch her soft lips with his in a firm, unhurried kiss. He ran his hands down her back, feeling her sun-warmed skin. She loved his touch and responded to his caress with an instant and surprising anticipation.

He reached lower, to her smooth rounded mounds, and pulled her toward him. She felt the full length of his warm hardness against her stomach, but the movement had unbalanced her. She tried to catch herself, but a stone gave way beneath her foot. She clutched at him for support, unbalancing him as his footing gave away. They fell into the water with a splash, then sat up, laughing.

"You're not hurt, are you?" Jondalar asked.

"No," she said, "but the water is cold and I was trying to ease in. Now that I'm wet, I think I'll go for a swim. Isn't that what we came here to do?"

"Yes, but that doesn't mean we can't do other things, too," he said. He noticed that the water reached to just under her arms, and her full breasts were floating, reminding him of the curving prows of a pair of boats with hard pink tips. He bent over and tickled a nipple with his tongue, feeling her warmth within the cool water.

She felt a shivery response and tilted her head back to let the sensation wash over her. He reached for her other breast, cupped it, then slid his hand back along her side and pulled her closer. She was feeling so sensitive, just the pressure of his palm sliding across her hard nipple sent new tingles of pleasure through her. He suckled the other, then let go and kissed her along her breast and on up her throat and neck. He blew softly in her ear, then found her lips. She opened her mouth slightly and felt the touch of his tongue, then his kiss.

"Come," he said, when they separated, getting up and extending a hand to help her up. "Let's go swimming."

He led her deeper into the pool, until the water reached her waist, then pulled her close to him, to kiss her again. She felt his hand between her legs, the coolness of the water

as he opened her folds, and a stronger sensation when he
found her hard little node and rubbed it.

She let the feeling course through her. Then, she thought,
This is happening too fast. I'm almost ready. She took a deep
breath, then slipped out of his grasp and, with a laugh,
splashed him.

"I think we should swim," she said, and reached out for
a few strokes. The swimming hole was small, enclosed on
the opposite side by a submerged island covered with a dense
reed bed. Once across it, she stood up and faced him. He
smiled and she felt the force of his magnetism, of his need,
of his love, and wanted him. He swam toward her as she
started swimming back toward the beach. When they met, he
turned and followed her.

Where the water became shallow, he stood up and said,
"All right, we did our swimming," then took her hand and
led her out of the water to the beach. He kissed her again
and felt her pull him closer, and she seemed to melt in his
arms as her breasts and stomach and thighs pressed against
his body.

"Now it's time for other things," he said.

Her breath caught in her throat, and he watched her eyes
dilate. Her voiced quivered slightly as she tried to speak.
"What other things?" she asked, with an attempt at a teasing
smile.

He dropped down on the ground cover and held up his
hand to her. "Come here and I'll show you."

She sat down next to him. He pushed her back kissing
her, then, with no other preliminary, he moved to cover her,
and down, pushed her legs apart, and ran his warm tongue
up her cool wet folds. Her eyes opened wide for an instant
as she shivered at the sudden throbbing rush that pulsed
through her, feeling it deep inside. Then she felt a sweet
pulling, as he suckled at her place of Pleasures.

He wanted to taste her, to drink her, and he knew she
was ready. His own excitement grew as he felt her respond,
and his loins ached with need as his large, slightly curving
manhood swelled to its fullest. He nuzzled, nibbled, suckled,
manipulating her with his tongue, then reached to taste her
inside, and savored it. For all his need, he wished he could
go on forever. He loved to Pleasure her.

She felt the excited frenzy growing inside her, and she

moaned, then cried out as she felt the peak rising, almost reaching its crest.

If he allowed it, he could have let himself release without even entering her, but he loved that feeling of her when he was inside, too. He wished there was some way he could do it all at once.

She reached for him and lifted up to meet him as the clamorous storm within her rose, and then almost without warning, suddenly erupted. He felt her wetness and warmth, then raised himself and moving up, found her welcome entrance and, with a strong surging push, filled it completely. His eager manhood was so ready, he wasn't sure how much longer he could wait.

She called out his name, reaching for him, wanting him, arching to his push. He plunged in again and felt her full embrace. Then, shuddering and groaning, he backed out, feeling the exquisite pull in his loins as his sensitive organ incited sensations deep within him. Then suddenly he was there, he could wait no more and as he pushed in again, felt the burst of Pleasures overtake him. She cried out with him, as her fierce delight overflowed.

He made a few last strokes; then he collapsed on top of her, both of them resting from the exhilarating arousal and tempestuous release. After a while, he lifted his head and she reached up to kiss him, conscious of the smell and taste of herself, which always reminded her of the incredible feelings he could evoke in her.

"I thought I wanted to make this last, take a long time, but I was so ready for you."

"That doesn't mean it can't last, you know," he said, and watched a slow smile grow.

Jondalar rolled off to his side, then sat up. "This rocky beach is not very comfortable," he said. "Why didn't you tell me?"

"I didn't notice, but now that you mention it, there is a stone jabbing my hip, and another under my shoulder. I think we should find a softer place . . . for you to lie on," she said with a sly grin and a glint in her eye. "But first, I'd like to go for a real swim. Maybe there's a deeper channel nearby."

They waded back into the river, swam the short distance of the pool, then continued upstream, breaking through the shallow, muddy reed bed. On the other side the water was suddenly cooler, then the ground under their feet dropped off and they found themselves in an open channel that wound through the reeds.

Ayla reached out and pulled ahead of Jondalar, but he exerted himself and caught up. They were both strong swimmers, and were soon having a friendly competition, racing along the open channel as it twisted and turned through the tall reeds. They were so evenly matched, that the smallest advantage could put one or the other into the lead. Ayla happened to be ahead when they reached a split with both new channels curving so sharply that, when Jondalar looked up, Ayla was out of sight.

"Ayla! Ayla! Where are you?" he called. There was no answer. He called out again, starting up one of the channels. It twisted around on itself, and all he could see were reeds; every place he turned, just walls of tall reeds. In a sudden panic, he called out again, "Ayla! Where in the Mother's cold underworld are you?"

Suddenly he heard a whistle, the one Ayla used to call Wolf. A wave of relief washed over him, but it sounded much farther away than he thought it should have. He whistled back and heard her reply, then started swimming back along the channel. He reached the place where the channel split, then turned up the other fork.

It also turned back on itself and into another channel. He felt a strong current take him, and suddenly he was heading downstream. But ahead he saw Ayla swimming hard against the pull of the stream, and he swam to meet her. She kept going when he came abreast, afraid the current would take her back down the wrong channel again if she stopped. He turned around and swam upstream beside her. When they reached the fork, they stopped to rest, treading water.

"Ayla! What were you thinking of? Why didn't you make sure I knew which way you were going?" Jondalar scolded in a loud voice.

She smiled at him, knowing now that his anger was a release of tension caused by his fear and worry. "I was just trying to keep ahead of you. I didn't know that channel would turn back on itself so quickly, or that the current would be so strong. I was carried downstream before I realized it. Why is it so strong?"

His tension vented, and relieved that she was safe, Jondalar's anger quickly dissipated. "I'm not sure," he said. "It is strange. Maybe we're close to the main channel, or the land under the water is dropping off here."

"Well, let's go back. This water is cold, and I'm ready for that sunny beach," Ayla said.

Letting the current help them, their swim back was more leisurely. Though it was not as strong as the pull of the other channel, it moved them along. Ayla turned to float on her back, and she watched the green reeds slipping by and the clear blue vault above. The sun was still in the eastern sky, but high.

"Do you recall where we came into this channel, Ayla?" Jondalar asked. "It all looks so much the same."

"There were three tall pines in a row on the riverbank, the middle one bigger. They were behind some hanging willows," she said, then turned over to swim again.

"There are a lot of pines along the water here. Maybe we should head for the shore. We might have gone past them," he said.

"I don't think so. The pine on the downstream side of the big one had a funny bent shape. I haven't seen it yet. Wait . . . up ahead . . . there it is, see it?" she said, moving toward the reed bed.

"You're right," Jondalar said. "Here's where we came through. The reeds are bent."

They clambered back across the reeds to the small pool, which now felt warm. They walked out onto the little spit of stony ground with a feeling of coming home.

"I think I'll start a fire and make some tea," Ayla said, running her hands down her arms to push the water off. She gathered up her hair and squeezed the water out, then headed for their pack baskets, gathering a few sticks of wood along the way.

"Do you want your clothes?" Jondalar asked, dropping more wood.

"I'd rather dry off a little first," she said, noting that the horses were grazing on the steppes nearby, but not seeing any sign of Wolf. She felt a twinge of worry, but it wasn't the first time he had gone off alone for half a day. "Why don't you spread out the ground cover on that sunny patch of grass. You can relax while I make the tea."

Ayla got a good fire going while Jondalar got some water. Then she selected the dried herbs from her store of them, thinking about them carefully. She thought alfalfa tea would be good, since it was generally stimulating and refreshing, with some borage flowers and leaves, which made a healthful tonic, and gillyflowers for sweetness and a mild spicy taste. For Jondalar, she also chose some of the deep red male catkins from alder trees that she had collected very early in the spring. She remembered having mixed feelings when she picked them, thinking of her Promise to mate with Ranec, but all the while wishing it was with Jondalar instead. She felt a warm glow of happiness as she added the catkins to his cup.

When it was done, she carried the two cups of tea to the patch of grass where Jondalar was relaxing. Part of the ground cover he had spread out was in the shade already, but she was just as glad. The heat of the day had already warmed away the chill of the swim. She handed him a cup and sat down beside him. They rested together companionably, sipping the refreshing drinks, not saying much, watching the horses standing together head to back, flicking flies away from each other's faces with their tails.

When he finished, Jondalar lay back, his hands behind his head. Ayla was glad to see him more relaxed and not pushing to be up and going right away. She put her cup down, then stretched out on her side beside him, putting her head in the hollow below his shoulder, and her arm across his chest. She closed her eyes, breathing in his man scent, and felt him put his arm around her and his hand moving across her hip, in an unconscious gentle caress.

She turned her head and kissed his warm skin, then blew her breath toward his neck. He felt a slight shiver and closed his eyes. She kissed him again, then raised up and pressed a series of nibbling little kisses up his shoulder and neck. Her kisses tickled him almost more than he could bear, but it gave him such excruciating tingles of excitement, he resisted moving and forced himself to lie still.

She kissed his neck and throat, and his jaw, feeling the stubble of whiskers on her lips; then she lifted herself up until she reached his mouth and moved across his lips from one side to the other with her soft nibbles. When she reached the other side, she pulled back and looked down at him. His eyes were closed, but he had an expression of anticipation. Finally he opened his eyes and saw her leaning over him and smiling with absolute delight, her hair still damp and hanging over one shoulder. He wanted to reach for her, crush her to him, but he smiled back.

She bent down and explored his mouth with her tongue, so lightly he could hardly feel it, but the breeze blowing across the wetness sent unbelievable shivers through him. Finally, when he thought he could stand it no longer, she kissed him, firmly. He felt her tongue seeking entrance and opened his mouth to receive her. Slowly she explored inside his lips, and under his tongue, and the ribbed roof of his mouth, testing, touching, tickling, then barely kissed his lips with her light little nibbles until he couldn't stand it. He reached up and grabbed her head and brought her to him as he lifted his head to give her a firm, strong, satisfying kiss.

When he dropped his head back and let go, she was grinning mischievously. She had made him react, and they both knew it. As he watched her, being so pleased with herself, he was pleased, too. She was feeling innovative, playful, and he wondered what other delights she had in store for him. A surge of sensation pulsed through him at the thought. This could turn out to be interesting. He smiled and waited, watching her with his startling, deep blue eyes.

She leaned across and kissed his mouth again, and his neck and shoulders and chest, then his nipples. Then, in a sudden shift, she got up on her knees at his side and leaned over him the other way, reached down and grasped his enlarged organ. As she took as much as she could hold into her warm mouth, he felt her moist warmth enclose the sensitive end of his manhood, and go farther. She pulled back slowly, creating suction, and he felt a pulling that seemed to draw from some deep internal place and extend throughout every part of him. He closed his eyes and let himself feel the growing enjoyment, as she moved her hands and warm, pulling mouth up and down his long shaft.

She probed the end with her exploring tongue, then made rapid circles around it, and he began to want her with more urgency. She reached down to take the soft pouch below his member in her hand, and gently—he had told her to always be gentle there—felt the two mysterious, soft, round pebbles within. She wondered about them, what they were for, and felt they were important in some way. As her warm hands cupped his tender sac, he felt a different sensation, pleasurable but with a touch of concern for this sensitive place, which seemed to stimulate him in another way.

She pulled away then and looked at him. His intense pleasure in her and what she was doing showed on his face and in his eyes as he smiled at her, encouraging her. She was enjoying the process of pleasuring him. It stimulated her in a different, but deep and exciting way, and she understood a little why he so loved to Pleasure her. She kissed him then, a long lingering kiss, then pulled back and put her leg over him, straddling him, facing his feet.

Sitting on his chest, she bent over and took his hard throbbing member in her two hands, one above the other. Though he was hard, extended, his skin felt soft, and when she held it in her mouth, he felt smooth and warm. She made her soft nibbling kisses down its length. When she reached the base, she reached farther down for his pouch, and took it gently in her mouth, feeling the firm roundnesses inside.

He shuddered as jolts of unexpected Pleasure eddied through him. It was almost too much. Not only the tumultuous sensations he was feeling, but the sight of her. She had lifted up to reach him, and with her legs straddling him, he could see her moist, deep pink petals and folds, and even her delicious opening. She let go of his pouch and moved back to take his exciting, throbbing manhood into her mouth to suckle again, when she suddenly felt him move her back a little farther. Then, with an unexpected shock of excitement, his tongue had found her folds, and the place of her Pleasures.

He explored her eagerly, completely, using his hands and his mouth, suckling, manipulating, feeling the joy of Pleasuring her, and at the same time, the excitement she caused within him as she rubbed him back and forth while she suckled him.

She was ready quickly and could not hold back, but he was trying to, straining not to let go just yet. He could easily have given in, but he wanted more, so when she stopped as her charging senses overcame her, arching back and crying out, he was glad. He felt her wetness, then gritted his teeth as he struggled for control. Without their earlier Pleasures, he was sure he would not have been able to, but he held back and reached a plateau just before he peaked.

"Ayla, move around the other way! I want all of you," he said.

She nodded, understanding. And, wanting all of him, too,

she backed off and then straddled him the other way. Lifting up, she eased his fullness into herself, and then lowered down. He moaned and called her name, over and over, feeling her deep warm well receive him. She felt pressures in sensitive different places as she moved up and down, guiding the direction of the hard fullness inside her.

At the plateau he had reached, his need was not quite as urgent. He could take a little time. She leaned forward, in yet another, slightly different position. He pulled her closer so he could reach her enticing breasts, held one to his mouth, and suckled hard; then he reached for the other, and finally, holding them together, both at the same time. As always, when he suckled her breasts, he felt the quivering excitement deep and low inside her.

She could feel herself building again as she moved up and down and back and forth on him. He was rising above the plateau, feeling his stronger urges coming over him again, and when she sat back, he grasped her hips and helped guide her movements, pushing up and pulling down. He felt a surge as she lifted up, and then, suddenly, he was there. She moved down on him again, and he cried out with the quaking tremor that rose from deep in his loins in a towering eruption, as she moaned and shuddered with the burst that roared within her.

Jondalar guided her up and down a few more times, then pulled her down on him and kissed her nipples. Ayla quivered once more, then collapsed on him. They lay still, breathing hard, trying to catch their breaths.

Ayla was just beginning to breathe easy when she felt something wet on her cheek. For a moment she thought it was Jondalar, but it was cold as well as wet, and there was a different, though not unfamiliar, smell. She opened her eyes and looked into the grinning teeth of a wolf. He nosed at her again, and then between them.

"Wolf! Get away from here!" she said, pushing his cold nose and wolfish breath away, then rolled over on her side beside the man. She reached up and grabbed Wolf's ruff and pulled her fingers through his fur. "But I am glad to see you. Where have you been all day? I was getting a little worried." She sat up and held his head in her two hands and put her forehead down on his, then turned toward the man. "I wonder how long he's been back."

"Well, I'm glad you taught him not to bother us. If he had interrupted us in the middle of that one, I'm not sure what I would have done to him," Jondalar said.

He got up, then helped her up. Taking her in his arms, he looked down at her. "Ayla, that was . . . what can I say? I don't begin to have the words to tell you."

She saw such a look of love and adoration in his eyes, she had to blink back tears. "Jondalar, I wish I had words, but I don't even know any Clan signs that would show you what I feel. I don't know if there are any."

"You just did show me, Ayla, in much more than words. You show me every day, in so many ways." Suddenly he pulled her to him and held her close, feeling his throat constrict. "My woman, my Ayla. If I ever lost you . . ."

Ayla felt a quiver of fear at his words, but she only held him tighter.

"Jondalar, how do you always know what I really want?" Ayla asked. They were sitting in the golden glow of the fire, sipping tea, watching sparks from the pitchy pine wood pop and send showers of sparks up into the night air.

Jondalar was feeling more rested, contented, and at ease than he had for some time. They had fished in the afternoon—Ayla showed him how she tickled a fish out of the water by hand—then she found soapwort and they had bathed and washed their hair. He had just finished a wonderful meal of some of the fish, plus the slightly fishy-tasting eggs of marsh birds, a variety of vegetables, a doughy cattail biscuit cooked on hot rocks, and a few sweet berries.

He smiled at her. "I just pay attention to what you tell me," he said.

"But, Jondalar, the first time, I thought I wanted to make it last, but you knew better than I what I really wanted. And then later, you knew I wanted to Pleasure you, and you let me, until I was ready for you again. And you knew when I was ready for you. I didn't tell you."

"Yes, you did. Just not with words. You taught me how to speak like the Clan does, with signs and motions, not words. I just try to understand your other signs."

"But I didn't teach you any signs like that. I don't really know any. And you knew how to give me Pleasures before you ever learned how to speak in the language of the Clan."

She was frowning with seriousness in trying to understand, which brought a smile to his face.

"That's true. But there is an unspoken language among people who speak, much more than they may realize."

"Yes, I've noticed that," Ayla said, thinking how much she was able to understand about people they met just by paying attention to the signs they made without knowing it.

"And sometimes you learn how to . . . do some things just because you want to, so you pay attention," he said.

She had been looking into his eyes, seeing in them the love he felt for her and the delight he seemed to be taking in her questions, and she noticed the unfocused look that came over him when he spoke. He stared into space as though he were seeing something far away for a moment, and she knew he was thinking of someone else.

"Especially when the one person you want to learn from is willing to teach you," she said. "Zolena taught you well."

He flushed, stared at her with shocked surprise, then looked away, disturbed.

"I've learned much from you, too," she added, knowing her remark had troubled him.

He seemed unable to look directly at her. When he finally did, his forehead was knotted in a frown. "Ayla, how did you know what I was thinking?" he asked. "I mean, I know you have some special Gifts. That's why the Mamut took you into the Mammoth Hearth when you were adopted, but sometimes you seem to know my thoughts. Did you take those thoughts from my head?"

She was sensing his concern and something more distressing, almost a fear of her. She had encountered a similar fear from some of the Mamutoi at the Summer Meeting when they thought she had some uncanny abilities, but most of it was misunderstanding. Like thinking she had some special control over animals, when all she did was find them when they were babies and raise them as her own.

But ever since the Clan Gathering, something had changed. She hadn't meant to drink any of the special root mixture that she made for the mog-urs, but she couldn't help it, and she hadn't meant to go into that cave and find the mog-urs, it just happened. When she saw them all sitting in a circle in that alcove deep in the cave and . . . fell into the black void that was inside her, she thought she was lost forever and would never find her way back. Then, somehow, Creb had reached inside her and had spoken to her. Since then, there had been times when she did seem to know things that she couldn't explain. Just like when Mamut took her with him when he Searched, and she felt herself rise up and follow him across the steppes. But as she looked at Jondalar and saw the strange way he was looking at her, a fear welled up inside her, a fear that she could lose him.

She looked at him in the light of the fire, then looked down. There could be no untruths . . . no lying between them. Not that she could deliberately say something that wasn't true, anyway, but not even the understood "refraining from speaking" that the Clan allowed for the sake of privacy, could come between them now. Even at the risk of losing him if she told him the truth, she had to tell him and try to find out what was troubling him. She looked directly at him then, trying to find words to begin.

"I did not know your thoughts, Jondalar, but I could guess them. Weren't we just talking about the unspoken signs that are made by people who speak with words? You make them, too, you know, and I . . . I look for them, and many times I know what they mean. Maybe because I love you so much and want to know you, I pay attention to you all the time." She looked away for a moment, and added, "That's what women of the Clan are trained to do."

She looked at him. There was some relief in his expression, and curiosity, as she continued. "It's not just you. I wasn't raised with . . . my kind of people, and I'm used to seeing meaning in the signs people make. It's helped me to learn about people I meet, though it was very confusing at first because people who talk with words often say one thing, but their unspoken signs mean something else. When I finally learned that, I began to understand more than the words people said. That's why Crozie wouldn't wager with me anymore when we played the Knucklebone games. I always knew which of her hands she was holding the marked bone in by the way she held them."

"I wondered about that. She was considered very good at the game."

"She was."

"But how did you know . . . how could you know I was thinking about Zolena? She's Zelandoni now. That's usually how I think of her, not the name she had when she was young."

"I was watching you, and your eyes were saying that you loved me, and that you were happy with me, and I was feeling wonderful. But when you talked about wanting to learn certain things, for a moment, you didn't see me. It was like you were looking far away. You told me about Zolena before, about the woman who taught you . . . your gift . . . the way you can make a woman feel. We had just been talking about that, too, so I knew that's who you must have been thinking about."

"Ayla, that's remarkable!" he said with a big, relieved grin. "Remind me never to try to keep a secret from you. Maybe you can't take thoughts from someone's head, but you can certainly do the next thing to it."

"There is something else you should know, though," she said.

Jondalar's frown returned. "What?"

"Sometimes I think I may have . . . some kind of Gift. Something happened to me when I was at the Clan Gathering, the time I went with Brun's clan, when Durc was a baby. I did something I wasn't supposed to. I didn't mean to, but I drank the liquid I made for the mog urs, and then happened to find them in the cave. I wasn't looking for them. I don't even know how I got in that cave. They were . . ." She got a chill and couldn't finish. "Something happened to me. I got lost in the darkness. Not in the cave, the darkness inside. I thought I was going to die, but Creb helped me. He put his thoughts inside my head . . ."

"He what?"

"I don't know how else to explain it. He put his thoughts inside my head, and ever since then . . . sometimes . . . it's like he changed something in me. Sometimes I think I might have some kind of . . . Gift. Things happen that I don't understand, and can't explain. I think Mamut knew."

Jondalar was quiet for a while. "So he was right to adopt you to the Mammoth Hearth, then, for more than just your healing skills."

She nodded. "Maybe. I think so."

"But you didn't know my thoughts just now?"

"No. The Gift is not like that, exactly. It's more like going with Mamut when he Searched. Or, like going to deep places, and far places."

"Spirit worlds?"

"I don't know."

Jondalar looked into the air over her head, considering the implications. Then he shook his head, looked at her with a grim smile. "I think it must be the Mother's joke on me," he said. "The first woman I loved was called to Serve Her, and I didn't think I'd ever love again. And now when I have found a woman to love, she turns out to be destined to Serve Her. Will I lose you, too?"

"Why should you lose me? I don't know if I'm destined to Serve Her. I don't want to Serve anyone. I just want to be with you, and share your hearth, and have your babies," Ayla objected vociferously.

"Have *my* babies?" Jondalar said, surprised at her choice of words. "How can you have my babies? I won't have babies, men don't have children. The Great Mother gives children to women. She may use a man's spirit to create them, but they're not his. Except to provide for, when his mate has them. Then they are the children of his hearth."

Ayla had talked about it before, about men starting the new life growing inside a woman, but he hadn't fully realized, then, that she truly was a daughter of the Mammoth Hearth. That she could visit spirit worlds, and might be destined to Serve Doni. Maybe she did know something.

"You can call my babies children of your hearth, Jondalar. I want my babies to be the children of your hearth. I just want to be with you, always."

"I want that, too, Ayla. I wanted you, and your children, even before I met you. I just didn't know I would find you. I only hope the Mother doesn't start any growing inside you until we get back."

"I know, Jondalar," Ayla said. "I would rather wait, too."

Ayla took their cups and rinsed them out, then finished her preparations for an early start, while Jondalar packed everything except their sleeping furs. They cuddled together, pleasantly tired. The Zelandonii man watched the woman beside him breathing quietly, but sleep eluded him.

My children, he was thinking. Ayla said her babies would be my children. Were we making life begin when we shared Pleasures today? If any new life started from that, then it would have to be very special, because those Pleasures were . . . better than any . . . ever . . .

Why were they better? It isn't as though I never did any of those things before, but with Ayla, it's different . . . I never get tired of her . . . she makes me want her more and more . . . just thinking about her makes me want her again . . . and she thinks I know how to Pleasure her . . .

But what if she gets pregnant? She hasn't yet . . . maybe she can't. Some women can't have children. But she did have a son. Could it be me?

I lived with Serenio for a long time. She didn't get pregnant all the time I was there, and she had a child before. I might have stayed with the Sharamudoi if she'd had children . . . I think. Just before I left, she said she thought she might be pregnant. Why didn't I stay? She said she didn't want to be mated to me, even though she loved me, because I didn't love her the same way. She said I loved my brother more than any woman. But I did care for her, maybe not the way I love Ayla, but if I had really wanted to, I think she would have mated me. And I knew it then. Did I use it as an excuse to leave? Why did I leave? Because Thonolan left and I was worried about him? Is that the only reason?

If Serenio was pregnant when I left, if she had another child, would it have been started from the essence of my manhood? Would it be . . . my child? That's what Ayla would say. No, that's not possible. Men don't have children, unless the Great Mother uses a man's spirit to make one. Of my spirit, then?

When we get there, at least I'll know if she had a baby. How would Ayla feel about it, if Serenio has a child that might somehow be a part of me? I wonder what Serenio will think when she sees Ayla? And what will Ayla think of her?

13

Ayla was eager to be up and moving the next morning, though it was no less sultry than it had been the day before. As she struck sparks with flint from her firestone, she wished she didn't have to bother with a fire. The food she had set by the night before and some water would have been enough for their morning meal, and thinking about the Pleasures she and Jondalar had shared, she wished she could forget about Iza's magic medicine. If she didn't drink her special tea, maybe she could find out if they had started a baby. But Jondalar got so upset at the idea of her getting pregnant on this Journey, that she had to drink the tea.

The young woman didn't know how the medicine worked. She just knew that if she drank a couple of bitter swallows of a strong decoction of golden thread every morning until her moon time, and a small bowl of the liquid from boiled antelope sage root each day that she was bleeding, she didn't get pregnant.

It would not be so hard to take care of a baby while they were traveling, but she didn't want to be alone when she gave birth. She didn't know if she would have lived through Durc's birth if Iza hadn't been there.

Ayla slapped a mosquito on her arm, then checked her supply of herbs while the water was heating. She had enough of the ingredients of her morning tea to last a while, which was just as well, since she had not noticed any of those plants growing around the marsh. They liked higher elevations and drier conditions. Checking the pouches and packages within her worn otter-skin medicine bag, she decided she had adequate quantities of most of the medicinal herbs that she needed in case of emergency, though she would have liked to replace some of last year's harvest with fresher plants. Fortunately she hadn't had much occasion to use her healing herbs so far.

Shortly after they started traveling west again, they came to a fairly large, fast stream. As Jondalar unfastened the pack baskets that hung down quite low on Racer's flanks, and loaded them into the bowl boat mounted on the travois, he took the time to study the rivers. The small river joined the Great Mother at a sharp angle, from upstream.

"Ayla, do you notice how this tributary comes into the Mother? It just goes straight in and flows downstream without even spreading out. I think this is the cause of that fast current we got caught in yesterday."

"I think you are right," she said, seeing what he meant. Then she smiled at the man. "You like to know the reasons for things, don't you?"

"Well, water doesn't suddenly start running fast for no reason. I thought there had to be an explanation."

"You found it," she said.

Ayla thought Jondalar seemed to be in a particularly good mood as they continued on after crossing the river, and that made her happy. Wolf was staying with them rather than wandering off and that pleased her, too. Even the horses seemed more spirited. The rest had been good for them. She was feeling alert and rested as well and, perhaps because she had just checked her medicines, she was particularly aware of the details of the plant and animal life of the great river mouth and the adjacent grassland they were traveling through. Though it was subtle, she noticed slight changes.

Birds were still the dominant form of wildlife around them, with those of the heron family most prevalent, but the abundance of other fowl was only less by comparison. Large flocks of pelicans and beautiful mute swans flew overhead, and many kinds of raptors, including black kites and white-tailed eagles, honey buzzards, and hawklike hobbies. She saw greater numbers of small birds hopping, flying, singing, and flashing their brilliant colors: nightingales and warblers, blackcaps, whitethroats, red-breasted flycatchers, golden orioles, and many other varieties.

Little bitterns were common in the delta, but the elusive, well-camouflaged marsh birds were heard more often than seen. They sang their characteristic, rather hollow, grunting notes all day, and more intensely with the coming of evening. But when anyone approached, they held their long beaks straight up and blended so well into the reeds among which they nested that they seemed to disappear. She saw many flying over the waters hunting for fish, however. Bitterns were quite distinctive in flight. Their coverts—the small feathers along the front of the wings and just over the base of the tail, which covered the quill ends of the larger flight feathers—were quite pale, and presented a strong contrast to their dark wings and back.

But the marshlands also accommodated a surprising number of animals that required a variety of different environments: roe deer and wild boars in the woods; hares, giant hamsters, and giant deer on the fringes, for example. As they rode, they noticed many creatures they hadn't seen for a while and pointed them out to each other: saiga antelope racing past plodding aurochs; a small tabby-striped wildcat stalking a bird and watched by a spotted leopard in a tree; a family of foxes with their kits; a couple of fat badgers; and some unusual polecats with white, yellow, and brown marbled coats. They saw otters in the water, and minks, along with their favorite food, muskrats.

And there were insects. The large yellow dragonflies winging past at great speed, and delicate damselflies in glowing blues and greens decorating the drab flower spikes of plantains were the beautiful exceptions to the irritating swarms that suddenly appeared. It seemed to happen in one day, though the ample moisture and warmth in the sluggish side streams and fetid pools had been nursing the tiny eggs all along. The first clouds of small gnats had appeared in the morning, hanging over the water, but the dry grassland nearby was still free of them, and they were forgotten.

By evening it was impossible to forget them. The gnats

burrowed into the heavy, sweat-soaked coats of the horses, buzzed around their eyes, and crept into their mouths and nostrils. The wolf fared little better. The poor animals were beside themselves with agony from the millions of mites. The annoying insects even got into the hair of the humans, and both Ayla and Jondalar found themselves spitting and rubbing their eyes to get rid of the tiny beasts as they rode. The swarms of gnats were thicker closer to the delta, and they began to wonder where they would camp for the night.

Jondalar spied a grassy hill on their right, and he thought the elevation might give him a broader view. They rode to the top of the rise and looked down at the sparkling water of an oxbow lake. It lacked the lush growth of the delta—and the stagnant pools that fostered the emerging imagoes—but a few trees and some brush lined the edges, bracketing a wide, inviting beach.

Wolf started down at a run, and the horses followed with no urging. It was all the woman and man could do to stop them long enough to lift off the pack baskets and unhitch Whinney's travois. They all splashed into the clear water in a rush that was slowed only by the resistance of the water. Even nervous Wolf, who disliked crossing rivers, showed no hesitation as he paddled around in the lake.

"Do you think he's finally starting to like water?" Ayla asked.

"I hope so. We have many more rivers to cross."

The horses dipped their heads to drink, snorted and blew water out of their noses and mouths, and then went back to the shallows. They dropped down on the muddy bank to roll and scratch themselves, and Ayla couldn't help laughing out loud at their grimacing faces and their eyes rolling and flashing in sheer delight. When they got up they were coated with mud, but when it dried, sweat, dead skin, insect eggs, and other causes of itching fell away with the dust.

They camped on the edge of the lake and started out early the next day. By evening they wished they could find another campsite as pleasant. A wave of mosquitoes followed the hatching of the gnats, raising red itching bumps that forced Ayla and Jondalar to don protective, and heavier, clothing, though it felt uncomfortably warm after being accustomed to the bare minimum. Neither of them was quite sure when the flies appeared. There had always been a few horseflies around, but now it was the smaller biting flies that suddenly increased. Even though it was a warm evening, they crawled into their sleeping furs early, just to escape the flying hordes.

They did not break camp until late morning the next day, not until after Ayla had searched for herbs that could be used to soothe their bites and to make insect repellents. She found brownwort, with its loose spike of strangely shaped brown flowers, in a damp and shady place near the water, and she collected the whole plants to make into a wash, for their skin-healing and itch-relieving properties. When she saw the large leaves of plantain she picked them to add to the solution; they were excellent for healing anything from bites to boils, even severe ulcers and wounds. From farther out on the steppes where it was dryer, she gathered wormwood flowers to add as a general antidote for poisons and toxic reactions.

She was quite pleased to find bright yellow marigolds for their antiseptic and quick-healing virtues, to take the sting out of bites, and because they were so effective in keeping insects away when a strong solution was splashed on. And growing at the sunny edge of the woods, she found wild marjoram, which was not only a good insect repellent when made into an infusion for an external wash, but drinking it as a tea gave a person's sweat a spicy odor that gnats, fleas, and most flies found distasteful. She even tried to get the horses and Wolf to drink some, though she wasn't sure how successful she was.

Jondalar watched her preparations, asking her questions and listening to her explanations with interest. When his irritating bites were relieved and he was feeling better, it occurred to him how lucky he was to be traveling with someone who could do something about insects. He would have just had to put up with them if he were alone.

By midmorning they were on their way again, and the changes Ayla had noticed before increased dramatically. They were seeing less marsh and more water, with fewer islands. The northern arm of the delta was losing its network of meandering waterways and all becoming one. Then, with little warning, the northern and one of the middle arms of the great river delta came together, doubling the size of the channel, and creating an enormous body of running water. A short distance beyond, the river increased again as the southern arm, which had joined with the other main channel, combined with the rest, bringing together all four arms to form a single deep channel.

The great waterway had received hundreds of tributaries and the runoff of two ice-mantled ranges as she swept across the breadth of a continent, but the granite stumps of ancient mountains had blocked her seaward passage farther south. Finally, unable to resist the inexorable pressures of the advancing river, they were finally broached, but the obdurate bedrock yielded reluctantly. The Great Mother, hemmed in by the narrow passage, gathered up her flowing outskirts for one brief length before making a sharp turn and debouching through the massive delta into the expectant sea.

It was the first time that Ayla had seen the full magnitude of the enormous river, and though he had been that way before, Jondalar had seen it from a different perspective. They were stunned, held by the sight. The awesome expanse seemed more like a flowing sea than a river, the shimmering, roiling surface betraying but a hint of the great power hidden within its depths.

Ayla noticed a broken branch moving toward them, hardly more than a stick carried along by the deep, swift current, but something about it caught her attention. It took longer than she expected to reach them, and as it drew near, she caught her breath in surprise. It was not a branch at all; it was a complete tree! As it floated serenely by, Ayla stared in wonder at one of the largest trees she had ever seen.

"This is the Great Mother River," Jondalar said.

He had traveled her entire length once before, and he knew the distance she had traveled, the terrain she had crossed, and the Journey still ahead of them. Though Ayla didn't entirely comprehend all the implications, she did understand that, gathered together in one place for the last time, at the end of her long Journey, the vast, deep, powerful Mother River had reached her culmination; this was as Great as she would ever be.

They continued upstream beside the brimming waterway, leaving the steamy river mouth behind, and with it many of the insects that plagued them, and they discovered that they were leaving the open steppes as well. The broad grasslands and flat marshes gave way to undulating hills covered with extensive woodlands interspersed with green meadows.

It was cooler in the shade of the open woods. This was such a welcome change that when they came upon a large

lake surrounded by trees near a beautiful green meadow, they
were tempted to stop and make camp though it was only the
middle of the afternoon. They rode alongside a creek toward
a sandy shore, but as they neared, Wolf began a low growl
deep in his throat and, with hackles raised, assumed a defensive posture. Both Ayla and Jondalar scanned the area, trying
to see what was disturbing the animal.

"I don't see anything wrong," Ayla said, "but there is
something here that Wolf doesn't like."

Jondalar looked at the inviting lake once more. "It's early
to make camp, anyway. Let's just go on," he said, turning
Racer aside and heading back toward the river. Wolf stayed
behind a while longer, then caught up with them.

As they rode through the pleasant wooded regions, Jondalar was just as happy that they decided not to stop early at
the lake. During the afternoon, they passed several more lakes
of various sizes; the area was full of them. He thought he
should have known that from his previous passage down the
river, until he remembered that he and Thonolan had come
downstream in a Ramudoi boat, only stopping at the edge of
the river occasionally.

But more than that, he felt that there ought to be people
living in such an ideal location, and he tried to remember if
any of the Ramudoi had talked about other River People living downstream. He didn't bring up any of his thoughts to
Ayla, though. If they weren't making themselves known,
they didn't want to be seen. He couldn't help but wonder,
however, what had caused Wolf to react so defensively.
Could it have been the scent of human fear? Hostility?

As the sun was beginning its descent behind the mountains that loomed large in front of them, they stopped at a
smaller lake that was a catch basin for several rivulets coming
from higher ground. An outlet led directly to the river, and
large trout and river-dwelling salmon had swum upstream into
the lake.

Ever since they reached the river and added fish on a
regular basis to their diet, Ayla had occasionally worked on
a net she was weaving, similar to the kind Brun's clan had
used to catch large fish from the sea. She had to make the
cordage first, and she tried out several kinds of plants that
had stringy, fibrous parts. Hemp and flax seemed to work
particularly well, though hemp was rougher.

She felt she had a large enough section of netting to try

it out in the lake, and, with Jondalar holding one end and she the other, they started some distance out and walked back toward the shore pulling the net between them. When they pulled in a couple of big trout, Jondalar became even more interested, and he wondered if there was a way to attach a handle to the netting so one person could catch a fish without wading into the water. The thought stayed on his mind.

In the morning they headed for the mountain ridges strung out ahead through a rare, rich, and diverse woodland. The trees, a wide assortment of deciduous and coniferous varieties, that, like the plants of the steppes, were distributed in a mosaic pattern of distinctive woods, broken by meadows and lakes, and in some lowlands, peat bogs or marshes. Certain trees grew in pure stands or in association with other trees or vegetation depending on minor variations in climate, elevation, availability of water, or soil, which could be loamy or sandy or sand mixed with clay, or several other combinations.

Evergreen trees preferred north-facing slopes and sandier soils and, where the moisture was sufficient, grew to great heights. A dense forest of huge spruces, soaring to a hundred sixty feet, occupied a lower slope that blended into pines that seemed to reach the same height but, though tall at a hundred thirty feet, were growing on the higher ground just above. Tall stands of deep green fir made way for thick communities of high, fat, white-barked birch. Even willows reached over seventy-five feet.

Where the hills faced south and the soil was moist and fertile, large-leaved hardwoods also attained amazing heights. Clusters of giant oaks with perfectly straight trunks and no spreading branches, except for a crown of green leaves at the top, climbed to over a hundred forty feet. Immense linden and ash trees reached nearly the same height, with magnificent maples not far behind.

In the distance ahead, the travelers could see the silvery leaves of white poplars mixed in with a stand of oaks, and when they reached the place, they found the oak woods alive with breeding tree sparrows nesting in every conceivable cranny. Ayla even found nests of the sparrows with eggs and young birds in them, built inside the nests of magpies and buzzards, that were themselves inhabited by eggs and young. There were also many robins in the woods, but their young were already fledged.

On the slanted hillsides, where breaks in the leafy canopy allowed more sunlight to reach the ground, undergrowth was luxuriant, with flowering clematis and other lianas often trailing down from the high branches of the canopy. The riders approached a stand of elms and white willows covered with vines climbing up their trunks and trailing plants hanging down. There they found the nests of many spotted eagles and black storks. They passed aspens quivering over dewberries and thick sallows near a stream. A mixed stand of majestic elms, elegant birches, and fragrant lindens marching up a hillside, overshadowed a thicket of edibles that they stopped to gather: raspberries, nettles, hazel brush with not-quite-ripe hazelnuts, just the way Ayla liked them, and a few stone pines bearing rich, hard-shelled pine nuts within their cones.

Farther on, a stand of hornbeams crowded out beeches, only to be replaced by them again later on—and one fallen giant hornbeam, thickly covered with a yellow-orange coating of honey mushrooms, set Ayla to picking in earnest. The man joined her in collecting the delicious edible fungi she found, but it was Jondalar who discovered the bee tree. With the help of a smoky torch and his axe, he climbed a makeshift ladder made from the fallen trunk of a fir with the stumps of sturdy branches still attached, and he braved a few stings to collect some honeycombs. They gobbled up most of the rare treat then and there, eating the beeswax and a few bees along with it, laughing like children at the sticky mess they made of themselves.

These southern regions had long been the natural preserves of temperate trees, plants, and animals, crowded out by the dry, cold conditions of the rest of the continent. Some pine species were so ancient that they had even seen the mountains grow. Nurtured in small areas favorable to their survival, the relict species were available, when the climate changed again, to spread quickly into lands newly open to them.

The man and woman, with the two horses and the wolf, continued their westward direction beside the broad river, heading toward the mountains. Details were becoming sharper, but the snowy ridges were an ever-present sight, and their progress toward them was so gradual that they hardly noticed that they were getting closer. They made occasional forays into the hills of the wooded countryside to the north, which could be rugged and steep, but for the most part they stayed close to the level plain near the trench of the river. The terrains were different, but the wooded plains had many plants and trees in common with the mountains.

The travelers realized they had come to a major change in the character of the river when they reached a large tributary rushing down from the highlands. They crossed it with the help of the bowl boat, but shortly afterward they came upon another fast river just as they were making a swing around to the south, where the Great Mother River had come from after skirting the lower end of the range. The river, unable to climb the northern highlands, had made a sharp turn and broached the ridge to reach the sea.

The bowl boat proved its usefulness again in crossing the second tributary, though they had to travel upstream from the confluence along the adjoining river until they found a less turbulent place to cross. Several other smaller streams entered the Mother just below the turn. Then, following the left bank around, the journeyers made a slight jog to the west and another swing back around. Though the great river was still on their left, they were no longer facing mountains. The range was now on their right and they were looking due south at dry open steppes. Far ahead, distant purple prominences hugged the horizon.

Ayla kept watching the river as they traveled upstream. She knew that all the tributaries were carried downstream and that the great river was now less full than it had been. The broad expanse of running water did not appear any different, yet she felt that the waters of the Great Mother were diminished. It was a feeling that went deeper than knowing, and she kept trying to see if the immense river had altered in any noticeable way.

Before long, however, the huge river's appearance did change. Buried deep beneath the loess, the fertile soil that had begun as rock dust ground fine by the huge glaciers and strewn by wind, and the clays, sands, and gravels deposited over millennia by running water, was the ancient massif. The enduring roots of archaic mountains had formed a stable shield so unyielding that the intractable granite crust, which had been forced against it by the inexorable movements of the earth, had buckled and risen into the mountains whose icy caps now glistened in the sun.

The hidden massif extended under the river, but an exposed ridge, worn down with time though still high enough to block the river's exodus to the sea, had forced the Great Mother to veer north, seeking an outlet. Finally, the ungiving rock grudgingly surrendered a narrow passage, but before she gathered herself together with its tight constraints, the huge river had run parallel to the sea across the level plain, languidly spread out into two arms interlinked by meandering channels.

The relict forest was left behind as Ayla and Jondalar rode south into a region of flat landscape and low rolling hills covered with standing hay, next to a huge river marsh. The countryside resembled the open steppes beside the delta, but it was a hotter, drier land with areas of sand dunes, mostly stabilized by tough, drought-resistant grasses, and fewer trees even near water. Brush, primarily wormwood, wood sage, and aromatic tarragon, dominated the stands of woody growth that were trying to force a meager existence from the dry soil, sometimes crowding out the dwarfed and contorted pines and willows that clung close to the banks of streams.

The marshland, the often-flooded area between the arms of the river, was second in size only to the great delta and as rich with reeds, swamps, water plants, and wildlife. Low islands with trees and small green meadows were enclosed by muddy yellow main channels or side lanes of clear water filled with fish, often unusually large.

They were riding through an open field quite near the water when Jondalar reined in Racer to a halt. Ayla pulled up beside him. He smiled at her puzzled expression, but before she spoke he silenced her with a finger to his lips and pointed toward a clear pool. Underwater plants could be seen waving to the motion of unseen currents. At first she saw nothing unusual; then, gliding effortlessly out of the green-tinged depths, an enormous and beautiful golden carp appeared. On another day they saw several sturgeon in a lagoon; the giant fish were fully thirty feet long. Jondalar was reminded of an embarrassing incident involving one of the tremendously large fish. He thought about telling Ayla, then changed his mind.

Reedbeds, lakes, and lagoons along the river's meandering course invited birds to nest, and great flocks of pelicans glided by on uplifting currents of warm air, barely flapping their broad wings. Toads and edible frogs sang their evening chorus, and sometimes provided a meal. Small lizards skittering over muddy banks were ignored by the passing travelers, and snakes were avoided.

There seemed to be more leeches in these waters, making them more wary and selective of the places they chose for swimming, though Ayla was intrigued by the strange creatures that attached themselves and drew blood without their knowing it. But it was the smallest of the creatures that were the most troublesome. With the swampy marsh nearby, there were also insects to plague them, more it seemed than before, sometimes forcing them and the animals into the river just to get relief.

The mountains to the west pulled back as they neared the southern end of the range, putting a wider sweep of plains between the great river they were following and the line of craggy crests marching south with them on their left flank. The snow-covered chain ended in a sharp bend, where another branch of the range, going in an east-west direction and defining the southern boundary, met the branch beside them. Near the farthest southeast corner, two high peaks jutted above all the rest.

Continuing south along the river and moving farther away from the major range, they gained the perspective of distance. Looking back, they began to see the full extent of the long line of lofty crests going west. Ice glistened on the highest tors, while snow mantled their steep sides and covered the adjoining ridges in white—a constant reminder that the short season of summer heat on the southern plains was only a brief interlude in a land ruled by ice.

After leaving the mountains behind, the view of the west seemed vacant; uninterrupted arid steppes presented a featureless plain as far as they could see. Without the variety of the forested hills to change the pace, or the rugged heights to break their view, one day blended into another with little change as they followed the left bank of the marshy waterway south. At one place the river came together for a time, and they could see steppes and a richer growth of trees on the opposite side, though there were still islands and reed beds within the great stream.

Before the day was over, however, the Great Mother was spreading out again. Following her, the journeyers continued south, veering only slightly west. As they drew closer, the distant purple hills gained altitude and began to exhibit their own character. In contrast to the sharp peaks of the north, the mountains to the south, though they reached summits high enough to keep a blanket of snow and ice until well into summer, were rounded, giving the appearance of uplands.

The southern mountains also affected the course of the river. When the travelers neared them, they noticed the great stream changing, with a pattern they had seen before. Meandering channels came together and straightened, then joined with others, and finally with the main arms. Reed beds and islands disappeared and the several channels formed one deep, broad channel as the huge waterway came sweeping around a wide bend toward them.

Jondalar and Ayla followed her around the inside turn until they were again facing west, toward the sun setting in a deep red hazy sky. There were no clouds that Jondalar could see, and he wondered what was causing the vibrant uniform color that reflected off the craggy pinnacles to the north, the rugged uplands across the river, and tinged the rippling water with the hue of blood.

They continued upstream along the left bank, looking for a good place to camp. Ayla found herself studying the river again, intrigued by the magnificent stream. Several tributaries of various sizes, some rather large, had flowed into the broad river from both sides, each contributing to her prodigious volume downstream. Ayla understood that the Great Mother was smaller now, by the volume of each river they had passed, but she was so vast that it was still hard to see any diminishing of her tremendous capacity. Yet at some deep level the young woman felt it.

Ayla woke before dawn. She loved the mornings, when it was still cool. She made her bitter-tasting contraceptive medicine, then readied a cup of tarragon-and-sage tea for the sleeping man and another for herself. She drank it watching the morning sun wake up the mountains to the north. It began with the first pink hint of predawn defining the two icy peaks, spreading slowly at first, reflecting a rosy glow in the east. Then suddenly, even before the edge of the glowing ball of fire sent a tentative gleam above the horizon, the blazing mountaintops heralded its coming.

When the woman and man started out again, they expected to see the great river spread out; so they were surprised when she remained within a single wide channel. A few brush-covered islands formed within the broad stream, but she didn't split into separate waterways. They were so used to seeing her meandering across the level grasslands in a wide unruly path that it seemed strange to see the enormous flood contained for any distance. But the Great Mother invariably took the lowest path as she wound her way around and between high mountains across the continent. The river flowed east through the southernmost plains of her long passage. The low ground was at the foot of the eroded mountains, which constrained and defined her right bank.

On her left bank, between the river and the sharply folded glistening crests of granite and slate to the north, lay a platform, a foreland of limestone, primarily, covered with a mantle of loess. It was a rough and rugged land subject to violent extremes. Harsh black winds from the south desiccated the land in summer; high pressure over the northern glacier hurled frigid blasts of freezing air across the open space in winter; fierce gale storms rising in the sea frequently bore down from the east. The occasional soaking rains and the fast-drying winds, along with the temperature extremes, caused the limestone underlying the porous loess soil to fracture, which created steeply scarped faces on flat open plateaus.

Tough grasses survived on the dry windy landscape, but trees were almost entirely absent. The only woody vegetation were certain kinds of brush that could withstand both arid heat and searing cold. An occasional thin-branched tamarisk bush, with its feathery foliage and spikes of tiny pink flowers, or a buckthorn, with black round berries and sharp thorns, dotted the landscape, and even a few small, bushy, black currant shrubs could be seen. Most prevalent were several varieties of artemisia, including a wormwood unknown to Ayla.

Its black stalks looked bare and dead, but when she picked some, thinking it would make fuel for a fire, she discovered it was not dry and brittle but green and living. After a brief wet squall, loose-toothed leaves with a silvery down on the underside uncurled and grew out from the stalks and numerous small yellowish flowers, like tightly cupped centers of daisies, appeared on branching spikes. Except for its darker stems, it resembled the more familiar, lighter-colored species that often grew alongside fescue and crested hair grass, until

the wind and sun dried the plains. Then it once again
appeared lifeless and dead.

With its variety of grasses and brush, the southern plains
supported hosts of animals. None they hadn't seen on the
steppes farther north, but in different proportions, and some
of the more cold-loving species, such as the musk-ox, never
ventured so far south. On the other hand, Ayla had never
seen so many saiga antelope in one place before. They were
a widespread animal, seen almost everywhere on the open
plains, but were not usually very numerous.

Ayla stopped and was watching a herd of the strange,
clumsy-looking animals. Jondalar had gone to investigate an
inlet in the river with some slender tree trunks stuck into the
bank that looked out of place. There were no trees on this
side of the river, and the arrangement seemed purposeful.
When he caught up, she seemed to be looking off in the
distance.

"I couldn't tell for sure," he said. "Those logs might
have been put there by some River People; someone could
tie a boat there. But it could be driftwood from upstream,
too."

Ayla nodded, then pointed toward the dry steppes. "Look
at all those saigas."

Jondalar didn't see them at first. They were the color of
the dust. Then he saw the outline of their straight horns with
coiled ridges, tipped slightly forward at the ends.

"They remind me of Iza. The spirit of the Saiga was her
totem," the woman said, smiling.

The saiga antelopes always made Ayla smile, with their
long overhanging noses and peculiar gait, which did not hin-
der their speed, she noted. Wolf liked to chase them, but
they were so fast that he seldom got very close to them, at
least not for long.

These saiga seemed to favor the black-stemmed wormwood in particular, and they banded together in much larger
than usual herds. A small herd of ten or fifteen animals was
common, usually females, with one and often two young;
some mothers were not much more than a year old themselves. But in this region the herds were numbering more
than fifty. Ayla wondered about the males. The only time
she saw them in any abundance was during their rutting sea-

son, when each tried to Pleasure as many females as he could, as many times as he could. Afterward there were always carcasses of male saigas to be found. It was almost as though the males wore themselves out with Pleasures, and for the rest of the year left the sparse feed they commonly ate for the females and the young.

There were also a few ibex and mouflon on the plains, often preferring to stay near the steep scarped faces, which the wild goats and sheep could climb with ease. Huge herds of aurochs were scattered over the land, most of them with solid-color coats of a deep reddish black, but a surprising number of individuals had white spots, some quite large. They saw faintly spotted fallow deer, red deer, and bison, and many onagers. Whinney and Racer were aware of most of the four-legged grazers, but the onagers, in particular, caught their attention. They watched the herds of horselike asses and sniffed long at their similar piles of dung.

There was the usual complement of small grassland animals: susliks, marmots, jerboas, hamsters, hares, and a crested porcupine species that was new to the woman. Keeping their numbers in check were the animals that preyed on the rest. They saw small wildcats, larger lynxes, and huge cave lions, and they heard the laughing cackle of hyenas.

In the days that followed, the great river changed her course and direction often. While the landscape on the left bank, through which they were traveling, remained much the same—grassy low rolling hills and flat plains with sharp-edged scarp faces and jagged mountains behind—they noticed that the opposite bank became more rugged and diverse. Tributary rivers cut deep valleys, and trees climbed the eroded mountains, occasionally covering an entire slope right down to the water's edge. The indented foothills and rough terrain, which defined the south bank, contributed to the broad curves swinging in every direction, even back on itself, but overall her course was eastward toward the sea.

Within the mighty turns and twists, the great body of water flowing toward them did spread out and break up into separate channels, but it did not develop into a marshland like the delta again. It was simply a huge river or, over more level ground, a meandering series of large parallel streams with richer brush and greener grass nearer the water.

Though it had sometimes seemed annoying, Ayla missed the chorus of marsh frogs, though the flutey trill of variegated toads was still a refrain in the aleatoric medley of night music. Lizards and steppe vipers took their place and along with them the distinctively beautiful demoiselle cranes, who thrived on the reptiles, as well as insects and snails. Ayla enjoyed watching a pair of the long-legged birds, bluish-gray with black heads and white tufts of feathers behind each eye, feeding their young.

She did not, however, miss the mosquitoes. Without their marshy breeding ground, those bothersome biting insects had largely disappeared. That was not true of the gnats. Clouds of them still plagued the wayfarers, particularly the furry ones.

"Ayla! Look!" Jondalar said, pointing out a simple construction of logs and planks at the edge of the river. "This is a boat landing. This was made by River People."

Though she did not know what a boat landing was, it was obviously not an accidental arrangement of materials. It had been purposely constructed for some human use. The woman felt a surge of excitement. "Does that mean there are people around here?"

"Probably not right now—there's no boat at the landing—but not far. This must be a place that is used frequently. They wouldn't go to the trouble of making a landing if they didn't use it a lot, and they wouldn't use a place that was far away very often."

Jondalar studied the landing for a moment, then looked upstream and across the river. "I'm not certain, but I'd say whoever built this lives on the other side of the river, and they land here when they cross. Maybe they come over to hunt, or collect roots, or something."

Proceeding upriver, they both kept looking across the wide stream. Except in general, they hadn't paid much attention to the territory on the other side until now, and it occurred to Ayla that there may have been people over there that they hadn't noticed before. They had not gone far when Jondalar caught a movement on the water, some distance upstream. He stopped to verify his sighting.

"Ayla, look over there," he said when she stopped beside him. "That could be a Ramudoi boat."

She looked and saw something, but she wasn't sure what she was seeing. They urged the horses on. When they got closer, Ayla saw a boat unlike anything she had ever seen before. She was only familiar with boats made in the Mamutoi style, hide-covered frames made in the shape of a bowl like the one that was mounted on the travois. The one she saw on the river was made of wood and came to a point in front. It held several people in a row. As they drew abreast, Ayla noticed more people on the opposite shore.

"Hola!" Jondalar called out, waving his arm in greeting. He shouted some other words in a language that was unfamiliar to her, though there seemed to be a vague similarity to Mamutoi.

The people in the boat did not respond, and Jondalar wondered if he had not been heard, though he thought they had seen him. He called out again, and this time he was sure they had heard him, but they did not wave back. Instead they began paddling for the other side as fast as they could.

Ayla noticed that one of the people on the opposite shore had seen them, too. He ran toward some other people and pointed across the river at them, then he and some of the others left in a hurry. A couple of people stayed until the boat reached shore; then they left.

"It's the horses, again, isn't it?" she said.

Jondalar thought he saw a tear glisten. "It wouldn't have been a good idea to cross the river here, anyway. The Cave of Sharamudoi that I know live on this side."

"I suppose so," she said, signaling Whinney to move on. "But they could have crossed in their boat. They could at least have answered your greeting."

"Ayla, think how strange we must look, sitting on these horses. We must seem like something from some spirit world with four legs, and two heads," he said. "You can't blame people for being afraid of something they don't know."

Ahead, across the water, they could see a spacious valley that dropped down from the mountains nearly to the level of the mighty stream beside them. A sizable river rushed through the middle of it and entered the Great Mother with a turbulence that sent eddies in both directions and broadened her width. Adding to the play of countercurrents, just beyond the tributary the southern range that bounded the river's right bank curved back around.

In the valley, near the confluence of the two rivers, but up on a slope, they saw several dwellings made of wood, obviously a settlement. Standing around them were the people who lived there, gaping at the travelers passing by across the river.

"Jondalar," Ayla said. "Let's get off the horses."

"Why?"

"So those people will at least see that we look like people, and the horses are just horses, not some two-headed creatures with four legs," she said. Ayla dismounted and began walking in front of the mare.

Jondalar nodded, threw his leg over, and leaped down. Taking hold of the lead rope, he followed her. But the woman had just started out when the wolf ran up to her and greeted her in his customary way. He jumped up, put his paws on her shoulders, licked her, and nuzzled her jaw, gently, with his teeth. When he got down, something, perhaps a scent wafting across the wide river, made him conscious of the people who were watching. He went to the edge of the bank and, lifting his head, began a series of yips that led into a heart-stopping ululation of wolf song.

"Why is he doing that?" Jondalar said.

"I don't know. He hasn't seen anyone else for a long time, either. Maybe he's glad to see them and wants to greet them," Ayla said. "I would, too, but we can't cross over to their side very easily, and they won't come over here."

Ever since leaving behind the deep curve of the river that had changed their direction toward the setting sun, the travelers had been bearing slightly south in their generally westward advance. But beyond the valley, where the mountains angled back, they began heading due west. They were as far south as they would go on their Journey, and it was the hottest season of the year.

During the highest days of summer, with an incandescent sun scourging the shadeless plains, even when ice as thick as mountains covered a quarter of the earth, the heat could be oppressive in the southern stretches of the continent. A strong, hot, unceasing wind that wore on their nerves made it worse. The man and woman, riding side by side, or walking the scorching steppes to let the horses rest, fell into a routine that made traveling, if not easy, at least possible.

They awakened with the first glimmer of dawn glistening off the highest peaks to the north and, after a light breakfast of a hot tea and cold food, were on their way before the day was fully light. As the sun rose higher, it struck the open steppes with such intensity that shimmering heat waves issued from the earth. A patina of dehydrating sweat gleamed the deeply tanned skin of the humans and soaked the fur of Wolf and the horses. The wolf's tongue lolled out of his mouth as he panted with the heat. He had no urge to run off on his own to explore or hunt but kept pace with Whinney and Racer, who plodded along, their heads hanging low. Their passengers drooped listlessly, allowing the horses to proceed at their own speed, talking little during the suffocating heat of midday.

When they could not take it any longer, they looked for a level beach, preferably near a clear backwater or slow-moving channel of the Great Mother. Even Wolf did not resist the slower currents, though he still hesitated a bit when a river ran fast. When the humans he was traveling with turned toward the river, dismounted, and began to unfasten the baskets, he raced ahead and bounded into the water first. If it was a tributary river, they usually plunged into the cool refreshing water, crossing before removing pack basket or travois harness.

After feeling revived by their swim, Ayla and Jondalar looked for what was available to eat, if they didn't have enough left over or hadn't found something along the way. Food was abundant, even on the hot, dusty steppes, and particularly in the cool watery element—if one knew where and how to get it.

They nearly always managed to catch fish when they wanted to, using Ayla's or Jondalar's methods or a combination of the two. If the situation called for it, they used Ayla's long net, walking in the water and holding it between them. Jondalar had devised a handle for some of her netting, creating a kind of dip net. He wasn't entirely happy with it yet, but it was useful in certain circumstances. He also fished with a line and gorge—a piece of bone he had sharpened to a keen tapered point on both ends and tied in the middle with a strong cord. Pieces of fish, meat, or earthworms were threaded onto it for bait. Once it was swallowed, a quick jerk usually caused the gorge to lodge sideways in the throat of the fish with a point sticking in each side.

Sometimes Jondalar caught rather large fish with the gorge, and after losing one of these he made a gaff to help bring others in. He started with the forking branch of a tree, cut off just below the joint. The longer arm of the fork was used as the handle; the shorter one was sharpened into a backward point and used as a hook to haul the fish in. There were some small trees and high brush near the river, and the first gaffs he made worked, but he never seemed to find a sturdy enough forking branch to last very long. The weight and struggles of a big fish often broke it, and he kept looking for stronger wood.

He passed by the antler the first time he saw it, registering its existence and that it had probably been shed by a three-year-old red deer, but not really paying attention to its shape. But the antler stayed on his mind, until he suddenly remembered the backward-pointing brow tine, and then he went back to get it. Antlers were tough and hard, and very difficult to break, and it was just the right size and shape. With a little sharpening, it would make an excellent gaff.

Ayla still fished by hand on occasion, the way Iza had taught her. It amazed Jondalar to watch her. The process was simple, he kept telling himself, though he hadn't been able to master it. It just took practice, and skill, and patience—infinite patience. Ayla looked for roots or driftwood or rocks that overhung the bank, and then for fish that liked to rest in those places. They always faced upstream, into the oncoming current, moving swim muscles and fins just enough to keep them in one place, so they would not be swept away by the current.

When she saw a trout or small salmon, she entered the water downstream, let her hand dangle in the river, then waded slowly upstream. She moved even more slowly when she got closer to the fish, trying not to stir the mud or disturb the water, which could cause the resting swimmer to dart away. Carefully, from the rear, she slipped her hand underneath it, touching lightly, or tickling, which the fish didn't seem to notice. When she reached the gills, she grabbed hold swiftly and scooped the fish out of the water onto the bank. Jondalar usually ran to get it before it flopped back into the river.

Ayla also discovered freshwater mussels, similar to the ones that were in the sea near the cave of Brun's clan. She looked for plants like pigweed, salt bush, and coltsfoot, high in natural salt, to restore their somewhat depleted reserves, along with other roots, leaves, and seeds that were beginning to ripen. Partridges were common on the open grassland and scrub near the water, with family coveys joining to form large flocks. The plump birds were good eating and not too hard to catch.

They rested during the worst heat of the day, after noon, while the food for their main meal cooked. With only stunted trees near the river, they set up their tent as a lean-to awning to provide a little shade from the searing heat of the open landscape. Late in the afternoon, when it started to cool down, they continued on their way. Riding into the setting sun, they used their conical woven hats to screen their eyes. They began looking for a likely place to stop for the night as the glowing orb dipped below the horizon, setting up their simple camp in twilight, and occasionally, when the moon was full and the steppes ablaze with its cool glow, they rode on into the night.

Their evening meal was fairly light, often food saved from midday with perhaps the addition of a few fresh vegetables, grains, or meat, if some had been encountered along the way. Something that could be eaten quickly and cold was prepared for morning. They usually fed Wolf, too. Though he foraged for himself at night, he had developed a taste for cooked meat and even enjoyed grains and vegetables. They seldom set up the tent, though the warm sleeping rolls were welcome. The nights cooled rapidly, and morning often brought a misty haze.

Occasional summer thunderstorms and drenching rains brought an unexpected and usually welcome cooling shower, though sometimes the atmosphere was even more oppressive afterward, and Ayla hated the thunder. It reminded her too much of the sound of earthquakes. The sheet lightning that crackled across the heavens, lighting the night sky, always filled them with awe, but it was the lightning that struck close that bothered Jondalar. He hated to be out in the open when it came, and he always felt like crawling into his sleeping roll and pulling the tent over him, though he resisted the urge and never would admit it.

As time passed, besides the heat, it was the insects that they noticed most. Butterflies, bees, wasps, even flies and a few mosquitoes were not particularly bothersome. It was the smallest of them all, the clouds of gnats, that gave them the most trouble. But if the people were bothered, the animals were miserable. The persistent creatures were everywhere, into eyes, noses, and mouths, and the sweaty skin under the shaggy coats.

Steppe horses usually migrated north during the summer. Their thick fur and compact bodies were adapted to the cold, and while there were wolves on the southern plains—no predator was more widespread—Wolf came from northern stock. Over time, wolves that lived in the southern regions had made several adaptations to the extreme conditions of the south, with its hot, dry summers, and winters that were nearly as cold as the land closer to the glaciers, but could also see much heavier snow. For example, they shed their fur in far greater amounts when the weather warmed, and their panting tongues cooled them more efficiently.

Ayla did everything she could for the suffering animals, but even daily dunkings in the river and various medications did not rid them entirely of the tiny gnats. Open running sores infested with their quick-maturing eggs grew larger despite the medicine woman's treatments. Horses and Wolf alike shed handfuls of hair, leaving bare spots, and their thick rich coats became matted and dull.

Applying a soothing wash to a sticky open sore near one of Whinney's ears, Ayla said, "I'm sick of this hot weather, and these terrible gnats! Will it ever be cool again?"

"You may wish for this heat before this trip is through, Ayla."

Gradually, as they continued traveling upstream beside the great river, the rugged uplands and high peaks of the north angled closer, and the eroded chain of mountains to the south increased in elevation. In all the twists and turns of their generally westward direction, they had been heading just slightly north. They veered then toward the south, before making a sharp turn that began taking them northwest, then arced around to the north, and finally even east for a distance before curving around a point and going northwest again.

Though he couldn't exactly say why—there weren't any particular landmarks he could positively identify—Jondalar felt a familiarity with the landscape. Following the river would take them northwest, but he was sure it would curve back around again. He decided, for the first time since they had reached the great delta, to leave the security of the Great Mother River and ride north beside a tributary, into the foothills of the high, sharp-peaked mountains that were now much closer to the river. The route they followed up the feeder river gradually turned northwest.

Ahead the mountains were coming together; a ridge joining the long arc of the ice-topped northern range was closing in on the eroded southern highlands, which had become sharper, higher, and icier, until they were separated by only a narrow gorge. The ridge had once held back a deep inland sea that had been surrounded by the soaring chains. But over the vast millennia the outlet that spilled out the yearly accumulation of water began to wear down the limestone, sandstone, and shale of the mountains. The level of the inland basin was slowly lowered to match the height of the corridor that was being ground out of the rock until, eventually, the sea was drained, leaving behind the flat bottom that would become a sea of grass.

The narrow gorge hemmed in the Great Mother River with rugged, precipitous walls of crystalline granite. And volcanic rock which once had been outcrops and intrusions in the softer more erodable stone of the mountains, soared up on both sides. It was a long gateway through the mountains to the southern plains and ultimately to Beran Sea, and Jondalar knew there was no way to walk beside the river as she went through the gorge. There was no choice but to go around.

14

Except for the absence of the voluminous flow, the terrain was unchanged when they first turned aside and began following the small stream—dry, open grassland with stunted brush close by the water—but Ayla experienced a sense of loss. The broad expanse of the Great Mother River had been their constant companion for so long, that it was disconcerting not to see her comforting presence there beside them, showing them the way. As they proceeded toward the foothills and gained altitude, the brush filled out, became taller and leafier, and extended farther out into the plains.

The absence of the great river affected Jondalar, too. One day had blended into another with reassuring monotony as they traveled beside her productive waters in the natural warmth of summer. The predictability of her lavish abundance had lulled him into complacency and blunted his anxious worries about getting Ayla home safely. After turning away from the bountiful Mother of rivers, his concerns returned, and the changing countryside made him think about the landscape ahead. He began to consider their provisions and wonder if they had enough food with them. He wasn't as sure about the easy availability of fish in the smaller waterway, and even less certain of foraging in the wooded mountains.

Jondalar wasn't as familiar with the ways of woodland wildlife. Animals of the open plains tended to congregate in herds and could be seen from a distance, but the fauna that lived in the forest were more solitary, and there were trees and brush to conceal them. When he had lived with the Sharamudoi, he had always hunted with someone who understood the region.

The Shamudoi half of the people liked to hunt the high tors for chamois, and they knew the ways of bear, boar, forest bison, and other elusive woodland prey. Jondalar recalled that Thonolan had developed a preference for hunting in the mountains with them. The Ramudoi moiety, on the other hand, knew the river and hunted its creatures, especially the giant sturgeon. Jondalar had been more interested in the boats and learning the ways of the river. Though he had climbed the mountains with the chamois hunters on occasion, he didn't care much for heights.

Sighting a small herd of red deer, Jondalar decided that it would be a good opportunity to procure a supply of meat to see them through the next few days until they reached the Sharamudoi, and perhaps bring some with them to share. Ayla was eager when he suggested it. She enjoyed hunting and they hadn't done much of it recently, except for bringing down a few partridges and other small game, which she usually did with her sling. The Great Mother River had been so giving, it hadn't been necessary to hunt much.

They found a place to set up their camp near the small river, left their pack baskets and the travois, and started off in the direction of the herd with their spear-throwers and spears. Wolf was excited; they were changing their routine, and the spears and throwers signaled their intentions to him. Whinney and Racer seemed friskier, too, if only because they were no longer carrying pack baskets or dragging poles.

This group of red deer was a bachelor herd, and the antlers of the ancient elk were thick with velvet. By fall, in time for the rutting season, when the branching horns had reached their full growth for the year, the soft covering of skin and nourishing blood vessels would dry up and peel off—with help from the deer rubbing them against trees or rocks.

The woman and man stopped to appraise the situation. Wolf was full of anticipation, whining and making false starts. Ayla had to command him to stay still, so he wouldn't chase after and scatter the herd. Jondalar, glad to see him settle down, gave a passing thought of admiration at the way Ayla had trained him, then turned back to study the deer. Sitting astride the horse gave the man an overall view, and another advantage he would not have had on foot. Several of the antlered animals had stopped feeding, aware of the presence of the newcomers, but horses were not threatening. They were fellow grazers that were usually tolerated or ignored, if they were not signaling fear. Even with the presence of human and wolf, the deer were not yet concerned enough to run.

Looking over the herd to decide which one to try for, Jondalar was tempted by a magnificent stag with a commanding rack who seemed to be looking directly at him, as though assessing the man in return. Perhaps if he'd been with a band of hunters needing food for a whole Cave, and wanting to show off their prowess, he might have considered going after the majestic animal. But the man was sure that when autumn brought their season of Pleasures, many females would be eager to join the herd that chose him. Jondalar couldn't bring himself to kill such a proud and beautiful animal just for a little meat. He selected another deer.

"Ayla, see the one near the tall bush? On the edge of the herd?" The woman nodded. "He seems to be in a good position to break away from the others. Let's try for him."

They talked over their strategy, then separated. Wolf watched the woman on the horse closely and, at her signal, sprang forward toward the deer she indicated. Ayla, on the mare, was close on his heels. Jondalar was coming around from the other side, spear and thrower ready.

The deer sensed danger, and so did the rest of the herd. They were bounding away in all directions. The one they had chosen leaped away from the attacking wolf and the charging woman, straight at the man on the stallion. He came so close that Racer shied back.

Jondalar had been ready with his spear, but the stallion's quick move spoiled his aim and distracted him. The stag changed direction, trying to get away from the horse and human blocking his way, only to find a huge wolf in his path. In fear, the deer leaped to the side, away from the snarling predator, and dashed between Ayla and Jondalar.

As the deer made another bound, Ayla shifted weight as she took aim. Whinney, understanding the signal, pounded after him. Jondalar recovered his balance and hurled his spear at the fleeing stag, just as Ayla loosed hers.

The proud antlers jerked once, and then again. Both spears landed with great force, almost simultaneously. The large stag tried to leap away again, but it was too late. The spears had found their mark. The red deer faltered, then fell in midstride.

The plains were empty. The herd had disappeared, but the hunters didn't notice, as they jumped off their horses beside the stag. Jondalar took his bone-handled knife out of its sheath, grabbed the velveted antlers, pulled the head back, and slit the throat of the large ancient elk. They stood silently and watched the blood pool around the head of the stag. The dry earth absorbed it.

"When you return to the Great Earth Mother, give Her our thanks," Jondalar said to the red deer lying dead upon the ground.

Ayla nodded agreement. She was accustomed to this ritual of his. Jondalar said similar words every time they killed an animal, even a small one, but she sensed it was never done by rote, just to be saying it. There was feeling and reverence in his words. His thanks were genuine.

The low, rolling plains gave way to steep hills, and birch trees appeared among the brush, then woods of hornbeam and beech with oak intermixed. At the lower elevations, the region resembled the wooded hills they had traveled beside near the delta of the Great Mother River. Climbing higher, they began to see fir and spruce and a few larch and pine among the huge deciduous trees.

They came to a clearing, an open, rounded knoll somewhat higher than the surrounding woodland. Jondalar halted to get his bearings, but Ayla was stopped by the view. They were higher in altitude than she realized. Toward the west, looking down over the tops of trees, she could see the Great Mother River in the distance, all her channels gathered together again, winding through a deep gorge of sheer rocky walls. She understood now why Jondalar had turned aside to find a way around.

"I've been on a boat in that passage," he said. "It's called the Gate."

"The Gate? You mean like a gate you'd make for a surround? To close the opening and trap animals inside?" Ayla asked.

"I don't know. I never asked, but maybe that is where the name came from. Although it's more like the fence you'd build on both sides leading up to the gate. It goes on for quite a distance. I wish I could take you on it." He smiled. "Maybe I will."

They headed north toward the mountain, downhill off the knoll for a space, then leveled out. In front of them, like an immense wall, was a long line of huge trees, the beginning of a deep, dense, mixed forest of hardwood and evergreens. The moment they stepped within the shade of the high canopy of leaves, they found themselves in a different world. It took a few moments for their eyes to adjust from the bright sun to the dim silent umbra of the primeval forest, but they felt the cool damp air immediately and smelled the rich dank luxuriance of growth and decay.

Thick moss covered the ground in a seamless blanket of green and climbed over boulders, spread over the rounded shapes of ancient trees long fallen, and circled disintegrating standing stumps and living trees impartially. The large wolf running ahead jumped up on a mossy log. He broke through the ancient rotted core that was slowly dissolving back into the soil, exposing writhing white grubs surprised by the light of day. The man and woman soon dismounted to make it easier to find their way across a forest floor littered with the remnants of life and its regenerating offspring.

Seedlings sprouted from mossy rotting logs, and saplings vied for a place in the sun where a lightning-struck tree had taken several more down with it. Flies buzzed around the nodding, pink-flowered spikes of wintergreen in the bright rays that reached the forest floor through a break in the canopy. The silence was uncanny; the smallest sounds were amplified. They spoke in whispers for no reason.

Fungus was rampant; mushrooms of every variety could be found almost anyplace they looked. Leafless herbs like beechdrops, lavender toothwort, and various bright-flowered small orchids, often without green leaves, were everywhere, growing from the roots of other living plants or their decaying remains. When Ayla saw several small, pale, waxy, leafless stems with nodding heads she stopped to collect some.

"This will help soothe Wolf's and the horses' eyes," she explained, and Jondalar noticed a warm, sad smile playing across her face. "It's the plant Iza used for my eyes when I cried."

While she was at it, she picked some mushrooms that she was certain were edible. Ayla never took chances: she was very careful about mushrooms. Many varieties were delicious, many were not very tasty but not harmful, some were good as medicine, some would make a person mildly sick, a few could help one see spirit worlds, and a few were deadly. And some of them could be easily confused with others.

They had trouble moving the travois with its widely spaced poles through the forest. It kept getting caught between trees growing close together. When Ayla first developed the simple but efficient method of utilizing the strength of Whinney to help her transport objects too heavy for her to carry by herself, she devised a way for the horse to climb the steep narrow path to her cave by bringing the poles closer together. But with the bowl boat mounted on it, they couldn't move the long poles, and it was difficult getting around objects while dragging them. The travois was very effective over rough terrain, it did not get stuck in holes or ditches or mud, but it needed an open landscape.

They struggled for the rest of the afternoon. Jondalar finally untied the bowl boat entirely and dragged it himself. They were beginning to think seriously of leaving it behind. It had been more than helpful in crossing the many rivers and smaller tributaries that had flowed into the Great Mother, but they weren't sure if it was worth the trouble it was taking to get it through the thick growth of trees. Even if there were many more rivers ahead, they could certainly get across them without the boat, and it was slowing them down.

Darkness caught them still in the forest. They set up camp for the night, but they both felt uneasy and more exposed than in the middle of the wide steppes. Out in the open, even in the dark, they could see something: clouds, or stars, silhouettes of moving shapes. In the dense forest, with the massive trunks of tall trees that were able to hide even large creatures, the dark was absolute. The amplifying silence that had seemed uncanny when they entered the wooded world

was terrifying in the deep woods at night, though they tried
not to show it.

The horses were tense, too, and crowded close to the
known comfort of fire. Wolf stayed at camp as well. Ayla
was glad, and as she gave him a serving of their meal,
thought she would have kept him close in any case. Even
Jondalar was glad; having a large friendly wolf nearby was
reassuring. He could smell things, sense things, that a human
could not.

The night was colder in the damp woods, with a clammy,
sticky sort of humidity, so heavy it felt almost like rain. They
crawled into their sleeping furs early, and though they were
tired they talked long into the night, not quite ready to trust
sleeping.

"I'm not sure we should bother with that bowl boat anymore," Jondalar commented. "The horses can wade across
the small streams without getting much of anything wet. With
deeper rivers, we can lift the pack baskets to their backs,
instead of letting them hang down."

"I tied my things to a log once. After I left the Clan and
was looking for people like me, I came to a wide river. I
swam across it pushing the log," Ayla said.

"That must have been hard to do, and maybe more dangerous, not having your arms free."

"It was hard, but I had to get across, and I couldn't think
of any other way," Ayla said.

She was quiet for a while, thinking. The man, lying
beside her, wondered if she had fallen asleep; then she
revealed the direction her thoughts had taken.

"Jondalar, I'm sure we have already traveled much farther than I did before I found my valley. We have come a
long way, haven't we?"

"Yes, we have come a long way," he replied, a little
guarded in his answer. He shifted to his side and raised up
on one arm so he could see her. "But we are still a long way
from my home. Are you tired of traveling already, Ayla?"

"A little. I would like to rest for a while. Then I'll be
ready to travel again. As long as I'm with you, I don't care
how far we have to go. I just didn't know this world was so
big. Does it ever end?"

"To the west of my home, the land ends at the Great
Waters. No one knows what lies beyond that. I know another
man who says he has traveled even farther, and has seen

great waters in the east, though many people doubt him. Most people travel a little, but few travel very far, so they find it hard to believe the stories of long Journeys, unless they see something that convinces them. But there are always a few who travel far." He made a disparaging chuckle. "Though I never expected to be one. Wymez traveled around the Southern Sea and found there was more land even farther to the south."

"He also found Ranec's mother and brought her back. It's hard to doubt Wymez. Have you ever seen anyone else with brown skin like Ranec's? Wymez had to travel far to find a woman like that," Ayla said.

Jondalar looked at the face glowing in the firelight, feeling a great love for the woman beside him, and a great worry. This talk of long Journeys made him think about the long way they still had to go.

"In the north, the land ends in ice," she continued. "No one can go beyond the glacier."

"Unless they go by boat," Jondalar said. "But I'm told that all you will find is a land of ice and snow, where white spirit bears live, and they say there are fish bigger than mammoths. Some of the western people claim there are shamans powerful enough to Call them to the land. And once they are beached, they can't go back, but . . ."

There was a sudden crashing among the trees. The man and woman both jumped with fright, then lay perfectly still, not uttering a sound. Hardly even breathing. A low, rumbling growl came from Wolf's throat, but Ayla had her arm around him and wasn't about to let him go. There was more thrashing about, and then silence. After a while Wolf stopped his rumbling, too. Jondalar wasn't sure if he'd be able to sleep at all that night. He finally got up to put a log on the fire, grateful that he had earlier found some good-size broken limbs that he could chop with his small ivory-hafted stone axe into pieces.

"The glacier we have to cross isn't in the north, is it?" Ayla asked after he came back to bed, her mind still on their Journey.

"Well, it's north of here, but not as far as that wall of ice to the north. There is another range of mountains west of these, and the ice we must cross is on a highland north of them."

"Is it hard to cross ice?"

"It's very cold, and there can be terrible blizzards. In spring and summer it melts a little and the ice gets rotten. Big cracks split open. If you fall in a deep crack, no one can get you out. In winter, most of the cracks fill with snow and ice, though it can still be dangerous."

Ayla shivered suddenly. "You said there's a way around. Why do we have to cross the ice?"

"It's the only way we can avoid fla . . . Clan country."

"You were going to say flathead country."

"It's just the name I've always heard, Ayla," Jondalar tried to explain. "It's what everyone calls it. You're going to have to get used to that word, you know. That is what most people call them."

She ignored the comment, and went on, "Why do we have to avoid them?"

"There's been some trouble." He frowned. "I don't even know if those northern flatheads are the same as your Clan." He stopped, then went on. "But they didn't start the trouble. On our way here, we heard of a band of young men who were . . . harassing them. They are Losadunai, the people who live near that plateau glacier."

"Why do the Losadunai want to cause trouble with the Clan?" Ayla was puzzled.

"It's not the Losadunai. Not all of them. They don't want trouble. It's just this band of young men. I guess they think it's fun, or at least that's how it started."

Ayla thought that some people's idea of fun didn't sound like much fun to her, but it was their Journey that she couldn't get off her mind, and how much farther they had to go. From the way Jondalar talked, they weren't even close yet. She decided that it might be best not to think too far ahead. She tried to put it out of her mind.

She stared up into the night and wished she could see the sky through the high canopy. "Jondalar, I think I see stars up there. Can you see them?"

"Where?" he said, looking up.

"Over there. You have to look straight up and back a little. See?"

"Yes . . . Yes, I think I do. It's nothing like the Mother's path of milk, but I do see a few stars," Jondalar said.

"What's the Mother's path of milk?"

"That's another part of the story about the Mother and Her child," he explained.

"Tell me it."

"I'm not sure if I can remember. Let's see, it goes something like . . ." He began to chant the rhythm without words, then came in at the middle of a verse.

Her blood clotted and dried into red-ochred soil,
But the luminous child made it all worth the toil.

The Mother's great joy.
A bright shining boy.

Mountains rose up spouting flames from their crests,
She suckled Her son from Her mountainous breasts.
He suckled so hard, and the sparks flew so high,
The Mother's hot milk laid a path through the sky.

"That's it," he concluded. "Zelandoni would be pleased that I remembered."

"That's wonderful, Jondalar. I love the sound of it, the way the sound of it feels." She closed her eyes, repeating the verses to herself aloud a few times.

Jondalar listened, and was reminded of how quickly she could memorize. She repeated it exactly right after only one hearing. He wished his memory was as good and his knack for picking up language as quick as hers.

"It's not really true, is it?" Ayla asked.

"What isn't true?"

"That the stars are the Mother's milk."

"I don't think they are really milk," Jondalar said. "But I think there is truth in what the story means. The whole story."

"What does the story mean?"

"It tells about the beginnings of things, how we came to be. That we were made by the Great Earth Mother, out of Her own body; that She lives in the same place as the sun and the moon, and is the Great Earth Mother to them as She is to us; and that the stars are a part of their world."

Ayla nodded. "There could be some truth in that," she said. She liked what he said, and thought that maybe, someday, she would like to meet this Zelandoni and ask her to tell the whole story. "Creb told me the stars were the hearths of the people who live in the spirit world. All the people who have returned, and all the people not yet born. And the home of the spirits of the totems."

"There could be truth in that, too," Jondalar said. Flat-heads really must be almost human, he thought. No animal would think like that.

"He once showed me where my totem's home was, the Great Cave Lion," Ayla said and, stifling a yawn, she rolled over on her side.

Ayla tried to see the way ahead, but huge, moss-covered trunks of trees blocked her view. She kept climbing, not sure where she was going or why, just wishing she could stop and rest. She was so tired. If she could just sit down. The log ahead looked inviting, if she could reach it, but it always seemed another step farther. Then she was on top of it, but it gave way beneath her, collapsing into rotten wood and wriggling grubs. She was falling through it, clawing at the earth, trying to climb back up.

Then the dense forest was gone, and she was clambering up the steep side of a mountain through an open woods along a familiar path. At the top was a high mountain meadow where a small family of deer fed. Hazelnut bushes grew against the rock of a mountain wall. She was afraid, and there was safety behind the bushes, but she couldn't find the way in. The opening was blocked by the hazelnut bushes, and they were growing, growing to the size of huge trees, with mossy trunks. She tried to see the way ahead, but all she could see were the trees, and it was getting dark. She was afraid, but then, in the distance, she saw someone moving through the deep shade.

It was Creb. He was standing in front of the opening of a small cave, blocking her way, his hand signs saying she couldn't stay. This was not her place. She had to leave, to find another place, the place where she belonged. He tried to tell her the way, but it was dark and she couldn't quite see what he was saying, only that she had to keep going. Then he stretched out his good arm and pointed.

When she looked ahead, the trees were gone. She started climbing again, toward the opening of another cave. Though she knew she had never seen it before, it was a strangely familiar cave, with an oddly misplaced boulder silhouetted against the sky above it. When she looked back, Creb was leaving. She called out to him, pleading with him.

"Creb! Creb! Help me! Don't go!"

"Ayla! Wake up! You're dreaming," Jondalar said, shaking her gently.

She opened her eyes, but the fire had gone out and it was dark. She clung to the man.

"Oh, Jondalar, it was Creb. He was blocking the way. He wouldn't let me in—he wouldn't let me stay. He was trying to tell me something, but it was so dark I couldn't see. He was pointing toward a cave, and something about it looked familiar, but he wouldn't stay."

Jondalar could feel her shaking in his arms as he held her close, comforting her with his presence. Suddenly she sat up. "That cave! The one he was blocking, that was my cave. That was where I went after Durc was born, when I was afraid they wouldn't let me keep him."

"Dreams are hard to understand. Sometimes a zelandoni can tell you what they mean. Maybe you are still feeling bad about leaving your son," the man said.

"Maybe," she said. She did feel bad about leaving Durc, but if that was what her dream meant, why was she dreaming it now? Why not after she stood on the island looking across Beran Sea, trying to see the peninsula, and cried her final goodbye to him. There was something about it that made her feel there was more to her dream than that. Finally she settled down and they both dozed off for a while. When she woke again, it was daylight, though they were still in the shaded gloom of the forest.

Ayla and Jondalar started north in the morning on foot, with the travois poles lashed together, and then fastened across the middle of the round boat. With each of them carrying an end, they could lift the poles and the boat over and around obstacles much more easily than trying to drag them behind the horse. It gave the horses a rest, too, with only the pack baskets to carry and their own feet to worry about. But after a while, without the guiding hand of the man on his back, Racer had a tendency to wander off to browse a little on the green leaves of young trees, since there hadn't been much pasture. He took a detour to the side and back a ways when he smelled the grass in a small clearing where a strong wind had blown down several trees, allowing sunlight in.

Jondalar, tired of going after him, tried for a time to hold on to both Racer's lead rope and his end of the poles, but it was hard to watch where Ayla was going to lift the poles out of the way, to watch his own footing, and to be careful that he wasn't leading the young horse into a hole, or something worse. He wished that Racer would follow him without rein or harness the way Whinney followed Ayla. Finally, when Jondalar accidentally shoved his end of the poles and jabbed Ayla rather hard, she came up with a suggestion.

"Why don't you tie Racer's lead rope to Whinney?" she said. "You know she'll follow me, and she'll watch her own footing, and won't lead Racer astray, and he's used to following her. Then you won't have to be concerned about him wandering off, or getting into some other kind of trouble, and you'll only have to worry about your end of the poles."

He stopped for a moment, frowning, then suddenly broke into a big grin. "Why didn't I think of that?" he said.

Though they had been gaining in elevation slowly, when the land began to get noticeably steeper the forest changed character rather abruptly. The woodland thinned out, and they quickly left the large deciduous hardwood trees behind. Fir and spruce became the primary trees, with the remaining hardwoods, even those of the same variety, much smaller.

They reached the top of a ridge and looked out over it onto a wide plateau that dropped down gently and then extended nearly level for quite some distance. A mostly coniferous forest of dark green fir, spruce, and pine, accented by a scattering of larch, with needles turning golden, dominated the plateau. It was set off by bright greenish-gold high meadows, and splashed with blue and white tarns, reflecting the clear sky above and the clouds in the distance. A fast river partitioned the space, fed by a rampaging falls cascading down the mountainside at the far end. Rising up beyond the tableland, and filling the sky, was the breathtaking vista of a high peak capped in white, partially masked by the clouds.

It seemed so close that Ayla felt she could almost reach out and touch it. The sun behind her illuminated the colors and shapes of the mountain stone; light tan rock jutting out from pale gray walls; nearly white faces contrasting with the dark gray of strangely regular columns that had emerged from the fiery core of the earth and cooled to the angled form of their basic crystal structure. Shimmering above that was the beautiful blue-green ice of a true glacier, frosted with snow that still lingered on the highest reaches. And while they watched, as if by magic, the sun and the rain clouds created a glowing rainbow and stretched it in a great arc over the mountain.

The man and woman gazed in wonder, drinking in the beauty and the serenity. Ayla wondered if the rainbow was meant to tell them something, if only that they were welcome. She noticed that the air she was breathing was deliciously cool and fresh, and she breathed with relief to be away from the deadening heat of the plains. Then she suddenly realized that the swarming bothersome gnats were gone. As far as she was concerned, she wouldn't have needed to go a step farther than this plateau. She could have made her home right there.

She turned to face the man, smiling. Jondalar was stunned for a moment by the sheer force of her emotions, her pleasure in the beauty of the place, and her desire to stay, but he felt it as pleasure in her beauty and desire for her. He wanted her that instant, and it showed in his rich blue eyes and his look of love and yearning. Ayla felt his force, a reflection of her own, but transmuted, and amplified through him.

Mounted on their horses, they stared into each other's eyes, transfixed by something they could not explain but felt the force of: their evenly matched, though unique, emotions; the power of a charisma each possessed, aimed at the other; and the strength of their mutual love. Unthinking, they reached out to each other—which the horses misinterpreted. Whinney started walking downhill and Racer followed. The movement brought the woman and man back to an awareness of where they were. Feeling an inexplicable warmth and tenderness, and just a touch foolish because they didn't quite know what had happened, they smiled at each other with a look that held a promise, and they continued down the hill, turning northwest to follow the plateau.

The morning that Jondalar thought they might reach the Sharamudoi settlement brought a crisp breath of frost to the air, foretelling the changing of seasons, and Ayla welcomed it. As they rode through the wooded hillsides, she could almost believe she had been there before, if she hadn't known better. For some reason, she kept expecting to recognize a landmark. Everything seemed so familiar: the trees, the plants, the slopes, the lay of the land. The more she saw, the more at home she felt.

When she saw hazelnuts, still on the tree in their green prickly casings, but nearly ripe, the way she liked them, she had to stop and pick some. As she cracked a few with her teeth, suddenly it struck her. The reason she felt that she knew the area, that it felt like home, was that it resembled the mountainous region at the tip of the peninsula, around the cave of Brun's clan. She had grown up in a place very much like this.

The area was becoming more familiar to Jondalar, too, with good reason, and when he found a clearly marked trail that he recognized, descending toward a path that led to the outside edge of a cliff face, he knew they weren't far. He could feel the excitement growing inside him. When Ayla found a big thorny briar mound, high in the middle with long prickly runners, and branches weighted down with ripe, juicy blackberries, he felt an edge of irritation that she wanted to delay their arrival just to pick some.

"Jondalar! Stop. Look. Blackberries!" Ayla said, sliding off Whinney and rushing to the briar patch.

"But we're almost there."

"We can bring them some." Her mouth was full. "I haven't had blackberries like this since I left the Clan. Taste them, Jondalar! Have you ever tasted anything so sweet and good?" Her hands and mouth were purple from picking small handfuls and popping them all in her mouth at one time.

Watching her, Jondalar suddenly laughed. "You should see yourself," he said. "You look like a little girl, full of berry stains and all excited." He shook his head and chuckled. She didn't answer. Her mouth was too full.

He picked some, decided that they were very sweet and good, and picked some more. After a few more handfuls, he stopped. "I thought you said we were going to pick some to take to them. We don't even have anything to put them in."

Ayla stopped for a moment, then smiled. "Yes, we do," she said, taking off her sweat-stained, woven conical hat, and looking for some leaves to line it. "Use your hat."

They had each filled a hat nearly three-quarters full when they heard Wolf give a warning growl. They looked up and saw a tall youth, almost a man, who had come along the trail, gaping at them and the wolf who was so near, eyes open wide with fear. Jondalar looked again.

"Darvo? Darvo, is it you? It's me, Jondalar. Jondalar of the Zelandonii," he said, striding toward the lad.

Jondalar was speaking a language Ayla wasn't familiar with, though she heard some words and tones that were reminiscent of Mamutoi. She watched the expression on the young man's face change from fear, to puzzlement, to recognition.

"Jondalar? Jondalar! What are you doing here? I thought you went away and were never coming back," Darvo said.

They rushed toward each other and threw their arms around each other; then the man backed off and looked at him, holding him by the shoulders. "Let me see you! I can't believe how you've grown!" Ayla stared at the young man, drawn to the sight of another person after not seeing one for so long.

Jondalar hugged him again. Ayla could see the genuine affection they shared, but after the first rush of greeting, Darvo seemed a little embarrassed. Jondalar understood the sudden reticence. Darvo was, after all, nearly a man now. Formal hugs of greeting were one thing, but exuberant displays of unrestrained affection, even for someone who had been like the man of your hearth for a time, were something else. Darvo looked at Ayla. Then he noticed the wolf she was holding back, and his eyes opened wide again. Then he saw the horses standing quietly nearby, with baskets and poles hanging on them, and his eyes opened even wider.

"I think I'd better introduce you to my . . . friends," Jondalar said.

"Darvo of the Sharamudoi, this is Ayla of the Mamutoi," Jondalar said.

Ayla recognized the cadence of the formal introduction, and enough of the words. She signaled Wolf to stay, then walked toward the boy, with both hands outstretched, palms up.

"I am Darvalo of the Sharamudoi," the young man said, taking her hands, and he said it in the Mamutoi language. "I welcome you, Ayla of the Mamutoi."

"Tholie has taught you well! You are speaking Mamutoi as though you were born to it, Darvo. Or do I say Darvalo now?" Jondalar said.

"I am called Darvalo, now. Darvo is a child's name," the youngster said; then he suddenly flushed. "But you can call me Darvo, if you want. I mean, that's the name you know."

"I think Darvalo is a fine name," Jondalar said. "I'm glad you kept up the lessons with Tholie."

"Dolando thought it would be a good idea. He said I would need the language when we go to trade with the Mamutoi next spring."

"Would you, perhaps, like to meet Wolf, Darvalo?" Ayla said.

The young man knitted his brows in consternation. In his whole life, he never expected to meet a wolf face to face, and he never wanted to. But Jondalar isn't afraid of him, Darvalo thought, and the woman isn't either . . . she's kind of a strange woman . . . she talks a little strange, too. Not wrong, but not quite like Tholie, either.

"If you reach your hand over here, and let him smell it, it will give Wolf a chance to know you," Ayla said.

Darvalo wasn't sure if he wanted his hand to be so close to the wolf's teeth, but he didn't think there was any way he could back out now. He tentatively reached forward. Wolf sniffed his hand, then unexpectedly he licked it. His tongue was warm and wet, but it certainly didn't hurt. In fact, it was rather nice. The youngster looked at the animal and the woman. She had an arm carelessly, and comfortably, draped around the wolf's neck, and she was petting his head with the other hand. What did it feel like to pet a living wolf on the head, he wondered?

"Would you like to feel his fur?" Ayla asked.

Darvalo looked surprised; then he reached out to touch, but Wolf moved to sniff him and he pulled back.

"Here," Ayla said, taking his hand and putting it firmly on the Wolf's head. "He likes to be scratched, like this," she said, showing him.

Wolf suddenly noticed a flea, or the tentative scratchings reminded him of one. He sat back on his haunch and, with a spasm of rapid motion, scratched behind his ear with his hind leg. Darvalo smiled. He had never seen a wolf in such a funny position, scratching fast and furious.

"I told you he likes to be scratched. So do the horses," Ayla said, signaling Whinney forward.

Darvalo glanced at Jondalar. He was just standing and smiling, like there was nothing strange at all about a woman who scratched wolves and horses.

"Darvalo of the Sharamudoi, this is *whinny*." Ayla said Whinney's name as a soft nicker, the way she had first named the horse, and when she said it, she sounded exactly like a horse. "That's her real name, but sometimes we just call her Whinney. It's easier for Jondalar to say."

"Can you talk to horses?" Darvalo said, completely overwhelmed.

"Anyone can talk to a horse, but a horse doesn't listen to everyone. You have to get to know each other first. That's why Racer listens to Jondalar. He got to know Racer when he was just a baby."

Darvalo spun around to look at Jondalar and took two steps back. "You are sitting on that horse!" he said.

"Yes, I'm sitting on this horse. That's because he knows me, Darvo. I mean, Darvalo. He even lets me sit on his back when he runs, and we can go very fast."

The young man looked like he was ready to run himself, and Jondalar swung a leg over and slid down. "About these animals, you could help us, Darvo, if you're willing," he said. The boy looked petrified and ready to bolt. "We've been traveling a long time, and I'm really looking forward to a visit with Dolando and Roshario, and everyone, but most people get a little nervous when they first see the animals. They aren't used to them. Would you walk in with us, Darvalo? I think if everyone sees that you aren't afraid to stand next to the animals, they might not be so worried, either."

The youth relaxed a little. That didn't seem so difficult. After all, he was already standing next to them, and wouldn't everyone be surprised to see him walking in with Jondalar and the animals? Especially Dolando and Roshario . . .

"I almost forgot," Darvalo said. "I told Roshario I would get some blackberries for her, since she can't pick them anymore."

"We have blackberries," Ayla said, at the same time that Jondalar said, "Why can't she pick them?"

Darvalo looked from Ayla to Jondalar. "She fell down the cliff to the boat dock and broke her arm. I don't think it will ever be right. It wasn't set."

"Why not?" they both asked.

"There was no one to set it."

"Where's Shamud? Or your mother?" Jondalar asked.

"Shamud died, last winter."

"I'm sorry to hear that," the man interjected.

"And my mother is gone. A Mamutoi man came to visit Tholie not long after you left. He's kin, a cousin. I guess he liked my mother, and he asked her to be his mate. She surprised everyone and left to go live with the Mamutoi. He asked me to come, too, but Dolando and Rosharia asked me to stay with them. So I did. I am Sharamudoi, not Mamutoi," Darvalo explained. Then he looked at Ayla and blushed. "Not that there's anything wrong with being Mamutoi," he added hastily.

"No, of course not," Jondalar said, a frown of worry on his face. "I understand how you feel, Darvalo. I am still Jondalar of the Zelandonii. How long ago did Rosharia fall?"

"Summer Moon, about now," the boy said.

Ayla looked at Jondalar with a questioning glance.

"About this phase of last moon," he explained. "Do you think it's too late?"

"I won't know until I see her," Ayla said.

"Ayla is a healer, Darvalo. A very good healer. She might be able to help," Jondalar said.

"I wondered if she was shamud. With those animals and all." Darvalo paused for a moment, looking at the horses and the wolf, and nodded. "She must be a very good healer." He stood up a little taller for his thirteen years. "I'll walk in with you so no one will be afraid of the animals."

"Will you carry these blackberries for me, too? So I can stay close to Wolf and Whinney. They are sometimes afraid of people, too."

15

Darvalo led the way downhill along the path through the open wooded landscape. At the bottom of the slope they came to another path and turned right, down a more gradual incline. The new trail was a runoff for excess water during the spring melt and in rainier seasons, and though the sometime creek bed was dry at the end of a hot summer, it was rocky, which made walking difficult.

Though horses were animals of the plains, Whinney and Racer were surefooted in the mountain terrain. They had learned at a young age to negotiate the steep narrow trail up to Ayla's cave in the valley. But she still worried that the horses might injure themselves because of the unstable footing, and she was glad when they turned up another path that came from someplace downhill and continued on. The new trail was well used and wide enough in most places for two people to walk side by side, though not two horses.

After traversing the side of a steep grade and around to the right, they reached a sheer rock wall. When they came to a talus slope, Ayla felt a sense of familiarity. She had seen similar accumulations of sharp rocky debris at the base of steep walls in the mountains where she grew up. She even noticed the large white horn-shaped flowers of a stout plant with jagged leaves. The members of the Mammoth Hearth she had met called the unpleasant-smelling plant thorn-apple, because of its spiny green fruit, but it brought back memories from her childhood. It was datura. Creb and Iza had both used it, but for different purposes.

The place was familiar to Jondalar because he had collected gravel from the loose pile of scree to line paths and fireplaces. He felt a wave of anticipation, knowing they were close. Once across the rocky sliding slope, the trail had been evened out with a covering of the rock chips as it wound around the foot of the soaring wall. Ahead they could see sky between the trees and brush, and Jondalar knew they were approaching the edge of the cliff.

"Ayla, I think we should take the poles and the pack baskets off the horses here," the man said. "The path around the edge of this wall is not all that wide. We can come back and get them later."

After everything was unloaded, Ayla, following the young man, walked a short distance along the wall toward the open sky. Jondalar, trailing behind to watch, smiled when she reached the edge of the cliff and looked down—then stepped back quickly. She grabbed for the wall, feeling a touch of vertigo, then edged forward and looked out again. Her jaw dropped in amazement.

Far below, down the sheer cliff, was the same Great Mother River they had been following, but Ayla had never viewed her from this perspective. She had seen all the branches of the river contained in a single channel, but it had always been from the level of a bank that was not much higher than the water itself. The urge to look down and watch from this height was compelling.

The often spread-out and meandering river was gathered together between walls of rock that soared straight out of the water from roots that extended deep into the earth. As the deep undercurrent raced elements of itself that moved against rock, the constrained force of the Great Mother River rolled by with silent power, undulating with an oily fluency of heaving swells folding and spilling over themselves. Though many more tributaries would be added before the magnificent river would attain her full capacity, even this far from the delta, she had already reached such an enormous size that the decrease was hardly noticeable, especially looking down upon her full measure of moving water.

An occasional pinnacle of soaring stone broke the surface in midstream, parting the waters with curls of foam, and while she watched, a log, finding its way blocked, bumped its way around one of them. Hardly noticed was a construction of wood directly below, close to the cliff. When she finally looked up, Ayla scanned the mountains on the other side. Though still rounded, they were taller and steeper than they had been downstream, nearly matching the height of the sharper peaks on her side. Separated only by the width of the river, the two ranges had once been joined until the sharp edge of time and tide cut a path through.

Darvalo was waiting patiently for Ayla to take in her first sight of the dramatic entry to the home of his people. He had lived there all his life and took it for granted, but he had seen the reaction of strangers before. It gave him a sense of pride when people were so overwhelmed, and it made him look more closely, seeing it anew through their eyes. When the woman finally turned to him, he smiled, then led her around the edge of the mountain wall, along a path that had been laboriously enlarged from the narrow ledge it had once been. The path could accommodate two people abreast, if they walked close together, which made it wide enough for someone to carry wood, animals that had been hunted, and other supplies with relative ease, and for the horses.

When Jondalar approached the edge of the cliff, he felt the familiar ache in his groin from looking far down over empty space, the ache that he had never entirely gotten over in all the time he had lived there. It wasn't so bad that he couldn't control it, and he did appreciate the spectacular view, as well as the work it had taken to hack out even a short section of solid stone using only stone boulders and heavy stone axes, but it didn't change the sensation he invariably felt. Even so, this was better than the other commonly used way of entry.

Keeping Wolf close to her, and Whinney just behind, Ayla followed the youth around the wall. On the other side was a level, roughly U-shaped area of appreciable size. Once, in long ages past when the huge inland basin to the west was a sea, and beginning to empty itself through the defile being worn down through the mountain ridge, the level of the water

was much higher, and a sheltered bay had been formed. Now
it was a protected embayment, high above the river.

Green grass covered the ground in front, growing nearly
to the edge of the drop-off. About halfway back brush, huddling close to the sheer side walls, filled out, becoming small
trees that continued up the steep grade at the back. Jondalar
knew it was possible to climb the rear wall, though few people did. It was an inconvenient, roundabout exit that was
seldom used. On the near side, in the rounded corner at the
back, was a sandstone overhang, large enough to shelter several dwellings made of wood, making a comfortable, protected
living area.

Across, on the mossy green far side, was the prize posses-
sion of the site. A spring of pure water starting high up
trickled over rocks, splashed down ledges, and spilled over
a smaller sandstone overhang in a long narrow waterfall to a
pool beneath. It ran off along the opposite wall to the edge
of the cliff and down rocky outcrops to the river.

Several people had stopped what they were doing when
the procession, particularly the wolf and the horse, started
coming around the wall. By the time Jondalar was in, he saw
stunned apprehension on every face.

"Darvo! What are you bringing here?" a voice called
out.

"Hola!" Jondalar said, greeting the people in their language. Then, seeing Dolando, he handed Racer's lead rope to
Ayla and, putting an arm around Darvalo's shoulder, walked
toward the leader of the Cave.

"Dolando! It's me, Jondalar!" he said as he neared.

"Jondalar? Is it really you?" Dolando said, recognizing
the man, but still hesitant. "Where are you coming from?"

"East of here. I wintered with the Mamutoi."

"Who is that?" Dolando asked.

Jondalar knew the man must have been greatly disturbed
to have ignored the common forms of courtesy. "Her name
is Ayla, Ayla of the Mamutoi. The animals travel with us,
too. They answer to her, or to me, and none of them will
harm anyone," Jondalar said.

"Including the wolf?" Dolando asked.

"I touched the wolf's head and felt his fur," Darvalo
said. "He didn't even try to hurt me."

Dolando looked at the lad. "You touched him?"

"Yes. She says you just have to get to know them."

"He's right, Dolando. I would not come here with anyone, or anything, that would cause harm. Come and meet Ayla, and the animals. You will see."

Jondalar led the man back to the center of the field. Several other people followed. The horses had begun to graze, but they stopped at the approach of the group. Winney moved in closer to the woman and stood alongside Racer, whose lead rope Ayla still held. Her other hand was on Wolf's head. The huge northern wolf was standing beside Ayla, watching defensively, but was not overtly threatening.

"How does she make the horses unafraid of the wolf?" Dolando asked.

"They know they have nothing to fear from him. They have known him since he was a tiny cub," Jondalar explained.

"Why aren't they running away from us?" the leader asked next, as they drew near.

"They have always been around people. I was there when the stallion was born," Jondalar replied. "I was badly hurt, and Ayla saved my life."

Dolando stopped suddenly and looked hard at the man. "Is she a shamud?" he asked.

"She is a member of the Mammoth Hearth."

A short, rather plump young woman spoke up then. "If she is Mamut, where is her tattoo?"

"We left before she was fully trained, Tholie," Jondalar said, then smiled at her. The young Mamutoi woman hadn't changed a bit. She was just as direct and outspoken as ever.

Dolando closed his eyes and shook his head. "That's too bad," he said, his eyes speaking his despair. "Roshario fell and hurt herself."

"Darvo told me. He said Shamud died."

"Yes, last winter. I wish the woman was a competent healer. We sent a messenger to another Cave, but their shamud had gone on a trip. A runner has gone to a different Cave, upstream, but they are farther away, and I'm afraid it is already too late to do any good."

"The training she lacked was not as a healer. Ayla is a healer, Dolando. A very good one. She was trained by . . ." Suddenly Jondalar recalled one of Dolando's few blind spots. " . . . the woman who raised her. It's a long story, but believe me. She is competent."

They had reached Ayla and the animals, and she listened

and watched Jondalar attentively as he spoke. There were some similarities between the language he was speaking and Mamutoi, but it was more by observation that she sensed the meaning of his words and understood that he had been trying to convince the other man of something. Jondalar turned to her.

"Ayla of the Mamutoi, this is Dolando, leader of the Shamudoi, the land-living half of the Sharamudoi," Jondalar said in Mamutoi. He then changed to Dolando's language: "Dolando of the Sharamudoi, this is Ayla, Daughter of the Mammoth Hearth of the Mamutoi."

Dolando hesitated a moment, eying the horses and then the wolf. He was a handsome animal, standing watchfully and quietly beside the tall woman. The man was intrigued. He had never been so close to one before, only to a few skins. They didn't often hunt wolf, and he had only seen them from a distance or running for cover. Wolf looked up at him in a way that made Dolando think he was being evaluated in return, then turned back to observe the others. The animal didn't seem to be posing any threat, Dolando thought, and perhaps a woman who had such control over animals was a skilled shamud, regardless of her training. He offered both hands, palms open and up, to the woman.

"In the name of the Great Mother, Mudo, I welcome you, Ayla of the Mamutoi."

"In the name of Mut, the Great Earth Mother, I thank you, Dolando of the Sharamudoi," Ayla said, taking both his hands.

The woman has a strange accent, Dolando thought. She speaks Mamutoi, but it does have an odd quality. She doesn't exactly sound like Tholie. Maybe she's from a different region. Dolando knew enough Mamutoi to understand it. He had traveled to the end of the great river several times in his life to trade with them, and he had helped to bring back Tholie, the Mamutoi woman. It had been the least he could do for the Ramudoi leader, to help the son of his hearth mate the woman he was determined to have. Tholie had made sure that many people knew her language, and it had been useful on subsequent trading expeditions.

Dolando's acceptance of Ayla had opened the way for everyone to welcome Jondalar back and to meet the woman he had brought with him. Tholie stepped forward, and Jondalar smiled at her. In a complex way, through his brother's mating, they were kin, and he was fond of her.

"Tholie!" he said, smiling broadly as he took both of her hands in his. "I can't tell you how wonderful it is to see you."

"It is wonderful to see you, too. And you have certainly learned to speak Mamutoi well, Jondalar. I must admit there were times when I doubted if you would ever be fluent."

She let go of his hands to reach up and give him a welcoming hug instead. He bent over and, on impulse, because he was so happy to be there, he picked the short woman up to give her a proper embrace. Slightly disconcerted, she blushed, and it occurred to her that the tall, handsome, sometimes moody man had changed. She didn't recall that he was so spontaneously demonstrative with his affections in the past. When he put her down, she studied the man, and the woman he had brought, sure she had something to do with it.

"Ayla of the Lion Camp of the Mamutoi, meet Tholie of the Sharamudoi, formerly of the Mamutoi."

"In the name of Mut or Mudo, whatever you call Her, I welcome you, Ayla of the Mamutoi."

"In the name of the Mother of All, I thank you, Tholie of the Sharamudoi, and I am very happy to meet you. I have heard so much about you. Don't you have kin in the Lion Camp? I think Talut said you were related when Jondalar mentioned you," Ayla said. She sensed that the perceptive woman was studying her. If Tholie didn't know already, she would soon discover that Ayla had not been born to the Mamutoi.

"Yes, we are related. Not close, though. I came from a southern Camp. The Lion Camp is farther north," Tholie said. "I know them, though. Everyone knows Talut. He's hard not to know, and his sister, Tulie, is very much respected," Tholie said.

That is not a Mamutoi accent, she thought, and Ayla is not a Mamutoi name. I'm not even sure if it's an accent, just a strange way of saying some words. She speaks well, though. Talut always was one for taking people in. He even took in that complaining old woman, and her daughter who mated way beneath her status. I would like to know more about this Ayla, and those animals, she thought, then looked at Jondalar.

"Is Thonolan with the Mamutoi?" Tholie asked.

The pain in his eyes told her the answer before he said the words. "Thonolan is dead."

"I'm sorry to hear that. Markeno will be, too. I can't say I didn't expect it, though. His desire to live died with Jetamio. Some people can recover from tragedy, some cannot," Tholie said.

Ayla liked the way the woman expressed herself. Not without feeling, but open and direct. She was still very much a Mamutoi.

The rest of the Cave who were present greeted Ayla. She sensed reserved acceptance, but curiosity. Their greeting to Jondalar was much less restrained. He was family; there was no doubt that they considered him one of them, and he was warmly welcomed home.

Darvalo was still holding the hat-basket of blackberries, waiting until all the greetings were finished. He held them up to Dolando. "Here are some berries for Rosharo," he said.

Dolando noticed the unfamiliar basket; it was not made the way they made baskets.

"Ayla gave them to me," Darvalo continued. "They were picking blackberries when I met them. These were already picked."

Watching the young man, Jondalar suddenly thought of Darvalo's mother. He had not expected Serenio to be gone, and he was disappointed. He had truly loved her, in a way, and he realized that he had been looking forward to seeing her. Was she expecting a child when she left? A child of his spirit? Maybe he could ask Rosharo. She would know.

"Let's bring them to her," Dolando said, nodding a silent thanks to Ayla. "I'm sure she'll like them. If you want to come in, Jondalar, I think she's awake, and I know she will want to see you. Bring Ayla, too. She will want to meet her. It's hard on her. You know how she is. Always up and busy, always the first one to greet visitors."

Jondalar translated for Ayla, and she nodded her willingness. They left the horses grazing in the field, but she signaled Wolf to stay with her. She could tell that the carnivore still bothered people. Tame horses were strange but not considered dangerous. A wolf was a hunter, capable of inflicting harm.

"Jondalar, I think it's best if Wolf stays with me for now.

Will you ask Dolando if it is all right to bring him in? Tell him he's accustomed to being indoors," Ayla said, speaking Mamutoi.

Jondalar repeated her request, although Dolando had understood her, and, seeing his subtle reactions, Ayla suspected that he did. She would keep that in mind.

They walked to the back and under the sandstone shelf, past a central hearth that was obviously a gathering place, to a wooden structure that resembled a sloping tent. Ayla noticed its construction as they approached. A ridgepole was anchored in the ground at the back and supported by a pole in front. Tapered oak planks that had been split radially out of a large tree trunk were leaned against it, graduated in size from short at the back to long in front. When she got closer, she saw that the planks were fastened together with slender willow withes sewn through predrilled holes.

Dolando pushed back a yellow drape of soft leather and held it up while everyone entered. He tied it back to allow more light in. Inside, thin cracks of daylight could be seen between some of the planks, but leather skins lined the walls in places to ward off drafts, although there was not much wind within the baylike niche carved out of the mountain. There was a small fireplace near the front, with a shorter plank making a hole in the roof above it, but no rain cover. The overhang protected the dwelling from rain and snow. Along one wall toward the back was a bed, a wide wooden shelf, fastened to the wall on one side and supported by legs on the other, covered by stuffed leather padding and furs. In the dim light, Ayla could just make out a woman reclining on it.

Darvalo knelt beside the bed, holding out the berries. "Here are the blackberries I promised you, Rosario. But I didn't pick them. Ayla did."

The woman opened her eyes. She had not been sleeping, only trying to rest, but she did not know visitors had arrived. She didn't quite catch the name Darvalo had said.

"Who picked them?" she said in a weak voice.

Dolando, bent over the bed, put his hand on her forehead. "Rosario, look who's here! Jondalar has come back," he said.

"Jondalar?" she said, looking at the man who was kneeling beside her bed next to Darvalo. He almost winced at the pain he saw etched on her face. "Is it really you? Sometimes

I dream and think that I see my son, or Jetamio, and then I find out it's not true. Is it you, Jondalar, or are you a dream?"

"It's not a dream, Rosh," Dolando said. Jondalar thought he saw tears in his eyes. "He's really here. He brought someone with him. A Mamutoi woman. Her name is Ayla." He beckoned her forward.

Ayla motioned Wolf to stay, and she walked toward the woman. That she was suffering great pain was immediately apparent. Her eyes were glazed and had dark circles around them, making them seem sunken; her face was flushed with fever. Even from a distance and beneath the light covering, Ayla could see that her arm, between the shoulder and elbow, was bent in a grotesque angle.

"Ayla of the Mamutoi, this is Roshario of the Sharamudoi," Jondalar said. Darvalo moved over and Ayla took his place beside the bed.

"In the name of the Mother, you are welcome, Ayla of the Mamutoi," Roshario said, trying to rise, then giving up and lying back again. "I am sorry I cannot greet you properly."

"In the Mother's name, I thank you," Ayla said. "There is no need for you to get up."

Jondalar translated, but Tholie had included everyone to some degree in her language instructions, and she had laid a good groundwork for understanding Mamutoi. Roshario had understood the gist of Ayla's words, and she nodded.

"Jondalar, she's in terrible pain. I'm afraid it could be very bad. I want to examine her arm," Ayla said, shifting to Zelandonii so the woman wouldn't know how serious she thought the injury was, but it did not disguise the urgency in her voice.

"Roshario, Ayla is a healer, a daughter of the Mammoth Hearth. She would like to look at your arm," Jondalar said, then looked up at Dolando to make sure he did not disapprove. The man was willing to try anything that might help, so long as Roshario agreed.

"A healer?" the woman said. "Shamud?"

"Yes, like a shamud. Can she look?"

"I'm afraid it's too late to help, but she can look."

Ayla uncovered the arm. Some attempt had obviously been made to straighten it, and the wound had been cleaned and was healing, but it was swollen and bone protruded beneath the skin at an odd angle. Ayla felt the arm, trying to be as gentle as she could. The woman winced only when she lifted the arm to feel underneath but did not complain. She knew her examination was painful, but she needed to feel the bone under the skin. Ayla looked at Roshario's eyes, smelled her exhalations, felt the pulse in her neck and in her wrist, then sat back on her heels.

"It's healing, but it's not properly set. She may eventually recover, but I don't think she will have the use of that arm, or her hand, the way it is, and it will always cause her some pain," Ayla said, speaking the language they all understood to some extent. She waited for Jondalar to translate.

"Can you do anything?" Jondalar asked.

"I think so. It may be too late, but I would like to try to rebreak the arm where it is healing wrong, and set it right. The problem is that where a broken bone has mended, it is often stronger than the bone itself. It could break wrong. Then she'd have two breaks, and more pain for nothing."

There was silence after Jondalar's translation. Finally Roshario spoke.

"If it breaks wrong, it won't be any worse than it is now, will it?" It was more a statement than a question. "I mean, I won't have the use of it the way it is now, so another break won't make it any worse." Jondalar translated her words, but Ayla was already picking up the sounds and rhythms of the Sharamudoi language and relating it to Mamutoi. The woman's tone and expression conveyed even more. Ayla understood the essence of Roshario's statement.

"But you could go through a lot more pain and get nothing for it," Ayla said, guessing what Roshario's decision would be but wanting her to fully understand all the implications.

"I have nothing now," the woman said, not waiting for a translation. "If you are able to set it right, will I be able to use my arm then?"

Ayla waited for Jondalar to restate her words in the language she knew, to be sure the meaning was clear. "You may not have full use, but I think you will at least have some. No one can be certain, though."

Roshario did not hesitate. "If there is a chance that I might be able to use my arm again, I want you to do it. I don't care about pain. Pain is nothing. A Sharamudoi needs two good arms to climb down the trail to the river. What good is a Shamudoi woman if she can't even get down to the Ramudoi dock?''

Ayla listened to the translation of her words. Then, looking directly at the woman, she said, "Jondalar, tell her I will try to help her, but tell her also that it is not whether someone has two good arms that is most important. I knew a man with only one arm, and one eye, but he led a useful life, and he was loved and greatly respected by all his people. I don't think Roshario would do less. This much I know. She is not a woman who gives in easily. Whatever the outcome, this woman will continue to lead a useful life. She will find a way, and she will always be loved and respected.''

Roshario stared back at Ayla as she listened to Jondalar say her words. Then she tightened her lips slightly and nodded. She took a deep breath and closed her eyes.

Ayla stood up, already thinking about what she needed to do. "Jondalar, will you get my pack basket, the right-hand one. And tell Dolando I need some slender pieces of wood for splints. And firewood, and a good-size cooking bowl, but something he won't mind giving up. It won't be a good idea to use it for cooking again. It will be used to make a strong pain medicine.''

Her thoughts continued racing ahead. I'll need something that will make her sleep when the arm is rebroken, she was thinking. Iza would use datura. It's strong, but it would be best for the pain, and it would make her sleep. I have some dried, but fresh would be best . . . wait . . . didn't I see some recently? She closed her eyes trying to remember. Yes! I did!

"Jondalar, while you get my basket, I'm going to get some of that thorn-apple I saw on the way here," she said, reaching the entry in a few strides. "Wolf, come with me." She was halfway across the field before Jondalar caught up with her.

Dolando stood at the entrance to the dwelling watching Jondalar and the woman, and the wolf. Though he hadn't said anything, he had been very much aware of the animal. He noticed that Wolf stayed right beside the woman, matching her stride when she walked. He had observed the subtle hand signals Ayla made when she approached Roshario's bed, and he saw the wolf drop to his stomach, though his head was up and his ears alert, watching the woman's every

movement. When she left, he was up at her command, eager
to follow her again.

He watched until Ayla, and the wolf that she controlled
with such absolute assurance, turned the corner around the
end of the wall. Then he looked back at the woman on the
bed. For the first time since that horrible moment when Roshario slipped and fell, Dolando dared to feel a glimmer of
hope.

When Ayla returned, carrying a pack basket and the
datura plants she had washed in the pool, she found a square
wooden cooking box, which she decided to examine more
closely later, another one filled with water, a hot fire burning
in the fireplace with several smooth, rounded stones heating
in it, and some small sections of plank. She nodded her
approval to Dolando. She looked through the contents of the
pack basket until she found several bowls and her old otter-
skin medicine bag.

Using a small bowl, she measured a quantity of water
into the cooking box, added several whole datura plants,
including the roots, then splashed a few drops of water on
the cooking stones. Leaving them in the fire to heat further,
she emptied the contents of her medicine bag and selected a
few packets. As she was putting the rest back, Jondalar came
in.

"The horses are fine, Ayla, enjoying the grass in the
field, but I've asked everyone to stay away from them for
now." He turned to Dolando. "They can get skittish around
strangers, and I don't want anyone accidentally harmed. Later
we can get them used to everyone." The leader nodded. He
didn't think there was much he could say, one way or
another, right now. "Wolf doesn't look very happy outside,
Ayla, and some people seem a little alarmed by him. I really
think you should bring him in here."

"I would rather have him inside with me, but I thought
Dolando and Roshario might want him to wait out there."

"Let me talk to Roshario first. Then I think she can bring
the animal in," Dolando said, not waiting for a translation
and speaking a mixture of Sharamudoi and Mamutoi that Ayla
had no trouble grasping. Jondalar gave him a surprised look,
but Ayla just continued the conversation.

"I need to measure these on her for splints, too," she

said, holding out the small pieces of plank, "and then I want
you to scrape these planks until there are no splinters,
Dolando." She picked up a loose piece of rather crumbly
stone that was near the fireplace. "And rub them with this
sandstone until they are very smooth. Do you have some soft
skins I can cut up?"

Dolando smiled, though it was a bit grim. "That's what
we are known for, Ayla. We use the skin of the chamois,
and no one makes softer leather than the Shamudoi."

Jondalar watched them talking to each other with perfect
understanding, even though the language they used was not
exactly perfect and shook his head in wonder. Ayla must
have known Dolando could understand Mamutoi, and she was
already using some Sharamudoi—when had she learned the
words for "plank" and "sandstone"?

"I'll get some after I talk to Roshario," Dolando said.

They approached the woman on the bed. Dolando and
Jondalar explained that Ayla traveled with a wolf as a companion—they didn't bother to mention the horses just yet—
and that she wanted to bring him inside the dwelling.

"She has complete control over the animal," Dolando
said. "He answers to her commands and will not harm
anyone."

Jondalar shot him another look of surprise. Somehow,
more had been communicated between Dolando and Ayla
than he could account for.

Roshario quickly agreed. Although she was curious, it
didn't seem at all surprising that this woman should be able
to control a wolf. It only relieved her fears more. Jondalar
had obviously brought a powerful Shamud who knew she
needed help, just as their old Shamud had once known, many
years before, that Jondalar's brother, who had been gored by
a rhinoceros, needed help. She didn't understand how Those
Who Served the Mother knew these things; they just did, and
that was enough for her.

Ayla went to the entry and called Wolf in, then brought
him to meet Roshario. "His name is Wolf," she said.

In some way, when she looked into the eyes of the handsome wild creature, he seemed to sense her anguish and her
vulnerability. He lifted one paw to the edge of her bed. Then,
putting his ears down, he maneuvered his head forward, without being threatening in any way, and licked her face, whin-

ing almost as though he felt her pain. Ayla was suddenly
reminded of Rydag, and the close bond that had developed
between the sickly child and the growing wolf cub. Had that
experience taught him to comprehend human need and
suffering?

They were all surprised at the gentle action of the wolf,
but Roshario was overwhelmed. She felt that something
miraculous had happened, that could only bode well. She
reached over with her good arm to touch him. "Thank you,
Wolf," she said.

Ayla laid the pieces of plank bedside Roshario's arm,
then gave them to Dolando, indicating the size she wanted
them to be. When Dolando went out, she led Wolf to a corner
of the wooden dwelling, then checked the cooking stones
again and decided they were ready. She started to take a
stone out of the fire using two pieces of wood, but Jondalar
appeared with a bent wood tool especially designed with
enough spring to hold the hot cooking stones securely, and
he showed her how to use it. As she put several stones into
the cooking box to start the datura boiling, she looked at the
unusual container a little more closely.

She had never seen anything like it. The square box had
been made from a single plank, bent around kerfed grooves
that had been cut not quite all the way through for three of
the corners; it was fastened together with pegs at the fourth.
As it was bent, the square bottom was eased into a groove
cut the length of the plank. Designs had been carved around
the outside, and the lid with a handle fit over the top.

These people had so many unusual things made out of
wood. Ayla thought it would be interesting to see how they
were made. Dolando returned then with some yellow-colored
skins and gave them to her. "Will this be enough?" he asked.

"But these are too fine," she said. "We need soft, absorbent skins, but they don't have to be your best."

Jondalar and Dolando both smiled. "These are not our
best," Dolando said. "We would never offer these in trade.
There are too many imperfections in them. They are for
everyday use."

Ayla knew something about working skins and making
leather, and these were supple and smooth with an exquisitely
soft feel and texture. She was very impressed and wanted to
know more about them, but now was not the time. Using the

knife that Jondalar had made for her, with a thin sharp flint blade mounted in an ivory handle made of mammoth tusk, she cut the chamois skin into wide strips.

Then she opened one of her packets and poured into a small bowl a coarse powder of pounded dried spikenard roots, whose leaves rather resembled foxglove, but with yellow dandelionlike flowers instead. She added a bit of hot water from the cooking box. Since she was making a poultice to help the bone fracture mend, a little addition of datura would not hurt, and its numbing quality might help. But she also added pulverized yarrow, for its external painkilling and quick-healing properties. She fished out the stones and added more hot ones to the cooking box, to keep the decoction simmering, smelling it to check for potency.

When she decided it had reached the proper strength, she scooped out a bowlful to let it cool, then carried it to Roshario. Dolando was sitting beside her. Then she asked Jondalar to translate exactly what she said, so there would be no misunderstanding.

"This medicine will both dull the pain and make you sleep," Ayla said, "but it is very powerful, and it is dangerous. Some people cannot tolerate this strong a dosage. It will relax your muscles, so I can feel the bones inside, but you may pass your water, or mess yourself, because those muscles will also relax. A few people stop breathing. If that happens, you will die, Roshario."

Ayla waited for Jondalar to repeat her statement, then longer to make sure it was fully understood. Dolando was obviously upset.

"Do you have to use it? Can't you break her arm without it?" he asked.

"No. It would be too painful, and her muscles are too tight. They will resist and make it much harder to break in the right place. I have nothing else that will dull the pain as well. I cannot rebreak and set the bones without this, but you must know the danger. She will probably live if I do nothing, Dolando."

"But I will be useless, and live in pain," Roshario said. "That is not living."

"You will have pain, but that doesn't mean you will be useless. There are remedies to ease the pain, though they may take something from you. You may not be able to think as clearly," Ayla explained.

"So I will either be useless or mindless," Rosharío said. "If I die, will it be painless?"

"You will go to sleep and not wake up, but no one knows what may happen in your dreams. You may feel great fear or pain in your dreams. Your pain may even follow you to the next world."

"Do you believe pain can follow someone to the next world?" Rosharío asked.

Ayla shook her head. "No, I don't think that, but I don't know."

"Do you think I will die if I drink that?"

"I would not offer it to you if I thought you would die. But you may have unusual dreams. It is used by some, prepared another way, to travel to other worlds, spirit worlds."

Though Jondalar had been translating the exchange of communication, there was enough understanding between them that his words only clarified. Ayla and Rosharío felt they were talking directly to each other.

"Maybe you should not take the chance, Rosharío," Dolando said. "I don't want to lose you, too."

She looked at the man with loving tenderness. "The Mother will call one or the other of us to Her first. Either you will lose me, or I will lose you. Nothing we do can stop that. But if She is willing to let me spend more time with you, my Dolando, I don't want to spend it in pain, and useless. I would rather go quietly now. And you heard Ayla, it's not likely that I will die. Even if it doesn't work, and I'm no better off, at least I will know that I tried, and that will give me heart to go on."

Dolando, sitting on the bed beside her, holding her good hand, looked at the woman he had shared so much of his life with. He saw the determination in her eyes. Finally he nodded. Then he looked up at Ayla.

"You have been honest. Now I must be honest. I will not hold it against you if you fail to help her, but if she dies, you must leave here quickly. I cannot be certain that I will be able to keep from blaming you, and I don't know what I may do. Consider that before you begin."

Jondalar, translating, knew the losses Dolando had suffered: Rosharío's son, the son of his hearth, and the child of his heart, killed just as he had reached the full flush of his manhood; and Jetamio, the girl who had been like a daughter to Rosharío and had captured Dolando's heart as well. She had grown to fill the void left by the death of the first child after her own mother died. Her struggles to walk again, to overcome the same paralysis that had taken so many, gave her a character that endeared her to everyone, including Thonolan. It seemed so unfair that she should have been taken in the agonies of childbirth. He would understand if Dolando blamed Ayla if Roshario died, but he would kill him before he would let the man harm her. He wondered if Ayla was taking on too much.

"Ayla, perhaps you should reconsider," he said, speaking Zelandonii.

"Roshario is in pain, Jondalar. I have to try to help her, if she wants me to. If she is willing to accept the risks, I can do no less. There is always risk, but I am a medicine woman; it is what I am. I cannot change any more than Iza could."

She looked down at the woman lying on the bed. "I am ready, if you are, Roshario."

16

Ayla bent over the woman on the bed, holding the bowl of cooling liquid. She dipped her little finger into it to check the temperature, then put it down and, gracefully lowering herself to the ground in a cross-legged position, sat quietly for a moment.

Her thoughts were drawn back to her life with the Clan, and particularly to the training she had received from the skilled and knowledgeable medicine woman who had raised her. Iza had taken care of most ordinary illnesses and minor injuries with practical dispatch, but when she had to treat a serious problem—an especially bad hunting accident or a life-threatening illness—she asked Creb, in his capacity as Mogur, to call upon higher powers for their assistance. Iza was a medicine woman, but in the Clan, Creb was the magician, the holy man, who had access to the world of the spirits.

Among the Mamutoi and, from the way Jondalar talked, apparently among his people as well, the functions of medicine woman and Mogur were not necessarily separated. Those who healed often interceded with the spirit world, though not all of Those Who Served the Mother were equally well versed in every capacity that was open to them. The Mamut of the Lion Camp was much more like Creb. His interest was in things of the spirit and the mind. Though he did have knowledge of certain remedies and procedures, his healing abilities were relatively undeveloped, and it often fell to Talut's mate, Nezzie, to deal with the minor injuries and illnesses of the Camp. At the Summer Meeting, however, Ayla had met many skilled healers among the mamutii and had exchanged knowledge with them.

But Ayla's training had been of the practical kind. Like Iza, she was a medicine woman, a healer. She felt herself to be unknowledgeable in the ways of the spirit world, and she wished at that moment she had someone like Creb to call on. She wanted, and felt she needed, the assistance of any powers greater than herself that would be willing to help. Though Mamut had begun to train her in the understanding of the spiritual realm of the Great Mother, she was still most familiar with the spirit world she grew up with, particularly her own totem, the spirit of the Great Cave Lion.

Though it was a Clan spirit, she knew it was powerful, and Mamut had said that the spirits of all animals, indeed all spirits, were part of the Great Earth Mother. He had even included her protective Cave Lion totem in the ceremony when she was adopted, and she knew how to ask for help from her totem. Even though she wasn't Clan, Ayla thought, perhaps the spirit of her Cave Lion would help Roshario.

Ayla closed her eyes and began to make the beautiful flowing motions of the most ancient, sacred, silent language of the Clan, the one known by all the clans, used to address the world of the spirits.

"Great Cave Lion, this woman, who was chosen by the powerful totem spirit, is grateful to have been chosen. This woman is grateful for the Gifts that have been given, and most grateful for the Gifts inside, for the lessons learned and the knowledge gained.

"Great Powerful Protector, who is known to choose males who are worthy and need great protection, but who chose this woman and marked her with the totem sign when she was only a girl, this woman is grateful. This woman knows not why the spirit of the Great Cave Lion of the Clan chose a girlchild, and one of the Others, but this woman is grateful that she was found worthy, and this woman is grateful for the protection of the great totem.

"Great Totem Spirit, this woman who has asked before for guidance, would now ask for assistance. The Great Cave Lion guided this woman to learn the ways of a medicine woman. This woman knows healing. This woman knows remedies for illness and injury, knows teas and washes and poultices and other medicines from plants, this woman knows treatments and practices. This woman is grateful for the knowledge, and grateful for the unknown knowledge of medicine that the Totem Spirit may guide to this woman. But this woman knows not the ways of the spirit world.

"Great Spirit of the Cave Lion, who dwells with the stars in the world of the spirits, the woman lying here is not Clan; the woman is one of the Others, as is this woman you chose, but help is asked for the woman. The woman suffers great pain, but the pain that is inside is worse. The woman would suffer the pain, but the woman fears that without both arms, the woman would be useless. The woman would be a good woman, would be a useful woman. This medicine woman would help the woman, but the help could be dangerous. This woman would ask the assistance of the spirit of the Great Cave Lion, and any spirits the Great Totem would choose, to guide this woman, and to help the woman lying here."

Rosario, Dolando, and Jondalar were as silent as Ayla, as she performed her unusual actions. Of the three, Jondalar was the only one who knew what she was doing, and he found himself watching the other two as much as Ayla. Though his knowledge of the Clan language was rudimentary—it was far more complex than he imagined—he did understand that she was asking for help from the spirit world.

Jondalar simply did not see some of the finer nuances of a method of communicating that had been developed upon an entirely different basis than any verbal language. It was impossible to fully translate anyway. At best, any translation to words seemed simplistic, but he did think her graceful motions were beautiful. He recalled that there was a time when he might have been embarrassed over her actions, and he smiled to himself now at his foolishness, but he was curious about how Rosario and Dolando would interpret Ayla's behavior.

Dolando was perplexed and a little disturbed, since her

actions were completely unfamiliar. His concern was for Roshario, and anything strange, even if it might be for a good purpose, felt slightly threatening. When Ayla was through, Dolando looked at Jondalar with a questioning expression, but the younger man only smiled.

The injury had debilitated Roshario, leaving her weak and feverish, not enough to make her delirious, but drained and disoriented, and more open to suggestion. She had found herself focusing on the unknown woman and was strangely moved. She didn't have the least idea what Ayla's movements meant, but she did appreciate their flowing gracefulness. It was as though the woman were dancing with her hands, indeed with more than her hands. She evoked a subtle beauty with her motions. Her arms and shoulders, even her body, seemed integral parts of her dancing hands, responding to some internal rhythm that had a definite purpose. Though she didn't understand it any more than she understood how Ayla had known she needed her help, Roshario was certain it was important, and that it had something to do with her calling. She was Shamud; that was sufficient. She had knowledge beyond the ken of ordinary people, and anything that seemed mysterious only added to her credibility.

Ayla picked up the cup and got up on her knees beside the bed. She tested the liquid again with her smallest finger, then smiled at Roshario.

"May the Great Mother of All watch over you, Roshario," Ayla said, then lifting the woman's head and shoulders up enough for her to drink comfortably, she held the small bowl to the woman's mouth. It was a bitter, rather foetid brew, and Roshario made a face, but Ayla encouraged her to drink more until she finally consumed the entire bowlful. Ayla lowered her back down gently and smiled again to reassure the injured woman, but she was already watching for telltale signs of its effect.

"Let me know when you feel sleepy," Ayla said, although it would just confirm other indications she was noting, such as changes in the size of her pupils, the depth of her breathing.

The medicine woman could not have said that she had administered a drug that inhibited the parasympathetic nervous system and paralyzed the nerve endings, but she could detect the effects, and she had enough experience to know if they were appropriate. When Ayla noticed Roshario's eyelids drooping sleepily, she felt her chest and her stomach, to monitor the relaxation of the smooth muscles of her alimentary tract, though she would not have described it that way, and watched her breathing closely to note the response of her lungs and bronchial tree. When she was sure the woman was sleeping comfortably, and in no apparent danger, Ayla stood up.

"Dolando, it is best that you leave now. Jondalar will stay and help me," she said in a firm though quiet voice, but her assured and competent manner gave her authority.

The leader started to object, but he recalled that Shamud never allowed close loved ones around, either, simply refusing to help in any way until the person left. Perhaps that was how all of them were, Dolando thought, as he took a long look at the sleeping woman, then left the dwelling.

Jondalar had watched Ayla take command in similar situations before. She seemed to forget herself entirely in her concentration on an ailing or suffering person, and without thought directed others to do whatever was necessary. It did not occur to her to question her prerogative to aid someone who needed her help, and as a result no one questioned her.

"Even if she's sleeping, it is not easy to watch someone break the bone of a person you love," Ayla said to the tall man who loved her.

Jondalar nodded, and he wondered if that was why Shamud had not let him stay when Thonolan was gored. It had been a frightening wound, a gaping, ragged puncture that almost made Jondalar sick when he first saw it, and though he thought he wanted to stay, it probably would have been difficult to watch Shamud doing whatever he had to do. He wasn't entirely sure he even wanted to stay and help Ayla, but there was no one else. He took a deep breath. If she could do it, he could at least try to help.

"What do you want me to do?" he said.

Ayla was examining Roshario's arm, seeing how far it would straighten, and how she reacted to such manipulation. She mumbled and moved her head from side to side, but it seemed to be in response to some dream or inner prompting, not directly because of pain. Ayla prodded deeply then, digging into the flaccid muscle, trying to locate the position of the bone. When she was finally satisfied, she asked Jondalar to come, catching a glimpse of Wolf watching intensely from his place in the corner.

"First, I will want you to support her arm at the elbow, while I try to break it where it is joining wrong," she said. "After it is broken, I will have to pull on it hard to straighten and fit it back together properly. With her muscles so lax, the bones of a joint could be pulled apart, and I might dislocate an elbow or a shoulder, so you will have to hold her firmly, and perhaps pull the other way."

"I understand," he said; at least he thought he did.

"Make sure you are in a comfortable, steady position, straighten her arm and support her elbow up about this far, and let me know when you are ready," Ayla directed.

He held her arm and braced himself. "All right, I'm ready," he said.

With both hands, one on either side of the break that bent it at an unnatural angle, Ayla took hold of Rosario's upper arm, gripping it experimentally in several places, feeling for the protruding ends of the ill-knit bone under the skin and muscle. If it had healed too well, she would never be able to break the jointure with her bare hands, and would have to attempt some other far less controllable means, or perhaps not be able to rebreak it properly at all. Standing over the bed to get the best leverage, she took a deep breath, then exerted a quick, hard pressure against the bend with her two strong hands.

Ayla felt the snap. Jondalar heard a sickening crack. Rosario jumped spasmodically in her sleep, and then quieted again. Ayla prodded through the muscle for the newly broken bone. The bone scar tissue had not cemented the fracture too firmly yet, perhaps because in its unnatural position the bone had not been joined in a way that encouraged healing. It was a good clean break. She breathed a sigh of relief. That part was done. She wiped the sweat off her brow with the back of her hand.

Jondalar was watching her with amazement. Though only partly healed, it took very strong hands to break a bone like that. He had always loved her sheer physical strength ever since he was first aware of it in her valley. He realized that she needed strength living alone as she did, and thought that having to do everything for herself had probably encouraged more muscle development, but he hadn't known how strong she really was.

Ayla's strength came not only from being forced to exert herself just to survive when she lived in the valley; it had been developing from the time she was first adopted by Iza. The ordinary tasks that were expected of her had become a conditioning process. Simply to keep up at the minimum level of competence for a woman of the Clan, she had become an exceptionally strong woman of the Others.

"That was good, Jondalar. Now I want you to brace yourself again, and hold her arm here at the shoulder," Ayla said, showing him. "You must not let go, but if you feel yourself slipping, tell me right away." Ayla realized that the bone had resisted healing in the wrong shape, making it somewhat easier to break than if it had been set straight for that length of time, but the muscle and tendon had healed much more. "When I straighten this arm, some of the muscle will tear, just as it did when it was first broken, and the sinews will be stretched. Muscle and sinew will be hard to force, and will cause her pain later, but it must be done. Tell me when you are ready."

"How do you know about this, Ayla?"

"Iza taught me."

"I know she taught you, but how do you know this? About rebreaking a bone that has started to heal?"

"Once Brun took his hunters on a hunt to a distant place. They were gone a long time, I don't remember how long. One of the hunters broke his arm shortly after they started out, but he refused to return. He tied it to his side and hunted with one arm. When he returned, Iza had to make it right," Ayla explained, quickly.

"But how could he do it? Go on like that with a broken arm?" Jondalar asked, looking incredulous. "Wouldn't he have been in great pain?"

"Of course he was in great pain, but not much was made of it. Men of the Clan would rather die than admit to pain. That's how they are; it's how they are trained," Ayla said. "Are you ready now?"

He wanted to ask more, but this was not the time. "Yes, I'm ready."

Ayla took a firm hold of Roshario's arm just above the elbow, while Jondalar held her below the shoulder. With slow but steady force, Ayla started pulling back, not only straightening, but working it around to avoid bone rubbing against bone and perhaps crushing it, and to keep the ligaments from tearing. At one point it had to be stretched slightly beyond its original shape to get it into a normal position.

Jondalar didn't know how she kept up the forceful, controlled tension when he could barely hold on. Ayla strained with the exertion, perspiration running down her face, but she could not stop now. For the bone to be right, it needed to be straightened in a steady, smooth movement. But once she got beyond the slight overstretch, past the broken end of the bone, the arm settled into the proper position, almost of its own accord. She felt it fall into place, carefully eased the arm to the bed, and finally let go.

When Jondalar looked up, she was shaking, her eyes were closed and she was breathing hard. Maintaining control under tension had been the most difficult part, and she was struggling now to control her own muscles.

"I think you did it, Ayla," he said.

She took a few more deep breaths, then looked at him and smiled, a broad, happy smile of victory. "Yes, I think I did," she said. "Now I need to put on the splints." She carefully felt along the straight, normal-looking arm again. "If it heals right, if I haven't done any damage to her arm while it was without feeling, I think she will be able to use it, but she is going to be very bruised and it will swell up."

Ayla dipped the strips of chamois skin in the hot water, placed the spikenard and yarrow on it, wrapped it loosely around the arm, then told Jondalar to ask Dolando if he had the splints ready.

When Jondalar stepped out of the dwelling, a crowd of faces greeted him. Not only Dolando, but all the rest of the Cave, both Shamudoi and Ramudoi, had been keeping a vigil in the gathering place around the large hearth. "Ayla needs the splints, Dolando," he said.

"Did it work?" the Shamudoi leader asked, handing him the pieces of smoothed wood.

Jondalar thought he should wait for Ayla to say, but he smiled. Dolando closed his eyes, took a long deep breath, and shuddered with relief.

Ayla placed the splints in position and wrapped more chamois strips around them. The arm would swell, and the poultice would have to be replaced. The splints were to hold the arm in place so Rosharío's movements would not disturb the fresh break. Later, when the swelling went down and she wanted to move about, birchbark, dampened with hot water, would mold to her arm and dry into a rigid cast.

She checked the woman's breathing again, and the pulses

in her neck and wrist, listened to her chest, lifted her eyelids, then went to the entrance of the dwelling.

"Dolando, you can come in now," she said to the man who was just outside the door.

"Is she all right?"

"Come and see for yourself."

The man went in and knelt down beside the sleeping woman, staring at her face. He watched her through several breaths, assuring himself that she was breathing, then finally looked at her arm. Under the dressings, the outline looked straight and normal.

"It looks perfect! Will she be able to use her arm again?"

"I have done what I can. With the help of the spirits and the Great Earth Mother, she should be able to use it. It may not be with the full use she had before, but she should be able to use it. Now, she must sleep."

"I am going to stay here with her," Dolando said, trying to convince her with his authority, though he knew if she insisted, he would leave.

"I thought you might want to," she said, "but now that it's done, there is something I would like."

"Ask. I will give you anything you want," he said, not hesitating, but wondering what she would demand of him.

"I would like to wash. Can the pool be used for swimming and washing?"

It was not what he had expected her to say, and he was taken aback for a moment. Then he noticed for the first time that her face was stained with blackberry juice, her arms were scratched from thorny briars, her clothes were worn and dirty, and her hair was disheveled. With a look of chagrin, and a wry smile, he said, "Roshario would never forgive me for my lack of hospitality. No one has so much as offered you a drink of water. You must be exhausted after your long travels. Let me get Tholie. Anything you want, if we have it, it is yours."

Ayla rubbed the saponin-rich flowers between her wet hands until a foam developed; then she worked it into her hair. The foam from ceanothus wasn't as rich as soaproot lather, but this was a final washing and the pale blue petals left a pleasant mild scent. The nearby area and the plants had been so familiar that Ayla was sure she'd be able to find some plant that they could use to wash with, but she was pleasantly surprised to find both soaproot and ceanothus when they went to get the pack baskets and travois with the bowl boat. They had stopped to check on the horses, and Ayla told herself she would spend some time combing Whinney later, partly to see to her coat, but also for the reassurance.

"Are there any foaming flowers left?" Jondalar asked.

"Over there, on the rock near Wolf," Ayla said. "But that's the last of them. We can pick more next time, and some extra to dry and take with us would be nice." She ducked under the water to rinse.

"Here are some chamois skins to dry yourselves with," Tholie said, approaching the pool. She had several of the soft yellow hides in her arms.

Ayla hadn't seen her come. The Mamutoi woman had tried to stay as far away from the wolf as possible, circling around and approaching from the open end of the site. A little girl of three or four, who had been walking behind, clung to her mother's leg and stared at the strangers with big eyes and a thumb in her mouth.

"I left a snack for you inside," Tholie said, putting the toweling skins down. Jondalar and Ayla had been given a bed inside the dwelling that she and Markeno used when they were on land. It was the same shelter that Thonolan and Jetamio had shared with them, and Jondalar had a few bad moments when they first entered, remembering the tragedy that had caused his brother to leave, and ultimately to die.

"But don't spoil your appetite," Tholie added. "We are having a big feast tonight, in honor of Jondalar's return." She did not add that it was also in honor of Ayla for helping Roshario. The woman was still sleeping, and no one wanted to tempt fate by saying it out loud before it was known that she would wake up, and would recover.

"Thank you, Tholie. For everything," Jondalar said. Then he smiled at the little girl. She put her head down and hung back behind her mother even more, but she continued to stare at Jondalar. "It looks like the last of the red from the burn on Shamio's face has faded. I don't see even a hint of it."

Tholie picked the girl up, giving Jondalar a chance to see her better. "If you look very closely, you can see where the burn was, but it's hardly noticeable. I'm grateful, the Mother was kind to her."

"She is a beautiful child," Ayla said, smiling at them and looking at the little girl with genuine longing. "You are so lucky. Someday I would like to have a daughter like her." Ayla started walking out of the pool. It was refreshing, but almost too cool to stay in for very long. "Did you say her name was Shamio?"

"Yes, and I do feel lucky to have her," the young mother said, putting the child down. Tholie couldn't resist the compliment to her offspring, and she smiled warmly at the tall, beautiful woman, who was not, however, what she claimed to be. Tholie had resolved to treat her with reserve and caution until she learned more.

Ayla picked up a skin and began drying herself. "This is so soft, and nice to dry with," she said, then stretched it around herself and tucked an end in at the waist. She picked up another to dry her hair, then wrapped it around her head. She had noticed Shamio watching the wolf, clinging to her mother but obviously curious. Wolf was interested in her, too, all but squirming with anticipation, but staying where he was told. She signaled the animal to her side, then got down on one knee and put her arm around him.

"Would Shamio like to meet Wolf?" Ayla asked the girl. When she nodded, Ayla glanced up at her mother for approval. Tholie looked apprehensively at the huge animal with the sharp teeth. "He won't hurt her, Tholie. Wolf loves children. He grew up with the children of Lion Camp."

Shamio had already let go of her mother and taken a tentative step toward them, fascinated by the creature that had been looking at her with equal fascination. The child watched him with unsmiling, solemn eyes, while the wolf whined with eagerness. Finally she took another step forward and reached for him with two hands. Tholie gasped, but the sound was drowned out by Shamio's giggles when Wolf licked her face. She pushed his eager muzzle away, grabbed a handful of fur, then lost her balance and fell over him. The wolf waited patiently for the girl to get up, then licked her face again, to another string of delighted giggles.

"C'mon, Wuffie," the girl said, grabbing him by the fur of his neck and pulling to make him come with her, already claiming him as her very own living toy.

Wolf looked at Ayla, and yipped a short puppy bark. She hadn't yet signaled his release. "You can go with Shamio, Wolf," she said, giving him the sign he was waiting for. She could almost believe that the look he gave her was gratitude, but there was no mistaking his delight as he followed the girl. Even Tholie smiled.

Jondalar had been watching the interaction with interest while he dried himself off. He picked up their clothes and walked toward the sandstone overhang with the two women. Tholie was keeping an eye on Shamio and Wolf, just in case, but she, too, was intrigued with the tame animal. She was not the only one. Many people were watching the girl and the wolf. When a boy a little older than Shamio approached, he was also greeted with a wet invitation to join them. Just then, two other children came out of one of the dwellings, tussling over some wooden object. The smaller one threw it to keep the other from getting it, which Wolf took as a signal that they wanted to play one of his favorite games. He raced after the carved stick, brought it back and laid it on the ground, his tongue panting and his tail waving, ready to play again. The boy picked it up and threw it again.

"I think you must be right—he's playing with them. He must like children," Tholie said. "But why should he like to play? He's a wolf!"

"Wolves and people are alike in some ways," Ayla said. "Wolves like to play. From the time they are cubs, siblings in a litter play, and the half-grown and adult wolves love to play with the little ones. Wolf didn't have any siblings when I found him; he was the only one left, and he barely had his eyes open. He didn't grow up in a wolf pack, he grew up playing with children."

"But look at him. He's so tolerant, even gentle. I'm sure when Shamio pulls on his fur, it must hurt. Why does he put up with it?" Tholie asked, still trying to understand.

"It's natural for a grown wolf to be gentle with the little ones of a pack, so it wasn't hard to teach him to be careful, Tholie. He's especially gentle with small children and babies and will tolerate almost anything from them. I didn't teach him that, that's just how he is. If they get too rough, he'll move away, but he goes back later. He won't put up with as much from older children, and he seems to know the difference between one of them accidentally hurting him and one who is being purposely hurtful. He has never really harmed anyone, but he will nip a little—give a little pinch with his teeth—to remind an older child, who is pulling on his tail or yanking his fur, that some things hurt."

"The idea of anyone, particularly a child, even thinking of pulling a wolf's tail is hard to imagine . . . or it would have been until today," Tholie said. "And I wouldn't have believed that I'd ever see the day that Shamio would play with a wolf. You have . . . made some people think, Ayla . . . Ayla of the Mamutoi." Tholie wanted to say more, to ask some questions, but she didn't exactly want to accuse the woman of lying, not after what she had done for Roshario, or at least seemed to have done. No one knew for sure, yet.

Ayla sensed Tholie's reservations, and she was sorry about them. It placed an unspoken strain between them, and she liked the short, plump Mamutoi woman. They walked a few steps in silence, watching Wolf with Shamio and the other children, and Ayla thought again how much she would like to have a daughter like Tholie's . . . a daughter next time, not a son. She was such a beautiful little girl, and her name matched her.

"Shamio is a beautiful name, Tholie, and unusual. It sounds like a Sharamudoi name, but also like a Mamutoi name," Ayla said.

Tholie could not resist smiling again. "You're right. Not everyone knows it, but that's what I was trying to do. She would be called Shamie if she were Mamutoi, although that isn't a name that would likely be found in any Camp. It comes from the Sharamudoi language, so her name is both. I may be Sharamudoi now, but I was born to the Red Deer Hearth, a line of high status. My mother insisted on a good Bride Price for me from Markeno's people, though he wasn't even Mamutoi. Shamio can be as proud of her Mamutoi background as she will be of her Sharamudoi heritage. That's why I wanted to show both in her name."

Tholie stopped as a thought occurred to her. She turned to look at the visitor. "Ayla is an unusual name, too. What Hearth were you born to?" she said, thinking, There, now I'd like to hear you explain that name.

"I was not born Mamutoi, Tholie. I was adopted by the Mammoth Hearth," Ayla said, glad that the woman had brought out the questions that had obviously been bothering her.

Tholie was certain she had caught the woman in a lie. "People are not adopted by the Mammoth Hearth," she asserted. "That is the Hearth of the mamutii. People choose

the way of the spirits, and may be accepted by the Mammoth
Hearth, but they are not adopted.''

"That is the usual way, Tholie, but Ayla was adopted,''
Jondalar interjected. "I was there. Talut was going to adopt
her into his Lion Hearth, but Mamut surprised everyone, and
adopted her into the Mammoth Hearth, as his own. He saw
something in her—that's why he was training her. He claimed
she was born to the Mammoth Hearth, whether she was born
a Mamutoi or not.''

"Adopted to the Mammoth Hearth? From outside?'' Tholie said, surprised, but she did not doubt Jondalar. After all,
she knew him and he was kin, but she was even more interested. Now that she no longer felt so constrained to be watchful and cautious, her natural forthright curiosity rose to the
surface. "Who were you born to, Ayla?''

"I don't know, Tholie. My people died in an earthquake
when I was a girl not much more than Shamio's age. I was
raised by the Clan,'' Ayla said.

Tholie had never heard of any people called the Clan.
They must be one of those eastern tribes, she thought. That
would explain a lot. No wonder she has such a strange accent,
though she does speak the language well, for an outsider.
That Old Mamut of the Lion Camp was a wise and canny
old, old man, she mused. He had always been old, it seemed.
Even when she was a girl, no one could remember when he
was young, and no one doubted his insights.

With a mother's natural instinct, Tholie glanced around
to check on her child. Noticing Wolf, she thought once again
about how strange it was that an animal would prefer associ-
ating with people. Then she looked the other way at the
horses grazing quietly and contentedly in the field so near to
their living site. Ayla's control over the animals was not only
surprising, it was interesting because they seemed so devoted
to her. The wolf seemed to adore her.

And look at Jondalar. He was obviously captivated by the
beautiful blond woman, and Tholie didn't think it was just
because she was beautiful. Serenio had been beautiful, and
there had been countless attractive women who had tried their
best to interest him in a serious attachment. He had been
closer to his brother, and Tholie recalled wondering if any
woman would ever reach his heart, but this woman had. Even
without her apparent healing skills, she seemed to possess

some unusual quality. Old Mamut must have been right. It probably was her destiny to belong to the Mammoth Hearth.

Inside the dwelling, Ayla combed out her hair, tied it back with a piece of soft leather thong, and put on the clean tunic and short pants she had been keeping aside in case they met some people, so she would not have to wear her stained traveling clothes for visiting. Then she went to check on Roshario. She smiled at Darvalo, who was sitting listlessly outside the dwelling, and she nodded to Dolando when she entered and approached the woman lying on the bed. She examined her briefly, just to make sure she was all right.

"Should she still be sleeping?" Dolando asked, with a worried frown.

"She's fine. She will sleep a while longer yet." Ayla looked at her medicine bag, then decided that it would be a good time to gather some fresh ingredients for a reviving tea to help bring Roshario out of the datura-induced sleep when she did begin to awaken. "I saw a linden tree on my way here. I want some flowers for a tea for her and, if I can find them, a few other herbs. If Roshario wakes up before I get back, you can give her a little water. Expect her to be bewildered and a bit dizzy. The splints should hold her arm straight, but don't let her move it too much."

"Will you be able to find your way?" Dolando asked. "Maybe you should take Darvo with you."

Ayla was sure she would have no trouble finding her way, but she decided to take the lad with her anyway. In all the concern for Roshario, he had been somewhat neglected, and he was worried about the woman, too.

"Thank you, I will," she said.

Darvalo had overheard the conversation and was standing and ready to go with her, looking pleased to be useful.

"I think I know where that linden tree is," he said. "There are always a lot of bees around it this time of year."

"That's the best time to gather the flowers," Ayla said, "when they smell like honey. Do you know where I can find a basket to carry them back?"

"Roshario stores her baskets back here," Darvalo said, showing Ayla to a storage space behind the dwelling. They selected a couple.

As they stepped out from under the overhang, Ayla noticed Wolf watching her, and she called him. She did not

feel comfortable leaving the wolf alone with these people just
yet, though the children complained when he left. Later,
when everyone felt more familiar with the animals, it might
be different.

Jondalar was in the field with the horses and two men.
Ayla walked toward them to tell him where she was going.
Wolf ran ahead and they all turned to watch when he and
Whinney rubbed noses, while the mare whickered a greeting.
Then the canine struck a playful pose and yipped a puppy
bark at the young stallion. Racer lifted his head in a neigh
and pawed the ground, returning the playful gesture. Then
the mare approached Ayla and put her head across her shoulder. The woman put her arms around Whinney's neck, and
they leaned against each other in a familiar posture of comfort
and reassurance. Racer took a few paces forward and nuzzled
them both, wanting contact, too. She hugged his neck, then
patted and stroked him, realizing that they all welcomed each
other's familiar presence in this place of so many strangers.

"I should introduce you, Ayla," Jondalar said.

She faced the two men. One was nearly as tall as Jondalar, but thinner, the other was shorter, and older, but their
similarity was striking, nonetheless. The shorter one stepped
forward first, with both hands outstretched.

"Ayla of the Mamutoi, this is Carlono, Ramudoi leader
of the Sharamudoi."

"In the name of Mudo, Mother of All in water and on
land, I welcome you, Ayla of the Mamutoi," Carlono said,
taking both of her hands. He spoke Mamutoi even better than
Dolando, a result of several trading missions to the mouth of
the Great Mother River, as well as Tholie's coaching.

"In the name of Mut, I thank you for your welcome,
Carlono of the Sharamudoi," she replied.

"Soon you must come down to our dock," Carlono said,
thinking, What a strange accent she has. I don't believe I've
ever heard one like that, and I've heard many. "Jondalar told
me he promised you a ride in a proper boat, not one of those
oversize Mamutoi bowls."

"I shall be pleased," Ayla said, offering one of her brilliant smiles.

Carlono's thoughts were diverted from consideration of
her speech mannerism to appreciation of her. This woman
Jondalar has brought certainly is a beauty. She suits him, he
decided.

"Jondalar has told me of your boats, and about hunting sturgeon," Ayla continued.

Both men laughed, as though she had made a joke, and they looked at Jondalar, who smiled, too, although he turned slightly red.

"Did he ever tell you how he hunted half a sturgeon?" the tall young man said.

"Ayla of the Mamutoi," Jondalar interjected, "this is Markeno of the Ramudoi, the son of Carlono's hearth, and Tholie's mate."

"Welcome, Ayla of the Mamutoi," Markeno said, informally, knowing she had been greeted with the proper ritual many times. "Have you met Tholie? She will be pleased you are here. She misses her Mamutoi kin sometimes." His command of his mate's language was almost perfect.

"Yes, I've met her, and Shamio, too. She is a beautiful little girl."

Markeno beamed. "I think so, too, though one is not supposed to say that of the daughter of one's own hearth." Then he turned to the youngster. "How is Rosharia, Darvo?"

"Ayla has fixed her arm," he said. "She is a healer."

"Jondalar told us she set the break properly," Carlono said, careful to be noncommittal. He would wait to see how well her arm healed.

Ayla noticed the Ramudoi leader's response, but she thought it was understandable, given the circumstances. No matter how well they liked Jondalar, she was a stranger, after all.

"Darvalo and I are going to gather some herbs I noticed on the way here, Jondalar," she said. "Rosharia is still sleeping, but I want to make a drink for her when she wakes. Dolando is with her. I don't like the look of Racer's eyes, either. Later I'll look for more of those white plants to help him, but I don't want to take the time now. You might try rinsing them with cool water," she said. Then, smiling at everyone, she signaled Wolf, nodded to Darvalo, and headed for the edge of the embayment.

The view from the path at the end of the wall was no less spectacular than it had been the first time she saw it. She had to catch her breath as she looked down, but she could not resist doing it. She allowed Darvalo to lead the way and was glad she did when he showed her a shortcut he knew. The wolf explored the area around the path, busily chasing after intriguing scents, then rejoining them. The first few times Wolf suddenly reappeared, he startled the youth, but as they continued, Darvalo began to get used to his comings and goings.

The large old linden tree announced its presence long before they reached it with a rich fragrance, reminiscent of honey, and the droning hum of bees. The tree came into view around a turn in the path and revealed the source of the luscious aroma, small green-and-yellow flowers dangling from oblong, winglike bracts. The bees were so busy collecting nectar that they didn't bother with the people who disturbed them, though the woman had to shake some bees out of the blossoms they cut. The insects just flew back to the tree and found others.

"Why is this especially good for Rosh?" Darvalo asked. "People always make linden tea."

"It does taste good, doesn't it? But it's helpful, too. If you're upset, or nervous, or even angry, it can be very soothing; if you're tired, it wakes you up, lifts your spirits. It can make a headache go away and calm an upset stomach. Roshario will be feeling all of those things, because of the drink that made her go to sleep."

"I didn't know it would do all that," the youngster said, looking again at the familiar spreading tree with smooth dark brown bark, impressed that something so ordinary had qualities that made it so much more than it seemed.

"There is another tree I would like to find, Darvalo, but I don't know the name in Mamutoi," Ayla said. "It's a small tree, sometimes growing as brush. It has thorns on it, and the leaves are shaped a little like a hand with fingers. It has clusters of white flowers earlier in the summer, and about now, round red berries."

"It's not a rosebush you want, is it?"

"No, but that's a good guess. The one I want usually grows bigger than a rosebush, but the flowers are smaller, and the leaves are different."

Darvalo frowned with concentration, then suddenly smiled. "I think I know what you mean, and there are some not far from here. In spring, we always pick the leaf buds and eat them when we walk by."

"Yes, that sounds like the one. Can you take me to it?"

Wolf was not in sight, so Ayla whistled. He appeared almost instantly, looking at her with eager anticipation. She signaled him to follow. They walked for a short while until they came to a stand of hawthorne.

"That's exactly what I was looking for, Darvalo!" Ayla said. "I wasn't sure if my description was clear enough."

"What does this do?" he asked as they were picking berries and some leaves.

"It's for the heart, restores, strengthens it, and stimulates, makes it beat hard—but it's gentle, for a healthy heart. It's not for someone with a weak heart, who needs a strong medicine," Ayla said, trying to find words to explain so that the youngster would understand what she knew from observation and experience. She had learned from Iza in a language and way of teaching that were difficult to translate. "It is also good to mix with other medicines. It stimulates them, makes them work better."

Darvalo was deciding that it was fun to gather stuff with Ayla. She knew all kinds of things that no one else did, and she didn't mind telling him at all. On the way back, she stopped at a dry sunny bank and cut some pleasant-smelling purple hyssop flowers. "What does that do?" he asked.

"It cleans the chest, helps breathing. And this," she said, picking some soft, downy leaves of mouse-eared hawkweed that were nearby, "stimulates everything. It's stronger, and doesn't taste too good, so I'll only use a little. I want to give her something pleasant to drink, but this will clear her mind, make her feel alert."

On the way back, Ayla stopped once more, to gather a large bunch of pretty pink gillyflowers. Darvalo expected to learn more medical lore when he asked what they were for.

"Just because they smell nice, and add a sweet, spicy flavor. I'll use some for the tea, and I'll put some in water by her bed, to make her feel good. Women like pretty, nice-smelling things, Darvalo, especially when they are sick."

He decided he liked pretty, nice-smelling things, too, like Ayla. He liked the way she always called him Darvalo, and not Darvo, the way everyone else did. Not that he minded so much when Dolando or Jondalar called him that, but it was nice to hear her use his grown-up name. Her voice sounded nice, too, even if she did say some words a little funny. All it did was make you pay attention to her when she talked, and after a while think about what a nice voice she had.

There was a time when he wished more than anything

that Jondalar would mate his mother and stay with the Sharamudoi. His mother's mate had died when he was young, and
there had never been a man who lived with them until the
tall Zelandonii man came. Jondalar had treated him like a
son of his hearth—he had even begun to teach him to work
the flint—and Darvalo had felt hurt when the man left.

He had hoped Jondalar would come back, but he never
really expected it. When his mother left with that Mamutoi
man, Gulec, he was sure there would be no reason for the
Zelandonii man to stay if he did come back. But now that
he had come, and with another woman, his mother didn't
need to be there. Everyone liked Jondalar, and, especially
since Roshario's accident, everybody talked about how much
they needed a healer. He was sure Ayla was a good one.
Why couldn't they both stay? he thought.

"She woke up once," Dolando said the instant Ayla
entered the dwelling. "At least I think she did. She might
have just been thrashing in her sleep. She has quieted down
and is sleeping again now."

The man was relieved to see her, though it was clear that
he did not want to make it obvious. Unlike Talut, who had
been completely open and friendly, and whose leadership was
based on the strength of his character, his willingness to listen, accept differences, and work out compromises . . . and
a voice loud enough to get the attention of a noisy group in
the midst of a heated argument . . . Dolando reminded her
more of Brun. He was more reserved, and though he was a
good listener who considered a situation carefully, he did not
like to reveal his feelings. But Ayla was used to interpreting
the subtle mannerisms of such a man.

Wolf came in with her, and he went to his corner even
before she signaled. She put down her basket of herbal flowers to check on Roshario, then spoke to the worried man.
"She'll be waking up soon, but I should have time to prepare
a special tea for her to drink when she does."

Dolando had noticed the fragrance of the flowers as soon
as Ayla entered, and the steaming liquid she made from them
had a warm floral scent when she brought a cup for him as
well as the woman on the bed.

"What is this for?" he asked.

"I made it to help Roshario wake up, but you might find
it refreshing, too."

He sipped it, expecting a light flowery essence, and was

surprised as a subtly sweet taste rich with character and flavor filled his mouth. "This is good!" he said. "What's in it?"

"Ask Darvalo. I think he'd be pleased to tell you."

The man nodded, understanding her implied suggestion. "I should pay more attention to him. I've been so worried about Roshario, I haven't thought of anything else, and I'm sure he's been worried about her, too."

Ayla smiled. She was beginning to perceive the qualities that made him the leader of this group. She liked the quickness of his mind and was fast growing to like him. Roshario made a sound, and their attention was suddenly diverted to her.

"Dolando?" she said in a weak voice.

"I'm here," he said, and the tenderness in his voice brought a lump to Ayla's throat. "How are you feeling?"

"A little dizzy, and I had the strangest dream," she said.

"I have something for you to drink." The woman made a face, remembering the last drink she had been given. "You will like this, I think. Here, smell it," Ayla said, bringing the cup down so that the delicious aroma was near her nose. The frown faded, and the medicine woman lifted Roshario's head and brought the cup to her lips.

"That is nice," Roshario said after a few sips, then drank some more. She lay back when she finished it and closed her eyes, but soon opened them. "My arm! How is my arm?"

"How does it feel?" Ayla said.

"It's a little painful, but not as much and in a different way," she said. "Let me see it." She craned to look at her arm, then tried to sit up.

"Let me help you," Ayla said, propping her up.

"It's straight! My arm looks right. You did it," the woman said. Then tears filled her eyes as she lay back down. "Now I won't have to be a useless old woman."

"You may not have full use of it," Ayla cautioned, "but it is set correctly now and has a chance to heal right."

"Dolando, can you believe it? Everything is going to be fine now," she sobbed, but her tears were of joy and relief.

17

Be careful now," Ayla said, helping Roshario to ease forward toward Jondalar and Markeno, who were stooped down on either side of her beside her bed. "The sling will support your arm and hold it in place, but keep it close to you."

"Are you sure she should get up so soon?" Dolando asked Ayla, frowning with worry.

"I'm sure," Roshario said. "I've been in this bed too long as it is. I don't want to miss Jondalar's welcoming celebration."

"So long as she doesn't tire herself too much, it will probably be good for her to get up and be with everyone for a while," Ayla said. Then she turned to Roshario. "But not too long. Rest is the best healer now."

"I just want to see everyone being happy for a change. Every time someone came in to see me, they looked so sorry for me. I want them to know I'm going to be all right," the woman said, easing off the bed into the waiting arms of the two young men.

"Steady now, watch the sling," Ayla said. Roshario put

her good arm around Jondalar's neck. "All right, together, lift her up."

With the woman between them, the two men stood up, moving forward a little so they could straighten up under the sloping roof of the dwelling. They were close to the same height, and they carried her easily. Though Jondalar was more obviously muscular, Markeno was a powerful young man. His strength was disguised by his more slender build, but rowing boats and handling the huge sturgeon the Ramudoi regularly hunted had given his flat, wiry muscles plenty of use.

"How do you feel?" Ayla asked.

"Up in the air," Rosharid said, smiling at each man in turn. "It's a different view from up here."

"Are you ready, then?"

"How do I look, Ayla?"

"Tholie did a good job of combing and fixing your hair; I think you look fine," Ayla said.

"The washing you both gave me made me feel better, too. I didn't even feel like combing or washing before. That must mean I'm better," Rosharid said.

"Some of it is the pain medicine I gave you. It will wear off. Be sure to tell me as soon as you start to feel very much pain. Don't try to be brave about it. And let me know when you begin to get tired, too," Ayla said.

"I will. I'm ready now."

"Look who's coming!" "It's Rosharid!" "She must be better," several voices exclaimed as the woman was carried from the dwelling.

"Put her down over here," Tholie said. "I've made a place for her."

At some time in the past, a large piece of sandstone had broken off the overhang and lodged near the gathering circle. Tholie had placed a bench against it and covered it with furs. The men took Rosharid there and lowered her carefully.

"Are you comfortable?" Markeno asked after they had settled her on the padded seat.

"Yes, yes, I'm fine," Rosharid said. She was unaccustomed to so much doting attention.

The wolf had followed them out of the dwelling, and, as soon as she was seated, he found a spot and lay down beside her. Rosharid was surprised, but when she saw the way he looked at her, and noticed how he watched everyone who approached, she had the strange but distinct feeling that he thought he was protecting her.

"Ayla, why is that wolf staying around Roshario? I think you should make him go away from her," Dolando said, wondering what the animal could want with a woman who was still so weak and vulnerable. He knew that wolf packs often hunted the old, sick, and weak members of a herd.

"No, don't make him go," Roshario said, reaching over with her good hand and patting his head. "I don't think he means to harm me, Dolando. I think he's watching out for me."

"I think he is, too, Roshario," Ayla said. "There was a boy at the Lion Camp, a weak, sickly child, but Wolf had a special attachment to him and was very protective. I think he senses that you are weak now, and he wants to protect you."

"Wasn't that Rydag?" Tholie said. "The one Nezzie adopted who was . . ."—she paused, suddenly remembering Dolando's strong and unreasonable feelings—". . . an outsider."

Ayla was aware of her hesitation and knew she had not said what she originally intended to say. She wondered why.

"Is he still with them?" Tholie asked, unaccountably flustered.

"No," Ayla said. "He died, early in the season, at the Summer Meeting." Rydag's death still upset and saddened her, and it showed.

Tholie's curiosity vied with her sense of discretion; she wanted to ask more questions, but this was not the time to ask questions about that particular child. "Isn't anyone else hungry? Why don't we eat?" she said.

After everyone had their fill, including Roshario, who didn't eat much, though it was more than she had eaten in one meal in some time, people gathered around the fire with cups of tea or lightly fermented dandelion wine. It was time to tell stories, recount adventures, and, especially, to learn more about the visitors and their unusual traveling companions.

The full complement of Sharamudoi were there, except those few who happened to be away: the Shamudoi, who lived on the land in the high embayment throughout the year, and their river-dwelling kin, the Ramudoi. During the warmer seasons the River People lived on a floating dock moored just below, but in winter they moved up to the high terrace and shared the dwellings of ceremonially joined cross-cousins. The dual couples were considered to be as closely related as mates, and the children of both families were treated as siblings.

It was the most unusual arrangement of closely related groups that Jondalar knew of, but it worked well for them because of their kinship ties and a unique reciprocal relationship that was mutually beneficial. There were many practical and ritual bonds between the two moieties, but primarily the Shamudoi contributed the products of the land and a safe place during rough weather, while the Ramudoi provided the produce of the river and skilled water transportation.

The Sharamudoi thought of Jondalar as kin, but he was kin only through his brother. When Thonolan fell in love with a Shamudoi woman, he had accepted their ways and had chosen to become one of them. Jondalar had lived with them just as long and felt they were family. He had learned and accepted their ways, but he had never gone through any ritual joining in his own right. In his heart he could not give up his identity with his own people, could not make the decision to settle with them permanently. Though his brother had become Sharamudoi, Jondalar was still Zelandonii. The evening conversation began, understandably, with questions about his brother.

"What happened after you left here with Thonolan?" Markeno asked.

As painful as it might be to talk about, Jondalar knew Markeno had a right to know. Markeno and Tholie had become cross-tied with Thonolan and Jetamio; Markeno was as close in kinship as he, and he was a brother born of the same mother. Briefly he told how they had traveled downriver in the boat Carlono had given them, some of their close calls, and their meeting with Brecie, the Mamutoi headwoman of Willow Camp.

"We're related!" Tholie said. "She is a close-cousin."

"I learned that later, when we lived with Lion Camp, but she was very good to us even before she knew we were kin," Jondalar said. "That was what made Thonolan decide to go north and visit other Mamutoi Camps. He talked about hunting mammoth with them. I tried to talk him out of it, tried to convince him to come back with me. We had reached the end of the Great Mother River, and that's as far as he always said he wanted to go.'' The tall man closed his eyes, shook his head as if trying to deny the fact, then bowed his head in anguish. The people waited, sharing his pain.

"But it wasn't the Mamutoi,'' he continued after a while. "That was an excuse. He just couldn't get over Jetamio. All he wanted was to follow her to the next world. He told me he was going to travel until the Mother took him. He was ready, he said, but he was more than ready. He wanted to go so much that he took chances. That's why he died. And I wasn't paying attention either. It was stupid of me to follow him when he went after that lioness who stole his kill. If it hadn't been for Ayla, I would have died with him.''

Jondalar's last comments piqued everyone's curiosity, but no one wanted to ask questions that would force him to further relive his grief. Finally Tholie broke the silence. "How did you meet Ayla? Were you near Lion Camp?''

Jondalar looked up at Tholie and then at Ayla. He had been speaking in Sharamudoi and he wasn't sure how much she had understood. He wished she knew more of the language so she could tell her own story. It was not going to be easy to explain, or rather to make the explanation believable. The more time that passed, the more unreal it all seemed, even to him, but when Ayla told it, it seemed easier to accept.

"No. We didn't know Lion Camp then. Ayla was living alone, in a valley several days' journey away from Lion Camp,'' he said.

"Alone?'' Roshario asked.

"Well, not entirely alone. She shared her small cave with a couple of animals, for company.''

"Do you mean she had another wolf like this one?'' the woman asked, reaching over to pat the animal.

"No. She didn't have Wolf then. She got him while we were living at Lion Camp. She had Whinney.''

"What is a Whinney?''

"Whinney is a horse.''

"A horse? You mean she had a horse, too?''

"Yes. That one, right over there,'' Jondalar said, pointing to the horses standing in the field, silhouetted against the red-streaked evening sky.

Roshario's eyes opened big with surprise, which made everyone else smile. They had all gone through their initial shock, but she hadn't noticed the horses before. "Ayla lived with those two horses?"

"Not exactly. I was there when the stallion was born. Before that, she lived with just Whinney . . . and the cave lion," Jondalar finished, almost under his breath.

"And the what?" Roshario changed to her less than perfect Mamutoi. "Ayla, you should tell us. Jondalar's confused, I think. And maybe Tholie will translate for us."

Ayla had caught bits and pieces of the conversation, but she looked to Jondalar for clarification. He looked absolutely relieved.

"I'm afraid I haven't been very clear, Ayla. Roshario wants to hear it from you. Why don't you tell them about living in your valley with Whinney, and Baby, and how you found me," he said.

"And why were you living alone in a valley?" Tholie added.

"It is a long story," Ayla said, taking a deep breath. The people settled back with smiles. That was exactly what they wanted to hear, a long, interesting new story. She took a sip of her tea and thought about how to begin. "I told Tholie, I don't remember who my people were. They were lost in an earthquake when I was a little girl, and I was found and raised by the Clan. Iza, the woman who found me, was a medicine woman, a healer, and she began to teach me healing when I was very young."

Well, that explained how the young woman could have such skill, Dolando thought, while Tholie was translating. Then Ayla picked up her narrative.

"I lived with Iza and her brother, Creb; her mate had died in the same earthquake that took my people. Creb was like the man of the hearth; he helped her raise me. She died a few years ago, but before she did, Iza told me I should leave and look for my own people. I didn't go, I couldn't leave . . ." Ayla hesitated, trying to decide how much to tell. ". . . Not then, but after . . . Creb died . . . I had to leave."

Ayla paused and took another sip of her tea while Tholie restated her words, having a little trouble with the strange names. The telling had brought back the powerful emotions of that time, and Ayla needed to regain her composure.

"I tried to find my own people, as Iza had told me to do," she continued, "but I didn't know where to look. I searched from early spring until well into summer, without finding anyone. I began to wonder if I ever would, and I was getting tired of traveling. Then I came to a small green valley in the middle of the dry steppes with a stream running through it, even a nice little cave. It had everything I needed . . . except people. I didn't know if I would find anyone, but I did know winter would be coming and if I wasn't ready for it, I would never live through it. I decided to stay in the valley until the next spring.''

The people had become so involved with her story, they were speaking out, nodding in agreement, saying she was right, it was the only thing to do. Ayla explained how she trapped a horse in a pit trap, discovered it was a nursing mare, and later saw a pack of hyenas going after the little filly. "I couldn't help myself," she said. "She was just a baby, and so helpless. I chased the hyenas away and brought her to live in my cave with me. I'm glad I did. She shared my loneliness, and she made it more bearable. She became a friend.''

The women, at least, could understand being drawn to a helpless baby, even if it was a baby horse. The way Ayla explained it made it seem perfectly reasonable, even if no one had ever heard of adopting an animal before. But it wasn't only the women who were captivated. Jondalar was watching the people. Women and men were equally enthralled, and he realized that Ayla had become a good storyteller. Even he was caught up, and he knew the story. He watched her closely, trying to see what made her so compelling, and he noticed that she used subtle but evocative gestures as well as words.

It wasn't a conscious effort or done for any particular effect. Ayla grew up communicating in the Clan way, and it was natural for her to describe with motions as well as with words, but when she first used birdcalls and the nickers and neighs of horses, it surprised her listeners. Living alone in her valley, hearing only the animal life in the vicinity, she began to mimic them, and she learned to reproduce their sounds with uncanny fidelity. After the first shock, her amazingly realistic animal sounds added a fascinating dimension.

As her story unfolded, especially when she told how she began riding and training the horse, even Tholie could hardly wait to finish translating Ayla's words so she could hear the rest. The young Mamutoi woman spoke both languages very well, though she could not begin to reproduce the whinny of a horse, or the birdcalls made with unnerving accuracy, but it wasn't necessary. People were getting a sense of what Ayla said, in part because the languages were similar, but also because of her expressive delivery. They understood the sounds when it was appropriate, but they waited for Tholie's translation to catch what they missed.

Ayla anticipated Tholie's words as much as everyone else, but for an entirely different reason. Jondalar had observed with awe her ability to learn new languages quickly when he first started teaching her to speak his, and he wondered how she did it. He didn't know her skill with language was derived from a unique set of circumstances. In order to exist among people who learned from the memories of their ancestors, that were stored from birth in their huge brains as a kind of evolved and conscious form of instinct, the girl of the Others had been forced to develop her own memorizing abilities. She had trained herself to remember quickly so she would not be considered so stupid by the rest of her clan.

She had been a normal, talkative little girl before she was adopted, and though she had lost most of her vocal language when she began to speak as the Clan did, the patterns were set. Her driving need to relearn verbal speech so she could communicate with Jondalar had added impetus to a natural ability. Once begun, the process she had unconsciously used was further developed when she went to live with the Lion Camp and had to learn yet another language. She could memorize vocabulary after one hearing, though syntax and structure took a little longer. But the language of the Sharamudoi was close to Mamutoi in structure, and many words were similar. Ayla listened carefully to Tholie's translation of her words, because as she was relating her story, she was learning their language.

As fascinating as her story of adopting a baby horse was, even Tholie had to stop and ask her to repeat herself when Ayla talked about finding the injured cave lion cub. Perhaps loneliness might drive someone to live with a grass-eating horse, but a gigantic carnivore? A full-grown male cave lion, walking on all fours, could nearly reach the height of the smallish steppe horses, and was more massive. Tholie wanted to know how she could even consider taking in a lion cub.

"He wasn't so big then, not even the size of a small wolf, and he was a baby . . . and he was hurt."

Though Ayla had meant to describe a smaller animal, people glanced toward the canine beside Roshario. Wolf was of northern stock, and big even for that large breed. He was the biggest wolf any of them had ever seen. The idea of taking in a lion that size did not appeal to many.

"The word she named him meant 'baby,' and she called him that even after he was full grown. He was the biggest Baby I ever saw," Jondalar added, which brought chuckles.

Jondalar smiled, too, but then told a more sobering fact. "I thought that was humorous, too, later, but there was nothing funny about the first time I saw him. Baby was the lion that killed Thonolan, and almost killed me." Dolando looked apprehensively at the wolf beside his woman again. "But what else can you expect when you walk into a lion's den? Though we had watched his mate leave and didn't know Baby was in there, it was a stupid thing to do. As it turned out, I was lucky that it happened to be that particular lion."

"What do you mean, 'lucky'?" Markeno asked.

"I was badly mauled and unconscious, but Ayla was able to stop him before he killed me," Jondalar said.

Everyone turned back to the woman. "How could she stop a cave lion?" Tholie asked.

"The same way she controls Wolf and Whinney," Jondalar said. "She told him to stop, and he did."

Heads were shaking in disbelief. "How do you know that's what she did? You said you were unconscious," someone called out.

Jondalar looked to see who the speaker was. It was a young River man he had known, though not well. "Because I saw her do the same thing later, Rondo. Baby came to visit her once when I was still recovering. He knew I was a stranger, and perhaps he remembered when Thonolan and I went into his den. Whatever the reason, he did not want me near Ayla's cave, and he immediately sprang to attack. But she stepped in front of him and told him to stop. And he did it. It was almost funny the way he pulled himself short in the middle of a leap, but at the time I was too scared to notice."

"Where's the cave lion now?" Dolando asked, looking at the wolf and wondering if the lion followed her, too. He was not particularly interested in being visited by a lion, no matter how well she might control him.

"He has made his own life," Ayla said. "He stayed with

me until he was grown. Then, like some children, he left to find a mate, and he probably has several by now. Whinney left me for a while, too, but she came back. She was pregnant when she returned."

"What about the wolf? Do you think he will leave someday?" Tholie asked.

Ayla caught her breath. It was a question that she had refused to consider. It had come to her mind more than once, but she always pushed it aside, not even wanting to acknowledge it. Now it was said, out in the open, and waiting for an answer.

"Wolf was so young when I found him, I think he grew up believing that the people of Lion Camp were his pack," she said. "Many wolves stay with their pack, but some wolves leave and become loners until they find another loner for a mate. Then a new pack starts. Wolf is still young, hardly more than a cub. He looks older because he's so big. I don't know what he will do, Tholie, but I worry about it sometimes. I don't want him to leave."

Tholie nodded. "Leaving is difficult, both for the one who leaves, and the ones that are left behind," she said, thinking about her own difficult decision to leave her people to live with Markeno. "I know how I felt. Didn't you say you left those people who raised you? What did you call them? Clan? I never heard of those people. Where do they live?"

Ayla glanced at Jondalar. He was sitting perfectly still, full of tension, with a strange expression on his face. He was very nervous about something, and suddenly she wondered if he was still ashamed of her background and the people who had raised her. She thought he was over those feelings now. She was not ashamed of the Clan. In spite of Broud and the anguish he had caused her, she had been cared for and loved even though she had been different, and she had loved in return. With a little feeling of anger, and a prickly touch of pride, she decided that she was not going to deny those people she had loved.

"They live on the peninsula in Beran Sea," Ayla replied.

"The peninsula? I didn't know there were people living on the peninsula. That's flathead territory . . ." Tholie stopped. It couldn't be, could it?

Tholie wasn't the only one who had seen the implications. Rosario had gasped and was furtively watching Dolando, trying to see if he had made any connections, but not wanting it to seem that she had noticed anything out of the ordinary. The strange names she mentioned, the ones that were so hard to pronounce, could they be names she had given some other kind of animals? But she said the woman who raised her had taught her healing medicine. Could there have been some woman living with them? What woman would choose to live with them, especially if she knew healing? Would a shamud live with flatheads?

Ayla was noticing the strange reactions of some of the people, but when she glanced at Dolando and saw him staring at her, she felt a shiver of dread. He did not seem to be the same man, the controlled leader who had cared for his woman with such tenderness. He was not looking at her with the grateful relief her healing skill had invoked, or even with the wary acceptance of their first meeting. Instead, she detected a deeply buried pain and saw a distancing; a menacing hard anger filled his eyes as though he could not see clearly, but only through the red haze of rage.

"Flatheads!" he exploded. "You lived with those filthy, murderous animals! I'd like to kill every one of them. And you lived with them. How could any decent woman live with them?"

His fists were clenched as he started to come for her. Both Jondalar and Markeno jumped up to hold him back. Wolf was standing in front of Roshario, teeth bared, a deep low growl in his throat. Shamio started to cry, and Tholie picked her up and held her protectively close. Under most circumstances, she would never fear for her daughter around Dolando, but he was not rational about flatheads, and at the moment he seemed to be in the grip of an uncontrollable madness.

"Jondalar! How dare you bring a woman like that here!" Dolando said, trying to shake off the restraining hold of the tall blond man.

"Dolando! What are you saying?" Roshario said, trying to get up. "She helped me! What difference does it make where she grew up? She helped me!"

The people who had gathered for Jondalar's welcoming were stunned, gaping with shock, and had no idea what to do. Carlono got up to help Markeno and Jondalar and to try to calm his coleader.

Ayla was stunned, too. Dolando's virulent reaction was so completely unexpected that she was at a loss. She saw Roshario attempting to get up, trying to push aside the wolf, who was standing defensively in front of her, as confused as everyone else by the commotion, but determined to protect the woman he saw as his charge. She should not get up, Ayla thought, hurrying toward the woman.

"Get away from my woman. I don't want her tainted with your filth," Dolando shouted, struggling to free himself from the men trying to hold him back.

Ayla stopped. Though she wanted to help Roshario, she didn't want to cause more trouble with Dolando. What is wrong with him? she wondered. Then she noticed that Wolf looked ready to attack, and she signaled him to come to her. That was the last thing she needed, for the wolf to cause anyone harm. Wolf was obviously struggling with himself. He wanted either to stand his ground or jump into the fray, but he did not want to back away from it; yet everything was confusing. Ayla's second signal was accompanied by her whistle, and that decided him. He ran to her, then stood defensively in front of her.

Though he spoke Sharamudoi, Ayla was aware that Dolando had been shouting about flatheads and directing angry words at her, but the meaning had not been entirely clear. While she was waiting there with the wolf, suddenly she got a clear sense of his ravings and began to feel angry herself. The people of the Clan were not filthy murderers. Why was he so enraged by the thought of them?

Roshario had gotten up and was trying to approach the struggling men. Tholie gave Shamio to someone nearby and ran to help her.

"Dolando! Dolando, stop it!" Roshario said. Her voice seemed to reach him; his struggles eased, though the three men still held him.

Dolando looked angrily at Jondalar. "Why did you bring her here?"

"Dolando, what's wrong with you? Look at me!" Roshario said. "What would have happened if he hadn't? Ayla was not the one who killed Doraldo."

He looked at Roshario and for the first time seemed to see the weak, drawn woman with her arm in a sling. A quick spasm shook him, and, like shedding water, the irrational fury left him. "Rosharo, you shouldn't be up," he said, reaching for her, but he found himself restrained. "You can let me go," he said to Jondalar with a voice of cold anger.

The Zelandonii man dropped his hold. Markeno and Carlono waited until they were sure he was not struggling before they released him, but they stayed nearby, just in case.

"Dolando, you have no call to be angry with Jondalar," Rosharo said. "He brought Ayla because I needed her. Everyone is upset, Dolando. Come and sit down and show them you are all right."

She saw a stubborn look in Dolando's eye, but he went with her back to the bench and sat beside her. A woman brought them both some tea, then walked over to the place where Ayla, Jondalar, Carlono, and Markeno were standing, along with Wolf.

"Would you like tea or a little wine?" she asked.

"You wouldn't happen to have some of that wonderful bilberry wine, Carolio?" he said. Ayla noticed her resemblance to both Carlono and Markeno.

"The new wine isn't ready, but there might be some left from last year. For you, too?" she said to Ayla.

"Yes, if Jondalar wants, I will try it. I don't think we met," she added.

"No," the woman said, as Jondalar was getting ready to jump in and make the introductions. "We don't need to be formal. We all know who you are, Ayla. I am Carolio, that one's sister." She indicated Carlono.

"I see the . . . likeness," Ayla said, searching for the word, and Jondalar suddenly realized she was speaking Sharamudoi. He looked at her in wonder. How did she learn it so fast?

"I hope you can overlook Dolando's outburst," Carolio said. "The son of his hearth, Rosharo's son, was killed by flatheads, and he hates all of them. Doraldo was a young man, a few years older than Darvo, and full of high spirits, just beginning his life. It was very hard on Dolando. He has never quite gotten over it."

Ayla nodded, but frowned. It was not usual for the Clan to kill the Others. What had the young man done? she wondered. She saw Rosharo motioning to her. Though Dolando's glare was not welcoming, she hurried toward the woman.

"You are tired?" she asked. "Is time you go to bed? Are you feeling pain?"

"A little. Not much. I'll go to bed soon, but not yet. I want to tell you how sorry I am. I had a son . . ."

"Carolio told me. She said he was killed."

"Flatheads . . ." Dolando mumbled under his breath.

"We may have all jumped to some conclusions," Roshario said. "You said you lived with . . . some people on the peninsula?" There was suddenly absolute silence.

"Yes," Ayla said. Then she looked at Dolando and took a deep breath. "The Clan. The ones you call flatheads, that is what they call themselves."

"How? They don't talk," a young woman called out. Jondalar saw it was the woman sitting next to Chalono, another young man he knew. She was familiar, but her name eluded him for the moment.

Ayla anticipated her unspoken comment. "They are not animals. They are people, and they do talk, but not with many words, though they use some. Their language is of signs and gestures."

"Is that what you were doing?" Roshario asked. "Before you put me to sleep? I thought you were dancing with your hands."

Ayla smiled. "I was talking to the spirit world, asking my totem spirit to help you."

"Spirit world? Talking with hands? What nonsense!" Dolando spat.

"Dolando," Roshario said, reaching for his hand.

"It's true, Dolando," Jondalar said. "I even learned some of it. All of Lion Camp did. Ayla taught us so we could communicate with Rydag. Everyone was surprised to find out he could talk that way, even if he couldn't say words right. It made them realize he was not an animal."

"You mean the boy Nezzie took in?" Tholie said.

"Boy? Are you talking about that abomination of mixed spirits that we heard some crazy Mamutoi woman took in?"

Ayla's chin went up. She was getting angry now. "Rydag was a child," she said. "He may have come from mixed spirits, but how can you blame a child for who he is? He didn't choose to be born that way. Don't you say it's the Mother who chooses the spirits? Then he was just as much a child of the Mother as anyone. What right do you have to call him an abomination?"

Ayla was glaring at Dolando, and everyone was staring at both of them, surprised at Ayla's defense, and wondering what Dolando's reaction would be. He looked as surprised as the others.

"And Nezzie is not crazy. She is a warm, kind, loving woman who took in an orphan child, and she didn't care what anyone thought," Ayla continued. "She was like Iza, the woman who took me in when I had no one, even though I was different, one of the Others."

"Flatheads killed the son of my hearth!" Dolando said.

"That may be, but it is not usual. The Clan would rather avoid the Others—that's how they think of people like us." Ayla paused, then she looked at the man who still suffered such anguish. "It is hard to lose a child, Dolando, but let me tell you about someone else who lost a child. She was a woman I met when many of the clans gathered—it was like a Summer Meeting, but they don't meet as often. She and some other women were out collecting food when suddenly several men came upon them, men of the Others. One of them grabbed her, to force her to have what you call Pleasures."

There were gasps among the people. Ayla was talking about a subject that was never discussed openly, though all but the very youngest had heard about it. Some mothers felt they should take their children away, but no one really wanted to leave.

"Women of the Clan do what men wish, they don't have to be forced, but the man who grabbed the woman couldn't wait. He wouldn't even wait for her to put her baby down. He grabbed her so roughly that the baby fell, and he didn't even notice. It wasn't until afterward, when he allowed her to get up, that she found her baby's head had hit a stone when it fell. Her baby was dead."

A few of the listeners had tears in their eyes. Jondalar spoke up. "I know those things can happen. I heard about some young men who live far to the west of here who liked to make sport with flatheads, several of them ganging up to force a clan woman."

"It happens around here, too," Chalono admitted.

The women looked at him with surprise that he said it, and most of the men avoided looking at him altogether, except Rondo, who was looking at him as though he were a worm.

"It's always the big thing boys talk about," Chalono said, trying to defend himself. "Not many of them do it any more, though, especially after what happened to Doral . . .'' He stopped suddenly, glanced around, then looked down, wishing he had never opened his mouth.

The following uneasy silence was broken when Tholie said, "Rosharo, you look very tired. Don't you think it's time you went back to bed?"

"Yes, I think I'd like to," she said.

Jondalar and Markeno hurried to help her, and everyone else took it as a signal to get up and leave. No one cared to linger around the last of the fire talking or gaming on this night. The two young men carried the woman into the dwelling while a stricken Dolando shuffled behind.

"Thank you, Tholie, but I think it would be better if I slept near Rosharo tonight," Ayla said. "I hope Dolando won't object. She's been through so much, and she is going to have a difficult night. In fact, the next few days will not be easy. The arm is already swelling, and she will be feeling some pain. I'm not sure she should have gotten up this evening, but she was so insistent I don't think I could have stopped her. She kept saying she was feeling good, but that was because the drink that made her sleep also stops deep pain, and it hadn't entirely worn off. I gave her something else besides, but it will all wear off tonight, and I would like to be there."

Ayla had just come into the dwelling after spending a little time currying and combing Whinney in the dying light of the sunset. It always relaxed her and made her feel better to be near and tend to the mare when she was upset. Jondalar had joined her there for a short time but had sensed that she wanted to be alone for a while, so after some pats and scratches and comforting words to the stallion, he had left them.

"Perhaps Darvo could stay with you," Jondalar suggested now. "He would probably sleep better. It bothers him to see her suffer."

"Of course," Markeno said. "I'll go get him. I wish I could convince Dolando to stay with us for a while, too, but I know he won't, especially after tonight. No one ever told him the full story of Doraldo's death."

"Maybe it's best that it all finally came out. Maybe he can finally put it aside now," Tholie said. "Dolando has been nursing a real hatred toward flatheads for a long time. It seemed fairly harmless, no one really cares that much for them anyway— I'm sorry, Ayla, but it is true.''

Ayla nodded. ''I know,'' she said.

''And we seldom have much contact. In most ways, he's a good leader,'' Tholie continued, ''except for anything to do with flatheads, and it's easy to work other people up about them. But such a strong hatred can't help but leave its mark. I think it's always worse on the person who does the hating.''

''I think it's time to get some rest,'' Markeno said. ''You must be exhausted, Ayla.''

Jondalar, Markeno, and Ayla, with Wolf at her heels, walked the few steps to the next dwelling together. Markeno scratched at the entrance flap and waited. Rather than calling out, Dolando came to the entrance and pushed the flap aside, then stood in the shadows of the entrance looking at them.

''Dolando, I think Rosahrio may have a hard night. I would like to stay near her,'' Ayla said.

The man looked down, then inside toward the woman on the bed. ''Come in,'' he said.

''I want to stay with Ayla,'' Jondalar said. He was determined not to leave her alone with the man who had threatened and raged at her, even if he did seem to have calmed down.

Dolando nodded and stepped aside.

''I came to ask Darvo if he'd like to spend the night with us,'' Markeno said.

''I think he should,'' Dolando said. ''Darvo, take your bedding and go with Markeno tonight.''

The boy got up, gathered up his pads and covers in his arms, and walked toward the opening. Ayla thought he looked relieved but not happy.

Wolf settled into his corner as soon as they entered. Ayla walked to the darkened rear to check on Rosahrio.

''Do you have a lamp or a torch, Dolando? I'd like a little more light,'' she said.

''And maybe some extra bedding,'' Jondalar added, ''or should I ask Tholie for some?''

Dolando would have preferred to be alone in the dark, but if Rosahrio woke up in pain, he knew the young woman would be able to help her much better than he could. From a shelf, he took down a shallow sandstone bowl that had been shaped by pecking and hitting it with another stone.

''The bedding is over here,'' he said to Jondalar. ''There

is some fat for the lamp in the box by the door, but I'll have to start a fire to light the lamp. It went out.''

"I'll start the fire," Ayla said, "if you'll tell me where your kindling and tinder are.''

He gave her the fire-starting materials she asked for, along with a round stick, black with charcoal on one end, and a flattish piece of wood with several round holes burned out of it from starting other fires, but she didn't use those. Instead, out of a pouch hanging from her belt, she withdrew two stones. Dolando watched with curiosity as she made a small pile of the dry, light shavings of wood and, hovering closely over it, hit one stone against the other. To his surprise, a large bright spark leaped from the stones and landed on the tinder, sending up a thin column of smoke. She bent close and blew, and the tinder burst into flame.

"How did you do that?" he asked, surprised and a little fearful. Anything so amazing, and unknown, always engendered a little fear. Was there no end to this woman's shamud magic? he wondered.

"It comes from the firestone," Ayla said, as she added a few sticks of kindling to keep the fire going, and then larger pieces of wood.

"Ayla discovered them when she was living in her valley," Jondalar said. "They were all over the rocky shore there, and I collected some extras. I'll show you how they work tomorrow, and give you one, so you will know what they look like. There may be some around here. As you can see, they make starting a fire much faster."

"Where did you say the fat was?" Ayla asked.

"In the box by the entrance. I'll get it. The wicks are there, too," Dolando said. He put a dollop of soft white tallow—fat that had been rendered in boiling water and skimmed after it cooled—into the stone bowl, stuck a twisted strand of dried lichen in it, next to the edge, then picked up a burning stick and lit it. It sputtered a bit; then a pool of oil started to form in the bottom of the bowl and was absorbed by the lichen, causing a steadier flame and more even light within the wooden structure.

Ayla put cooking stones in the fire, then checked the level in the wooden water box. She started outside with it, but Dolando took it and went out to get more water instead. While he was gone, Ayla and Jondalar put the bedding on a sleeping platform. Then Ayla selected some dried herbs from her medicine packets to make a relaxing tea for all of them. She put other ingredients in some of her own bowls to have it ready for Rosario when she woke up. Not long after Dolando brought in the water, she gave cups of tea to each of them.

They sat in silence, sipping the warm liquid, which was a relief to Dolando. He was afraid they would want him to make conversation, and he was in no mood for it. It wasn't a matter of mood to Ayla. She simply didn't know what to say. She had come for Rosario's sake, though she would have preferred not to be there at all. The prospect of spending the night within the dwelling of a man who had raged in anger against her was not pleasant, and she was grateful Jondalar had chosen to stay with her. Jondalar was also at a loss for words and had been waiting for someone else to say something. When no one did, he felt that silence, perhaps, was most appropriate.

With timing that almost seemed planned, just as they were finishing their tea, Rosario began to moan and thrash about. Ayla picked up the lamp and went to her. She put it down on a wooden bench that also served as a bedside table, moving aside a damp woven cup of spicy fragrant gillyflowers. The woman's arm was swollen and warm to the touch, even through the wrappings, which were now tighter. The light and Ayla's touch woke the woman. Her eyes, glazed with pain, focused on the medicine woman, and she tried to smile.

"I'm glad you are awake," Ayla said. "I need to take off the sling and loosen the wrappings and splints, but you were thrashing in your sleep, and you need to keep your arm still. I'll make a fresh poultice that should lessen the swelling, but I want to make you something for the pain, first. Will you be all right for a while?"

"Yes, you go and do what you need to. Dolando can stay and talk to me," Rosario said, looking past Ayla's shoulder to one of the men standing behind her. "Jondalar, don't you think you should help Ayla?"

He nodded. It was obvious that she wanted to talk to Dolando in private, and he was just as happy to leave them alone. He brought in more wood for the fire, and then more water, and a few more river-smoothed, large pebbles to use for heating the liquid. One of the cooking stones had cracked when it was transferred from the hot fire to the fresh, cold water Dolando had brought in for tea. As he watched Ayla preparing her medications, he heard the low murmur of voices from the rear of the dwelling. He was glad he could not hear what they were saying. When Ayla finished treating Roshario and making her more comfortable, they were all tired and ready for sleep.

Ayla was awakened in the morning by the delightful sound of children laughing and playing, and Wolf's wet nose. When she opened her eyes, Wolf looked toward the entrance, where the sounds were coming from. Then he looked back at her and whined.

"You want to go out there and play with those children, don't you?" she said. He whined again.

She lifted off her covers and sat up, noticing that Jondalar was sprawled out in sound sleep beside her. She stretched, rubbed her eyes, and glanced toward Roshario. The woman was still sleeping; she had many wakeful nights to make up for. Dolando, wrapped in a fur cover, was sleeping on the ground beside her bed. He, too, had spent many sleepless nights.

When Ayla got up, Wolf dashed to the entrance and stood there waiting for her, his whole body wriggling with anticipation. She pushed back the flap and quickly stepped outside, but told Wolf to stay. She did not want him scaring anyone by dashing into the middle of something without warning. She looked across and saw several children of various ages in the pool made by the waterfall along with several women, all taking a morning bath. She walked toward them with Wolf close to her side. Shamio squealed when she saw him.

"C'mon, Wuffie. You should take a bath, too," the girl said. Wolf whined, looking up at Ayla.

"Would anyone mind if Wolf got in the pool, Tholie? Shamio seems to want him to come in and play."

"I was just getting out," the young woman said, "but she can stay in and play with him, if the others don't mind."

When no one made an objection, Ayla gave him a signal. "Go ahead, Wolf," she said. The wolf bounded into the water, making a big splash, straight to Shamio.

A woman who was coming out of the water alongside Tholie smiled, then said, "I wish my children would mind as well as that wolf does. How do you make him do what you want?"

"It takes time. You have to go over it a lot, make him repeat what you want many times, and it can be difficult to make him understand at first, but once he learns something, he doesn't forget. He's really very smart," Ayla said. "I've been teaching him every day while we were traveling."

"Sounds like teaching a child," Tholie said, "but why a wolf? I never knew you could teach them to do anything, but why do you do it?"

"I know he can be frightening to people who don't know him, and I didn't want him to scare anyone," Ayla said. Watching Tholie come out of the pool and dry herself, Ayla was suddenly aware she was pregnant. Not too far along yet, and her plumpness concealed it when she was dressed, but she was definitely pregnant. "I think I'd like to wash, too, but first I have to pass water."

"If you follow that path up the back, you'll find a trench. It's quite a ways up, over the far wall so it runs off the other side when it rains, but it's closer than going around," Tholie said.

Ayla started to call Wolf, then hesitated. As usual, he had lifted his leg in the bushes—she had taught him to go outside of dwellings, but not to use special places. She watched the children playing with him and knew he would rather stay, but she wasn't sure if she should leave him. She was sure everything would be fine, but she didn't know how the mothers would feel.

"I think you can leave him for a while, Ayla," Tholie said. "I've seen him around the children, and you were right. They'd all be disappointed if you called him away so soon."

Ayla smiled. "Thank you. I'll be right back."

She started up the path that traversed in a diagonal across the steepest incline to one wall and then switchbacked toward the other. When she reached the far wall she climbed over it on steps made out of short sections of logs. These were held in place with stakes pounded into the ground in front of them, so they would not roll, and filled in behind with stones and dirt.

The trench and a level area in front of it, lined with a low fence of smooth round logs to sit across, had been dug out of the sloping ground on the other side of the wall. The smell and the buzzing flies made its purpose obvious, but the sunlight shining through the trees, and the sound of birds made it a pleasant place to linger when she found herself moving her bowels, as well. She saw a pile of dried moss on the ground nearby and guessed its use. It was not at all scratchy and quite absorbent. When she was through, she noticed that fresh dirt had recently been scattered over the bottom of the trench.

The path continued downhill and Ayla decided to follow it a ways. As she walked along, the region felt so much like the area around the cave where she grew up that she had the haunting feeling she had been there before. She would come upon a rock formation that seemed familiar, or a space opening out at the crest of a ridge, or similar vegetation. She stopped to pick a few hazelnuts off a bush growing against a rock wall, and she could not resist pushing aside the low branches to see if there was a small cave hidden behind it.

She found another large mound of blackberry bushes with long thorny runners reaching out, heavy with clumps of sweet ripe fruit. She stuffed herself with them and wondered what had happened to the berries she had picked the day before. Then she remembered eating some at the welcoming feast. She decided she'd have to come back and get more for Roshario. Suddenly she realized that she had to return. The woman might be waking up and need some attention. The woods had felt so familiar that Ayla had forgotten where she was for a moment. Roaming the hillsides, she had felt like a girl again, using the excuse of looking for Iza's medicinal plants to explore.

Perhaps because it was second nature anyway, or because she had always looked harder for plants on her way back so she'd have something to show for her forays, Ayla paid close attention to the vegetation. She almost shouted with excitement, and relief, when she noticed the small yellow vines with tiny leaves and flowers twined around other plants that were dead and dried, strangled by the golden threadlike vines.

That's it! That's golden thread, Iza's magic plant, she thought. That's what I need for my morning tea, so I won't start a baby growing. And there's a lot of it. I was running so low that I didn't know if I'd have enough to last for the whole Journey. I wonder if there's antelope sage root around here, too? There ought to be. I'll have to come back and look.

She found a plant with large basal leaves and wove them together with twigs for a makeshift gathering container, then picked as many of the small plants as she could, without depleting the area entirely. Iza had taught her long ago always to leave some from which the next year's growth would start.

On the way back, she took a small detour through a thicker, more shaded patch of forest, to look for more of the waxy white plant that would soothe the horses' eyes, though they did seem to be improving. She scanned the ground under the trees carefully. With so much that was familiar, it shouldn't have come as a surprise, but when she saw the green leaves of one particular kind of plant, she gasped and felt a cold chill go through her.

18

Ayla dropped to the moist ground and sat staring at the plants, breathing the rich forest air, while memories came flooding back. Even in the Clan the secret of the root was little known. The knowledge had belonged to Iza's line, and only those descended from the same ancestors—or the one to whom she had taught it—knew the complicated processing required to produce the final result. Ayla remembered Iza explaining the unusual method of drying the plant so that its properties would concentrate in the roots, and she recalled that they actually got stronger with long storage, if kept out of the light.

Though Iza had told her, carefully and repeatedly, how to make the drink from the dry roots, she couldn't let Ayla practice preparing it before she went to the Clan Gathering; it could not be used without proper ritual and, Iza had stressed, it was too sacred to throw away. That was why Ayla had drunk the dregs she had found in the bottom of Iza's ancient bowl, after she made it for the mog-urs, even though it was forbidden to women, so it wouldn't have to be thrown out. She wasn't thinking straight by then. There was so much going on, other beverages that clouded her mind, and the root drink was so powerful that even the little she had swallowed while making it had a strong effect.

She had wandered along narrow passages through the deep honeycombed caves, and by the time she saw Creb and the other mog-urs, she couldn't have retreated even if she'd tried. That was when it happened. Somehow Creb had known she was there, and he had taken her with them, back into the memories. If he hadn't, she would have been lost in that black void forever, but something happened that night that changed him. He wasn't The Mog-ur afterward, he had no heart for it anymore, until that last time.

She'd had some of the roots with her when she left the Clan. They were in her medicine bag in the sacred red-colored pouch, and Mamut had been very curious when she told him about them. But he didn't have the power of The Mog-ur, or perhaps the plant affected the Others differently. She and Mamut were both drawn into the black void and almost didn't return.

Sitting on the ground, staring at the seemingly innocuous plant that could be made into something so powerful, she recalled the experience. Suddenly she shivered with another chill and sensed a shadow of darkness, as though a cloud were passing overhead, and then she wasn't just remembering, she was reliving that strange Journey with Mamut. The green woods faded and dimmed as she felt herself drawn back into her memory of the darkened earthlodge. In the back of her throat she tasted the dark cool loam and growing fungus of ancient primeval forests. She sensed herself moving with great speed to the strange worlds she had traveled with Mamut, and she felt the terror of the black void.

Then faintly, from far away, she heard Jondalar's voice, full of agonized fear and love, calling to her, pulling her back and Mamut as well, by the sheer strength of his love and his need. In an instant she was back, feeling chilled to the bone in the warmth of late summer sunshine.

"Jondalar brought us back!" she said aloud. At the time she hadn't been aware of it. He was the one she had opened her eyes to, but then he was gone and Ranec was there instead bringing a hot drink to warm her. Mamut had told her that someone had helped them to return. She hadn't realized that it was Jondalar, but suddenly she knew, almost as though she was meant to know.

The old man had said he would never use the root again and warned her against it, but he also said that if she ever did, to make sure someone was there who could call her back. He'd told her the root was more than deadly. It could steal her spirit; she could be lost in the black void forever, and would never be able to return to the Great Earth Mother. It hadn't mattered then, anyway. She'd had no roots left. She had used the last of them with Mamut. But now, in front of her, there was the plant.

Just because it was there didn't mean she had to take it, she thought. If she left it, she would never have to worry that she might use it again and lose her spirit. She had been told the drink was forbidden to her, anyway. It was for mogurs who dealt with the spirit world, not medicine women who were only supposed to make it for them, but she had already drunk it, twice. And besides, Broud had cursed her; as far as the Clan was concerned, she was dead. Who was there to forbid her now?

Ayla didn't even ask herself why she was doing it when she picked up the broken branch and used it as a digging stick to carefully extract several of the plants without damaging the roots. She was one of the few people on earth who knew their properties and how to prepare them. She could not leave them. It wasn't that she had any particular intention of using them, which in itself was not unusual. She had many preparations of plants that might never be used, but this was different. The others had potential medicinal uses. Even the golden thread, Iza's magic medicine to fight off impregnating essences, was good for stings and bites when applied externally, but, as far as she knew, this plant had no other use. The root was spirit magic.

"There you are! We were beginning to worry," Tholie called out when she saw Ayla coming down the path. "Jondalar said if you didn't get back soon, he'd send Wolf after you."

"Ayla, what took you so long?" Jondalar said, before she could answer. "Tholie said you were coming right back." He had unthinkingly spoken Zelandonii, which let her know just how worried he had been.

"The path kept on going, and I decided to follow it a little farther. Then I found some plants I wanted," Ayla said, holding up the material she had collected. "This area is so much like the place I grew up. I haven't seen some of these since I left."

"What was so important about those plants that you had to collect them now? What is that one for?" Jondalar said, pointing to the golden thread.

Ayla understood him well enough, now, to know that the angry tone was the result of his concern, but his question caught her by surprise. "That's . . . that's for bites . . . and stings," she said, flustered, and embarrassed. It felt like a lie; even though her answer was perfectly true, it was not complete.

Ayla had been raised as a woman of the Clan, and Clan women could not refuse to answer a direct question, especially when posed by a man, but Iza had stressed very strongly never to tell anyone, particularly a man, what power the tiny golden threads held. Iza herself would not have been able to resist answering Jondalar's question fully, but she would never have had to. No man of the Clan would consider questioning a medicine woman about her plants or practices. Iza had meant that Ayla should never volunteer the information.

It was acceptable to refrain from mentioning, but Ayla knew that the allowance was meant for courtesy and to permit some measure of privacy, and she had gone beyond that. She was deliberately withholding information. She could administer the medicine, if she felt it was appropriate, but Iza had told her that it could be dangerous if people, especially men, realized that she knew how to defeat the strongest of spirits and prevent pregnancy. It was secret knowledge meant only for medicine women.

A thought suddenly occurred to Ayla. If it could prevent Her from blessing a woman, could Iza's magic medicine be stronger than the Mother? How could that be? But if She did create all the plants in the first place, She must have made it on purpose! She must have meant for it to be used to help women when it would be dangerous or difficult for them to become pregnant. But then why didn't more women know about it? Maybe they did. Since it grew so close, maybe these Sharamudoi women were familiar with it. She could ask, but would they tell her? And if they didn't know, how could she ask without telling them? But if the Mother meant it for women, wouldn't it be right to tell them? Ayla's mind raced with questions, but she had no answers.

"Why did you need to get plants for bites and stings now?" Jondalar said, his concern still showing in his eyes.

"I didn't meant to worry you," Ayla said, then smiled, "it's just that this area feels so much like home, I wanted to explore it."

Suddenly he had to smile, too. "And you found some blackberries for breakfast, didn't you? Now I know what took you so long. I never met anyone who loved blackberries more than you do." He had noticed her discomfiture, but he was delighted when he thought he had discovered why she seemed so reluctant to talk about her little side trip.

"Well, yes, I did have a few. Maybe we can go back later and pick some for everyone. They are so ripe and good now. There are some other things I want to look for, too."

"I have a feeling we're going to have all the blackberries we could want, with you around, Ayla," Jondalar said, kissing her purple-stained mouth.

He was so relieved that she was safe, and so pleased with himself to think that he had found her out and discovered her weakness for sweet berries, that she just smiled and let him think what he wanted. She did like blackberries, but her real weakness was him, and she suddenly felt such an overwhelming warmth of love for him that she wished they were alone. She wanted to hold him, and touch him, and Pleasure him, and feel him Pleasuring her the way he did so well. Her eyes showed her feelings, and his wonderful, exceptionally blue eyes returned them with added measure. She felt a tingling deep inside and had to turn away to settle herself.

"How is Roshario?" she said. "Is she awake yet?"

"Yes, and she says she's hungry. Carolio came up from the dock and is fixing something for us, but we thought we should wait until you came before she ate."

"I'll go and see how she is, and then I'd like to take a morning swim," Ayla said.

As she headed for the dwelling, Dolando pulled back the flap to come outside, and Wolf came bounding out. He jumped up on her, put his paws on her shoulders, and licked her jaw.

"Wolf, get down! My hands are full," she said.

"He seems glad to see you," Dolando said. He hesitated, then added, "I am, too, Ayla. Roshario needs you."

It was an acknowledgment of sorts, at least an admission that he did not want her to keep away from his mate, for all

his raving the night before. She had known it when he
allowed her into his dwelling, but he hadn't said it.

"Is there anything you need? Anything I can get for
you?" the man asked. He had noticed her hands were full.

"I'd like to dry these plants and need a rack," she said.
"I can make one, but for that I need some wood, and thongs
or sinew for lashings."

"I may have something better. Shamud used to dry plants
for his uses, and I think I know where his racks are. Would
you like to use one?"

"I think that would be perfect, Dolando," she said. He
nodded and strode away as she went inside. She smiled when
she saw Roshario sitting up on her bed. Putting the plants
down, she went to see her.

"I didn't know Wolf had come back in here," Ayla said.
"I hope he didn't bother you."

"No. He was watching out for me, I'm sure. When he
first came in—he knows how to get around the flap—he came
straight back here. After I patted him, he went and settled
down in that corner and just looked this way. That's his place
now, you know," Roshario said.

"Did you sleep well?" Ayla asked the woman, straightening her bed and propping her up with pads and furs to
make her more comfortable.

"Better than I have since I fell. Especially after Dolando
and I had a long talk," she said. She looked at the tall blond
woman, the stranger that Jondalar had brought with him, who
had stirred up their life and precipitated so much change in
such a short time. "He really didn't mean what he said about
you, Ayla, but he is upset. He has lived with Doraldo's death
for years, never able to really put it away. He didn't know
the full circumstances until last night. Now he's trying to
reconcile years of hatred, and violence, toward what he was
convinced were vicious animals, with all that came out about
them, including you."

"How about you, Roshario? He was your son," Ayla
said.

"I hated them, too, but then Jetamio's mother died, and
we took her in. She didn't take his place, exactly, but she
was so sick and needed so much care that I didn't have time
to dwell on his death. As I came to feel as though she was
my own daughter, I was able to let the memory of my son
rest. Dolando grew to love Jetamio, too, but boys are special

to men, especially boys born to their hearth. He couldn't get over the loss of Doraldo, just as he had reached manhood and had his life in front of him." Tears were glistening in Roshario's eyes. "Now Jetamio's gone, too. I was almost afraid to take Darvo in, for fear he would die young."

"It's never easy to lose a son," Ayla said, "or a daughter."

Roshario thought she saw a look of pain flash across the young woman's face as she got up and went to the fire to start preparations. When she came back, she brought her medicines in her interesting wooden bowls. The woman had never seen any quite like them. Most of their tools, utensils, and containers were decorated with carvings or paintings, or both, particularly Shamud's. Ayla's bowls were finely made, smooth and well shaped, but starkly plain. There were no decorations of any kind, except for the grain of the wood itself.

"Are you feeling much pain now?" Ayla asked as she helped Roshario lie down.

"Some, but not nearly as much as before," the woman said, as the young healer started to remove the wrappings.

"I think the swelling is down," Ayla said, studying the arm. "That's a good sign. I'll put the splints and a sling back on it for now, in case you want to get up for a while. I'll put another poultice on tonight. When there is no more swelling, I'll wrap it in birchbark, which you should keep on until the bone is healed; at least a moon and halfway into another," Ayla explained, as she deftly took away the damp chamois skin and looked at a spreading bruise caused by her manipulations the day before.

"Birchbark?" Roshario said.

"When it is soaked in hot water, it softens and is easy to shape and fit. It gets hard and stiff as it dries, and will hold your arm rigid so the bone will heal straight, even when you are up and moving around."

"You mean I'll be able to get up and do something, instead of just lying around?" Roshario said with a delighted grin.

"You will only have the use of one arm, but there's no reason you can't stand on both legs. It was the pain that kept you here."

Roshario nodded. "That's true."

"There is one thing I want you to try before I put the

wrappings back on. If you can, I want you to move your fingers; it might hurt a little."

Ayla tried not to show her concern. If there was some internal damage that prevented Roshario from moving her fingers now, it might be an indication that she would have only limited use of that arm. They were both watching her hand intently, and both smiled with relief when she moved her middle finger up, and then the rest of them.

"That's good!" Ayla said. "Now, can you curl your fingers?"

"I can feel that!" Roshario said as she flexed her fingers.

"Does it hurt too much to make a fist?" Ayla watched while she slowly closed her hand.

"It hurts, but I can do it."

"That's very good. How much can you move your hand? Can you bend it up at the wrist?"

Roshario grimaced with the effort and breathed in through her teeth, but she bent her hand forward.

"That's enough," Ayla said.

They both turned to look when they heard Wolf announce Jondalar's appearance with a single bark that sounded like a hoarse cough, and smiled when he entered.

"I came to see if there is anything I can do. Do you want me to help Roshario outside?" Jondalar asked. He had glanced at Roshario's exposed arm, then looked away quickly. The swollen, discolored thing did not look good to him.

"Nothing now, but sometime in the next few days I will need some wide strips of fresh birchbark. If you happen to see a good-size birch tree, keep it in mind so you can show me where it is. It's to hold her arm rigid while it's healing," Ayla replied while she wrapped it with splints.

"You never did tell me what all that finger moving was about, Ayla," Roshario said. "What did it mean?"

Ayla smiled. "It means that, with luck, the chances are good that you will have full use of your arm again, or close to it."

"That is indeed good news," Dolando said. He had heard her remark as he was coming into the dwelling holding one end of a drying rack. The other end was supported by Darvalo. "Will this do?"

"Yes, and thank you for bringing it inside. Some of the plants need to dry away from the light."

"Carolio says our morning meal is ready," the young man said. "She wants to know if you want to eat outside, since it's such a nice day."

"Well, I would," Rosario said, then turned to Ayla, "if you think it's all right."

"Just let me put the arm in a sling, and then you can walk out, if Dolando will give you a little support," Ayla said. The Shamudoi leader's smile was uncharacteristically broad. "And if no one minds, I would like to take a morning swim before I eat."

"Are you sure this thing is a boat?" Markeno said, helping Jondalar to prop the hide-covered round frame against the wall alongside the long poles. "How do you steer this bowl?"

"It's not as easy to control as your boats, but it's used mostly for crossing rivers, and the paddles work well enough to push it across. Of course with the horses, we just attached it to the pole drag and let them pull it," Jondalar said.

They both glanced across the field where Ayla was currying Whinney while Racer stood by. Jondalar had brushed the stallion's coat earlier and noticed that bare spots, where hair had fallen out on the hot plains, were filling in. Ayla had treated the eyes of both horses. Now that they were in a cooler, higher elevation away from the bothersome gnats, there was obvious improvement.

"It's the horses that are most surprising," Markeno said. "I never imagined they would willingly stay near people, but those two seem to enjoy it. Although I think I was more surprised by the wolf at first."

"You are more used to Wolf now. Ayla kept him close to her because she thought he would be more frightening to people than the horses."

They saw Tholie walking toward Ayla, with Shamio and Wolf running around her. "Shamio just loves him," Markeno said. "Look at her. I ought to be afraid, that animal could tear her apart, but he's not threatening at all. He's playing with her."

"The horses can be playful, too, but you can't imagine what it's like to ride on the back of that stallion. You can try it, if you want, though there isn't much room here for him to really run."

"That's all right, Jondalar. I think I'll stick to riding in boats," Markeno said. As a man appeared at the edge of the cliff, he added, "And here comes Carlono. I think it's time for Ayla to ride in one."

They all converged near the horses, then walked together toward the cliff and stood at the place where the small stream spilled over the edge into the Great Mother River below.

"Do you really think she ought to climb down? It's a long drop and it can be scary," Jondalar said. "It's even a little unsettling for me. I haven't done it in quite a while."

"You said you wanted to give her a ride in a real boat, Jondalar," Markeno said. "And she might want to see our dock."

"It's not that difficult," Tholie said. "There are footholds and ropes to hold on to. I can show her how."

"She doesn't have to climb down," Carlono said. "We can lower her in the supply basket, the same way we brought you up the first time, Jondalar."

"That might be best," Jondalar said.

"Come down with me and we'll send it up."

Ayla had listened to the discussion while she was looking down at the river and the precarious path they used to descend—the path Roshario had fallen down, though she had been completely familiar with it. She saw the sturdy knotted ropes that were secured to wooden pegs driven into narrow crevices in the rock, starting at the top where they stood. Part of the steep descent was washed by the stream as it fell, splashing from rock to ledge.

She watched Carlono step over the edge with practiced ease, grabbing a rope with one hand while his foot found the first narrow ledge. She saw Jondalar blanch a little, take a deep breath, then follow the man down, somewhat slower and more carefully. In the meantime, Markeno, with Shamio wanting to help, picked up a large coil of thick rope. The coil ended with a loop that had been woven into the end as an integral part and dropped over a heavy stake that was about midway between the walls at the edge of the embayment. The rest of the long cable was thrown over the cliff. Ayla wondered what kind of fiber they used to make their ropes. They were the heaviest cordage she had ever seen.

Shortly afterward, Carlono came back up carrying the other end of the cable. He walked toward a second stake not far from the first, then began hauling up the rope, neatly dropping it in a coil beside him. A large, shallow, basketlike object soon appeared at the edge of the cliff between the two stakes. Full of curiosity, Ayla went to take a closer look.

Like the ropes, the basket was extremely sturdy. The flat woven bottom, which was reinforced and stiffened with wooden planks, was shaped in a long oval with straight sides around the edge like a low fence. It was easily big enough to hold a person lying down, or a medium-size sturgeon with its head and tail over the front and back. The largest sturgeon, one of two varieties that lived only in the river and its major tributaries, reached thirty feet in length and weighed over three thousand pounds, and had to be cut into pieces to be hoisted up.

The supply basket was slung between two ropes that were threaded through and held in place by four rings made of fiber, two attached to each long side. Each rope went down through one ring, and up through the ring that was diagonally on the opposite side, crossing underneath. The four ends of the ropes were plaited together and formed into a large heavy loop above, and the rope that had been thrown over the edge was threaded through that loop.

"Just climb in, Ayla. We'll hold it steady and lower you down," Markeno said, putting on a pair of close-fitting, leather mittens, then wrapping the long end once around the second stake in preparation for lowering the basket.

When she hesitated, Tholie said, "If you'd rather just climb down, I'll show you how. I never did like to ride the basket."

Ayla looked at the steep climb again. Neither way looked very inviting. "I'll try the basket this time," she said.

Where the path down was located, the wall below the cliff was steep but sloped enough to make it climbable, barely; near the middle where the stakes were, the top of the cliff overhung the wall. Ayla climbed into the basket, sat down on the bottom, and held on to the edge with a white-knuckled grip.

"Are you ready?" Carlono asked. Ayla turned her head without letting go and nodded. "Lower her down, Markeno."

The young man loosened his grip as Carlono guided the supply basket over the edge. While Markeno let the rope slide through his leather-covered hands, controlling the descent with the help of the twist around the stake, the loop at the top of the basket skidded along the heavy rope and

Ayla, suspended in empty space over the dock, was slowly lowered.

Their device for transporting supplies and people between the deep ledge above and the dock below was simple but effective. It depended upon muscle power, but the basket itself, though sturdy, was relatively lightweight, making it possible for even one person alone to move fairly large loads. With additional people, quite heavy ones could be moved.

When she first dropped over the top of the cliff, Ayla shut her eyes and clung to the basket, hearing her heart pound in her ears. But as she felt herself dropping slowly, she peeked her eyes open, then looked around in open-mouthed wonder. It was a view from a perspective she had never seen before and would probably never see again.

Hanging out over the great moving river beside the steep wall of the gorge, Ayla felt that she was floating in air. The rock wall across the river was slightly more than a mile away, but it felt very close, though in places along the Gate the walls were much closer. It was a fairly straight stretch of river and, as she looked east and then west along its length, she could feel its power. When she had nearly reached the dock, she looked up and watched a white cloud appear over the edge of the wall, and she noticed two figures—one quite small—and the wolf, looking down at her. She waved. Then she landed with a slight bump while she was still looking up.

When she saw Jondalar's smiling face, she said, "That was exciting!"

"It is pretty spectacular, isn't it?" he said, helping her out.

A crowd of people was waiting for her, but she was more interested in the place than the people. She felt a swaying movement under her feet when she stepped out of the basket onto wooden planks, and she realized they were floating on water. It was a sizable dock, large enough to hold several dwellings of a construction similar to the ones under the sandstone ledge, plus open areas. There was a fire nearby, built on a slab of sandstone and surrounded by rocks.

Several of the interesting boats she had seen before, used by the people downstream—narrow and coming together in a sharp edge at the front and back—were tied to the floating construction. They were of various sizes, no two exactly the same, ranging from barely big enough to hold one person to long ones with several seats.

As she turned to look around, she saw two very large boats that startled her. The prows extended up to become the heads of strange birds, and the boats were painted with various geometric markings, which together gave the impression of feathers. Extra eyes were painted near the water line. The largest craft had a canopy over the middle section. When she looked at Jondalar to exclaim her amazement, his eyes were closed and his forehead creased with anguish, and she knew the large boat must have had something to do with his brother.

But neither of them had much time to pause or reconsider. They were moved along by the group, which was eager to show the visitor both their unusual craft and their boating expertise. Ayla noticed people scurrying up a ladderlike connection between the dock and the boat. When she was urged toward the foot of it, she understood that she was expected to do the same. Most of the people walked up the gangway, balancing easily even though the boat and the dock sometimes moved at cross-purposes, but Ayla was grateful for the hand Carlono extended to her.

She sat between Markeno and Jondalar under the canopy that extended from one side to the other, on a bench that could easily have accommodated more. Other people sat on benches in front and back, several of them taking up very long-handled paddles. Before she knew it, they had cast off the ropes that held them to the dock and were in the middle of the river.

Carlono's sister Carolio, singing out from the front of the boat in a strong high voice, began a rhythmic chant that rose above the liquid melody of the Great Mother River. Ayla watched with fascination as the rowers pulled against the powerful current, intrigued by the way they rowed in unison to the beat of the song, and she was surprised at how swiftly and smoothly they were propelled upstream.

At the bend in the river, the sides of the rocky gorge closed in. Between the soaring walls that reared out of the depths of the voluminous river, the sound of the water grew louder and more intense. Ayla could feel the air becoming cooler and damper, and her nostrils flared at the wet clear smell of the river and the living and dying of life within it, so different from the crisp dry aromas of the plains.

Where the gorge widened out again, trees grew on both sides down to the edge of the water. "This is beginning to look familiar," Jondalar said. "Isn't that the boat-making place ahead? Are we going to stop there?"

"Not this time. We'll keep going and turn around at Half-Fish."

"Half-Fish?" Ayla said. "What is that?"

A man sitting in front of her turned around and grinned. Ayla recalled that he was Carolio's mate. "You should ask him," he said, glancing at the man beside her. Ayla watched a red glow fill Jondalar's face as he blushed with embarrassment. "It's where he became half a Ramudoi man. Hasn't he told you about it?" Several people laughed.

"Why don't you tell it, Barono?" Jondalar said. "I'm sure it won't be the first time."

"Jondalar's right about that," Markeno said. "It's one of Barono's favorite stories. Carolio says she's tired of hearing it, but everyone knows that he can't stop telling a good story, no matter how many times he's told it."

"Well, you must admit, it was funny, Jondalar," Barono said. "But you should tell it."

Jondalar smiled in spite of himself. "To everyone else, maybe." Ayla was looking at him with a puzzled smile. "I was just learning to handle small boats," he began. "I had a harpoon—a spear for fish—with me, and started upriver, and then I noticed the sturgeon were on the move. I thought it might be my chance to get the first one, not thinking about how I would ever land a big fish like that alone, or what would happen in such a small boat."

"That fish gave him the ride of his life!" Barono said, unable to resist.

"I wasn't even sure I'd be able to spear one; I wasn't used to a spear with a cord attached," Jondalar continued. "I should have worried about what would happen if I did."

"I don't understand," Ayla said.

"If you are hunting on land and spear something, like a deer, even if you just wound it, and the spear falls out, you can trail it," Carlono explained. "You can't follow a fish in water. A harpoon has barbs that face backward and a strong cord attached, so once you spear a fish, the point with the cord stays in it so it doesn't get lost in the water. The other end of the cord can be fastened to the boat."

"The sturgeon he speared pulled him upstream, boat and all," Barono interrupted again. "We were on the shore back there, and we saw him going past, hanging on to the cord that was tied to the boat. I never saw anyone going so fast in my life. It was the funniest thing I ever saw. Jondalar thought he hooked the fish, but the fish had hooked him instead!"

Ayla was smiling along with everyone else.

"By the time the fish finally lost enough blood and died, I was pretty far upstream," Jondalar continued. "The boat was almost swamped, and I ended up swimming to the shore. In the confusion, the boat went downstream but the fish ended up in a backwater next to the land. I pulled it up on the shore. By then I was pretty cold, but I'd lost my knife and couldn't find any dry wood or anything to make fire. Suddenly a flathead . . . a Clan . . . youngster appeared."

Ayla's eyes opened with surprise. The story had taken on a new meaning.

"He led me to his fire. There was an older woman at his camp and I was shivering so much that she gave me a wolf-skin. After I warmed up, we went back to the river. The fl . . . the youngster wanted half the fish and I was glad to let him have it. He cut the sturgeon in half, longways, and took his half with him. Everybody who saw me go by came looking for me, and just about then they found me. Even if they laugh about it, I was more than happy to see them."

"It's still hard to believe that only one flathead carried off half that fish by himself. I remember it took three or four men to move the half fish he left behind," Markeno said. "That was a big sturgeon."

"Men of the Clan are strong," Ayla said, "but I didn't know there were any Clan people in this region. I thought they were all on the peninsula."

"There used to be quite a few on the other side of the river," Barono said.

"What happened to them?" Ayla asked.

The people in the boat were suddenly embarrassed, looking down and away. Finally Markeno said, "After Doraldo died, Dolando got a lot of people together and . . . went after them. After a while, most of them . . . were gone . . . I guess they went away."

"Show that to me again," Roshario said, wishing she could try it with her own hands. Ayla had put the birchbark cast on her arm that morning. Though it was not quite dry,

the strong, lightweight material was already rigid enough to
hold the arm securely, and Roshario was enjoying the greater
mobility it allowed her, but Ayla did not want her to attempt
to use the hand yet.

They were sitting with Tholie out in the sun amidst several soft chamois hides. Ayla had her sewing case out and
was showing them the thread-puller she had developed with
the help of the Lion Camp.

"First you have to cut holes with an awl into both pieces
of the leather you want to sew together," Ayla said.

"The way we always do," Tholie said.

"But you use this to pull the thread through the holes.
The thread goes through this tiny hole at the back end, then
when you put the point into the cuts in the leather, it pulls
the thread with it through both pieces that you want to join
together." A thought occurred to Ayla as she was demonstrating the ivory needle. If it was sharp enough, I wonder if the
thread-puller could make the hole, too? Leather can be tough,
though.

"Let me see it," Tholie said. "How do you get the thread
through the hole?"

"Like this, see?" Ayla said, showing her, then gave it
back. Tholie tried a few stitches.

"This is so easy!" she said. "You could almost do it
with one hand."

Roshario, watching closely, thought Tholie might be
right. Though she couldn't use her broken arm, if she could
use her hand just to hold the pieces together, with a thread-
puller like that, she might be able to sew with her good hand.
"I never saw anything like that. Whatever made you think
of it?" Roshario asked.

"I don't know," Ayla said. "It was just an idea I had
when I was having trouble trying to sew something, but a lot
of people helped. I think the hardest part was making a drill
out of flint small enough to make the tiny hole at the end.
Jondalar and Wymez worked on that."

"Wymez is Lion Camp's flint knapper," Tholie explained
to Roshario. "I understand he is very good."

"I know Jondalar is," Roshario said. "He worked out so
many improvements on the tools we use to make boats that
everyone was raving about him. Just little things, but it made
a big difference. He was teaching Darvo before he left. Jon-

dalar's good at teaching youngsters. Maybe he'll be able to show him more.''

"Jondalar said he learned much from Wymez," Ayla said.

"That may be, but you both seem to be good at thinking up better ways to do things," Tholie said. "This thread-puller of yours is going to make sewing a lot easier. Even when you know how, it's always hard to push a thread through holes with an awl, and that spear-thrower of Jonda-lar's has everyone excited. When you showed how good you are with it, you made people think that anyone could do it, though I don't think it's as easy as you made it seem. I think you must have practiced more than a little.''

Jondalar and Ayla had demonstrated the spear-thrower. It took a great deal of skill and patience to get close enough to a chamois to make a kill, and when the Shamudoi hunters saw how far a spear could be thrown with it, they were eager to try it on the elusive mountain antelopes. Several of the Ramudoi sturgeon hunters were so enthusiastic about it that they decided to adapt a harpoon to it, to see how it would work. In the discussion, Jondalar brought up his idea of a spear in two parts, with a long back shaft fletched with two or three feathers, and a smaller detachable front end tipped with a point. The potential was immediately understood, and several approaches were tried by both groups over the next few days.

Suddenly there was a commotion at the far end of the field. The three women looked up and saw several people hauling up the supply basket. Some youngsters were running toward them.

"They caught one! They caught one with the harpoon-thrower!" Darvalo shouted as he approached the women. "And it's a female!"

"Let's go see!" Tholie said.

"You go ahead. I'll catch up as soon as I put my thread-puller away.''

"I'll wait for you, Ayla," Rosharlo said.

By the time they joined the others, the first part of the sturgeon had been unloaded and the basket sent down again. It was a huge fish, too much to bring up at one time, but the best part had gone up first: nearly two hundred pounds of tiny black sturgeon eggs. It seemed propitious that the large

female was the result of the first sturgeon hunt with the new
weapon developed from Jondalar's spear-thrower.

Fish-drying racks were brought out to the end of the field,
and most of the people there were beginning to cut the great
fish into small pieces. The great mass of caviar, however,
was brought back to the living area. It was Roshario's responsibility to oversee its distribution. She asked Ayla and Tholie
to help her, and she dished out some for all of them to taste.

"I haven't eaten this in years!" Ayla said, taking another
bite. "It's always best when it's fresh from the fish, and
there's so much."

"And a good thing, too, or we wouldn't get to eat much
of it," Tholie said.

"Why not?" Ayla asked.

"Because sturgeon roe is one of the things we use to
make the chamois skin so soft," Tholie said. "Most of it is
used for that."

"I'd like to see how you make that skin so soft sometime," Ayla said. "I have always liked to work with leather
and furs. When I lived with the Lion Camp, I learned how
to color skins and made a really red one, and Crozie showed
me how to make white leather. I like your yellow color,
too."

"I'm surprised Crozie was willing to show you," Tholie
said. She looked significantly at Roshario. "I thought white
leather was a secret of the Crane Hearth."

"She didn't say it was a secret. She said her mother
taught her, and her daughter wasn't too interested in working
leather. She seemed pleased to pass the knowledge on to
someone."

"Well, since you were both members of Lion Camp, you
were the same as family," Tholie said, though she was quite
surprised. "I don't think she would have shown an outsider,
any more than we would. The Sharamudoi method of treating
chamois is a secret. Our skins are admired and have a high
trade value. If everyone knew how to make them, they would
not be as valuable, so we don't share it," Tholie said.

Ayla nodded, but her disappointment showed. "Well, it
is nice, and the yellow is so bright and pretty."

"The yellow comes from bog myrtle, but we don't use
it for its color. That just happens. Bog myrtle helps to keep
the hides soft even after they get wet," Roshario volunteered.

She paused, then added, "If you stayed here, Ayla, we could teach you to make yellow chamois skin."

"Stayed? How long?"

"As long as you want; as long as you live, Ayla," Rosh-ario said, giving her an earnest look. "Jondalar is kin; we think of him as one of us. It wouldn't take much for him to become Sharamudoi. He has even helped to make a boat already. You said you weren't mated yet. I'm sure we could find someone willing to cross-couple with you, and then you could be mated here. I know you would be welcome among us. Ever since our old Shamud died, we've needed a healer."

"We would be willing to cross-couple," Tholie said. Although Rosharia's offer was spontaneous, it seemed entirely appropriate the moment she mentioned it. "I'd have to talk to Markeno, but I'm sure he'd agree. After Jetamio and Tho-nolan, it's been hard to find another couple we wanted to join with. Thonolan's brother would be perfect. Markeno has always liked Jondalar, and I would enjoy sharing a dwelling with another Mamutoi woman." She smiled at Ayla. "And Shamio would love having her 'Wuffie' around all the time."

The offer caught Ayla by surprise. When she fully grasped the meaning, she was overwhelmed. She felt tears begin to sting. "Rosharia, I don't know what to say. It has felt like home here since I first came. Tholie, I would love to share with you . . ." The tears overflowed.

The two Sharamudoi women felt the contagion of tears and blinked them back, smiling at each other as though they had conspired in a wonderful plan.

"As soon as Markeno and Jondalar come back, we'll tell them," Tholie said. "Markeno will be so relieved . . ."

"I don't know about Jondalar," Ayla said. "I know he wanted to come here. He even gave up taking a shorter way just to see you, but I don't know if he will want to stay. He says he wants to go back to his people."

"But we are his people," Tholie said.

"No, Tholie. Even though he was here as long as his brother, Jondalar is still Zelandonii. He could never quite let go of them. I thought that might have been why his feelings for Serenio were not as strong," Rosharia said.

"That was Darvalo's mother?" Ayla asked.

"Yes," the older woman said, wondering how much Jon-dalar had told her about Serenio, "but since it's obvious how he feels about you, maybe, after all this time, his ties to his own people are weaker. Haven't you traveled enough? Why should you make such a long Journey when you can have a home right here?''

"Besides, it's time for Markeno and me to choose a cross-couple . . . before winter, and before . . . I didn't tell you, but the Mother has blessed me again . . . and we should join before this one comes.''

"I thought as much. That's wonderful, Tholie,'' Ayla said. Then her eyes unfocused in a dreamy look. "Maybe, someday, I'll have a baby to cuddle . . .''

"If we are cross-mates, the one I'm carrying would be yours, too, Ayla. And it would be nice to know there was someone around who could help, just in case . . . although I didn't have any trouble at all birthing Shamio.''

Ayla thought that she would like to have a baby of her own someday, Jondalar's baby, but what if she couldn't? She had been careful to drink her morning tea every day, and she had not gotten pregnant, but what if it wasn't the tea? What if she just wasn't able to make a baby start? Wouldn't it be wonderful to know that Tholie's children would be hers and Jondalar's? It was true, too, that the area nearby was so much like the region around the cave of Brun's clan, that it felt like home. The people were nice . . . although she wasn't sure of Dolando. Would he really want her to stay? And she wasn't sure about the horses. It was nice to be able to let them rest, but would there be enough feed to last the winter? And was there a big enough place to run?

Most important, what about Jondalar? Would he be willing to give up his Journey back to the land of the Zelandonii and settle here instead?

19

Tholie walked to the front of the large fireplace and stood silhouetted against the red glow of dying embers and evening sky framed by the high side walls of the embayment. Most of the people were still in the gathering space just under the sandstone overhang, finishing the last of their blackberries or sipping a favorite tea or slightly foaming, newly fermented berry wine. Their feast of fresh sturgeon had begun with their first, and only, taste of caviar from the female caught earlier. The balance of the oily fish eggs would be put to more mundane use in the making of soft chamois skins.

"I want to say something, Dolando, while we're all gathered together here," Tholie said.

The man nodded, although it wouldn't have mattered. Tholie continued without waiting for his acknowledgment.

"I think I can speak for everyone when I say how glad we are to have Jondalar and Ayla here," she said. Several people spoke out in agreement. "We were all worried about Rosharo, not only because of the pain she was suffering, but because we feared she would lose the use of her arm. Ayla changed that. Roshario says she feels no more pain and, with luck, there is a good chance that she will have full use of her arm again.''

There was a chorus of positive comments expressing gratitude and invocations for good luck.

"We owe our kinsman, Jondalar, thanks too,'' Tholie went on. "When he was here before, his ideas for changes in the tools we use were a big help, and now he has shown us his thrower, and the result is this feast.'' Again the group made vocal expressions of affirmation. "In the time he has lived with us, he has hunted both sturgeon and chamois, but he has never said whether he prefers the water or the land. I think he would make a good River man . . .''

"You're right, Tholie. Jondalar's a Ramudoi!'' one man shouted out. "Or at least half of one!'' Barono added, to an uproar of laughter. "No, no, he's been learning about the water, but he knows the land,'' a woman said. "That's right! Ask him! He threw a spear before he cast his first harpoon, he's a Shamudoi!'' an older man added. "He even likes women who hunt!''

Ayla glanced up to see who had made the last comment. It was a young woman, a little older than Darvalo, named Rakario. She liked to be around Jondalar all the time, which annoyed the young man. He had complained that she was always in the way.

Jondalar was smiling broadly at the good-humored argument. The commotion was a demonstration of the friendly competition between the moieties; a rivalry within the family that added a little excitement but was never allowed to go beyond well-understood limits. Jokes, bragging, and a certain level of insults were permissible, but anything that might unduly offend or cause real anger was quickly squelched, with both sides joining forces to calm tempers and alleviate hurt feelings.

"As I said, I think Jondalar would make a good River man,'' Tholie continued when everyone had settled down, "but Ayla is most familiar with the land, and I'd like to encourage Jondalar to stay with the land hunters, if he is willing and they will accept him. If Jondalar and Ayla would stay and become Sharamudoi, we would make an offer to cross-mate with them, but since Markeno and I are Ramudoi, they would have to be Shamudoi.''

There was a great outburst of excitement among the people, with encouraging remarks and even congratulations directed at the two couples.

"That's a wonderful plan, Tholie," Carolio said.

"It was Roshario who gave me the idea," Tholie said.

"But what does Dolando think about accepting Jondalar, and Ayla, a woman who was raised by the ones who live on the peninsula?" Carolio asked, looking directly at the Shamudoi leader.

There was a sudden silence. Everyone knew the implications of her question. After his violent reaction to Ayla, would Dolando be willing to accept her? Ayla had hoped his angry raving would be forgotten and wondered why Carolio had brought it up, but she had to do it. It was her responsibility.

Carlono and his mate had originally been cross-coupled with Dolando and Roshario, and together they had founded this particular group of Sharamudoi when they and a few others moved away from their rather crowded birthplace. Positions of leadership were usually conferred by informal consensus, and they were the natural choice. In practice, a leader's mate usually took on the responsibilities of a co leader, but Carlono's woman had died when Markeno was quite young. The Ramudoi leader never formally mated again and his twin sister, Carolio, who had stepped in to care for the boy, began to take on the duties of a leader's mate as well. As time went on, she was accepted as coleader, and, as such, it was her duty to ask the question.

The people knew Dolando had allowed Ayla to continue treating his woman, but Roshario had needed help and Ayla was obviously helping her. That did not necessarily mean he would want her around permanently. He could be merely controlling his feelings for the time being, and even though they needed a healer, Dolando was one of their own. They did not want to take in a stranger who might cause a problem for their leader and possible dissension within the group.

While Dolando was considering his answer, Ayla's stomach churned up a lump in her throat. She had the uneasy feeling that she had done something wrong and was being judged for it. Yet she knew it wasn't for anything she had done. She became upset and a little angry, and she wanted to get up and walk away. The wrong thing was being who she was. The same kind of thing had happened with the Mamutoi. Is this how it would always be? Is this what would

happen with Jondalar's people? Well, she thought, Iza and
Creb and Brun's clan had taken care of her, and she wasn't
going to deny the ones she loved, but she felt isolated and
vulnerable.

Then she sensed someone had moved quietly to her side.
She turned and smiled gratefully at Jondalar and felt better,
but she knew it was still a trial, and that he was waiting to
see how it would come out. She had been watching him
closely, and she knew what his answer to Tholie's offer
would be. But Jondalar was waiting for Dolando's response
before he framed his own reply.

Suddenly, in the middle of the tension, there was a peal
of laughter from Shamio. Then she and several other children
came rushing out of one of the dwellings with Wolf in their
midst.

"Isn't it amazing how that wolf plays with children?"
Rosario said. "A few days ago I would never have believed
that I could watch an animal like that in the middle of children that I love and not be afraid for their lives. Perhaps
that's something to remember. When you get to know an
animal that you once hated and feared, it's possible to
become very fond of it. I think it's better to try to understand
than to blindly hate."

Dolando had been quietly pondering how to respond to
Carolio's question. He knew what he was being asked, and
how much rested on his answer, but he was not quite sure
how to frame what he thought and felt. He smiled at the
woman he loved, grateful that she knew him so well. She
had sensed his need and shown him a way to reply.

"I have blindly hated," he began, "and I have blindly
taken the lives of those I hated, because I thought they had
taken the life of one that I loved. I thought they were vicious
animals and I wanted to kill them all, but it did not bring
Doraldo back. Now I learn they did not deserve such hate.
Animals or not, they were provoked. I must live with that,
but . . ."

Dolando stopped, started to say something about those
who knew more than they had told him, yet aided him in his
rampages . . . then he changed his mind.

"This woman," he went on, looking at Ayla, "this healer
says she was raised by them, trained by those I thought were
vicious animals, those I hated. Even if I still hated them, I

could not hate her. Because of her, Roshario has been given back to me. Maybe it is time to try to understand.

"I think Tholie's idea is a good one. I would be happy if the Shamudoi accepted Ayla and Jondalar."

Ayla felt the relief wash over her. Now she truly understood why this man had been chosen by his people to lead them. In their day-to-day lives, they had come to know him well, and they knew the basic quality of the man.

"Well, Jondalar?" Roshario said. "What do you say? Don't you think it's time to give up this long Journey of yours? It's time to settle, time to set up your own hearth, time to give the Mother a chance to bless Ayla with a baby or two."

"I cannot find words to tell you how grateful I am," Jondalar began, "that you would welcome us, Roshario. I feel that the Sharamudoi are my people, my kin. It would be very easy to make a home here among you, and you tempt me with your offer. But I must return to the Zelandonii"— he hesitated for a moment—"if only for Thonolan's sake."

He paused, and Ayla turned to look at him. She had known he would refuse, but that was not what she expected him to say. She noticed a subtle, nearly indiscernible nod, as though he'd thought of something else. Then he smiled at her.

"When he died, Ayla gave Thonolan's spirit what comfort she could for his Journey through the next world, but his spirit was not laid to rest, and I am afraid, I have a feeling, that he wanders lost and alone, trying to find his way back to the Mother."

His remark surprised Ayla, and she watched him closely as he continued.

"I cannot leave it like that. Someone needs to help him find his way, but I know of only one who might know how: Zelandoni, a shamud, a very powerful shamud, who was there when he was born. Perhaps, with the help of Marthona—his mother and mine—Zelandoni might be able to find his spirit and guide it on the right path."

Ayla knew that wasn't the reason he wanted to return, at least not the main reason. She sensed that what he said was perfectly true but, she suddenly realized, like the answer she had given him when he asked her about the golden thread plant, it was not complete.

"You've been gone a long time, Jondalar," Tholie said, her disappointment clear. "Even if they could help him, how do you know if your mother, or this Zelandoni, are still alive?"

"I don't know, Tholie, but I have to try. Even if they can't help, I think Marthona and the rest of his kin would like to know how happy he was here, with Jetamio, and you and Markeno. My mother would have liked Jetamio, I'm sure, and I know she would like you, Tholie." The woman tried not to show it, but she could not help being pleased by his comment, even if she was disappointed. "Thonolan made a great Journey—and it always was his Journey. I only followed along to look out for him. I want to tell about his Journey. He traveled all the way to the end of the Great Mother River, but even more important, he found a place here, with people who loved him. It is a story that deserves to be told."

"Jondalar, I think you are still trying to follow your brother, to look out for him even in the next world," Roshario said. "If that is what you must do, we can only wish you well. I think Shamud would have told us that you must follow your own path."

Ayla considered what Jondalar had done. The offer made by Tholie and the Sharamudoi, to become one of them, was not made lightly. It was generous and very much an honor, and for those reasons it was hard to refuse without offending. Only a strong need to fulfill a higher goal, to follow a more compelling quest, could make the rejection acceptable. Jondalar chose not to mention that even though he thought of them as kin, they were not the kin he was homesick for, but his incomplete truth had provided a graceful and face-saving refusal.

In the Clan, not mentioning was acceptable to allow an element of privacy in a society where it was difficult to hide anything, because emotions and thoughts could be discerned so easily from postures, expressions, and subtle gestures. Jondalar had chosen to show a necessary consideration. She had the feeling that Roshario had suspected the truth, that she had accepted his excuse for the same reason that he had given it. The subtlety was not lost on Ayla, but she wanted to think about it, and she realized that generous offers could have more than one side to them.

"How long will you stay, Jondalar?" Markeno asked.

"We have traveled farther than I thought we would by now. I did not expect to get here until fall. I think, because of the horses, we are moving faster than I expected," he explained, "but we still have a long way to go, and there are difficult obstacles ahead. I would like to leave as soon as we can."

"Jondalar, we can't leave so soon," Ayla interjected. "I can't go until Roshario's arm is healed."

"How long will that take?" Jondalar said with a frown.

"I told Roshario her arm would have to be held rigid in that birchbark for a moon and halfway into the next," Ayla said.

"That's too long. We can't stay that long!"

"How long can we stay?" Ayla asked.

"Not very long at all."

"But who will take the bark off? Who will know when the time is right?"

"We have sent a runner for a shamud," Dolando offered. "Wouldn't another healer know?"

"I suppose so," Ayla said, "but I would like to talk to this shamud. Jondalar, can't we stay at least until he comes?"

"If it's not too long, but maybe you should consider telling Dolando or Tholie what to do, just in case."

Jondalar was brushing Racer, and it seemed that the stallion's coat was growing in and thickening fast. He thought he had detected a decided nip in the air that morning, and the stallion seemed particularly frisky.

"I think you are as eager as I am to be moving, aren't you, Racer?" he said. The horse flicked his ears in Jondalar's direction at the sound of his name, and Whinney tossed her head and nickered. "You want to go, too, don't you, Whinney? This really isn't a place for horses. You need more open country to run in. I think I should remind Ayla of that."

He gave Racer a final slap on the rump, then headed back toward the overhang. Roshario seems much better, he thought when he noticed the woman sitting alone near the large fireplace, sewing with one hand, using one of Ayla's threadpullers. "Do you know where Ayla is?" he asked her.

"She and Tholie went off with Wolf and Shamio. They said they were going to the boat-making place, but I think Tholie wanted to show Ayla the Wishing Tree and make an

offering for an easy birth and a healthy baby. Tholie is beginning to show her blessing,'' Roshario said.

Jondalar hunkered down beside her. ''Roshario, there is
something I've been meaning to ask you,'' he said, ''about
Serenio. I felt terrible leaving her like I did. Was she . . .
happy, when she left here?''

''She was upset, and very unhappy at first. She said you
offered to stay, but she told you to go with Thonolan. He
needed you more. Then Tholie's cousin unexpectedly arrived.
He's like her in many ways, says what he thinks.''

Jondalar smiled. ''That's the way they are.''

''He looks like her, too. He's a good head shorter than
Serenio, but strong. He made up his mind in a hurry, too.
He took one look at her and decided she was the one for
him—he called her his 'beautiful willow tree,' the Mamutoi
word for it. I never thought he would convince her, I almost
told him not to bother—not that anything I said would have
stopped him—but I thought it was hopeless, that she'd never
be satisfied with anyone else after you. Then one day I saw
them laughing together, and I knew I was wrong. It was like
she came to life after a long winter. She blossomed. I don't
think I've seen her so happy since her first man, when she
had Darvo.''

''I'm glad for her,'' Jondalar said. ''She deserves to be
happy. I was wondering, though, when I left . . . she said
she thought the Mother might have blessed her. Was Serenio
pregnant? Had she started a new life, maybe from my spirit?''

''I don't know, Jondalar. I remember when you left she
said she thought she might be. If she was, it would be a
special blessing on her new mating, but she never told me.''

''But what do you think, Roshario? Did she look like she
was? I mean, can you tell just from looking that soon?''

''I wish I could tell you for sure, Jondalar, but I don't
know. I can only say she could have been.''

Roshario studied him closely, wondering why he was so
curious. It wasn't as if the child was born to his hearth—he
had given up that claim when he left—although if she had
been pregnant, the baby Serenio would have by now was
likely to be of his spirit. Suddenly she smiled at the idea of
a son of Serenio, grown to the size of Jondalar, born to the
hearth of the short Mamutoi man. Roshario thought it would
probably please him.

Jondalar opened his eyes to the rumpled bedding of the empty place beside him. He pushed the covers aside, sat up on the edge of the bed platform, yawned and stretched. Looking around, he realized he must have slept late. Everyone else was up and gone. There had been talk around the fire the night before of chamois hunting. Someone had seen them moving down from the high crags, which meant the season for hunting the sure-footed mountain-goat-like antelopes would soon begin.

Ayla had been excited about going on a chamois hunt, but when they went to bed and talked to each other in quiet tones, as they often did, Jondalar had reminded her that they had to leave soon. If the chamois were coming down, it meant it was getting cold in the high meadows, which signaled a turn of the seasons. They had a long way to travel yet, and they needed to be on their way.

They hadn't argued, exactly, but Ayla had indicated she didn't want to go. She talked about Rosharia's arm, and he knew she wanted to hunt chamois. In fact, he felt sure that she wanted to stay with the Sharamudoi, and he wondered if she was trying to delay their departure in the hope that he would change his mind. She and Tholie were already fast friends, and everyone seemed to like her. It pleased him that she was so well liked, but it was going to make the leaving more difficult, and the longer they stayed, the harder it would get.

He lay awake far into the night, thinking. He wondered if they should stay, for her sake, but then, they could have stayed with the Mamutoi just as well. He finally came to the conclusion that they would have to leave as soon as possible, within the next day or two. He knew Ayla was not going to be happy about it, and he wasn't sure how to tell her.

He got up, put on his trousers, and started toward the entrance. Pushing aside the drape, he stepped outside and felt a sharp cool wind on his bare chest. He was going to need warmer clothes, he thought, hurrying to the place where the men passed their morning water. Instead of the cloud of colorful butterflies that usually fluttered nearby—he had wondered why they should be so attracted to the strong-smelling place—he suddenly noticed a colorful leaf fluttering down, and then he saw that most of those left on the trees were starting to turn.

Why hadn't he noticed that before? The days had passed so quickly and the weather had been so pleasant that he hadn't paid attention to the changing season. He suddenly recalled that they were facing south in a southern region of the land. It could be much later into the season than he thought, and much colder to the north, where they were heading. As he hurried back to the dwelling, he was more determined than ever that they had to leave very soon.

"You're awake," Ayla said, entering with Darvalo while Jondalar was dressing. "I was coming to get you before all the food was put away."

"I was just putting something warm on. It's cool out there," he said. "It will soon be time to let my beard grow."

Ayla knew he was telling her more than his words said. He was still talking about the same thing they had talked about the night before; the season was changing and they had to be on their way. She didn't want to talk about it.

"We should probably unpack our winter clothes and make sure they are undamaged, Ayla. Are the pack baskets still at Dolando's?" he said.

He knows they are. Why is he asking me? You know why, Ayla said to herself, trying to think of something to change the subject.

"Yes, they are," Darvalo said, trying to be helpful.

"I need a warmer shirt. Do you remember what basket my winter clothes were in, Ayla?"

Of course she did. So did he.

"The clothes you are wearing now aren't anything like the ones you wore when you first came, Jondalar," Darvalo said.

"These were given to me by a Mamutoi woman. When I came before, I was still wearing my Zelandonii clothes."

"I tried on the shirt you gave me this morning. It's still too big for me, but not as much," the young man said.

"Do you still have that shirt, Darvo? I've almost forgotten what it looks like."

"Do you want to see it?"

"Yes. Yes, I would," Jondalar said.

In spite of herself, Ayla was curious, too.

They walked the few steps to Dolando's wooden shelter. From a shelf above his bed, Darvalo took down a carefully wrapped package. He untied the cord, opened the soft leather wrapping, and held up the shirt.

It was unusual, Ayla thought. The decorative patterns, as well as the longer style and looser cut were not at all like the Mamutoi clothing she was used to. One thing surprised her more than anything else. It was decorated with black-tipped white ermine tails.

It even looked strange to Jondalar. So much had happened since he had last worn that shirt, it seemed almost quaint, old-fashioned. He hadn't worn it much in the years he lived with the Sharamudoi, preferring to dress like the others, and though it was only a few moons longer than a year since he had given it to Darvo, it felt like ages since he had seen clothing from his homeland.

"It's supposed to fit loose, Darvo. You wear it belted. Go ahead and put it on. I'll show you. Do you have something to tie around you?" Jondalar said.

The young man pulled the highly decorated and patterned tunic-style leather shirt over his head, then handed Jondalar a long leather thong. The man told Darvo to stretch up, then belted it fairly low, almost at the hips, so that it bloused in a way that made the ermine tails hang free.

"See? It's not so big on you, Darvo," Jondalar said. "What do you think, Ayla?"

"It's unusual, I've never seen a shirt like that. But I think it looks fine, Darvalo," she said.

"I like it," the young man said, holding out his arms and looking down, trying to see how it looked. Maybe he'd wear it the next time they went to visit the Sharamudoi downriver. She might like it, that girl he'd noticed.

"I'm glad I had a chance to show you how to wear it . . ." Jondalar said, "before we left."

"When are you leaving?" Darvalo asked, looking startled.

"Tomorrow, or the day after at the latest," Jondalar said, looking straight at Ayla. "As soon as we can get ready."

"The rains may have started on that side of the mountains," Dolando said, "and you remember what the Sister is like when she's flooding."

"I hope it won't be as bad as that," Jondalar said. "We'd need one of your big boats to cross."

"If you want to go by boat, we would take you to the Sister," Carlono said.

"We need to get more bog myrtle, anyway," Carolio added, "and that's where we go for it."

"I would be happy to go up the river in your boat, but I don't think the horses can ride in one," Jondalar said.

"Didn't you say they can swim across rivers? Maybe they could swim behind the boat," Carlono suggested. "And the wolf could ride."

"Yes, horses can swim across a river, but it's a long way to the Sister, several days as I recall," Jondalar said, "and I don't think they could swim upriver for such a long distance."

"There is a way over the mountains," Dolando said. "You'll have to do a little backtracking, then go up and around one of the lower peaks, but the trail is marked and it will, eventually, take you close to where the Sister joins the Mother. There is a high ridge just to the south that makes it easy to see even from a distance, once you reach the lowland to the west."

"But would that be the best place to cross the Sister?" Jondalar asked, remembering the wide swirling waters from the last time.

"Perhaps not, but from there you can follow the Sister north until you find a better place, although she's not an easy river. Her feeders come down out of the mountains hard and fast, her current is much swifter than the Mother's, and she's more treacherous," Carlono said. "A few of us once went upstream on her for almost a moon. She stayed swift and difficult the whole time."

"It's the Mother I need to follow to get back, and that means crossing the Sister," Jondalar said.

"Then I'll wish you well."

"You'll need food," Rosharo said, "and I have something I'd like to give you, Jondalar."

"We don't have much room to take anything extra," Jondalar said.

"It is for your mother," Rosharo said, "Jetamio's favorite necklace. I saved it to give to Thonolan, if he came back. It won't take much room. After her mother died, Jetamio needed to know she belonged somewhere. I told her to remember she was always Sharamudoi. She made the necklace out of chamois teeth and the backbones of a small sturgeon, to represent the land and the river. I thought your mother might want something that belonged to her son's chosen woman."

"You're right. She would," Jondalar said. "Thank you. I know it will mean a great deal to Marthona."

"Where is Ayla? I have something to give her, too. I hope she will have room for it," Rosharia said.

"She's in with Tholie, packing," Jondalar said. "She doesn't really want to leave, yet, not until your arm is healed. But we really can't wait any longer."

"I'm sure I'll be fine." Rosharia fell into step beside him as they walked toward the dwellings. "Ayla took off the old birchbark and put on a fresh piece yesterday. Except that it's smaller from not using it, my arm seems healed, but she wants me to keep this on for a while longer. She says once I start using my arm again, it will fill out."

"I'm sure it will."

"I don't know what is taking the runner and the Shamud so long to get here, but Ayla has explained what to do, not only to me, but to Dolando, Tholie, Carolio, and several others. We'll manage without her, I'm sure—although we would rather you both stayed. It's not too late to change your mind . . ."

"It means more to me than I can tell you, Rosharia, that you would welcome us so willingly . . . especially with Dolando, and Ayla's . . . upbringing . . ."

She stopped and looked at the tall man. "That's bothered you, hasn't it?"

Jondalar felt the red heat of embarrassment. "It did," he admitted. "It really doesn't anymore, but knowing how Dolando felt about them, that you would still accept her, makes it . . . I can't explain it. It relieves me. I don't want her to be hurt. She's been through enough."

"She's stronger for it, though." Rosharia studied him, noted the frown of concern, the troubled look in his stunning blue eyes. "You've been gone a long time, Jondalar. You've known many people, learned other customs, other ways, even other languages. Your own people may not know you anymore—you are not even the same person you were when you left here—and they will not be quite the people you remember. You will think of each other as you were, not as you are now."

"I've worried so much about Ayla, I hadn't thought of

that, but you are right. It has been a long time. She might
fit in better than I. They will be strangers, and she will learn
about them very quickly, the way she always does . . .''

"And you will have expectations," Rosharia said, starting toward the wooden shelters again. Before they entered,
the woman stopped again. "You will always be welcome
here, Jondalar. Both of you."

"Thank you, but it's such a long way to travel. You have
no idea how long, Rosharia."

"You're right. I don't. But you do, and you are used to
traveling. If you should ever decide that you want to come
back, it won't seem so long."

"For someone who never dreamt of making a long Journey, I have already traveled more than I want," Jondalar
said. "Once I get back, I think my Journeying days will be
over. You were right when you said it was time to settle, but
it might make getting used to home easier knowing that I
have a choice."

When they pushed the entrance flap aside, they found
only Markeno inside. "Where's Ayla?" Jondalar asked.

"She and Tholie went to get the plants she was drying.
Didn't you see them, Rosharia?"

"We came from the field. I thought she was here," Jondalar said.

"She was. Ayla's been telling Tholie about some of her
medicines. After she looked at your arm yesterday, and
started explaining what to do for you, they've been talking
about nothing but plants, and what they are good for. That
woman knows a lot, Jondalar."

"I know it! I don't know how she remembers it all."

"They went out this morning and came back with basket-
fuls. All kinds. Even tiny yellow threads of plants. Now she's
explaining how to prepare them," Markeno said. "It's a
shame you are leaving, Jondalar. Tholie is going to miss
Ayla. We're all going to miss you both."

"It's not easy to go, but . . .''

"I know. Thonolan. That reminds me. I want to give you
something," Markeno said, rummaging through a wooden
box filled with various tools and implements made of wood,
bone, and horn.

He pulled out an odd-looking object made of the primary
branch of an antler, with the tines cut away and a hole just
below the fork where they had joined. It was carved with

decorations, but not the geometric and stylized forms of birds and fish typical of the Sharamudoi. Instead, very beautiful and lifelike animals, deer and ibex, were inscribed around the handle. Something about it gave Jondalar a chill. When he looked closer, it became a chill of recognition.

"This is Thonolan's spear-shaft straightener!" he said. How many times had he watched his brother use that tool, he thought. He even remembered when Thonolan got it.

"I thought you might want it, to remember him. And I thought, maybe it would be helpful when you search for his spirit. Besides, when you put him . . . his spirit . . . to rest, he might want to have it," Markeno said.

"Thank you, Markeno," Jondalar said, taking the sturdy tool and examining it with wonder and reverence. It had been so much a part of his brother, it brought back flashes of memory. "This means a lot to me." He hefted it, shifted it for balance, feeling in its weight the presence of Thonolan. "I think you might be right. There is so much of him in this, I can almost feel him."

"I have something to give Ayla, and this seems to be the time for it," Roshario said, going out. Jondalar joined her.

Ayla and Tholie looked up quickly when they entered Roshario's dwelling, and for a moment the woman had the strange feeling that they were intruding on something personal or secret, but smiles of welcome dispelled it. She walked to the back and took a package off a shelf.

"This is for you, Ayla," Roshario said, "for helping me. I wrapped it so it would stay clean on your Journey. You can always use the wrapping for a towel, later."

Ayla, looking surprised and pleased, untied the cord and unfolded soft chamois skins to reveal more of the yellow leather, beautifully decorated with beads and quills. She lifted it up and caught her breath. It was the most beautiful tunic she had ever seen. Folded under it was a pair of women's trousers, fully decorated on the front of the legs and around the bottom in a pattern matching the tunic.

"Roshario! This is beautiful. I have never seen anything so beautiful. It's too beautiful to wear," Ayla said. Then she put the garments down and hugged the woman. For the first time since she arrived, Roshario noticed Ayla's strange accent, particularly in the way she said certain words, but she didn't find it unpleasant.

"I hope it fits. Why don't you try it on so we can see?"
Rosario said.

"Do you really think I should?" Ayla said, almost afraid
to touch it.

"You have to know if it will fit, so you can wear it when
you and Jondalar are mated, don't you?"

Ayla smiled at Jondalar, excited and happy about the outfit, but she refrained from mentioning that she already had a
mating tunic, given to her by Talut's mate, Nezzie of the
Lion Camp. She couldn't exactly wear both of them, but
she would find a very special occasion for the beautiful new
outfit.

"I have something for you, too, Ayla. Not nearly as
beautiful, but useful," Tholie said, giving her a handful of
soft leather straps that she had tucked away in a pouch that
dangled from her waist.

Ayla held them up and avoided looking at Jondalar. She
knew exactly what they were. "How did you know I needed
fresh straps for my moon time, Tholie?"

"A woman can always use some new ones, especially
when she's traveling. I have some nice absorbent padding for
you, too. Rosario and I talked about it. She showed me the
outfit she had made for you, and I wanted to give you something beautiful, too, but you can't take much with you when
you travel. So I started to think about what you might need,"
Tholie said, explaining her very practical gift.

"It's perfect. You couldn't have given me something I
needed, or wanted, more. You are so thoughtful, Tholie,"
Ayla said, then turned her head and blinked her eyes. "I'm
going to miss you."

"Come now, you're not leaving yet. Not until tomorrow
morning. There's plenty of time for tears then," Rosario
said, though her own eyes threatened to overflow.

That evening, Ayla emptied both her pack baskets and
had everything she wanted to take with her spread out, trying
to decide how to pack it all, including the quantities of food
they had been given. Jondalar would take some of it, but he
didn't have much room, either. They had discussed the bowl
boat several times, trying to decide if its usefulness in crossing rivers was worth the effort it would take to move it across
the wooded mountain slopes. They finally decided to take it,
but not without misgivings.

"How are you going to fit all that in only two baskets?"

Jondalar asked, looking at a pile of mysterious bundles and packages, all carefully wrapped, and worried about taking too much. "Are you sure you need it all? What's in that package?"

"All my summer clothes," Ayla said. "That's the one I'll leave behind if I have to, but I will need clothes to wear next summer. I'm just glad I don't have to pack winter clothes anymore."

"Hhmmm!" he grunted, not able to fault her reasoning, but still concerned about the load. He scanned the pile and noticed a package that he knew he had seen before. She'd been carrying it since they left, but he still didn't know what was in it. "What's that one?"

"Jondalar, you're not being much help," Ayla said. "Why don't you take these squares of traveling food Carolio gave us and see if you can find room in your pack basket for them?"

"Easy, Racer. Settle down," Jondalar said, pulling down on the lead rope and holding it in close while he patted the stallion's cheek and stroked his neck, trying to calm him. "I think he knows we're ready and he's eager to go."

"I'm sure Ayla will be along soon," Markeno said. "Those two have become very close in the short time you've been here. Tholie was crying last night, wishing you would stay. To tell you the truth, I'm sorry to see you go, too. We looked around, and we talked to several people, but we just hadn't found anyone we wanted to share with, until you came. We do need to make a commitment soon. Are you sure you don't want to change your mind?"

"You don't know how hard this decision has been for me, Markeno. Who knows what I'll find when I get there. My sister will be grown up and probably won't remember me. I have no idea what my older brother will be doing, or where he'll be. I just hope my mother is still alive," Jondalar said, "and Dalanar, the man of my hearth. My close-cousin, the daughter of his second hearth, ought to be a mother by now, but I don't even know if she has a mate. If she has, I probably won't know him. I really won't know anyone anymore, and I feel so close to everyone here. But I have to go."

Markeno nodded. Whinney nickered softly, and they both

looked up. Roshario, Ayla, and Tholie, who was holding Shamio, were coming out of his dwelling. The little girl struggled to get down when she saw Wolf.

"I don't know what I'm going to do about Shamio when that wolf is gone," Markeno said. "She wants him around all the time. She'd sleep with him if I'd let her."

"Maybe you can find a wolf cub for her," Carlono said, joining them. He had just come up from the dock.

"I hadn't thought of that. It wouldn't be easy, but maybe I could get one cub from a wolf den," Markeno mused. "At least I could promise her to try. I'm going to have to tell her something."

"If you do," Jondalar said, "I'd make sure it's a young one. Wolf was still nursing when his mother died."

"How did Ayla feed him without a mother to give him milk?" Carlono asked.

"I wondered that myself," Jondalar said. "She said a baby can eat whatever its mother eats, but it has to be softer and easier to chew. She cooked up broth, soaked a piece of soft leather in it, and let him suck it, and she cut meat up into tiny pieces for him. He eats anything we eat now, but he still likes to hunt for himself sometimes. He even flushes game for us, and he helped us get that elk we brought with us when we came."

"How do you get him to do what you want him to?" Markeno asked.

"Ayla spends a lot of time at it. She shows him and goes over it again and again until he gets it right. It's surprising how much he can learn, and he's so eager to please her," Jondalar said.

"Anyone can see that. Do you think it's just her? After all, she is shamud," Carlono said. "Could just anybody make animals do what he wants?"

"I ride on Racer's back," Jondalar said, "and I'm not shamud."

"I wouldn't be too sure of that," Markeno said, then laughed. "Remember, I've seen you around women. I think you could make any one of them do whatever you wanted."

Jondalar flushed. He hadn't really thought about that for a while.

As Ayla walked toward them, she wondered about his red face, but then Dolando joined them, coming from around the wall.

"I'll go with you part of the way to show you the trails and the best way over the mountains," he said.

"Thank you. That will be a help," Jondalar said.

"I'll go along, too," Markeno said.

"I would like to come," Darvalo said. Ayla looked in his direction and saw that he was wearing the shirt Jondalar had given him.

"So would I," Rakario said.

Darvalo looked at her with an annoyed frown, expecting to see her staring at Jondalar, but she was looking at him instead, with an adoring smile. Ayla watched his expression change from annoyance, to puzzlement, to understanding, and then to a surprised blush.

Almost everyone had congregated in the middle of the field to say farewell to their visitors, and several others voiced a wish to walk along with them for part of the way.

"I won't be going," Roshario said, looking at Jondalar and then Ayla, "but I wish you were staying. I wish you both good Journey."

"Thank you, Roshario," he said, giving the woman a hug. "We may need your good wishes before we are through."

"I need to thank you, Jondalar, for bringing Ayla. I don't even want to think about what would have happened to me if she hadn't come." She reached for Ayla's hand. The young medicine woman took it, and then the other hand still in the sling, and squeezed both of them, pleased to feel the strength in the grip of both hands in return. Then they hugged.

There were several other goodbyes, but most of the people planned to follow along the trail for at least a short way.

"Are you coming, Tholie?" Markeno asked, falling into step beside Jondalar.

"No." Her eyes glistened with tears. "I don't want to go. It won't be any easier to say goodbye on the trail than it will be right here." She went up to the tall Zelandonii man. "It's hard for me to be nice to you right now, Jondalar. I've always been so fond of you, and I liked you even more after you brought Ayla here. I wanted so much for you and her to stay, but you won't do it. Even though I understand why you won't, it doesn't make me feel very good."

"I'm sorry you feel so bad, Tholie," Jondalar said. "I wish there was something I could do to make you feel better."

"There is, but you won't do it," she said.

It was so like her to say exactly what she was thinking. It was one of the things he liked about her. You never had to guess what she really meant. "Don't be angry at me. If I could stay, nothing would please me more than to join with you and Markeno. You don't know how proud you made me feel when you asked us, or how hard it is for me to leave right now, but something pulls me. To be honest, I'm not even sure what it is, but I have to go, Tholie." He looked at her with his startling blue eyes full of genuine sorrow, concern, and caring.

"Jondalar, you shouldn't say such nice things and look at me like that. It makes me want you to stay even more. Just give me a hug," Tholie said.

He bent down and put his arms around the young woman, and he felt her shaking with her effort to control her tears. She pulled away and looked at the tall blond woman beside him.

"Oh, Ayla. I don't want you to go," she said with a huge sob as they fell into each other's arms.

"I don't want to leave, I wish we could stay. I'm not sure why, but Jondalar has to go, and I have to go with him," Ayla said, crying as hard as Tholie. Suddenly the young mother broke away, picked up Shamio, and ran back toward the shelters.

Wolf started to go after them. "Stay here, Wolf!" Ayla commanded.

"Wuffie! I want my Wuffie," the little girl cried out, reaching toward the shaggy, four-legged carnivore.

Wolf whined and looked up at Ayla. "Stay, Wolf," she said. "We are leaving."

20

Ayla and Jondalar stood in a clearing that commanded a broad view of the mountain, feeling a sense of loss and loneliness as they watched Dolando, Markeno, Carlono, and Darvalo walking back down the trail. The rest of the large crowd that had started out with them had dropped back by twos and threes along the way. When the last four men reached a turn in the trail, they turned and waved.

Ayla returned their wave in a "come back" motion with the back of her hand toward them, suddenly overcome by the knowledge that she would never see the Sharamudoi again. In the short time she had known them, she had come to love them. They had welcomed her, asked her to stay, and she could have lived with them gladly.

This leaving reminded her of their departure from the Mamutoi early in the summer. They, too, had welcomed her, and she had loved many of them. She could have been happy living with them, except that she would have had to live with the unhappiness she had caused Ranec, and when she left, there had been the excitement of going home with the man

she loved. There were no undercurrents of unhappiness
among the Sharamudoi, which made the parting all the more
difficult, and though she loved Jondalar and had no doubt
that she wanted to go with him, she had found acceptance
and friendships that were hard to end with such finality.

Journeys are full of goodbyes, Ayla thought. She had
even made her last farewell to the son she had left with the
Clan . . . though if she had stayed there, someday she might
have been able to go with the Ramudoi in a boat back down
the Great Mother River to the delta. Then, perhaps, she could
have made a trek around to the peninsula, to look for the
new cave of her son's clan . . . but there was no point in
thinking about it anymore.

There would be no more opportunities to return, no more
last chances to hope for. Her life took her in one direction,
her son's life led him in another. Iza had told her "find your
own people, find your own mate." She had found acceptance
among her own kind of people and she had found a man to
love who loved her. But for all she had gained, there were
losses. Her son was one of them; she had to accept that fact.

Jondalar felt desolate as well, watching the last four turning back toward their home. They were all friends he had
lived with for several years and had known well. Though
their relationship was not through his mother and her ties, he
felt they were as much kin as his own blood. In his commitment to return to his original roots, they were family he
would never see again, and that saddened him.

When the last of the Sharamudoi that had seen them off
moved out of sight, Wolf sat on his haunches, lifted his head,
and gave voice to a few yips that led to a full, throaty howl,
shattering the tranquillity of the sunny morning. The four
men appeared again on the trail below and waved one last
time, acknowledging the wolf's farewell. Suddenly there was
an answering howl from one of his own kind. Markeno
looked to see which direction the second howl came from
before they started back down the trail. Then Ayla and Jondalar turned and faced the mountain with its glistening peaks
of blue-green glacial ice.

Though not as high as the range to the west, the mountains in which they were traveling had been formed at the
same time, in the most recent of the mountain-building
epochs—recent only in relation to the ponderously slow
movements of the thick stony crust floating on the molten

core of the ancient earth. Uplifted and folded into a series of parallel ridges during the orogeny that had brought the whole continent into sharp relief, the rugged terrain of this farthest east expansion of the extensive mountain system was clothed with verdant life.

A skirt of deciduous trees formed a narrow band between the plains below, still warmed by the vestiges of summer, and the cooler heights. Primarily oak and beech with horn-beam and maple also prominent, the leaves were already changing into a colorful tapestry of reds and yellows accented by the deep evergreen of spruce at the higher edge. A cloak of conifers, which included not only spruce, but yew, fir, pine, and the deciduous-needled larch, starting low, climbed to the rounded shoulders of lower prominences and covered the steep sides of higher peaks with subtle variations of green that shaded to the yellowing larch. Above the timberline was a collar of summer-green alpine pasture that turned white with snow early in the season. Capping it was the hard helmet of blue-tinged glacial ice.

The heat that had brushed the southern plains below with the ephemeral touch of the short hot summer was already fading, giving way to the grasping clutch of cold. Though a warming trend had been moderating its worst effects—an interstadial period lasting several thousands of years—the glacial ice was regrouping for one last assault on the land before the retreat would be turned to a rout thousands of years later. But even during the milder lull before the final advance, glacial ice not only coated low peaks and mantled the flanks of high mountains, it held the continent in its grip.

In the rugged forested landscape, with the added hindrance of hauling the round boat on the pole drag, Ayla and Jondalar walked more than they rode the horses. They hiked up sharply pitched slopes, over ridges, across loose patches of scree, and down the steep sides of dry gullies, caused by the spring runoff of melting snow and ice, and the heavy fall rains of the southern mountains. A few of the deep ditches had water at the bottom, oozing through the mulch of rotting vegetation and soft loam, which sucked at the feet of humans and animals alike. Others carried clear streams, but all would soon be filled again with the tempestuous outflow of the downpours of autumn.

At the lower elevations, in the open forest of broad-leaved trees, they were impeded by undergrowth, forcing their way through or finding a way around brush and briars. The stiff canes and thorny vines of the delicious blackberries were a formidable barrier that tore at hair, clothes, and skin as well as hides and fur. The warm shaggy coats of the steppe horses, adapted for living on cold open plains, were easily caught and tangled, and even Wolf took his share of burrs and twigs.

They were all glad when they finally reached the elevation of evergreens, whose relatively constant shade kept the undergrowth to a minimum, although on the steep slopes where the canopy was not as dense, the sun did filter through more than it would have on level ground, allowing some brush to grow. It was not much easier to ride in the thick forest of tall trees, with the horses having to pick their way around the wooded obstacles and passengers dodging low-hanging branches. They camped the first night in a small clearing on a knoll surrounded by needled spires.

It was approaching evening of the second day before they reached the timberline. Finally free of entangling brush and past the obstacle course of taller trees, they set up their tent beside a fast, cold brook on an open pasture. When the burdens were removed from the horses, they were eager to graze. Though their customary coarser dry fodder of the lower, hotter elevations was adequate, the sweet grass and alpine herbs of the green meadow were a welcome treat.

A small herd of deer shared the pasture, the males busily rubbing their antlers on branches and outcrops to free them of the soft coating of skin and nourishing blood vessels called velvet in preparation for the fall rut.

"It will soon be their season for Pleasures," Jondalar commented as they were setting up the fireplace. "They are getting ready for the fights, and the females."

"Is fighting a Pleasure for males?" Ayla asked.

"I never thought of it that way, but it may be for some," he acknowledged.

"Do you like to fight with other men?"

Jondalar frowned as he gave the question serious consideration. "I've done my share. Sometimes you get drawn into it, for one reason or another, but I can't say I liked it, not if it's serious. I don't mind wrestling or other competitions, though."

"Men of the Clan don't fight with each other. It's not allowed, but they do have competitions," Ayla said. "Women do, too, but they are a different kind."

"How are theirs different?"

Ayla paused to think about it. "The men compete in what they do; the women in what they make," she said, then smiled, "including babies, though that is a very subtle competition, and nearly everyone thinks she is the winner."

Farther up the mountain, Jondalar noticed a family of mouflon, and he pointed out the wild sheep with huge horns that curled around close to their heads. "Those are the real fighters," Jondalar said. "When they run at each other and bang their heads together, it sounds almost like a clap of thunder."

"When stags and rams run at each other with their antlers or horns, do you think they are really fighting? Or are they competing?" Ayla asked.

"I don't know. They can hurt each other, but they don't very often. Usually one just gives up when another one shows he is stronger, and sometimes they just strut around and bellow, and don't fight at all. Maybe it is more competition than actual fight." He smiled at her. "You do ask interesting questions, woman."

A fresh cool breeze turned chilly as the sun dipped below the edge of vision. Earlier in the day, light siftings of snow had drifted down and melted in the open sunny spaces, but some had accumulated in the shady nooks, forecasting the possibility of a cold night, and heavier snows to come.

Wolf disappeared shortly after their hide shelter was set up. When he hadn't returned by dark, Ayla felt anxious about him. "Do you think I should whistle to call him back?" she asked as they were getting ready to settle down for the night.

"It's not the first time he's gone off to hunt by himself, Ayla. You're just used to him being around because you kept him close to you. He'll be back," Jondalar said.

"I hope he's back by morning," Ayla said, getting up to look around, trying in vain to see into the dark beyond their campfire.

"He's an animal; he knows his way. Come back and sit down," he said. He put another piece of wood on the fire and watched the sparks rising into the sky. "Look at those stars. Did you ever see so many?"

Ayla looked up and a feeling of wonder came over her. "It does seem like a lot. Maybe it's because we're closer up here, and we're seeing more of them, especially the smaller ones . . . or are they farther away? Do you think they go on and on?"

"I don't know. I never thought about it. Who could ever know?" Jondalar asked.

"Do you think your Zelandoni might?"

"She might, but I'm not sure she'd tell. There are some things only meant for Those Who Serve the Mother to know. You do ask the strangest questions, Ayla," Jondalar said, feeling a chill. Though he wasn't sure it was from the cold, he added, "I'm getting cold, and we need to get an early start. Dolando said the rains could begin any time. That could mean snow up here. I'd like to be down from here before that."

"I'll be right there. I just want to make sure Whinney and Racer are all right. Maybe Wolf is with them."

Ayla was still worried when she crawled into their sleeping furs, and she was slow to fall asleep as she strained to hear any sound that might be the animal returning.

It was dark, too dark to see beyond the many, many stars that were streaming out of the fire into the night sky, but she kept looking. Then two stars, two yellow lights in the dark moved together. They were eyes, the eyes of a wolf who was looking at her. He turned and started walking away and she knew he wanted her to follow, but when she started after him, her path was suddenly blocked by a huge bear.

She jerked back in fear when the bear got up on his hind legs and growled. But when she looked again, she discovered it wasn't a real bear. It was Creb, the Mog-ur, dressed in his bearskin cloak.

In the distance she heard her son calling out to her. She looked beyond the great magician and saw the wolf, but it wasn't just a wolf. It was the spirit of the Wolf, Durc's totem, and it wanted her to follow. Then the Wolf spirit turned into her son, and it was Durc who wanted her to follow. He called out to her once more, but when she tried to go to him, Creb blocked her way again. He pointed to something behind her.

She turned and saw a path leading up to a cave, not a deep cave, but an overhanging shelf of light-colored rock in the side of a cliff and above it an odd boulder that seemed frozen in the act of falling over the edge. When she looked back, Creb and Durc were gone.

•   •   •

"Creb! Durc! Where are you?" Ayla called out, bolting up.

"Ayla, you're dreaming again," Jondalar said, sitting up, too.

"They're gone. Why wouldn't he let me go with them?" Ayla said, with tears in her eyes and a sob in her voice.

"Who's gone?" he said, taking her in his arms.

"Durc is gone, and Creb wouldn't let me go with him. He blocked the way. Why wouldn't he let me go with him?" she said, crying in his arms.

"It was a dream, Ayla. It was only a dream. Maybe it means something, but it was just a dream."

"You're right. I know you're right, but it felt so real," Ayla said.

"Have you been thinking about your son, Ayla?"

"I guess I have," she said. "I've been thinking I'll never see him again."

"Maybe that's why you dreamed about him. Zelandoni always said when you have a dream like that, you should try to remember everything about it, and that someday you might understand it," Jondalar said, trying to see her face in the dark. "Go back to sleep now."

They both lay awake for some time, but finally they dozed off again. When they woke up the next morning, the sky was overcast and Jondalar was anxious to be on their way, but Wolf had still not returned. Ayla whistled for him periodically as they struck their tent and repacked their gear, but he still did not appear.

"Ayla, we need to go. He'll catch up with us, just like he always does," Jondalar said.

"I'm not going until I know where he is," she said. "You can go or wait here. I'm going to look for him."

"How can you look for him? That animal could be anywhere."

"Maybe he went back down. He did like Shamio," Ayla said. "Maybe we should go back to look for him."

"We're not going back! Not after we've come this far."

"I will if I have to. I'm not going until I find Wolf," she said.

Jondalar shook his head as Ayla started backtracking. It was obvious she was adamant. They could have been well on their way by now if it wasn't for that animal. As far as he was concerned, the Sharamudoi could have him!

Ayla kept whistling for him as she went along, and suddenly, just as she was starting back into the woods, he appeared on the other side of the clearing and raced toward her. He jumped up on her, almost knocking her over, put his paws on her shoulder, and licked her mouth, gently biting her jaw.

"Wolf! Wolf, there you are! Where have you been?" Ayla said, grabbing his ruff, rubbing her face next to his, and putting her teeth on his jaw to greet him in return. "I was so worried about you. You shouldn't run off like that."

"Do you think we can get started now?" Jondalar said. "The morning is half gone."

"At least he did come, and we didn't have to go all the way back," Ayla said, leaping up on Whinney's back. "Which way do you want to go? I'm ready."

They rode across the pasture without speaking, irritated with each other, until they came to a ridge. Riding alongside, they looked for a way over it and finally came to a steep grade with sliding gravel and boulders. It appeared very unstable, and Jondalar continued trying to find another way. If it had been just them, they might have been able to climb over at several places, but the only way that seemed at all passable for the horses was the slope of sliding rock.

"Ayla, do you think the horses can climb that? I don't think there's any other way, except going down and trying to find some way around," Jondalar said.

"You said you didn't want to go back," she said, "especially for an animal."

"I don't, but if we have to, we have to. If you think it's too dangerous for the horses, we won't try it."

"What if I thought it was too dangerous for Wolf? Would we leave him behind then?" Ayla said.

To Jondalar, the horses were useful, and though he liked the wolf, the man simply did not think it was necessary to delay their passage for him. But it was obvious that Ayla did not agree, and he had sensed an undercurrent of division between them, a feeling of strain probably because she wanted to stay with the Sharamudoi. He thought that once they put some distance between them, she would look forward to reaching their destination, but he didn't want to make her more unhappy than she was.

"It's not that I wanted to leave Wolf behind. I just thought he would catch up with us, like he has before,"

Jondalar said, although he had been nearly ready to leave him.

She sensed there was something more to it than he said, but she didn't like to have the distance of disagreement between them, and now that Wolf had come back, she was relieved. With her anxiety gone, her anger dissipated. She dismounted and started climbing up the slope to test it. She wasn't altogether certain the horses could make it, but he'd said they would look for another way if they couldn't.

"I'm not sure, but I think we should try it, Jondalar. I don't think it's quite as bad as it seems. If they can't make it, then we can go back and see if we can find some other way," she said.

It actually wasn't quite as unstable as it appeared. Although there were a few bad moments, they were both surprised at how well the horses negotiated the slope. They were glad to put it behind them, but as they continued to climb, they encountered other difficult areas. In their mutual concern for each other and the horses, they were talking comfortably again.

The slope was easy for Wolf. He had run up to the top and back down again while they were carefully leading the horses up. When they reached the top, Ayla whistled for him and waited. Jondalar watched her and it occurred to him that she seemed much more protective toward the animal. He wondered why, thought about asking her, changed his mind afraid she would get angry, then decided to bring it up anyway.

"Ayla, am I wrong, or are you more concerned about Wolf than you were? You used to let him come and go. I wish you'd tell me what's troubling you. You were the one who said we shouldn't keep things from each other."

She took a deep breath and closed her eyes, her forehead wrinkled in a frown. Then she looked up at him. "You're right. It's not that I was keeping it from you. I've been trying to keep it from myself. Remember those deer down there, that were rubbing the velvet off their antlers?"

"Yes." Jondalar nodded.

"I'm not sure, but it might be the season of Pleasures for wolves, too. I don't even want to think about it, for fear that would make it happen, but Tholie brought it up when I was talking about Baby leaving to find his own mate. She asked me if I thought Wolf would leave someday, like Baby did.

I don't want Wolf to leave, Jondalar. He's almost like a child to me, like a son.''

"What makes you think he will?"

"Before Baby left, he would go off for longer and longer times. First a day, then several days, and sometimes, when he came back, I could see he had been fighting. I knew he was looking for a mate. And he found one. Now, every time Wolf goes, I'm afraid he's looking for a mate,'' Ayla said.

"So that's it. I'm not sure we can do anything about it, but is it likely?'' Jondalar asked. Unbidden came the thought that he wished it was. He didn't want her to be unhappy, but more than once the wolf had delayed them or caused tension between them. He had to admit that if Wolf found a mate and went off with her, he would wish him well and be glad he was gone.

"I don't know,'' Ayla said. "So far, he's come back every time, and he seems happy to be traveling with us. He greets me like he thinks we are his pack, but you know how it is with Pleasures. It is a powerful Gift. The need can be very strong.''

"That's true. Well, I don't know if there is anything you can do about it, but I'm glad you told me.''

They rode together in silence for a while, up another high meadow, but it was a companionable silence. He was glad she had told him. At least he understood her strange behavior a little better. She had been acting like an overly concerned mother, though he was glad she didn't normally. He'd always felt sorry for the boys whose mothers didn't want them to do things that might be a little dangerous, like going deep in a cave, or climbing high places.

"Look, Ayla. There's an ibex,'' Jondalar said, pointing to a nimble and beautiful goatlike animal with long curved horns. It was perched on a precipitous ledge high up on the mountain. "I have hunted those before. And look over there. Those are chamois!''

"Are those really the animal the Shamudoi hunt?'' Ayla asked as she watched the antelope relative of the wild mountain goat, with smaller upright horns, gamboling across inaccessible peaks and scarp faces of rock.

"Yes. I've gone with them.''

"How can anybody hunt animals like that? How do you reach them?''

"It's a matter of climbing up behind them. They tend to

look down all the time for danger, so if you can get above them, you can usually get close enough for a kill. You can see why the spear-thrower would be a great advantage," Jondalar explained.

"It makes me appreciate that outfit Roshario gave me even more," Ayla said.

They continued their climb and by afternoon were just below the snowline. Sheer walls reared up on both sides of them with patches of ice and snow not far above. The top of the slope ahead was outlined with blue sky and seemed to lead to the very edge of the world. As they topped the rise, they halted and looked. The view was spectacular.

Behind them was a clear vista of their climb up the mountain from the treeline. Below that the evergreen-carpeted slopes cushioned the hard rock and disguised the rough terrain they had struggled over. To the east they could even see the plain below with its braided ribbons of water flowing sluggishly across it, which surprised Ayla. The Great Mother River seemed hardly more than a few trickles from their vantage point on the frigid mountaintop, and she couldn't quite believe that ages ago they had sweltered in the heat traveling beside her. In front of them was a view of the next mountain ridge somewhat below and the deep valley of feathery green spires that separated them. Looming close above were the glimmering icebound peaks.

Ayla looked around in awe, her eyes glistening with wonder, moved by the grandeur and beauty of the sight. In the chill, sharp air, puffs of steam escaping her mouth made every excited breath perceptible.

"Oh, Jondalar, we are higher than everything. I have never been so high. I feel like we're on the very top of the world!" she said. "And it's so . . . so beautiful, so exciting."

As the man watched her expressions of wonder, her sparkling eyes, her beautiful smile, his own enthusiasm for the dramatic panorama was fired by her sheer excitement, and he was moved with immediate desire for her.

"Yes, so beautiful, so exciting," he said. Something in his voice sent a shiver through her and made her turn away from the extraordinary view to look at him.

His eyes were such an impossibly rich shade of blue, it seemed for a moment that he had stolen two small pieces of the deep, luminous blue sky, and filled them with his love and wanting. She was caught by them, captured by his ineffable charm, whose source was as unknowable to her as the magic of his love, but which she could not—and did not want to—deny. Just his desire for her had always been his "signal." For Ayla, it was not an act of will but a physical reaction, a need as strong and driving as his own.

Without being aware that she moved, Ayla was in his arms, feeling his strong embrace and his warm and eager mouth on hers. There was certainly no lack of Pleasures in her life; they shared that Gift of the Mother regularly, with great enjoyment, but this moment was exceptional. Perhaps it was the excitement of the setting, but she felt a heightened awareness of every sensation. Every place she felt the pressure of his body on hers, a tingling coursed through her; his hands on her back, his arms around her, his thighs against hers. The bulge in his groin, felt through the thicknesses of fur-lined winter parkas, seemed warm, and his lips on hers gave her an indescribable sense of wanting him never to stop.

The instant he released her and stepped back enough to unfasten the closures of her outer garment, her body ached with the desire and expectation of his touch. She could hardly wait, yet she did not want him to hurry. When he reached under her tunic to cup her breast, she was glad his hands were cold for the contrasting shock to the heat she felt inside. She gasped when he squeezed a hard nipple, feeling fires that raised goosebumps as they raced through her to the place deep inside that burned with wanting more.

Jondalar sensed her powerful reactions and felt a corresponding increase in his own heat. His member surged erect and pulsed with its fullness. He felt her smooth warm tongue reaching inside his mouth and suckled it. Then he released it to seek the soft warmth of hers, and he suddenly felt an overwhelming desire to taste the warm salt and feel the moist folds of her other opening, but he did not want to stop kissing her. He wished he could have all of her all at once. He took both breasts in his hands, played with both nipples, squeezing, rubbing, then lifted her tunic and took one in his mouth and suckled hard, feeling her push against him and hearing her moan with pleasure.

He felt a throbbing and imagined his full manhood being inside her. They kissed again and she felt the strength of her need and her wanting grow. She was hungry for his touch, his hands, his body, his mouth, his manhood.

He was pushing her parka off, and she shrugged out of it, delighting in the cold wind that felt hot with his mouth on hers and his hands on her body. He untied the drawstring of her leggings; she felt them being pulled down, and off. Then they were both down on her parka, and his hands were caressing her hips, and her stomach, and the inside of her thighs. She opened to his touch.

He moved down between her legs, and the warmth of his tongue as he tasted her shot spikes of excitement through her. She was so sensitive, her reactions so powerful, it was almost unbearable, unbearably stimulating.

He sensed her strong and immediate response to his light touch. Jondalar had been trained as a flint knapper, a maker of stone tools and hunting weapons, and was among the most skilled because he was sensitive to the stone with its fine and subtle variations. Women responded to his perception and sensitive handling the way a fine piece of flint did, and both brought out the best in him. He sincerely loved to see a fine tool emerge from a good piece of flint under his deft touch, or to feel a woman aroused to her full potential, and he had spent a great deal of time practicing both.

With his natural inclination and genuine desire to be aware of a woman's feelings, particularly Ayla's, at that most intimate of moments, he knew that a featherlight touch would arouse her more, at that moment, though a different technique might be suitable later.

He kissed the inside of her thigh, then ran his tongue up and noticed that chill bumps appeared. In the cold wind, he felt her shiver, and though she had her eyes closed and did not object, he could see she was covered with gooseflesh. He got up and took off his own parka to cover her but left her bare below the waist.

Although she hadn't minded, his fur-lined outer garment, still warm from his body and filled with his masculine scent, felt wonderful. The contrast of the cold wind blowing across the skin of her thighs, wet from his tongue, made her shiver with delight. She felt the warm wetness moisten her folds, and the instant shiver from the cold filled her with a fierce heat. With a moan, she arched up to him.

With both hands, he held her folds apart, admired the beautiful pink flower of her feminine self and, unable to restrain himself, warmed the cooling petals with his wet tongue, savoring the taste of her. She felt the warmth, then the cold, and quivered in response. This was a new feeling, not something he had done before. He was using the very air of the mountaintop as a means to bring her Pleasure, and at some inner level she marveled.

But as he continued, the air was forgotten. With stronger pressure and the familiar provocation of his mouth and hands, stimulating, encouraging, inciting her senses to respond, she lost all sense of where she was. She felt only his mouth sucking, his tongue licking and prodding her place of Pleasure, his knowing fingers reaching inside, and then only the rising tide within her reaching a crest, and washing over her, while she reached for his manhood and guided it to her well. She pushed up as he filled it.

He sunk his shaft deeply, closing his eyes as he felt her warm, moist embrace. He waited a moment, then pulled back and felt the caress of her deep tunnel, and pushed in again. He plunged in, retracted, each stroke bringing him closer, the pressure inside him building. He heard her moan, felt her rise to him, and then he was there, and he exploded with the release of wave after wave of Pleasure.

In the silence, only the wind spoke. The horses had waited patiently; the wolf had watched with interest, but had learned to contain his more active curiosity. Finally Jondalar lifted himself, rested on his arms, and looked down at the woman he loved.

"Ayla, what if we started a baby?" he asked.

"Don't worry, Jondalar. I don't think we did." She was grateful she had found more of her contraceptive plants, and she was tempted to tell him, as she had told Tholie. But Tholie had been so shocked at first, even though she was a woman, that Ayla didn't dare mention it. "I'm not certain, but I don't think this would be a time when I could get pregnant," she said, and it was true she wasn't absolutely certain.

Iza did have a daughter, eventually, even though she had taken the contraceptive tea for years. Perhaps the special plants lost their effectiveness after long use, Ayla thought, or maybe Iza forgot to take it, though that was unlikely. Ayla wondered what would happen if she stopped drinking her morning tea.

Jondalar hoped she was right, although a small part of him wished she wasn't. He wondered if there would ever be a child at his hearth, a child born of his spirit, or perhaps, of his own essence.

It was a few days before they reached the next ridge, which was lower, not much above the timberline, but from it they had their first sight of the broad western steppes. It was a crisp clear day, though it had snowed earlier, and in the far distance they glimpsed another, higher range of ice-encrusted mountains. On the plains below they saw a river flowing south into what appeared to be a great swollen lake.

"Is that the Great Mother River?" Ayla asked.

"No. That's the Sister, and we have to cross her. I'm afraid it will be the hardest crossing of our whole Journey," Jondalar explained. "See over there, toward the south? Where the water is all spread out so that it looks like a lake? That's the Mother, or rather where the Sister joins her—or tries to. She backs up and overflows, and the currents are treacherous. We won't try our crossing there, but Carlono said she's a turbulent river even upstream."

As it turned out, the day they looked down toward the west from the second ridge was the last clear day. They woke the following morning to a brooding, overcast sky that drooped so low it merged with fog rising from depressions and hollows. Mist hung palpably in the air and gathered into miniature droplets on hair and fur. The landscape was draped with an insubstantial shroud that allowed trees and rocks to materialize out of indistinct shapes only as they drew near.

In the afternoon, with an unexpected and resounding roar of thunder, the sky opened, lit only heartbeats before by a sudden shaft of lightning. Ayla jerked with surprise, and she shivered with dread as bright flashes of white branching light played with the mountaintops behind them. But it wasn't the lightning that scared her, it was the anticipation of the explosive noise it presaged.

She recoiled each time she heard a distant rumble or a nearby rolling boom, and it seemed with each burst of thunder that the rain came down harder, as though frightened out of the clouds by the noise. As they worked their way down the west-facing slope of the mountains, rain fell in sheets as thick as waterfalls. Streams filled and overflowed, and rivulets spilling over ledges became gushing torrents. The footing grew slick and dangerous in places.

They were both grateful for their Mamutoi rain parkas, made of dehaired deer hides, Jondalar's from megaceros, the giant deer of the steppes, and Ayla's from the northern reindeer. They were worn over their fur parkas, when the weather was cold, or over their regular tunics when it was warmer. The exterior surfaces were colored with red and yellow ochres. The mineral pigments had been mixed with fats, and the color was worked into the hides with a special burnishing tool made of rib bone that brought the garments to a hard, shiny luster that was also quite water repellent. Even wet, it provided some protection, but the burnished, fat-soaked finish was unable to entirely resist the soaking deluge.

When they stopped for the night and put up the tent, everything was damp, even their sleeping furs, and no fire was possible. They brought wood into their tent, mostly the dead lower branches of conifers, hoping it would dry overnight. In the morning the rains still poured and their clothes were still damp, but using a firestone and the tinder she had with her, Ayla managed to get a small fire going, enough to boil a little water to make a warming tea. They ate only the square compressed cakes of traveling food Rosario had given them, which were a variation of the commonly made, filling, nutritious, compact food that could sustain a person indefinitely even if that was all he ate. It consisted of some variety of meat that was dried then ground up and mixed with fat, usually some dried fruit or berries, and occasionally partially cooked grains or roots.

The horses were standing outside the tent impassively, their heads drooping and water dripping from long winter fur, and the bowl boat had fallen over and was half-full of water. They were ready to leave it and the dragging poles behind. The travois that had been so useful for hauling loads across the open grasslands, and with the addition of the round boat effective for transporting their gear across rivers, had been an encumbrance in the rugged, forested mountains. It had hampered and slowed their travel, and it could even be dangerous going down difficult slopes in the pouring rain. If Jondalar hadn't known that for most of the rest of their Journey the passage would still be across plains, he would have left it long before.

They unfastened the boat from the poles and poured out the water, turning the boat upside down and eventually lifting it over them. Standing underneath, holding the round boat above their heads, they looked at each other and grinned. For a moment they were out of the rain. It hadn't occurred to them that the boat that held them out of the water of a river could also be a roof to keep off the rain. Not while they were moving, perhaps, but they could at least get out of the rain for a short time when it pelted down in earnest.

But that discovery didn't solve the problem of how they were going to transport it. Then, as though they both thought of it at the same time, they lifted the bowl boat over Whinney's back. If they could find a way to hold it in place, it could help to keep their tent and two of the pack baskets dry. Using the poles and some cordage, they worked out a way to support the boat across the patient mare's back. It was somewhat awkward, and they knew it would be too wide, occasionally, requiring either finding another way around, or lifting it off, but they didn't think it would be any more trouble than it had been before, and it might provide some benefit.

They haltered and packed the horses, but with no intention of riding them. Instead, the heavy wet leather tent and ground cloth were draped over Whinney's back, and the round boat was hoisted over them, supported by crossed poles. A heavy tarp made of mammoth hide, which Ayla had used to cover the pack basket in which she carried the food, was draped across Racer's back to cover both his baskets.

Before they started out, Ayla spent some time with Whinney, reassuring and thanking her, using the special language she had developed in the valley. It didn't occur to Ayla to question whether Whinney actually understood her. The language was familiar and calming, and the mare definitely responded to certain sounds and movements as signals.

Even Racer perked his ears, tossed his head, and nickered as she talked, and Jondalar assumed she was communicating with the horses in some special way that he was incapable of grasping, even though he understood a little of it. It was part of the mystery of her that kept him fascinated.

Then they started down the rough terrain in front of the horses, leading the way. Wolf, who had spent the night inside the tent and had not been as soaked to begin with, soon looked even worse than the horses. His usually thick and fluffy fur was plastered to his body, seeming to diminish his size and showing the outlines of bone and sinewy muscle. The damp fur parkas of the man and woman were warm enough, if not completely comfortable, especially with the wet and matted fur inside the hoods. After a while water trickled down their necks, but there was little they could do about it. As the dreary skies continued to leak, Ayla decided that rain was her least favorite kind of weather.

It rained during the next few days almost constantly, all the way down the side of the mountain. When they reached the tall conifers, there was some protection under the canopy, but they left most of the trees behind them where a broad terrace leveled out, though the river was still far below them. Ayla began to realize that the river she had seen from above must be much farther and even bigger than she thought. Though it had slacked up occasionally, the rain did not stop, and without the protection of the trees, scant though it was, they were wet and miserable, but they gained one advantage. They were able to ride the horses, at least part of the time.

They rode west down a series of loess terraces that fell off from the mountains, the higher ones dissected by countless small streams filled and overflowing with drainage from the highland, the result of the deluge that poured from the sky. They slogged through mud and crossed several swirling waterways rushing down from the heights. Then they dropped down to another terrace and unexpectedly came upon a small settlement.

The rough wooden shelters, little more than lean-tos, obviously put together quickly, looked ramshackle, but they offered some protection from the constantly falling water and were a welcome sight to the travelers. Ayla and Jondalar hurried toward them. They dismounted, conscious of the fear that the tame animals might cause people to feel, and called out in Sharamudoi, hoping it would be a familiar language. But there was no answer, and when they looked closer, it was obvious that no one was about.

"I'm sure the Mother realizes we need shelter. Doni will not object if we go in," Jondalar said, stepping inside one of the shacks and looking around. It was completely empty, except for a leather thong hanging from a peg, and its dirt floor was sloppy mud where a stream had run through it before it was diverted. They went out and headed for the largest one.

As they approached it, Ayla became aware that something important was missing. "Jondalar, where is the donii? There is no figure of the Mother guarding the entrance."

He looked around and nodded. "This must be a temporary summer camp. They did not leave a donii because they did not call upon Her to protect it. Whoever built these doesn't expect them to last the winter. They have abandoned this place, gone and taken everything with them. They probably moved to higher ground when the rains began.''

They entered the larger structure and found it was more substantial than the other. There were unfilled cracks in the walls, and the rain leaked through the roof in several places, but the rough wooden floor was raised above the level of the sticky mud, and a few pieces of wood were scattered near a hearth built up with stones to floor height. It was the driest, most comfortable place they had seen for days.

They went out, unharnessed the travois, and brought the horses in. Ayla started a fire while Jondalar went into one of the smaller structures and began tearing wood from the dry inner walls for firewood. By the time he returned, she had strung heavy cordage across the room from pegs she found in the wall, and she was draping wet clothes and bedding over them. Jondalar helped her spread the tent across a rope, but they had to bunch it up to avoid a steady stream from a leak.

"We ought to do something about the leaks in the roof," Jondalar said.

"I saw cattails growing nearby," Ayla said. "It wouldn't take long to weave the leaves into mats that we could cover the holes with."

They went out to gather the tough, rather stiff, cattail leaves to patch the leaking roof, both cutting down an armload of the plants. The leaves that were wrapped around the stem averaged about two feet long, about an inch or more in width, tapering to a point. Ayla had been teaching Jondalar the basics of weaving, and after watching her to see the method she was using to make square sections of flat mats, he began to make one like them. Ayla looked down at her work, smiling to herself. She couldn't help it. She still felt a sense of surprise that Jondalar was able to do woman's work, and she was delighted by his willingness. With both of them working, they soon had as many patches made as there were leaks.

The structures were made of a rather thin thatch of reeds fastened to a basic frame of long tree trunks, not much more than saplings, lashed together. Though not made of planks, they were similar to the A-shaped dwellings made by the Sharamudoi, except the ridgepole did not slope and they were asymmetrical. The side with the entrance opening, facing the river, was nearly vertical; the opposite side leaned against it at a sharp angle. The ends were closed, but they could be propped up somewhat like awnings.

They went out and attached the mats, tying them down with lengths of the tough, stringy cattail leaves. There were two leaks near the peak that were difficult to reach even with Jondalar's six-foot-six-inch height, and they did not think the structure would bear the weight of either of them. They decided to go back inside and try to think of a way to patch them, remembering at the last moment to fill a waterbag and some bowls with water for drinking and cooking. When Jondalar reached up and blocked one of the leaks with his hand, it finally occurred to them to fasten the patch from the inside.

After they covered the entrance with the mammoth hide tarp, Ayla looked around the darkened interior, lit only by the fire that was starting to warm the place, feeling snug. The rain was outside and they were inside a place that was dry and warm, though it was starting to get steamy as the wet things began to dry, and there was no smokehole in the summer dwelling. The smoke from fires had usually escaped through the less-than-airtight walls and ceiling, or the ends, which were often left open in warmer weather. But the dried grass and reeds had expanded with the moisture, making it harder for smoke to escape, and it began to accumulate along the ridgepole at the ceiling.

Though horses were accustomed to being out in the elements and usually preferred it, Whinney and Racer had been raised around people and were used to sharing human habitations, even darkened smoky ones. They stayed at the end that Ayla had decided would be their place, and even they seemed glad to be out of the waterlogged world. Ayla put cooking rocks in the fire; then she and Jondalar rubbed down the horses and Wolf, to help them dry.

They opened all the packages and bundles to see if anything had been damaged by the excess moisture, found dry clothes and changed into them, and sat by the fire drinking hot tea, while a soup, made from the compressed traveling food, was cooking. When the smoke began to fill the upper levels of the dwelling, they broke holes through the light thatch of both ends near the top, which cleared it out and added a little more light.

It felt good to relax. They hadn't realized how tired they

were, and before it was even fully dark, the woman and man crawled into their still slightly damp sleeping furs. But as tired as he was, Jondalar could not go to sleep. He remembered the last time he had faced the swift and treacherous river called the Sister, and in the dark he felt a chill of dread at the thought of having to cross her with the woman he loved.

21

Ayla and Jondalar stayed at the abandoned summer camp through the next day, and the next. By the morning of the third day, the rain finally slacked off. The dull, solid gray cloud cover broke up, and by afternoon bright sunlight beamed through the blue patches stitched between fleecy white clouds. A brisk wind puffed and sputtered from one direction and then another, as if trying out different positions unable to decide which would best suit the occasion.

Most of their things were dry, but they opened the ends of the dwelling to let the wind blow through to dry completely the last few heavy pieces and air everything out. Some of their leather items had stiffened. They would need working and stretching, though regular use would probably be sufficient to make them supple again, but they were essentially undamaged. Their woven pack baskets, however, were another matter. They had dried misshapen and badly frayed, and a rotting mildew had developed. The moisture had softened them, and the weight of their contents had caused them to sag and the fibers to pull apart and break.

Ayla decided she would have to make new ones, even though the dried grasses, plants, and trees of autumn were not the strongest or best materials to use. When she told Jondalar, he brought up another problem.

"Those pack baskets have been bothering me, anyway," he said. "Every time we cross a river deep enough for the horses to have to swim, if we don't take them off, the baskets get wet. With the bowl boat and the pole drag, it hasn't been much of a problem. We just put the baskets in the boat, and as long as we're in open country, it's easy enough to use the drag. Most of the way ahead is open grassland, but there will be some woods and rough country. Then, just like in these mountains, it might not be so easy to drag those poles and the boat. Sometime we may decide to leave them behind, but if we do, we need pack baskets that won't get wet when the horses have to swim a river. Can you make some like that?"

Now it was Ayla's turn to frown. "You're right, they do get wet. When I made the pack baskets, I didn't have to cross many rivers, and those I did weren't very deep." She wrinkled her forehead in concentration; then she remembered the pannier she had first devised. "I didn't use pack baskets in the beginning. The first time I wanted Whinney to carry something on her back, I made a big, shallow basket. Maybe I can work out something like that again. It would be easier if we didn't ride the horses, but . . ."

Ayla closed her eyes, trying to visualize an idea she was getting. "Maybe . . . I could make pack baskets that could be lifted up to their backs while we're in the water. . . . No, that wouldn't work if we were riding at the same time . . . but . . . maybe, I could make something the horses could carry on their rumps, behind us . . ." She looked at Jondalar. "Yes, I think I can make carriers that will work."

They gathered reed and cattail leaves, osier willow withes, long thin spruce roots, and whatever else Ayla saw that she thought could be used as material for baskets or for cordage to construct woven containers. Trying various approaches and fitting it on Whinney, Ayla and Jondalar worked on the project all day. By late afternoon they had made a sort of pack-saddle basket that was sufficient to hold Ayla's belongings and traveling gear, that could be carried by the mare while she was riding, and that would stay reasonably dry when the horse was swimming. They started immediately on another one for Racer. His went much faster because they had worked out the method and the details.

In the evening the wind picked up and shifted, bringing a sharp norther that was fast blowing the clouds south. As twilight turned to dark, the sky was almost clear, but it was much colder. They planned to leave in the morning, and both of them decided to go through their things to lighten their load. The pack baskets had been bigger and it was a tighter fit in the new pack-saddle carriers. No matter how they tried to arrange it, there just wasn't as much room. Some things had to go. They spread everything out that both of them were carrying.

Ayla pointed to the slab of ivory on which Talut had carved the map showing the first part of their Journey. "We don't need that anymore. Talut's land is far behind us," she said, feeling a touch of sadness.

"You're right, we don't need it. I hate to leave it, though," Jondalar said, grimacing at the thought of getting rid of it. "It would be interesting to show the kind of maps the Mamutoi make, and it reminds me of Talut."

Ayla nodded with understanding. "Well, if you have the room, take it, but it isn't essential."

Jondalar glanced at Ayla's array spread out on the floor, and picked up the mysterious wrapped package he had seen before. "What is this?"

"It's just something I made last winter," she said, taking it out of his hands and looking away quickly as a flush rose to her face. She put it behind her, shoving it under the pile of things she was taking. "I'm going to leave my summer traveling clothes, they're all stained and worn anyway, and I'll be wearing my winter ones. That gives me some extra room."

Jondalar looked at her sharply, but he made no further comment.

It was cold when they awoke the next morning. A fine cloud of warm mist showed every breath. Ayla and Jondalar hurriedly dressed, and after starting a fire for a morning cup of hot tea, they packed their bedding, eager to be off. But when they went outside, they stopped and stared.

A thin coat of shimmering hoarfrost had transformed the surrounding hills. It sparkled and glinted in the bright morning sun with an unusual vividness. As the frost melted, each drop of water became a prism reflecting a brilliant bit of rainbow in a tiny burst of red, green, blue, or gold, which flickered from one color to another when they moved and saw the spectrum from a different angle. But the beauty of the frost's ephemeral jewels was a reminder that the season of warmth was little more than a fleeting flash of color in a world controlled by winter, and the short hot summer was over.

When they were packed and ready to go, Ayla looked back at the summer camp that had been such a welcome refuge. It was even more dilapidated, since they had torn down parts of the smaller shelters to fuel their fireplace, but she knew the flimsy temporary dwellings wouldn't last much longer anyway. She was grateful they had found them when they did.

They continued west toward the Sister River, dropping down a slope to another level terrace, though they were still high enough in elevation to see the wide grasslands of the steppes on the other side of the turbulent waterway they were approaching. It gave them a perspective of the region as well as showing the extent of the river floodplain ahead. The level land that was usually under water during times of flood was about ten miles across, but broader on the far bank. The foothills of the near side limited the floodwaters' normal expansion, though there were elevations, hills and bluffs, across the river, too.

In contrast to the grasslands, the floodplain was a wilderness of marshes, small lakes, woods, and tangled undergrowth with the river churning through it. Though it lacked meandering channels, it reminded Ayla of the tremendous delta of the Great Mother River, but on a smaller scale. The sallows and seasonal brush that seemed to be growing out of the water along the edges of the swiftly flowing stream indicated both the amount of flooding caused by the recent rains and the sizable portion of land already given up to the river.

Ayla's attention was brought back to her immediate surroundings when Whinney's gait suddenly changed, caused by her hooves sinking into sand. The small streams that had cut across the terraces above had become deeply entrenched riverbeds between shifting dunes of sandy marl. The horses floundered as they proceeded, kicking up fountains of loose, calcium-rich soil with each step.

Near evening, as the setting sun, nearly blinding in its intensity, approached the earth, the man and woman, trying to shade their eyes, peered ahead, looking for a place to make camp. Drawing nearer to the floodplain, they noticed that the fine shifting sand was developing a slightly different character. Like the upper terraces, it was primarily loess—rock dust created by the grinding action of the glacier and deposited by the wind—but occasionally the river's flooding was extreme enough to reach their elevation. The clayey silt that was added to the soil hardened and stabilized the ground. When they began to see familiar steppe grasses growing beside the stream they were following, one of the many that were racing down the mountain toward the Sister, they decided to stop.

After they set up their tent, the woman and man went in separate directions to hunt for their dinner. Ayla took Wolf, who ran ahead and in a short time flushed up a covey of ptarmigan. He pounced on one as Ayla whipped out her sling and brought down another that thought it had reached the safety of the sky. She considered allowing Wolf to keep the bird he had caught, but when he resisted giving it up at once, she decided against it. Though one fat fowl could certainly have satisfied both her and Jondalar, she wanted to reinforce to the wolf the understanding that, when she expected it, he would have to share his kills with them, because she didn't know what lay ahead.

She didn't fully reason it out, but the nippy air had made her realize that they would be traveling during the cold season into an unknown land. The people she had known, both the Clan and the Mamutoi, seldom traveled very far during the severe glacial winters. They settled into a place that was secure from bitter cold and wind-driven blizzards, and they ate food they had stored. The idea of traveling in winter made her uneasy.

Jondalar's spear-thrower had found a large hare, which they decided to save for later. Ayla wanted to roast the birds on a spit over a fire, but they were camped on the open steppes, beside a stream with only scanty brush beside it. Looking around, she spied a couple of antlers, unequal in size and obviously from different animals, that had been discarded the previous year. Though antler was much harder to break than wood, with Jondalar's help, sharp flint knives, and the small axe he kept in his belt, they broke them apart. Ayla used part to skewer the birds, and the broken-off tines became forks to support the spit. After all the effort, she decided she would keep them to use again, especially since antler was slow to catch fire.

She gave Wolf his share of the cooked fowl, along with a portion of some large reed roots she had dug from a backwater ditch beside the stream, and the meadow mushrooms that she recognized as edible and tasty. After their evening meal, they sat next to the fire and watched the sky grow dark. The days were getting shorter, and they weren't as tired at night, especially since it was so much easier riding the horses across the open plains than it had been making their way over the wooded mountains.

"Those birds were good," Jondalar said. "I like the skin crisp like that."

"This time of year, when they're so nice and fat, that's the best way to cook them," Ayla said. "The feathers are changing color already, and the breast down is so thick. I wanted to take it with us. It would make a nice soft filling for something. Ptarmigan feathers make the lightest and warmest bedding, but I don't have room for them."

"Maybe next year, Ayla. The Zelandonii hunt ptarmigan, too," Jondalar said, as a gentle encouragement, something for her to anticipate at the end of their Journey.

"Ptarmigan were Creb's favorite," Ayla said.

Jondalar thought she seemed sad, and when she said nothing more, he kept on talking, hoping it would take her mind off whatever was bothering her. "There's even one kind of ptarmigan, not around our Caves, but south of us, that doesn't turn white. All year it looks like a ptarmigan does in summer, and it tastes like the same kind of bird. The people who live in that region call it a red grouse, and they like to use the feathers on their headwear and clothes. They make special costumes for a Red Grouse ceremony, and they dance with the bird's movements, stamping their feet and everything, like the males do when they are trying to entice the females. It's part of their Mother Festival." He paused, but when she still had no comment to make, he continued, "They hunt the birds with nets, and get many at one time."

"I got one of these with my sling, but Wolf got the other one," Ayla said. When she said nothing more, Jondalar decided she just didn't feel like talking, and they sat in silence for a while, watching the fire consume brush and dried dung that had redried after the rains enough to burn. Finally she

spoke again. "Remember Brecie's throwing stick? I wish I
knew how to use something like that. She could bring down
several birds at one time with it."

The night cooled quickly, and they were glad for the tent.
Though Ayla had seemed unusually silent, full of sadness
and remembering, she was warmly responsive to his touch,
and Jondalar soon stopped worrying about her quiet mood.

In the morning the air was still brisk, and the condensed
moisture had brought a ghostly shimmer of frost to the land
again. The icy stream was cold but invigorating when they
used it to wash. They had buried Jondalar's hare, encased in
its furry hide, under the hot coals to cook overnight. When
they peeled off the blackened skin, the rich layer of winter
fat just underneath had basted the usually lean and often
stringy meat, and slow cooking within its natural container
made it moist and tender. It was the best time of the year to
hunt the long-eared animals.

They rode side by side through the tall ripe grass, not
rushing but keeping a steady pace, talking occasionally. Small
game was plentiful as they headed toward the Sister, but the
only large animals they saw all morning were across the river
in the distance: a small band of male mammoths, heading
north. Later in the day they saw a mixed herd of horses and
saiga antelope, also on the other side. Whinney and Racer
noticed them, too.

"Iza's totem was the Saiga," Ayla said. "That was a
very powerful totem for a woman. Even stronger than Creb's
birth totem, the Roe Deer. Of course, the Cave Bear had
chosen him and was his second totem before he became Mog-
ur."

"But your totem is the Cave Lion. That's a much more
powerful animal than a saiga antelope," Jondalar said.

"I know. It's a man's totem, a hunter's totem. That's
why it was so hard for them to believe it, at first," Ayla
said. "I don't really remember, but Iza told me that Brun
even got angry at Creb when he named it at my adoption
ceremony. That's why everyone was sure I would never have
any children. No man had a totem powerful enough to defeat
the Cave Lion. It was a big surprise when I got pregnant
with Durc, but I'm sure it was Broud who started him, when
he forced me." She frowned at the unpleasant thought. "And

if totem spirits have something to do with starting babies, Broud's totem was the Woolly Rhinoceros. I remember the Clan hunters talking about a woolly rhino that killed a cave lion, so it could have been strong enough, and, like Broud, they can be mean.''

"Woolly rhinos are unpredictable and can be vicious," Jondalar said. "Thonolan was gored by one not far from here. He would have died then if the Sharamudoi hadn't found us." The man closed his eyes with the painful memory, letting Racer carry him along. They didn't speak for a while, then he asked, "Does everyone in the Clan have a totem?"

"Yes," Ayla replied. "A totem is for guidance and protection. Each clan's mog-ur discovers every new baby's totem, usually before the end of the birthing year. He gives the child an amulet with a piece of the red stone inside it at the totem ceremony. The amulet is the totem spirit's home."

"You mean like a donii is a place for the Mother spirit to rest?" Jondalar asked.

"Something like that, I think, but a totem protects you, not your home, although it is happier if you live in a place that's familiar. You have to keep your amulet with you. It is how your totem spirit recognizes you. Creb told me that the spirit of my Cave Lion would not be able to find me without it. Then I would lose his protection. Creb said if I ever lost my amulet, I would die," Ayla explained.

Jondalar hadn't understood the full implications of Ayla's amulet before, or why she was so protective of it. He had occasionally thought she carried it too far. She seldom took it off, except to bathe or swim, and sometimes not even then. He had supposed it was her way of clinging to her Clan childhood, and he hoped she would someday get over it. Now he realized there was more to it than that. If a man of great magical power had given him something, and told him he would die if he ever lost it, he would be protective of it, too. Jondalar no longer doubted that the holy man of the Clan, who had raised her, possessed true power derived from the spirit world.

"It's also for the signs your totem leaves for you if you make the right decision about something important in your life," Ayla continued. A nagging worry that had been bothering her suddenly struck her with more force. Why hadn't her totem given her a sign to confirm that she had made the right choice when she decided to go with Jondalar to his home? She had not found a single object that she could interpret as a sign from her totem since they left the Mamutoi.

"Not very many Zelandonii have personal totems," Jondalar said, "but some do. It's usually considered lucky. Willomar has one."

"He's your mother's mate, right?" Ayla asked.

"Yes. Thonolan and Folara were both born to his hearth, and he always treated me as though I was."

"What is his totem?"

"It's the Golden Eagle. The story is told that when he was a baby, a golden eagle swooped down and picked him up, but his mother grabbed him before he could be taken away. He still bears the scars from the talons on his chest. Their zelandoni said that the eagle recognized him as his own and came for him. That's how they knew it was his totem. Marthona thinks that's why he likes to travel so much. He can't fly like the eagle, but he has a need to see the land."

"That's a powerful totem, like the Cave Lion, or the Cave Bear," Ayla commented. "Creb always said that powerful totems were not easy to live with, and it's true, but I have been given so much. He even sent you to me. I think I have been very lucky. I hope the Cave Lion will be lucky for you, Jondalar. He is also your totem now."

Jondalar smiled. "You've said that before."

"The Cave Lion chose you, and you have the scars to prove it. Just as Willomar was marked by his totem."

Jondalar looked thoughtful for a moment. "Perhaps you are right. I hadn't thought of it that way."

Wolf, who had been off exploring, suddenly appeared. He yipped to get Ayla's attention, then fell into place beside Whinney. She watched him, tongue lolling out of the side of his mouth, ears perked up, running with the wolf's usual untiring, ground-covering pace through the standing hay, which sometimes hid him from view. He seemed so happy and alert. He loved to go off and explore on his own, but he always returned, which made her happy. Riding with the man and the stallion beside her made her happy, too.

"From the way you always talk about him, I think your brother must have been like the man of his hearth," Ayla said, resuming the conversation. "Thonolan liked to travel, too, didn't he? Did he look like Willomar?"

"Yes, but not as much as I resemble Dalanar. Everyone remarks on it. Thonolan had a lot more of Marthona in him,"

Jondalar smiled, "but he was never chosen by an eagle, so that doesn't explain his travel urge." The smile faded. "My brother's scars were from that unpredictable woolly rhinoceros." He was thoughtful for a while. "But then Thonolan always was a bit unpredictable. Maybe it was his totem. It didn't seem to be very lucky for him, although the Sharamudoi did find us, and I never saw him as happy as he was after he met Jetamio."

"I don't think the Woolly Rhino is a lucky totem," Ayla said, "but I think the Cave Lion is. When he chose me, he even gave me the same marks the Clan uses for a Cave Lion totem, so Creb would know. Your scars are not Clan marks, but they are clear. You were marked by a Cave Lion."

"I definitely do have the scars to prove that I was marked by your cave lion, Ayla."

"I think the spirit of the Cave Lion chose you so that your totem spirit would be strong enough for mine, so that someday I will be able to have your children," Ayla said.

"I thought you said it was a man who made a baby start growing inside a woman, not spirits," Jondalar said.

"It is a man, but maybe spirits need to help. Since I have such a strong totem, the man who is my mate would need a strong one, too. So maybe the Mother decided to tell the Cave Lion to choose you, so we can make babies together."

They rode together in silence again, thinking their own thoughts. Ayla was imagining a baby that looked like Jondalar, except a girl, not a boy. She didn't seem to be lucky with sons. Maybe she'd be able to keep a daughter.

Jondalar was thinking about children, too. If it was true that a man started life with his organ, they had certainly given a baby plenty of chances to start. Why wasn't she pregnant?

Was Serenio pregnant when I left? he thought. I'm glad she found someone to be happy with, but I wish she had said something to Roshario. Are any children in the world in some way a part of me? Jondalar tried to think of the women he had known and remembered Noria, the young woman of Haduma's people with whom he shared First Rites. Both Noria and the old Haduma herself had seemed convinced that his spirit had entered her and that a new life had begun. She was supposed to give birth to a son with blue eyes like his. They were even going to name him Jondal. Was it true? he wondered. Had his spirit mixed with Noria's to begin a new life?

But Haduma's people didn't live so far away, and in the right direction, to the north and west. Maybe they could stop for a visit, except, he suddenly realized, he didn't really know how to find them. They had come to where he and Thonolan had been camped. He knew their home Caves were not only west of the Sister, they were west of the Great Mother River, but he didn't know where. He did recall that they sometimes hunted in the region between the two rivers, but that was of little help. He would probably never know if Noria had that baby.

Ayla's thoughts had turned from waiting until they reached Jondalar's home before they started having children, to his people, and what they were like. She wondered if they would find her acceptable. She felt a little more confident, after meeting the Sharamudoi, that there would be a place for her somewhere, but she wasn't sure if it would be with the Zelandonii. She remembered that Jondalar had reacted with strong revulsion when he first discovered she had been raised by the Clan, and then she recalled his strange behavior the previous winter while living with the Mamutoi.

Some of it was because of Ranec. She came to know that before they left, though she hadn't understood it in the beginning. Jealousy was not a part of her upbringing. Even if they had felt such an emotion, no man of the Clan would ever show jealousy over a woman. But part of Jondalar's strange behavior also stemmed from his concern about how his people would accept her. She knew now that, though he loved her, he had been ashamed of her living with the Clan and, especially, he had been ashamed of her son. True, he did not seem concerned anymore. He was protective of her and not at all uneasy when her Clan background came out when they were with the Sharamudoi, but he must have had some reason for feeling that way in the first place.

Well, she loved Jondalar and wanted to live with him, and besides, it was too late now to change her mind, but she hoped she had done the right thing in coming with him. She wished once again that her Cave Lion totem would give her a sign so that she would know she had made the right decision, but no sign seemed to be forthcoming.

As the travelers neared the turbulent expanse of water at the confluence of the Sister River with the Great Mother River, the loose, crumbly marls—sands and clays rich in calcium—of the upper terraces gave way to gravels and loess soils on the low levels.

In that wintry world, glaciered mountain crests filled streams and rivers during the warmer season with meltwater. Near the end of the season, with the addition of heavy rains that accumulated as snow in the higher elevations, which sharp temperature changes could release suddenly, the swift streams became torrential floods. With no lakes on the western face of the mountains to hold back the gathering deluge in a natural reservoir and dole the outpour in more measured tribute, the increasing tide fell over itself down the steep slopes. The cascading waters gouged sand and gravel out of the sandstones, limestones, and shales of the mountains, which was washed down to the mighty river and deposited on the beds and floodplains.

The central plains, once the floor of an inland sea, occupied a basin between two massive mountain ranges on the east and west and highlands to the north and south. Almost equal in volume to the burgeoning Mother as she neared their meeting, the swollen Sister held the drainage of part of the plains, and the entire western face of the mountain chain that curved around in a great arc toward the northwest. The Sister River raced along the lowest depression of the basin to deliver her offering of floodwater to the Great Mother of Rivers, but her surging current was rebuffed by the higher water level of the Mother, already filled to capacity. Forced back on herself, she dissipated her offertory in a vortex of countercurrents and destructive spreading overflow.

Near midday, the man and woman approached the marshy wilderness of half-drowned underbrush and occasional stands of trees with their lower trunks beneath the water. Ayla thought the similarity to the soggy marshland of the eastern delta grew stronger as they drew closer, except that the currents and countercurrents of the joining rivers were swirling maelstroms. With the weather much cooler, the insects were less bothersome, but the carcasses of bloated, partially devoured, and rotting animals that had been caught up by the flood collected their share. To the south, a massif with densely forested slopes was rising out of a purple mist caused by the surging eddies.

"Those must be the Wooded Hills Carlono told us about," Ayla said.

"Yes, but they are more than hills," Jondalar said. "They are higher than you think, and they extend for a long way. The Great Mother River flows south until she reaches that barrier. Those hills turn the Mother east."

They rode around a large quiet pool, a backwater that was separated from the moving waters, and stopped at the eastern edge of the swollen river, somewhat upstream from the confluence. As Ayla stared across the mighty flood at the other side, she began to understand Jondalar's warnings about the difficulty of crossing the Sister.

The muddy waters, swirling around the slender trunks of willows and birches, tore loose those trees whose roots were not as securely anchored into the soil of low islands that were surrounded by channels in drier seasons. Many trees were pitched at precarious angles, and naked branches and boles that had been wrenched from upstream woods were trapped in muck along the banks or circled in a dizzy dance in the river.

Ayla silently wondered how they would ever get across the river, and she asked, "Where do you think we should cross?"

Jondalar wished the large Ramudoi boat that had rescued Thonolan and him a few years before would appear and take them to the other side. The reminder of his brother again brought a piercing stab of grief, but also a sudden concern for Ayla.

"I think it's obvious we can't cross here," he said. "I didn't know it would be this bad so soon. We'll have to go upstream to look for an easier place to attempt it. I just hope it doesn't rain again before we find it. Another rainstorm like the last one, and this whole floodplain will be under water. No wonder that summer camp was abandoned."

"This river wouldn't go up as high as that, would it?" Ayla asked, her eyes open wide.

"I don't think it would, yet, but it might. All the water falling on those mountains will eventually end up here. Besides, flash floods could easily come down the stream that ran so near the camp. And probably do. Frequently. I think we should hurry, Ayla. This is not a safe place to be if it starts to rain again," Jondalar said, looking up at the sky. He urged the stallion to a gallop and kept to such a fast pace that Wolf was hard pressed to keep up with them. After a while he slowed down again, but not to the leisurely pace they had maintained before.

Jondalar stopped occasionally and studied the river and its far bank before continuing north, glancing at the sky anxiously. The river did seem narrower in some places and wider in others, but it was so full and broad that it was hard to tell for sure. They rode until it was nearly dark without finding a suitable crossing place, but Jondalar insisted that they ride to higher ground to make camp for the night, and they halted only when it became too dark to travel safely.

"Ayla! Ayla! Wake up!" Jondalar said, shaking her gently. "We have to get moving."

"What? Jondalar! What's wrong?" Ayla said.

She was usually awake before him, and she felt disconcerted to be awakened so early. When she moved the sleeping fur aside, she felt a chill breeze, and then she noticed the tent flap was open. The diffused radiance of seething clouds was outlined by the opening, providing the only illumination inside their sleeping quarters. She could barely make out Jondalar's face in the dim gray light, but it was enough to see that he was worried, and she shivered with foreboding.

"We have to go," Jondalar said. He had hardly slept all night. He couldn't exactly say why he felt they had to get across the river as soon as possible, but the feeling was so strong that it gave him a knot of fear in the pit of his stomach, not for himself, but for Ayla.

She got up, not asking why. She knew he would not have awakened her if he didn't think their situation was serious. She dressed quickly, then got out her fire-making kit.

"Let's not take the time for a fire this morning," Jondalar said.

She frowned, then nodded and poured out cold water for them to drink. They packed while eating cakes of traveling food. When they were ready to leave, Ayla looked for Wolf, but he was not in camp.

"Where is Wolf," Ayla said, a note of desperation in her voice.

"He's probably hunting. He'll catch up with us, Ayla. He always does."

"I'll whistle for him," she said, then pierced the early morning air with the distinctive sound she used to call him.

"Come on, Ayla. We need to go," Jondalar said, feeling a familiar irritation over the wolf.

"I'm not going without him," she said, whistling again louder, giving the tone more urgency.

"We have to find a place to cross this river before the rain starts, or we might not get across," Jondalar said.

"Can't we just keep on going upstream? This river is bound to get smaller, isn't it?" she argued.

"Once it starts to rain, it will only get bigger. Even upstream it will be bigger than it is here now, and we don't know what kind of rivers will be coming down off those mountains. We could easily get caught by a flash flood. Dolando said they were common once the rains started. Or we could be stopped by a large tributary. Then what do we do? Climb back up the mountain to get around it? We need to get across the Sister while we can," Jondalar said. He mounted the stallion and looked down at the woman standing beside the mare with the travois trailing behind her.

Ayla turned her back and whistled again.

"We have to go, Ayla."

"Why can't we wait a little while? He'll come."

"He's only an animal. Your life is more important to me than his."

She turned around and looked up at him, then looked back down, frowning deeply. Was it as dangerous to wait as Jondalar thought? Or was he just being impatient? If it was, shouldn't his life be more important to her than Wolf's, too? Just then, Wolf loped into sight. Ayla breathed a sigh of relief and braced as he jumped up to greet her, putting his paws on her shoulders and licking her jaw. She climbed up to Whinney's back, using one of the travois poles to assist her. Then, signaling Wolf to stay close, she followed Jondalar and Racer.

There was no sunrise. The day just kept getting imperceptibly lighter, but never bright. The cloud cover hung low, giving the sky a uniform gray, and there was a cool dampness in the air. Later in the morning they stopped to rest. Ayla made a hot tea to warm them, then a rich soup out of a cake of traveling food. She added lemony sorrel leaves and wild rose hips, after removing the seeds and the sharp bristly hairs from inside, and a few leaves from the tips of the clump of field roses growing nearby. For a while, the tea and the warm soup seemed to relieve Jondalar's concerns, until he noticed darker clouds gathering.

He urged her to pack her things quickly, and they started

out again. Jondalar anxiously watched the sky to note the progress of the oncoming storm. He watched the river, too, looking for a place to cross. He hoped for some abatement of the swift churning current: a wider, shallower spot, or an island or even a sandbar between the two banks. Finally, fearing the storm would not hold off much longer, he decided they would have to take a chance, though the tumultuous Sister looked no different than it had all along. Knowing that once the rains began, the situation would only get worse, he headed toward a section of bank that offered fairly easy access. They stopped and dismounted.

"Do you think we should try to ride the horses across?" Jondalar asked, glancing nervously at the threatening sky.

Ayla studied the racing river and the debris it carried along. Often large whole trees floated by, along with many broken ones, that had been washed down from stands higher in the mountains. She shuddered when she noticed a large, bloated deer carcass, its antlers caught and entwined in the branches of a tree that was lodged near the shore. The dead animal made her fear for the horses.

"I think it would be easier for them to cross if we are not on their backs," she said. "I think we should swim beside them."

"That's what I thought," Jondalar said.

"But we'll need a rope to hold on," she said.

They got out short lengths of rope, then checked over the harnesses and baskets to make sure their tent, food, and few precious belongings were secure. Ayla unhitched the travois from Whinney, deciding it might be too dangerous for her to try to swim the tumultuous river in full harness, but they did not want to lose the poles and bowl boat, if they could help it.

With that in mind, they bound the long poles together with cordage. While Jondalar fastened one end to the side of the bowl boat, Ayla secured the other end to the harness that was used to hold on Whinney's pack-saddle basket. She used a slip knot that could readily be released if she felt it was necessary. Then, to the flat braided cord that went down around behind the mare's front legs and up across her chest, used to hold Ayla's riding blanket on the mare, the woman attached another rope, much more securely.

Jondalar attached a similar rope to Racer, then he took off his boots, his inner foot-coverings, and his heavy outer clothes and furs. When soaked, they would weigh him down, making swimming all but impossible. He wrapped them together and piled them on top of the pack saddle, but he kept his under tunic and leggings on. Even when wet, the leather would provide some warmth. Ayla did the same.

The animals sensed the urgency and anxiety of the humans and were disturbed by the roiling water. The horses had shied away from the dead deer, and they were prancing around with short steps, tossing their heads and rolling their eyes, but their ears were perked up and alertly forward. Wolf, on the other hand, had gone to the edge of the water to investigate the deer, but he didn't go in.

"How do you think the horses will do, Ayla?" Jondalar asked, as big sloppy raindrops began to fall.

"They're nervous, but I think they'll be all right, especially since we will be with them, but I'm not so sure about Wolf," Ayla said.

"We can't carry him across. He has to make it on his own—you know that," Jondalar said. But seeing her distress, he added, "Wolf's a strong swimmer, he should be all right."

"I hope so," she said, kneeling down to give the wolf a hug.

Jondalar noticed that the raindrops were falling thicker and faster. "We better get started," he said, taking hold of Racer's halter directly, since the lead rope was fastened farther back. He closed his eyes for a moment and wished for good luck. He thought of Doni, the Great Earth Mother, but he couldn't think of anything to promise Her in return for their safety. He made a silent request for help in crossing the Sister anyway. Though he knew he would someday, he did not want to meet the Mother just yet, but even more, he did not want to lose Ayla.

The stallion tossed his head and tried to rear as Jondalar led him toward the river. "Easy now, Racer," the man said. The water was cold as it swirled around his bare feet, and up his covered calves and thighs. Once in the water, Jondalar let go of Racer's halter, giving him his head, and he wrapped the dangling rope around his hand, relying on the sturdy young stallion to find his way across.

Ayla wrapped the rope that was attached at the top of the mare's withers around her hand several times, tucking the end in and around, and she closed her fist tightly to hold it.

Then she started in behind the tall man, walking beside Whinney. She pulled on the other rope, the one that was fastened to the poles and boat, making sure it did not get tangled as they entered the river.

The young woman felt the cold water and the tug of the strong current immediately. She looked back toward the land. Wolf was still on the riverbank, advancing and retreating, whining anxiously, hesitant to enter the fast-moving river. She called to him, encouragingly. He paced back and forth, looking at the water and the widening distance between him and the woman. Suddenly, just as the rain began to fall in earnest, he sat down and howled. Ayla whistled to him and, after a few more false starts, he finally plunged in and started paddling toward her. She turned her attention back to the horse and the river ahead.

The rain, coming down harder, seemed to flatten out the choppy waves in the distance, but nearby the wild water was even more cluttered with debris than she had thought. Broken trunks and branches swirled around or bumped into her, some still with leaves, others waterlogged and almost hidden. The bloated animals were worse, often torn open by the violence of the flood that had caught them and swept them down the mountain and into the muddy river.

She saw several birch mice and pine voles. A large ground squirrel was harder to recognize; its pale brown pelt was dark and the thick fluffy tail was plastered down. A collared lemming, long white winter hair, lank but shiny, growing out through fur of summer gray that looked black, showed the bottom of its feet already covered with white fur. It had probably come from high on the mountain near the snow. The large animals showed more damage. A chamois floated past with a horn broken off and the fur gone from half its face, exposing pinkish muscle. When she saw the carcass of a young snow leopard, she looked back again for Wolf, but he was not in sight.

She noticed, however, that the rope dragging behind the mare was hauling along a snag as well as the poles and boat. The broken stump with spreading roots was adding an unnecessary burden and slowing Whinney down. Ayla pulled and tugged on the rope, trying to bring it closer to her, but it suddenly came loose by itself. A small forked branch was still clinging, but it was nothing to worry about. She was concerned about not seeing any sign of Wolf, even though she was so low in the water that she couldn't see much. It upset her, especially since there was nothing she could do about it. She whistled for him once, but she wondered if he would hear it above the noise of the rushing water.

She turned back and took a critical look at Whinney, worried that the heavy snag might have tired her, but she was still swimming strongly. Ayla looked ahead and was relieved to see Racer with Jondalar bobbing along beside him. She kicked and pulled with her free arm, trying not to be a greater burden than she had to be. But as they continued, more and more she just hung on to the rope, beginning to shiver. She began to feel that it was taking an unreasonably long time to cross the river. The opposite shore still seemed so far ahead. The shivering wasn't too bad at first, but with more time in the cold water, it became more intense and wouldn't stop. Her muscles were becoming very tense, and her teeth were chattering.

She looked back for Wolf again, but she still did not see him. I should go back for him, he's so cold, she thought, as she shivered violently. Maybe Whinney can turn around and go back. But when she tried to speak, her jaw was so tense and chattering that she could not get the words out. No, Whinney shouldn't have to go. I'll do it. She tried to unwrap the rope from around her hand, but it was tight and tangled, and her hand was so numb that she could hardly feel it. Maybe Jondalar can go back for him. Where is Jondalar? Is he in the river? Did he go back for Wolf? Oh, there's a log caught up in the rope again. I have to . . . something . . . pull something . . . take rope away . . . heavy for Whinney.

Her shivering had stopped, but her muscles were so tense that she couldn't move. She closed her eyes to rest. It felt so good to close her eyes . . . and rest.

22

Ayla was almost unconscious when she felt the solid stones of the riverbed under her. She tried to stumble to her feet as Whinney dragged her across the rocky bottom, taking a few steps onto a beach of smooth round stones at a bend in the river. Then she fell. The rope, still tightly wrapped around her hand, jerked her around and halted the horse.

Jondalar, too, had shivered through the first stages of hypothermia while crossing the river, but he had reached the opposite shore sooner than she, before he became too uncoordinated or irrational. She would have made it across more quickly, but so much debris had gotten caught up in Whinney's rope that it had slowed the horse considerably. Even Whinney was beginning to suffer from the cold river before the slip knot, though swollen from the water, finally worked itself loose, freeing her from the encumbering weight.

Unfortunately, when he first reached the other side, the cold had affected Jondalar enough so that he wasn't entirely coherent. He pulled his outer fur parka over his wet clothing and started out to look for Ayla, on foot, leading the stallion, but he headed in the wrong direction along the river's edge. The exercise warmed him and cleared away the confusion. They had both been carried downstream for some distance, but since she had taken longer to get across, she had to be farther downriver. He turned around and walked back. When Racer nickered and he heard an answering whinny, he started to run.

When Jondalar saw Ayla, she was lying on her back on the rocky shore, beside the patient mare, her arm held up by the rope entangled around her hand. He rushed to her, his heart racing with fear. After first making sure she was still breathing, he gathered her up in his arms and held her close, tears filling his eyes.

"Ayla! Ayla! You're alive!" he cried. "I was so afraid you were gone. But you're so cold!"

He had to get her warm. He loosened the rope from her hand and picked her up. She stirred and opened her eyes. Her muscles were tense and rigid, and she could hardly speak, but she was straining to say something. He bent closer.

"Wolf. Find Wolf," she said in a hoarse whisper.

"Ayla, I have to take care of you!"

"Please. Find Wolf. Lose too many sons. Not Wolf, too," she said through a clenched jaw.

Her eyes were so full of sorrow and pleading that he couldn't refuse. "All right. I'll look for him, but I have to get you into a shelter first."

It was raining hard as he carried Ayla up a gentle slope. It leveled out in a small terrace with a stand of willows, some brush and sedge, and, near the back, a few pines. He looked for a flat place with no water running across it, then quickly set up the tent. After putting down the mammoth hide on top of the ground cover for extra protection from the saturated soil, he brought Ayla in, then the packs, and laid out their sleeping furs. He stripped off her wet clothes and his own as well, put her between the furs, and crawled in with her.

She wasn't quite unconscious, but in a dazed stupor. Her skin was cold and clammy, her body stiff. He tried to cover her with his body to warm her. When she began to shiver again, Jondalar breathed a little easier. It meant she was warming inside, but with the beginnings of a return to more awareness, she also remembered Wolf, and irrationally, almost wildly, she insisted that she was going to find him.

"It's my fault," she said through chattering teeth. "I told

him to jump in the river. I whistled. He trusted me. I have to find Wolf." She struggled to get up.

"Ayla, forget about Wolf. You don't even know where to begin to look," he said, trying to hold her down.

Shivering and sobbing hysterically, she tried to get out of the sleeping furs. "I've got to find him," she cried.

"Ayla, Ayla, I'll go. If you stay here, I'll go look for him," he said, trying to convince her to stay under the warm furs. "But promise me you will stay here, and stay covered."

"Please find him," she said.

He quickly put on dry clothes and his outer parka. Then he took out a couple of squares of traveling food, full of energy-rich fat and protein. "I'm going now," he said. "Eat this, and stay in the furs."

She grabbed his hand as he turned to go. "Promise me you will search for him," she said, looking into his troubled blue eyes. She was still shivering, but she seemed to be talking with more ease.

He looked back into her gray-blue eyes, full of worry and pleading and clutched her to him, hard and close. "I was so afraid you were dead."

She held on to him, reassured by his strength, and his love. "I love you, Jondalar, I would never want to lose you, but, please, find Wolf. I couldn't bear to lose him. He's like . . . a child . . . a son. I can't give up another son." Her voice cracked and tears filled her eyes.

He pulled back and looked down at her. "I'll look for him. But I can't promise I'll find him, Ayla, and even if I do, I can't promise he'll be alive."

A look of fear and horror filled her eyes; then she closed them and nodded. "Just try to find him," she said, but as he started to move away, she clung to him.

He wasn't sure if he had really planned to search for the wolf when he first started to get up. He had wanted to get some wood for a fire to get some warm tea or soup into her and see to the horses, but he had promised. Racer and Whinney were standing within the grove of willows, their riding blankets and Racer's halter still on, but the sturdy animals seemed fine for the moment, so he headed down the slope.

He didn't know which direction to go when he reached the river, but he finally decided to try downstream. Pulling his hood down farther to keep off the rain, he started hiking along the bank, checking through piles of driftwood and concentrations of debris. He found many dead animals and saw as many carnivores and scavengers, both four-legged and winged, feasting on the river's leavings, even a pack of southern wolves, but none that looked like Wolf.

Finally he turned around and headed back. He would go upstream a way, but he doubted if he'd have any better luck. He didn't really expect to find the animal, and he realized that it saddened him. Wolf could be troublesome sometimes, but he had developed a real affection for the intelligent beast. He would miss him, and he knew Ayla would be distraught.

He reached the rocky shore where he had found Ayla and walked around the bend, not sure how far he ought to go in the other direction, especially when he noticed that the river was rising. He decided they would move the tent farther away from the river as soon as Ayla was fit to travel. Maybe I ought to forget about looking upstream and make sure she is all right, he said to himself, hesitating. Well, maybe I'll go a short distance; she'll ask if I searched in both directions.

He started up the river, working his way around a pile of logs and branches, but when he saw the majestic silhouette of an imperial eagle gliding on outstretched wings, he stopped and watched with awe. Suddenly the large, graceful bird folded his powerful wings and dropped rapidly to the bank of the river, then swooped up again with a large suslik hanging from its talons.

A little farther on, where the bird had found its meal, a healthy tributary, widening into a slight delta, added its share to the waters of the Sister. He thought he saw something familiar on the wide stretch of sandy beach where they came together, and he smiled with recognition. It was the bowl boat, but when he looked closer, he frowned and started running toward it. Beside the boat, Ayla was sitting in the water holding Wolf's head in her lap. A wound above his left eye was still seeping blood.

"Ayla! What are you doing here? How did you get here?" he stormed, more in fear and worry than in anger.

"He's alive, Jondalar," she said, shaking with cold and at the same time sobbing so hard that she was almost incoherent. "He's hurt, but he's alive."

After Wolf had jumped into the river, he swam toward Ayla, but when he reached the lightweight, empty bowl boat skimming over the water, he rested his paws across the poles that were attached to it. He stayed there with the familiar objects, letting the buoyant boat and poles support him. It wasn't until the slip knot came loose, and the boat and poles started careening wildly over the choppy waves, that he was slammed into the heavy, waterlogged tree trunk. By then they were almost at the other side. The boat skittered up on the sandy bank, dragging the poles with the wolf draped across them partially out of the water. The blow had stunned him, but being half-submerged in cold water was worse. Even wolves were subject to hypothermia and death from exposure.

"Come on, Ayla, you're shivering again. We have to get you back. Why did you come out? I told you I'd look for him," Jondalar said. "Here, I'll take him." He lifted the wolf from her lap and then tried to help her up.

After a few steps, he knew they were going to have a difficult time making it back to the tent. Ayla was hardly able to walk, and the wolf was a large, heavy animal. His waterlogged fur added even more weight. The man could not carry both of them, and he knew Ayla would never let him leave Wolf and come back for him later. If only he could whistle for the horses the way Ayla did . . . but why couldn't he? Jondalar had developed a whistle for Racer, but he hadn't really worked very hard at training him to respond. He'd never had to. The young stallion always came with his dam when Ayla called Whinney.

Maybe Whinney would come to him if he whistled. At least he could try. He mimicked Ayla's signal, hoping he had managed to come close enough, but, just in case they didn't respond, he was determined to keep going. He shifted Wolf in his arms, and he tried to put an arm around Ayla to give her more support.

They hadn't even reached the pile of driftwood and he was already tiring from the effort. He was holding his own exhaustion off by sheer effort of will. He, too, had swum the mighty river, and then had carried Ayla up the slope and set up the tent. And then he had tramped up and down the riverbank searching for the wolf. When he heard a neigh, he looked up. Relief and joy flooded through him at the sight of the two horses.

He laid the wolf across Whinney's back, since she had carried him before and was used to it; then he helped Ayla up on Racer and led him toward the rocky beach. Whinney followed. Ayla, shivering in her wet clothes as the rain began to pour down harder, had trouble staying on the horse when they started up the slope. But, taking it slowly, they made it back to the tent near the grove of trees.

Jondalar helped Ayla down and got her into the tent, but hypothermia was making her irrational again and she was getting hysterical about the wolf. He had to bring him in immediately, then had to promise he would dry him off. He searched through the packs for something with which to rub him down. But when she wanted to bring him into their sleeping roll, he adamantly refused, though he did find a cover for him. While she sobbed uncontrollably, he helped Ayla undress and wrapped her with the furs.

He went out again, removed Racer's halter and the riding blankets from both horses, patted them gratefully, and gave them some words of thanks. Even though horses normally lived outside in all kinds of weather, and were adapted to the cold, he knew they didn't care much for rain, and he hoped they would not suffer for it. Then, finally, Jondalar went into the tent, undressed, and crawled in beside the violently shaking woman. Ayla huddled close to Wolf, while Jondalar cuddled her back, wrapping himself around her. After a time, with the warming body of a wolf on one side and the man on the other, the woman's shaking stopped, and they both gave in to their exhaustion and fell asleep.

Ayla woke up to a wet tongue licking her face. She pushed Wolf away, smiling with joy, then hugged him. Holding his head between her hands, she looked at his wound closely. The rain had washed the dirt away from the injury, and he had stopped bleeding. Though she wanted to treat him with some medicines later, he seemed fine for now. It wasn't so much the bump on the head, but the cold river that had weakened him. Sleep and warmth had been the best medicine. She became conscious that Jondalar had his arms around her, even though he was sleeping, and she lay still being held and holding Wolf, listening to the rain drumming on the tent.

She was remembering bits and pieces of the day before: stumbling through the brush and driftwood, searching the riverbank for Wolf; her hand hurting because the rope wrapped around it had become so tight; Jondalar carrying her. She smiled at the thought of him so close to her, then remembered watching him set up the tent. She felt a little ashamed that she had not helped him more, even though she had been so rigid with cold that she couldn't move.

Wolf wriggled out of her constraining hold and went out, nosing his way around the tent flap. She heard Whinney nicker and, with a feeling of joy, almost answered her, but then she remembered Jondalar sleeping. She began to worry about the horses out in the rain. They were used to dry weather, not this wet, soggy rain. Even freezing cold was fine if it was dry. But she recalled that she had seen horses, so some must live in this region. Horses did have undercoats that were thick, dense, and warm even when wet. She supposed they could cope with it, so long as it didn't rain all the time.

She realized that she didn't like the heavy autumn rains that fell in this southern region, though she had welcomed the long wet northern springs, with their warming mists and drizzles. The cave of Brun's clan was south, and it had rained quite a lot in autumn, but she didn't remember such drenching downpours. The southern regions were not all the same. Ayla thought about getting up, but before she got around to it, she went back to sleep.

When she awoke the second time, the man beside her was stirring. As she lay in the furs, there was a difference she couldn't quite place. Then she realized the sound of the rain had stopped. She got up and went outside. It was late afternoon and rather more cool than it had been, and she wished she had put on something warm. She passed her water near a bush, then walked toward the horses that were grazing on sedge grass near the willows where a creek ran through. Wolf was with them. They all came toward her as she approached, and she spent some time stroking and scratching and talking to them. Then she went back in the tent, and into the sleeping furs beside the warm man.

"You're cold, woman!" he said.

"And you're nice and warm," she said, snuggling up to him.

He wrapped his arms around her and nuzzled her neck, relieved that her warmth was returning so quickly. It had taken so long for her to warm up after being chilled by the water. "I don't know what I could have been thinking of, letting you get so wet and cold," Jondalar said. "We shouldn't have tried to cross that river."

"But Jondalar, what else could we do? You were right. As hard as it was raining, we would have had to cross some river, and it would have been worse trying to get across one that was coming down the mountain," she said.

"If we had left the Sharamudoi sooner, we would have missed the rain. Then the Sister wouldn't have been nearly as hard to cross," Jondalar said, continuing to berate himself.

"But it was my fault we didn't leave sooner, and even Carlono thought we would make it here before the rains."

"No, it was my fault. I knew what this river was like. If I had made the effort, we would have left earlier. And if we had left that boat behind, it wouldn't have taken so long to get over the mountain, or slowed you down in the river. I was so stupid!"

"Jondalar, why are you blaming yourself?" Ayla asked. "You are not stupid. You could not foresee what would happen. Not even One Who Serves the Mother can do it very well. It's never clear. And we did make it. We're here now, and everyone is all right, thanks to you, including Wolf. We even have the boat, and who knows how useful that might still be."

"But I almost lost you," he said, burying his head in her neck and clutching her so hard that it hurt, though she did not stop him. "I can't tell you how much I love you. I care about you so much, but the words that say it are so small. They are not enough to say what I feel for you." He held her close as if he thought that by holding her tight enough, he could somehow make her part of him, and would therefore never lose her.

She held him tightly, too, loving him and wishing she could do something to relieve his anguish and suddenly overwhelming need. Then she realized she knew what to do. She breathed in his ear and kissed his neck. His response was immediate. He kissed her with a fierce passion, caressing her arms and molding her breasts in his hands, sucking on her nipples with a hungry need. She put her leg around him, and rolled him over on top of her, then opened her thighs. He backed away, prodding and groping with his full member, trying to find her opening. She reached down and helped to guide him in, and she found herself as eager for him as he was for her.

As he plunged in and felt the warm embrace of her deep well, he moaned with the sudden indescribable sensation. All his nightmarish thoughts and fearful worries fled for the moment as the sensuous joy of this wondrous Gift of Pleasure from the Mother filled him, leaving no room for any other thoughts except his love for her. He pulled out, and then he felt her motion match his as they came together again. Her response incited stronger passions in him.

As they backed away and drew together again, he felt so right that she didn't think at all. His body and hers flowed apart and back together in a rhythmic pattern that she gave herself up to completely as it grew faster, glorying in the senses of that moment. Individual fires of feeling raced through her, centering deep within, as they moved back and forth.

He was feeling himself build with volcanic power, waves of excitement washing over him, engulfing him, and then almost before he knew it, bursting through with sweet release. As he moved the last few times, he felt a few aftershocks from the violent eruption, and then the warm and glowing feeling of utter relaxation.

He lay on top of her, catching his breath after the sudden and powerful exertion. She closed her eyes with contentment. After a time he rolled off and cuddled next to her, as she backed into him. Nesting together like two ladles, they lay quietly, happily entwined together.

After quite a long time, Ayla said softly, "Jondalar?"

"Hmmm?" he mumbled. He was in a pleasant, languorous state, not sleepy, but not wanting to move.

"How many more rivers like that will we have to cross?" she asked.

He reached over and kissed her ear. "None."

"None?"

"None, because there are no other rivers quite like the Sister," Jondalar explained.

"Not even the Great Mother River?"

"Not even the Mother is as fast and treacherous, or as dangerous as the Sister," he said, "but we won't be crossing the Great Mother River. We'll stay on this side most of the way to the plateau glacier. When we get close to the ice, there are some people I'd like to visit who live on the other side of the Mother. But that's a long way from here, and by then she will be little more than a mountain stream." He rolled over on his back. "Not that we don't have some good-size rivers to get across yet, but across these plains, the

Mother branches into many channels that split off and join
again. By the time we see her all together again, she will be
so much smaller that you'll hardly recognize her as the Great
Mother River.''

"Without all the water from the Sister, I'm not sure if
I'd recognize her,'' Ayla said.

"I think you would. As big as the Sister is, when they
join, the Mother is still bigger. There is a major river that
feeds from the other side just before the Wooded Hills that
turn her east. Thonolan and I met some people who took us
across on rafts at that place. Several more feeders come in
from the big mountains to the west, but we'll be going north
up the center plain, and we won't even see them.''

Jondalar sat up. The conversation had put him in the
mood to think about getting on their way, although they
wouldn't be leaving until the following morning. He was
rested and relaxed, and he didn't feel like staying in bed
anymore.

"We won't be crossing many rivers at all until we reach
the highlands to the north,'' he continued. "At least, that's
what Haduma's people told me. They say there are a few
hills, but it's pretty flat country. Most of the rivers we'll see
will be channels of the Mother. They say she wanders all over
the place through here. It's good hunting grounds, though.
Haduma's people cross the channels all the time to hunt
here.''

"Haduma's people? I think you told me about them, but
you never said much,'' Ayla said, getting up as well, and
reaching for her pack-saddle basket.

"We didn't visit with them long, just long enough for
a . . .'' Jondalar hesitated, thinking about the First Rites he
had shared with the pretty young woman, Noria. Ayla noticed
a strange expression, as though he was slightly embarrassed,
but also pleased with himself. ". . . Ceremony, a festival,''
he finished.

"A festival to honor the Great Earth Mother?'' Ayla
asked.

"Ah . . . yes, as a matter of fact. They asked me . . .
ah, they asked Thonolan and me, to share it with them.''

"Are we going to visit Haduma's people?'' Ayla said
from the opening, holding a Sharamudoi chamois skin to dry
herself with after she washed in the creek by the willows.

"I'd like to, but I don't know where they live,'' Jondalar

said. Then, seeing her puzzled expression, he quickly explained. "Some of their hunters found our camp, and then they sent for Haduma. She was the one who decided to have the festival, and she sent for the rest." He paused, thinking back. "Haduma was quite a woman. She was the oldest person I've ever met. Even older than Mamut. She's the mother of six generations." At least I hope so, he thought. "I really would like to see her again, but we can't take the time to look for them. I imagine she's dead by now, anyway, although her son, Tamen, would still be alive. He was the only one who spoke Zelandonii."

Ayla went out, and Jondalar was feeling a strong need to pass his water. He quickly pulled his tunic over his head and went outside, too. While he was holding his member, watching the steaming arc of strong-smelling yellow water pouring on the ground, he wondered if Noria ever did have the baby Haduma said she would, and if that organ he was holding was responsible for it.

He noticed Ayla heading toward the willows with only the chamois skin thrown over her shoulders. He supposed he ought to go and wash, too, although he'd had his fill of cold water today. It wasn't that he wouldn't get into it, if he had to, crossing the river, for example, but it hadn't seemed that washing frequently in cold water was so important when he was traveling with his brother.

And it wasn't that Ayla ever said anything to him, but since she never let cold water stop her, he felt he could hardly use that as an excuse to avoid washing himself—and he had to admit he liked the fact that she usually smelled so fresh. But sometimes she actually broke through ice to reach water, and he wondered how she stood it so cold.

At least she was up and around. He had thought they might have to make camp for several days, as chilled as she was, or even that she might get sick. Maybe all that cold washing has made her accustomed to cold water, he said to himself. Maybe a little washing wouldn't hurt me, either. He came to the realization that he had been watching the way her bare bottom peeked below the edge of the hide, moving back and forth enticingly as she walked.

Their Pleasures had been exciting and more satisfying than he would have imagined, considering how quickly they were over, but as he watched Ayla drape the soft skin over a branch and wade into the creek, he had an urge to start all

over again, only this time he would Pleasure her slowly,
lovingly, enjoying every part of her.

The rains continued intermittently as they started across
the lowland plains nestled between the Great Mother River
and the tributary that nearly matched her in size, the Sister.
They headed northwest, although their route was far from
direct. The central plains resembled the steppes to the east
and were in fact an extension of them, but the rivers traversing the ancient basin from north to south played a dominant
role in the character of the land. The frequently changing,
branching, and widely meandering course of the Great Mother
River, in particular, created enormous wetlands with the vast
dry grasslands.

Oxbow lakes developed in the sharply curved bends of
the larger channels that sprawled over the land, and the
marshes, wet meadows, and lush fields that gave diversity to
the magnificent steppes were a haven to unbelievable numbers
and varieties of birds, but they also caused detours for land-
bound travelers. The diversity of the skies was complemented
by a rich plant life and a variegated population of animals
that paralleled that of the eastern grasslands, but was more
concentrated, as though a larger landscape had shrunk while
its community of living creatures remained the same size.

Surrounded by mountains and highlands that funneled
more moisture to the land, the central plains, especially in
the south, were also more wooded, often in subtle ways.
Rather than stunted dwarfs, the brush and trees that crowded
close to watercourses were often full size and filled out. In
the southeastern section, near the broad turbulent confluence,
bogs and swamps stood in valleys and hollows, and these
became enormous during flood seasons. Small soggy fen
woods of alder, ash, and birch mired the unwary between
knolls capped with groves of willow, occasionally spiced with
oak and beech, while pines took root in sandier soils.

Most soils were either a mixture of rich loess and black
loams or sands and alluvial gravels, with an occasional outcrop of ancient rock interrupting the flat relief. Those isolated
highlands were usually forested with conifers, which sometimes extended down to the plains, providing a place for
several species of animals that could not live on the open
ground exclusively; life was richest at the margins. But with

all the complexity, the primary vegetation was still grass. Tallgrass and short steppe grasses and herbs, feather grasses and fescues, the central steppic plains were an extraordinarily rich, abundantly productive grassland blowing in the wind.

As Ayla and Jondalar left the southern plains and approached the cold north, the season seemed to progress more quickly than usual. The wind in their faces carried a hint of the earth-chilling cold of its source. The inconceivably massive accumulation of glacial ice, stretching over vast areas of northern lands, lay directly in front of them, within a walking distance much less than they had already traveled.

With the changing season, the increasing force of the icy air held a deep undercurrent of its potential power. The rains diminished and finally ceased altogether as ragged streaks of white replaced the thunderheads, the clouds torn to shreds by the strong steady winds. Sharp blasts tore the dry leaves from deciduous trees and scattered them in a loose carpet at their feet. Then, in a sudden change of mood, a sudden updraft lifted the brittle skeletons of summer growth, churned them around furiously and, tiring of the game, resettled them in another place.

But the dry, cold weather was more to the travelers' liking, familiar, even comfortable with their fur-lined hoods and parkas. Jondalar had been told correctly; hunting was easy in the central plains and the animals were fat and healthy after a summer of eating. It was also the time of year when many grains, fruits, nuts, and roots were ripe for harvesting. They had no need to use their emergency traveling food, and they even replenished supplies they had used when they killed a giant deer, then decided to stop and rest for a few days while they dried the meat. Their faces glowed with vigorous health and the happiness of being alive and in love.

The horses were rejuvenated, too. It was their milieu, the climate and conditions to which they had been adapted. Their heavy coats fluffed out with winter growth, and they were frisky and eager each morning. The wolf, nose pointed into the wind, picking up scents familiar to the deep instinctive recesses of his brain, loped contentedly along, made occasional forays on his own, then suddenly appeared again, looking smug, Ayla thought.

River crossings presented no problems. Most waterways ran parallel to the north-south direction of the Great Mother River, though they splashed through some that crossed the plain, but the patterns were unpredictable. The channels meandered so widely they weren't always sure if a stream running across their path was a turn in the river or one of the few streams coming down from higher ground. Some parallel channels ended abruptly in a westerly flowing stream that, in turn, emptied into another channel of the Mother.

Though they sometimes had to detour from their northerly direction because of a wide swing of the river, it was the kind of open grassland that made traveling on horseback such an advantage over traveling on foot. They made exceptionally good time, covering such long distances each day that they made up for previous delays. Jondalar was pleased to think that they were even compensating, somewhat, for his decision to take the long way around so they could visit the Sharamudoi.

The crisp, cold, clear days gave them a wide panoramic view, obscured only by morning mists when the sun warmed the condensed moisture from the night to above freezing. To the east now were the mountains they had skirted when they followed the great river across the hot southern plains, the same mountains over whose southwest corner they had climbed. The glistening glaciered peaks moved imperceptibly closer as the range curved toward the northwest in a great arc.

On their left, the highest chain of mountains on the continent, bearing a heavy crown of glacial ice that reached halfway down its flanks, marched in ridges from east to west. The towering, shining peaks loomed in the purple distance as a vaguely sinister presence, an apparently insurmountable barrier between the travelers and their ultimate destination. The Great Mother River would take them around the broad northern face of the range to a relatively small glacier that covered, with an armor of ice, an ancient rounded massif at the northwestern end of the alpine foreland of the mountains.

Lower and closer, beyond a grassy plain broken up by pine woods, another massif rose. The granite highland overlooked steppe meadows and the Mother, but gradually decreased as they continued north, blending into the rolling hills that continued all the way to the foothills of the western mountains. Fewer and fewer trees broke the openness of the grassy landscape, and those that did began to take on the familiar dwarfed contortions of trees sculptured by wind.

Ayla and Jondalar had traveled nearly three quarters of the entire distance, from south to north, of the immense central plains before the first snow flurries began.

"Jondalar, look! It's snowing!" Ayla said, and her smile was radiant. "It's the first snow of winter." She had been smelling snow in the air, and the first snow of the season always seemed special to her.

"I can't understand why you look so happy about it," he said, but her smile was contagious and he couldn't help smiling back. "You're going to be very tired of snow, and ice, before we see the last of it, I'm afraid."

"You're right, I know, but I still love the first snow." After a few more paces, she asked, "Can we make camp soon?"

"It's only a little past noon," Jondalar said, looking puzzled. "Why are you talking about making camp already?"

"I saw some ptarmigan a little while ago. They have started to turn white, but with no snow on the ground, they are easy to see right now. They won't be after it snows, and they always taste so good this time of year, especially the way Creb liked them, but it takes a long time to cook them that way." She was remembering, looking off into the distance. "You have to dig a hole in the ground, line it with rocks, and build a fire in it, then put the birds in, all wrapped in hay, cover them up, and then wait." The words had tumbled out of her mouth so fast, she almost tripped over them. "But it's worth the wait."

"Slow down, Ayla. You're all excited," he said, smiling with amusement and delight. He loved to watch her when she was filled with such enthusiasm. "If you are sure they will be that delicious, then I guess we ought to make an early camp, and go hunt ptarmigan."

"Oh, they will be," she said, looking at Jondalar with a serious expression, "but you've eaten them that way. You know how they taste." Then she noticed his smile and realized he had been playing with her. She pulled her sling out of her waistband. "You make camp, I'll hunt ptarmigan, and if you'll help me dig the hole, I'll even let you taste one," she said, grinning as she urged Whinney on.

"Ayla!" Jondalar called before she got very far. "If you

leave me the pole drag, I'll have camp all set up for you, 'Woman Who Hunts.' ''

She looked startled. "I didn't know you remembered what Brun named me when he allowed me to hunt," she said, returning and stopping in front of him.

"I may not have your Clan's memories, but I do remember some things, especially about the woman I love," he said, and he watched her full, lovely smile make her even more beautiful. "Besides, if you help me decide where to set up, you'll know where to come back and bring those birds."

"If I didn't see you, I would track you, but I will come and leave the drag. Whinney can't turn very fast with it."

They rode until they saw a likely place to make a camp, near a stream with a level area for the tent, a few trees, and, most important to Ayla, a rocky beach with stones that could be used for her ground oven.

"I might as well help set up camp, since I'm here," Ayla said, dismounting.

"Go hunt your ptarmigan. Just tell me where you want me to start digging a hole," Jondalar said.

Ayla paused, then nodded. The sooner the birds were killed, the sooner she could start cooking them, and they would take some time to cook, and maybe to hunt. She walked over the area and picked a spot that looked right for the ground oven. "Over here," she said, "not too far from these stones." She scanned the beach, deciding that she might as well pick out some nice round stones for her sling while she was there.

She signaled Wolf to come with her and backtracked along their trail, looking for the ptarmigan she had sighted. Once she started looking for the fat birds, she saw several species that resembled them. She was tempted first by the covey of gray partridges she saw pecking at the ripe seeds of ryegrass and einkorn wheat. She identified the surprisingly large number of young by their slightly less defined markings, not by their size. Though the middle-size stocky birds laid as many as twenty eggs in a clutch, they were usually subject to such heavy predation that not many survived to adulthood.

Gray partridges were also flavorful, but Ayla decided she would continue on, keeping their location in mind in case she didn't find the ptarmigan she had a taste for. A flock, several family coveys, of smaller gregarious quails startled her as they took to wing. The rotund little birds were tasty, too, and if she had known how to use a throwing stick that could bring down several at one time, she might have tried for them.

Since she had decided to pass by the others, Ayla was glad to see the usually well camouflaged ptarmigan near the place she had seen them before. Though they still showed some patterning on their backs and wings, their predominantly white feathers made them stand out against the grayish ground and dark gold dry grass. The fat, stocky birds had already grown winter feathers on their legs, extending even to their feet for both warmth and for use as snowshoes. Though quail often traveled longer distances, both partridge and ptarmigan, the grouse that turned white in snow, normally stayed within a general area close to their birthplace, migrating only a short distance between winter and summer ranges.

In the way of that wintry world, which allowed close associations of living things whose habitats would at other times be far apart, each had its niche and both would stay on the central plains through the winter. While the partridge kept to the windblown open grassland, eating seeds and roosting at night in trees near rivers and highlands, the ptarmigan would stay in the drifting snow, burrowing out snow caves to keep warm, and living on twigs, shoots, and buds of brush, often varieties containing strong oils that were distasteful or even poisonous to other animals.

Ayla signaled Wolf to stay while she picked out two stones from her pouch and readied her sling. From Whinney's back, she sighted on one nearly white bird and hurled the first stone. Wolf, understanding her motion as a signal, dashed for another bird at the same time. With a burst of wings and loud squawks of protest, the rest of the covey of heavy birds took to the air, their large flight muscles beating strongly. Their normal camouflaged markings on the ground made a startling change in the air when erect plumage displayed distinct patterns, making it easier for others of their kind to follow and keep together in a flock.

After the impetus of the first surge of activity and sudden flash of feathers, the flight of the ptarmigan eased into a long glide. With a pressure and movement of her body that was second nature, Ayla signaled Whinney to follow the birds, while she prepared to throw a second stone. The young woman grabbed the sling on the downstroke, slid her hand

down to the loose end, and, with a smooth practiced action
that moved with the motion, she brought it back to her throwing hand and dropped the second stone in the pocket before
she let go. Though she sometimes took an extra swing for
the first cast, she seldom required the buildup of momentum
for her second throw.

Her ability to cast stones so quickly was such a difficult
skill that, had she asked, she would have been told it was
impossible. But there was no one for her to ask, no one to
tell her it couldn't be done, so Ayla had taught herself the
double-stone technique. Over the years she had perfected it,
and she was very accurate with both stones. The bird she had
aimed for on the ground never took flight. As the second bird
came falling out of the sky, she quickly grabbed two more
stones, but by then the flock was out of reach.

Wolf trotted up with a third in his mouth. Ayla slid off
the mare and at her signal the wolf dropped the ptarmigan at
her feet. Then he sat down, looking up at her, pleased with
himself, a soft white feather clinging to the side of his mouth.

"That was good, Wolf," she said, grabbing his winter-
thickened ruff and touching her forehead to his. Then she
turned to the horse. "This woman appreciates your help,
Whinny," she said in her special language that was partly
Clan signs and soft horse nickers. The horse lifted her head,
snorted, and stepped closer to the woman. Ayla held the
mare's head up and blew into her nostrils, exchanging scents
of recognition and friendship.

She wrung the neck of one bird that wasn't dead; then,
using some tough grass, she tied the feathered feet of the
birds together. She mounted the horse and draped them across
the pack-saddle basket behind her. On her way back, she
came upon the partridges again, and she couldn't resist trying
for a couple of them as well. With two more stones, she got
two more birds, but she missed on her try for a third. Wolf
got one, and this time she let him keep his.

She thought she would cook them all at once to compare
both kinds of fowl. She would save the leftovers for the next
day or two. Then she began to think about what she might
stuff the cavities with. If they had been nesting, she would
have used their own eggs, but she had used grains when she
lived with the Mamutoi. It would take a long time to pick
enough grains, though. Harvesting wild grains was a time-
consuming process best done with a group of people. The

big ground roots might be good, maybe with wild carrots and onions.

Thinking about the meal she was going to prepare, the young woman wasn't paying much attention to her surroundings, but she could hardly help noticing when Whinney came to a complete halt. The mare tossed her head and neighed, then stood perfectly still, but Ayla could feel her tension. The horse was actually shaking, and the woman understood why.

23

Ayla sat on Whinney's back staring ahead, feeling an unaccountable apprehension, a fear welling up inside that sent a chill up her spine. She closed her eyes and shook her head to dispel the sensation. After all, there was nothing to fear. Opening her eyes, she looked again at the large herd of horses in front of them. What was so fearsome about a herd of horses?

Most of the horses were looking in their direction, and Whinney's attention was just as intensely focused on the other members of her species as they were on her. Ayla signaled Wolf to stay, noticing that he was very curious and overly eager to investigate. Horses, after all, were often prey to wolves, and the wild ones wouldn't like it if he got too close.

As Ayla studied the herd more closely, not quite sure what they or Whinney would do, she realized that it was not one, but two different herds. Dominating the area were the mares with their young, and Ayla assumed that the one standing aggressively forward of the others was the lead mare. In the background was a smaller herd of bachelors. Suddenly she noticed one standing between them, and then she couldn't help staring. It was the most unusual horse she had ever seen.

Most horses were variations of Whinney's shade of dun yellow, some tending more to tans, some more pale. Racer's dark brown coloring was unusual, she had never seen another horse as dark, but the coloring of the herd stallion was just as strange in the other direction. She had never seen a horse as light. The mature, well-formed stallion approaching warily was pure white!

Before he noticed Whinney, the white had been keeping the other males at bay, making it clear that, if they didn't come too close, they might be tolerated since it was not the season for horses to mate, but he was the only one who had the right to mingle with the females. The sudden appearance of a strange female, however, piqued his interest, and it caught the attention of the rest of the horses as well.

Horses, by nature, were social animals. They liked to associate with other horses. Mares in particular tended to form permanent relationships. But unlike the pattern of most herding animals, where the daughters remained with their mothers in close kinship groups, horses generally formed herds of unrelated mares. Young females usually left their natal group when they were fully mature, at about two years old. They did establish dominance hierarchies, which brought privileges and benefits to mares of high rank, and to their young—including first access to water and the best feeding areas—but their attachments were cemented by mutual grooming and other friendly activities.

Although they playfully sparred with each other when they were colts, it was not until the young male horses joined the mature stallions, at about four years old, that they began training in earnest for the day when they would fight for the right to mate. Although they groomed each other in the bachelor herd, vying for dominance was the major activity. Beginning with pushing and shoving, and ritualized defecating and sniffing, the contests escalated, especially during the spring rutting season, to rearing, biting necks, striking at knees, and kicking out hind legs toward faces, heads, and chests. It was only after several years in such associations that males were able to steal young females or displace an established herd male.

As an unattached female who had wandered into their range, Whinney was the object of intense interest on the part of both the female herd and the individual bachelors. Ayla decided she didn't like the way the herd stallion was moving toward them, so proud and forceful, as though he was about to make a claim.

"You don't have to stay anymore, Wolf," she said, giving him a sign that released him, and she watched while he stalked. To Wolf, it was a whole herd of Racers and Whinneys, and he wanted to play with them. Ayla was sure that his actions would not pose a serious threat to the horses. He could not bring down such a strong animal alone, anyway. That would have required a pack of wolves, and packs seldom attacked mature animals in the prime of health.

Ayla urged Whinney to start back to the camp. The mare hesitated for a moment, but her habit of obeying the woman was stronger than her interest in the other horses. She started walking, but slowly, and with continual hesitations. Then Wolf dashed into the herd. He was having fun chasing them, and Ayla was glad to see them scatter. It drew their attention away from her Whinney.

When Ayla arrived back at camp, everything was ready for her. Jondalar had just finished erecting the three poles to keep the food they carried out of the reach of most of the animals that might be interested in it. The tent was up, the hole was dug and lined with rocks, and he had even used some stones to make a boundary for the fireplace.

"Look at that island," he told her as she dismounted. He pointed to a stretch of land, built of accumulated silt, in the middle of the river with sedge, reeds, and several trees growing on it. "There's a whole flock of storks over there, black ones and white ones. I watched them land," he said with a pleased smile. "I kept wishing you would come. It was a sight worth seeing. They were diving and soaring, even flipping over. They just folded their wings and dropped from the sky to land; then when they were almost down, they opened their wings. It looked like they were heading south. They'll probably leave in the morning."

Ayla looked across the water at the large, long-billed, long-legged, stately birds. They were actively feeding, walking or running on the land or in the shallow water, snapping at anything that moved with their long, strong beaks, taking fish, lizards, frogs, insects, and earthworms. They even ate carrion, judging from the way they went after the remains of a bison washed up on the beach. The two species were quite similar in general shape, though different in coloring. The white storks had black-edged wings and there were more of them; the black storks had white underparts, and most of them were in the water after fish.

"We saw a big herd of horses on the way back," Ayla said, reaching for the ptarmigan and partridges. "A lot of mares and young ones, but a male was close by. The herd stallion is white."

"White?"

"As white as those white storks. He didn't even have black legs," she said, unfastening the thongs of the pack-saddle basket. "You'd never see him in snow."

"White is rare. I've never seen a white horse," Jondalar said. Then, thinking back to Noria and the First Rites ceremony, he recalled the white horsehide hanging on the wall behind the bed, decorated with the red heads of immature great spotted woodpeckers. "But I did once see the hide of a white horse," he said.

Something about the tone of his voice made Ayla look closer. He saw her look, blushed a little as he turned away to lift the carrier basket off Whinney, then felt compelled to explain further.

"It was during the . . . ceremony with the Hadumai."

"Are they horse hunters?" Ayla asked. She folded the riding blanket, then picked up the birds and walked to the edge of the river.

"Well, they do hunt horses. Why?" Jondalar asked, walking along with her.

"Remember Talut telling us about hunting the white mammoth? It was very sacred to the Mamutoi because they are the Mammoth Hunters," Ayla said. "If the Hadumai use a white horsehide during ceremonies, I wondered if they thought horses were special animals."

"It's possible, but we weren't with them long enough to know," Jondalar said.

"But they do hunt horses?" she asked, starting to pluck the feathers from the birds.

"Yes, they were hunting horses when Thonolan met them. They weren't very happy with us at first, because we had scattered the herd they were after, but we didn't know."

"I think I will put Whinney's halter on tonight, and tie

her next to the tent," Ayla said. "If there are horse hunters out there, I'd rather have her close by. And besides, I didn't like the way that white stallion was coming for her."

"You may be right. Maybe I should stake Racer down, too. I wouldn't mind seeing that white stallion, though," Jondalar said.

"I'd rather not see him again. He was too interested in Whinney. But he is unusual, and beautiful. You're right, white is rare," Ayla said. Feathers were flying as she pulled them out with rapid movements. She paused for a moment. "Black is rare, too," she said. "Do you remember when Ranec said that? I'm sure he meant himself as well, even though he was brown, not really black."

Jondalar felt a pang of jealousy at the mention of the name of the man Ayla almost mated, even though she had come away with him instead. "Are you sorry you did not stay with the Mamutoi and mate with Ranec?" he asked.

She turned and looked at him directly, her hands stopping her task. "Jondalar, you know the only reason I Promised Ranec was that I thought you didn't love me anymore, and I knew he did . . . but, yes, I am a little sorry. I could have stayed with the Mamutoi. If I had not met you, I think I could have been happy with Ranec. I did love him, in a way, but not the way I love you."

"Well, that's an honest answer, anyway," he said, frowning.

"I could have stayed with the Sharamudoi, too, but I want to be where you are. If you need to return to your home, then I want to go with you," Ayla continued, trying to explain. Noticing his frown, she knew it wasn't quite the answer he wanted to hear.

"You asked me, Jondalar. When you ask, I will always tell you what I feel. When I ask, I want you to tell me how you feel. Even if I don't ask, I want you to tell me if something is wrong. I don't ever want that kind of misunderstanding we had last winter to come between us, where I don't know what you mean, and you won't tell me, or you guess that I feel something, but you don't ask. Promise me that you will always tell me, Jondalar."

She looked so serious and so earnest that it made him want to smile with affection. "I promise, Ayla. I would never want to go through a time like that again, either. I couldn't stand it when you were with Ranec, especially when I could see why any woman would be interested in him. He was funny, and friendly. And he was a fine carver, a true artist. My mother would have liked him. She likes artists and carvers. If things had been different, I would have liked him myself. He reminded me of Thonolan, in a way. He may have looked different, but he was just like the Mamutoi, outspoken, confident.''

"He was a Mamutoi," Ayla said. "I do miss the Lion Camp. I miss the people. We haven't seen many people on this Journey. I didn't know how far you had traveled, Jondalar, or how much land there is. So much land and so few people.''

As the sun moved closer to the earth, the clouds over the high mountains to the west were reaching up to embrace the fiery orb and glowing pink in their excitement. The brightness settled into the brilliant enveloping display, then faded into darkness while Ayla and Jondalar finished their meal. Ayla got up to put the extra birds away; she had cooked much more than they could eat. Jondalar put cooking stones back in the fire in preparation for their evening tea.

"They were delicious," Jondalar said. "I'm glad you wanted to stop early. It was worth it.''

Ayla happened to glance toward the island, and, with a gasp, her eyes opened wide. Jondalar heard her startled intake of breath, and looked up.

Several people carrying spears had appeared out of the gloom and stepped into the edge of the light by the fire. Two of them wore capes of horsehide, with the dried head still attached and worn over the head like a hood. Jondalar stood up. One of the men pulled his horse-head hood back and walked toward him.

"Zel-an-don-yee!" the man said, pointing at the tall blond man. Then he slapped himself on the chest. "Hadumai! Jeren!" He was grinning broadly.

Jondalar looked closely, then grinned back. "Jeren! Is that you? Great Mother, I can't believe it! It is you.''

The man started talking in a language just as unintelligible to Jondalar as his was to Jeren, but the friendly smiles were understood.

"Ayla!" Jondalar said, motioning her over. "This is Jeren. He's the Hadumai hunter who stopped us when we were heading the other way. I can't believe it!" Both were still grinning with delight. Jeren looked at Ayla, and his smile took on an appreciative gleam as he nodded at Jondalar.

"Jeren, this is Ayla, Ayla of the Mamutoi," Jondalar said, making formal introductions. "Ayla, this is Jeren, one of Haduma's people."

Ayla held out both her hands. "Welcome to our camp, Jeren of Haduma's people," she said.

Jeren understood the intent, although it wasn't a customary greeting among his people. He put his spear into a holder slung across his back, took both her hands, and said, "Ayla," knowing it was her name, but not comprehending the rest of the words. He slapped himself on the chest again. "Jeren," he said, then added some unfamiliar words.

Then the man jerked with sudden apprehension. He had seen a wolf move to Ayla's side. Seeing his reaction, Ayla immediately knelt down and put an arm around the wolf's neck. Jeren's eyes opened with surprise.

"Jeren," she said, standing up and making the motions of a formal introduction. "This is Wolf. Wolf, this is Jeren, one of Haduma's people."

"Wolf?" he said, his eyes still full of concern.

Ayla put her hand in front of Wolf's nose, as if letting him smell her scent. Then she knelt down beside the wolf and put her arm around him again, demonstrating her closeness and lack of fear. She touched Jeren's hand, then put her hand to Wolf's nose again, showing him what she wanted him to do. Hesitantly Jeren extended his hand toward the animal.

Wolf touched it with his cold wet nose and pulled back. He had been through a similar introduction many times when they had stayed with the Sharamudoi, and he seemed to understand Ayla's intention. Then Ayla took Jeren's hand and, looking up at him, guided it toward the wolf's head to let him feel the fur, showing him how to stroke Wolf's head. When Jeren looked at her with a smile of acknowledgment and petted Wolf's head on his own accord, she relaxed.

Jeren turned around and looked at the others. "Wolf!" he said, making a gesture toward him. He said some other things, then spoke her name. Four men stepped into the light of the fire. Ayla made welcoming motions to come and sit.

Jondalar, who had been watching, was smiling his approval. "That was a good idea, Ayla," he said.

"Do you think they're hungry? We have a lot of food left," she said.

"Why don't you offer it and see."

She took out a platter made of mammoth ivory that she had used for the birds they had eaten, picked up something that looked like a wilted bundle of hay, and opened it to reveal a whole cooked ptarmigan. She held it out toward Jeren and the rest. The aroma preceded it. Jeren went to break off a leg and he found a tender and juicy piece of meat in his hand. The smile on his face after tasting it encouraged the others.

Ayla brought out a partridge as well, served out the stuffing of roots and grains onto a makeshift assortment of bowls and smaller plates, some woven, some made of ivory, and one of wood. She left the men to divide up the meat as they wanted, while she got out a large wooden bowl, one she had made, and filled it with water for tea.

The men looked much more relaxed after the meal, even when Ayla brought Wolf to sniff them. As they all sat around the fire holding cups of tea, they tried to communicate beyond the level of smiling friendliness and hospitality.

Jondalar started. "Haduma?" he asked.

Jeren shook his head and looked sad. He made a motion toward the ground with his hand that Ayla sensed meant she had returned to the Great Earth Mother. Jondalar understood as well that the old woman he had grown so fond of was gone.

"Tamen?" he asked.

Smiling, Jeren nodded in an exaggerated fashion. Then he pointed to one of the others and said something that included Tamen's name. A young man, hardly more than a boy, smiled at them, and Jondalar saw a similarity to the man he had known.

"Tamen, yes," Jondalar said, smiling and nodding. "Tamen's son, or perhaps grandson, I think. I wish Tamen were here," he said to Ayla. "He knew some Zelandonii, and we could talk a little. He made a long Journey there when he was a young man."

Jeren looked around the camp, then at Jondalar, and said, "Zel-an-don-yee . . . Ton . . . Tonolan?"

This time Jondalar shook his head and looked sad. Then, thinking about it, he made the motion toward the ground. Jeren looked surprised, but he nodded and said a word that was a question. Jondalar didn't understand, and he looked at Ayla. "Do you know what he's asking?"

Though the language was unfamiliar, there was a quality about most languages she had heard that felt familiar. Jeren said the word again, and something about his expression or his tone gave her an idea. She held her hand in the shape of a claw and growled like a cave lion.

The sound she made was so realistic that all the men gaped at her with shocked surprise, but Jeren nodded with understanding. He had asked how Thonolan died, and she had told him. One of the other men said something to Jeren. When Jeren responded, Jondalar heard another familiar name, Noria. The one who asked smiled at the tall blond man, pointed at him, and then at his own eye, and smiled again.

Jondalar felt a flush of excitement. Maybe it meant that Noria did have a baby with his blue eyes. But then he wondered if it was just that the hunter had heard of the man with the blue eyes who had celebrated First Rites with her? He couldn't be sure. The other men were pointing at their eyes and smiling. Were they smiling about a baby with blue eyes? Or grinning about Pleasures with a blue-eyed man?

He thought about saying Noria's name and rocking his arms as though he were holding a baby, but then he glanced at Ayla and held back. He hadn't said anything to her about Noria, or about the announcement Haduma had made the next day that the Mother had blessed the ceremony and that the young woman would have a child, a boy named Jondal, who would have eyes like his. He knew that Ayla wanted a child of his . . . or of his spirit. How would she feel about it if she knew Noria already had one? If he were Ayla, he would probably be jealous.

Ayla was making motions indicating that the hunters should sleep near the fire. Several nodded and got up to get their sleeping rolls. They had stashed them downriver before they approached the fire they had smelled, hoping it was a friendly fire, but not sure. But when Ayla saw them heading around the tent, toward the place where she had staked the horses, she ran in front of the men and held up her hand to stop them. They looked at each other with questioning glances when she disappeared into the dark. When they started to leave again, Jondalar made a motion to wait. They smiled and nodded acquiescence.

Their expression changed to one of fear when Ayla reappeared leading two horses. She stood between the two animals and tried to explain with motions and even the expressive Clan gestures that these were special horses that should not be hunted, but neither she nor Jondalar was sure they understood. Jondalar was even concerned that they might think she had some unique powers to Call horses and had brought these expressly for them to hunt. He told Ayla that he thought a demonstration might help.

He got a spear from inside the tent and made motions with it as though he were going to stab Racer, but Ayla stood barring the way with her arms held up and crossed in front of her, shaking her head emphatically. Jeren scratched his head and the other men looked puzzled. Finally Jeren nodded, took one of his own spears out of the holder on his back, aimed it toward Racer, and then stabbed it into the ground. Jondalar didn't know if the man thought Ayla was telling them not to hunt those two horses, or not to hunt horses at all, but some point had been understood.

The men slept near their fire that night but were up just after first light. Jeren said some words to Ayla that Jondalar vaguely remembered referred to appreciation for food. The visitor smiled at the woman when Wolf sniffed at him and allowed himself to be petted again. She tried to invite them to share their morning meal, but they left quickly.

"I wish I had known some of their language," Ayla said. "It was nice to visit, but we couldn't talk."

"Yes, I wish we could have, too," Jondalar said, sincerely wishing that he had found out whether Noria ever did have a baby, and if it had his blue eyes.

"In the Clan, different clans used some words in their everyday language that weren't always understood by everyone, but everyone knew the silent language of gestures. You could always communicate," Ayla said. "Too bad the Others don't have a language everyone can understand."

"It would be helpful, especially when you are on a Journey, but it's hard for me to imagine a language that everyone would understand. Do you really think that people of the Clan everywhere can understand the same sign language?" Jondalar asked.

"It's not like a language they have to learn. They are born with it, Jondalar. It is so ancient that it is in their memories, and their memories go back to the beginning. You can't imagine how far back that is," Ayla said.

She shivered with a chill of fear as she remembered the time that Creb, to save her life, had taken her back with them, against all tradition. By the unwritten law of the Clan, he should have let her die. But to the Clan, she was dead, now. It occurred to her how ironic that was. When Broud had cursed her with death, he shouldn't have. He didn't have a good reason. Creb did have a reason; she had broken the most powerful taboo of the Clan. Perhaps he should have made sure that she died, but he didn't.

They began striking camp and stowing their tent, sleeping rolls, cooking utensils, ropes, and other equipment in the pack-saddle baskets, with the efficiency of unspoken routine. Ayla was filling waterbags at the river when Jeren and his hunters returned. With smiles and many words of what were obviously profuse thanks, the men presented Ayla with a package wrapped in a piece of fresh aurochs hide. She opened it to find the tender rump, butchered from a recent kill.

"I am grateful, Jeren," Ayla said, and she gave him the beautiful smile that always made Jondalar melt with love. It seemed to have a similar affect on Jeren, and Jondalar smiled inwardly when he saw the dazed expression on the man's face. It took Jeren a moment to collect himself; then he turned to Jondalar and began talking, trying very hard to communicate something. He stopped when he saw he was not being understood, and he talked to the other men. Then he turned back to Jondalar.

"Tamen," he said, and began walking toward the south and motioning for them to follow. "Tamen," he repeated, beckoning and adding some other words.

"I think he wants you to go with him," Ayla said, "to see that man you know. The one who speaks Zelandonii."

"Tamen, Zel-an-don-yee. Hadumai," Jeren said, beckoning both of them.

"He must want us to visit. What do you think?" Jondalar said.

"Yes, I think you're right," Ayla said. "Do you want to stop and visit?"

"It would mean going back," Jondalar said, "and I don't know how far. If we had met them farther south, I wouldn't have minded stopping for a little while on the way, but I hate to go back now that we've come this far."

Ayla nodded. "You'll have to tell him, somehow."

Jondalar smiled at Jeren, then shook his head. "I'm

sorry," he said, "but we need to go north. North," he repeated, pointing in that direction.

Jeren looked distressed, shook his head, then closed his eyes as if trying to think. He walked toward them and took a short staff out of his belt. Jondalar noticed the top of it was carved. He knew he had seen one like it before, and he tried to remember where. Jeren cleared a space on the ground, then drew a line with the staff, and another crossing it. Below the first line, he drew a figure that vaguely resembled a horse. At the end of the second line pointing toward the channel of the Great Mother River, he drew a circle with a few lines radiating from it. Ayla looked more closely.

"Jondalar," she said, with excitement in her voice, "when Mamut was showing me symbols and teaching me what they meant, that was a sign for 'sun.' "

"And that line points in the direction of the setting sun," Jondalar said, pointing west. "Where he drew the horse, that must be south." He indicated the direction when he said it.

Jeren was nodding vigorously. Then he pointed north and frowned. He walked to the north end of the line he had drawn and stood facing them. He lifted his arms and crossed them in front of him, in the same way that Ayla had done when she was trying to tell Jeren not to hunt Whinney and Racer. Then he shook his head no. Ayla and Jondalar looked at each other and back at Jeren.

"Do you think he's trying to tell us not to go north?" Ayla asked.

Jondalar felt a dawning recognition of what Jeren was trying to communicate. "Ayla, I don't think he just wants us to go south with him and visit. I think he's trying to tell us something more. I think he's trying to warn us not to go north."

"Warn us? What could be north that he would warn us against?" Ayla said.

"Could it be the great wall of ice?" Jondalar wondered.

"We know about the ice. We hunted mammoth near it with the Mamutoi. It's cold, but not really dangerous, is it?"

"It does move," Jondalar said, "over many years, and sometimes it even uproots trees with the changing seasons, but it doesn't move so fast that you can't get out of its way."

"I don't think it's the ice," Ayla said. "But he's telling us not to go north, and he seems very concerned."

"I think you're right, but I can't imagine what could be

so dangerous,'' Jondalar said. "Sometimes people who don't travel much beyond their own range imagine that the world outside their territory is dangerous, because it's different.''

"I don't think Jeren is a man who fears very much,'' Ayla said.

"I have to agree," Jondalar said, then faced the man. ''Jeren, I wish I could understand you.''

Jeren had been watching them. He guessed from their expressions that they had understood his warning, and he was waiting for their response.

"Do you think we should go with him and talk to Tamen?'' Ayla asked.

"I hate to turn back and lose time now. We still have to reach that glacier before the end of winter. If we keep going, we should make it easily, with time to spare, but if anything happens to delay us, it could be spring and melting, and too dangerous to cross,'' Jondalar said.

"So we'll keep going north," Ayla said.

"I think we should, but we will be watchful. I just wish I knew what I should be watching for." He looked at the man again. "Jeren, my friend, I thank you for your warning," he said. "We will be careful, but I think we should keep on going." He pointed south, then shook his head and pointed north.

Jeren, trying to protest, shook his head again, but he finally gave up and nodded acceptance. He had done what he could. He went to talk to the other man in the horse-head cape, spoke for a moment, then returned and indicated they were going.

Ayla and Jondalar waved as Jeren and his hunters left. Then they finished up their packing and, with some reservations, started out toward the north.

As the Journeyers traveled across the northern end of the vast central grassland, they could see the terrain ahead was changing; the flat lowlands were giving way to rugged hills. The occasional highlands that had interrupted the central plain were connected, though partly submerged beneath the soil in the midland basin, to great broken blocks of faulted sedimentary rock running in an irregular backbone from northeast to southwest through the plain. Relatively recent volcanic eruptions had covered the highlands with fertile soils that nurtured forests of pine, spruce, and larch on the upper reaches, with birch and willows on the lower slopes, while brush and steppe grass grew on the dry lee sides.

As they started up into the rugged hills, they found themselves having to backtrack and work their way around deep holes and broken formations that blocked their way. Ayla thought the land seemed more barren, though with the deepening cold she wondered if it might be the changing season that gave that impression. Looking back from the heightened elevation, they gained a new perspective of the land they had crossed. The few deciduous trees and brush were bare of leaves, but the central plain was covered with the dusty gold of dry standing hay that would feed multitudes through the winter.

They sighted many large grazing animals, in herds and individually. Horses seemed most prevalent to Ayla, perhaps because she was especially conscious of them, but giant deer, red deer, and, particularly as they reached the northern steppes, reindeer were also abundant. The bison were gathering into large migratory herds and heading south. During one whole day, the great humpy beasts with huge black horns moved over the rolling hills of the northern grassland in a thick, undulating carpet, and Ayla and Jondalar stopped often to watch. The dust rose to cast an obscuring pall over the great moving mass, the earth shook with the pounding hooves of their passage, and the combined roar of the multitude of deep rolling grunts and bawls growled like thunder.

They saw mammoths less often, usually traveling north, but even from a distance the giant woolly beasts commanded attention. When not driven by the demands of reproduction, male mammoths tended to form small herds with loose ties for companionship. Occasionally one would join a female herd and travel with it for a while, but whenever the Journeyers noticed a lone mammoth, it was invariably male. The larger permanent herds were of closely related females; a grandmother, the old and wily matriarch who was their leader, and sometimes a sister or two, with their daughters and grandchildren. The female herds were easy to identify because their tusks tended to be somewhat smaller and less curved, and there were always young ones with them.

Though also impressive when they were sighted, woolly rhinoceroses were most rare and least social. They didn't, as a rule, herd together. Females kept to small family groups and, except during mating, males were solitary. Neither mammoths nor rhinoceroses, except for the young and the very old, had much to fear from four-legged hunters, not even the huge cave lion. The males in particular could afford to be solitary; the females needed the herds to help protect their young.

The smaller woolly musk-oxen, however, who were goat-like creatures, all banded together for protection. When they were under attack, the adults usually packed themselves into a circular phalanx facing outward, with the young ones in the middle. A few chamois and ibex made an appearance as Ayla and Jondalar climbed higher in the hills; they often dropped down to lower ground with the approach of winter.

Many of the small animals were secure for the winter in their nests burrowed deep in the ground, surrounded by stores of seeds, nuts, bulbs, roots, and, in the case of pikas, piles of hay that they had cut and dried. The rabbits and hares were changing color, not to white, but to a lighter mottled shade, and on a wooded knoll they saw a beaver and a tree squirrel. Jondalar used his spear-thrower to get the beaver. Besides the meat, the fatty beaver tail was a rare and rich delicacy, roasted by itself on a spit over the fireplace.

They usually used the spear-throwers for the larger game they hunted. They were both quite accurate with the weapons, but Jondalar had more power, could throw farther. Ayla often brought down the smaller animals with her sling.

Though they didn't hunt them, they noticed that otter, badger, polecat, marten, and mink were also numerous. The carnivores—foxes, wolves, lynxes, and larger cats—found sustenance in small game or the other herbivores. And though they seldom fished on this leg of their Journey, Jondalar knew there were sizable fish in the river, including perch, pike, and very big carp.

Toward evening they saw a cave with a large opening and decided to investigate it. As they approached, the horses did not show any nervousness, which the humans took to be a good sign. Wolf sniffed around with interest when they entered the cave, obviously curious, but no hackles were raised. Seeing the unconcerned behavior of the animals, Ayla felt confident that the cave was empty, and they decided to camp for the night.

After building a fire, they made a torch to explore a little deeper. Near the front were many signs that the cave had been used before. Jondalar thought the scrapes on the walls were either from a bear or a cave lion. Wolf smelled out droppings nearby but they were so dry and old that it was hard to tell what animal had made them. They found large, dry leg bones that had been partly eaten. The way they were broken and the teeth marks made Ayla think cave hyenas had cracked them with their extremely powerful jaws. She shuddered with repugnance at the thought.

Hyenas were no worse an animal than any other. They scavenged the carcasses that had died naturally and the kills of others, but so did other predators, including wolves, lions, and humans, and hyenas were also effective pack hunters. That didn't matter, Ayla's hatred of them was irrational. To her they represented the worst of all that was bad.

But the cave had not been used recently. All the signs were old, including the charcoal in a shallow pit from the fire of some other human visitor. Ayla and Jondalar went into the cave for some distance, but it seemed to go on forever, and beyond the dry front opening there were no signs of use. Stone columns, seeming to grow up from the floor or down from the ceiling and sometimes meeting in the middle, were the only inhabitants of the cool damp interior.

When they came to a bend, they thought they heard running water from deep within, and they decided to turn back. They knew the makeshift torch would not last long, and neither of them wanted to go beyond sight of the fading light from the entrance. They walked back touching the limestone walls and were glad to see the drab gold of dry grass and brilliant golden light outlining clouds in the west.

As they rode deeper into the highlands north of the great central plain, Ayla and Jondalar noticed more changes. The terrain was becoming pocked with caves, caverns, and sinkholes that ranged from bowl-shaped dips covered with grass, to inaccessible drop-offs that fell to great depths. It was a peculiar landscape that made them feel vaguely uneasy. While surface streams and lakes were rare, they sometimes heard the eerie sound of rivers running underground.

Unknown creatures of warm ancient seas were the cause of that strange and unpredictable land. Over untold millennia, the sea floors grew thick with their settling shells and skeletons. After even longer eons, the sediment of calcium hardened, was lifted high by conflicting movements of the earth, and became rocks of calcium carbonate, limestone. Underlying great stretches of land, most of the earth's caves were formed out of limestone because, given the right conditions, the hard sedimentary rock will dissolve.

In pure water, it is hardly soluble at all, but water that is even slightly acid attacks limestone. During warmer seasons and when climates were humid, circulating ground water, bearing carbonic acid from plants and charged with carbon dioxide, dissolved vast quantities of the carbonate rock.

Flowing along flat bedding planes and down minute cracks at the vertical joints in the thick layers of the calcareous stone, the ground water gradually widened and deepened the fissures. It carved jagged pavements and intricate grooves as it carried the dissolved limestone away, to escape in seepages and springs. Forced to lower levels by gravity, the acidic water enlarged underground cracks into caves. Caves became caverns and stream channels, with narrow vertical shafts opening into them, and eventually joined with others to become entire subterranean water systems.

The dissolving rock below the ground had a profound effect on the land above it, and the landscape, called karst, displayed unusual and distinctive features. As caves became larger, and their tops extended closer to the surface, they collapsed, creating steep-walled sinkholes. Occasional remnants of the cavern roofs left natural bridges. Streams and rivers running along the surface would suddenly disappear into the sinkholes and flow underground, sometimes leaving valleys that had been formed earlier by rivers, high and dry.

Water was becoming harder to find. Running water quickly sank into cavities and potholes in the rocks. Even after a heavy rainfall, the water disappeared almost instantly, with no rivulets or streams running across the ground. Once the travelers had to go to a small pool at the bottom of a sinkhole for the precious fluid. Another time, water suddenly appeared in a large spring, flowed across the surface for a while, then disappeared underground again.

The ground was barren and rocky, with thin surface soil that exposed underlying rock. Animal life was scarce as well.

Except for some mouflon, with their tightly curled wool coats thickened for winter, and heavy curling horns, the only animals they saw were a few rock marmots. The quick, wily little creatures were adept at evading their many predators. Whether it was wolves, arctic foxes, hawks, or golden eagles, a high-pitched whistle from a lookout sent them scurrying into small holes and caves.

Wolf tried to follow them in pursuit, to no avail, but since long-legged horses were not normally perceived as dangerous, Ayla managed to down a few with her sling. The furry little rodents, fattened for winter hibernation, tasted much like rabbit, but they were small, and for the first time since the previous summer, they often fished the Great Mother River for their dinner.

At first their uneasiness made Ayla and Jondalar very careful traveling through the karst landscape, with its strange formations, caves, and holes, but familiarity lessened their concern. They were walking to give the horses a rest. Jondalar had Racer on a long lead but let him stop to graze a mouthful of the sparse dry grass now and then. Whinney was doing the same, biting off a mouthful, then following Ayla, though she was not using the halter.

"I wonder if the danger Jeren was trying to warn us about was this barren land full of caves and holes," Ayla was saying. "I don't like it much here."

"No, I don't either. I didn't know it would be like this," Jondalar said.

"Haven't you been here before? But I thought you came this way," the woman said, looking surprised. "You said you followed the Great Mother River."

"We did follow the Great Mother River, but we stayed on the other side. We didn't cross until we were much farther south. I thought it would be easier to stay on this side coming back, and I was curious about this side. The river makes a very sharp turn not far from here. We were heading east then, and I wondered about the highland that forced her south. I knew this would be the only chance I'd ever have to see it."

"I wish you had told me before."

"What difference does it make? We're still following the river."

"But I thought you were familiar with this area. You don't know any more about it than I do." Ayla wasn't quite sure why it bothered her so much, except that she had counted on him to know what to expect, and now she found that he didn't. It made her feel nervous about the strange place.

They had been walking along, involved in the conversation that was edging toward a grievance, if not an argument, and not paying much attention to where they were going. Suddenly Wolf, who had been trotting alongside of Ayla, yipped and nudged her leg. They both turned to look and stopped short. Ayla felt a sudden surge of fright, and Jondalar blanched.

24

The woman and man looked toward the ground ahead and saw nothing. The land in front of them had ceased to be there. They had nearly stepped over the edge of a precipice. Jondalar felt the familiar tightening in his groin as he stared down at the steep drop-off, but he was surprised to see that far below was a long, flat green field, with a stream running through it.

The floors of big sinkholes were usually covered with a deep layer of soil, the insoluble residue of the limestone, and some of the deep sinkholes joined together and opened out into elongated depressions, creating large areas of land deep below the normal surface. With both soil and water, the vegetation below was rich and inviting. The problem was that neither of them could see any way to get down to the green meadow at the bottom of the steep-sided hole.

"Jondalar, there's something wrong about this place," Ayla said. "It's so dry and barren, hardly anything can live up here; down there is a beautiful meadow with a stream and trees, but nothing can reach it. Any animal that tried would die in the fall. It's all mixed up. It feels wrong.''

"It does feel wrong. And maybe you're right, Ayla. Maybe this is what Jeren was trying to warn us about. There's not much here for hunters, and it's dangerous. I've never known of a place where you had to worry about falling over a cliff when you're just walking across the land.''

Ayla bent down, grabbed Wolf's head with both her hands, and touched her forehead to his. "Thank you, Wolf, for warning us when we weren't paying attention,'' she said. He whined his affection and licked her face in response.

They backed up and led the the horses around the deep hole, without saying much. Ayla couldn't even remember what was so important about the argument they almost had. She only thought that they should never have gotten so distracted that they didn't even see where they were going.

As they continued north, the river on their left began flowing through a gorge that was becoming deeper as the rocky cliffs got higher. Jondalar wondered whether they should try to follow close to the water or keep to the highland above, but he was glad they were following the river's course and not attempting to cross it. Rather than valleys with grassy slopes and broad floodplains, in karst regions the large rivers that could be seen from the surface tended to flow in steep-sided limestone gorges. As difficult as it was to use waterways as travel routes with no stream edge to walk along, it was even harder to get across them.

Remembering the great gorge farther south, with long stretches where there were no banks, Jondalar decided to stay on the highland. As they continued to climb, he was relieved to see a long thin stream of water falling down the face of the rock into the water of the river below. Although the waterfall was across the river, it meant some water was available on the higher ground, even though most of it quickly disappeared into the cracks of the karst.

But karst was also a landscape with many caves. They were so frequent that Ayla and Jondalar, and the horses, spent the next two nights protected from the weather by stone walls, without having to put up the tent. After examining several, they began to develop a sense about which openings in the rock were likely to be suitable for them.

Although water-filled caverns deep underground were

continuing to increase in size, most enterable caves near the surface were no longer growing larger. Instead, the space inside was decreasing, sometimes rapidly when the general conditions were wet, though hardly changing at all during dry spells. Some caves could only be entered in dry weather; they would fill up during heavy rains. Some, though always open, had running streams covering the floors. The travelers looked for dry caves, usually somewhat higher up, but water, along with limestone, had been the instrument that had shaped and sculpted all of them.

Rainwater, slowly seeping through the rock of the roof, absorbed the dissolved limestone. Each drip of calcareous water, even the tiniest droplet of moisture in the air, was saturated with calcium carbonate in solution, which was redeposited inside the cave. Though usually pure white, the hardened mineral could be beautifully translucent, or mottled and shaded with gray, or faintly colored with tints of red or yellow. Pavements of travertine were created, and immovable draperies festooned the walls. Icicles of stone hanging from the ceiling strained with each wet drop to meet their counterparts growing slowly from the floor. Some were joined in thin-waisted columns, which grew thicker with time in the ever-changing cycle of the living earth.

The days were getting noticeably colder and windier, and Ayla and Jondalar were glad for the prevalence of caves to break the chill of the wind. They usually checked potential shelters to make sure they were not occupied by four-legged inhabitants before they moved in, but they found they could rely on the keener senses of their traveling companions to warn them of danger. Without saying so, or consciously considering it, they depended on the smell of smoke to tell them if there were human occupants—humans were the only animals that used fire—but they encountered no one, and even other animal species were rare.

Therefore, they were surprised when they came to a region that was unusually lavish in vegetation, at least compared with the rest of the barren, rocky landscape. Limestone was not all the same. It varied greatly in how easily it dissolved, and in the proportion that was insoluble. As a result, some areas of limestone karst were fertile, with meadows and

trees growing beside normal streams that flowed on the surface. Sinking lands and caves and underground rivers did
exist in those areas, but they were rarer.

When they came upon a herd of reindeer grazing in a
field of dry standing hay, Jondalar looked at Ayla with a
smile, then pulled out his spear-thrower. Ayla nodded in
agreement and urged Whinney to follow the man and the
stallion. With nothing around but a few small animals, hunting had been poor, and as the river was by then far below
in the gorge, they hadn't been able to fish. They had been
subsisting essentially on dried food and emergency traveling
rations, even sharing some with the wolf. The horses were
hard pressed, too. The scraggly grass that managed to grow
in the thin soil had been barely sufficient for them.

Jondalar slit the throat to bleed the small-antlered doe
they killed. Then they lifted the carcass into the bowl boat
attached to the travois and looked for a place to camp nearby.
Ayla wanted to dry some of the meat and render the animal's
winter fat, and Jondalar was looking forward to a good piece
of roast haunch and some tender liver. They thought they'd
stay a day or so, especially with the meadow nearby. The
horses needed the feed. Wolf had discovered an abundance
of small creatures, voles, lemmings, and pikas, and had gone
off to hunt and explore.

When they noticed a cave tucked into a hillside, they
headed for it. It was a little smaller than they would have
liked, but it seemed sufficient. They dropped the pole drag
and unloaded the horses to let them enjoy the meadow, put
the packs beside the cave, and dragged the travois over themselves, then spread out to collect woody brush and dried dung.

Ayla was looking forward to making a meal with fresh
meat and was thinking about what to cook with it. She gathered some dried seed heads and grains from the meadow
grasses, and handfuls of the tiny black seeds from the pigweed that was growing beside a small stream somewhat north
of the cave. When she returned, Jondalar had already started
the fire, and she asked him to go to the stream and fill up
the waterbags.

Wolf arrived before the man came back, but when the
animal approached the cave, he bared his teeth and snarled
menacingly. Ayla felt the hairs on the back of her neck rise.

"Wolf, what is it?" she said, unconsciously reaching for
her sling and picking up a stone, although her spear-thrower

was just as close. The wolf stalked slowly into the cave, his throat rumbling with a deep snarl. Ayla followed behind, ducking her head to enter the small dark opening in the rock, and she wished she had brought a torch. But her nose told her what her eyes could not see. It had been many years since she had smelled that odor, but she would never forget it. Suddenly her mind pictured that first time so long ago.

They were in the foothills of the mountains not far from the Clan Gathering. Her son was riding on her hip, supported by his carrying cloak, and though she was young and one of the Others, she was walking in the medicine woman's position. They had all stopped in their tracks and were staring at the monstrous cave bear, nonchalantly scratching his back against the bark of the tree.

Though the huge creature, twice the size of ordinary brown bears, was the most revered totem of all the Clan, the young people of Brun's clan had never seen a living one. There were none left in the mountains near their cave, though dry bones attested to the fact that there once had been. For the powerful magic they contained, Creb had retrieved the few tufts of hair that had been caught in the bark after the cave bear finally lumbered off, leaving only his distinctive smell behind.

Ayla signaled Wolf and backed out of the cave. She noticed the sling in her hand and tucked it in her waist tie with a wry face. What good was a sling against a cave bear? She was just grateful that the bear had begun his long sleep and hadn't been disturbed by her intrusion. She quickly threw dirt on the fire and stamped it out, then picked up her pack-saddle basket and moved it away from the cave. Fortunately they hadn't unpacked very much. She went back for Jondalar's pack and then dragged the travois by herself. She had just picked up her pack again to move it farther away when Jondalar appeared with the full waterbags.

"What are you doing, Ayla?" he asked.

"There's a cave bear in that cave," she said. At his look of apprehension, she added, "He's started his long sleep, I think, but they sometimes move if they are disturbed early in winter, at least that's what they said."

"Who said?"

"The hunters of Brun's clan. I used to watch them when they talked about hunting . . . sometimes," Ayla explained. Then she grinned. "Not just sometimes. I watched as often as I could, especially after I started practicing with my sling. The men usually didn't pay attention to a girl busying herself nearby. I knew they would never teach me, and watching when they exchanged hunting stories was a way to learn. I thought they might be angry if they found out what I was doing, but I didn't know how severe the punishment would be . . . until later."

"I guess if anyone would, the Clan would know about cave bears," Jondalar said. "Do you think it's safe to stay around here?"

"I don't know, but I don't think I want to," she said.

"Why don't you call Whinney. We have time before it gets dark to find another place."

After spending the night in their tent out in the open, they started out early in the morning, wanting to put still more distance between themselves and the cave bear. Jondalar didn't want to take the time to dry the meat, and he convinced Ayla that the temperature was cold enough for it to keep. He was in a hurry to get out of the region altogether. Where there was one bear, there were usually more.

But when they reached the top of a ridge, they stopped. In the sharp, clear, cold air, they could see in all directions, and the view was spectacular. Directly east, a snow-covered mountain of somewhat lower elevation rose in the foreground, drawing attention to the eastern range, closer now and curving around them. Though not exceptionally tall, the glaciered mountains reached their highest point to the north, rising to form a line of jagged white peaks, shadowed with hints of glacier blue against the deep azure sky.

The icy northern mountains were in the broad outer belt of the curving arc; the travelers were in the innermost arc, in the foothills of the range that encompassed them, standing on a ridge that stretched across the northern end of the ancient basin that formed the central plain. The great glacier, the densely packed cake of solid ice that had spread down from the north until it covered nearly a quarter of the land, ended in a mountainous wall that was hidden just beyond the far peaks. Toward the northwest, highlands that were lower but closer dominated the horizon. Shimmering in the distance the northern glacial ice could be glimpsed hovering like a pale horizon above the nearer heights. The huge range of much higher mountains to the west was lost in clouds.

The distant mountains that surrounded them were magnificent, but the most heart-stopping sight was closer at hand. Down below, in the deep gorge, the course of the Great Mother River had changed direction. It was now coming from the west. As Ayla and Jondalar stared down from the ridge and looked upstream at the wavering course of the river, they, too, felt as though they had reached a turning point.

"The glacier we have to cross is due west of here," Jondalar said, his voice taking on a faraway tone that matched his thoughts, "but we'll follow the Mother and she'll veer a little to the northwest after a while, then southwest again until we reach it. It's not a huge glacier and, except for a higher region in the northeast, nearly flat once we get up to it, like a big high plain made out of ice. After we get across it, we'll head slightly southwest again, but essentially, from here on, we'll be traveling west all the way home."

In breaking through the ridge of limestone and crystalline rock, the river, as though hesitating, unable to make up her mind, jogged north, then dipped south, and then north again, forming a lobe that the river traced, before finally heading south through the plain.

"Is that the Mother?" Ayla asked. "All of her, I mean, not just a channel?"

"That's all of her. She's still a good-size river, but nothing like she was," Jondalar conceded.

"We've been beside her for quite a while, then. I didn't know that. I'm used to seeing the Great Mother River so much more full, when she isn't all spread out. I thought we were following a channel. We've crossed feeders that were greater," Ayla said, feeling a little disappointed that the enormous swollen Mother of rivers had become just another large waterway.

"We're up high. She looks different from here. There is more to her than you think," he said. "We have some large tributaries to cross yet, and there will be stretches where she breaks into channels again, but she will keep getting smaller." Jondalar stared toward the west in silence for a time; then he added, "This is just the beginning of winter.

We should make it to the glacier in plenty of time . . . if nothing happens to delay us.''

The Journeyers turned west along the high ridge, following the outside bend of the river. The elevation continued to increase on the north side of the river until they were looking down from a high point above the little southward lobe. The drop-off toward the west was quite steep, and they headed north down a slightly more gradual slope through scattered brush. At the bottom, a tributary that curled around the base of the lofty prominence from the northeast cut a deep gorge. They traced it upstream until they found a crossing. It was only hilly on the other side, and they rode beside the feeder until they reached the Great Mother again, then continued west.

In the broad central plain there had been only a few tributaries, but they were now in an area where many rivers and streams fed the Mother from the north. They came upon another large tributary later in the day and their legs got wet in the crossing. It was not like crossing rivers in the warm summertime, when it didn't matter if they got a little wet. The temperature was dipping down to freezing at night. They were chilled by the icy-cold water, and they decided to camp on the far bank to get warm and dry.

They continued due west. After passing through the hilly terrain, they reached the lowland again, a marshy grassland, but not like the wetlands downstream. These were on acid soils, and more swampy than marshy, with moors of sphagnum mosses that in places were compacting into peat. They discovered the peat would burn when they made camp one day and inadvertently built a fire on top of a dry patch of it. The following day they collected some on purpose for their next fires.

When they came to a large, fast tributary that fanned into a broad delta at its confluence with the Mother, they decided to follow it upstream a short distance to see if they could find an easier place to cross. They reached a fork where two rivers converged, followed the right branch, and came to another fork where yet another river joined. The horses easily waded across the smaller river, and the middle fork, though larger, wasn't too difficult. The land between the middle and the left fork was a boggy lowland with sphagnum moors, and it was difficult going.

The last fork was deep, and there was no way to cross it without getting wet, but on the other side they disturbed a megaceros with an enormous rack of palmate antlers and decided to go after him. The giant deer, with his long legs, easily outdistanced the stocky horses, although Racer and Wolf gave him a good run. Whinney, hauling the pole drag, couldn't keep up, but the exercise had put them all in a good mood.

Jondalar, red-faced and windblown, his fur hood thrown back, was smiling when he came back. Ayla felt an unexplainable pang of love and longing as he rode up. He had let his pale yellow beard grow, as he usually did in winter, to help keep his face warm, and she always did like him with a beard. He liked to call her beautiful, but in her mind, he was beautiful.

"That animal can sure run!" he said. "And did you see that magnificent rack? One of his antlers must be twice as big as I am!"

Ayla was smiling, too. "He was magnificent, and beautiful, but I'm glad we didn't get him. He was too big for us, anyway. We couldn't take all that meat, and it would have been a shame to kill him when we didn't need it."

They rode back to the Mother, and even though their clothes had dried on them somewhat, they were glad to make camp and change. They made a point of hanging their damp clothing near the fire so it could dry further.

The next day they started out heading west; then the river veered toward the northwest. Some distance beyond, they could see another high ridge. The high prominence that reached all the way to the Great Mother River was the farthest northwest finger, the last they would see, of the great chain of mountains that had been with them almost from the beginning. The range had been west of them then, and they had traveled around its broad southern end following the lower course of the Great Mother River. The whitened mountain peaks had marched along to the east of them in a great curving arc, as they rode up the central plain beside the river's winding middle course. Going west along the Mother's upper course, the ridge ahead was the last outlier.

No tributaries joined the long river until they were almost

up to the ridge, and Ayla and Jondalar realized they must have been between channels again. The river that joined from the east at the foot of the rocky promontory was the other end of the northern channel of the Mother. From there the river flowed between the ridge and a high hill across the water, but there was enough lowland riverbank to ride around the base of the high rocky point.

They crossed another large tributary just on the other side of the ridge, a river whose great valley marked the separation between the two groups of mountain ranges. The high hills to the west were the farthest eastern foreland of the enormous western chain. As the ridge fell behind them, the Great Mother River separated again into three channels. They followed the outer bank of the northernmost stream through the steppes of a smaller northern basin that was a continuation of the central plain.

In the times when the central basin had been a great sea, this wide river valley of grassy steppes, along with the swampy bogs and moors of the riverside wetlands and the grasslands to the north of them, were all inlets to that ancient inland body of water. The inner curve of the eastern mountain chain contained lines of weakness in the hard crust of the earth that became the vents for great outpourings of volcanic material. That material, combined with the ancient sea deposits and the windblown loess, created a rich and fertile soil. But only the skeletal wood of winter gave evidence of it.

The bony fingers and leafless limbs of a few birch trees near the river rattled in the rapacious wind from the north. Dry brushwood, reeds, and dead ferns lined the banks, where crusts of ice were forming that would thicken and build up jagged levees; the beginning of spring ice floes. On the northern faces and higher ground of the rolling hills in the valley divide, the wind combed billowing fields of gray standing hay with rhythmic strokes, while dark evergreen boughs of spruce and pine swayed and shivered in erratic gusts that found their way around to the protected south-facing sides. Powdery snow churned around, then settled lightly on the ground.

The weather had definitely turned cold, but snow flurries were not a problem. The horses, the wolf, and even the people were accustomed to the northern loess steppes with its dry cold and light winter snows. Only in heavy snow, that could bog down and tire the horses, and make feed harder to

find, would Ayla begin to worry. She had another worry at
the moment. She had seen horses in the distance, and Whinney and Racer had noticed them, too.

When he happened to look back, Jondalar thought he saw
smoke coming from the high hill across the river from the
last ridge they had edged around earlier. He wondered if there
were people nearby, but he did not see smoke again though
he turned around to check several times.

Toward evening, they followed a small feeder upstream
through an open woodland of bare-branched willows and
birch, to a stand of stone pines. Frosty nights had given a
still pond nearby a transparent layer of ice on top, and had
frozen the edges of the little creek, but it still ran freely in
the center, and they set up camp beside it. A dry snow blew
down and dusted the north-facing slopes with white.

Whinney had been agitated ever since they had seen the
horses in the distance, which in turn made Ayla nervous.
She decided to put the halter on her mare that evening, and
she fastened it with a long tether to a sturdy pine. Jondalar
tied Racer's lead rope to a tree near her. Then they collected
deadfall and snapped off the dead branches still attached to
the trunks of the pine trees underneath the living branches;
"women's wood" Jondalar's people had always called it. It
was available on most coniferous trees, and even in the wettest of conditions it was usually dry. It could be collected
without having to use an axe or even a knife. They built the
fire just outside the entrance of the tent and left the flap open
to heat it inside.

A varying hare, already turned white, dashed through
their camp when, by sheer chance, Jondalar happened to be
checking the heft of his spear-thrower with a new spear he'd
been working on for the past few evenings. He threw almost
by instinct, but he was surprised when the shorter spear with
a smaller point, made out of flint not bone, found its mark.
He walked over, picked up the hare, and tried to pull out the
shaft. When it didn't come easily, he took out his knife, cut
out the point, and was pleased to see that the new spear was
undamaged.

"Here's meat for tonight," Jondalar said, handing the
hare to Ayla. "It almost makes me wonder if this one didn't
come by just to help me test the new spears. They're light
and easy. You'll have to try one out."

"I think it's more likely that we camped in the middle of

his regular run," Ayla said, "but that was a good throw. I would like to try the light spear. Right now, though, I think I'll start this cooking and see what I can find for the rest of our meal."

She cleaned out the entrails but did not skin the hare, so the winter fat would not be lost. Then she skewered it on a sharpened willow branch and propped it up over the fire between two forked sticks. Next, though she had to break the ice to dig them out, Ayla collected several cattail roots, and the rhizomes from some dormant licorice fern. She pounded both of them together with a rounded stone in a wooden bowl with water to extract the tough, stringy fibers, then let the white starchy pulp settle in the bottom of the bowl while she looked through her supplies to see what else she had.

When the starch had settled and the liquid was almost clear, she carefully poured off most of it and added dried blue elderberries. While she waited for them to plump up and absorb more of the water, she stripped away the outer bark of a birch tree, scraped off some of the soft, sweet, edible cambium layer underneath, and added it to her root-starch-and-berry mixture. She gathered cones of the stone pines, and when she put them on the fire, she was pleased to see that several of them still had large, hard-shelled pine nuts in them that the heat had helped to crack.

When the hare was cooked, she broke off some of the blackened skin and rubbed the inside on a few stones she had put in the fire, to spread some fat on them. Then she took small handfuls of the doughy root starch, mixed with the berries, the sweet, flavorful licorice-fern root stalk, and the sweetening and thickening sap from the birch cambium, and dropped them on the hot rocks.

Jondalar had been watching her. She could still surprise him with her extensive knowledge of growing things. Most people, particularly women, knew where to find edible plants, but he had never met anyone who knew so much. When she had several of the doughy, unleavened biscuits cooked, he took a bite out of one.

"This is delicious!" he said. "You really are amazing, Ayla. Not very many people can find growing food to eat in the cold of winter."

"It's not the cold of winter yet, Jondalar, and not so hard to find things to eat now. Wait until the ground is frozen solid," Ayla said, then took the hare off the spit, peeled back the crispy charcoaled skin, and put the meat on the mammoth-ivory platter, from which they both would eat.

"I think you could find something to eat even then," Jondalar said.

"But maybe not plants," she said, offering him a tender leg of hare.

When they finished the hare and the cattail-root biscuits, Ayla gave the leftovers to Wolf, including the bones. She started their herb tea steeping, adding some birch cambium for the wintergreen flavor, then took the pine cones out of the edge of the fire. They sat by the fire for a while, sipping their tea and eating pine nuts, cracked with rocks or sometimes with their teeth. After their meal, they made preparations for an early start, checked to make sure the horses were all right, then settled into their warm furs for the night.

Ayla looked down the corridor of a long, winding cave, and the line of fires that were showing the way cast light upon beautiful draped and flowing formations. She saw one that resembled the long flowing tail of a horse. As she approached, the dun-yellow animal nickered and swished its dark tail, seeming to beckon her closer. She started to follow, but the rocky cave grew dark, and the stalagmites crowded in.

She looked down to see where she was going, and when she looked up, it wasn't a horse that was beckoning, after all. It seemed to be a man. She strained to see who it was, and was startled to see Creb stepping out of the shadows. He motioned her on, urging her to hurry and come with him; then he turned and limped away.

She started to follow him, then heard a horse whinny. When she turned around to look for the yellow mare, the dark tail disappeared into a herd of dark-tailed horses. She ran after them, but they turned into flowing stone and then into a jumble of stone columns. When she looked back, Creb was disappearing down a dark tunnel.

She ran after him, trying to catch up with him, until she came to a fork, but she didn't know which branch Creb had taken. She was in a panic, looking at one and then the other. Finally she started up the right fork, and she found a man standing in the middle of it, blocking her way.

*It was Jeren! He was filling the entire passage, standing
with his legs apart and his arms crossed in front of him,
shaking his head no. She pleaded with him to let her get by,
but he didn't understand. Then, with a short, carved staff, he
pointed toward the wall behind her.*

*When she turned to look, she saw a dark yellow horse
running and a yellow-haired man running after. Suddenly the
herd surrounded the man, hid him from sight. Her stomach
churned into a knot of fear. As she ran to him, she heard
horses whinnying, and Creb was at the mouth of the cave,
beckoning with great urgency, telling her to hurry, before it
was too late. Suddenly the pounding hooves of horses were
louder. She heard whinnying, neighing, and, with a sinking
feeling of horror and panic, the sound of a horse screaming.*

Ayla bolted awake. Jondalar was up, too. There was a
commotion outside the tent, horses neighing and hooves
stamping. They heard Wolf snarling, then a yelp of pain.
They threw back their covers and rushed out of the tent.

It was very dark, with only a sliver of a moon, which
shed little light, but there were more horses in the pine woods
than the two they had left there. They could tell from the
sounds, though they couldn't see anything. As she ran toward
the sounds of horses, Ayla tripped on an exposed root and
fell heavily to the ground, knocking the wind out of her.

"Ayla! Are you all right?" Jondalar said, searching for
her in the dark. He'd only heard her fall.

"Here I am," she said, her voice hoarse, trying to catch
her breath. She felt his hands on her, and she tried to get
up. When they heard the sounds of horses racing off into the
night, she pulled herself up and they ran toward the place
where the horses were tied. Whinney was gone!

"She's gone," Ayla cried. She whistled and called her
name. There was an answering whinny in the distance.

"That's her! That's Whinney! Those horses, they've
taken her. I have to get her back!" The woman started after
the horses, stumbling through the woods in the dark.

Jondalar caught up to her in a few strides. "Ayla, wait!
We can't go now, it's dark. You can't even see where you're
going."

"But I have to get her back, Jondalar!"

"We will. In the morning," he said, taking her in his arms.

"They'll be gone by then," the woman wailed.

"But it'll be light then, and we'll see their tracks. We'll follow them. We'll get her back, Ayla. I promise, we'll get her back."

"Oh, Jondalar. What will I do without Whinney? She's my friend. For a long time, she was my only friend," Ayla said, giving in to the logic of his argument, but breaking down into tears.

The man held her and let her cry for a moment, then said, "Right now, we need to see if Racer is gone, too, and find Wolf."

Ayla suddenly remembered hearing the wolf yelp in pain, and she grew concerned for him and for the young stallion. She whistled once for Wolf, and then she made the sound she used to call the horses.

They heard a whinny first, and then a whine. Jondalar went to find Racer, while Ayla followed the sound of the wolf in pain until she found him. She reached down to comfort the animal and felt something wet and sticky.

"Wolf! You're hurt." She tried to pick him up to carry him to the fireplace, where she could restart the fire and see. He yelped in pain as she staggered under his weight. Then he struggled out of her arms, but stayed up on his own legs, and though she knew it cost him some effort, he walked back to their camp on his own.

Jondalar also returned to the camp, leading Racer, while Ayla was stirring up the fire. "His rope held," the man announced. He had gotten into the habit of using sturdy ropes to hold the stallion, who had always been a little harder for him to handle than Whinney was for Ayla.

"I'm so glad he's safe," the woman said, hugging the stallion's neck, then stepping back to look him over more closely, just to make sure. "Why didn't I use a stronger rope, Jondalar?" Ayla said, angry with herself. "If I had been more careful, Whinney wouldn't have gotten away." Her relationship with the mare was closer. Whinney was a friend, who did what she wanted because the horse wanted to, and Ayla only used a light tether to keep the horse from wandering too far afield. It had always been enough.

"It wasn't your fault, Ayla. The herd wasn't after Racer.

They wanted a mare, not a stallion. Whinney wouldn't have gone if the horses hadn't made her go.''

"But I knew those horses were out there, and I should have realized they might come for Whinney. Now she's gone, and even Wolf is hurt.''

"Is it very bad?'' Jondalar asked.

"I don't know,'' Ayla said. "It hurts him too much when I touch him to be certain, but I think his rib is either badly bruised or broken. He must have gotten kicked. I'll give him something for pain, and I'll try to find out for sure in the morning . . . before we look for Whinney.'' Suddenly she reached out for the man. "Oh, Jondalar, what if we don't find her? What if I've lost her forever?'' she cried.

25

"Look, Ayla," Jondalar said, bending down on one knee to examine the ground that was covered with the imprint of horse hooves. "The whole herd must have been here last night. The trail is clear. I told you it would be easy to track them once it got light."

Ayla looked down at the tracks, then up toward the northeast in the direction they seemed to be heading. They were near the edge of the small woods, and she could see far into the distance across the open grassy plain, but as hard as she tried, she could not see a single horse. She found herself thinking, The tracks are plain enough here, but who knows how long we will be able to follow them?

The young woman had not slept at all after she had been awakened by the commotion and discovered that her beloved friend was gone. The moment the sky lightened, shading from ebony to indigo, she was up, though it was still too dark to see any distinctive features on the land. She had stirred up the fire and started water boiling for tea while the heavens transformed, shifting through a monochromatic spectrum of gradually paler shades of blue.

Wolf had crept near her while she was staring into the flames, but he had to whine to get her attention. She had taken the opportunity to examine him closely. Though he had winced when she prodded deeply, she was grateful to find no broken bones. A bruise was bad enough. Jondalar had gotten up soon after the morning tea was ready, still well before it was light enough to search for signs.

"Let's hurry and leave right away, so they don't get too far ahead of us," Ayla said. "We can pile everything into the bowl boat and . . . no . . . we can't do that." She suddenly realized that, without the mare she wanted to find, they couldn't just pack up and go. "Racer doesn't know how to pull the pole drag, so we can't take it or the bowl boat. We can't even take Whinney's pack-saddle basket."

"And if we're going to have any chance to catch up with that herd, we'll have to ride double on Racer. That means we can't even take his pack-saddle. We'll have to cut our load down to bare necessities," Jondalar said.

They stopped to digest the new situation the loss of Whinney had put them in. Both of them realized there were some hard decisions to make.

"If we take just the sleeping rolls and the ground cover, which could be used as a low tent, and roll them up together, that should fit on Racer's back behind us," Jondalar suggested.

"A low tent should be enough," Ayla agreed. "That's all we ever took when we went with the hunters of our clan. We used a stick to prop up the front, and rocks or heavy bones that we found to weigh it down around the edges." She began to remember the times that she and several women accompanied the men when they went hunting. "The women had to carry everything except the hunting spears, and we had to move fast to keep up, so we traveled light."

"What else did you take? How light do you think we can travel?" Jondalar asked, his curiosity piqued.

"We'll need the fire-making kit and some tools. A chopper to cut wood to burn, and to break up the bones of any animals we might need to butcher. We can burn dried dung and grass, too, but we should have something to cut the stems. A knife to skin animals, and a sharp one to cut meat," she began. Ayla was remembering not only the times that she accompanied the hunters, but the time she traveled alone after she left the clan.

"I'll wear my belt with the loops for holding my axe, and my ivory-handled knife," Jondalar said. "You should wear yours, too.

"A digging stick is always a help, and it can be used to prop up the tent. Some extra warm clothes in case it turns really cold and extra foot-coverings," the woman continued.

"An extra pair of boot liners. That's a good idea. Under tunics and pants, fur mitts, and we can always wrap our sleeping furs around us, if we have to."

"A waterbag or two . . ."

"We can tie those to our belts, too, and with enough cord to make a loop to go over the arm, we can wear them close to the body if it gets too cold, so they won't freeze."

"I'll need my medicine bag, and maybe I should take the sewing kit—it doesn't take much room—and my sling."

"Don't forget the spear-throwers and spears," Jondalar added. "Do you think I should take any flint-knapping tools, or flint blanks, in case a knife or something breaks?"

"Whatever we take, it should be no more than I can carry on my back . . . or could if I had a carrying basket."

"If anyone carries anything on his back, I think it should be me," Jondalar said, "but I don't have my backframe."

"I'm sure we can make a back-carrier of some kind, probably out of one of the pack-saddles and some rope or thong, but how can I sit behind you if you're wearing it?" Ayla asked.

"But I'm going to sit behind . . ." They looked at each other and smiled. They even had to decide how to ride, and both of them had made their own assumptions. It was the first time Ayla had smiled all morning, Jondalar noticed.

"You have to guide Racer, so I have to be in back," Ayla said.

"I can guide him with you in front of me," the man said, "but if you are behind you won't be able to see anything but my back. I don't think you'd be happy if you couldn't see ahead, and we both need to be watching the trail. It may be harder to follow over hard ground or where there are other tracks to confuse it, and you are a good tracker."

Ayla's smile widened. "You're right, Jondalar. I don't know if I could stand it if I couldn't see ahead." She understood that he had been worrying about following the trail left

by the horses, just as she had, and had even considered her
feelings. Tears suddenly filled her eyes with the love she
felt overflowing inside her, and then the tears overflowed to
match.

"Don't cry, Ayla. We'll find Whinney."

"I wasn't crying about Whinney. I was thinking how
much I love you, and the tears just came out."

"I love you, too," he said, reaching for her, feeling a
constriction in his own throat.

Suddenly, she was in his arms, sobbing on his shoulder,
and the tears that came were for Whinney as well. "Jondalar,
we've got to find her."

"We will. We'll just keep looking until we do. Now,
how about fixing up a backpack for me. Something that can
hold the spear-throwers and some spears on the outside,
where they will be easy to reach."

"That shouldn't be too hard. We'll have to take dried
traveling food, of course," Ayla said, wiping her eyes with
the back of her hand.

"How much do you think we'll need?" he asked.

"It depends. How long will we be gone?" she asked.

The question stopped them both. How long would they
be gone? How long would it take them to find Whinney and
get her back?

"It probably won't take more than a few days to track
the herd and find her, but perhaps we should take enough for
half a moon cycle," Jondalar said.

Ayla paused, thinking of the counting words. "That's
more than ten days, maybe as much as three hands, fifteen
days. Do you think it will take that long?"

"No, I don't think so, but it's best to be prepared,"
Jondalar said.

"We can't leave this camp alone for that long," Ayla
said. "Some kind of animal will come and tear it apart,
wolves or hyenas or wolverines or bears . . . no, bears are
sleeping, but something. They'll chew up the tent, the bowl
boat, anything leather, and the extra food. What will we do
with everything we have to leave behind?"

"Maybe Wolf could stay behind and watch the camp?"
Jondalar said, wrinkling his forehead. "Wouldn't he stay if
you told him to? He's hurt, anyway. Wouldn't it be better
for him not to travel?"

"Yes, it would be better for him, but he won't stay. He

would for a while, but he'd come looking for us if we didn't get back within a day or so."

"Maybe we could tie him close to the camp . . ."

"No! He would hate that, Jondalar!" Ayla exclaimed. "You wouldn't like to be made to stay someplace that you didn't want to be! Besides, if wolves or something did come, they could attack him and he wouldn't be able to fight, or run out of their way. We'll just have to think of some other way to protect our things."

They walked back to their camp in silence, Jondalar a little chagrined and Ayla worried, but both of them still trying to resolve the problem of what to do with their gear while they were gone. As they approached the tent, Ayla remembered something.

"I have an idea," she said. "Maybe we could put everything in the tent and close it up. I still have some of that wolf repellent I made to keep Wolf from chewing on things. I could soften it up and spread it on the tent. That might keep some animals away."

"It might, for a while at least, until the rains washed it away, and that could take some time, but it wouldn't keep out the ones that tried to dig or burrow under it." Jondalar paused. "Why couldn't we gather everything together and wrap it up with a tent? Then you could put your repellent on it . . . but we shouldn't just leave it out."

"No, I think we have to get it up, off the ground, like we do with the meat," Ayla said, then more excited, "Maybe we could put it up on the poles. And cover it with the bowl boat, to keep the rain away."

"That's a good idea!" Jondalar said, then paused again. "But those poles could be knocked over by a cave lion, or even a determined pack of wolves or hyenas." He looked around trying to think, and he noticed a large clump of brambles with long leafless canes full of sharp thorns spreading out from the middle. "Ayla," he said, "do you think we could poke the three poles through the middle of those brambles, tie them together about halfway up, put our tent bundle on top of that, and cover it all with the bowl boat?"

Ayla's smiled broadened as he talked. "I think we could carefully cut some of those canes so we could get close enough to get the poles in and tied, and put everything on top, then weave them back in with the others. Small animals would still be able to get to it, but most of them are sleeping, or staying in their nests, and those sharp thorns would probably keep the bigger animals away. Even lions will avoid sharp thorns. Jondalar, I think it would work!"

Selecting the few items they could take required thought and consideration. They decided to take a little extra flint and a few essential tools to work it with, some extra rope and cordage, and as much food as they could pack. In sorting through her things, Ayla located the special belt and the mammoth-tusk dagger that Talut had given to her at the ceremony when she was adopted by the Lion Camp. The belt had thin leather thongs threaded through it that could be pulled out into loops for carrying things, in particular the dagger, although the carrying belt could also be used to hold many other useful objects close at hand.

She tied the belt around her hips, over her outer fur tunic, then took the dagger out and turned it over in her hands, wondering if she should take it. Though its point was very sharp, it was more ceremonial than practical. Mamut had used one like it to cut her arm, and then, with the blood he had drawn, to mark the ivory plaque that he had worn around his neck, counting her among the Mamutoi.

She had also watched a similar dagger used to make tattoos, by cutting fine lines in the skin with the point. Black charcoal from ash wood was then put into the resulting wounds. She didn't know that ash trees produced a natural antiseptic that inhibited infection, and it was unlikely that the Mamut who told her knew exactly why it worked. She only knew that it had been strongly impressed on her never to use anything but burned ash wood to darken the scar when making a tattoo.

Ayla put the dagger back in its rawhide sheath and left it there. Then she picked up another leather sheath that protected the extremely sharp flint blade of a small ivory-handled knife Jondalar had made for her. She put it through a loop in her belt, and then she put the handle of the hatchet he had given her through yet another loop. The stone head of the small axe was also wrapped in leather to protect it.

She decided that there was no reason the belt couldn't hold her spear-thrower. Then she tucked her sling through it, and she finally tied on the pouch that held stones for her sling. She felt weighted down, but it was a convenient way to carry things when they had to travel with very little. She added her spears to the ones Jondalar had already put in the carrier of the backpack.

It took longer than they had thought to decide what to take, and even more time to safely stow everything they were leaving behind. Ayla felt anxious over the delay, but by noon they were finally mounted and leaving.

When they started out, Wolf loped along beside them, but he soon lagged behind, obviously in some pain. Ayla worried about him, not sure how far or how fast he could travel, but she decided she would have to let him follow at his own pace, and if he couldn't keep up, he would have to catch up when they stopped. She was torn by concern for both animals, but Wolf was nearby and, though injured, she felt confident that he would recover. Whinney could be anywhere, and the longer they delayed, the farther away she might be.

They followed the trail of the herd more or less northeast for some distance; then the tracks of the horses inexplicably changed direction. Ayla and Jondalar overshot the turn and thought for a moment that they had lost the trail. They turned back, but it was late afternoon by the time they found it again, going east, and it was near nightfall when they came to a river.

It was evident that the horses had crossed, but it was getting too dark to see the hoofprints and they decided to camp beside the river. The question was, which side? If they crossed now, their wet clothes would probably dry before morning, but Ayla was afraid Wolf would not be able to find them if they crossed the water before he caught up with them. They decided to wait for him and set up their camp where they were.

With their minimal gear, the camp felt bare and depressing. They hadn't seen any more than tracks the whole day. Ayla was beginning to worry that they might be following the wrong herd, and she was worried about Wolf. Jondalar tried to ease her anxieties, but when Wolf hadn't appeared by the time the night sky was filled with stars, her concern for him grew. She waited up quite late, but when Jondalar finally convinced her to join him in their sleeping furs, she still couldn't go to sleep, though she was tired. She had almost dozed off when she felt a cold wet nose nuzzle her.

"Wolf! You made it! You're here! Jondalar, look! Wolf is here," Ayla cried, feeling him wince under her hugs. Jondalar felt relieved and glad to see him, too, though he told himself his happiness was mostly for Ayla's sake. At least she might get some sleep. But first she got up to give the animal the share she had saved for him of their meal, a stew made of dried meat, roots, and a cake of traveling food.

Earlier, she had mixed dried willowbark tea into a bowl of water she had put aside for him, and he was thirsty enough to lap it up, painkilling medication and all. He curled up beside their sleeping roll and Ayla fell asleep with one arm around him, while Jondalar cuddled close and put an arm around her. In the freezing cold but clear night, they slept in their clothes, except for their boots and fur outer garments, and they didn't bother with setting up the low tent.

Ayla thought Wolf seemed better in the morning, but she took more willowbark out of her otter-skin medicine bag and added a cup of the decoction to his food. They all had to face crossing the cold river, and she wasn't sure how it would affect the animal's injury. It might chill him too much, but on the other hand, the cold water might actually relieve the healing wound, and the internal bruising.

But the young woman wasn't any too eager to get her clothing wet. It wasn't the dousing of cold water so much— she had often bathed in colder water—it was the idea of wearing wet trousers and footwear in the near-freezing air. When she started to wrap the upper leather of her high-topped moccasinlike boots around her calf, she suddenly changed her mind.

"I'm not going to wear these into the water," she declared. "I'd rather go barefoot and get my feet wet. At least I'd have dry footwear to put on when we get across."

"That may not be a bad idea," Jondalar said.

"In fact, I'm not even going to wear these," Ayla said, pulling off her trousers and standing there bare from her tunic down—which made Jondalar smile and want to do something else besides chase horses. But he knew Ayla was too concerned about Whinney to think about dallying.

As funny as it might look, he had to admit it was an intelligent thought. The river wasn't exceptionally large, though it did look swift. They could cross the water riding double on Racer, with bare legs and feet, then put dry clothes on when they reached the other side. It would not only be more comfortable, it would keep them from a prolonged chill.

"I think you're right, Ayla. It's better not to get these wet," he said, pulling off his leg-coverings.

Jondalar put on the backpack, and Ayla held the sleeping roll, just to make sure it wouldn't get wet. The man felt a little silly getting up on the horse with his lower half bare, but feeling Ayla's skin between his legs made him forget it. The obvious result of his thoughts was not lost on her. If she hadn't been so filled with her need to hurry, she, too, could have been tempted to stay a little longer. In the back of her mind she thought that some other time they might ride double again, just for fun, but this was not the time for fun.

The water was icy cold when the brown stallion entered the stream, breaking through the crust of ice near the edge. Though the river was swift, and soon deep enough to wet their legs to midway up their thighs, the horse did not lose his footing; it was not so deep that he had to swim. Racer's two riders tried to curl their legs out of the water at first, but soon felt numbed to the cold river. About halfway across, Ayla turned around to look for Wolf. He was still on the bank, pacing back and forth, avoiding the initial plunge, as he often did. Ayla whistled to encourage him on, and she saw him finally jump in.

They reached the opposite shore without incident, except for feeling cold. The chill wind blowing on their wet legs when they dismounted didn't help. After pushing most of the water off with their hands, they hurried to put on their pants and moccasin-boots, with liners of downy chamois wool felted together—a departing gift from the Sharamudoi, for which they were more than grateful at that moment. Their legs and feet tingled with the returning warmth. When Wolf reached the shore, he climbed on the bank and shook himself. Ayla checked him over to satisfy herself that he was none the worse for the cold swim.

They located the trail easily and remounted the young stallion. Wolf again tried to keep up, but he soon lagged behind. Ayla worriedly watched him falling farther and farther back. That he had found them the night before eased her fears a little, and she consoled herself with the knowledge that he had often run off hunting or exploring on his own and had always caught up with them again. She hated to leave him behind, but they had to find Whinney.

It was midafternoon before they finally caught sight of

horses in the distance. As they drew nearer, Ayla strained to find her friend amidst the others. She thought she caught a glimpse of a familiar hay-colored coat, but she couldn't be sure. There were too many other horses with coats that were similar, and when the wind carried their scent to the herd, they raced away.

"Those horses have been hunted before," Jondalar remarked. But he was glad that he caught himself in time before he voiced his next thought out loud: There must be people in this region who like horsemeat. He didn't want to upset Ayla even more. The herd soon outdistanced a young stallion that was carrying two passengers, but they continued to follow the trail. It was all they could do for now.

The herd turned south, for some reason only they knew, heading back toward the Great Mother River. Before long, the ground began to slope up. The land became rugged and rocky, and the grass more sparse. They continued until they came to a broad field high above the rest of the landscape. When they caught sight of water sparkling below, they realized they were on a plateau on top of the prominence they had skirted around the base of a few days before. The river they had crossed hugged its western face before joining the Mother.

As the herd started to graze, they moved in closer.

"There she is, Jondalar!" Ayla said with excitement, pointing to a particular animal.

"How can you be sure? Several of those horses have a similar color."

Though her coloration was similar to others, the woman knew the particular conformation of her friend too well to doubt it. She whistled and Whinney looked up. "I told you. It is her!"

She whistled again, and Whinney started toward her. But the lead mare, a large, graceful animal with a darker than usual, grayish-gold coat, saw the newest addition to the herd moving away from the fold and moved in to head her off. The herd stallion joined in to help. He was a big, stunning, cream-colored horse with a high-standing silver mane, a gray stripe down his back, and a flowing silvery tail that looked almost white when he swished it. His lower legs were silver-gray, too. He nipped at Whinney's hocks and herded her toward the rest of the females, who were watching with nervous interest; then he cantered back to challenge the younger stallion. He pawed the ground, then reared and neighed, daring Racer to fight.

The young brown stallion backed away, intimidated, and could not be coaxed to move in closer, much to the frustration of his human companions. From a safe distance, he neighed to his dam, and they heard Whinney's familiar answering nicker. Ayla and Jondalar dismounted to discuss the situation.

"What are we going to do, Jondalar?" Ayla wailed. "They won't let her go. How are we going to get her?"

"Don't worry, we will," he said. "If necessary, we'll use the spear-throwers, but I don't think we'll have to."

His assurance calmed her, and she hadn't thought of the spear-throwers. She didn't want to kill any horses if she didn't have to, but she'd do anything to get Whinney back. "Do you have a plan?" she asked.

"I'm pretty sure this herd has been hunted before, so they have some fear of people. That gives us an advantage. The herd stallion probably thinks Racer was trying to challenge him. He and that big mare were trying to keep him from stealing one of their herd. So we have to keep Racer away," Jondalar began. "Whinney will come when you whistle for her. If I can distract the stallion, you can help her avoid the mare until you get close enough to get on her back. Then, if you shout at the big mare, or even poke her with your spear if she crowds in on Whinney, I think she'll keep her distance until you ride away."

Ayla smiled, feeling relieved. "It sounds easy enough. What will we do with Racer?"

"There was a rock a little ways back with a couple of bushes growing near it. I can tether him to one of them. It wouldn't hold if he really fought it, but he's used to being tied, and I think he'll stay there." Taking the young stallion's lead rope, Jondalar started back with long strides.

When they reached the rock, Jondalar said, "Here, take your spear-thrower and a spear or two." Then he slipped off the backpack. "I'm going to take this off and leave it for now. It limits my movement." He took his own thrower and spears out of the holder. "Once you get Whinney, you can get Racer and come back for me."

The highland angled in a northeast-to-southwest direction, with a gradual incline on the north that became somewhat steeper toward the east. At the southwestern end, it jutted up like a precipice. On the western side, facing the river they had crossed earlier, it fell off sharply enough, but toward the south and the Great Mother River there was a high precipice with a sheer drop. As Ayla and Jondalar walked back toward the horses, the day was clear, and the sun was high in the sky, though well past its zenith. They looked over the steep western edge, then shied back from it, afraid that a misstep or a stumble might carry them down.

When they got closer to the grazing herd, they stopped and tried to find Whinney. The herd—mares, foals, and yearlings—was grazing in the middle of a field of waist-high dry grass; the herd stallion was off to one side, somewhat away from the others. Ayla thought she saw her horse far back, toward the south. She whistled, the dun-yellow mare's head came up, and Whinney started toward them. With his spear-thrower in hand and a spear in place ready to go, Jondalar slowly edged toward the cream-colored stallion, attempting to get between him and the herd, while Ayla walked toward the mares, determined to reach Whinney.

While she was working her way toward the mare, some of the horses stopped grazing and looked up, but they weren't looking at her. She had a sudden feeling that something was not right. She turned around to look for Jondalar, and she saw a wisp of smoke, and then another. It was the smell of smoke she had noticed. The field of dry grass was ablaze in several places. Suddenly, through the haze of the smoke, she saw figures running toward the horses, shouting and brandishing torches! They were chasing the horses toward the edge of the field, toward the sharp drop-off, and Whinney was among them!

The horses were beginning to panic, but among the high-pitched sounds she thought she heard a familiar neigh coming from another direction. Looking north, she spied Racer with his lead rope dragging behind, running toward the herd. Why did he have to break loose now? And where was Jondalar? The air was filled with more than smoke. She could feel the tension and smell the contagious fear of the horses as they started moving away from the fire.

Horses were jostling around her, and she couldn't see Whinney anymore, but Racer was coming toward her, running fast, caught up in the panic. She whistled loud and long, then made a dash for him. He slowed and turned in her direction, but his ears were laid flat back and his eyes were rolling with fear. She reached him and grabbed for the rope dangling from his halter, yanking his head around. He screamed and reared as horses dodged around him. The rope burned as he yanked it through Ayla's hands, but she held on, and when his forefeet touched the ground, she grabbed his mane and leaped up on his back.

Racer reared again. Ayla was nearly thrown, but she held on. The horse was still full of fear, but he was used to a weight on his back. There was a comfort in it, and in the familiar woman. He settled down to a run, but it was difficult for her to control the horse Jondalar had trained. Though she had ridden Racer a few times and knew the signals that had been developed for the horse, she was not accustomed to guiding with reins or a rope. The man had used both with equal ease, and the stallion knew the confidence of his usual rider. He did not respond well to Ayla's first tentative attempts, but she was looking for Whinney while trying to settle him down, and she was distracted by her anxious need to find her friend.

Horses were running, crowding together all around her, neighing, whinnying, screaming, and their fear was strong in her nostrils. She whistled again, loud and piercing, but she wasn't sure if she could be heard above the din, and she knew the urge to run was powerful.

Suddenly, in the haze of dust and smoke, Ayla saw a horse slow, try to turn away and resist the urgings of the panicked horses racing past her, communicating their fear of the fire. Though her coat was the color of the choking air, Ayla knew it was Whinney. She whistled again to encourage her, and she saw her beloved mare stop, undecided. The instinct to run with the herd was strong in her, but that whistle had always meant safety, security, love, and she was not as frightened of the fire. She had been raised with the smell of smoke nearby. It had only signaled the proximity of people.

Ayla saw Whinney standing her ground while other horses brushed close or bumped her while trying to avoid her. The woman urged Racer forward. The mare started to turn back toward the woman, but a light-colored horse suddenly appeared, seemingly out of the dust. The big herd stallion tried to head her off, screaming a warning challenge at Racer, even in his panic, trying to keep his new mare away from the younger male. This time Racer screamed a response, then

pranced and pawed the ground and started for the bigger
animal, forgetting in all the excitement that he was too young
and inexperienced to fight a mature stallion.

Then, for some reason—a sudden change of mind or contagion of fear—the stallion wheeled and pounded away.
Whinney started to follow, and Racer rushed to overtake her.
As the herd raced closer and closer to the edge of the cliff
and the sure death waiting below, the mare with a coat the
color of sun-ripened hay and the young brown stallion she
had foaled, with the woman on his back, were being carried
along with them! With fierce determination, Ayla pulled
Racer to a stop in front of his dam. He whinnied with fear,
wanting to run in panic with the rest of the horses, but he
was held in check by the woman and the commands he was
trained to obey.

Then all the horses had passed her by. As Whinney and
Racer stood shivering with fear, the last of the herd disappeared over the edge of the cliff. Ayla shuddered at the distant sound of neighing, screaming, whinnying horses, and
then she was stunned by the silence. Whinney and Racer and
she, herself, could have been with them. She breathed deeply
at the close call, then looked around for Jondalar.

She didn't see him. The fire was moving south but east;
the wind was blowing away from the southwestern edge of
the field—but the flames had served their purpose. She looked
in all directions, but Jondalar was nowhere in sight. Ayla and
the two horses were alone on the smoking field. She felt a
lump of fear and anxiety rise in her throat. What happened
to Jondalar?

She slid off Racer and, still holding his lead rope, leaped
easily onto Whinney's back, then headed back to the place
where they had separated. She scanned the area carefully,
walking back and forth, looking for tracks, but the ground
was covered with hoofprints. Then, out of the corner of her
eye, she spied something and ran to see what it was. With
her heart pounding in her throat, she picked up Jondalar's
spear-thrower!

Looking more closely, she saw footprints, obviously
many people, but distinctive among them were the imprints
of Jondalar's large feet encased in his well-worn boots. She
had seen those prints too many times at their campsites to be
mistaken. Then she saw a dark spot on the ground. She

reached down to touch it and pulled back a fingertip red with blood.

Her eyes opened wide, and fear caught in her throat. Standing where she was, so as not to disturb the signs, she carefully looked around, trying to piece together some sense of what had happened. She was an experienced tracker, and to her trained eye, it soon became clear that someone had hurt Jondalar and dragged him away. She followed the tracks north for a while. Then she took note of her surroundings, so she could pick up the trail again, mounted Whinney, with Racer's lead firmly in hand, and turned west to retrieve the backpack.

As she rode toward the west, she was scowling, and the hard angry frown expressed exactly how she felt, but she had to think things out and decide what to do. Someone had hurt Jondalar and taken him away, and no one had the right to do that. Perhaps she didn't understand all the ways of the Others, but that was one thing she knew. She knew something else, too. She didn't know how yet, but she was going to get him back.

She was relieved when she saw the backpack still leaning against the rock, just as they'd left it. She dumped everything out of it and made a few adjustments so Racer could carry it on his back, then began to repack. She had left off her carrying belt that morning—it had felt rather clumsy—and stuffed everything into the backpack. She lifted the belt and examined the sharp ceremonial dagger that was still in the loop, accidentally pricking herself with the point. She stared at the tiny drop of blood beading up, and for some strange reason she felt like crying. She was alone again. Someone had taken Jondalar away.

Suddenly she put the belt on again and stuffed her dagger, knife, hatchet, and hunting weapons back into it. He wasn't going to be gone for long! She packed the tent on Racer's back, but she kept the sleeping roll with her. Who could tell what kind of weather she might run into? She kept a waterbag, too. Then she took out a cake of traveling food and sat down on the rock. It wasn't so much that she was hungry, but she knew she had to keep her strength up if she was going to follow the trail and find Jondalar.

The other nagging worry that had been bothering her besides the missing man, was the missing wolf. She couldn't leave to find Jondalar until she found Wolf. He was more than just an animal companion that she loved, he could be essential in following the trail. She hoped he would appear before nightfall, and she wondered if she could backtrack over their trail until she found him. But what if he was hunting? She might miss him. As impatient as it made her feel, she decided it was best to wait.

She tried to think about what she could do, but she couldn't even think of possible courses of action. The very act of hurting someone and taking him away was so alien to her that it was hard to think beyond it. It seemed such an unreasonable, illogical thing to do.

Intruding on her thoughts she heard a whine and then a yip. She turned to see Wolf running toward her, obviously happy to see her. She was greatly relieved.

"Wolf!" she cried with joy. "You made it, and much earlier than yesterday. Are you better?" After greeting him affectionately, she examined him and was glad when she confirmed again that although he was definitely bruised, nothing was broken, and he seemed much improved.

She decided to leave immediately, so she could pick up the trail while it was still light. She tied Racer's lead to a strap that held Whinney's riding blanket on, then mounted the mare. Calling Wolf to follow her, she started back toward the trail, then rode all the way to the place where she had found his footprints along with the others, his spear-thrower, and the spot of blood, now a slightly brownish stain on the ground. She dismounted to examine the place again.

"We have to find Jondalar, Wolf," she said. The animal looked at her quizzically.

She lowered herself and, sitting comfortably on her haunches, looked more closely at the footprints, making an effort to identify individuals so she could estimate how many there were, and to commit the size and shapes of them to memory. The wolf waited, sitting on his haunches and staring at her, sensing something unusual and important. Finally she pointed to the bloodstain.

"Someone hurt Jondalar and carried him away. We need to find him." The wolf sniffed the blood, then wagged his tail and yipped. "That's Jondalar's footprint," she said, pointing to the distinctive large impression among the smaller ones. Wolf again sniffed where she pointed, then looked at her, as if waiting for her next move. "They took him away," she said, indicating the other imprints of human feet.

Suddenly she stood up and walked over to Racer. She took Jondalar's spear-thrower out of the pack on Racer's back and knelt to let the wolf sniff it. "We have to find Jondalar, Wolf! Someone took him away, and we're going to get him back!"

26

Jondalar slowly became aware that he was awake, but caution made him lie still until he could sort out what was wrong, because something most certainly was. For one thing, his head was throbbing. He opened his eyes a crack. There was only dim light, but enough to see the cold, hard-packed dirt he was lying on. Something felt dry and caked on the side of his face, but when he attempted to reach up and find out what it was, he discovered that his hands were tied together behind his back. His feet were tied together, too.

He rolled to his side and looked around. He was inside a small round structure, a kind of wooden frame covered with skins, which he sensed was inside a larger enclosure. There were no sounds of wind, no drafts, no billowing of the hides as there would have been if he had been outside, and though it was cool, it wasn't freezing. And he suddenly realized that he was no longer wearing his fur parka.

Jondalar struggled to sit up, and a wave of dizziness washed over him. The throbbing in his head localized to a sharp pain above his left temple, near the dry, caked residue.

He stopped when he heard the sound of voices drawing near. Two women were speaking an unfamiliar language, though he thought he detected a few words that sounded vaguely Mamutoi.

"Hello out there. I'm awake," he called out, in the language of the Mammoth Hunters. "Will someone come and untie me? These ropes aren't necessary. I'm sure there has been a misunderstanding. I mean no harm." The voices stopped for a moment, then continued, but no one either answered or came.

Jondalar, lying facedown on the dirt, tried to remember how he had gotten there, and what he might have done that would have prompted someone to tie him up. In his experience, the only time people were tied up was when they behaved wildly and tried to hurt someone. He recalled a wall of fire—and horses racing toward the drop-off at the edge of the field. People must have been hunting the horses, and he'd been caught up in the middle of it.

Then he remembered seeing Ayla riding Racer, but having trouble controlling him. He wondered how the stallion had ended up in the middle of the stampeding herd when he had left him tied to a bush.

Jondalar had almost panicked then, afraid the horse would respond to his herding instinct and follow the others over the edge, taking Ayla with him. He remembered running toward them with his spear ready in his spear-thrower. As much as he loved that brown stallion, he would have killed Racer before allowing him to carry Ayla over the cliff. That was the last thing he remembered, except for a fleeting recollection of a sharp pain before everything went dark.

Someone must have hit me with something, Jondalar thought. It was a hard blow, too, because I don't remember anything about being brought here, and my head still hurts. Did they think I was spoiling their hunting strategy? The first time he'd met Jeren and his hunters, it had been under similar circumstances. He and Thonolan had inadvertently run off a herd of horses the hunters had been driving toward a trap. But Jeren had understood, once he got over his anger, that it wasn't intentional, and they had become friends. I didn't spoil the hunt of these people, did I?

He tried again to sit up. Bracing himself on his side, he pulled his knees up, then strained to roll and bob up into a sitting position. It took a few tries and left his head throbbing from the effort, but he finally succeeded. He sat with his eyes closed, hoping the pain would soon subside. But as it eased off, his concern for Ayla and the animals grew. Had Whinney and Racer been swept over the edge with the herd, and had Racer taken Ayla with him?

Was she dead? He felt his heart beat with fear just thinking about it. Were they all gone, Ayla and the horses? What about Wolf? When the injured animal finally reached the field, he would find no one. Jondalar imagined him sniffing around, trying to follow a trail that went nowhere. What would he do? Wolf was a good hunter, but he was hurt. How well could he hunt for himself with his injury? He would miss Ayla and the rest of his "pack." He wasn't used to living alone. How would he get along? What would happen when he came up against a pack of wild wolves? Would he be able to defend himself?

Isn't anyone going to come? I'd like a drink of water, Jondalar thought. They must have heard me. I'm hungry, too, but mostly thirsty. His mouth felt drier and drier, and his craving for water grew stronger. "Hey, out there! I'm thirsty! Can't someone bring a man a drink of water?" he shouted. "What kind of people are you? Tying a man up and not even giving him a drink of water!"

No one answered. After shouting a few more times, he decided to save his breath. It was only making him more thirsty, and his head still hurt. He considered lying down, but it had taken so much effort to get up that he wasn't sure if he could do it again.

As more time passed, he began to feel morose. He was weak, bordering on delirious, and he imagined the worst, vividly. He convinced himself that Ayla was dead, and both the horses as well. When he thought of Wolf, he pictured the poor beast wandering alone, injured and unable to hunt, looking for Ayla and open to attack by local wolves or hyenas or some other animal . . . better, perhaps, than dying of starvation. He wondered if he was going to be left to die of thirst, and then almost hoped he would, if Ayla was gone. Identifying with the plight he envisioned for the wolf, the man decided that he and Wolf must be the last surviving members of their unusual band of travelers, and that they would soon be gone.

He was pulled out of his despair by the sound of people approaching. The entrance flap of the small structure was thrown back, and through the opening he saw a figure standing, feet apart and hands on hips, silhouetted by torchlight. She issued a sharp command. Two women entered the enclosed space, walked to either side of him, lifted him up, and dragged him out. They propped him up on his knees in front of her, his hands and feet still bound. His head was throbbing again, and he leaned unsteadily against one of the women. She pushed him away.

The woman who had ordered him to be brought forward looked down at him for a moment or two and then she laughed. It was harsh and dissonant, a demented, jarring curse of a sound. Jondalar recoiled involuntarily and felt a shudder of fear. She spoke a few sharp words at him. He didn't understand, but he tried to straighten up and look at her. His vision blurred, and he weaved unsteadily. The woman scowled, barked more orders, then turned on her heel and stalked out. The women who were holding him up dropped him and followed her, along with several others. Jondalar toppled over on his side, dizzy and weak.

He felt the bindings on his feet being cut, and then water was poured on his mouth. It almost choked him, but he tried eagerly to swallow some. The woman who was holding the waterbag spoke a few words in tones of disgust, and then she thrust the bladder of liquid at an older man. He came forward and held the waterbag to Jondalar's mouth, then tipped it up, not more gently, exactly, but with more patience, so that Jondalar could swallow and finally slake his ravenous thirst.

Before he was fully satisfied, the woman impatiently spat out a word, and the man took the water away. Then she pulled Jondalar to his feet. He staggered with dizziness as she pushed him ahead, out of the shelter, and in with a group of other men. It was cold, but no one offered him his fur parka or even untied his hands so he could rub them together.

But the cool air revived him, and he noticed that some of the other men had their hands tied behind their backs, too. He looked more closely at the people among whom he had been thrust. They were all ages, from young men—more like boys actually—to oldsters. All of them looked thin, weak, and dirty, with tattered, inadequate clothes and matted hair. A few had untended wounds, full of dried blood and dirt.

Jondalar tried to speak to the man standing next to him in Mamutoi, but he just shook his head. Jondalar thought he didn't understand, so he tried Sharamudoi. The man looked away just as a woman holding a spear came and threatened Jondalar with it, barking a sharp command. He didn't know her words, but her actions were plain enough, and he wondered if the reason the man had not spoken was that he didn't understand him, or if he had, had not wanted to speak.

Several women with spears spaced themselves around the group of men. One of them shouted some words and the men started walking. Jondalar used the opportunity to look around and try to get a sense of where he was. The settlement, consisting of several rounded dwellings, felt vaguely familiar, which was strange because the countryside was totally unknown to him. Then he realized it was the dwellings. They resembled Mamutoi earthlodges. Though they were not exactly the same, they appeared to be constructed in a similar fashion, probably using the bones of mammoths as structural supports that were covered with thatch, then sod and clay.

They started walking uphill, which afforded Jondalar a broader view. The countryside was mostly grassy steppeland or tundra—treeless plains on land with frozen subsoil that thawed to a black mucky surface in summer. Tundra was able to support only dwarfed herbs, but in spring their conspicuous blossoms added color and beauty, and they fed musk-oxen, reindeer, and other animals that could digest them. There were also stretches of taiga, low-growing evergreen trees so uniform in height that their tops could have been sheared off by some gigantic cutting tool, and in fact they were. Icy winds driving needles of sleet or sharp bits of gritty loess cut short any individual twig or tip that dared to strive above its brethren.

As they trudged higher, Jondalar saw a herd of mammoths grazing far to the north, and somewhat closer, reindeer. He knew horses roamed nearby—the people had been hunting them—and he guessed that bison and bear frequented the region in the warmer seasons. The land resembled his own country more than it did the dry grassy steppes to the east, at least in the types of plants that grew, although the dominant vegetation was different, and probably the proportional mix of animals, too.

Out of the corner of his eye, Jondalar caught movement to the left. He turned in time to see a white hare dash across the hill chased by an arctic fox. As he watched, the large rabbit suddenly bounded in another direction, passing by the partially decomposed skull of a woolly rhinoceros, then scooted into its hole.

Where there are mammoths and rhinoceroses, Jondalar thought, there are cave lions, and with the other herding animals, probably hyenas, and certainly wolves. Plenty of meat and fur-bearing animals, and food that grows. This is a bountiful land. Making such an assessment was second nature to him, as it was to some degree to most people. They lived off the land, and careful observations about its resources were necessary.

When the group reached a high, level place on the side of the hill, they stopped. Jondalar looked down the hillside and saw that the hunters who lived in this area had a unique advantage. Not only could the animals be seen from a distance, the vast and various herds that roamed the land had to pass through a narrow corridor below that lay between steep walls of limestone and a river. They would be easy to hunt right here. It made him wonder why they had been hunting horses near the Great Mother River.

A keening wail brought Jondalar's attention back to his immediate surroundings. A woman with long, stringy, disheveled gray hair was being supported by two somewhat younger women as she wailed and cried in obvious grief. Suddenly she broke free, fell on her knees, and draped herself over something on the ground. Jondalar edged forward to get a closer look. He was a good head taller than most of the other men, and with a few steps he understood the woman's grief.

This was obviously a funeral. Stretched out on the ground were three people—young, probably late teens or early twenties, he guessed. Two of them were definitely male; they were bearded. The biggest one was probably the youngest. His light facial hair was still somewhat sparse. The gray-haired woman was sobbing over the body of the other male, whose brown hair and short beard were more apparent. The third one was fairly tall but thin, and something about the body and the way it lay made him wonder if that person had had some physical problem. He could see no facial hair, which made him think it was a woman at first, but it also could have been a rather tall young man who shaved, just as easily.

The details of clothing were not much help. They were

all dressed in leg coverings and loose tunics that disguised distinguishing characteristics. The clothes appeared to be new, but lacked decoration. It was almost as though someone didn't want them recognized in the next world and had attempted to make them anonymous.

The gray-haired woman was lifted, almost dragged—though not roughly—away from the body of the young man by the two women who had tried to support her. Then another woman stepped forward, and something about her made Jondalar look again. Her face was strangely skewed, oddly unsymmetrical, with one side seemingly pushed back and slightly smaller than the other. She made no attempt to hide it. Her hair was light-colored, perhaps gray, pulled back and piled up into a bun on top of her head.

Jondalar thought she was about his mother's age, and she moved with the same grace and dignity, although there was no physical resemblance to Marthona. In spite of her slight deformity, the woman was not unattractive, and her face commanded attention. When she caught his eye, he realized he had been staring, but she looked away first, rather quickly, he thought. As she began to speak, he realized that she was conducting the funeral ceremony. She must be a mamut, he thought, a woman who communicates with the spirit world, a zelandonii for these people.

Something made him turn and look to the side of the congregation. Another woman was staring at him. She was tall, quite muscular and strong featured, but a handsome woman with light brown hair and, interestingly, very dark eyes. She did not turn away when he looked at her, but appraised him quite frankly. She had the size and shape, the general appearance of a woman that he would ordinarily be attracted to, he thought, but her smile made him uneasy.

Then he noticed she was standing with her legs apart and her hands on her hips, and suddenly he knew who she was: the woman who had laughed so menacingly. He fought an urge to move back and hide among the other men, knowing he couldn't even if he tried. He was not only a head taller, he was far healthier and more muscular than they. He would be conspicuous no matter where he stood.

The ceremony seemed rather perfunctory, as if it were an unpleasant necessity, rather than a solemn, important occasion. With no burial shrouds, the bodies were simply carried to a single shallow grave one at a time. They were limp when they were picked up, Jondalar noted. They could not have been dead very long; no stiffness had set in yet and there was no smell. The tall, thin body went in first, placed on its back, and powdered red ochre was sprinkled on the head and, strangely, over the pelvis, the powerful generative area, making Jondalar wonder if, perhaps, it was indeed a woman.

The other two were handled differently, but even more strangely. The brown-haired male was put in the common grave, to the left of the first corpse from Jondalar's viewpoint, but on the figure's right, and placed on his side, facing the first body. Then his arm was stretched out so that his hand rested on the red-ochred pubic region of the other. The third body was almost thrown into the grave, facedown, on the right side of the body that had been put in first. Red ochre was also sprinkled on both of their heads. The sacred red powder was obviously meant for protection, but for whom? And against what? Jondalar wondered.

Just as the loosely piled dirt was being scooped back into the shallow grave, the gray-haired woman broke loose again. She ran to the grave and threw something in it. Jondalar saw a couple of stone knives and a few flint spear points

The dark-eyed woman strode forward, clearly incensed. She cracked an order to one of the men, pointing at the grave. He cringed but did not move. Then the shaman stepped forward and spoke, shaking her head. The other woman screamed at her in anger and frustration, but the shaman stood her ground and continued to shake her head. The woman pulled back and slapped her face with the back of her hand. There was a collective gasp, and then the angry woman stalked off, with a coterie of spear-carrying females following her.

The shaman did not acknowledge the blow, not even to put her hand to her cheek, though Jondalar could see the growing redness even from where he stood. The grave was hurriedly filled in, with soil that had several pieces of loose charcoal and partially burned wood mixed in. Large bonfires must have burned here, Jondalar thought. He glanced down at the narrow corridor below. With dawning insight, it occurred to him that this high ground was a perfect lookout from which fires could be used to signal when animals—or anything else—approached.

As soon as the bodies were covered, the men were marched back down the hill and taken to an area surrounded

by a high palisade of trimmed tree trunks placed side by side
and lashed together. Mammoth bones were piled against a
section of the fence, and Jondalar wondered why. Perhaps
the bones helped to prop it up. He was separated from the
others and taken back to the earthlodge, then shoved toward
the small, circular, hide-covered enclosure again. But before
he went in, he noted how it was made.

The sturdy frame was constructed of poles made from
slender trees. The thicker butt ends had been buried in the
ground; the tops were bent together and joined. Leather hides
covered the frame on the outside, but the entrance flap he
had seen from inside was barred on the outside with a gatelike
closure that could be secured shut with lashings.

Once inside, he continued his examination of the structure. It was completely bare, lacking even a sleeping pallet.
He could not stand up straight, except in the very middle,
but he bent over to get close to the side, then walked slowly
around the small, dark space, studying it very carefully. He
noticed that the hides were old and torn, some in such shreds
that they seemed almost rotten, and they had been only
roughly sewn together, as though done in a hurry. There were
gaps at the seams through which he could see some of the
area beyond his cramped quarters. He lowered himself to the
ground and sat watching the entrance of the earthlodge, which
was open. A few people walked past, but none entered.

After a time, he began to feel an urge to pass his water.
With his hands tied, he could not even bare his member to
relieve himself. If someone didn't come and untie him soon,
he would wet himself. Besides that, his wrists were getting
raw where the ropes were rubbing. He was getting angry.
This was ridiculous! It had gone far enough!

"Hey, out there!" he shouted. "Why am I being held
like this? Like an animal in a trap? I have done nothing to
harm anyone. I need my hands free. If someone doesn't untie
me soon, I will wet myself." He waited for a while, then
shouted again. "Someone out there, come and untie me!
What strange kind of people are you?"

He stood up and leaned against the structure. It was well
made, but it gave a little. He stepped back and, aiming with
his shoulder, ran into the framing, trying to break it down.
It gave a little more, and he rammed it again. With a feeling
of satisfaction, he heard a piece of wood crack. He stepped

back, ready to try again, when he heard people running into the earthlodge.

"It's about time someone came! Let me out of here! Let me out of here now!" he shouted.

He heard the rustlings of someone unlashing the gate. Then the entrance flap was thrown back to reveal several women holding spears aimed at him. Jondalar ignored them and pushed his way out of the opening.

"Untie me!" he said, turning to the side so they could see him raising up the hands that were tied behind his back. "Get these ropes off me!"

The older man who had helped him drink water stepped forward. "Zelandonii! You . . . far . . . away," he said, obviously struggling to remember the words.

Jondalar hadn't realized that in his anger, he had been speaking in his native tongue. "You speak Zelandonii?" he said to the man with surprise, but his overwhelming need came first. "Then tell them to get these ropes off me before I make a mess all over myself!"

The man spoke to one of the women. She answered, shaking her head, but he spoke again. Finally she took a knife out of a sheath at her waist, and with a command that made the rest of the women surround him with pointing spears, she stepped forward and motioned him around. He turned his back to her and waited while she hacked at his bindings. They must need a good flint knapper around here, he couldn't help but think. Her knife is dull.

After what seemed forever, he felt the ropes fall away. Immediately he reached to unfasten his closure flap, and, too much in need to be embarrassed, he pulled out his organ and frantically looked for a corner or some out-of-the-way place to go. But the spear-holding women would not let him move. In anger and defiance, he purposely turned to face them and, with a great sigh of relief, let his water come.

He watched them all as the long yellow stream slowly emptied his bladder, steaming as it hit the cold ground and raising up a strong smell. The woman in command seemed appalled, though she tried not to show it. A couple of the women turned their heads or averted their eyes; others stared in fascination, as if they'd never seen a man pass his water before. The older man was trying very hard not to smile, though he couldn't hide his delight.

When Jondalar was through, he tucked himself back in and then faced his tormentors, determined not to let them tie his hands again. He addressed himself to the man. "I am Jondalar of the Zelandonii, and I am on a Journey."

"You Journey far, Zelandonii. Maybe . . . too far."

"I have traveled much farther. I wintered last year with the Mamutoi. I am returning home now."

"That's what I thought I heard you speaking before," the old man said, shifting into the language in which he was much more fluent. "There are a few here who understand the language of the Mammoth Hunters, but the Mamutoi usually come from the north. You came from the south."

"If you heard me speaking before, why didn't you come? I'm sure there's been some misunderstanding. Why was I tied up?"

The old man shook his head, Jondalar thought with sadness. "You will find out soon enough, Zelandonii."

Suddenly the woman interrupted with a spate of angry words. The old man started to limp away, leaning on a staff.

"Wait! Don't go! Who are you? Who are these people? And who is that woman who told them to take me here?" Jondalar asked.

The old man halted and looked back. "Here, I am called Ardemun. The people are the S'Armunai. And the woman is . . . Attaroa."

Jondalar missed the emphasis that had been put on the name of the woman. "S'Armunai? Where have I heard that name before . . . wait . . . I remember. Laduni, the leader of the Losadunai . . ."

"Laduni is leader?" Ardemun said.

"Yes. He told me about the Sarmunai when we were traveling east, but my brother didn't want to stop," Jondalar said.

"It's well you didn't, and too bad you are here now."

"Why?"

The woman in command of the spear holders interrupted again with a sharp order.

"Once I was a Losadunai. Unfortunately, I made a Journey," Ardemun said as he limped out of the earthlodge.

After he left, the woman in command said some sharp words to Jondalar. He guessed that she wanted to lead him someplace, but he decided to feign complete ignorance.

"I don't understand you," Jondalar said. "You'll have to call Ardemun back."

She spoke to him again, more angrily, then poked her spear at him. It broke the skin, and a line of blood trickled down his arm. Anger flared in his eyes. He reached over and touched the cut, then looked at his bloody fingers.

"That wasn't necess—" he started to say.

She interrupted with more angry words. The other women circled him with their weapons as the woman walked out of the earthlodge; then they prodded Jondalar to follow. Outside, the cold made him shiver. They went past the palisaded enclosure, and though he couldn't see in, he sensed that he was being watched through the cracks by those inside. The whole idea puzzled him. Animals were sometimes driven into surrounds like that, so they couldn't get away. It was a way of hunting them, but why were people kept there? And how many were in there?

It's not all that large, he thought, there can't be too many in there. He imagined how much work it must have taken to fence in even a small area with wooden stakes. Trees were scarce on the hillside. There was some woody vegetation in the form of brush, but the trees for the fence had to come from the valley below. They had to chop the trees down, trim them of branches, carry them up the hill, dig holes deep enough to hold them upright, make rope and cord, and then tie the trees together with it. Why had these people been willing to put forth so much effort for something that made so little sense?

He was led toward a small creek, largely frozen over, where Attaroa and several women were overseeing some young men who were carrying large, heavy mammoth bones. The men all looked half-starved, and he wondered where they found the strength to work so hard.

Attaroa eyed him up and down once, her only acknowledgment of him, then ignored him. Jondalar waited, still wondering about the behavior of these strange people. After a while he became chilled, and he began moving around, jumping up and down and beating his arms trying to warm himself. He was getting more and more angry at the stupidity of it all, and, finally deciding he wasn't going to stand there any longer, he turned on his heel and started back. In the earthlodge, at least he'd be out of the wind. His sudden move-

ment caught the spear wielders by surprise, and when they put
up their phalanx of points, he pushed them aside with his arm
and kept on going. He heard shouts, which he ignored.

He was still cold when he got inside the earthlodge. Looking around for something to warm himself, he strode to the
round structure, ripped off the leather cover, and wrapped it
around him. Just then several women burst in, brandishing their
weapons again. The woman who'd pricked him before was
among them, and she was obviously furious. She lunged at him
with her spear. He ducked aside and grabbed for it, but they
were all stopped in their tracks by harsh and sinister laughter.

"Zelandonii!" Attaroa sneered, then spoke other words
that he didn't understand.

"She wants you to come outside," Ardemun said. Jondalar hadn't noticed him near the entrance. "She thinks you are
clever, too clever. I think she wants you where she can have
her women surround you."

"What if I don't want to go outside?" Jondalar said.

"Then she'll probably have you killed here and now."
The words were said by a woman, speaking in perfect Zelandonii, without even a trace of an accent! Jondalar shot a look
of surprise in the direction of the speaker. It was the shaman!
"If you go outside, Attaroa will probably let you live a little
longer. You interest her, but eventually she'll kill you anyway."

"Why? What am I to her?" Jondalar asked.

"A threat."

"A threat? I've never threatened her."

"You threaten her control. She'll want to make an example of you."

Attaroa interrupted, and though Jondalar didn't understand her, the barely restrained fury of her words seemed to
be directed at the shaman. The older woman's response was
reserved but showed no fear. After the exchange, she spoke
again to Jondalar. "She wanted to know what I said to you.
I told her."

"Tell her I'll come outside," he said.

When the message was relayed, Attaroa laughed, said
something, then sauntered out.

"What did she say?" Jondalar asked.

"She said she knew it. Men will do anything for one
more heartbeat of their miserable lives."

"Perhaps not anything," Jondalar said, starting out, then
he turned back to the shaman. "What is your name?"

"I am called S'Armuna," she said.

"I thought you might be. Where did you learn to speak my language so well?"

"I lived among your people for a time," S'Armuna said, but then she cut off his obvious desire to know more. "It's a long story."

Though the man had rather expected to be asked to give his identity in return, S'Armuna simply turned her back. He volunteered the information. "I am Jondalar of the Ninth Cave of the Zelandonii," he said.

S'Armuna's eyes opened with surprise. "The Ninth Cave?" she said.

"Yes," he said. He would have continued to name his ties, but he was stopped by the look on her face, though he could not fathom its meaning. A moment later her expression showed nothing, and Jondalar wondered if he had imagined it.

"She's waiting," S'Armuna said, leaving the earthlodge.

Outside, Attaroa was sitting on a fur-covered seat on a raised platform of earth, which had been dug from the floor of the large semisubterranean earthlodge just behind her. She was opposite the fenced area, and, as he walked past it, Jondalar sensed again that he was being watched through the cracks.

As he drew near, he was sure the fur on her seat was from a wolf. The hood of her parka, thrown back off her head, was trimmed with wolf fur, and around her neck she wore a necklace made primarily of the sharp canine teeth of wolves, although there were some from arctic fox, and at least one cave-bear tooth. She was holding a carved staff similar to the Speaking Staff Talut had used when there were issues to be discussed or arguments to be resolved. That stick had helped to keep the talk orderly. Whoever held it had the right to speak, and when someone else had something to say, it was necessary first to ask for the Speaking Staff.

Something else was familiar about the staff she held, though he couldn't quite place it. Could it be the carving? It bore the stylized shape of a seated woman, with an enlarging series of concentric circles representing breasts and stomach, and a strange triangular head, narrow at the chin, with a face of enigmatic designs. It wasn't like Mamutoi carving, but he felt he'd seen it before.

Several of her women surrounded Attaroa. Other women

he hadn't noticed before, only a few of them with children, were standing nearby. She observed him for a while; then she spoke, looking at him. Ardemun, standing off to the side, began a stumbling translation into Zelandonii. Jondalar was about to suggest that he speak Mamutoi, but S'Armuna interrupted, said something to Attaroa, then looked at him.

"I will translate," she said.

Attaroa made a sneering comment that made the women around her laugh, but S'Armuna did not translate it. "She was speaking to me," was all she said, her face impassive. The seated woman spoke again, this time to Jondalar.

"I speak now as Attaroa," S'Armuna said, beginning to translate. "Why did you come here?"

"I did not come here voluntarily. I was brought here, tied up," Jondalar said, while S'Armuna translated almost simultaneously. "I am on my Journey. Or I was. I don't understand why I was tied up. No one bothered to tell me."

"Where did you come from?" Attaroa said through S'Armuna, ignoring his comments.

"I wintered last year with the Mamutoi."

"You lie! You came from the south."

"I came the long way around. I wanted to visit kin who live near the Great Mother River, at the south end of the eastern mountains."

"Again you lie! The Zelandonii live far to the west of here. How can you have kin to the east?"

"It is not a lie. I traveled with my brother. Unlike the S'Armunai, the Sharamudoi welcomed us. My brother mated a woman there. They are my kin through him."

Then, full of righteous indignation, Jondalar continued. It was the first chance he'd had to speak to someone who was listening. "Don't you know those on a Journey have rights of passage? Most people welcome visitors. They exchange stories, share with them. But not here! Here I was hit on the head and though I was injured, my wound was left untreated. No one gave me water or food. My fur parka was taken from me, and it was not given back even when I was made to go out."

The more he spoke, the angrier he got. He had been very badly treated. "I was brought outside in the cold and left standing. No other people on my long Journey have ever treated me like this. Even animals of the plains share their pasture, their water. What kind of people are you?"

Attaroa interrupted him. "Why did you try to steal our meat?" She was fuming, but she tried not to show it. Although she knew everything he said was true, she didn't like being told that she was somehow less than others, especially in front of her people.

"I wasn't trying to steal your meat," Jondalar said, denying the accusation vigorously. S'Armuna's translation was so smooth and quick and Jondalar's need to communicate so intense, that he almost forgot his interpreter. He felt he was talking directly with Attaroa.

"You are lying! You were seen running into that herd we were after with a spear in your hand."

"I am not lying! I was only trying to save Ayla. She was on the back of one of those horses, and I couldn't let them carry her along."

"Ayla?"

"Didn't you see her? She is the woman I have been traveling with."

Attaroa laughed. "You were traveling with a woman who rides on the backs of horses? If you are not a traveling storyteller, you have missed your calling." Then she leaned forward and, jabbing her finger at him for emphasis, said, "Everything you've said is untrue. You are a liar and a thief!"

"I am neither a liar nor a thief! I have told the truth and I have stolen nothing," Jondalar said with conviction. But in his heart he couldn't really blame her for not believing him. Unless someone had seen Ayla, who would believe that they had traveled by riding on the backs of horses? He began to worry about how he would ever convince Attaroa that he wasn't lying, that he had not intentionally interfered with their hunt. If he'd known the full extent of his plight, he would have been more than concerned.

Attaroa studied the tall, muscular, handsome man standing in front of her, wrapped in the hides he had torn from his cage. She noticed that his blond beard was a shade darker than his hair and that his eyes, an unbelievably vivid shade of blue, were compelling. She felt strongly attracted to him, but the very strength of her response dredged up painful memories long suppressed and provoked a powerful but strangely twisted reaction. She would not allow herself to be attracted to any man, because to have feelings for one might give him control over her—and never again would she allow anyone, particularly a man, to have control over her.

She had taken his parka and left him standing in the cold
for the same reason she had withheld food and water. Depri-
vation made men easier to control. While they still had the
strength to resist, it was necessary to keep them tied. But the
Zelandonii man, wrapped in those hides he was not supposed
to have, showed no fear, she thought. Look at him standing
there, so sure of himself.

He was so defiant and cocky, he had even dared to criti-
cize her in front of everyone, including the men in the Holding. He did not cringe, or plead, or hurry to please her as
they did. But she vowed that he would before she was
through with him. She was determined to bring him down.
She would show them all how to handle a man like that, and
then . . . he would die.

But before I break him, she said to herself, I will play
with him for a while. Besides, he's a strong man, and he'll
be hard to control if he decides to resist. He's suspicious
now, so I need to make him lower his guard. He needs to
be weakened. S'Armuna will know of something. Attaroa
beckoned to the shaman and spoke to her privately. Then she
looked at the man and smiled, but the smile held such malice
that it sent a chill up his spine.

Jondalar not only threatened her leadership, he threatened
the fragile world that her sick mind had led her to create. He
even threatened her tenuous hold on reality, which had
recently been stretched very thin.

"Come with me," S'Armuna said when she left Attaroa.

"Where are we going?" Jondalar asked, as he stepped in
beside her. Two women with spears followed behind.

"Attaroa wants me to treat your wound."

She led Jondalar to a dwelling on the far edge of the
settlement, similar to the big earthlodge that Attaroa had been
seated near, but smaller and more dome-shaped. A low, narrow entrance led through a short passageway to another low
opening. Jondalar had to bend over and walk bent-kneed for
a few paces, then step down three stairs. No one, except a
child, could enter her dwelling easily, but once inside, the
man was able to stand to his full height with room to spare.
The two women who had followed stayed outside.

After his eyes adjusted to the dim interior, he noticed a
bed platform against the far wall. It was covered with a white
fur of some kind . . . the rare and unusual white animals
were held sacred among his people and, he had discovered

in his travels, by many others as well. Dried herbs hung from roof supports and racks, and many of the baskets and bowls on shelves along the walls probably contained more. Any mamut or zelandoni could have moved in and been completely at home, except for one thing. Among most people, the hearth or dwelling place of the One Who Served the Mother was a ceremonial area, or adjacent to one, and the larger space was also where visitors stayed. But this was not a spacious and inviting area for activities and visitors. It had a closed and secretive feeling. Jondalar felt sure that S'Armuna lived alone and that other people seldom entered her domain.

He watched her stir up the fire, add dried dung and a few sticks of wood, and pour water into a blackened, pouchlike container, formerly the stomach of an animal, attached to a frame of bone. From a basket on one of her shelves, she added a small handful of some dried material, and when the water began to soak through the container, she moved it directly over the flames. As long as there was liquid in it, even if it was boiling, the pouch could not catch fire.

Though Jondalar did not know what it was, the odor that rose from the pot was familiar and, strangely, made him think of home. With a sudden flash of memory, he knew why. It was a smell that had often emanated from a zelandoni's fire. They used the decoction to wash wounds and injuries.

"You speak the language very well. Did you live among the Zelandonii long?" Jondalar asked.

S'Armuna looked up at him and seemed to consider her reply. "Several years," she said.

"Then you know that the Zelandonii welcome their visitors. I don't understand these people. What could I possibly have done to deserve such treatment?" Jondalar said. "You shared the hospitality of the Zelandonii—why don't you explain to them about rights of passage and courtesy to visitors? It's really more than a courtesy, it's an obligation."

S'Armuna's only response was a sardonic glance.

He knew he wasn't handling the situation well, but he was still so incredulous over his recent experiences that he found himself with an almost childish need to explain how things should be, as if that would put them right. He decided to try another approach.

"I wonder, since you lived there so long, if you knew my mother. I am the son of Marthona . . ." He would have continued, but the expression on her somewhat misshapen face stopped him. She registered such shock that it contorted her features even more.

"You are the son of Marthona, born to the hearth of Joconan?" she finally said, more as a question.

"No, that's my brother Joharran. I was born to Dalanar's hearth, the man she mated later. Did you know Joconan?"

"Yes," S'Armuna said, looking down, then turning her attention back to the skin pot that was almost boiling.

"Then you must have known my mother, too!" Jondalar was excited. "If you knew Marthona, then you know I'm not a liar. She would never put up with that in a child of hers. I know it sounds unbelievable—I'm not even sure I'd believe it, if I didn't know better—but the woman I was traveling with was sitting on the back of one of those horses that was being chased over the cliff. It was one she raised from a foal, not one that really belonged to that herd. Now I don't even know if she's alive. You must tell Attaroa I'm not lying! I've got to look for her. I've got to know if she's still alive!"

Jondalar's impassioned plea elicited no response from the woman. She did not even look up from the pouch of boiling water she was stirring. But, unlike Attaroa, she did not doubt him. One of Attaroa's hunters had come to her with a story about seeing a woman riding on one of the horses, afraid because she thought it was a spirit. S'Armuna thought there could be something to Jondalar's story, but she wondered whether it was real or supernatural.

"You did know Marthona, didn't you?" Jondalar asked, walking to the fire to get her attention. He had gotten her to respond before by invoking his mother.

When she looked up, her face was impassive. "Yes, I knew Marthona, once. I was sent, when I was young, to be trained by the Zelandoni of the Ninth Cave. Sit here," she said. Then she moved the frame back from the fire, turned away from him, and reached for a soft skin. He winced when she washed his injury with the antiseptic solution she had prepared, but he was sure her medicine was good. She had learned it from his people.

After it was clean, S'Armuna looked closely at his wound. "You were stunned for a while, but it is not serious. It will heal by itself." She averted her eyes, then said, "But you probably have a headache. I will give you something for it."

"No, I don't need anything now, but I am still thirsty. All I really want is some water. Is it all right if I drink from your waterbag?" Jondalar said, walking over to the large damp bladder of water, from which she had filled the pot. "I'll refill it for you, if you'd like. Do you have a cup I can use?"

She hesitated, then got a cup from a shelf.

"Where can I fill your waterbag?" he asked when he was through. "Is there a favorite place nearby?"

"Don't worry about the water," she said.

He walked closer and looked at her, realizing she was not going to let him walk freely, not even for water. "We weren't trying to hunt the horses they were after. Even if we had been, Attaroa should have known we would have offered something to compensate. Although with that whole herd driven off the cliff, there should have been plenty. I just hope Ayla isn't with them. S'Armuna, I need to go and look for her!"

"You love her, don't you?" S'Armuna asked.

"Yes, I love her," he said. He saw her expression change again. There was an element of gloating bitterness, but something softer, too. "We were on our way back to my home to be mated, but I also need to tell my mother about the death of my younger brother, Thonolan. We started out together, but he . . . died. She will be very unhappy. It's hard to lose a child."

S'Armuna nodded but made no comment.

"That funeral earlier, what happened to those youngsters?"

"They weren't much younger than you are," S'Armuna said, "old enough to make some wrong decisions for themselves."

Jondalar thought she looked distinctly uncomfortable. "How did they die?" he asked.

"They ate something that was bad for them."

Jondalar didn't believe she was quite telling the truth, but before he could say more, she handed him his hide coverings and led him back out to the two women who had been guarding the entrance. They marched on either side of him, but this time he was not taken back to the earthlodge. Instead he was led to the fenced enclosure, and the gate was opened just enough to push him inside.

27

Ayla sipped tea at her after-noon campfire and stared, unseeing, across the grassy landscape. When she had stopped to let Wolf rest, she noticed a large rock formation outlined against the blue sky to the northwest, but as the conspicuous limestone hill faded into mists and clouds in the distance, it receded from memory as her thoughts focused inward, worrying about Jondalar.

Between her tracking skills and Wolf's keen nose, they had managed to follow the trail that she felt sure was left by the people who had taken Jondalar. After making a gradual descent off the highland, traveling north, they had turned west until they reached the river she and Jondalar had crossed earlier, but they did not cross over. They turned north again, along the river, leaving a trail that was easier to follow.

Ayla camped the first night beside the flowing stream and continued tracking the next day. She wasn't sure how many people she was following, but she occasionally saw several sets of footprints on the muddy banks of the river, a couple of which she was beginning to recognize. None of them, however, were Jondalar's large prints, and she began to wonder if he was still with them.

Then she recalled that occasionally something large was put down, flattening the grass or leaving an impression in the dust or damp ground beneath it, and she remembered seeing that sign, along with the tracks and other signs, from the beginning. It wouldn't have been horsemeat, she reasoned, because the horses had been driven over the edge and this load had been carried down from the top. She decided it had to be the man who was being carried on some kind of litter, which caused her both worry and relief.

If they'd had to carry him, it must mean he couldn't walk himself, so the blood she had found did indicate a serious injury, but they certainly would not bother to carry him if he was dead. She drew the conclusion that he was still alive but seriously hurt, and she hoped they were taking him someplace where his injuries could be treated. But why would anyone hurt him in the first place?

Whoever she was following had been moving fast, but the trail was getting colder and she knew she was falling behind. The telltale signs showing the way they had gone were not always easy to find, which slowed her down, and even Wolf had some trouble keeping up. Without the animal, she wasn't sure if she could have tracked them this far, especially over areas of rocky ground, where the subtle marks of their passing were all but nonexistent. But more than that, she didn't want to let Wolf out of her sight and risk losing him, too. Nonetheless, she felt an anxious need to hurry, and she was grateful that he seemed better each day.

She had awakened that morning with a strong sense of foreboding, and she was glad to see that Wolf seemed eager to start out, but by afternoon she could tell he was tiring. She decided to stop and make a cup of tea to let him rest and give the horses time to graze.

Not long after starting out again she came to a fork in the river. She had easily crossed a couple of small streams flowing down from the highlands, but she wasn't sure if she should cross the river. She hadn't seen tracks for some time, and she didn't know whether to take the east fork or make the crossing and follow the west one. She kept to the east for a while, weaving back and forth, trying to find the trail, and just before nightfall she saw an unusual sight that clearly showed her the way to go.

Even in the failing light, she knew the posts sticking out of the water had been put there for a purpose. They had been pounded into the riverbed near several logs that were lodged into the bank. From the time she spent with the Sharamudoi, she recognized the construction as a rather simple docking place for some kind of watercraft. Ayla started to make her camp beside it, then changed her mind. She didn't know anything about the people she was following, except that they had hurt Jondalar and then taken him with them. She did not want such people to come upon her unawares, while she was sleeping and vulnerable. She chose a place around a bend in the river instead.

In the morning she carefully examined the wolf before entering the river. Though not especially wide, the water was cold and deep, and he would have to swim it. His bruises were still tender to the touch, but he was very much improved, and he was eager to go. He seemed to want to find Jondalar as much as she did.

Not for the first time, she decided to remove her leggings before getting on Whinney's back, so they would not get wet. She didn't want to take the time to worry about drying clothes. Much to her surprise, Wolf did not hesitate to enter the water. Instead of pacing back and forth on the bank, he jumped in and paddled after her, as though he no more wanted to let her out of his sight than she wanted to let him out of hers.

When they reached the other side, Ayla moved out of the way to avoid the spray from the animals shaking off excess moisture while she donned her legwear. She checked the wolf again, just to satisfy herself, though he showed no discomfort when he shook himself vigorously and then began searching for the trail. Somewhat downstream of their landing, Wolf discovered the watercraft that had been used by the ones she was tracking to make the crossing, hidden in some brush and trees that grew near the water. It took her a while, however, to understand it for what it was.

She had assumed the people would use a boat, something similar to the Sharamudoi boats—beautifully crafted dugouts with gracefully pointed prows and sterns, or perhaps like the more pedestrian but practical bowl boat that she and Jondalar used. But the contrivance Wolf found was a platform of logs, and she was unfamiliar with a raft. Once she understood its purpose, she thought it was rather clever, if somewhat ungainly. Wolf sniffed around the crude craft curiously. When he came to a certain place, he stopped and made a low growl deep in his throat.

"What is it, Wolf?" Ayla said. Looking more closely, she found a brown stain on one of the logs and felt a touch of panic drain her face. It was dried blood, she was sure, probably Jondalar's blood. She patted the canine's head. "We'll find him," she said, to reassure herself as much as the wolf, but she wasn't at all sure that they would find him alive.

The trail leading from the landing ran between fields of tall dry grass intermixed with brush and was much easier to follow. The problem was that it was so well used that she couldn't be sure it had been taken by the ones she was pursuing. Wolf was in the lead, for which Ayla was soon more than grateful. They had not been on the path long when he stopped in his tracks, wrinkling his nose and baring his teeth in a snarl.

"Wolf? What is it? Is someone coming?" Ayla said, even as she turned Whinney off the path and headed for some thick brush, signaling Wolf to follow. She slid off the mare's back as soon as they were screened by the tall, bare branches and grass, grabbed Racer's lead rope to guide him behind the mare, since he was wearing the pack, and hid between the horses herself. She knelt on one knee and put an arm around Wolf's neck to keep him quiet, then waited.

Her assessment was not wrong. Before long, two young women ran past, obviously heading for the river. She signaled Wolf to stay and then, using the stealth she had learned when tracking carnivores as a girl, she followed them back, creeping close through the grass, then hiding behind some brush to watch.

The two women talked to each other as they uncovered the raft, and though the language was unfamiliar, she noticed a similarity to Mamutoi. She wasn't quite able to understand them, but she thought she caught the meaning of a word or two.

The women pushed the log platform almost into the water, then retrieved two long poles that had been underneath it. They fastened one end of a large coil of rope around a tree, then climbed on. As one began to pole across the river, the other played out the rope. When they were near the other side, where the current was not as swift, they started poling upstream until they reached the docking place. With ropes fastened to the raft, they secured it to the poles sticking up from the water and stepped off to the logs stuck into the bank. Leaving the raft, they started running back the way Ayla had just come.

She returned to the animals, thinking about what to do. She felt sure the women would be returning soon, but "soon" could be this day, or the next, or the one after. She wanted to find Jondalar as soon as possible, but she didn't want to continue following the trail and have them catch up with her. She was also reluctant to approach them directly until she knew more about them. She finally decided to look for a place to wait for them where she could watch them coming without being seen.

She was pleased that her wait was not too long. By afternoon she saw the two women returning, along with several other people, all carrying litters of butchered meat and sections of horse. They were moving surprisingly fast in spite of their loads. When they drew nearer, Ayla realized there was not a single man in the hunting party. All the hunters were women! She watched them load the meat on the raft, then pole across using the rope for a guide. They hid the raft after unloading it, but they left the guide rope strung across the river, which puzzled her.

Ayla was again surprised at how fast they traveled as they started up the trail. Almost before she knew it, they were gone. She waited some time before she followed, and she kept well behind.

Jondalar was appalled at the conditions inside the fence. The only shelter was a rather large, crude lean-to, which offered scant protection from rain or snow, and the fence of posts, itself, which blocked the wind. There were no fires, little water, and no food available. The only people within the Holding were male, and they showed the effects of the poor conditions. As they came out of the shelter to stand and stare at him, he saw that they were thin, dirty, and ill-clad. None of them had sufficient clothing for the weather, and they probably had to huddle together in the lean-to in an attempt to keep warm.

He recognized one or two from the walk up to the funeral, and he wondered why the men and boys were living in such a place. Suddenly several puzzling things came together: the attitude of the women with spears, the strange comments of Ardemun, the behavior of the men walking to the funeral, the reticence of S'Armuna, the belated examination of his wounds, and their generally harsh treatment of him. Maybe it wasn't the result of a misunderstanding that would be cleared up as soon as he convinced Attaroa that he wasn't lying.

The conclusion he was forced to seemed preposterous, but the full realization struck him with the force to shatter his disbelief. It was so obvious that he wondered why it had taken him so long to see it. The men were kept here against their will by the women!

But why? It was such a waste to keep people inactive like this when they could all be contributing to the welfare and benefit of the entire community. He thought of the prosperous Lion Camp of the Mamutoi, with Talut and Tulie organizing the necessary activities of the Camp for the benefit of everyone. They all contributed, and they still had plenty of time to work on their own individual projects.

Attaroa! How much was her doing? She was obviously the headwoman or leader of this Camp. If she wasn't entirely responsible, at the least, she seemed determined to maintain the peculiar situation.

These men should be hunting and collecting food, Jondalar thought, and digging storage pits, making new shelters and repairing old ones; contributing, not huddling together trying to keep warm. No wonder these people were out hunting horses this late in the season. Did they even have enough food stored to last through the winter? And why did they hunt so far away when they had such a perfect hunting opportunity so close at hand?

"You're the one they call the Zelandonii man," one of the men said, speaking Mamutoi. Jondalar thought he recognized him as one whose hands had been tied when they marched up to the funeral.

"Yes. I am Jondalar of the Zelandonii."

"I am Ebulan of the S'Armunai," he said, then added sardonically, "In the name of Muna, the Mother of All, let me welcome you to the Holding, as Attaroa likes to call this place. We have other names: the Men's Camp, the Mother's Frozen Underworld, and Attaroa's Man Trap. Take your pick."

"I don't understand. Why are you . . . all of you, here?"
Jondalar asked.

"It's a long story, but essentially we were all tricked,
one way or another," Ebulan said. Then, with an ironic grimace, he continued, "We were even tricked into building
this place. Or most of it."

"Why don't you just climb over the wall and get out?"
Jondalar said.

"And get pierced by Epadoa and her spear-stickers?"
another man said.

"Olamun is right. Besides, I'm not sure how many could
make the effort, anymore," Ebulan added. "Attaroa likes to
keep us weak . . . or worse."

"Worse?" Jondalar said, frowning.

"Show him, S'Amodun," Ebulan said to a tall, cadaver-
ously thin man with gray matted hair and a long beard that
was almost white. He had a strong, craggy face with a long,
high-bridged beak of a nose and heavy brows that were
accented by his gaunt face, but it was his eyes that captured
the attention. They were compelling, as dark as Attaroa's,
but rather than malice they held depths of ancient wisdom,
mystery, and compassion. Jondalar wasn't sure what it was
about him, some quality of carriage or demeanor, but he
sensed that this was a man who commanded great respect,
even in these wretched conditions.

The old man nodded and led the way to the lean-to. As
they neared, Jondalar could see that a few people were still
inside. As he ducked under the sloping roof, an overpowering
stench assaulted him. A man was lying on a plank that might
have been torn from the roof, and he was covered with only
a ripped piece of hide. The old man pulled back the cover
and exposed a putrefying wound in his side.

Jondalar was aghast. "Why is this man here?"

"Epadoa's spear-stickers did that," Ebulan said.

"Does S'Armuna know about this? She could do something for him."

"S'Armuna! Hah! What makes you think she would do
anything?" said Olamun, who was among those who had
followed them. "Who do you think helped Attaroa in the
first place?"

"But she cleaned the wound on my head," Jondalar said.

"Then Attaroa must have plans for you," Ebulan said.

"Plans for me? What do you mean?"

"She likes to put the men who are young and strong enough to work, as long as she can control them," Olamun said.

"What if someone doesn't want to do her work?" Jondalar asked. "How can she control them?"

"By withholding food or water. If that doesn't work, by threatening kin," Ebulan said. "If you know that the man of your hearth or your brother will be put in the cage without food or water, you'll usually do what she wants."

"The cage?"

"The place you were kept," Ebulan said. Then he smiled wryly. "Where you got that magnificent cloak." Other men were smiling, too.

Jondalar looked at the ragged hide he had torn from the structure inside the earthlodge and wrapped around him.

"That was a good one!" Olamun said. "Ardemun told us how you almost broke down the cage, too. I don't think she expected that."

"Next time, she make stronger cage," said another man. It was obvious that he was not entirely familiar with the language. Ebulan and Olamun were so fluent that Jondalar had forgotten that Mamutoi was not the native language of these people. But apparently others knew some, and most seemed to understand what was being said.

The man on the ground moaned, and the old man knelt to comfort him. Jondalar noticed a couple of other figures stirring, farther back under the lean-to.

"It won't matter. If she doesn't have a cage, she'll threaten to hurt your kin to make you do what she wants. If you were mated before she became headwoman, and were unlucky enough to have a son born to your hearth, she can make you do anything," Ebulan said.

Jondalar didn't like the implication, and he frowned deeply. "Why should it be unlucky to have a son born to your hearth?"

Ebulan glanced toward the old man. "S'Amodun?"

"I will ask if they want to meet the Zelandonii," he said.

It was the first time S'Amodun had spoken, and Jondalar wondered how a voice so deep and rich could emanate from so spare a man. He went to the back of the lean-to, bending down to talk to the figures huddled in the space where the slanting roof reached the ground. They could hear the deep mellow tones of his voice, but not his words, and then the sound of younger voices. With the old man's help, one of the younger figures got up and hobbled toward them.

"This is Ardoban," the old man announced.

"I am Jondalar of the Ninth Cave of the Zelandonii, and in the name of Doni, the Great Earth Mother, I greet you, Ardoban," he said with great formality, holding out both his hands to the youngster, somehow feeling that the boy needed to be treated with dignity.

The boy tried to stand straighter and take his hands, but Jondalar saw him wince with pain. He started to reach for him to support him, but caught himself.

"I really prefer to be called Jondalar," he said, with a smile, trying to gloss over the awkward moment.

"I called Doban. Not like Ardoban. Attaroa always say Ardoban. She wants me say S'Attaroa. I not say anymore."

Jondalar looked puzzled.

"It's hard to translate. It's a form of respect," Ebulan said. "It means someone held in the highest regard."

"And Doban does not respect Attaroa anymore."

"Doban hate Attaroa!" the youngster said, his voice rising to the edge of tears as he tried to turn away and hobble back. S'Amodun waved them out as he helped the youngster.

"What happened to him?" Jondalar asked after they were outside and somewhat away from the lean-to.

"His leg was pulled until it became dislocated at the hip," Ebulan said. "Attaroa did it, or rather, she told Epadoa to do it."

"What!" Jondalar said, his eyes open wide in disbelief. "Are you saying she purposely dislocated the leg of that child? What kind of abomination is this woman?"

"She did the same thing to the other boy, and Odevan's younger."

"What possible justification can she even give to herself for doing such a thing?"

"With the younger one, it was to make an example. The boy's mother didn't like the way Attaroa was treating us, and she wanted her mate back at her hearth. Avanoa even managed to get in here sometimes and spend the night with him, and she used to sneak extra food to us. She's not the only woman who does that sometimes, but she was stirring up the other women, and Armodan, her man, was . . . resisting Attaroa, refusing to work. She took it out on the boy. She said at seven years he was old enough to leave his mother and live with the men, but she dislocated his leg first."

"The other boy is seven years?" Jondalar said, shaking his head and shuddering with horror. "I have never heard of anything so terrible."

"Odevan is in pain, and he misses his mother, but Ardoban's story is worse." It was S'Amodun who spoke. He had left the lean-to and just joined the group.

"It's hard to imagine anything worse," Jondalar said.

"I think he suffers more from the pain of betrayal than from the physical pain," S'Amodun said. "Ardoban thought of Attaroa as his mother. His own mother died when he was young and Attaroa took him in, but she treated him more like a favored plaything than a child. She liked to dress him in girl's clothes and adorn him with silly things, but she fed him well, and she often gave him special tidbits. She even cuddled him, sometimes, and took him to her bed to sleep with her when she was in the mood. But when she got tired of him, she'd push him out and make him sleep on the ground. A few years ago, Attaroa began to think people were trying to poison her."

"They say that's what she did to her mate," Olamun interjected.

"She made Ardoban taste everything before she ate it," the old man continued, "and when he got older, she tied him up, sometimes, convinced he was going to run away. But she was the only mother he knew. He loved her and tried to please her. He treated the other boys the same way she treated the men, and he began telling the men what to do. Of course, she encouraged him."

"He was insufferable," Ebulan added. "You'd think the whole Camp belonged to him, and he made the other boys' lives miserable."

"But what happened?" Jondalar asked.

"He reached the age of manhood," S'Amodun said. Then, seeing Jondalar's puzzled look, he explained. "The Mother came to him in his sleep in the form of a young woman and brought his manhood to life."

"Of course. That happens to all young men," Jondalar said.

"Attaroa found out," S'Amodun explained, "and it was as though he had purposely turned into a man just to displease her. She was livid! She screamed at him, called him terrible names, then banished him to the Men's Camp, but not before she had his leg dislocated.''

"With Odevan, it was easier," Ebulan said. "He was younger. I'm not even sure if they originally intended to tear his joint loose. I think they just wanted to make his mother and her mate suffer by listening to his screams, but once it happened, I think Attaroa thought it would be a good way to disable a man, make him easier to control.''

"She had Ardemun as an example," Olamun said.

"Did she dislocate his leg, too?" Jondalar asked.

"In a way," S'Amodun said. "It was an accident, but it happened when he was trying to get away. Attaroa would not allow S'Armuna to help him, although I believe she wanted to.''

"But it was harder to disable a boy of twelve years. He fought and screamed, but it did no good," Ebulan said. "And I will tell you, after listening to his agony, no one here could be angry with him anymore. He more than paid for his childish behavior.''

"Is it true that she has told the women that all children, including the one that is expected, if they are boys, will have their legs dislocated?" Olamun asked.

"That's what Ardemun said," Ebulan confirmed.

"Does she think she can tell the Mother what to do? Force Her to make only girl babies?" Jondalar asked. "She is tempting her fate, I think.''

"Perhaps," Ebulan said, "but it will take the Mother Herself to stop her, I'm afraid.''

"I think the Zelandonii may be right," S'Amodun said. "I think the Mother has already tried to warn her. Look how few babies have been born in the last several years. This latest outrage of hers, injuring children, may be more than She will stand for. Children are supposed to be protected, not harmed.''

"I know Ayla would never stand for it. She wouldn't stand for any of this," Jondalar said. Then, remembering, he frowned and lowered his head. "But I don't even know if she's alive.''

The men glanced at each other, hesitant to speak, though they all thought the same question. Finally Ebulan found his voice. "Is that the woman you claimed could ride on the backs of horses? She must be a woman of great powers if she can control horses like that.''

"She wouldn't say so.'' Jondalar smiled. ''But I think she has more 'power' than she will acknowledge. She doesn't ride all horses. She only rides the mare that she raised, although she has ridden my horse, too. But he's a little harder to control. That was the problem . . .''

"You can ride horses, too?'' Olamun said in tones of disbelief.

"I can ride one . . . well, I can ride hers, too, but . . .''

"Are you saying that the story you told Attaroa is true?'' Ebulan said.

"Of course it's true. Why would I make up something like that?'' He looked at the skeptical faces. ''Maybe I'd better start at the beginning. Ayla raised a little filly . . .''

"Where did she get a filly?'' Olamun asked.

"She was hunting and killed its dam, and then she saw the foal.''

"But why would she raise it?'' Ebulan asked.

"Because it was alone, and she was alone . . . and that's a long story,'' Jondalar sidestepped, ''but she wanted company and decided to take in the filly. When Whinney grew up—Ayla named the horse Whinney—she gave birth to a colt, just about the time we met. She showed me how to ride and gave me the colt to train. I named him Racer. That's a Zelandonii word that means a fast runner, and he likes to run fast. We have traveled all the way from the Mamutoi Summer Meeting, around the southern end of those mountains to the east, riding those horses. It really doesn't have anything to do with special powers. It's a matter of raising them from the time they are born, just like a mother would take care of a baby.''

"Well . . . if you say so,'' Ebulan said.

"I say so because it's true,'' Jondalar countered, then decided it was worthless to pursue the subject. They would have to see it to believe it, and it was unlikely that they ever would. Ayla was gone, and so were the horses.

Just then the gate opened and they all turned to see. Epadoa entered first along with a few of her women. Now that he knew more about her, Jondalar studied the woman who had actually caused such great pain to the two children. He wasn't sure who was more of an abomination, the one who conceived of the idea or the one who carried it out. Though he had no doubt that Attaroa would have done it herself, it was evident that something was wrong with her. She was not whole. Some dark spirit must have touched her and stolen a vital part of her being—but what about Epadoa? She seemed sound and whole, but how could she be and still be so cruel and unfeeling? Was she also lacking some essential part?

To everyone's surprise, Attaroa herself came in next.

"She never comes in here," Olamun said. "What can she want?" Her unusual behavior frightened him.

Behind her came several women carrying steaming trays of cooked meat along with tightly woven baskets of some delicious-smelling rich and meaty soup. Horsemeat! Have the hunters returned? Jondalar wondered. He hadn't eaten horsemeat for a long time, the thought of it didn't usually appeal to him, but at that moment it smelled delicious. A large, full waterbag with a few cups was also carried in.

The men watched the arriving procession avidly, but none of them moved anything except his eyes, afraid to do anything that might cause Attaroa to change her mind. They feared that it might be another cruel trick, to bring it in and show them and then take it away.

"Zelandonii!" Attaroa said, making the word sound like a command. Jondalar looked at her closely as he approached. She seemed almost masculine . . . no, he decided, not exactly that. Her features were strong and sharp, but cleanly defined and well shaped. She was actually beautiful, in her way, or could have been, if she had not been so hard. But there was cruelty in the set of her mouth, and the lack in her soul showed in her eyes.

S'Armuna appeared at her side. She must have come in with the other women, he thought, though he hadn't noticed her before.

"I now speak for Attaroa," S'Armuna said in Zelandonii.

"You have a lot to answer for, yourself," Jondalar said. "How could you allow it? Attaroa lacks reason, but you do not. I hold you responsible." His blue eyes were icy with outrage.

Attaroa spoke angrily to the shaman.

"She does not want you to speak to me. I am here to translate for her. Attaroa wants you to look at her when you speak," S'Armuna said.

Jondalar looked at the headwoman and waited while she spoke. Then S'Armuna began the translation.

"Attaroa is speaking now: How do you like your new . . . accommodations?"

"How does she expect me to like them?" Jondalar said to S'Armuna, who avoided his look and spoke to Attaroa.

A malicious smile played across the headwoman's face. "I'm sure you've heard many things about me already, but you should not believe everything you hear."

"I believe what I see," Jondalar said.

"Well, you saw me bring food in here."

"I don't see anyone eating it, and I know they are hungry."

Her smile broadened when she heard the translation. "They shall, and you must, too. You will need your strength." Attaroa laughed out loud.

"I'm sure I will," Jondalar said.

After S'Armuna translated, Attaroa left abruptly, signaling the woman to follow.

"I hold you responsible," Jondalar said to S'Armuna's retreating back.

As soon as the gate closed, one of the guard women said, "You'd better come and get it, before she changes her mind."

The men rushed for the platters of meat on the ground. As S'Amodun passed by, he stopped. "Be very careful, Zelandonii. She has something special in mind for you."

The next few days passed slowly for Jondalar. Some water, but little additional food was brought in, and no one was allowed out, not even to work, which was very unusual. It made the men uneasy, especially since Ardemun was also kept inside the Holding. His knowledge of several languages had made Ardemun first a translator and then a spokesman between Attaroa and the men. Because of his lame, dislocated leg, she felt he posed no threat and, further, would not be able to run away. He was given more freedom to move around the Camp, and he often brought back bits of information about the life outside the Men's Camp and occasionally extra food.

Most of the men passed the time playing games and gambling for future promises, using as playing pieces small sticks

of wood, pebbles, and even some broken pieces of bone from
meat they had been given. The legbone from the shank of
horsemeat had been put aside, after it was stripped clean and
cracked for the marrow, for just such a possible purpose.

Jondalar spent the first day of his confinement examining
in close detail and testing the strength of the entire fence that
surrounded them. He found several places that he thought he
could have broken through or climbed over, but through the
cracks Epadoa and her women could be seen diligently guarding them, and the terrible infection of the man with the wound
deterred him from such a direct approach. He also looked
over the lean-to, thinking of several things that could be done
to repair it and make it more weatherproof . . . if only he'd
had the tools and materials.

By mutual consent, one end of the enclosed space, behind
a jumble of stones—the only other feature beside the lean-to
in their barren confinement—had been set aside for passing
water and eliminating their wastes. Jondalar became nauseat-
ingly aware of the smell permeating the entire enclosure on
the second day. It was worse near the lean-to, where the
putrefying flesh of morbid infection added its malodorous
aroma, but at night he had no choice. He huddled together
with the others for warmth, sharing his makeshift cloak with
those who had even less to cover them.

In the days that followed, his sensitivity to the odor
dulled, and he hardly noticed his hunger, but he did seem to
feel the cold more and was dizzy and light-headed occasionally. He wished for some willowbark for his headache, too.

The circumstances began to change when the man with
the wound finally died. Ardemun went to the gate and asked
to speak to Attaroa or Epadoa, so the body could be removed
and buried. Several men were let out for the purpose, and
later they were told that all who could would attend the burial
rites. Jondalar was almost ashamed by the excitement he felt
at the thought of getting out of the Holding, since the reason
for the temporary release was a death.

Outside, long shadows of a late afternoon sun spread
across the ground, highlighting features of the distant valley
and river below, and Jondalar felt an almost overwhelming
sense of the beauty and grandeur of the open landscape. His
appreciation was interrupted by a prick of pain on his arm.
He looked down with annoyance at Epadoa and three of her
women surrounding him with spears, and it took a large mea-

sure of self-control to prevent himself from pushing them out of his way.

"She wants you to put your hands behind your back so they can tie them," Ardemun said. "You can't go if your hands are not tied."

Jondalar scowled, but he complied. As he followed Ardemun, he thought about his predicament. He wasn't even sure where he was, or how long he had been here, but the thought of spending any more time cooped up in that Holding, with nothing but the fence to look at, was more than he could bear. One way or another, he was getting out, and soon. If he didn't, he could foresee a time when he might not be able to. A few days without food was no great problem, but if it continued for very long, it could become one. Besides, if there was any chance at all that Ayla was still alive, hurt perhaps, but still alive, he had to find her fast. He didn't know yet how he was going to accomplish it, he only knew he was not going to stay there very much longer.

They walked some distance, crossing a stream and getting wet feet along the way. The perfunctory funeral was over quickly, and Jondalar wondered why Attaroa bothered with a burial ceremony at all when she showed no concern for the man while he was alive. If she had, he might not have died. He had not known the man, he didn't even know his name, he had only seen him in his suffering—unnecessary suffering. Now he was gone, walking in the next world, but free from Attaroa. Perhaps that was better than spending years looking at the inside of a fence.

As short as the ceremony was, Jondalar's feet were cold from standing in wet footwear. On the way back, he paid more attention to the small waterway, trying to find a stepping-stone or a way across that would keep his feet dry. But when he looked down, he didn't care. Almost as though it were intended, he saw two stones next to each other at the edge of the stream. One was a small but adequate nodule of flint; the other was a roundish stone that looked as though it would just fit in his hand—the perfect shape for a hammerstone.

"Ardemun," he said to the man in back of him, then spoke in Zelandonii. "Do you see these two stones?" He indicated them with his foot. "Can you get them for me? It's very important."

"That is flint?"

"Yes, and I'm a flint knapper."

Suddenly Ardemun appeared to trip, and he fell down heavily. The crippled man had trouble getting up, and a woman with a spear approached. She spoke sharply to one of the men, who offered his hand to help him up. Epadoa marched back to see what was holding up the men. Ardemun got to his feet just before she arrived, and he stood contritely apologetic while she railed at him.

When they got back, Ardemun and Jondalar went to the end of the Holding, where the stones were, to pass their water. When they returned to the lean-to, Ardemun told the men that the hunters had returned with more meat from the horse kill, but something had happened while the second group was returning. He didn't know what it was, but it was causing some commotion among the women. They were all talking, but he hadn't been able to overhear anything specific.

That evening, food and water were brought to the men again, but not even the servers were allowed to stay and slice the meat. It had been precut into chunks and left for the men on a few logs, with no conversation. The men talked about it while they were eating.

"Something strange is going on," Ebulan said, switching to Mamutoi so Jondalar could understand. "I think the women were ordered not to speak to us."

"That doesn't make sense," Olamun said. "If we did know something, what could we do about it?"

"You're right, Olamun. It doesn't make sense, but I agree with Ebulan. I think the women were told not to speak," S'Amodun said.

"Maybe this is the time, then," Jondalar said. "If Epadoa's women are busy talking, maybe they won't notice."

"Notice what?" Olamun said.

"Ardemun managed to pick up a piece of flint . . ."

"So that's what it was all about," Ebulan said. "I couldn't see anything that would make him trip and fall."

"But what good is a piece of flint?" Olamun said. "You have to have tools to make it into anything. I used to watch the flint knapper, before he died."

"Yes, but he also picked up a hammerstone, and there is some bone around here. It's enough to make a few blades and shape them into knives and points, and a few other tools—if it's a good piece of flint."

"You're a flint knapper?" Olamun said.

"Yes, but I'm going to need some help. Some noise to cover up the sound of stones hitting stones," Jondalar said.

"But even if he can make some knives, what good will they be? The women have spears," Olamun said.

"For one thing, they're good for cutting the rope off someone whose hands are tied," Ebulan said. "I'm sure we can think of a competition or game that will cover up the noise. The light is almost gone, though."

"There should be enough. It won't take me long to make the tools and the points. Then tomorrow I can work inside the lean-to, where they can't see. I'll need that legbone and those logs, and maybe a piece of a plank from the lean-to. It would help if I had some sinew, but thin strips of leather should work. And, Ardemun, if you find any feathers while you are out of the Holding, I could use them."

Ardemun nodded, then said, "You're going to make something that will fly? Like a throwing spear?"

"Yes, something that will fly. It will take careful whittling and shaping, and that will take some time. But I think I can make a weapon that might surprise you," Jondalar said.

28

The next morning, before Jondalar began further work on the flint tools, he talked to S'Amodun about the two injured youngsters. He had thought about it the night before, and, recalling how Darvo had taken to flint knapping even as a young boy, he felt that if they could be taught a craft, like flint knapping, they could lead independent and useful lives even though they were crippled.

"With Attaroa as headwoman, do you really think they will ever have the opportunity?" S'Amodun asked.

"She allows Ardemun more freedom; she might feel that the two boys will not be a threat, either, and let them out of the Holding more often. Even Attaroa might be persuaded to see the logic of having a couple of toolmakers around. Her hunters' weapons are poorly made," Jondalar said. "And who knows? She may not be a leader much longer."

S'Amodun eyed the blond stranger speculatively. "I wonder if you know something I don't," he said. "In any case, I will encourage them to come and watch you."

Jondalar had worked outside the evening before, so the

sharp chips that broke off in the process of knapping the flint would not be scattered around their only shelter. He had picked a spot somewhat behind the stone pile near the place where they passed their wastes. Because of the smell, it was the end of the enclosure that the guards tended to avoid, and was watched the least.

The blade-shaped pieces he had quickly detached from the flint core were at least four times as long as they were wide with rounded ends, and these were the blanks from which other tools would be made. The edges were razor sharp as they were cleaved from the flint core, sharp enough to cut through tough leather as if it were congealed fat. The blades were so sharp, in fact, that often the edges had to be dulled so the tool could be handled without cutting the user.

Inside the lean-to the following morning, the first thing Jondalar did was to select a place under a crack in the roof, so he would have sufficient light to work by. Then he cut off a piece of leather from his makeshift cloak and spread it out on the ground to catch the inevitable sharp bits of flint debris. With the two lame boys and several others seated around him, he proceeded to demonstrate how a hard oval stone and a few pieces of bone could be used to make tools of flint, which in turn could be used to shape and make things out of leather, wood, and bone. Though they had to be careful not to draw attention to their activity, getting up occasionally to maintain a normal routine, then coming back and huddling together for warmth, which also served to block the view of their guards, they all watched with fascination.

Jondalar picked up a blade and examined it critically. There were several different tools he wanted to make, and he was trying to decide which of them would lend itself best to this particular blank. One long, sharp edge was nearly straight, the other wavered somewhat. He started by dulling the uneven edge by scraping the hammerstone across it a few times. He left the other edge as it was. Then, with the long tapered end of a broken legbone, he pressure-flaked the rounded end, breaking off carefully controlled small chips until it was a point. If he'd had sinew, or glue, or pitch, or a number of other materials with which to attach it, he could have added a handle, but when he was through, it was an adequate knife as it was.

As the tool was passed around and tested on the hair of an arm or bits of leather, Jondalar picked up another blade blank. Both edges of it dipped in to a narrow waist near the middle. Applying careful pressure with the knobby, rounded end of the legbone, he broke off only the sharpest edge of both lengths, which dulled them only slightly but, more important, strengthened them, so this piece could be used as a scraper to shape and smooth a piece of wood or bone. He showed how it was used and passed it around, too.

With the next blank, he dulled both edges so the tool could be handled easily. Then, with two carefully placed blows at one end of it, he detached a couple of spalls, leaving a sharp, chisellike point. To demonstrate its use, he cut a groove into a piece of bone, then went over the groove many times, making it deeper and deeper and creating a little pile of curled shavings. He explained how a shaft, or a point, or a handle, could be cut out with roughly the desired shape, then finished by scraping or smoothing.

Jondalar's demonstration was almost a revelation. None of the boys or younger men had ever seen an expert flint-knapping toolmaker work, and few of the older men had ever seen one so skilled. In the few moments of twilight the night before, he had managed to cleave off nearly thirty usable blanks from the single nodule of flint before the flint core was too small to work. By the next day, most of the men had used one or more of the tools he made from them.

Then he tried to explain the hunting weapon he wanted to show them. Some of the men seemed to understand him immediately although they invariably questioned the accuracy and speed he claimed for a spear thrown with a spear-thrower. Others couldn't seem to grasp the concept of it at all, but it didn't matter.

Having good serviceable tools in their hands, and working on something constructive with them, gave the men a sense of purpose. And doing anything that opposed Attaroa, and the conditions she had forced upon them, lifted the despair of the Men's Camp and fostered the hope that it might be possible, someday, to regain control of their own destiny.

Epadoa and her guards sensed a change in attitude over the next few days, and she felt sure something was going on. The men seemed to walk with a lighter step, and they smiled too much, but as hard as she looked, she couldn't see anything different. The men had been extremely careful to hide not only the knives and scrapers and chisels Jondalar had made, and the objects they were making, but even the waste products of their efforts. The smallest flint chip or spall, the tiniest curled shaving of wood or bone, was buried inside the lean-to and covered with a roof plank or a piece of leather.

But the greatest change of all was in the two crippled boys. Jondalar not only showed the youngsters how the tools were made, he made special tools for them, and then showed them both how to use them. They stopped hiding in the shadows of the lean-to and began to get acquainted with the other, older boys in the Holding. Both idolized the tall Zelandonii, Doban in particular, who was old enough to comprehend more, though he was reluctant to show it.

For as long as he could remember, living with the disturbed and irrational Attaroa, Ardoban had always felt helpless, completely at the mercy of circumstances beyond his control. In a tiny corner of his being, he had always expected something terrible to happen to him, and after the excruciatingly painful and terrifying trauma of his experience, he was convinced that his life would only get worse. He often wished he were dead. But watching someone take two stones that he found near a stream and with them, using the skill of his hands and the knowledge in his mind, offer the hope of changing his world, made a deep impression. Doban was afraid to ask—he still couldn't trust anyone—but more than anything, he wanted to learn to make tools out of stone.

The man sensed his interest and wished that he had more flint, so he could begin to teach him, at least to get him started. Did these people go to any kind of Summer Meetings or Gatherings, he wondered, where ideas and information and goods could be exchanged? There had to be some flint knappers in the region who could train Doban. He needed to learn a skill like that, where being lame wouldn't matter.

After Jondalar made a sample spear-thrower out of wood, to show them what it looked like and how to make it, several of the men began to make copies of the strange implement. He also made flint spear points from some of the blanks, and out of the strongest leather they had he cut thin strips for bindings to fasten them with. Ardemun even found the ground nest of a golden eagle and brought back some good flight feathers. The only thing lacking were the shafts for the spears.

Trying to make one out of the scanty materials that were available, Jondalar cut a fairly long, thin piece out of a plank with the sharp chisel tool. He used it to show the younger

men how to fasten the point and attach the feathers, and he
demonstrated how to hold the spear-thrower and the basic
technique for using it, without actually casting the spear. But
cutting a spear shaft out of a plank was a long and tedious
job, and the wood was dry and brittle, with no spring, and
it broke easily.

What he needed were young, straight saplings, or reasonably long branches that could be straightened; though for that
he needed the heat of a fire. He felt so frustrated stuck in the
Holding. If only he could get out and look for something
with which to make shafts. If only he could convince Attaroa
to let him out. When he mentioned his feelings to Ebulan as
they were getting ready to sleep, the man looked at him
strangely, started to say something, then shook his head,
closed his eyes, and turned away. Jondalar thought it was a
strange reaction, but he soon forgot about it and fell asleep
thinking about the problem.

Attaroa had been thinking about Jondalar, too. She was
looking forward to the diversion he would give her through
the long winter, gaining control over him, and seeing him do
her bidding, showing everyone that she was more powerful
than the tall, handsome man. Then, when she was through
with him, she had other plans for him. She had been wondering if he was ready to be let out and set to work. Epadoa
had told her that she thought something was going on inside
the Holding, and that the stranger was involved, but she
hadn't yet discovered what it was. Perhaps it was time to
separate him from the other men for a while, Attaroa thought,
maybe put him back in the cage. It was a good way to keep
them all unsettled.

In the morning she told her women that she wanted a
work crew, and to include the Zelandonii man. Jondalar was
glad just to be getting out where he could see something
besides bare earth and desperate men. It was the first time
he had been allowed outside the Holding to work, and he
had no idea what she planned to have him do, but he hoped
he would have an opportunity to look for young, straight
trees. Finding a way to get them into the Holding would be
another problem.

Later in the day, Attaroa strode out of her earthlodge,
accompanied by two of her women and S'Armuna, and wear-

ing—flaunting—Jondalar's fur parka. The men had been carrying mammoth bones that had been brought earlier from some other place, and they were piling them up where Attaroa wanted. They had worked all morning and into the afternoon with nothing to eat and little to drink. Even though he was out of the Holding, he had not been able to look for potential spear shafts, much less think of a way of cutting them down and bringing them back. He was watched too closely and given no time to rest. He was not only frustrated, he was tired, and hungry, and thirsty, and angry.

Jondalar put down one end of the legbone that he and Olamun were carrying, then stood up and faced the approaching women. As Attaroa neared, he noticed how tall she was, taller than many men. She could have been very attractive. What had happened to make her hate men so much? he wondered. When she spoke to him, her sarcasm was clear, though he didn't understand her words.

"Well, Zelandonii, are you ready to tell us another story like your last? I'm ready to be entertained," S'Armuna translated, complete with sarcastic intonation.

"I did not tell you a story. I told you the truth," Jondalar said.

"That you were traveling with a woman who rides on the backs of horses? Where is this woman, then? If she has the power you say, why hasn't she come to claim you?" Attaroa said, standing with her hands on her hips, as though to face him down.

"I don't know where she is. I wish I did. I'm afraid she went over the cliff with the horses you were hunting," Jondalar said.

"You lie, Zelandonii! My hunters saw no woman on the back of a horse, and no body of a woman was found with the horses. I think you have heard that the penalty for stealing from the S'Armunai is death, and you are trying to lie your way out of it," Attaroa said.

No body was found? Jondalar was elated in spite of himself when S'Armuna translated, feeling a surge of hope that Ayla might still be alive.

"Why do you smile when I have just told you that the penalty for stealing is death? Do you doubt that I will do it?" Attaroa said, pointing to him, and then to herself for emphasis.

"Death?" he said, then paled. Could someone be put to

death for hunting food? He had been so happy to think that
Ayla might still be alive that he hadn't really comprehended
what she had said. When he did, his anger returned. "Horses
were not given to the S'Armunai alone. They are here for all
of Earth's Children. How can you call hunting them stealing?
Even if I had been hunting the horses, it would have been
for food."

"Ha! See, I've caught you in your lies. You admit you
were hunting the horses."

"I did not! I said, 'Even if I had been hunting the horses.'
I didn't say that I was." He looked at the translator. "Tell
her, S'Armuna. Jondalar of the Zelandonii, son of Marthona,
former leader of the Ninth Cave, does not lie."

"Now you say you are the son of a woman who was a
leader? This Zelandonii is an accomplished liar, covering one
lie about a miraculous woman with another about a woman
leader."

"I've known many women who were leaders. You are
not the only headwoman, Attaroa. Many Mamutoi women
are leaders," Jondalar said.

"Coleaders! They share leadership with a man."

"My mother was a leader for ten years. She became
leader when her mate died, and she shared it with no one.
She was respected by both women and men, and gave the
leadership over to my brother Joharran willingly. The people
did not wish it."

"Respected by women and men? Listen to him! You
think I don't know men, Zelandonii? You think I was never
mated? Am I so ugly no man would have me?"

Attaroa was nearly screaming at him, and S'Armuna was
translating almost simultaneously, as though she knew the
words the headwoman would be saying. Jondalar could
almost forget that the shaman was speaking for her, it seemed
as though he were hearing and understanding Attaroa herself,
but the shaman's unemotional tone gave the words a strange
detachment from the woman who was behaving so belliger-
ently. A bitter, deranged look came into her eyes as she
continued to harangue Jondalar.

"My mate was the leader here. He was a strong leader,
a strong man." Attaroa paused.

"Many people are strong. Strength doesn't make a
leader," Jondalar said.

Attaroa didn't really hear him. She wasn't listening. Her

pause was only to hear her own thoughts, to gather her own memories. "Brugar was such a strong leader that he had to beat me every day to prove it." She sneered. "Wasn't it a shame that the mushrooms he ate were poisonous?" Her smile was malignant. "I beat his sister's son in a fair fight to become leader. He was a weakling. He died." She looked at Jondalar. "But you are no weakling, Zelandonii. Wouldn't you like a chance to fight me for your life?"

"I have no desire to fight you, Attaroa. But I will defend myself, if I must."

"No, you will not fight me, because you know I would win. I am a woman. I have the power of Muna on my side. The Mother has honored women; they are the ones who bring forth life. They should be the leaders," Attaroa said.

"No," Jondalar said. Some of the people watching flinched when the man disagreed so openly with Attaroa. "Leadership doesn't necessarily belong to one who is blessed by the Mother any more than it does to one who is physically strong. The leader of the berry pickers, for instance, is the one who knows where the berries grow, when they will be ripe, and the best way to pick them." Jondalar was working up to a harangue of his own. "A leader has to be dependable, trustworthy; leaders have to know what they are doing."

Attaroa was scowling. His words had no effect on her, she listened only to her own counsel, but she didn't like the scolding tone of his voice, as though he thought he had the right to speak so freely, or to presume to tell her anything.

"It doesn't matter what the task is," Jondalar continued. "The leader of the hunt is the one who knows where the animals will be and when they will be there; he is the one who can track them. He's the one most skilled at hunting. Marthona always said leaders of people should care about the people they lead. If they don't, they won't be leaders for very long." Jondalar was lecturing, venting his anger, oblivious to Attaroa's glowering face. "Why should it matter if they are women or men?"

"I will not allow men to be leaders anymore," Attaroa interrupted. "Here, men know that women are leaders, the young ones are raised to understand it. Women are the hunters here. We don't need men to track or lead. Do you think women cannot hunt?"

"Of course women can hunt. My mother was a hunter before she became leader, and the woman I traveled with was one of the best hunters I know. She loved to hunt and was very good at tracking. I could throw a spear farther, but she was more accurate. She could knock a bird out of the sky or kill a rabbit on the run with a single stone from her sling.''

"More stories!" Attaroa snorted. "It's easy enough to make claims for a woman that doesn't exist. My women didn't hunt; they weren't allowed to. When Brugar was leader, no women were even allowed to touch a weapon, and it was not easy for us when I became leader. No one knew how to hunt, but I taught them. Do you see these practice targets?

Attaroa pointed to a series of sturdy posts stuck in the ground. Jondalar had noticed them in passing before, though he hadn't known what they were for. Now he saw a large section of a horse carcass hanging from a thick wooden peg near the top of one. A few spears were sticking out of it.

"All the women must practice every day, and not just jabbing the spears hard enough to kill—throwing them, too. The best of them become my hunters. But even before we learned to make and use spears, we were able to hunt. There is a certain cliff north of here, near the place I grew up. People there chase horses off that cliff at least once every year. We learned to hunt horses like that. It is not so difficult to stampede horses off a cliff, if you can entice them up."

Attaroa looked at Epadoa with obvious pride. "Epadoa discovered how much horses like salt. She makes the women save the water they pass and uses it to lead the horses along. My hunters are my wolves," Attaroa said, smiling in the direction of the women with spears who had gathered around.

They took evident pleasure in her praise, standing taller as she spoke. Jondalar hadn't paid much attention to their clothing before, but now he realized that all of the hunters wore something that came from a wolf. Most of them had a fringe of wolf fur around their hoods and at least one wolf tooth, but often more, dangling around their necks. Some of them also had a fringe of wolf fur around the cuffs of their parkas, or the hem, or both, plus additional decorative panels. Epadoa's hood was entirely wolf fur, with a portion of a wolf's head, with fangs bared, decorating the top. Both the hem and cuffs of her parka were fringed, wolf paws hung down from her shoulders in front, and a bushy tail hung behind from a center panel of wolf skin.

"Their spears are their fangs, they kill in a pack, and

bring the food back. Their feet are their paws, they run steady all day, and go a long way," Attaroa said in a rhythmic meter that he felt sure had been repeated many times. "Epadoa is their leader, Zelandonii. I wouldn't try to outsmart her. She is very clever."

"I'm sure she is," Jondalar said, feeling outnumbered. But he also couldn't help feeling a touch of admiration for what they had accomplished, starting with so little knowledge. "It just seems such a waste to have men sitting idle when they could be contributing, too, helping to hunt, helping to gather food, making tools. Then the women alone wouldn't have to be working so hard. I'm not saying women cannot do it, but why should they have to do it all, for both men and women?"

Attaroa laughed, the harsh, demented laugh that gave him a chill. "I have wondered the same thing. Women are the ones who produce new life; why do we need men at all? Some of the women don't want to give men up yet, but what good are they? For Pleasures? It's men who get the Pleasure. Here we don't worry about giving men Pleasures anymore. Instead of sharing a hearth with a man, I have put women together. They share the work, they help each other with their children, they understand each other. When there are no men around, the Mother will have to mix the spirits of women, and only female children will be born."

Would it work? Jondalar wondered. S'Amodun had said that very few babies had been born in the last few years. Suddenly he remembered Ayla's idea that it was the Pleasures that men and women shared that started new life growing inside a woman. Attaroa had kept the women and men separated. Could that be why there were so few babies?

"How many children have been born?" he asked, out of curiosity.

"Not many, but some, and where there are some, there can be more."

"Have they all been girls?" he asked then.

"The men are still too close. It confuses the Mother. Soon enough all the men will be gone; then we will see how many boy babies are born," Attaroa said.

"Or how many babies are born at all," Jondalar said. "The Great Earth Mother made both women and men, and like Her, women are blessed to give birth to both male and female, but it is the Mother Who decides which man's spirit is mingled with the woman's. It is always a man's spirit. Do you really think you can alter what She has ordained?''

"Don't try to tell me what the Mother will do! You are not a woman, Zelandonii," she said contemptuously. "You just don't like to be told how worthless you are, or perhaps you don't want to give up your Pleasures. That's it, isn't it?''

Suddenly Attaroa changed her tone, affecting a purr of attraction. "Do you want Pleasures, Zelandonii? If you will not fight me, what will you do to gain your freedom? Ah, I know! Pleasures. For such a strong, handsome man, Attaroa might be willing to give you Pleasures. But can you give Attaroa Pleasures?''

S'Armuna's change to speaking about the woman, rather than as her, made him suddenly aware that all the words he had heard had been translated. It was one thing to speak as the voice of Attaroa the headwoman, it was quite another to speak as the voice of Attaroa the woman. S'Armuna could translate the words; she just couldn't take on the intimate persona of the woman. As S'Armuna continued to translate, Jondalar heard both of them.

"So tall, so fair, so perfect, he could be the mate of the Mother Herself. Look, he is even taller than Attaroa, and not many men are. You have given many women Pleasure, haven't you? One smile from the big, tall, handsome man with his blue, blue eyes and women clamor to climb into his furs. Do you Pleasure them all, Zelandonii man?''

Jondalar refused to answer. Yes, there was once a time when he enjoyed Pleasuring many women, but now he only wanted Ayla. A wrenching pain of grief threatened to overcome him. What would he do without her? Did it matter if he lived or died?

"Come, Zelandonii, if you give Attaroa great pleasure, you can have your freedom. Attaroa knows you can do it.'' The tall, attractive headwoman walked seductively toward him. "See? Attaroa will give herself to you. Show everyone how a strong man gives a woman Pleasures. Share the Gift of Muna, the Great Earth Mother, with Attaroa, Jondalar of the Zelandonii.''

Attaroa put her arms around his neck and pressed herself against him. Jondalar did not respond. She tried to kiss him, but he was too tall for her, and he would not bend down. She was not used to a man who was taller; it wasn't often that she had to reach up to a man, especially one she could not bend. It made her feel foolish and flamed her anger.

"Zelandonii! I am willing to couple with you, and give you a chance for your freedom!"

"I won't share the Mother's Gift of Pleasures under these circumstances," Jondalar said. His quiet, controlled voice belied his great anger, but did not hide it. How did she dare to insult the Mother like that? "The Gift is sacred, meant to be shared with willingness and joy. Coupling like this would be contemptuous of the Mother. It would defile Her Gift and anger Her just as much as taking a woman against her will. I choose the woman I want to couple with, and I have no desire to share Her Gift with you, Attaroa."

Jondalar might have responded to Attaroa's invitation, but he knew it was not genuine. He was an exciting, handsome man to most women. He had gained skill at pleasing them, and experience in the ways of mutual attraction and invitation. For all her sinuous walking, there was no warmth to Attaroa, and she gave him no spark of desire. He sensed that even if he had tried, he could not have pleased her.

But Attaroa looked stunned when she heard the translation. Most men had been more than willing to share the Gift of Pleasures with the handsome woman to gain their freedom. Visitors unfortunate enough to pass through her territory and get caught by her hunters had usually jumped at the chance to get away from the Wolf Women of the S'Armunai so easily. Though some had hesitated, doubtful and wondering what she was up to, none had ever refused her outright. They soon found out they were right to doubt.

"You refuse . . ." the headwoman sputtered, unbelieving. The translation was spoken without feeling, but her reaction was clear enough. "You refuse Attaroa. How dare you refuse!" she screamed, then turned to her Wolf Women. "Strip him and tie him to the practice target."

That had been her intention all along, just not so soon. She had wanted Jondalar to keep her occupied through the whole long, dreary winter. She enjoyed tantalizing men with promises of freedom in exchange for Pleasures. To her, it was the height of irony. From that point, she led them into further acts of humiliation or degradation, and she usually managed to get them to do whatever she wanted before she was ready to play her final game. They would even strip

themselves when she told them she would let them go if they
did, hoping it would please her enough.

But no man could give Attaroa Pleasure. She had been
used badly when she was a girl, and she had looked forward
to mating the powerful leader of another group. Then she
discovered that the man she had joined with was worse than
the situation she had left behind. His Pleasures were always
done with painful beatings and humiliation, until she finally
rebelled and caused his painful, humiliating death. But she
had learned her lesson too well. Warped by the cruelty she
received, she could not feel Pleasure without causing pain.
Attaroa cared little for sharing the Mother's Gift with men,
or even women. She gave herself Pleasures watching men
die slow and painful deaths.

When there was a long time between visitors, Attaroa had
even played with S'Armunai men, but after the first two or
three fell to her "Pleasures," they knew her game and would
not play it. They just pleaded for their lives. She usually, but
not always, gave in to those who had a woman to plead their
case. Some of the women were not as cooperative—they
didn't understand it was for them that she needed to eliminate
men—but they could usually be controlled through the males
to whom they were tied, so she kept them alive.

Travelers ordinarily came during the warmer season. People seldom traveled very far in the cold of winter, especially
those on a Journey, and there had been fewer travelers lately,
none the previous summer. A few men, by a lucky fluke,
managed to escape, and some women ran away. They warned
others. Most people who heard the stories passed them on as
rumors, or fantastic tales of storytellers, but the rumors of
the vicious Wolf Women had been growing, and people were
staying away.

Attaroa had been delighted when Jondalar was brought
back, but he turned out to be worse than one of her own
men. He wouldn't go along with her game, and he didn't
even give her the satisfaction of watching him plead. If he
had, she might have even let him live a little longer, just to
savor the pleasure of seeing him bend to her will.

At her command, Attaroa's Wolf Women rushed Jondalar. He swung out wildly, knocking aside spears and landing
hard blows that would have telling aftereffects. His struggles
to get free were almost successful, but he was eventually
overwhelmed by sheer force of numbers. He continued to

fight while they cut the lashing closures of his tunic and trousers to strip him of his clothes. But they expected it and held sharp blades to his neck.

After they tore off his tunic and bared his chest, they tied his hands together with a length of slack rope between them, then lifted him up and hung him with his hands over his head from the high peg on the target post. He kicked while they pulled off his boots and trousers, landing a few strong blows that would leave bruises, but all his resistance only served to make the women want to get back at him. And they knew they could.

Once he was hanging naked from the post, they all stood back and looked him over with self-satisfied smirks, pleased with themselves. Big and strong as he was, his fighting had done him no good. Jondalar's toes touched the ground, but just barely, and it was clear that most men would have dangled there. It gave him some slight feeling of security to touch the earth, and he sent a vague, unvoiced appeal to the Great Earth Mother to somehow deliver him from this unexpected and fearful predicament.

Attaroa was interested in the massive scar on his upper thigh and groin. It had healed well. He had given no hint that he had sustained such a serious injury, no limping or favoring of that leg. If he was that strong, perhaps he would last longer than most. He might give her some enjoyment yet. She smiled at the thought.

Attaroa's detached appraisal gave Jondalar second thoughts. He felt a breeze raise goose bumps, and he shivered, but not only with the cold. When he looked up, he saw Attaroa smiling at him. Her face was flushed and her breathing fast; she looked pleased and strangely sensual. Her enjoyment was always greater if the man she Pleasured herself with was handsome. Attracted in her own way to the tall man with the unconscious charisma, she anticipated making this one last as long as possible.

He looked across at the fence made of poles, and he knew the men were watching through the cracks. He wondered why they hadn't warned him. It was obviously not the first time something like this had happened. Would it have done any good if they had? Would he have just anticipated with fear? Perhaps they thought he would be better off not knowing.

In truth, some of the men had talked about it. They all liked the Zelandonii and admired his toolmaking skills. With the sharp knives and tools that were his legacy, they each hoped they might find an opportunity to break away. They would always remember him for that, but each of them knew in his heart that if there was too long a time between visitors, Attaroa was likely to hang one of them from a target post. A couple of them had already been strung up once, and they knew that their abject pleadings would probably not move her to delay her deadly game again. They secretly cheered his refusal to give in to her demands, but they were afraid that any noise would call attention to themselves. Instead they watched in silence as the familiar scene unfolded, each of them feeling compassion and fear and a small stab of shame.

Not only her Wolf Women, but all the women of the Camp were expected to bear witness to the man's ordeal. Most of them hated to watch, but they feared Attaroa, even her hunters. They stood as far back as they dared. It made some of them sick, but if they did not appear, then any man they had spoken up for in the past was the next one chosen. Some women had tried to run away, and a few had managed it, but most were caught and brought back. If there were men in the Holding they cared about—mates, brothers, sons—as punishment, the women were made to watch them suffer days in the cage without food or water. And occasionally, though rarely, they were put in the cage themselves.

The women with boys were particularly fearful, not knowing what would become of their sons, especially after what she had done to Odevan and Ardoban, but the women who feared the most were the two with infants and the one who was pregnant. Attaroa was delighted with them, gave them special treats and asked after their welfare, but they each harbored a guilty secret and were afraid that if she ever found out, they would end up hanging from the target posts.

The headwoman stepped in front of her hunters and picked up a spear. Jondalar noticed it was rather heavy and clumsy and, in spite of himself, he thought about how he could make them a better one. But the poorly made thick point was nonetheless sharp and effective. He watched the woman take careful aim and noticed she was aiming low. She did not mean to kill, but to maim. He was conscious of his naked exposure to whatever pain she chose to inflict on him, and he fought an urge to lift his legs to try to protect himself. But then he'd be dangling, too, and he felt that would make him even more vulnerable, and would expose his fear.

Attaroa watched him through narrowed eyes, knowing that he feared her and enjoying it. Some of them begged. This one she knew would not, at least not immediately. She pulled her arm back as she prepared to make her throw. He closed his eyes and thought of Ayla, wondering if she was alive or dead, her body crushed and broken below a herd of horses at the bottom of the cliff. With a pain sharper than any spear could inflict, he knew that if she were dead, life had no meaning for him anyway.

He heard a *thunk* as a spear landed on the target, but above him, not low and painful. Suddenly he dropped to his heels as his arms were freed. He looked at his hands and saw that the short length of slack in the rope, which had been hung over the peg, was severed. Attaroa still held her spear in her hand. The spear he heard had not come from her. Jondalar looked up at the target pole and saw a neat, somewhat small, flint-tipped spear embedded beside the peg, its feathered end still quivering. The thin, finely made point had cut the cord. He knew that spear!

He turned back to look in the direction from which it had come. Directly behind Attaroa he saw movement. His vision became blurry as his eyes filled with tears of relief. He could hardly believe it. Could it really be her? Was she really alive? He glanced down to blink several times so he could see more clearly. Looking up, he saw four nearly black horse legs attached to a yellow horse with a woman on her back.

"Ayla!" he cried. "You're alive!"

29

Attaroa spun around to see who had thrown the spear. From the far edge of the field that was just outside the Camp, she saw a woman coming toward her riding on the back of a horse. The hood of the woman's fur parka was thrown back, and her dark blond hair and the horse's dun-yellow coat were so nearly the same color that the fearful apparition seemed truly of one flesh. Could the spear have come from the woman-horse? she wondered. But how could anyone throw a spear from that distance? Then she saw that the woman had another spear close at hand.

A chilling wash of fear crawled up Attaroa's scalp, the sensation of her hair rising, but the cold tingling terror that she felt at that moment had little to do with anything so material as spears. The apparition she saw was not a woman; of that she was certain. In a moment of sudden lucidity, she knew the full and unspeakable atrocity of her heinous acts, and she saw the figure coming across the field as one of the spirit forms of the Mother, a munai, this one an avenging spirit sent to exact retribution. In her heart, Attaroa almost welcomed Her; it would be a relief to have the nightmare of this life ended.

The headwoman was not alone in fearing the strange woman-horse. Jondalar had tried to tell them, but no one had believed him. No one had ever conceived of a human riding a horse; even seeing it, it was hard to believe. Ayla's sudden appearance struck each person individually. For some she was only intimidating because of the strangeness of a woman on horseback and their fear of the unknown; others looked upon her uncanny entrance as a sign of otherworldly power and were filled with foreboding. Many of them saw her as Attaroa did: their own personal nemesis, a reflection of their own consciences about their wrongdoings. Encouraged or forced by Attaroa, more than one had committed appalling brutalities, or allowed and abetted them, for which, in the quiet moments of the night, they felt deep shame or fear of retribution.

Even Jondalar wondered, for a moment, if Ayla had come back from the next world to save his life, convinced at that moment that if she had wanted to, she could. He watched her unhurried approach, studying every detail of her, carefully and lovingly, wanting to fill up his vision with a sight he had thought he would never see again: the woman he loved, riding the familiar mare. Her face was ruddy with cold and streamers of hair that had escaped the restraining thong at the nape of her neck whipped in the wind. Wispy clouds of warmed air streamed forth with each breath exhaled by both the woman and the horse, making Jondalar suddenly conscious of his exposed flesh and chattering teeth.

She was wearing her carrying belt over her fur parka and, in a loop of it, the dagger made from the tusk of a mammoth that had been a present from Talut. The ivory-handled flint knife he had made for her also dangled in its sheath, and he saw his hatchet in her belt, too. The worn otter skin of her medicine bag hung down her other side.

Riding the horse with easy grace, Ayla seemed dauntingly sure and confident, but Jondalar could see her tense readiness. She held her sling in her right hand, and he knew how swiftly she could let fly from that position. With her left hand, which he was sure held a couple of stones, she supported a spear, set in place on her spear-thrower and balanced diagonally across Whinney's withers from Ayla's right leg to the mare's left shoulder. More spears stuck up from a woven grass holder just behind her leg.

On her approach, Ayla had watched the tall headwoman's face reflecting her inner reactions, showing shock and fear, and the despair of her moment of clarity, but as the woman on horseback drew closer, dark and deranged shadows clouded the leader's mind again. Attaroa narrowed her eyes to watch the blond woman, then slowly smiled, a smile of twisted, calculating malice.

Ayla had never seen madness, but she interpreted Attaroa's unconscious expressions, and she understood that this woman who threatened Jondalar was someone to be wary of; she was a hyena. The woman on horseback had killed many carnivores and knew how unpredictable they could be, but it was only hyenas that she despised. They were her metaphor for the very worst that people could be, and Attaroa was a hyena, a dangerously malignant manifestation of evil who could never be trusted.

Ayla's angry glare was focused on the tall headwoman, though she was careful to keep an eye on the entire group, including the stunned Wolf Women, and it was fortunate that she did. When Whinney was within a few feet of Attaroa, in the periphery of her vision Ayla caught a stealthy movement off to the side. With motions so swift they were hard to follow, a stone was in her sling, whipped around, and flung.

Epadoa squawked with pain and grabbed her arm as her spear clattered to the frozen ground. Ayla could have broken a bone if she had tried, but she had deliberately aimed for the woman's upper arm and checked her force. Even so, the leader of the Wolf Women would have a very painful bruise for some time.

"Tell spear-women stop, Attaroa!" Ayla demanded.

It took Jondalar a moment to comprehend that she was speaking in a strange language because he found that he had understood her meaning. Then he was stunned when he realized that the words she spoke were in S'Armunai! How could Ayla possibly know how to speak S'Armunai? She had never heard it before, had she?

It surprised the headwoman, too, to hear a complete stranger address her by name, but she was more shocked to hear the peculiarity of Ayla's speech that was like the accent of another language, yet not. The voice aroused feelings

Attaroa had all but forgotten; a buried memory of a complex of emotions, including fear, which filled her with a disquieting unease. It reinforced her inner conviction that the approaching figure was not simply a woman on a horse.

It had been many years since she'd had those feelings. Attaroa hadn't liked the conditions that first provoked them, and she liked even less being reminded of them now. It made her nervous, agitated, and angry. She wanted to push the memory away. She had to get rid of it, destroy it completely, so it would never come back. But how? She looked up at Ayla sitting on the horse, and at that instant she decided it was the blond woman's fault. She was the one who had brought it all back, the memory, the feelings. If the woman was gone—destroyed—it would all go away and everything would be fine again. With her quick, if twisted, intelligence, Attaroa began to consider how she could destroy the woman. A sly, crafty smile spread across her face.

"Well, it seems the Zelandonii was telling the truth after all," she said. "You came just in time. We thought he was trying to steal meat, and we have barely enough for ourselves. Among the S'Armunai, the penalty for stealing is death. He told us some story about riding on horses, but you can understand why we found it so unbelievable . . ." Attaroa noticed her words were not being translated and stopped. "S'Armuna! You are not speaking my words," she snapped.

S'Armuna had been staring at Ayla. She recalled that one of the first hunters who had returned with the group carrying the man had revealed a frightening vision she'd had during the hunt, wanting her to interpret it. She told of a woman sitting on the back of one of the horses they were driving over the cliff, struggling to gain control of it, and finally making it turn back. When the hunters carrying the second load of meat talked about seeing a woman riding away on a horse, S'Armuna wondered at the meaning of the strange visions.

Many things had been bothering the One Who Served the Mother for some time, but when the man they brought in turned out to be a young man who seemed to have materialized out of her own past, and he told a story of a woman on horseback, it distressed her. It had to be a sign, but she had not been able to discern the meaning. The idea had preyed on S'Armuna's mind while she considered various interpretations of the recurring vision. A woman actually riding into their Camp on the back of a horse gave the sign unprecedented power. It was the manifestation of a vision, and the impact of it put her in a turmoil. She hadn't been giving her full attention to Attaroa, but a part of her had heard and she quickly translated the headwoman's words into Zelandonii.

"Death to a hunter as a punishment for hunting is not the way of the Great Mother of All," Ayla said in Zelandonii when she heard the translation, though she had understood the gist of Attaroa's statement. S'Armunai was so close to Mamutoi that she could understand much of it, and she had learned a few words, but Zelandonii was easier, and she could express herself better. "The Mother charges Her children to share food and offer hospitality to visitors."

It was when she was speaking in Zelandonii that S'Armuna noticed Ayla's speech peculiarity. Though she spoke the language perfectly, there was something . . . but there was no time to think about it now. Attaroa was waiting.

"That is why we have the penalty," Attaroa smoothly explained, though the anger she was fighting to control was evident to both S'Armuna and Ayla. "It discourages stealing so there will be enough to share. But a woman like you, so good with weapons, how could you understand the way it was for us when no woman could hunt. Food was scarce. We all suffered."

"But the Great Earth Mother provides more than meat for Her children. Certainly the women here know the foods that grow and can be gathered," Ayla said.

"But I had to forbid that! If I had allowed them to spend their time gathering, they would not have learned to hunt."

"Then your scarcity was of your own doing, and the choice of those who went along with you. That is not a reason to kill people who are not aware of your customs," Ayla said. "You have taken on yourself the Mother's right. She calls Her children to Her when She is ready. It is not your place to assume Her authority."

"All people have customs and traditions that are important, and if their ways are broken, some of them require a punishment of death," Attaroa said.

That was true enough; Ayla knew it from experience. "But why should your custom require a punishment of death for wanting to eat?" she said. "The Mother's ways must come before all other customs. She requires sharing of food, and hospitality to visitors. You are . . . discourteous and inhospitable, Attaroa.''

Discourteous and inhospitable! Jondalar fought to control a derisive laugh. More like murderous and inhuman! He had been watching and listening with amazement, and he was grinning with appreciation for Ayla's understatement. He remembered when she couldn't even understand a joke, much less make subtle insults.

Attaroa was obviously irritated; it was all she could do to contain herself. She had felt the barb of Ayla's ''courteous'' criticism. She had been scolded as if she were a mere child; a bad girl. She would have preferred the implied power of being called evil, a powerfully evil woman to be respected and greatly feared. The mildness of the words made her seem laughable. Attaroa noticed Jondalar's grin and glared at him balefully, certain that everyone watching wanted to laugh with him. She vowed to herself that he would be sorry, and so would that woman!

Ayla seemed to resettle herself on Whinney, but she had actually shifted her position unobtrusively in order to get a better grip on the spear-thrower.

''I believe Jondalar needs his clothes,'' Ayla continued, lifting the spear slightly, making it apparent that she held it without being overtly threatening. ''Don't forget his outer fur, the one you are wearing. And perhaps you should send someone into your lodge to get his belt, his mitts, his waterbag, his knife, and the tools he had with him.'' She waited for S'Armuna to translate.

Attaroa clenched her teeth but smiled, though it was more a grimace. She signaled Epadoa with a nod. With her left arm, the one that wasn't sore—Epadoa knew she would also have a bruise on her leg where Jondalar had kicked her—the woman who was the leader of Attaroa's Wolves picked up the clothes they had struggled so hard to pull off the man and dropped them down in front of him; then she went inside the large earthlodge.

While they waited, the headwoman suddenly spoke up, trying to assume a friendlier tone. ''You have traveled a long way, you must be tired—what did he say your name was? Ayla?''

The woman on horseback nodded, understanding her well enough. This leader cared little for formal introductions, Ayla noticed; not very subtle.

"Since you put such importance on it, you must allow me to extend the hospitality of my lodge. You will stay with me, won't you?"

Before either Ayla or Jondalar could respond, S'Armuna spoke up. "I believe it is customary to offer visitors a place with the One Who Serves the Mother. You are welcome to share my lodge."

While listening to Attaroa and waiting for the translation, the shivering man pulled on his trousers. Jondalar hadn't thought too much about how cold he was before, when his life was in immediate jeopardy, but his fingers were so stiff that he fumbled to tie knots in the severed cords that held his legwear on. Though it was torn, he was grateful to have his tunic, but he stopped for a moment, surprised, when he heard S'Armuna's offer. Looking up after he pulled the tunic over his head, he noticed that Attaroa was scowling at the shaman; then he sat down to put on his foot-coverings and boots as quickly as he could.

She will hear from me later, Attaroa thought, but she said, "Then you must allow me to share food with you, Ayla. We will prepare a feast, and you will be the honored guests. Both of you." She included Jondalar in her glance. "We have recently had a successful hunt, and I cannot allow you to leave, thinking too badly of me."

Jondalar thought her attempt at a friendly smile was ludicrous, and he had no desire either to eat their food or to stay in this encampment a moment longer, but before he could voice his opinion, Ayla answered.

"We will be happy to accept your hospitality, Attaroa. When do you plan to have this feast? I would like to make something to bring, but it is late in the day."

"Yes, it is late," Attaroa said, "and there are some things I will want to prepare, too. The feast will be tomorrow, but of course, you will share our simple meal tonight?"

"There are things I must do for my contribution to your feast. We will be back tomorrow," Ayla said. Then she added, "Jondalar still needs his outer fur, Attaroa. Of course, he will return the 'cloak' he was wearing."

The woman pulled the parka up over her head and gave it to the man. He smelled her female scent when he pulled it on, but he appreciated the warmth. Attaroa's smile was pure evil as she stood in the cold in her thin inner garment.

"And the rest of his things?" Ayla reminded her.

Attaroa glanced at the entrance to her lodge and motioned to the woman who had been standing there for some time. Epadoa quickly brought Jondalar's gear and put it on the ground some feet away from him. She was not happy about returning his things. Attaroa had promised some of them to her. She had particularly wanted the knife. She had never seen one so beautifully made.

Jondalar tied on his belt, then put his tools and implements in their places, hardly believing he had everything back. He had doubted if he'd ever see them again. For that matter, he had doubted that he'd ever leave alive. Then, to everyone's surprise, he leaped up behind the woman on the horse. This was one Camp he would be glad to see the last of. Ayla scanned the area, making sure no one was in a position to try to prevent them from leaving, or to cast a spear after them. Then she turned Whinney and left at a gallop.

"Follow them! I want them back. They aren't getting away that easily," Attaroa snarled to Epadoa, as she stomped into her lodge in a hot rage, shivering with cold.

Ayla kept Whinney at a fast pace until they were some distance away and heading down the hill. They slowed when they entered a wooded stretch at the bottom, near the river, then doubled back in the direction they had come, toward her camp, which was actually quite close to the S'Armunai settlement. Once they settled into a more steady pace, Jondalar became aware of Ayla's closeness, and he felt such an overwhelming gratitude to be with her again that it almost took his breath away. He put his arms around her waist and held her, feeling her hair on his cheek and breathing in her unique warm womanscent.

"You're here, with me. It's so hard to believe. I was afraid you were gone, walking in the next world," he said softly. "I'm so grateful to have you back, I don't know what to say."

"I love you so much, Jondalar," she replied. She leaned back, pressing herself even more into his arms, feeling such a relief to be with him again. Her love for him welled up and filled her to overflowing. "I found a bloodstain, and all the while I was following your trail, trying to find you, I never knew if you were alive or dead. When I realized they were carrying you, I thought you must be alive, but hurt bad enough that you couldn't walk. I was so worried, but the trail was not easy to follow, and I knew I was falling behind. Attaroa's hunters can travel very fast, for being on foot, and they knew the way.''

"You got here just in time. It's a good thing you arrived when you did. A little later and it would have been too late,'' Jondalar said.

"I didn't just get here.''

"You didn't? When did you arrive?''

"I came right after the second load of horsemeat. I was ahead of both of them at first, but the ones carrying the first load caught up with me at the river crossing. It was lucky that I saw two women going to meet them. I found a place to hide and waited for them to go past me, and followed them, but the hunters with the second load of meat were closer than I knew. I think they might have seen me, at least from a distance. I was riding at the time, and I rode away from the trail fast. Later I went back and followed again, but I was more careful, in case there was a third load.''

"That would explain the 'commotion' Ardemun was talking about. He didn't know what it was, he just knew everyone was nervous and talking after they brought in the second load. But if you've been here, why did you wait so long to get me out of there?'' Jondalar asked.

"I had to watch for a long time, waiting for a chance to get you out of that fenced keeping place—what do they call it, a Holding?''

Jondalar made a sound of assent. "Weren't you afraid someone would see you?''

"I've watched real wolves in their den; next to them, Attaroa's Wolves are noisy and easy to avoid. I was close enough to hear them talking most of the time. There's a knoll behind the Camp, up the hill. From there you can see the whole settlement and directly into that Holding. Behind it, if you look up, you can see three big white rocks in a row high in the hillside.''

"I noticed them. I wish I'd known you were there. It would have made me feel better every time I saw those white rocks.''

"I heard a couple of the women call them the Three Girls or maybe the Three Sisters,'' Ayla said.

"They call it the Camp of the Three Sisters,'' Jondalar said.

"I guess I don't know the language very well, yet."

"You know more than I do. I think you surprised Attaroa when you spoke in their language."

"S'Armunai is so much like Mamutoi that it's easy to get a sense of the words," Ayla said.

"I never thought to ask if the white rocks had a name. They make such a good landmark, it seems logical that they would be named."

"That whole highland is a good landmark. You can see it from a long way. At a distance it resembles a sleeping animal, even on this side. There's a place ahead with a good view, you'll see."

"I'm sure the hill must have a name, too, especially since it's such a good location for hunting, but I've only seen a little of it, when we went to funerals. There have been two of them, just in the time I've been here, and the first time they buried three young people," Jondalar said, ducking his head to avoid the bare branches of a tree.

"I followed you to the second funeral," Ayla said. "I thought I might be able to get you out then, but you were too closely watched. And then you found the flint and were showing everyone about spear-throwers," Ayla said. "I had to wait until the time was right, so I could surprise them. I'm sorry it took so long."

"How did you know about the flint? We thought we were careful," Jondalar said.

"I was watching you all the time. Those Wolf Women really aren't very good watchers. You would have seen that and found a way to get out yourself, if you hadn't gotten distracted with the flint. For that matter, they aren't very good hunters, either," she said.

"When you consider that they didn't know anything to start with, they haven't done badly. Attaroa said they didn't know how to use spears, so they had to chase animals," Jondalar said.

"They waste their time going all the way to the Great Mother River to chase horses off a cliff, when they could hunt better right here. Animals following this river have to go across a narrow stretch between the water and the highland, and you can easily see them coming," Ayla said.

"I saw that when we went to the first funeral. The place they were buried would be a good lookout, and someone has signaled with balefires from up there before, though I don't know how recently. I could see the charcoal from large fires," Jondalar commented.

"Instead of building surrounds for men, they could have made one to hold animals and chased them into that, even without spears," Ayla said, then pulled Whinney to a halt. "Look, there it is." She pointed to the limestone highland outlined against the horizon.

"It does look like an animal sleeping, and look, you can even see the three white stones, the Three Sisters," Jondalar said.

They rode in silence for a while. Then, as though he had been thinking about it, Jondalar said, "If it's so easy to get out of the Holding, why haven't the men done it?"

"I don't think they have really tried," Ayla said. "Maybe that's why the women have stopped watching so closely. But a lot of the women, even some of the hunters, don't want the men kept in there anymore. They are just afraid of Attaroa." Ayla stopped then. "This is where I have been camping," she said.

As if to confirm it, Racer nickered a greeting as they entered a small secluded space that was clear of brush. The young stallion was tied securely to a tree. Ayla had set up a minimal camp in the middle of the copse each night, but she had packed everything on Racer's back in the morning to be ready to leave immediately if it was necessary.

"You saved both of them from going over that cliff!" Jondalar said. "I didn't know if you had, and I was afraid to ask. The last thing I remember, before I was hit on the head, was seeing you on Racer's back, having some trouble controlling him."

"I had to get used to the rein, that's all. The biggest problem was that other stallion, but now he's gone and I'm sorry. Whinney came to my whistle as soon as they stopped herding her away from me," Ayla said.

Racer was just as glad to see Jondalar. He dropped his head, then flipped it up in greeting, and he would have walked to the man if he hadn't been tied. The stallion, his ears forward and his tail lifted high, whinnied to Jondalar with eager anticipation as he approached. Then he lowered his head to nuzzle the man's hand. Jondalar greeted the stallion like a friend he thought he would never see again, hugging, scratching, stroking, and talking to the animal.

He frowned when he thought of another question, one he almost hated to ask. "What about Wolf?"

Ayla smiled, then pierced the air with an unfamiliar whistle. Wolf came bounding out of the brush, so glad to see Jondalar that he couldn't keep still. He ran to him, wagging his tail, barked a little yip, then jumped up and put his paws on the man's shoulders and licked his jaw. Jondalar grabbed him by the ruff as he'd seen Ayla do so many times, roughed it up a bit, then pressed his forehead against the wolf's.

"He's never done that to me before," Jondalar said, surprised.

"He missed you. I think he wanted to find you as much as I did, and I'm not sure I would have been able to track you without him. We're quite a distance from the Great Mother River, and there were long stretches of rocky dry ground that showed no tracks. But his nose found the trail," Ayla said. Then she greeted the wolf.

"But he was waiting there in that brush all the time? And he didn't come until you signaled? It must have been hard to teach him that, but why did you?"

"I had to teach him to hide because I didn't know who might be coming here, and I didn't want them to know about him. They eat wolf meat."

"Who eats wolf meat?" Jondalar asked, wrinkling his nose with repugnance.

"Attaroa and her hunters."

"Are they that hungry?" Jondalar asked.

"Maybe they were once, but now they do it as a ritual. I watched them one night. They were initiating a new hunter, making a young woman part of their Wolf Pack. They keep it a secret from the other women, go away from the lodges to a special place. They had a live wolf in a cage and killed it, butchered it, then cooked it and ate it. They like to think they are getting the strength and cunning of the wolf that way. It would be better if they just watched wolves. They'd learn more," Ayla said.

No wonder she seemed so disapproving of the Wolf Women and their hunting skills, Jondalar thought, suddenly understanding why she didn't like them. Their initiation rites threatened her wolf. "So you taught Wolf to stay in hiding until you called him. That's a new whistle, isn't it?" he said.

"I'll teach it to you, but even if he does stay in hiding—

most of the time—when I tell him, I still worry about him. Whinney and Racer, too. Horses and wolves are the only animals I've ever seen Attaroa's women kill," she said, looking around at her beloved animals.

"You've learned a lot about them, Ayla," Jondalar said.

"I had to learn everything I could, so I could get you out of there," she said. "But maybe I learned too much."

"Too much? How could you learn too much?"

"When I first found you, I only thought about getting you out of that place, and then getting away from here as soon as we could, but now we can't go."

"What do you mean we can't go? Why not?" Jondalar said, frowning.

"We can't leave those children living in such terrible conditions, or the men, either. We have to get them out of that Holding," Ayla said.

Jondalar became worried. He had seen that determined look before. "It's dangerous to stay here, Ayla, and not just for us. Think what easy targets those two horses would make. They don't run away from people. And you don't want to see Wolf's teeth hanging around Attaroa's neck, do you? I want to help those people, too. I lived inside that place, and no one should have to live like that, especially children, but what can we do? We are only two people."

He did want to help them, but he feared that if they stayed, Attaroa might harm Ayla. He thought he had lost her, and now that they were back together he was afraid that if they stayed, he might really lose her. He was trying to find a strong reason to convince her to leave.

"We are not alone. There are more than the two of us who want to change things. We have to find a way to help them," Ayla said, then paused, thinking. "I think S'Armuna wants us to come back—that's why she offered her hospitality. We must go to that feast tomorrow."

"Attaroa has used poison before. If we go back there, we may never leave," Jondalar cautioned her. "She hates you, you know."

"I know, but we have to go back anyway. For the sake of the children. We won't eat, except what I bring, and only if it doesn't leave our sight. Do you think we should change our camp or stay here?" Ayla said. "I have a lot to do before tomorrow."

"I don't think moving will help. They will just trail us.

That's why we should leave now," Jondalar said, clasping
both her arms. He looked into her eyes, concentrating as if
trying to will her to change her mind. Finally he let her go,
knowing she wouldn't leave and that he would stay to help
her. In his heart it was what he wanted to do, but he had to
be convinced that he couldn't persuade her to go. He vowed
to himself that he would let nothing harm her.

"All right," he said. "I told the men you would never
stand for anyone being treated like that. I don't think they
believed me, but we will need help to get them out. I admit
I was surprised to hear S'Armuna suggest that we stay with
her," Jondalar said. "I don't think she does that very often.
Her lodge is small and out of the way. She is not set up to
accommodate visitors, but why do you think she wants us to
go back?"

"Because she interrupted Attaroa to ask. I don't think
that headwoman was happy about it. Do you trust S'Armuna,
Jondalar?"

The man stopped to think. "I don't know. I trust her
more than I trust Attaroa, but I guess that's not saying much.
Did you know S'Armuna knew my mother? She lived with
the Ninth Cave when she was young, and they were friends."

"So that's why she speaks your language so well. But if
she knows your mother, why didn't she help you?"

"I wondered that myself. Maybe she didn't want to. I
think something must have happened between her and Marthona. I don't remember that my mother ever talked about
knowing someone who came to live with them when she was
young, either. But I have a feeling about S'Armuna. She did
treat my injury, and though that's more than she's done for
most of the men, I think she wants to do more. I don't think
Attaroa will allow it."

They unpacked Racer and set up their camp, although
both of them felt uneasy. Jondalar started the fire while Ayla
began to prepare a meal for them. She started with the portions she usually estimated for both of them, but then she
remembered how little the men in the Holding had been given
to eat and decided to increase the quantity. Once he started
eating again, he was going to be very hungry.

Jondalar hunkered near the heat for a while after he had
the fire blazing, watching the woman he loved. Then he
walked over to her. "Before you get too busy, woman," he
said, taking her into his arms, "I've greeted a horse and a

wolf, but I haven't yet greeted the one who's most important to me."

She smiled in the way that always evoked a warm feeling of love and tenderness. "I'm never too busy for you," she said.

He bent down to kiss her mouth, slowly at first, but then all his fear and anguish at the thought of losing her suddenly overcame him. "I was so afraid I would never see you again. I thought you were dead." His voice cracked with a sob of strain and relief as he held her close. "Nothing Attaroa could have done to me would be worse than losing you."

He held her so tight she could hardly breathe, but she didn't want him to let her go. He kissed her mouth, then her neck, and he began to explore her familiar body with his knowing hands.

"Jondalar, I'm sure Epadoa is following us . . ."

The man pulled back and caught his breath. "You're right, this is not the right time. We'd be too vulnerable if they came upon us." He should have known better. He felt a need to explain. "It's just that . . . I thought I'd never see you again. It's like a Gift from the Mother to be here with you, and . . . well . . . the urge came over me to honor Her."

Ayla held him, wanting to let him know that she felt the same. The thought occurred to her that she had never heard him try to explain why he wanted her before. She didn't need an explanation. It was all she could do to keep herself from forgetting the danger they were in and giving in to her own desire for him. Then, as she felt her warmth for the man growing, she reconsidered their situation.

"Jondalar . . ." The tone of her voice caught his attention. "If you really think about it, we are probably so far ahead of Epadoa, it will take a while for her to track us here . . . and Wolf would warn us . . ."

As Jondalar looked at her and began to perceive her meaning, his frown of concern slowly eased into a smile, and his compelling blue eyes filled with his wanting and his love. "Ayla, my woman, my beautiful loving woman," he said, his voice husky with need.

It had been a long time, and Jondalar was ready, but he took the time to kiss her slowly and fully. The feel of her lips parting to give access to her warm mouth encouraged thoughts of other parting lips and warm moist openings, and he felt the strivings of his manhood in anticipation. It was going to be difficult to hold back enough to Pleasure her.

Ayla held him close, closing her eyes to think only of his mouth on hers, and his gently exploring tongue. She felt his turgid heat pressing against her, and her response was as immediate as his; an urge so strong that she didn't want to wait. She wanted to be closer to him, to be as close as only the feel of him within her could be. Keeping her lips on his, she slipped her arms down from around his neck to untie the waist closure of her fur leggings. She dropped them down, then reached for his ties.

Jondalar felt her fumbling with the knots he had had to tie in the leather thongs that had been cut. He straightened up, breaking their contact, smiled into eyes that were the blue-gray color of a certain fine-quality flint, unsheathed his knife, and cut through his lacings again. They needed to be replaced anyway. She grinned, then held up her lower garment long enough to take a few steps to the sleeping rolls, then dropped down on top of them. He followed her while she unlaced her boots, then untied his own.

Lying on their sides, they kissed again, as Jondalar reached beneath her fur parka and tunic for a firm breast. He felt her nipple harden in the middle of his palm, then pushed up her heavy garments to expose the tantalizing tip. It contracted with the cold, until he took it in his mouth. Then it warmed but did not relax. Not wanting to wait, she rolled to her back, pulling him with her, and opened to receive him.

With a feeling of joy that she was as ready as he was, he knelt between her warm thighs and guided his eager member into her deep well. Her moist warmth enveloped him, caressing his fullness as he entered her depths with a moaning sigh of pleasure.

Ayla felt him inside her, penetrating deeply, bringing him closer to the core of her being. She let herself forget everything except the warmth of him filling her as she arched to reach him. She felt him pulling back, caressing her from within, and then he filled her again. She cried out her welcome and delight as his long shaft withdrew and penetrated again, in just the right position so that each time he entered, his manhood rubbed against her small center of pleasure, sending shocks of excitement through her.

Jondalar was building quickly; for a moment he feared it was too quickly—but he could not have held back if he'd tried, and this time he didn't try. He let himself advance and retreat as his need directed, sensing her willingness in the rhythm of her motion matching his as he moved steadily faster. Suddenly, overpoweringly, he was there.

With an intensity that met his, she was ready for him. She whispered, "Now, oh now," as she strained to meet him. Her encouragement was a surprise. She had not done it before, but it had an immediate effect. With the next stroke, his building force reached an explosive rush and burst through in an eruption of release and pleasure. She was only a step behind, and, with a cry of exquisite delight, she reached her peak a moment later. A few more strokes and they both lay still.

Though it was over quickly, the moment had been so intense that it took the woman a while to come down from the culminating summit. When Jondalar, feeling his weight on her was becoming too much, rolled over and disengaged, she felt an inexplicable sense of loss and wished they could stay linked together longer. Somehow he completed her, and the full realization of how much she had feared for him, and missed his presence struck her with such poignancy that she felt tears sting her eyes.

Jondalar saw a transparent bead of water fall from the outside corner of her eye and run down the side of her face to her ear. He raised himself up and looked at her. "What's wrong, Ayla?"

"I'm just so happy to be with you," she said, as another tear welled up and quivered at the edge of her eye before it spilled over.

Jondalar reached for it with a finger and brought the salty drop to his mouth. "If you are happy, why are you crying?" he said, though he knew.

She shook her head, unable to speak at that moment. He smiled with the knowledge that she shared his powerful feelings of relief and gratitude that they were together again. He bent down to kiss her eyes, and her cheek, and finally her beautiful smiling mouth. "I love you, too," he whispered in her ear.

He felt a faint stirring in his manhood, and he wished they could start all over again, but this was not the time. Epadoa was certain to be trailing them, and sooner or later she would find them.

"There is a stream nearby," Ayla said. "I need to wash, and I might as well fill the waterbags."

"I'll go with you," the man said, partly because he still wanted to be close to her, and partly because he felt protective.

They picked up their lower garments and boots, then the waterbags, and walked to a fairly wide stream, nearly closed over with ice, leaving only a small section in the middle still flowing. He shivered with the shock of freezing water and knew he washed himself only because she did. He would have been content to let himself dry off in the warmth of his clothes, but if she had any opportunity at all, even in the coldest water, she always cleaned herself. He knew it was a ritual her Clan stepmother had taught her, although now she invoked the Mother with mumbled words spoken in Mamutoi.

They filled up the waterbags, and, as they walked back to their campsite, Ayla recalled the scene she had witnessed just before his lacings had been cut the first time.

"Why didn't you couple with Attaroa?" she asked. "You damaged her pride in front of her people."

"I have pride, too. No one is going to force me to share the Mother's Gift. And it wouldn't have made any difference. I'm sure it was her intention all along to make a target out of me. But now, I think you are the one who has to be careful. 'Discourteous and inhospitable' . . ." He chuckled; then he became more serious. "She hates you, you know. She'll kill us both, if she gets the chance."

30

As Ayla and Jondalar settled down for the night, both were wary of every sound they heard. The horses were staked nearby, and Ayla kept Wolf beside her bedroll, knowing he would warn her of anything unusual that he sensed, but she still slept poorly. Her dreams felt threatening, but amorphous and disorganized, with no messages or warnings that she could define, except that Wolf kept appearing in them.

She awoke as the first glimmerings of day broke through the bare branches of willow and birch to the east, near the stream. It was still dark in the rest of their secluded glen, but as she watched, she began to see thick-needled spruce and the longer needle-shafts of stone pine defined in the growing light. A fine powdering of dry snow had sprinkled down during the night, dusting evergreens, tangled brush, dry grass, and bedrolls with white, but Ayla was cozily warm.

She had almost forgotten how good it felt to have Jondalar sleeping beside her, and she stayed still for a while, just enjoying his nearness. But her mind would not stay still. She kept worrying about the day ahead and thinking over what she was going to make for the feast. She finally decided to get up, but when she tried to slip out of the furs, she felt Jondalar's arm tightening around her, holding her back.

"Do you have to get up? It's been so long since I've felt you beside me, I hate to let you go," Jondalar said, nuzzling her neck.

She settled back into his warmth. "I don't want to get up either. It's cold, and I'd like to stay here in the furs with you, but I need to start cooking something for Attaroa's 'feast,' and make your morning meal. Aren't you hungry?"

"Now that you mention it, I think I could eat a horse!" Jondalar said, eying the two nearby exaggeratedly.

"Jondalar!" Ayla said, looking shocked.

He grinned at her. "Not one of ours, but that is what I've been eating lately—when I've had anything at all. If I hadn't been so hungry, I don't think I would have eaten horsemeat, but when there is nothing else, you eat what you can get. And there's nothing wrong with it."

"I know, but you don't have to eat it anymore. We have other food," she said. They snuggled together for a moment longer, then Ayla pulled back the fur. "The fire has gone out. If you start a new one, I'll make our morning tea. We'll need a hot fire today, and a lot of wood."

For their meal the evening before, Ayla had prepared a larger than usual amount of a hearty soup from dried bison meat and dried roots, adding a few pine nuts from the cones of the stone pines, but Jondalar had not been able to eat as much as he thought. After she put the rest aside, she had taken out a basket of small whole apples, hardly bigger than cherries, which she had found while trailing Jondalar. They had frozen but were still clinging to a dwarfed clump of leafless trees on the south face of a hillside. She had cut the hard little apples in half, seeded them, then boiled them for a while with dried rose hips. She left the result overnight near the fire. By morning it had cooled and thickened from the natural pectin to a sauce of a jellylike consistency with bits of chewy apple skin.

Before she made their morning tea, Ayla added a little water to the soup that was left and put extra cooking stones in the fire to heat it for their breakfast. She also tasted the thickened apple mixture. Freezing had moderated the usual tart sourness of the hard apples and adding rose hips had imparted a reddish tinge and a tangy sweet flavor. She served a bowl to Jondalar along with his soup.

"This is the best food I've ever eaten!" Jondalar said after the first few bites. "What did you put in it to make it taste so good?"

Ayla smiled. "It's flavored with hunger."

Jondalar nodded, and between mouthfuls he said, "I suppose you're right. It makes me feel sorry for the ones still in the Holding."

"No one should have to go hungry when there is food available," Ayla said, her anger flaring for a moment. "It's another thing when everyone is starving."

"Sometimes, near the end of a bad winter, that can happen," Jondalar said. "Have you ever gone hungry?"

"I've missed a few meals, and favorite foods always seem to go first, but if you know where to look, you can usually find something to eat—if you are free to go looking!"

"I've known of people who starved because they ran out of food and didn't know where to find more, but you always seem to find something to eat, Ayla. How do you know so much?"

"Iza taught me. I think I've always been interested in food and things that grow," Ayla said, then paused. "I guess there was a time when I nearly starved, just before Iza found me. I was young, and I don't remember much about it." A fond smile of remembrance flitted across her face. "Iza said that she never knew anyone who learned to find food as fast as I did, especially since I was not born with the memories of where or how to look for it. She told me that hunger taught me."

After he finished devouring a second large serving, Jondalar watched Ayla sort through her carefully hoarded preserved food supplies and begin preparations for the dish she wanted to make for the feast. She had been thinking about what container she could cook in that would be large enough to make the amount she would need for the entire S'Armunai Camp, since they had cached most of their equipment and brought only bare essentials with them.

She took down their largest waterbag and emptied it into smaller bowls and cooking utensils, then separated the lining from the hide covering, which had been sewn together with the fur side out. The lining had been made from the stomach of an aurochs, which was not exactly waterproof, but seeped very slowly. The moisture was absorbed by the soft leather of the covering and wicked away by the hair, which kept the outside essentially dry. She cut open the top of the lining, tied it to a frame of wood with sinew from her sewing kit, then refilled it with water and waited until a thin film of moisture had seeped through.

By then the hot fire they had started earlier had burned down to searing coals, and she placed the mounted waterbag directly over them, making sure she had additional water close at hand to keep the skin pot filled. While she waited for it to boil, she started weaving a tight basket out of willow withes and yellowed grasses made flexible by moisture from the snow.

When bubbles appeared, she broke strips of lean dried meat and some fatty cakes of traveling food into the water to make a rich, meaty broth. Then she added a mixture of various grains. Later she planned to mix in some dry roots— wild carrots and starchy groundnuts—plus other pod and stem vegetables, and dried currants and blueberries. She flavored it all with a choice selection of herbs including coltsfoot, ramsons, sorrel, basil, and meadowsweet, and a bit of salt saved since they left the Mamutoi Summer Meeting, which Jondalar didn't even know she still had.

He had no desire to go very far, and he stayed nearby gathering wood, getting more water, picking grasses, and cutting willow withes for the baskets she was weaving. He was so happy to be with her that he didn't want to let her out of his sight. She was just as happy to be in his company again. But when the man noticed the large quantity of their food supplies she was using, he became concerned. He had just been through a very hungry time and was unusually aware of food.

"Ayla, a lot of our emergency food stores are in that dish. If you use up too much, it could leave us short."

"I want to make enough for all of them, the women and the men of Attaroa's Camp, to show them what they could have in their own storage if they work together," Ayla explained.

"Maybe I should take my spear-thrower and see if I can find fresh meat," he said with a worried frown.

She glanced up at him, surprised at his concern. By far, the majority of the food they had eaten on their Journey had been gleaned from the land they passed through, and most of the time, when they did dip into their stores, it was more for convenience than necessity. Besides, they had more food supplies stashed away with the rest of their things near the river. She looked at him closely. For the first time, she noticed that he was thinner, and she began to understand his uncharacteristic misgivings.

"That might be a good idea," she agreed. "Maybe you should take Wolf with you. He's good at finding and flushing out game, and he could warn you if anyone was near. I'm sure Epadoa and Attaroa's Wolf Women are looking for us."

"But if I take Wolf, who will warn you?" Jondalar said.

"Whinney will. She'll know if strangers are approaching. But I would like to leave here as soon as this is done and head back to the S'Armunai settlement."

"Will you be very long?" he asked, his forehead knotted deeper as he weighed his alternatives.

"Not too long, I hope, but I'm not used to cooking this much at one time, so I'm not sure."

"Maybe I should wait, and go hunting later."

"It's up to you, but if you stay here, I could use more wood," she said.

"I'll get you some wood," he decided. Looking around, he added, "And I'll pack up everything you're not using so we'll be ready to go."

It took Ayla longer than she expected, and around mid-morning, Jondalar did take Wolf to survey the area, more to make sure that Epadoa was not nearby than to look for game. He was a little surprised at how eager the wolf was to accompany him . . . once Ayla told him to go. He had always thought of the animal as hers alone and never considered taking Wolf along with him. The animal turned out to be good company, and he did flush something, but Jondalar decided to let him make a meal of the rabbit by himself.

When they came back, Ayla handed Jondalar a large hot serving of the delicious mixture she had prepared for the Camp. Though they usually ate no more than twice a day, as soon as he saw the bowl piled high with food, he realized that he was very hungry. She took some herself and gave a little to Wolf as well.

It was just after noon before they were ready to leave. While the food was cooking, Ayla had completed two rather steep-sided bowl-shaped baskets, both of good size but one somewhat larger than the other, and both were filled with the thick, rich combination. She had even added some oily pine nuts from the cones of the stone pines. She knew with their diet of mostly lean meat, it was the richness of fats and oils that would be most appealing to the people of the Camp. She also knew, without entirely understanding why, that it was what they needed the most, especially in winter, for warmth and energy, and, along with the grains, to make everyone feel full and satisfied.

Ayla covered the heaping bowls with inverted shallow baskets used as lids, lifted them to Whinney's back, and secured them in a roughly made holder of dry grass and willow withes that she had worked together quickly, since it would be used only once and then disposed of. Then they started back to the S'Armunai settlement, using a different route. On the way they discussed what to do with the animals once they reached Attaroa's Camp.

"We can hide the horses in the woods by the river. Tie them to a tree and walk the rest of the way," Jondalar suggested.

"I don't want to tie them. If Attaroa's hunters happened to find them, they'd be too easy to kill," Ayla said. "If they are free, at least they have a chance to get away, and they'll be able to come when we whistle. I would rather have them close by, where we can see them."

"In that case, the field of dry grass next to the Camp might be a good place for them. I think they would stay there without being tied. They usually stay close by if we put them where they have something to graze," Jondalar said. "And it would make a big impression on Attaroa and the S'Armunai if we both ride horses into the Camp. If they're like everyone else we've met, the S'Armunai are probably a little afraid of people who can control horses. They all think it has to do with spirits or magical powers or something, but as long as they're afraid, it gives us an edge. With only two of us, we need every advantage we can get."

"That's true," Ayla said, frowning, both because of her concerns for them and the animals, and because she hated the thought of taking advantage of the unfounded fears of the S'Armunai. It made her feel as if she were lying, but their lives were at stake, and very likely the lives of the boys and men in the Holding.

It was a difficult moment for Ayla. She was being

required to make a choice between two wrongs, but she was the one who had insisted that they return to help, even though it put their own lives in jeopardy. She had to overcome her ingrained compulsion to be absolutely truthful; she had to choose the lesser wrong, to adapt, if they were to have any chance of saving the boys and men of the Camp, and themselves, from the madness of Attaroa.

"Ayla," Jondalar said. "Ayla?" he repeated, when she had not responded to his question.

"Uh . . . yes?"

"I said, what about Wolf? Are you going to take him into the Camp, too?"

She paused to think about it. "No, I don't think so. They know about the horses, but they don't know about a wolf. Considering what they like to do with wolves, I don't see any reason why we should give them an opportunity to get too close to him. I'll tell him to stay in hiding. I think he will, if he sees me once in a while."

"Where will he hide? It's mostly open country around the settlement."

Ayla thought for a moment. "Wolf can stay where I was hiding when I watched you, Jondalar. We can go around from here to the uphill side. There are some trees and brush along a small stream leading up to the place. You can wait for me there with the horses; then we can go back around and ride into the Camp from another direction."

No one noticed them entering the field from the fringe of woods, and the first ones who saw the woman and man, each on a separate horse, cantering across the open land toward the settlement, had the feeling that they had simply appeared. By the time they reached Attaroa's large earthlodge, everyone who could had gathered to watch them. Even the men in the Holding were crowded behind the fence watching through the cracks.

Attaroa stood with her hands on her hips and her legs apart, assuming her attitude of command. Though she would never admit it, she was shocked and more than a little concerned to see them, and this time both on horses. The few times that anyone had ever gotten away from her, he had run as far and as fast as he could. No one had ever voluntarily come back. What power did these two possess that they felt

confident enough to return? With her underlying fear of repri-
sal from the Great Mother and Her world of spirits, Attaroa
wondered what the reappearance of the enigmatic woman and
the tall, handsome man might signify, but her words showed
none of her worry.

"So you did decide to come back," she said, looking to
S'Armuna to translate.

Jondalar thought the shaman seemed surprised, too, but
he sensed her relief. Before she translated Attaroa's words
into Zelandonii, she spoke to them directly.

"No matter what she says, I would advise you not to stay
in her lodge, son of Marthona. My offer is still open to both
of you," she said before repeating Attaroa's comment.

The headwoman eyed S'Armuna, sure she had spoken
more words than were necessary to translate. But without
knowing the language, she couldn't be sure.

"Why shouldn't we come back, Attaroa? Weren't we
invited to a feast in our honor?" Ayla said. "We have
brought our contribution of food."

As her words were translated, Ayla threw her leg over
and slid down from Whinney's back, then lifted the largest
bowl and set it on the ground between Attaroa and S'Armuna.
She picked up the basket cover, and the delicious aroma from
the huge mound of grains cooked with other foods made
everyone stare in wonder as their mouths watered. It was a
treat they had seldom enjoyed in recent years, especially in
winter. Even Attaroa was momentarily overwhelmed.

"There seems to be enough for everyone," she said.

"That is only for the women and children," Ayla said.
Then she took the slightly smaller woven bowl that Jondalar
had just brought and put it down beside the first. She lifted
the lid and announced, "This is for the men."

A murmuring undercurrent arose from behind the fence,
and from the women who had come out of their lodges, but
Attaroa was furious. "What do you mean, for the men?"

"Certainly when the leader of a Camp announces a feast
in honor of a visitor, it includes all the people? I presumed
that you were the leader of the entire Camp, and that I was
expected to bring enough for all. You are the leader of everyone, aren't you?"

"Of course I am the leader of everyone," Attaroa sputtered, caught at a loss for words.

"If you aren't ready yet, I think I should take these bowls

inside, so they don't freeze," Ayla said, picking up the larger bowl again and turning toward S'Armuna. Jondalar took the other.

Attaroa quickly recovered. "I invited you to stay in my lodge," she said.

"But I'm sure you are busy with preparations," Ayla said, "and I would not want to impose on the leader of this Camp. It is more appropriate for us to stay with the One Who Serves the Mother." S'Armuna translated, then added, "It is the way it is always done."

Ayla turned to go, saying to Jondalar under her breath, "Start walking toward S'Armuna's lodge!"

As Attaroa watched them go with the shaman, a smile of pure evil slowly altered her features, turning a face that could have been beautiful into a hideous, subhuman caricature. They were stupid to come back here, she thought, knowing that their return had given her the opportunity she wanted: her chance to destroy them. But she also knew she would have to catch them off guard. When she thought about it, she was glad to let them go with S'Armuna. It would get them out of the way. She wanted time to think and discuss plans with Epadoa, who had not yet returned.

For the time being, however, she would have to go along with this feast. She signaled one of the women, the one who had a baby girl and was a favorite, and told her to tell the other women to prepare some food for a celebration. "Make enough for everyone," the headwoman said, "including the men in the Holding."

The woman looked surprised, but she nodded and hurried away.

"I would guess you are ready for some hot tea," S'Armuna said, after she showed Ayla and Jondalar to their sleeping places, expecting Attaroa to come charging in any moment. But after they had drunk their tea without being disturbed, she relaxed a little. The longer Ayla and Jondalar were there without the headwoman objecting, the more it was likely they would be allowed to stay.

But as the tension of worrying about Attaroa eased, an uncomfortable silence descended on the three people seated around the hearth. Ayla studied the woman Who Served the

Mother, trying not to be too obvious. Her face had a peculiar skew, the left side was much more prominent than the right, and she guessed S'Armuna might even have some pain in the underdeveloped right jaw when she chewed. The woman did nothing to hide the abnormality, wearing her graying, light brown hair with straightforward dignity, pulled back and up in a smooth bun near the top of her head. For some inexplicable reason, Ayla felt drawn to the older woman.

Ayla could not help but notice, however, a hesitancy in her manner, and she sensed that S'Armuna was pulled by indecision. She kept glancing toward Jondalar as if she wanted to say something to him but found it hard to begin, as if she were trying to find a delicate way to broach a difficult subject.

Acting on instinct, Ayla spoke up. "Jondalar told me that you knew his mother, S'Armuna," she said. "I wondered where you learned to speak his language so well."

The woman turned to the visitor with a look of surprise. *His* language, she thought, not hers? Ayla almost felt the shaman's sudden, intense evaluation of her, but her return gaze was just as strong.

"Yes, I knew Marthona, and the man she mated as well."

It seemed as though she wanted to say more, but instead she was silent. Jondalar filled the void, eager to talk about his home and family, especially with someone who once knew them.

"Was Joconan leader of the Ninth Cave when you were there?" Jondalar asked.

"No, but I'm not surprised that he became leader."

"They say Marthona was almost a coleader, like a Mamutoi headwoman, I suppose. That's why, after Joconan died . . ."

"Joconan is dead?" S'Armuna interrupted. Ayla sensed her shock and noted an expression that showed something akin to grief. Then she seemed to gather her composure. "It must have been a difficult time for your mother."

"I'm sure it was, although I don't think she had much time to think about it, or to grieve too long. Everyone was pressing her to be leader. I don't know when she met Dalanar, but by the time she mated him, she had been leader of the Ninth Cave for several years. Zelandoni told me she was already blessed with me before the mating, so it should have been lucky, but they severed the knot a couple of years after

I was born, and he chose to leave. I don't know what happened, but sad stories and songs about their love are still recalled. They embarrass Mother."

It was Ayla who prompted him to continue, for her own interest, although S'Armuna's interest was also obvious. "She mated again, and had more children, didn't she? I know you had another brother."

Jondalar continued, directing his comments at S'Armuna. "My brother Thonolan was born to Willomar's hearth, and my sister Folara, too. I think that was a good mating for her. Marthona is very happy with him, and he was always very good to me. He used to travel a lot, go on trading missions for my mother. He took me with him sometimes. Thonolan, too, when he got old enough. For a long time I thought of Willomar as the man of my hearth, until I went to live with Dalanar and got to know him a little better. I still feel close to him, although Dalanar was also very kind to me, and I grew to love him, too. But everyone likes Dalanar. He found a flint mine, met Jerika, and started his own Cave. They had a daughter, Joplaya, my close-cousin."

It suddenly occurred to Ayla that if a man was as much responsible for starting a new life growing inside a woman as the woman was, then the "cousin" he called Joplaya was actually his sibling; as much a sister as the one named Folara. Close-cousin, he had called her; was that because they recognized it was a closer tie than the relationship to the children of a mother's sisters or the mates of her brothers? The conversation about Jondalar's mother had gone on while she pondered the implications of Jondalar's kin.

" . . . then my mother turned the leadership over to Joharran, although he insisted that she stay on as adviser to him," Jondalar was saying. "How did you happen to know my mother?"

S'Armuna hesitated for a while, staring into space as though she were seeing an image from the past; then slowly she began to speak. "I was little more than a girl when I was taken there. My mother's brother was leader here, and I was his favorite child, the only girl born to either of his two sisters. He had made a Journey when he was young and had learned of the renowned zelandonia. When it was felt that I had some talent or gift to Serve the Mother, he wanted me to be trained by the best. He took me to the Ninth Cave because your Zelandoni was First among those Who Serve the Mother.''

"That seems to be a tradition with the Ninth Cave. When I left, our Zelandoni had just been chosen First," Jondalar commented.

"Do you know the former name of the one who is First now?" S'Armuna asked, interested.

Jondalar made a wry smile, and Ayla thought she understood why. "I knew her as Zolena."

"Zolena? She's young to be First, isn't she? She was just a pretty little girl when I was there."

"Young, perhaps, but dedicated," Jondalar said.

S'Armuna nodded, then picked up the thread of her story. "Marthona and I were close to the same age, and the hearth of her mother was one of high status. My uncle and your grandmother, Jondalar, made an arrangement for me to live with her. He stayed just long enough to make sure I was settled." S'Armuna's eyes held a faraway look; then she smiled. "Marthona and I were like sisters. Even closer than sisters, more like twins. We liked the same things, and shared everything. She even decided to train to be zelandoni along with me."

"I didn't know that," Jondalar said. "Maybe that's where she gained her leadership qualities."

"Perhaps, but neither of us were thinking about leadership then. We were just inseparable, and wanted the same things . . . until it became a problem." S'Armuna stopped speaking then.

"Problem?" Ayla encouraged. "There was a problem with feeling so close to a friend?" She had been thinking about Deegie, and how wonderful it had been to have a good friend, if only for a little while. She would have loved knowing someone like that when she was growing up. Uba had been like a sister, but as much as she had loved her, Uba was Clan. No matter how close she felt, there were some things they could never understand about each other, such as Ayla's innate curiosity, and Uba's memories.

"Yes," S'Armuna said, looking at the young woman, suddenly aware of her unusual accent again. "The problem was that we fell in love with the same man. I think Joconan may have loved us both. Once he talked of a double mating, and I think Marthona and I would have been willing, but by then the old Zelandoni had died, and when Joconan went to the new one for advice, he told him to choose Marthona. I thought then it was because Marthona was so beautiful and her face wasn't twisted, but now I think it may have been because my uncle had told them he wanted me to come back. I didn't stay for their Matrimonial; I was too bitter and angry. I started back soon after they told me."

"You came back here alone?" Jondalar asked. "Across the glacier by yourself?"

"Yes," the woman said.

"Not many women make such long Journeys, especially by themselves. It was a dangerous and a brave thing to do, alone," Jondalar said.

"Dangerous, yes. I almost fell into a crevasse, but I'm not sure how brave it was. I think my anger sustained me. But when I got back, everything had changed; I had been gone for many years. My mother and aunt had moved north, where many other S'Armunai live, along with my cousins and brothers, and my mother had died there. My uncle was dead, too, and another man was leader, a stranger named Brugar. I'm not sure where he came from. He seemed charming at first, not handsome, but very attractive in a rugged sort of way, but he was cruel and vicious."

"Brugar . . . Brugar," Jondalar said, closing his eyes and trying to remember where he had heard the name. "Wasn't he Attaroa's mate?"

S'Armuna got up, suddenly very agitated. "Would anyone like more tea?" she asked. Ayla and Jondalar both accepted. She brought them each fresh hot cups of the herbal beverage, then got one for herself, but before she sat down, she addressed the visitors. "I've never told all this to anyone before."

"Why are you telling us now?" Ayla asked.

"So you will understand." She turned to Jondalar. "Yes, Brugar was Attaroa's mate. Apparently he began to make changes shortly after he became leader, and he started by making men more important than women. Small things at first. Women had to sit and wait until they were granted permission to speak. Women were not allowed to touch weapons. It didn't seem so serious at first, and the men were enjoying the power, but after the first woman was beaten to death as punishment for speaking her mind, the rest began to realize things were very serious. By then people didn't know what had happened or how to change things back. Brugar brought out the worst in men. He had a band of followers, and I think the others were scared not to go along.''

"I wonder where he ever got such ideas?'' Jondalar said.

With a sudden inspiration, Ayla asked, "What did this Brugar look like?''

"He was strong-featured, rugged, as I said, but very charming and appealing when he wanted to be.''

"Are there many people of the Clan, many flatheads, in this area?'' Ayla asked.

"There used to be, but not too many anymore. There are a lot more of them to the west of here. Why?''

"How do the S'Armunai feel toward them? Particularly those of mixed spirits?''

"Well, they are not considered abominations, the way they are among the Zelandonii. Some men have taken flathead women as mates, and the offspring are tolerated, but they are not well accepted by either side, as I understand it.''

"Do you think Brugar could have been born of mixed spirits?'' Ayla asked.

"Why are you asking all these questions?''

"Because I think he must have lived with, perhaps grown up with, the ones you call flatheads,'' Ayla replied.

"What makes you think so?'' the shaman asked.

"Because the things you describe are Clan ways.''

"Clan?''

"That's what 'flatheads' call themselves,'' Ayla explained, then began to speculate. "But if he could speak so well that he was charming, he could not have lived with them always. He probably was not born to them, but went to live with them later and, as a mixture, he would have been barely tolerated, and perhaps considered deformed. I doubt if he really understood their ways, so he would have been an outsider. His life was probably miserable.''

S'Armuna was surprised. She wondered how Ayla, a complete stranger, could know so much. "For someone you never met, you seem to know a great deal about Brugar.''

"Then he was born of mixed spirits?'' Jondalar said.

"Yes. Attaroa told me about his background, what she knew of it. Apparently his mother was a full mixture, half-human, half-flathead; she had been born to a full flathead mother,'' S'Armuna began.

Probably a child caused by some man of the Others who

forced her, Ayla thought, like the baby girl at the Clan Meeting who was promised to Durc.

"Her childhood must have been unhappy. She left her people when she was barely a woman, with a man from a Cave of the people who live to the west of here."

"The Losadunai?" Jondalar asked.

"Yes, I think that's what they are called. Anyway, not long after she ran away, she had a baby boy. That was Brugar," S'Armuna continued.

"Brugar, but sometimes called Brug?" Ayla interjected.

"How did you know?"

"Brug could have been his Clan name."

"I guess the man his mother ran away with used to beat her. Who knows why? Some men are like that."

"Women of the Clan are raised to accept that," Ayla said. "The men are not allowed to strike each other, but they can hit a woman to reprimand her. They are not supposed to beat them, but some men do."

S'Armuna nodded with understanding. "So perhaps in the beginning Brugar's mother took it for granted when the man she lived with hit her, but it must have gotten worse. Men like that usually do, and he started beating on the boy, too. That may have been what finally prompted her to leave. Anyway, she took him and ran away from her mate, back to her people," S'Armuna said.

"And if it was hard on her to grow up with the Clan, it must have been worse for her son, who was not even a full mixture," Ayla said.

"If the spirits mixed as expected, he would have been three parts human, and only one part flathead," S'Armuna said.

Ayla suddenly thought of her son, Durc. Broud is bound to make his life difficult. What if he turns out like Brugar? But Durc is a full mixture, and he has Uba to love him, and Brun to train him. Brun accepted him into the Clan when he was leader and Durc was a baby. He will make sure Durc knows the ways of the Clan. I know he would be capable of talking, if there was someone to teach him, but he may also have the memories. If he does, he could be full Clan, with Brun's help.

S'Armuna had a sudden inkling about the mysterious young woman. "How do you know so much about flatheads, Ayla?" she asked.

The question caught Ayla by surprise. She wasn't on her guard, as she would have been with Attaroa, and she wasn't prepared to evade it. Instead she blurted out the truth. "I was raised by them," she said. "My people died in an earthquake and they took me in."

"Your childhood must have been even more difficult than Brugar's," S'Armuna said.

"No. I think in a way it was easier. I wasn't considered a deformed child of the Clan; I was just different. One of the Others—which is what they call us. They didn't have expectations of me. Some of the things I did were so strange to them that they didn't know what to think of me. Except I'm sure some of them did think I was rather slow because I had such a hard time remembering things. I'm not saying it was easy growing up with them. I had to learn to speak their way, and I had to learn to live according to their ways, learn their traditions. It was hard to fit in, but I was lucky. Iza and Creb, the people who raised me, loved me, and I know that without them I would not have lived at all."

Nearly all of her statements raised questions in S'Armuna's mind, but the time was not appropriate to ask them. "It is a good thing that you have no mixture in you," she said, giving Jondalar a significant look, "especially since you are going to meet the Zelandonii."

Ayla caught the look, and she had an idea what the woman meant. She recalled the way Jondalar had first reacted when he discovered who had raised her, and it was even worse when he found out about her son of mixed spirits.

"How do you know she hasn't met them already?" Jondalar asked.

S'Armuna paused to consider the question. How had she known? She smiled at the man. "You said you were going home, and she said, 'his language,' not hers." Suddenly a thought came to her, a revelation. "The language! The accent! Now I know where I've heard it before. Brugar had an accent like that! Not quite as much as yours, Ayla, though he didn't speak his own language as well as you speak Jondalar's. But he must have developed that speech . . . mannerism—it isn't quite an accent—when he lived with the flatheads. There is something about the sound of your speech, and now that I hear it, I don't think I'll ever forget again."

Ayla felt embarrassed. She had worked so hard to speak correctly, but she had never been quite able to make some

sounds. For the most part, it had ceased to bother her when
people mentioned it, but S'Armuna was making such an issue
of it.

The shaman noticed her discomfiture. "I'm sorry, Ayla.
I don't mean to embarrass you. You really do speak Zelandonii very well, probably better than I do, since I've forgotten
so much. And it isn't really an accent you have. It's something else. I'm sure most people don't even notice. It's just
that you have given me such an insight into Brugar, and that
helps me to understand Attaroa."

"Helps you to understand Attaroa?" Jondalar asked. "I
wish I could understand how someone could be so cruel."

"She wasn't always so bad. I really grew to admire her
when I first came back, although I felt very sorry for her,
too. But in a way, she was prepared for Brugar as few women
could have been."

"Prepared? That's a strange thing to say. Prepared for
what?"

"Prepared for his cruelty," S'Armuna explained. "Attaroa
was used badly when she was a girl. She never said much
about it, but I know she felt her own mother hated her. I
learned from someone else that her mother did abandon her,
or so it was thought. She left and nothing was heard from
her again. Attaroa was finally taken in by a man whose mate
had died in childbirth, under very suspicious circumstances,
the baby with her. The suspicions were borne out when it
was discovered that he beat Attaroa and took her before she
was even a woman, but no one else wanted responsibility for
her. It was something about her mother, some question about
her background, but it left Attaroa to be raised with and
warped by his cruelty. Finally the man died, and some people
of her Camp arranged for her to be mated to the new leader
of this Camp."

"Arranged without her consent?" Jondalar asked.

"They 'encouraged' her to agree, and they brought her
to meet Brugar. As I said, he could be very charming, and
I'm sure he found her attractive."

Jondalar nodded agreement. He had noticed that she could
have been quite attractive.

"I think she looked forward to the mating," S'Armuna
continued. "She felt it would be a chance for a new beginning. Then she discovered the man with whom she had joined
was even worse than the one she had known before. Brugar's

Pleasures were always done with beatings, and humiliation, and worse. In his way, he did . . . I hesitate to say he loved her, but I think he did have feeling for her. He was just so . . . twisted. Yet she was the only one who dared to defy him, in spite of everything he did to her.''

S'Armuna paused, shook her head, and then continued. "Brugar was a strong man, very strong, and he liked to hurt people, especially women. I really think he enjoyed causing women pain. You said the flatheads don't allow men to hit other men, though they can hit women. That might have something to do with it. But Brugar liked Attaroa's defiance. She was a good deal taller than he was, and she is very strong herself. He liked the challenge of breaking down her resistance, and he was delighted when she fought him. It gave him an excuse to hurt her, which seemed to make her feel powerful.''

Ayla shuddered, recalling a situation not too dissimilar, and she felt a moment of empathy and compassion for the headwoman.

"He bragged about it to the other men, and they encouraged him, or at least they went along with him,'' the older woman said. "The more she resisted, the worse he made it for her, until she finally broke. Then he would want her. I used to wonder, if she had been complaisant in the beginning, would he have grown tired of her and stopped beating her?''

Ayla thought about that. Broud had grown tired of her when she stopped resisting.

"But somehow I doubt it,'' S'Armuna continued. "Later, when she was blessed and did stop fighting him, he didn't change. She was his mate, and as far as he was concerned, she belonged to him. He could do whatever he wanted to her.''

I was never Broud's mate, Ayla thought, and Brun wouldn't let him beat me, not after the first time. Though it was his right, the rest of Brun's clan thought his interest in me was strange. They discouraged his behavior.

"Brugar didn't stop beating her, even when Attaroa became pregnant?'' Jondalar asked, appalled.

"No, although he seemed pleased that she was going to have a baby,'' the woman said.

I became pregnant, too, Ayla thought. Her life and Attaroa's had many similarities.

"Attaroa came to me for healing,'' S'Armuna was contin-

uing, closing her eyes and shaking her head as if to dispel
the memory. "It was horrible, the things he did to her, I
cannot tell you. Bruises from beatings were the least of it."

"Why did she put up with it?" Jondalar asked.

"She had no other place to go. She had no kin, no
friends. The people of her other Camp had made it clear to
her that they didn't want her, and at first she was too proud
to go back and let them know that her mating to the new
leader was so bad. In a way, I knew how she felt," S'Armuna said. "No one beat me, although Brugar did try it
once, but I believed there was no other place for me to go,
even though I do have relatives. I was the One Who Served
the Mother, and I couldn't admit how bad things had become.
It would have seemed that I had failed."

Jondalar nodded his understanding. He, too, had once felt
that he was a failure. He glanced at Ayla, and he felt his
love for her warm him.

"Attaroa hated Brugar," S'Armuna continued, "but, in
a strange way, she may have loved him, too. Sometimes she
provoked him on purpose, I think. I wondered if it was
because when the pain was over, he would take her and, if
not love her, or even Pleasure her, at least make her feel
wanted. She may have learned to take a perverse kind of
Pleasure from his cruelty. Now she wants no one. She Pleasures herself by causing men pain. If you watch her, you can
see her excitement."

"I almost pity her," Jondalar said.

"Pity her, if you want, but do not trust her," the shaman
said. "She is insane, possessed by some great evil. I wonder
if you can understand? Have you ever been filled with such
rage that all reason leaves you?"

Jondalar's eyes were huge as he felt compelled to nod his
assent. He had felt such rage. He had beaten a man until he
was unconscious, and still he had been unable to stop.

"With Attaroa, it is as though she is constantly filled by
such a rage. She doesn't always show it—in fact, she is very
good at hiding it—but her thoughts and feelings are so full
of this evil rage that she is no longer able to think or to feel
the way ordinary people do. She is not human anymore,"
the shaman explained.

"Surely she must have some human feeling?" Jondalar
said.

"Do you recall the funeral shortly after you came here?" S'Armuna asked.

"Yes, three young people. Two men and I wasn't sure about the third, even though they were all dressed the same. I remember wondering what had caused their deaths. They were so young."

"Attaroa caused their deaths," S'Armuna said. "And the one you weren't sure of? That was her own child."

They heard a sound and turned as one toward the entrance of S'Armuna's earthlodge.

31

Ayoung woman stood in the entrance passage of the earthlodge, looking nervously at the three people within. Jondalar noticed immediately that she was quite young, hardly more than a girl; Ayla noticed that she was quite pregnant.

"What is it, Cavoa?" S'Armuna said.

"Epadoa and her hunters just returned, and Attaroa is yelling at her."

"Thank you for telling me," the older woman said, then turned back to her guests. "The walls of this earthlodge are so thick that it is hard to hear anything beyond them. Perhaps we should go out there."

They hurried out, past the pregnant young woman, who tried to pull back to let them by. Ayla smiled at her. "Not wait much more?" she said in S'Armunai.

Cavoa smiled nervously, then looked down.

Ayla thought she seemed frightened and unhappy, which was unusual for an expectant mother, but then, she reasoned, most women expecting their first were a little nervous. As soon as they stepped outside, they heard Attaroa.

". . . tell me you found where they camped. You missed your chance! You're not much of a Wolf Woman if you can't even track," the headwoman railed in loud derision.

Epadoa stood tight-lipped, anger flaring from her eyes, but made no reply. A crowd had gathered, not too closely, but the young woman dressed in wolf skins noticed that most of them had turned to look in another direction. She glanced to see what had commanded their attention, and she was startled at the sight of the blond woman coming toward them, followed, even more surprisingly, by the tall man. She had never known a man to return once he got away.

"What are you doing here?" Epadoa blurted.

"I told you. You missed your chance," Attaroa sneered. "They came back on their own."

"Why shouldn't we be here?" Ayla said. "Weren't we invited to a feast?" S'Armuna translated.

"The feast is not ready yet. Tonight," Attaroa said to the visitors, dismissing them curtly, then addressing her head Wolf Woman, "Come inside, Epadoa. I want to talk to you." She turned her back on all the watchers and entered her lodge. Epadoa stared at Ayla, a deep frown indenting her forehead; then she followed the headwoman.

After she was gone, Ayla looked out across the field a bit apprehensively. After all, Epadoa and the hunters were known to hunt horses. She felt relieved when she saw Whinney and Racer at the opposite end of the sloping field of dry brittle grass some distance away. She turned and studied the woods and brush on the uphill slope outside of the Camp, wishing she could see Wolf, yet glad that she could not. She wanted him to stay in hiding, but she did make a point of standing in plain sight looking in his direction, hoping that he could see her.

As the visitors walked back with S'Armuna toward her dwelling, Jondalar recalled a comment she had made earlier that had piqued his curiosity. "How did you keep Brugar away from you?" he asked. "You said he tried once to beat you like he did the other women; how did you stop him?"

The older woman halted and looked hard at the young man, then at the woman beside him. Ayla felt the shaman's indecision and sensed she was evaluating them, trying to decide how much to tell them.

"He tolerated me because I am a healer—he always

referred to me as a medicine woman," S'Armuna said, "but
more than anything, he feared the world of the spirits."

Her comments brought a question to Ayla's mind. "Medicine women have a unique status in the Clan," she said,
"but they are only healers. Mog-urs are the ones who communicate with the spirits."

"The spirits known to the flatheads, perhaps, but Brugar
feared the power of the Mother. I think he realized that She
knew the harm he did, and the evil that corrupted his spirit.
I think he feared Her retribution. When I showed him that I
could draw on Her power, he didn't bother me anymore,"
S'Armuna said.

"You can draw on Her power? How?" Jondalar asked.

S'Armuna reached inside her shirt and pulled out a small
figure of a woman, perhaps four inches high. Both Ayla and
Jondalar had seen many similar objects, usually carved out
of ivory, bone, or wood. Jondalar had even seen a few that
had been carefully and lovingly sculpted out of stone, using
only stone tools. They were Mother figures and, except for
the Clan, every group of people either of them had met, from
the Mammoth Hunters in the east to Jondalar's people to the
west, depicted some version of Her.

Some of the figures were quite rough, some were exquisitely carved; some were highly abstract, some were perfectly
proportional images of full-bodied mature women, except for
certain abstract aspects. Most of the carvings emphasized the
attributes of bountiful motherhood—large breasts, full stom-
achs, wide hips—and purposely deemphasized other characteristics. Often the arms were only suggested, or the legs
ended in a point, rather than feet, so the figure could be stuck
in the ground. And invariably they lacked facial features. The
figures were not meant to be a portrait of any particular
woman, and certainly no artist could know the face of the
Great Earth Mother. Sometimes the face was left blank, or
was given enigmatic markings, sometimes the hair was elabo-
rately styled and continued all around the head, covering the
face.

The only portrayal of a woman's face that either of them
had ever seen was the sweet and tender carving Jondalar had
made of Ayla when they were alone in her valley, not long
after they had met. But Jondalar sometimes regretted his
impulsive indiscretion. He had not meant it to be a Mother
figure; he had made it because he had fallen in love with

Ayla and wanted to capture her spirit. But he realized, after it was made, that it carried tremendous power. He feared it might bring her harm, particularly if it ever got into the hands of someone who wanted to have control over her. He was even afraid to destroy it, for fear that its destruction might harm her. He had decided to give it to her to keep safely. Ayla loved the small sculpture of a woman, with a carved face that bore a resemblance to her own, because Jondalar had made it. She never considered any power it might have; she just thought it was beautiful.

Although the Mother figures were often considered beautiful, they were not nubile young women made to appeal to some male canon of beauty. They were symbolic representations of Woman, of her ability to create and produce life from within her body, and to nourish it with her own bountiful fullness, and by analogy they symbolized the Great Mother Earth, Who created and produced all life from Her body, and nourished all Her children with Her wondrous bounty. The figures were also receptacles for the spirit of the Great Mother of All, a spirit that could take many forms.

But this particular Mother figure was unique. S'Armuna gave the munai to Jondalar. "Tell me what this is made of," she said.

Jondalar turned the small figure over in his hands, examining it carefully. It was endowed with pendulous breasts and wide hips, the arms were suggested only to the elbow, the legs tapered, and though a hairstyle was indicated, the face bore no markings. It was not much different in size or shape from many he had seen, but the material from which it was made was most unusual. The color was uniformly dark. When he tried, he could make no indentation in it with his fingernail. It was not made of wood or bone or ivory or antler. It was as hard as stone, but smoothly formed, with no indication or marks of carving. It was not any stone he knew.

He looked up at S'Armuna with a puzzled expression. "I have never seen anything like this before," he said.

Jondalar gave the figure to Ayla, and a shiver went through her at the moment she touched it. I should have taken my fur parka when we went out, she said to herself, but she could not help feeling that it was more than the cold that had made her feel such a sharp chill.

"That munai began as the dust of the earth," the woman stated.

"Dust?" Ayla said. "But this is stone!"

"Yes, it is now. I turned it to stone."

"You turned it to stone? How can you turn dust to stone?" Jondalar said, full of disbelief.

The woman smiled. "If I tell you, would it make you believe my power?"

"If you can convince me," the man retorted.

"I will tell you, but I won't try to convince you. You will have to convince yourself. I started with hard, dry clay from the river's edge and pounded it to dusty earth. Then I mixed in water." S'Armuna paused for a moment, wondering if she should say anything more about the mixture. She decided against it for now. "When it was the right consistency, it was shaped. Fire and hot air turned it to stone," the shaman stated, watching to see how the two young strangers would react, whether they would show disdain or be impressed, whether they would doubt or believe her.

The man closed his eyes trying to recall something. "I remember hearing . . . from a Losadunai man, I think . . . something about Mother figures made of mud."

S'Armuna smiled. "Yes, you could say we make munai out of mud. Animals, too, when we have need to call upon their spirits, many kinds of animals, bears, lions, mammoths, rhinos, horses, whatever we want. But they are mud only while they are being shaped. A figure made of the dust of the earth mixed with water, even after it has hardened, will melt in water back to the mud from which it was formed, then turn to dust, but after it is brought to life by Her sacred flame, it is forever changed. Passing through the Mother's searing heat makes the figures as hard as stone. The living spirit of the fire makes them endure."

Ayla saw the fire of excitement in the woman's eyes, and it reminded her of Jondalar's excitement when he was first developing the spear-thrower. She realized that S'Armuna was reliving the thrill of discovery, and it convinced her.

"They are brittle, even more than flint," the woman continued. "The Mother Herself has shown how they can be broken, but water will not change them. A munai made of mud, once touched by Her living fire, can stay outside in the rain and snow, can even soak in water and will never melt."

"You do indeed command the power of the Mother," Ayla said.

The woman hesitated an instant, then asked, "Would you like to see?"

"Oh, yes, I would," Ayla said at the same time as Jondalar replied, "Yes, I'd be very interested."

"Then come, I will show you."

"Can I get my parka?" Ayla said.

"Of course," S'Armuna said. "We should all put warmer clothes on, although if we were having the Fire Ceremony, it would be so hot that if you were anywhere near it, you would not need furs, not even on a day like this. Everything is nearly ready. We would have made the fire and begun the ceremony tonight, but it takes time, and the proper concentration. We'll wait until tomorrow. Tonight we have an important feast to attend."

S'Armuna stopped for a moment and closed her eyes, as though listening, or considering a thought that had occurred to her. "Yes, a very important feast," she repeated, looking straight at Ayla. Does she know the danger that threatens her? the shaman wondered. If she is who I think, she must.

They ducked into the shaman's lodge and slipped on their outer garments. Ayla noticed the young woman had left. Then S'Armuna led them some distance beyond her dwelling to the farthest edge of the settlement, toward a group of women working around a rather innocuous construction that resembled a small earthlodge with a sloped roof. The women were bringing dried dung, wood, and bone into the small structure, materials for a fire, Ayla realized. She recognized the pregnant young woman among them and smiled at her. Cavoa smiled shyly back.

S'Armuna went into the low entrance of the small structure, ducking her head, then turned and beckoned to the visitors when they held back, not sure if they were supposed to follow. Inside, a fireplace with lambent flames licking at glowing coals kept the small, somewhat circular anteroom quite warm. Separate piles of bone, wood, and dung filled almost the entire left half of the space. Along the right curved wall were several rough shelves, flattish shoulder and pelvic bones of mammoths supported by stones, displaying many small objects.

They moved closer and were surprised to see that the objects were figurines that had been shaped and molded out of muddy clay and left to dry. Several of the figures were of women, Mother figures, but some of them were not complete, just the distinguishing parts of women, the lower half of the body, including the legs, for example, or the breasts. On other shelves were animals, again not always in their complete form, heads of lions, and of bears, and the distinctive shapes of mammoths with high domed heads, humped withers, and sloping backs.

The figurines seemed to have been made by different people; some were quite crude, showing little artistic skill, other objects were sophisticated in concept and well made. Though neither Ayla nor Jondalar understood why the molders of the pieces made the particular shapes they did, they felt that each was inspired by some individual reason or feeling.

Opposite the entrance was a smaller opening that led to an enclosed space within the structure, which had been scooped out of the loess soil of a hillside. Except that it opened into the side, it reminded Ayla of a large ground oven, the kind that was dug into the earth, heated with hot rocks, and used to cook food, but she felt that no food had ever been cooked in this oven. When she went to look inside, she saw a fireplace within the second room.

From the bits of charred material in the ash, she realized bone was burned as fuel, and, looking closer, she recognized that it was a firepit similar to the ones used by the Mamutoi, but even deeper. Ayla looked around, wondering where the indrawing air vent was. In order to burn bone, a very hot fire was needed, which required that air be forced in. The Mamutoi firepits were fed by the constantly blowing wind outside, brought in through trench-vents that were controlled by dampers. Jondalar examined the interior of the second room closely and drew similar conclusions; from the color and hardness of the walls, he was sure that very hot fires had been sustained within the space for long periods of time. He guessed that the small clay objects on the shelves were destined for the same treatment.

The man had been right when he said he had never before seen anything like the Mother figure S'Armuna showed him. The figure, made by the woman standing in front of him, had not been manufactured by modifying—carving or shaping or polishing—a material that occurred naturally. It was made of ceramic, fired clay, and it was the first material ever created by human hand and human intelligence. The heating chamber was not a cooking oven, it was a kiln.

And the first kiln ever devised was not invented for the purpose of making useful waterproof containers. Long before pottery, small ceramic sculptures were fired into impermeable hardness. The figures they had seen on the shelves resembled animals and humans, but the images of women—no men were made, only women—and other living creatures were not considered actual portrayals. They were symbols, metaphors, meant to represent more than they showed, to suggest an analogy, a spiritual similarity. They were art; art came before utility.

Jondalar indicated the space that would be heated, and he said to the shaman, "This is the place where the Mother's sacred fire burns?" It was as much statement as question.

S'Armuna nodded, knowing he believed her now. The woman had known before she saw the place; it had taken the man a little longer.

Ayla was glad when the woman led them out of the place. She didn't know if it was the heat from the fire inside the small space, or the clay objects, or something else, but she had begun to feel quite uneasy. She sensed it could be dangerous in there.

"How did you discover this?" Jondalar asked, waving his arm to take in the entire complex of ceramic objects and kiln.

"The Mother led me to it," the woman said.

"I'm certain of that, but how?" he asked again.

S'Armuna smiled at his persistence. It seemed appropriate that a son of Marthona would want to understand. "The first idea came when we were building an earthlodge," she said. "Do you know how we make them?"

"I think so. Yours seem to be similar to the Mamutoi lodges, and we helped Talut and the others make an addition to Lion Camp," Jondalar said. "They started with the supporting frame made of mammoth bones, and over that attached a thick thatch of willow withes, followed by another thatch of grasses, and reeds. Then a layer of sod. On top of that they spread a coating slurry of river clay, which got very hard when it dried."

"That is essentially what we do," S'Armuna said. "It was when we were adding that last coating of clay that the Mother revealed the first part of Her secret to me. We were finishing up the final section, but it was getting dark, so we built a big fire. The clay slurry was thickening, and some of it was accidentally dropped in the fire. It was a hot fire, using a lot of bone for fuel, and we kept it going most of the night. In the morning, Brugar told me to clean out the fireplace, and I found some of the clay had hardened. I noticed, in particular, a piece that resembled a lion.''

"Ayla's protective totem is a lion," Jondalar commented.

The shaman glanced at her, then nodded as though to herself as she continued. "When I discovered that the lion figure didn't soften in water, I decided to try to make more. It took a lot of trying, and other hints from the Mother, before I finally worked it out.''

"Why are you telling us your secrets? Showing us your power?'' Ayla asked.

The question was so direct that it caught the woman off guard, but then she smiled. "Do not imagine I am telling you all my secrets. I am only showing you the obvious. Brugar thought he knew my secrets, too, but he soon learned.''

"I'm sure Brugar must have been aware of your trials," Ayla said. "You can't make a hot fire without everyone knowing about it. How were you able to keep secrets from him?''

"At first he didn't really care what I was doing, so long as I supplied my own fuel, until he saw some of the results. Then he thought he would make figures himself, but he did not know all that the Mother had revealed to me.'' The smile of the One Who Served showed her sense of vindication and triumph. "The Mother rejected his efforts with great fury. Brugar's figures burst apart with loud noises and broke into many pieces when he tried to fire them. The Great Mother flung them away with such speed that they caused painful injuries to the people close by. Brugar feared my power after that, and he stopped trying to control me.''

Ayla could imagine being inside the small anteroom with pieces of red-hot clay flying around at great speeds. "But that still doesn't explain why you are telling us so much about your power. It's possible that someone else who can understand the ways of the Mother could learn your secrets.''

S'Armuna nodded. She had almost expected as much from the woman, and she had already decided that complete openness would be the best course to follow. "You're right, of course. I do have a reason. I need your help. With this magic, the Mother has given me great power, even over

Attaroa. She fears my magic, but she is shrewd and unpredictable, and someday she will overcome her fear, I'm sure
of it. Then she will kill me.'' The woman looked at Jondalar.
''My death would not be very important, except to me. It's
the rest of my people, this whole Camp, that I fear the most
for. When you talked about Marthona passing the leadership
on to her son, it made me realize how bad things have
become. I know Attaroa would never willingly turn over leadership to anyone, and by the time she is gone, I'm afraid
there may be no Camp left.''

''What makes you so certain? If she is so unpredictable,
couldn't she just as easily grow tired of it all?'' Jondalar asked.

''I'm certain because she has already killed one person to
whom she might have passed on her leadership, her own
child.''

''She killed her child?!'' Jondalar said. ''When you said
Attaroa caused the death of the three young people, I assumed
it was an accident.''

''It was not an accident. Attaroa poisoned them, though
she doesn't admit to it.''

''Poisoned her own child! How could anyone kill her own
child?'' Jondalar said. ''And why?''

''Why? For plotting to help a friend. Cavoa, the young
woman you met. She was in love with a man and was planning to run away with him. Her brother was trying to help
them, too. All four were caught. Attaroa spared Cavoa only
because she was pregnant, but she has threatened that if the
baby is a boy, she will kill them both.''

''No wonder she seems so unhappy and afraid,'' Ayla
said.

''I must also be held responsible,'' S'Armuna said, the
blood draining from her face as she said the words.

''You! What did you have against those young people?''
Jondalar said.

''I had nothing against them. Attaroa's child was my acolyte, almost like my own child. I feel for Cavoa, hurt for
her, but just as surely as if I had fed them the poison myself,
I am responsible for their deaths. If it were not for me,
Attaroa would not have known where to get the poison and
how to use it.''

They could both see that the woman was obviously distraught, though she controlled it well.

''But to kill her own child,'' Ayla said, shaking her head

as if to rid herself of the idea. She was horror-stricken by the mere thought. "How could she?"

"I don't know. I will tell you what I do know, but it is a long story. I think we should go back to my lodge," S'Armuna suggested, looking around. She did not want to spend any more time talking about Attaroa in such a public place.

Ayla and Jondalar followed her back to her earthlodge, doffed their outdoor clothes, then stood by the fire while the older woman added more fuel and cooking stones for hot tea. When they were settled with the warming herbal drink, S'Armuna paused to collect her thoughts.

"It's hard to know where it all began, probably with the early difficulties of Attaroa and Brugar, but it didn't stop there. Even when Attaroa was far along in her pregnancy, Brugar continued to beat her. When she went into labor, he did not send for me. I only knew about it when I heard her crying out in pain. I went to her, but he refused to let me attend her when she gave birth. It was not an easy delivery, and he would allow nothing to help her with the pain. I am convinced he wanted to watch her suffer. Apparently the baby was born with some deformity. My guess is that it was caused by all the beatings he gave Attaroa, and though it wasn't obvious at birth, it soon became apparent that the spine of the child was bent and weak. I was never allowed to make an examination, so I'm not sure, but there may have been other problems," S'Armuna said.

"Was her child a boy or a girl?" Jondalar asked, realizing it hadn't been made clear.

"I don't know," S'Armuna declared.

"I don't understand. How can you not know?" Ayla said.

"No one did, except Brugar and Attaroa, and for some reason, they kept it a secret. Even as an infant, the child was never allowed to appear in public without clothes, the way most babies and young children are, and they chose a name with neither a male nor a female ending. The child was called Omel," the woman explained.

"Did the child never say?" Ayla asked.

"No. Omel kept the secret, too. I think Brugar may have threatened dire consequences to them both if the child's gender was ever revealed," S'Armuna said.

"There must have been some hint, especially as the child grew older. The body that was buried appeared to be of adult size," Jondalar said.

"Omel did not shave, but could have been a male late in developing, and it was hard to tell if breasts developed. Omel wore loose clothing that disguised the shape. Omel did grow to be quite tall for a female, in spite of the crooked spine, but quite thin. Perhaps it was because of the weakness, but Attaroa herself is very tall, and there was a certain delicacy there that men don't usually have."

"Did you have no sense of the child as it was growing up?" Ayla asked.

The woman is perceptive, S'Armuna thought, then nodded. "In my heart, I always thought of Omel as a girl, but perhaps that is what I wanted. Brugar wanted people to think of the child as male."

"You are probably right about Brugar," Ayla said. "In the Clan, every man wants his mate to have sons. He thinks of himself as less than a man if she doesn't have at least one. It means his totem spirit is weak. If the infant was a girl, Brugar might have been trying to hide the fact that his mate had given birth to a female," Ayla explained, then paused and considered a different point of view. "But deformed newborns are usually taken away and left exposed. So it could be that if the baby was born deformed, especially if it was a boy and unable to learn the necessary hunting skills required of a man, Brugar might have wanted to hide that."

"It's not easy to interpret his motivations, but whatever they were, Attaroa went along with him."

"But how did Omel die? And the two young men?" Jondalar asked.

"It's a strange, complicated story," S'Armuna said, not wanting to be rushed. "In spite of all the problems, and secrecy, the child became Brugar's favorite. Omel was the only person he never struck or tried to hurt in some way. I was glad, but I often wondered why."

"Did he suspect that he might have caused the deformity because he beat Attaroa so much before birth?" Jondalar asked. "Was he trying to make up for it?"

"Perhaps, but Brugar laid the blame on Attaroa. He often told her she was an inadequate woman who could not deliver a perfect baby. Then he'd become angry and beat her. But his beatings were no longer a prelude to Pleasures with his mate. Instead he demeaned Attaroa and showered affection on the child. Omel began to treat Attaroa the same way that he did, and as the woman felt more estranged, she became jealous of her own offspring, jealous of the affection Brugar showed the child, and even more of the love Omel felt for Brugar.''

"That would have been very hard to bear,'' Ayla said.

"Yes, Brugar had discovered a new way to cause Attaroa pain, but she wasn't the only one who suffered because of him,'' S'Armuna continued. ''As time went on, all the women were treated worse and worse, by Brugar and the other men. The men who tried to resist his ways were sometimes beaten, too, or they were forced out. Finally, after a particularly bad occasion that left Attaroa with a broken arm and several broken ribs from being jumped on and kicked, she rebelled. She swore she would kill him, and she begged me to give her something to do it with.''

"Did you?'' Jondalar asked, unable to restrain his curiosity.

"One Who Serves the Mother learns many secrets, Jondalar, often dangerous secrets, especially one who has studied with the zelandonia,'' S'Armuna explained. ''But those who are admitted into the Motherhood must swear by the Sacred Caves and the Elder Legends that the secrets will not be misused. One Who Serves the Mother gives up name and identity, and takes on the name and identity of her people, becomes the link between the Great Earth Mother and Her children, and the means by which Earth's Children communicate with the world of the spirits. Therefore, to Serve the Mother means to serve Her children as well.''

"I understand that,'' Jondalar said.

"But you may not understand that the people become engraved on the spirit of One Who Serves. The need to consider their welfare becomes very strong, second only to the needs of the Mother. It is often a matter of leadership. Not directly, usually, but in the sense of showing the way. One Who Serves the Mother becomes a guide to understanding, and to finding the meaning inherent in the unknown. Part of the training is to learn the lore, the knowledge to enable the One to interpret the signs, visions, and dreams sent to Her children. There are tools to help, and ways to seek guidance from the world of the spirits, but ultimately it all comes down to the One's own judgment. I wrestled with the thought of how best to Serve, but I'm afraid my judgment was clouded by my own bitterness and anger. I came back here hating men, and watching Brugar I learned to hate them more.''

"You said that you felt responsible for the death of the

three young people. Did you teach her about poisons?'' Jondalar asked, unable to let it go.

"I taught Attaroa many things, Marthona's son, but she was not training to be One Who Serves. However, she has a quick mind and is able to learn more than may be intended . . . but I also knew that.'' S'Armuna stopped then, stopped just short of admitting to a grievous transgression, making it clear, but allowing them to draw their own conclusions. She waited until she saw Jondalar frown with concern and Ayla nod in acknowledgment.

"In any case, I did help Attaroa establish her power over the men in the beginning—maybe I wanted power over them myself. In truth, I did more than that. I prodded and encouraged her, convinced her that the Great Earth Mother wanted women to lead, and I helped her to convince the women, or most of them. After the way they had been treated by Brugar and the men, it wasn't hard. I gave her something to put the men to sleep, and I told her to put it in their favorite drink— a brew they fermented from birch sap.''

"The Mamutoi make a similar drink,'' Jondalar commented, listening with amazement.

"When the men were sleeping, the women tied them up. They were glad to do it. It was almost a game, a way of getting back at the men. But Brugar never woke up. Attaroa tried to imply that he was just more susceptible to the sleeping liquid, but I'm sure she put something else in his drink. She said she wanted to kill him, and I believe she did. She all but admits it now, but, whatever the truth is, I was the one who led her to believe that women would be better off if the men were gone. I was the one who convinced her that if there were no men, the spirits of women would have to mix with the spirits of other women to create new life, and only girl children would be born.''

"Do you really think so?'' Jondalar asked, frowning.

"I think I almost persuaded myself that I did. I didn't actually say it—I didn't want to make the Mother angry— but I know I made her think so. Attaroa thinks the pregnancy of a few women proves it.''

"She is wrong,'' Ayla said.

"Yes, of course she is, and I should have known better. The Mother was not deluded by my ruse. I know in my heart that men are here because that is how the Mother planned it. If She didn't want men, She would not have made them.

Their spirits are necessary. But if the men are weak, their spirits are not strong enough for the Mother to use. That's why so few children have been born.'' She smiled at Jondalar. ''You are such a strong young man, I would not doubt that your spirit has already been used by Her.''

''If the men were freed, I think you would find they are more than strong enough to make the women pregnant,'' Ayla said, ''with no help from Jondalar.''

The tall blond man glanced at her and grinned. ''But I'd be more than happy to help,'' he said, knowing exactly what she meant, even if he wasn't entirely sure if he shared her opinion.

''And perhaps you should,'' Ayla said. ''I just said I didn't think it would be necessary.''

Jondalar suddenly stopped smiling. It occurred to him that no matter who was right, he had no reason to think he was capable of engendering a child.

S'Armuna looked at both of them, knowing they were making reference to something that she wasn't privy to. She waited, but when it became obvious that they were waiting for her, she continued. ''I helped her, and I encouraged her, but I didn't know it would be worse with Attaroa as leader than it was with Brugar. In fact, right after he was gone, it was better . . . for the women, at least. But not for the men, and not for Omel. Cavoa's brother understood; he was a special friend of Omel. That child was the only one who grieved for him.''

''It's understandable, under the circumstances,'' Jondalar said.

''Attaroa didn't see it that way,'' S'Armuna said. ''Omel was sure that Attaroa had caused Brugar's death, became very angry and defied her, and was beaten for it. Attaroa told me once that she only wanted to make Omel understand what Brugar had done to her and the other women. Although she didn't say it, I think she thought, or hoped, that once Brugar was gone, Omel would turn to her, love her.''

''Beatings are not likely to make someone love you,'' Ayla said.

''You're right,'' the older woman said. ''Omel had never been beaten before and hated Attaroa even worse after that. They were mother and child, but they couldn't stand to be near each other, it seemed. That's when I offered to take Omel as an acolyte.''

S'Armuna stopped, picked up her cup to drink, saw it was empty, then put it down. "Attaroa seemed glad that Omel was out of her lodge. But thinking back, I realized that she took it out on the men. In fact, ever since Omel left her lodge, Attaroa has been getting worse. She has become more cruel than Brugar ever was. I should have seen it before. Instead of keeping them apart, I should have tried to find ways to reconcile them. What will she do now that Omel is gone? Killed by her own hand?"

The woman stared into the dancing air above the fire as though she were seeing something that wasn't apparent to anyone else. "Oh, Great Mother! I've been blind!" she suddenly said. "She had Ardoban crippled and put in the Holding and I know she cared for that boy. And she killed Omel and the others."

"Had him crippled?" Ayla said. "Those children in the Holding? That was done on purpose?"

"Yes, to make the boys weak, and fearful," S'Armuna said, shaking her head. "Attaroa has lost all reason. I fear for us all." Suddenly she broke down and held her face in her hands. "Where will it end? All this pain and suffering I have wrought," she sobbed.

"It was not your doing alone, S'Armuna," Ayla said. "You may have allowed it, even encouraged it, but do not take it all on yourself. The evil is Attaroa's, and perhaps belongs, too, to those who treated her so badly." Ayla shook her head. "Cruelty mothers cruelty, pain breeds pain, abuse fosters abuse."

"And how many of the young ones that she has hurt will pass it on to the next generation?" the older woman cried out, as though in pain herself. She began rocking back and forth, keening with grief. "Which of the boys behind that fence has she condemned to carry on her terrible legacy? And which of the girls who look up to her will want to be like her? Seeing Jondalar here has reminded me of my training. Of all people, I should not have allowed it. That is what makes me responsible. Oh, Mother! What have I done?"

"The question is not what you have done. It is what you can do now," Ayla said.

"I must help them. Somehow, I must help them, but what can I do?"

"It is too late to help Attaroa, but she must be stopped. It is the children and men in the Holding we must help, but first they must be freed. Then we must think of how to help them.''

S'Armuna looked at the young woman, who seemed at that moment so positive and so powerful, and wondered who she really was. The One Who Served the Mother had been made to see the damage she had caused and to know she had abused her power. She feared for her own spirit, as well as for the life of the Camp.

There was silence in the lodge. Ayla got up and picked up the bowl used to brew tea. ''Let me make tea this time. I have a very nice mixture of herbs with me,'' she said. When S'Armuna nodded without saying a word, Ayla reached for her otter-skin medicine bag.

''I've thought about those two crippled youngsters in the Holding,'' Jondalar said. ''Even if they can't walk well, they could learn to be flint knappers, or something like that, if they had someone to train them. There must be someone among the S'Armunai who could teach them. Perhaps you could find someone at your Summer Meeting who would be willing.''

''We don't go to the Summer Meetings with the other S'Armunai anymore,'' S'Armuna said.

''Why not?'' he asked.

''Attaroa doesn't want to,'' S'Armuna said, speaking in a dull monotone. ''Other people had never been especially kind to her; her own Camp barely tolerated her. After she became leader, she didn't want anything to do with anyone else. Not long after she took over, some of the Camps sent a delegation, inviting us to join them. They had somehow heard that we had many women without mates. Attaroa insulted them and sent them away, and within a few years she had alienated everyone. Now, no one comes, not kin, not friends. They all avoid us.''

''Being tied to a target post is more than an insult,'' Jondalar said.

''I told you that she's getting worse. You aren't the first. What she did to you, she has done before,'' the woman said. ''A few years ago, a man came, a visitor, on a Journey. Seeing so many women apparently alone, he became arrogant and condescending. He assumed he would not only be welcome, but in great demand. Attaroa played with him, the way a lion will play with its prey; then she killed him. She enjoyed the game so much that she began detaining all visitors. She liked to make their life miserable, then make them promises, torment them, before getting rid of them. That was her plan for you, Jondalar.''

Ayla shuddered as she added some calming and soothing medicines to her ingredients for S'Armuna's tea. ''You were right when you said she is not human. Mog-ur sometimes told of evil spirits, but I always thought they were legends, stories to frighten children into minding, and to send a shiver through everyone. But Attaroa is no legend. She is evil.''

''Yes, and when no visitors came, she began toying with the men in the Holding,'' S'Armuna kept on, as though unable to stop once she had begun to tell what she had seen and heard, but kept inside. ''She took the stronger ones first, the leaders or the rebellious ones. There are getting to be fewer and fewer men, and the ones that are left are losing their will to rebel. She keeps them half-starved, exposed to the cold and weather. She puts them in cages or ties them up. They are not even able to clean themselves. Many have died from exposure and the bad conditions. And not many children are being born to replace them. As the men die, the Camp is dying. We were all surprised when Cavoa became pregnant.''

''She must have been going into the Holding to stay with a man,'' Ayla said. ''Probably the one she fell in love with. I'm sure you know that.''

S'Armuna did know, but she wondered how Ayla knew. ''Some women do sneak in to see the men, and sometimes they bring them food. Jondalar probably told you,'' she said.

''No, I didn't tell her,'' Jondalar said. ''But I don't understand why the women allow the men to be held.''

''They fear Attaroa. A few of them follow her willingly, but most would rather have their men back. And now she is threatening to cripple their sons.''

''Tell the women the men must be set free, or no more children will be born,'' Ayla said, in tones that sent a chill through both Jondalar and S'Armuna. They turned to stare. Jondalar recognized her expression. It was the distanced, somewhat objective way she looked when her mind was occupied with someone who was sick or injured, although in this case, he saw more than her need to help. He also saw in her a cold, hard anger he had not seen before.

But the older woman saw Ayla as something else, and she interpreted her pronouncement as a prophecy, or a judgment.

After Ayla served the tea, they sat in silence together, each deeply affected. Suddenly Ayla felt a strong need to go outside and breathe the clean, crisp, cold air, and she wanted to check on the animals, but as she quietly observed S'Armuna, she didn't think it was the best time to leave just yet. She knew the older woman had been devastated, and she sensed that she needed something of meaning to cling to.

Jondalar found himself wondering about the men he had left behind in the Holding, and what they were thinking. They no doubt knew he was back but had not been put back in with them. He wished he could talk to Ebulan and S'Amodun, and reassure Doban, but he needed some reassuring himself. They were on dangerous ground, and they hadn't done anything yet, except talk. Part of him wanted to get out of there as fast as possible, but the larger part of him wanted to help. If they were going to do something, he wished they would do it soon. He hated just sitting there.

Finally, out of desperation, he said, "I want to do something for those men in the Holding. How can I help?"

"Jondalar, you already have," S'Armuna said, feeling a need to plan some strategy herself. "When you refused her, it gave the men heart, but that by itself would not have been enough. Men have resisted her before, for a while, but this was the first time a man walked away from her, and even more important, came back," S'Armuna said. "Attaroa has lost face, and that gives others hope."

"But hope doesn't get them out of there," he replied.

"No, and Attaroa will not let them out willingly. No man leaves here alive, if she can help it, although a few have gotten away, but women don't often make Journeys. You are the first who has come this way, Ayla."

"Would she kill a woman?" Jondalar asked, unconsciously moving in closer to protect the woman he loved.

"It's harder for her to justify killing a woman, or even putting her in the Holding, although many of the women here are held against their will, though they have no fence around them. She has threatened the ones they love, and they are held by their feelings for their sons or mates. That's why your life is in danger," S'Armuna said, looking directly at Ayla. "You have no ties to this place. She has no hold over you, and if she succeeds in killing you, it will make it easier for her to kill other women. I'm telling you this not only to warn you, but because of the danger to the whole Camp.

You can both still get away, and perhaps that is what you should do.''

"No, I cannot leave," Ayla said. "How can I walk away from those children? Or those men? The women will need help, too. Brugar called you a medicine woman, S'Armuna. I don't know if you know what that means, but I am a medicine woman of the Clan.''

"You are a medicine woman? I should have known,'' S'Armuna said. She wasn't entirely sure what a medicine woman was, but she had gained such respect from Brugar after he had ranked her within that classification, that she had granted the position the highest significance.

"That is why I can't go," Ayla said. "It is not so much something I choose to do; it is what a medicine woman must do, it is what she is. It is inside. A piece of my spirit is already in the next world''—Ayla reached for the amulet around her neck—"given in exchange for the spirit obligation of those people who will need my help. It's difficult to explain, but I can't allow Attaroa to abuse them anymore, and this Camp will need help after the ones in the Holding are free. I must stay, as long as I need to.''

S'Armuna nodded, feeling that she understood. It was not an easy concept to explain. She equated Ayla's fascination with healing and compassionate need to help with her own feelings about being called to Serve the Mother, and she identified with the young woman.

"We will stay as long as we can," Jondalar amended, remembering that they still had to cross a glacier that winter. "The question is, how are we going to persuade Attaroa to let the men out?''

"She fears you, Ayla," the shaman said, "and I think most of her Wolf Women do, too. Those who don't fear you are in awe of you. The S'Armunai are horse-hunting people. We hunt other animals, too, including mammoths, but we know horses. To the north there is a cliff that we have driven horses over for generations. You cannot deny your control over horses is powerful magic. It is so powerful that it is hard to believe, even seeing it.''

"There is nothing mysterious about it," Ayla snorted. "I raised the mare from the time she was a foal. I was living alone, and she was my only friend. Whinney does what I want because she wants to, because we are friends,'' she said, trying to explain.

The way she said the name was the gentle nicker that was the sound made by a horse. Traveling alone with only Jondalar and the animals for so long, she had slipped back into the habit of saying Whinney's name in its original form. The nicker coming from the woman's mouth startled S'Armuna, and the very idea of being the friend of a horse was beyond comprehension. It didn't matter that Ayla had said it wasn't magic. She had just convinced S'Armuna that it was.

"Perhaps," the woman said. But she thought, No matter how simple you try to make it, you can't stop people from wondering who you really are, and why you have come here. "People want to think, and hope, that you have come to help them," she continued. "They fear Attaroa, but I think with your help, and Jondalar's, they may be willing to stand up to her and make her free the men. They may refuse to let her intimidate them anymore."

Ayla was again feeling a strong need to get out of the lodge, which was more uncomfortable. "All this tea," she said, standing up. "I need to pass water. Can you tell me where to go, S'Armuna?" After she listened to the directions, she added, "We need to see to the horses while we're out, make sure they are comfortable. Is it all right to leave these bowls here for a while?" She had lifted a lid and was checking the contents. "It's cooling off fast. It's too bad this can't be served hot. It would be better."

"Of course, leave it," S'Armuna said, picking up her cup and drinking the last of her tea as she watched the two strangers leave.

Perhaps Ayla wasn't an incarnation of the Great Mother, and Jondalar really was Marthona's son, but the idea that someday the Mother would exact Her retribution had been weighing heavily on the One Who Served Her. After all, she was S'Armuna. She had exchanged her personal identity for the power of the spirit world, and this Camp was her charge, all the people, women and men. She had been entrusted with the care of the spiritual essence of the Camp, and Her children depended on her. Looking from the view of outsiders, of the man who had served to remind her of her calling, and the woman with unusual powers, S'Armuna knew she had failed them. She only hoped it was still possible to redeem herself and to help the Camp recover a normal, healthy life.

32

S'Armuna stepped outside her lodge and watched the two visitors as they walked away toward the edge of the Camp. She saw that Attaroa and Epadoa, standing in front of the headwoman's lodge, had turned to watch them, too. The shaman was about to go back in when she noticed Ayla suddenly changing direction and heading for the palisade. Attaroa and her chief Wolf Woman also saw her veer, and both moved forward in quick strides to intercept the blond woman. They reached the fenced enclosure almost simultaneously. The older woman arrived a moment later.

Through the cracks, Ayla looked directly into the eyes and faces of silent watchers on the other side of the sturdy poles. On close inspection, they were a sorry sight, dirty and unkempt, and dressed in ragged skins, but even worse was the stench emanating from the Holding. It was not only malodorous; to the perceptive nose of the medicine woman it was revealing. Normal body odors of healthy individuals did not bother her, even a certain amount of normal bodily wastes was not offensive, but she smelled sickness. The foetid breath of starvation, the noisome filth of excrement resulting from stomach ailments and fever, the foul odor of pus from infected, suppurating wounds, and even the putrid rot of progressed gangrene, all assaulted her senses and infuriated her.

Epadoa stepped in front of Ayla, trying to block her view, but she had seen enough. She turned and confronted Attaroa. "Why are these people held here behind this fence, like animals in a surround?"

There was a gasp of surprise from the people who were watching when they heard the translation, and they held their breaths waiting for the headwoman's reaction. No one had ever dared to ask her before.

Attaroa glared at Ayla, who stared back with dauntless anger. They were nearly equal in height, though the dark-eyed woman was a shade taller. Both were physically strong women, but Attaroa was more muscular as a natural attribute of her heredity, while Ayla had flat and wiry muscles developed from use. The headwoman was somewhat older than the stranger, more experienced, crafty, and totally unpredictable; the visitor was a skilled tracker and hunter, quick to notice details, draw conclusions, and able to react swiftly on her judgments.

Suddenly Attaroa laughed, and the familiar manic sound sent a shiver through Jondalar. "Because they deserve it!" the headwoman said.

"No one deserves that kind of treatment," Ayla retorted, before S'Armuna had a chance to translate. The woman instead respoke Ayla's comment to Attaroa.

"What do you know? You were not here. You don't know how they treated us," the dark-eyed woman said.

"Did they make you stay outside when it was cold? Did they not give you food and clothing?" Some of the women who had gathered around looked a little uneasy. "Are you any better than they were if you treat them worse than you were treated?"

Attaroa did not bother to reply to the words repeated by the shaman, but her smile was harsh and cruel.

Ayla noticed movement beyond the fence, and she saw some of the men standing aside so the two boys who had been in the lean-to could limp to the front. All the others crowded around them. It angered her even more to see the injured youngsters, and other boys cold and hungry. Then she saw that some of the Wolf Women had entered the Holding with their spears. She felt such fury that she was hardly able to suppress it, and she addressed the women directly.

"And did these boys also treat you badly? What did they do to you to justify this?" S'Armuna made sure all could understand.

"Where are the mothers of these children?" she asked Epadoa.

The leader of the Wolf Women glanced at Attaroa after hearing the words in her own language, looking for some kind of direction, but the headwoman only looked back with her cruel smile, as though waiting to hear what she would say.

"Some are dead," Epadoa said.

"Killed when they tried to run away with their sons," one of the women from the crowd standing nearby said. "The rest are afraid to do anything for fear their children will be hurt."

Ayla looked and saw it was an old woman who had spoken, and Jondalar noticed it was the one who had grieved so loudly at the funeral of the three young people. Epadoa shot her a threatening look.

"What more can you do to me, Epadoa?" the woman said, stepping boldly to the forefront. "You've already taken my son, and my daughter will soon be gone, one way or another. I'm too old to care if I live or die."

"They betrayed us," Epadoa said. "Now they all know what will happen if they try to run away."

Attaroa gave no sign of approval or disapproval to indicate that Epadoa had voiced her own feelings. Instead, with a bored look, she turned her back on the tense scene and walked to her lodge, leaving Epadoa and her Wolf Women to guard the Holding. But she stopped and spun around when she heard a loud, shrill whistle. A fleeting expression of dread replaced her cold, cruel smile when she saw both horses, who had been almost out of sight at the far edge of the field, galloping toward Ayla. She quickly entered her earthlodge.

Feelings of stunned amazement filled the rest of the settlement as the blond woman, and the man with even lighter yellow hair, leaped on the backs of the animals and galloped away. Most of those remaining wished they could leave as quickly and easily, and many wondered if they would ever see the two again.

"I wish we could keep on going," Jondalar said, after
they had slowed down and he had pulled Racer up alongside
Ayla and Whinney.

"I wish we could, too," she said. "That Camp is so
unbearable; it fills me with anger and sadness. I'm even angry
about S'Armuna allowing it to go on for so long, though I
pity her and understand her remorse. Jondalar, how are we
going to free those boys and men?"

"We're going to have to work that out with S'Armuna,"
Jondalar said. "I think it's obvious that most of the women
want things to change, and I'm sure many of them would
help, if they knew what to do. S'Armuna will know who
they are."

They had entered the open woods from the field, and they
rode through its cover, though in places it was quite sparse,
toward the river and then back around to the place they had
left the wolf. As soon as they neared, Ayla signaled with a
soft whistle, and Wolf bounded out to greet them, almost
beside himself with happiness. He had been watching from
the place Ayla had told him to stay, and they both gave him
praise and attention for waiting. Ayla did notice he had
hunted and brought his kill back, which meant he had left
his hiding place at least for a while. It worried her, since
they were so close to the Camp and its Wolf Women, but
she found it hard to blame him. It made her all the more
determined, however, to get him away from the hunting
women who ate wolves as soon as possible.

They walked the horses quietly back toward the river, to
the grove where they had hidden their packs. Ayla got out
one of their few remaining cakes of traveling food, broke it
in two, and gave the larger piece to Jondalar. They sat amidst
the brush, eating their snack, glad to be away from the
depressing environment of the S'Armunai Camp.

Suddenly she heard a low rumbling growl from Wolf, and
the hair on the back of Ayla's neck stood on end.

"Someone's coming," Jondalar whispered, feeling a
quick rush of alarm at the sound.

Snapped to the sharp edge of awareness by the warning,
Ayla and Jondalar scanned the area, certain that Wolf's
keener senses had detected immediate danger. Noticing the
direction Wolf's nose was pointing, Ayla looked carefully

through the screen of brush and saw two women approaching. One of them, she was almost certain, was Epadoa. She tapped Jondalar's arm and pointed. He nodded when he saw them.

"You wait, keep horses quiet," she signed to him in the silent language of the Clan. "I make Wolf hide. I go stalk women, keep women away."

"I go," Jondalar signed, shaking his head.

"Women more listen to me," Ayla replied.

Jondalar nodded reluctantly. "I watch here with spearthrower," he said with gestures. "You take spear-thrower."

Ayla nodded in agreement. "And sling," she signaled back.

With silent stealth, Ayla circled around in front of the two women, then waited. As they slowly approached, she heard them talking.

"I'm sure they came this way after they left their campsite last night, Unavoa," the head Wolf Woman said.

"But they already came to our Camp since last night. Why are we still looking here?"

"They may come back this way, and even if they don't, we may find out something about them."

"Some people are saying they disappear, or turn into birds or horses when they leave," the younger Wolf Woman said.

"Don't be silly," Epadoa said. "Didn't we find where they camped last night? Why would they have to make a camp if they could turn into animals?"

She's right, Ayla thought. At least she uses her head and thinks, and she's not really so bad at tracking. She's probably even a decent hunter; it's too bad she's so close to Attaroa.

Ayla, crouching behind bare tangled brush and yellowed knee-high grass, watched as they drew closer. At a moment when both women were looking down, she silently stood up, holding her spear-thrower poised.

Epadoa started with surprise, and Unavoa jumped back and let out a little squeal of shock when they looked up and saw the blond stranger.

"You look for me?" Ayla said, speaking in their language. "I am here."

Unavoa appeared ready to break and run, and even Epadoa seemed nervous and frightened.

"We were . . . we were hunting," Epadoa said.

"No horses here to chase over edge," Ayla said.

"We weren't hunting horses."

"I know. You hunt Ayla and Jondalar."

Her sudden appearance, and the strange quality to the way Ayla said the words in their language, made her seem exotic, from someplace far away, perhaps even from another world. She made both women want nothing more than to get as far away as possible from this woman, who seemed endowed with attributes that were more than human.

"I think these two should return to their Camp, or they may miss the big feast tonight."

The voice came from the woods, and it was speaking Mamutoi, but both women understood the language and recognized that it was Jondalar who spoke. They looked back in the direction from which his voice had come and saw the tall blond man leaning nonchalantly against the bole of a large white-barked birch, holding his spear and spear-thrower ready.

"Yes. You are right. We don't want to miss the feast," Epadoa said. Prodding her speechless young companion, she wasted no time in turning around and leaving.

When they were gone, Jondalar could not resist cracking a big grin.

The sun was descending toward late afternoon of the short winter day when Ayla and Jondalar rode back to the S'Armunai Camp. They had changed Wolf's hiding place, leaving him somewhat closer to the settlement, since it would soon be dark, and people seldom went beyond the comfort of firelight at night, though Ayla still worried that he might be captured.

S'Armuna was just leaving her lodge as they dismounted at the edge of the field, and she smiled with relief when she saw them. In spite of their promises, she couldn't help wondering if they would return. After all, why should strangers put themselves in jeopardy to help people they didn't even know? Their own kin had not even come for the past several years to find out if all was well with them. Of course, friends and kin had not been made welcome the last time they came.

Jondalar removed Racer's halter so he would not be encumbered in any way, and both gave the horses friendly slaps on the rump to encourage them to move away from the Camp. S'Armuna walked over to meet the two.

"We are just finishing our preparations for the Fire Ceremony tomorrow. We always start a warming fire the night
before; would you like to come and warm up?" the woman
said.

"It is cold," Jondalar said. They both walked beside her
to the kiln on the other side of the Camp.

"I've found a way to heat the food you brought, Ayla.
You said it would be better warm, and I'm sure you are right.
It smells wonderful." S'Armuna smiled.

"How can you heat such a thick mixture in baskets?"

"I'll show you," the woman said, ducking into the anteroom of the small structure. Ayla followed her, with Jondalar
right behind. Although no fire burned in the small fireplace,
it was quite warm inside. S'Armuna went directly to the
opening of the second chamber and removed the mammoth
shoulder bone that was covering it. The air from inside was
hot, hot enough to cook, Ayla thought. She looked in and
saw that a fire had been started inside the chamber, and just
inside the opening, some distance from the fire itself, were
her two baskets.

"It does smell good!" Jondalar said.

"You have no idea how many people have been asking
when the feast is going to start," S'Armuna said. "They can
even smell it in the Holding. Ardemun came to me and asked
if the men are really going to get a share. It's not only this.
I'm surprised, but Attaroa did tell the women to prepare food
for a feast, and to make enough for everyone. I can't remember when we last had a real feast . . . but we haven't had
much reason to celebrate. It makes me wonder what we have
to celebrate tonight."

"Visitors," Ayla said. "You are honoring visitors."

"Yes, visitors," the woman said. "Remember, that was
her excuse to get you to come back. I must warn you. Do
not drink or eat any food that comes from a dish that she has
not eaten from first. Attaroa knows many harmful things that
can be disguised in food. If necessary, only eat what you
have brought. I have watched it carefully."

"Even in here?" Jondalar said.

"No one dares come in here without my permission," the
One Who Served the Mother said, "but outside of this
place, be very careful. Attaroa and Epadoa have had their
heads together most of the day. They are planning something."

"And they have many to help them, all the Wolf Women.
Who can we count on to help us?" Jondalar said.

"Nearly everyone else wants to see a change," S'Armuna
said.

"But who will help?" Ayla said.

"I think we can count on Cavoa, my acolyte."

"But she's pregnant," Jondalar said.

"All the more reason," the woman said. "All the signs
indicate that she will have a boy. She will fight for the life
of her baby, as well as her own. Even if she has a girl, the
chances are Attaroa won't let her live long once the baby is
weaned, and Cavoa knows it."

"What about the woman who spoke out today?" Ayla
said.

"That was Esadoa, Cavoa's mother. I'm sure you can
count on her, but she blames me as much as Attaroa for the
death of her son."

"I remember her at the funeral," Jondalar said. "She
threw something in the grave that made Attaroa angry."

"Yes, some tools for the next world. Attaroa had forbidden anyone to give them anything that might help them in
the world of the spirits."

"I think you stood up to her."

S'Armuna shrugged as if to pass it off. "I told her once
the tools were given, they could not be taken back. Not even
she dared to retrieve them."

Jondalar nodded. "I'm sure all the men in the Holding
would help," he said.

"Of course, but first we have to get them out," S'Armuna
said. "The guards are being especially watchful. I don't think
anyone could even sneak in right now. In a few days, perhaps. That will give us time to talk to the women quietly.
When we know how many we can count on, then we can
work out a plan to overpower Attaroa and the Wolf Women.
We're going to have to fight them, I'm afraid. That's the
only way we'll get the men out of the Holding."

"I think you're right," Jondalar said, looking grim.

Ayla shook her head in sorrow at the thought. There had
been so much pain in this Camp already that the idea of
fighting, of causing more trouble and pain, was distressing.
She wished there was some other way.

"You said you gave Attaroa something to make the men

sleep. Couldn't you give something to Attaroa and her Wolf Women to make them sleep?'' Ayla asked.

"Attaroa is wary. She will not eat or drink anything that isn't first tasted by someone else. That was what Doban did once. Now, I think she'll just pick out one of the other children,'' S'Armuna said, glancing outside. "It's almost dark. If you are ready, I think it's time for the feast to begin.''

Ayla and Jondalar each picked up one of the baskets from the inner chamber; then the One Who Served closed it up again. Once outside, they could see that a big bonfire had been started in front of Attaroa's earthlodge.

"I wondered if she was going to invite you in, but it appears the feast is going to be eaten outside, in spite of the cold,'' S'Armuna said.

As they approached, bearing their baskets, Attaroa turned to face them. "Since you wanted to share this feast with the men, it seemed right to eat out here, so you can watch them,'' she said. S'Armuna translated, although Ayla understood the woman perfectly, and even Jondalar knew enough of their language to get the meaning of her words.

"But it is hard to see them in the dark. It would help if you built another fire on their side,'' Ayla said.

Attaroa paused a moment, then laughed, but she made no move to comply with the request.

The feast seemed to be an extravagant affair with many dishes, but the food was primarily lean meat with hardly any fat, very few vegetables or grains or filling starchy roots, and no dried fruit or hint of sweetness, not even from the inner bark of a tree. There was some of the lightly fermented brew made from birch sap, but Ayla decided she would not drink it, and she was pleased to see a woman coming around and pouring hot herb tea into cups for those who wanted it. She'd had experience with Talut's brew and knew it could cloud her judgment; tonight she wanted all her wits about her.

All in all, it was a rather meager feast, Ayla thought, although the people of the Camp would not have agreed. The food was more like the kind that might be left at the end of the season, not what should have been available in the middle of winter. A few furs had been scattered around Attaroa's raised platform near the large fire for the guests. The rest of the people were bringing their own to sit upon while they ate.

S'Armuna led Ayla and Jondalar toward Attaroa's fur-covered platform, and they stood waiting until the head-woman swaggered to her place. She was dressed in all her wolf-fur finery and necklaces of teeth, bone, ivory, and shell, decorated with bits of fur and feathers. Most interesting to Ayla was the staff she held, which was made from a straight-ened mammoth tusk.

Attaroa commanded that the food be served and, with a pointed look at Ayla, ordered that the share set aside for the men be taken into the Holding, including the bowl Ayla and Jondalar had provided. Then she sat down on her platform. Everyone else took it as a signal to sit down on their furs. Ayla noticed that the raised seat put the headwoman in an interesting position. She was above everyone else, which enabled her to see over the heads of the others and also to look down on them. Ayla recalled that there had been times when people had stood on logs or rocks when they had some-thing to say to a group that they wanted everyone to hear, but it had always been a temporary position.

It was a powerful placement Attaroa had created, Ayla realized, as she observed the unconscious postures and ges-tures of the people around. Everyone seemed to express toward Attaroa the attitude of deference that the women of the Clan did when they sat in silence in front of a man, waiting for the tap on the shoulder that gave them the right to make their thoughts known. But there was a difference that was hard to characterize. In the Clan, she never sensed resentment from the women, which she felt here, or lack of respect from the men. It was just the way things were done, inherent behavior, not forced or coerced, and it served to make sure that both parties were paying close attention to the communication between them, which was expressed primarily with signs and gestures.

While they were waiting to be served, Ayla tried to get a better look at the headwoman's staff. It was similar to the Speaking Staff used by Talut and the Lion Camp, except the carvings were very unusual, not at all like Talut's staff, yet they seemed so familiar. Ayla recalled that Talut brought out the Speaking Staff for various occasions including ceremon-ies, but particularly during meetings or arguments.

The Speaking Staff invested the one who held it with the right to speak, and allowed each person to make a statement, or express a point of view without interruption. The next person with something to say then asked for the staff. In principle, only the one holding the Speaking Staff was supposed to talk, although at Lion Camp, especially in the midst of a heated discussion or argument, people didn't always wait their turn. But with some reminding, Talut was usually able to get the people to abide by the principle, so that everyone who wanted to was given a chance to have a say.

"That is a most unusual and beautifully carved Speaking Staff," Ayla said. "May I see it?"

Attaroa smiled when she heard S'Armuna's translation. She moved it toward Ayla and closer to the firelight, but she did not give it up. It was soon obvious that she had no intention of letting it go at all, and Ayla sensed that the headwoman was using the Speaking Staff to invest herself with its power. As long as Attaroa held it, anyone who wanted to speak had to request permission from her, and by extension, other actions—when to serve the food, or when to begin eating, for example—waited on her permission. Like her raised platform, Ayla realized, it was a means of affecting, and controlling, the way People behaved toward her. It gave the younger woman much to think about.

The staff itself was quite unusual. It was not newly carved, that much was obvious. The color of the mammoth ivory had begun to turn creamy, and the area where it was usually held was gray and shiny, caused by the accumulated dirt and oils of the many hands that had held it. It had been used by many generations.

The design carved into the straightened tusk was a geometric abstraction of the Great Earth Mother, formed by concentric ovals to shape the pendulous breasts, rounded belly, and voluptuous thighs. The circle was the symbol for all, everything, the totality of the known and unknown worlds, and symbolized the Great Mother of All. The concentric circles, especially the way they were used to suggest the important motherly elements, reinforced the symbolism.

The head was an inverted triangle, with the point forming the chin, and the base, curved slightly into a domelike shape, at the top. The downward-pointing triangle was the universal symbol for Woman; it was the outward shape of her generative organ and therefore also symbolized motherhood and the Great Mother of All. The area of the face contained a horizontal series of double parallel bars, joined by laterally incised lines going from the pointed chin up to the position of the eyes. The larger space between the top set of double horizontal lines and the rounded lines that paralleled the curved top was filled in with three sets of double lines that were perpendicular, joining where eyes would usually be.

But the geometric designs were not a face. Except that the inverted triangle was placed in the position of a head, the carved markings would not even have suggested a face. The awesome countenance of the Great Mother was too much for an ordinary human to behold. Her powers were so great that Her look alone could overwhelm. The abstract symbolism of the figure on Attaroa's Speaking Staff conveyed that sense of power with subtlety and elegance.

Ayla remembered from the training she had begun with Mamut the deeper meaning of some of the symbols. The three sides of the triangle—three was Her primary number—represented the three major seasons of the year, spring, summer, and winter, although two additional minor seasons were also recognized, fall and midwinter, the seasons which signaled changes to come, making five. Five, Ayla had learned, was Her hidden, power number, but the three-sided, inverted triangles were understood by everyone.

She recalled the triangular shapes on the bird-woman carvings, representing the transcendent Mother changing into Her bird shape, that Ranec had made . . . Ranec . . . Suddenly, Ayla remembered where she had seen the figure on Attaroa's Speaking Staff before. Ranec's shirt! The beautiful, creamy white, soft leather shirt that he had worn at her adoption ceremony. It had been stunning partly because of its unusual style with its tapered body and wide flaring sleeves, and because the color looked so good with his brown skin, but mostly because of its decoration.

It had been embroidered with brightly dyed porcupine quills and threads of sinew with an abstract Mother figure that could have been copied directly from the carving on the staff that Attaroa held. It had the same concentric circles, the same triangular head; the S'Armunai must be the distant relatives of the Mamutoi that Ranec's shirt had originally come from, she realized. If they had taken the northern route that Talut had suggested, they would have had to pass by this Camp.

When they had left, Nezzie's son, Danug, the young man who was growing into the image of Talut, had told her that someday he would make a Journey to the Zelandonii to visit her and Jondalar. What if Danug did decide to make such a Journey when he got a few years older, and what if he came this way? What if Danug, or any other Mamutoi, got caught by Attaroa's camp and came to harm? The thought strengthened her resolve to help these people put an end to Attaroa's power.

The headwoman pulled back the staff Ayla had been studying and turned to her with a wooden bowl. "Since you are our honored visitor, and since you have provided an accompaniment to this feast that is collecting so many compliments," Attaroa said, her tone heavy with sarcasm, "let me offer you a taste of the specialty of one of our women." The bowl was full of mushrooms, but since they were cut up and cooked, there was no way to identify the variety.

S'Armuna translated, adding a cautionary, "Be careful."

But Ayla needed neither the translation nor the warning. "I don't want any mushrooms right now," she said.

Attaroa laughed when she heard Ayla's words repeated, as though she had expected such an answer. "Too bad," she said, dipping into the bowl with her hand and lifting out a large mouthful. When she had swallowed enough to speak, she added, "These are delicious!" She ate several more mouthfuls, then handed the bowl to Epadoa, smiled knowingly, and downed her cup of birch brew.

As the meal progressed, she drank several more cups and was beginning to show the effects; she was becoming loud and insulting. One of the Wolf Women who'd been left guarding the Holding—they had exchanged places with other guards so that everyone could share in the feast—approached Epadoa, who then came to Attaroa and spoke to her in a whisper.

"It seems Ardemun wants to come out and bring thanks from the men for this feast," Attaroa said, and she laughed with derision. "I'm sure I am not the one they want to thank. It is our most honored visitor." She turned to Epadoa. "Bring the old man out."

The guard went back and soon Ardemun was limping toward the fire from the gate of the wooden fence. Jondalar was surprised at how glad he was to see him, and he realized that he hadn't seen any men since he had left the Holding. He wondered how they all were.

"So the men want to thank me for this feast?" the headwoman said.

"Yes, S'Attaroa. They asked me to come and tell you."

"Tell me, old man, why do I have trouble believing you?"

Ardemun knew better than to reply. He simply stood there, looking down at the ground, as though he wished he could disappear.

"Worthless! He's worthless! No fight in him at all," Attaroa spat with disgust. "Just like all of them. They're all worthless." She turned to Ayla. "Why do you keep yourself tied to that man?" she said, indicating Jondalar. "Are you not strong enough to be free of him?"

Ayla waited until S'Armuna translated, which gave her time to consider her answer. "I choose to be with him. I lived alone long enough," Ayla replied.

"What good will he be to you when he becomes weak and feeble like Ardemun there," Attaroa said, casting a sneering glance at the old man. "When his tool is too limp to give you Pleasure, he'll be as worthless as the rest of them."

Again Ayla waited for the older woman, though she understood the headwoman. "No one stays young forever. There is more to a man than his tool."

"But you should get rid of that one; he won't last long." She motioned toward the tall blond man. "He looks strong, but it's all show. He did not have the strength to take Attaroa, or perhaps he was just afraid." She laughed and swallowed another cupful of brew, then turned to Jondalar. "That was it! Admit it, you fear me. That's why you couldn't take me."

Jondalar also understood her, and it made him angry. "There is a difference between fear and lack of desire, Attaroa. You cannot force desire. I did not share the Mother's Gift because I did not want you," Jondalar said.

S'Armuna glanced at Attaroa and cringed before she began the translation, almost forcing herself not to modify his words.

"That's a lie!" Attaroa screamed, incensed. She stood up and hovered over him. "You feared me, Zelandonii. I could see it. I've fought men before, and you were even afraid to fight me."

Jondalar stood up, too, and Ayla with him. Several of her women closed in around them.

"These people are our guests," S'Armuna said, also getting up. "They were invited to share our feast. Have we forgotten how to treat visitors?"

"Yes, of course. Our guests," Attaroa said scornfully. "We must be courteous and hospitable to visitors, or the woman won't think well of us. I'll show you how much I care what she thinks of us. You both left here without my permission. Do you know what we do to people who run away from here? We kill them! Just like I will kill you," the headwoman screeched, as she lunged for Ayla with a sharpened pointed fibula of a horse in her hand, a formidable dagger.

Jondalar tried to intercede, but Attaroa's Wolf Women had surrounded him, and their spear points were pushed to his chest, stomach, and back so hard that they had pierced the skin and drawn blood. Before he knew it, his hands were tied behind his back, as Attaroa knocked Ayla down, straddled her, and raised a dagger to her throat, without a hint of the drunkenness she had shown before.

She had planned it all along, Jondalar realized. While they had been talking, trying to think of ways to blunt Attaroa's power, she had been planning to kill them. He felt so stupid, he should have known. He had sworn to himself he would protect Ayla. Instead he was watching helplessly, full of fear for her, while the woman he loved tried to fight off her attacker. That was why everyone feared Attaroa. She killed without hesitation or remorse.

Ayla had been taken completely by surprise. She'd had no time to reach for a knife or a sling, or anything, and she was not experienced in fighting with people. She had never fought anyone in her life. But Attaroa was on top of her, with a sharp dagger in her hand, trying to kill her. Ayla grabbed the headwoman's wrist and struggled to hold her arm away. Ayla was strong, but Attaroa was both strong and cunning, and she was pushing down, against Ayla's resistance, forcing the sharp tip toward Ayla's throat.

Instinctively, Ayla rolled over at the last moment, but the dagger grazed her neck, leaving a line of red welling up, before the weapon was plunged halfway into the ground. And Ayla was still pinned by the woman whose demented anger added to her strength. Attaroa yanked the dagger out of the ground, then hit the blond woman, stunning her, straddled her once again, and pulled back to plunge her dagger down.

33

Jondalar closed his eyes, unable to watch the violent final moment of Ayla's life. His own life would have no meaning to him when she was gone . . . So why was he standing there afraid of threatening spears when he didn't care if he lived or died? His hands were tied, but his legs weren't. He could run over there and maybe knock Attaroa away.

He heard a commotion near the gate of the Holding at the instant he decided to ignore the sharp spears and try to help Ayla. The noise from the Holding distracted his guards as he unexpectedly lurched forward, pushed aside their spears, and ran toward the two women struggling on the ground.

Suddenly a dark blur dashed past the watching people, brushed against his leg, and leaped at Attaroa. The momentum of the attack knocked the headwoman backward as sharp fangs clamped around her throat, tearing through the skin. The headwoman found herself on her back on the ground, trying to fight off a fury of snarling teeth and fur. She managed to make a stab into the heavy, furry body before she dropped the dagger, but it only evoked a deadly snarl and a tighter grip of the viselike jaws pressing together in a stranglehold that cut off her air.

Attaroa tried to scream as she felt darkness overcoming her, but at that moment a sharp canine tooth severed an artery, and the sound that emerged was a horrible, suffocating gurgle. Then, the tall, handsome woman fell limp and fought no more. Still snarling, Wolf shook her, making sure there was no more resistance.

"Wolf!" Ayla cried, overcoming her shock and sitting up. "Oh, Wolf."

As the wolf let go, blood spurted from the severed artery and sprayed him. He crept toward Ayla with his tail tucked between his legs, whining apologetically, asking for her approval. The woman had told him to stay in hiding, and he knew he had acted against her wishes. When he saw the attack and understood that she was in danger, he had sprung to her defense, but now he wasn't sure how his misbehavior would be received. More than anything, he hated being scolded by this woman.

Ayla opened her arms and reached for him. Quick to realize that he had acted correctly and was forgiven for his transgression, he rushed to her with joy. She hugged him, burying her face in his fur, while tears of relief ran from her eyes.

"Wolf, you saved my life," she sobbed. He licked her, staining her face with Attaroa's warm, wet blood that was still on his muzzle.

The people of the Camp backed away from the scene, staring open-mouthed with incomprehension and wonder at the blond woman who was holding in her arms a large wolf that had just killed another woman in a furious assault. She had addressed the animal with the Mamutoi word for *wolf*, but it was similar to their own name for the meat-eating hunter, and they knew she was talking to him, just as though he could understand her, the same way she talked to the horses.

No wonder this stranger had shown no fear of Attaroa. Her magic was so powerful that she could not only make horses do her bidding, she could command wolves! The man had not shown concern either, they realized, when they saw him drop to his knees beside the woman and the wolf. He had even ignored the spears of the Wolf Women, who had also stepped back a few paces and stood gaping. Suddenly

they saw a man behind Jondalar, and he had a knife! Where
did the knife come from?

"Let me cut these cords for you, Jondalar," Ebulan said,
slashing the bindings.

Jondalar glanced around as he felt his hands come free.
Other men were mixed through the crowd, and more were
coming from the direction of the Holding. "Who let you
out?"

"You did," Ebulan said.

"What do you mean? I was tied up."

"But you gave us the knives . . . and the courage to
try," Ebulan said. "Ardemun sneaked up behind the guard
at the gate and hit her with his staff. Then we cut the cords
that kept the gate closed up. Everyone was watching the fight,
and then the wolf came . . ." His voice trailed off and he
shook his head as he watched the woman and the wolf.

Jondalar didn't notice that the man was too overcome to
continue. Something else was more important. "Are you all
right, Ayla? Did she hurt you?" he said, taking both the
woman and the wolf in his arms. The animal turned from
licking Ayla to licking him.

"A little scratch on the neck. It's nothing," she said,
clinging to the man and the excited wolf, "and I think Wolf
was cut, but it doesn't seem to bother him."

"I would never have let you come back here if I'd thought
she would try to kill you, Ayla, right here at the feast. But
I should have known. I was stupid not to realize how dangerous she was," he said, holding her close.

"No, you're not stupid. It didn't even occur to me that
she would try to attack me, and I didn't know how to defend
myself. If it hadn't been for Wolf . . ." They both looked
at the animal, full of gratitude.

"I have to admit, there have been times on this Journey
when I wanted to leave Wolf behind, Ayla. I thought he was
an extra burden, making our travels more difficult. When I
found that you had gone to look for him after crossing the
Sister, I was so angry. The thought that you had put yourself
in jeopardy for this animal upset me."

Jondalar took the wolf's head in both his hands and
looked him straight in the eyes. "Wolf, I promise, I will
never leave you behind. I would risk my life to save yours,
you glorious, furious beast," the man said, roughing his fur
and rubbing behind his ears.

Wolf licked Jondalar's neck and face, and with his jaws, he grasped the exposed and trusting throat and jaw of the man, and held it gently, showing his affection. Wolf felt nearly as strongly about Jondalar as he did about Ayla, and he growled contentedly at the attention and approval he was getting from both of his humans.

But the people who were watching made sounds of wonder and awe to see the man expose his vulnerable throat to the animal. They had watched that same wolf grab the throat of Attaroa with those powerful jaws and kill her, and to them Jondalar's action bespoke magic, unimaginable control over the spirits of animals.

Ayla and Jondalar stood up with the wolf between them, while the people watched with some trepidation, not sure what to expect next. Several of them looked toward S'Armuna. She stepped toward the visitors, eying the wolf warily.

"We are finally free of her," she said.

Ayla smiled; she could see the woman's anxiety. "Wolf won't hurt you," she said. "He attacked only to protect me."

S'Armuna noticed that Ayla didn't translate the name of the animal into Zelandonii, and she sensed that the word was used as a personal name for the animal. "It is appropriate that her end should come from a wolf. I knew you were here for a reason. We are no longer clutched in her grip, held by her madness," the woman said. "But what do we do now?" The question was rhetorical, spoken more to herself than to any of the listeners.

Ayla looked down at the still body of the woman who had only moments before been so malevolently, but vibrantly alive, and it made her conscious of how fragile a thing life was. Except for Wolf, it could have been her lying dead on the ground. She shuddered at the thought. "I think someone should take this headwoman away and prepare her for burial." She spoke in Mamutoi so that more people would understand without the need for translation.

"Does she deserve burial? Why not throw her body to the carrion eaters?" It was a male voice that had spoken.

"Who speaks?" Ayla asked.

Jondalar knew the man who stepped forward, somewhat hesitantly. "I am called Olamun."

Ayla nodded in recognition. "You have a right to feel angry, Olamun, but Attaroa was driven to violence by the violence done to her. The evil in her spirit is eager to carry it on, to leave you with a legacy of her violence. Give it up. Don't let your rightful anger make you fall prey to the trap her restless spirit has set. It is time to break the pattern. Attaroa was human. Bury her with the dignity she was not able to find in life, and let her spirit rest.''

Jondalar was surprised by her response. It was the kind of answer a Zelandoni might make, wise and restrained.

Olamun nodded with acquiescence. ''But who will bury her? Who will prepare her? She has no kin,'' he said.

''That is the responsibility of the One Who Serves the Mother,'' S'Armuna said.

''Perhaps with the help of those who followed her in this life,'' Ayla suggested. The body was obviously too heavy for the older woman to handle alone.

Everyone turned to face Epadoa and the Wolf Women. They seemed to press together as though to draw strength from each other.

''And then follow her to the next world,'' another male voice said. There were shouts of agreement from the crowd, and a surge toward the women hunters. Epadoa stood her ground, brandishing her spear.

Suddenly one young Wolf Woman stepped away from the others. ''I never asked to be a Wolf Woman. I just wanted to learn to hunt so I wouldn't have to be hungry.''

Epadoa glared at her, but the young woman looked back defiantly.

''Let Epadoa find out what it's like to be hungry,'' the male voice said again. ''Let her go without food until she reaches the next world. Then her spirit will be hungry, too.''

The people surging toward the hunters, and toward Ayla, brought a warning snarl from Wolf. Jondalar quickly knelt to quiet him, but his reaction did have the effect of making the people back away. They looked at the woman and the animal with some trepidation.

Ayla didn't ask who had spoken that time. ''Attaroa's spirit still walks among us,'' Ayla said, ''encouraging violence and revenge.''

''But Epadoa must pay for the evil she has done.'' Ayla saw the mother of Cavoa stepping forward. Her young, pregnant daughter stood just behind her, offering moral support.

Jondalar got up and stood beside Ayla. He could not help thinking that the woman had a right to retribution for the death of her son. He looked to S'Armuna. The One Who

Served the Mother ought to be answering, he thought, but she, too, was waiting for Ayla to reply.

"The woman who killed your son has already gone to the next world," Ayla said. "Epadoa should pay for the evil she has done."

"She has more than that to pay for. What about the harm she did to these boys?" It was Ebulan who spoke. He stood back to let Ayla see two youngsters leaning on a cadaverous old man.

Ayla was startled when she saw the man; for an instant she thought she was looking at Creb! He was tall and thin, where the holy man of the Clan had been short and stocky, but his craggy face and dark eyes held the same kind of compassion and dignity, and he obviously commanded the same kind of esteem.

Ayla's first thought was to offer him the Clan gesture of respect by sitting at his feet and waiting for him to tap her shoulder, but she knew the action would be misunderstood. Instead, she decided to offer him the regard of formal courtesy. She turned to the tall man beside her.

"Jondalar, I cannot properly address this man without an introduction," she said.

He was quick to understand her sensitivity. He, too, had felt awed by the man. He stepped forward and led Ayla to him. "S'Amodun, most respected of the S'Armunai, may I introduce Ayla, of the Lion Camp of the Mamutoi, Daughter of the Mammoth Hearth, Chosen by the spirit of the Cave Lion, and Protected by the Cave Bear."

Ayla was surprised that Jondalar had added the last part. No one had ever named the Cave Bear as her protector, but when she considered it, she thought it might be true, at least through Creb. The Cave Bear had chosen him—it was the totem of Mog-ur—and Creb had been in her dreams so much that she was sure he was guiding and protecting her, perhaps with the help of the Great Cave Bear of the Clan.

"S'Amodun of the S'Armunai welcomes the Daughter of the Mammoth Hearth," the old man said, holding out both of his hands. He was not alone in singling out the Mammoth Hearth as the most impressive of her relationships. Most of the people there understood the importance of the Mammoth Hearth to the Mamutoi; it named her the equivalent of S'Armuna, One Who Served the Mother.

The Mammoth Hearth, of course, thought S'Armuna. It

cleared up many questions she'd had. But where was her tattoo? Weren't those accepted to the Mammoth Hearth marked with a tattoo?

"I am happy you welcome, Most Respected S'Amodun," Ayla said, speaking in S'Armunai.

The man smiled. "You have learned much of our language, but you just said something twice. My name is Amodun. S'Amodun means 'Most Respected, Amodun,' or 'Greatly Honored,' or whatever you think of to mean singled out for special notice," he said. "It is a title imposed by the will of the Camp. I am not sure why I have earned it."

She knew why. "I thank you, S'Amodun," Ayla said, looking down and nodding with gratitude. Up close, he reminded her even more of Creb, with his deep, dark, luminous eyes, prominent nose, heavy brows, and generally strong features. She had to consciously overcome her Clan training—women were not supposed to stare directly at men—to look up and talk to him. "I would ask you a question," she said, speaking in Mamutoi, in which she was more fluent.

"I will answer if I can," he replied.

She looked at the two boys who stood on either side of him. "The people of this Camp want Epadoa to pay for the evil she has done. These boys, in particular, have suffered great harm at her hands. Tomorrow I will see if I can do anything to help them, but what retribution should Epadoa pay for carrying out the wishes of her leader?"

Involuntarily most people glanced at the body of Attaroa, still sprawled where Wolf had left her; then their eyes were drawn to Epadoa. The woman stood straight and unflinching, ready to accept her punishment. In her heart, she had known that someday she would have to pay.

Jondalar looked at Ayla, a little awed. She had done exactly the right thing, he thought. No matter what she might have said, even with the fearful respect she had gained, the words of a stranger would never be accepted by these people as willingly as the words of S'Amodun.

"I think Epadoa should pay for her evil," the man said. Many people nodded with satisfaction, particularly Cavoa and her mother. "But in this world, not the next. You were right when you said it was time to break the pattern. There has been too much violence and evil in this Camp for too long.

The men have suffered greatly in recent years, but they did harm to the women first. It is time to end it.''

"Then what retribution will Epadoa pay?'' the grieving mother asked. "What will be her punishment?''

"Not punishment, Esadoa. Restitution. She should give back as much as she has taken, and more. She can start with Doban. No matter what the Daughter of the Mammoth Hearth may be able to do for him, it is unlikely that Doban will ever recover fully. He will suffer ill effects for the rest of his life. Odevan will suffer, too, but he has a mother, and kin. Doban has no mother, no kin to care for him, no one to take responsibility for him, or see to it that he is trained in some craft or skill. I would make Epadoa responsible for him, as if she were his mother. She may never love him and he may hate her, but she should be held accountable.''

There were nods of approval. Not everyone agreed, but someone had to take care of Doban. Although everyone had felt his pain, he had not been well liked when he lived with Attaroa, and no one wanted to take him in. Most people felt that if they objected to S'Amodun's idea, they might be asked to open their lodges to him.

Ayla smiled. She thought it was a perfect solution, and though there might be hatred and lack of trust in the beginning, warmth could grow into the relationship. She had known S'Amodun was wise. The idea of restitution seemed much more helpful than punishment, and it gave her an idea.

"I would offer another suggestion,'' she said. "This Camp is not well stocked for winter, and by spring everyone may suffer hunger. The men are weak, and they have not hunted for some years. Many may have lost their skills. Epadoa and the women she has trained are the best hunters of this Camp. I think it would be wise for them to continue to hunt, but they must share the meat with everyone.''

People were nodding. The thought of facing hunger was not appealing.

"As soon as any of the men are able, and want to start hunting, it should be Epadoa's responsibility to help them, hunt with them. The only way to avoid facing hunger next spring is if the women and the men work together. Every Camp needs the contribution of both to thrive. The rest of the women, and the older or weaker men, should gather whatever foods they can find.''

"It's winter! There is nothing to gather now," one of the young Wolf Women said.

"There is not much to be found in winter, that's true, and what there is will require work to harvest, but food can be found, and whatever there is will help," Ayla said.

"She's right," Jondalar said. "I have seen and eaten food that Ayla has found, even in winter. You even ate some of it tonight. She gathered the pine nuts from the stone pines near the river."

"Those lichens that reindeer like can be eaten," one of the older women said, "if you cook them right."

"And some of the wheats, and millets, and other grasses still bear seed heads," Esadoa said. "They can be collected."

"Yes, but be careful of ryegrass. It can foster a growth that is harmful, often fatal. If it looks and smells bad, it's probably full of ergot, and it should be avoided," Ayla advised. "But certain edible berries and fruits stay on the bush well into winter—I even found a tree with a few apples still clinging to it—and the inner bark of most trees can be eaten."

"We'd need knives to cut down to it," Esadoa said. "The ones we have aren't very good."

"I will make you some," Jondalar volunteered.

"Will you teach me to make knives, Zelandon?" Doban suddenly asked.

The question pleased him. "Yes, I will show you how to make knives, and other tools, too."

"I'd like to learn more about that, too," Ebulan said. "We will need weapons to hunt."

"I'll show anyone who wants to learn, or at least get you started. It takes many years to gain real skill. Perhaps next summer, if you go to a S'Armunai Meeting, you will find someone to continue your training," Jondalar said.

The youngster's smile turned to a frown; he knew the tall man would not be staying.

"But I'll help you all I can," Jondalar said. "We've had to make many hunting weapons on this Journey."

"What about that . . . stick that throws spears . . . like the one she used to free you?" It was Epadoa who had spoken, and everyone turned to stare. The head Wolf Woman had not spoken before, but her comments reminded them of the long and accurate cast Ayla had made to release Jondalar from the target post. It had seemed so miraculous that most people didn't consider that it was a skill that could be learned.

"The spear-thrower? Yes, I'll show anyone who is interested how to use it."

"Including the women?" Epadoa asked.

"Including the women," Jondalar said. "When you learn to use good hunting weapons, you won't have to go to the Great Mother River to chase horses off a cliff. You have one of the best hunting spots I've ever seen, right here down by the river."

"Yes, we do," Ebulan said. "I especially remember them hunting mammoths. When I was a boy, they used to post a lookout and light signal fires when anything was seen."

"I thought as much," Jondalar said.

Ayla was smiling. "I think the pattern is breaking. I don't hear Attaroa's spirit talking anymore," she said, stroking Wolf's fur. Then she spoke to the head Wolf Woman. "Epadoa, I learned to hunt four-legged hunters when I first started, including wolves. Wolf hides can be warm and useful for hoods, and a wolf that seriously threatens ought to be killed, but you would learn more from watching living wolves than from trapping and eating them after they are dead."

All the Wolf Women looked at each other with guilty expressions. How had she known? Among the S'Armunai, wolf meat was prohibited, and it was considered particularly bad for women.

The chief hunter studied the blond woman, trying to see if there was more to her than there appeared. Now that Attaroa was dead, and she knew she would not be killed for her actions, Epadoa felt a release. She was glad it was over. The headwoman had been so compelling that the young hunter had become enamored and did many things to please her that she didn't like thinking about. Many of these things had bothered her even while she did them, though she had not admitted it, even to herself. When she saw the tall man, while they were hunting horses, she had hoped that if she brought him back for Attaroa to toy with, she might spare one of their own men from the Holding.

She hadn't wanted to hurt Doban, but she was afraid that if she didn't do as Attaroa commanded, the headwoman would kill him, as she had killed her own child. Why had this Daughter of the Mammoth Hearth selected S'Amodun rather than Esadoa to pronounce judgment on her? It was a choice that had spared her life. It wouldn't be easy living in this Camp any longer. Many people hated her, but she was grateful for the chance to redeem herself. She would take care of the boy, even if he hated her. She owed him that much.

But who was this Ayla? Had she come to break the grip of Attaroa on the Camp as everyone seemed to think? What about the man? What magic did he have that spears couldn't touch him? And how did the men in the Holding get knives? Had he been responsible for that? Did they ride horses because that was the animal the Wolf Women had hunted most, even though the rest of the S'Armunai were as much mammoth hunters as their kin, the Mamutoi? Was the wolf a spirit wolf, come to revenge his kind? One thing she knew. She would never hunt a wolf again, and she was going to stop calling herself a Wolf Woman.

Ayla walked back toward the dead leader and saw S'Armuna. The One Who Served the Mother had watched everything but said little, and Ayla remembered her anguish and remorse. She spoke to her in quiet, private tones.

"S'Armuna, even if the spirit of Attaroa is finally leaving this Camp, it won't be easy to change old ways. The men are out of the Holding—I'm glad they managed to free themselves, they will remember it with pride—but it will be a long time before they forget Attaroa and the years they were held in there. You are the one who can help, but it will be a heavy responsibility."

The woman nodded her head in acquiescence. She felt she had been given the chance to make right her abuse of the Mother's power; it was more than she had hoped for. The first thing to do was to bury Attaroa and put her behind them. She turned to the crowd.

"There is food left. Let us finish this feast together. It is time to tear down the fence that was raised between the men and women of this Camp. Time to share food together, and fire, and the warmth of community. Time for us to come back together as a whole people, with neither one more than the other. Everyone has skills and abilities, and with each person contributing and helping, this Camp will thrive."

The women and men nodded in agreement. Many had found the mates from whom they had long been separated; the others joined to share food and fire, and human company.

"Epadoa," S'Armuna called, as the people were getting their food. When the woman walked over to her, she said, "I think it is time to move Attaroa's body away and prepare her for burial."

"Shall we take her to her lodge?" the hunting woman said.

S'Armuna thought. "No," she said. "Take her to the Holding and put her in the lean-to. I think the men should have the warmth of Attaroa's earthlodge tonight. Many are weak and sick. We may need it for some time. Do you have another place to sleep?"

"Yes. When I could get away from Attaroa, I had a place with Unavoa in the lodge she shares."

"You might consider moving in with her for now, if that's agreeable to her, and you."

"I think we would both like that," Epadoa said.

"Later, we'll work something out with Doban."

"Yes," Epadoa said, "we will."

Jondalar watched Ayla as she walked with Epadoa and the hunters with the body of the headwoman, and he felt proud of her and a little surprised. Somehow Ayla had assumed the wisdom and the stature of Zelandoni herself. The only time he had seen Ayla assume control of a situation before was when someone was hurt, or sick, and in need of her special skills. Then, when he thought of it, he realized that these people were hurt and sick. Perhaps it wasn't so strange that Ayla would know what to do.

In the morning Jondalar took the horses and brought back the necessities they had taken when they left the Great Mother River and went to get Whinney. It seemed so long ago, and it made him realize that their Journey had been considerably delayed. They had been so far ahead of the distance he thought they would have to cover to reach the glacier that he had been sure they would make it in plenty of time. Now they were well into winter, and they were farther away.

This Camp did need help, and he knew Ayla would not leave until she had done everything she felt she could. He had promised to help, too, and he was excited about the prospect of teaching Doban and the others to work the flint, and the ones who wanted, to use the spear-thrower, but a small knot of worry had begun. They had to cross that glacier

before the spring melt made it too treacherous, and he wanted
to get under way again, soon.

S'Armuna and Ayla worked together to examine and treat
the boys and men of the Camp. Their help was too late for
one man. He died in Attaroa's lodge the first night out of the
Holding, of gangrene so advanced that both legs were already
dead. Most of the rest needed treatment for some injury or
illness, and they were all underfed. They also smelled of the
sickness of the Holding and were unbelievably filthy.

S'Armuna decided to delay firing of the kiln. She didn't
have time, and the feeling was wrong for it, though she did
think it could be a powerful healing ceremony at the right
moment. They used the inner fire chamber to heat water for
bathing and treating of wounds instead, but the treatment that
was needed most was food and warmth. After the healers had
administered whatever help they could, those who were not
in serious difficulty and had mothers or mates, or other kin
to live with, moved back in with them.

It was the youngsters, the ones who were nearing or
barely into adolescence, that made Ayla particularly angry.
Even S'Armuna was appalled. She had closed her eyes to the
severity of their situation.

That evening, after another meal shared together, Ayla
and S'Armuna described some of the problems they had
found, explaining general needs and answering questions. But
the day had been long, and Ayla finally said she had to rest.
As she stood up to leave, someone asked a last question about
one of the youngsters. When Ayla replied, another woman
made a comment about the evil headwoman, laying all blame
at Attaroa's feet, and self-righteously absolving herself of all
responsibility. It raised Ayla's ire, and she made an announcement that came out of the deep anger that had been
growing all day.

"Attaroa was a strong woman, with a strong will, but no
matter how strong a person is, two people, or five people, or
ten people are stronger. If all of you had been willing to
resist her, she could have been stopped long before this.
Therefore, you are all, as a Camp, women and men, partly
responsible for the suffering of these children. And I will tell
you now, any of those youngsters, or even any of the men,
who suffer for a long time as a result of this . . . this abomination"—Ayla struggled to contain her fury—"must be cared
for by this whole Camp. You are all responsible for them,

for the rest of their lives. They have suffered, and in their suffering have become the chosen of Muna. Anyone who refuses to help them will answer to Her."

Ayla turned and left, and Jondalar followed, but her words carried more weight than she could know. Most people already felt that she was not an ordinary woman, and many were saying that she was an incarnation of the Great Mother Herself; a living munai in human form, who had come to take Attaroa and set the men free. What else could explain horses that came at her whistle? Or a wolf, huge even for his own large northern breed, following her wherever she went and sitting quietly at her command? Wasn't it the Great Earth Mother Who had given birth to the spirit forms of all the animals?

According to the rumors, the Mother had created both women and men for a reason, and She had given them the Gift of Pleasures to honor Her. The spirits of both men and women were necessary to make new life, and Muna had come to make it clear that anyone trying to create Her children some other way was an abomination to Her. Hadn't She brought the Zelandonii to show them how She felt? A man who was the embodiment of Her lover and mate? Taller and more handsome than most men, and light and fair like the moon. Jondalar was noticing a difference in the way the Camp was acting toward him, which made him uneasy. He didn't much like it.

There had been so much to do the first day, even with both healers and help from most of the Camp, that Ayla put off the special treatment she wanted to try on the boys with the dislocations. S'Armuna had even delayed the burial of Attaroa. The following morning a site was selected and the grave was dug. A simple ceremony conducted by the One Who Served finally returned the headwoman to the bosom of the Great Mother Earth.

A few even felt some grief. Epadoa had not expected to feel anything, and yet she did. Because of the way most of the Camp felt, she couldn't express it, but Ayla could see from her body language, her postures and expressions, that she was struggling with it. Doban also exhibited strange behavior, and she guessed he was trying to deal with his own mixed emotions. For most of his young life, Attaroa had been the only mother he knew. He had felt betrayed when she turned on him, but her love had always been erratic, and he couldn't entirely let go of his feelings for her.

Grief needed to be released. Ayla knew that from her own losses. She had planned to try to treat the boy right after the burial, but she wondered if she should wait longer. This might not be the right day for it, but maybe having something else to concentrate on would be better for both of them. She approached Epadoa on the way back to the Camp.

"I'm going to try to reset Doban's dislocated leg, and I'm going to need help. Will you assist me?"

"Won't it be painful for him?" Epadoa said. She recalled only too well his screams of pain, and she was beginning to feel protective of him. He was, if not her son, at least her charge, and she took it seriously. Her life, she was sure, depended on it.

"I will put him to sleep. He won't feel it, though he will have some pain when he wakes up, and he will have to be moved very carefully for some time," Ayla explained. "He won't be able to walk."

"I will carry him," Epadoa said.

When they got back to the big lodge, Ayla explained to the boy that she wanted to try to straighten his leg. He pulled away from her, looking very nervous, and when he saw Epadoa coming into the lodge, his eyes filled with fear.

"No! She's going to hurt me!" Doban screamed at the sight of the Wolf Woman. If he could have run away, he would have.

Epadoa stood straight and stiff beside the bed platform he was sitting on. "I will not hurt you. I promise you, I will never hurt you again," she said. "And I will never let anyone else hurt you, not even this woman."

He glanced up at her, apprehensive, but wanting to believe her. Desperately wanting to believe her.

"S'Armuna, please make sure he understands what I am going to say," Ayla said. Then she stooped down until she could look into his frightened eyes.

"Doban, I'm going to give you something to drink. It won't taste very good, but I want you to drink it all anyway. After a while, you will begin to feel very sleepy. When you feel like it, you can lie down right here. While you are asleep, I'm going to try to make your leg a little better, put it back the way it was. You won't feel it because you will be sleeping. When you wake up, you will feel some pain, but it may feel better in a way, too. If it hurts too much, tell me, or S'Armuna, or Epadoa—someone will be here with you all the time—and she will give you something to drink that will make the pain go away a little. Do you understand?"

"Can Zelandon come here to see me?"

"Yes, I will get him now, if you want."

"And S'Amodun?"

"Yes, both of them, if you want."

Doban looked up at Epadoa. "And you won't let her hurt me?"

"I promise. I won't let her hurt you. I won't let anyone hurt you."

He looked at S'Armuna, then back at Ayla. "Give me the drink," he said.

The process was not unlike the resetting of Roshario's broken arm. The drink both relaxed his muscles and put him to sleep. It took sheer physical strength to pull the leg straight, but when it slipped back into place, it was obvious to everyone. There had been some breakage, Ayla realized, and it would never be entirely right, but his body looked almost normal again.

Epadoa moved back into the large earthlodge, since most of the men and boys had moved in with their kin, and she stayed near Doban almost constantly. Ayla noticed the tentative beginnings of trust developing between them. She was sure that was exactly what S'Amodun had envisioned.

They went through a similar procedure with Odevan, but Ayla feared his healing process would be more difficult and that his leg would have a tendency to pop out and become dislocated more easily in the future.

S'Armuna was impressed and a little in awe of Ayla, privately wondering if the rumors about her might not have some truth in them. She seemed like an ordinary woman, talked and slept and shared Pleasures with the tall, fair man, like any other woman, but her knowledge of the plant life that grew in the earth, and their medical properties in particular, was phenomenal. Everyone talked about it; S'Armuna gained prestige by association. And though the older woman learned not to fear the wolf, it was almost impossible to see him around Ayla and not believe that she controlled his spirit. When he wasn't following her, his eyes were. It was the same with the man, although he wasn't as obvious about it.

The older woman didn't notice the horses as much because they were left to graze most of the time—Ayla said she was glad to give them the rest—but S'Armuna did see the two people ride them. The man rode the brown stallion easily enough, but seeing the young woman on the back of the mare made one think they were of the same flesh.

But though she wondered, the One Who Served the Mother was skeptical. She had been trained by the Zelandonia, and she knew that such ideas were often encouraged. She had learned, and often employed, ways to misdirect people, to lead them into believing what she, and they, wanted to believe. She didn't think of it as trickery—no one was more convinced of the rightness of her calling—but she used the means at her disposal to smooth the way and persuade others to follow. People could often be helped by such means, especially some of those whose problems and illnesses had no discernible cause, except, perhaps, curses by powerful evil people.

Though she herself was not willing to accept all the rumors, S'Armuna did not discourage them. The people of the Camp wanted to believe that anything Ayla and Jondalar said was a pronouncement from the Mother, and she used their belief to set in place some necessary changes. When Ayla talked about the Mamutoi Council of Sisters and Council of Brothers, for example, S'Armuna organized the Camp to set up similar Councils. When Jondalar mentioned finding someone from another Camp to continue the training in flint-toolmaking that he had begun, she instigated plans to send a delegation to several other S'Armunai Camps to renew ties with kin and reestablish friendships.

On a night that fell so cold and clear the stars blazed from the heavens, a group of people were clustered outside the entrance of the former headwoman's large earthlodge, which was becoming a center for community activities after it had served as a place for healing and recovery. They were talking about the mysterious twinkling lights in the sky, and S'Armuna was answering questions and offering interpretations. She had to spend so much time in the place—healing with medicines and ceremonies, and gathering with people to make plans and discuss problems—that she had begun to move some of her things in, and she often left Ayla and Jondalar alone in her small lodge. The arrangement was starting to resemble other Camps and Caves that Ayla and Jondalar knew, with the lodging of the One Who Served the Mother acting as a focus and gathering place for the people.

After the two visitors left the stargazers, with Wolf at their heels, someone asked S'Armuna about the wolf that followed Ayla everywhere. The One Who Served the Mother pointed to one of the bright lights in the sky. "That is the Wolf Star," was all she said.

The days passed quickly. As the men and boys began to recover and no longer needed her as a medicine woman, Ayla went out with those who were collecting the sparse winter foods. Jondalar got caught up in teaching his craft and showing how to make spear-throwers and hunt with them. The Camp began to accumulate more supplies of a variety of foods that were easy to preserve and store in the freezing weather, particularly meat. At first there had been some difficulties in getting accustomed to the new arrangements, with the men moving into lodges that the women considered theirs, but they were working it out.

S'Armuna felt that the timing was right to fire the figures in the kiln, and she had talked about establishing a new Firing Ceremony with her two visitors. They were at the kiln lodge, gathering some of the fuel she had collected over the summer and fall to burn for her firing, for medical purposes, and for everyday uses. She explained that they would have to gather more fuel and it would be a lot of work.

"Can you make some tree-cutting tools, Jondalar?" she asked.

"I'll be glad to make some axes, and mauls and wedges, whatever you want, but green trees don't burn well," he said.

"I will be burning mammoth bone, too, but we have to get the fire good and hot first, and it has to burn for a long time. It takes a great deal of fuel for a Firing Ceremony."

As they came out of the small lodge, Ayla looked across the settlement at the Holding. Although people had been using bits and pieces of it, they hadn't torn it down. She had mentioned at one time that the poles could be used for a hunting surround, a corral into which animals could be chased. The people of the Camp tended to avoid using the wood after that, and now that they had all become accustomed to it, they almost didn't see it.

Suddenly Ayla said, "You don't need to cut down trees.

Jondalar can make wood-cutting tools to cut up the wood of the Holding.''

They all saw the fence in a new way, but S'Armuna saw even more. She began to see the outlines of her new ceremony. "That's perfect!" she said. "The destruction of that place to create a new and healing ceremony! Everyone can take part, and everyone will be glad to see it go. It will mark the new beginning for us, and you'll be here, too.''

"I'm not sure about that,'' Jondalar said. "How long will it take?''

"It's not something that can be hurried. It's too important.''

"That's what I thought. We have to be leaving soon,'' he said.

"But it will soon be the coldest part of winter,'' S'Armuna objected.

"And not long after that, the spring melt. You've crossed that glacier, S'Armuna. You know it can only be crossed in winter. And I promised some Losadunai that I would visit their Cave on the way back and spend a little time with them. Though we couldn't stay long, it would be a good place to stop and prepare for the crossing.''

S'Armuna nodded. "Then I will use the Firing Ceremony to ease your leaving as well. There are many of us who had hoped you would stay, and all will feel your absence.''

"I had hoped to see a firing,'' Ayla said, "and Cavoa's baby, but Jondalar is right. It's time for us to leave.''

Jondalar decided to make the tools for S'Armuna immediately. He had located a supply of good flint nearby, and, with a couple of others, he went to get some that could be made into axes and wood-cutting implements. Ayla went into the small lodge to gather together their belongings and see what else they might need. She had spread everything out when she heard a noise at the entrance. She looked up to see Cavoa.

"Am I bothering you, Ayla?'' she asked.

"No, come in.''

The young, very pregnant woman entered and eased herself down on the edge of a sleeping platform, across from Ayla. "S'Armuna told me you are leaving.''

"Yes, in a day or so.''

"I thought you were going to stay for the firing.''

"I wanted to, but Jondalar is anxious to go. He says we must cross a glacier before spring.''

"I made something that I was going to give you after the

firing," Cavoa said, taking a small leather package out of her shirt. "I'd still like to give it to you, but if it gets wet, it won't last." She handed the package to Ayla.

Inside the package was a small head of a lioness powerfully modeled out of clay. "Cavoa! This is beautiful. More than beautiful. It is the essence of a cave lioness. I didn't know you were so skilled."

The young woman smiled. "You like it?"

"I knew a man, a Mamutoi man, who was a carver of ivory, a very fine artist. He showed me how to see things that are carved and painted, and I know he would love this," Ayla said.

"I have carved figures out of wood, ivory, antler. I've been doing it as long as I can remember. That's why S'Armuna asked me to train with her. She has been so wonderful to me. She tried to help us . . . She was good to Omel, too. She let Omel keep the secret and never made demands, the way some would have. Many people were so curious." Cavoa looked down and seemed to be struggling to hold back tears.

"I think you miss your friends," Ayla said gently. "It must have been difficult for Omel to keep a secret like that."

"Omel had to keep that secret."

"Because of Brugar? S'Armuna said she thought he might have threatened great harm."

"No, not because of Brugar, or Attaroa. I didn't like Brugar, and I remember how he blamed her for Omel, even though I was little, but I think he feared Omel more than Omel feared him, and Attaroa knew why."

Ayla sensed what was bothering Cavoa. "And you knew, too, didn't you?"

The young woman frowned. "Yes," she whispered; then she looked into Ayla's eyes. "I was hoping you would be here when the time comes. I want everything to be right with my baby, not like . . ."

It wasn't necessary to say more, or to explain in detail. Cavoa feared that her baby might be born with some abnormality, and naming an evil only gave it power.

"Well, I'm not leaving yet, and who knows? It appears to me that you could have that baby any time," Ayla said. "Perhaps we will still be here."

"I hope so. You have done so much for us. I only wish you had come before Omel and the others . . ."

Ayla saw tears glittering in her eyes. "You miss your

friends, I know, but soon you will have a brand-new baby all your own. I think that may help. Have you thought about a name?''

"I didn't for a long time. I knew there wouldn't be much point in thinking about a boy's name, and I didn't know if I'd be allowed to name a girl. Now, if it's a boy, I don't know whether to name it after my brother, or . . . another man I knew. But if it's a girl, I want to name it for S'Armuna. She helped me to see . . . him . . .'' A sob of anguish interrupted her words.

Ayla took the young woman in her arms. Grief needed to be expressed. It was good for her to get it out. This Camp was still full of grief that had to come out. Ayla hoped the ceremony that S'Armuna planned would help. When her tears finally abated, Cavoa pulled back and wiped her eyes with the side of her hand. Ayla looked around for something to give her to dry her tears, and she opened up a package she had carried with her for years to let the young woman use the soft leather wrapping. But when Cavoa saw what was inside, her eyes opened wide in disbelief. It was a munai, a small figure of a woman carved out of ivory, but this munai had a face, and the face was Ayla's!

She averted her eyes, as though she had seen something she shouldn't have, dried her eyes, and quickly left. Ayla frowned as she wrapped the carving Jondalar had made of her back in the soft leather. She knew it had frightened Cavoa.

She tried to put it out of her mind as she packed their few things. She picked up the pouch that held their firestones, and she emptied it to see how many of the grayish-yellow metallic pieces of iron pyrite they had left. She wanted to give one to S'Armuna, but she didn't know how plentiful they would be near Jondalar's home, and she wanted to have some for gifts to his kin. She decided to part with one, but only one, and she selected a good-size nodule, then put the rest away.

When Ayla went out, she noticed Cavoa leaving the large earthlodge as she entered. She smiled at the young woman, who smiled nervously back, and when she went in, she thought S'Armuna looked at her strangely. Jondalar's carving had created some worry, it seemed. Ayla waited until another person had left the lodge, and S'Armuna was alone.

"I have something I want to give you before I leave. I discovered this when I was living alone in my valley," she said, opening her palm to show her the stone. "I thought you might be able to make use of it for your Fire Ceremony."

S'Armuna looked at it, then looked up at Ayla questioningly.

"I know it doesn't look like it, but there is fire inside this stone. Let me show you."

Ayla went to the fireplace, got out the tinder they used, and arranged small shavings of wood loosely around dried cattail fluff. She placed sticks of kindling nearby, then bent down low and struck the iron pyrite with flint. A large hot spark was drawn off and fell on the tinder, and when she blew on it, a small flame miraculously appeared. She added kindling to keep it going, and when she looked up she saw the stunned woman gaping at her incredulously.

"Cavoa told me she saw a munai with your face, and now you make fire appear. Are you . . . who they say you are?"

Ayla smiled. "Jondalar made that carving, because he loved me. He said he wanted to capture my spirit, and then he gave it to me. It's not a donii, or a munai. It's just a token of his feeling, and I will be happy to show you how to make fire appear. It's not me, it's something in the firestone."

"Should I be here?" The voice came from the entrance, and both women turned to look at Cavoa. "I forgot my mitts and came back for them."

S'Armuna and Ayla looked at each other. "I don't see why not," Ayla said.

"Cavoa is my acolyte," S'Armuna remarked.

"Then I'll show both of you how the firestone works," Ayla said.

When she had gone through the process again and let them both try it, they were feeling more relaxed, though they were no less amazed at the properties of the strange stone. Cavoa even felt brave enough to ask Ayla about the munai.

"That figure I saw . . ."

"Jondalar made it for me, not long after we met. It was meant to show his feeling for me," Ayla explained.

"You mean, if I wanted to show a person how important I think that person is, I could make a carving of that person's face?" Cavoa said.

"I don't see why not," Ayla said. "When you make a munai, you know why you are making it. You have a special feeling inside you about it, don't you?"

"Yes, and certain rituals go along with it," the young woman said.

"I think it's the feeling you put into it that makes the difference."

"So I could carve someone's face, if the feeling I put into it was good."

"I don't think there would be anything wrong with that at all. You are a very fine artist, Cavoa."

"But, perhaps, it would be best," S'Armuna cautioned, "if you did not make the whole figure. If you just made the head, there would be no confusion."

Cavoa nodded in agreement; then both of them looked at Ayla, as though waiting for her approval. In the recesses of their private thoughts, both women still wondered who this visitor really was.

Ayla and Jondalar woke the next morning with every intention of leaving, but outside the lodge a dry snow was blowing so fiercely that it was hard even to see across the settlement.

"I don't think we'll be leaving today, not with a blizzard in the making," Jondalar said, though he hated the thought of the delay. "I hope it blows over soon."

Ayla went to the field and whistled for the horses, to make sure they were all right. She was relieved to see them appear out of the haze of wind-driven snow, and she led them to an area nearer the Camp that was protected from the wind. As she walked back, her mind was on their return trip to the Great Mother River, since she was the one who knew the way. She didn't hear her name whispered at first.

"Ayla!" The whisper was louder. She looked around and saw Cavoa on the far side of the small lodge, staying out of view and beckoning to her.

"What is it, Cavoa?"

"I want to show you something, to see how you like it," the young woman said. When Ayla got close, Cavoa took off her mitt. In her hand was a small roundish object, the color of mammoth ivory. She placed it carefully in Ayla's palm. "I just finished it," she said.

Ayla held it up and smiled with a look of wonder. "Cavoa! I knew you were good. I didn't know you were this good," she said, carefully examining the small carving of S'Armuna.

It was just the head of the woman, no hint of a body, not even a neck, but there was no doubt who the carving was meant to depict. The hair was pulled up into a bun near the top of the head, and the narrow face was slightly skewed, with one side somewhat smaller than the other, yet the beauty and the dignity of the woman were evident. It seemed to emanate from within the small work of art.

"Do you think it's all right? Do you think she'll like it?" Cavoa said. "I wanted to make something special for her."

"I would like it," Ayla said, "and I think it expresses your feeling for her very well. You have a rare and wonderful Gift, Cavoa, but you must be sure to use it well. There could be great power in it. S'Armuna was wise to choose you as her acolyte."

By evening, a howling blizzard was raging, making it dangerous to move more than a few feet beyond the entrance of a lodge. S'Armuna was reaching for a bunch of dried greenery hanging from the rack near the entryway, planning to add it to a new batch of herbs she was mixing together for a potent drink she was preparing for the Fire Ceremony. The fire in the fireplace was burning low, and Ayla and Jondalar had just gone to bed. The woman planned to retire as soon as she finished.

Suddenly a blast of cold air and a flurry of snow accompanied the opening of the heavy drape stretched across the entrance to the anteroom. Esadoa pushed through the second drape in evident distress.

"S'Armuna! Hurry! It's Cavoa! Her time has come."

Ayla was out of bed pulling on clothes before the woman could reply.

"She picked a good night for it," S'Armuna said, maintaining calm, in part to soothe the agitated expectant grandmother. "It will be all right, Esadoa. She won't have the baby before we reach your lodge."

"She's not in my lodge. She insisted on going out in this storm to the big lodge. I don't know why, but she wants to have the baby there. And she wants Ayla to come, too. She says it's the only way to be sure the baby will be all right.''

S'Armuna frowned with concern. ''No one is there tonight, and it wasn't wise for her to go out in this weather.''

''I know, but I couldn't stop her,'' Esadoa said, starting back out.

''Wait a moment,'' S'Armuna said. ''We might as well all go together. You can get lost going from one lodge to the next in a storm like this.''

''Wolf won't let us get lost,'' Ayla said, signaling the animal, who had been curled up beside their bed.

''Would it be inappropriate for me to come?'' Jondalar said. It wasn't so much that he wanted to be there for the birthing as that he was worried about Ayla going out in the blizzard. S'Armuna looked at Esadoa.

''I don't mind, but should a man be at a birthing?'' Esadoa said.

''There is no reason why not,'' S'Armuna said, ''and it might be a good thing to have a man nearby since she has no mate.''

They all braved the brunt of the wind together as the three women and the man went out into the howling gale. When they reached the big lodge, they found the young woman huddled over a cold, empty fireplace, her body tense with pain and a look of fear in her eyes. She brightened with relief when she saw her mother arrive with the others. Within moments, Ayla had a fire lit—much to the surprise of Esadoa— Jondalar was back outside getting snow from a drift to melt for water, Esadoa found the bedding that had been put away and arranged it on a bed platform, and S'Armuna was selecting various herbs that she might need from the supply she had brought there before.

Ayla settled the young woman, arranging everything so she could sit up comfortably or lie down if she chose, but she waited for S'Armuna and then both examined her. After reassuring Cavoa and leaving her with her mother, the two healers walked back to the fireplace and spoke quietly with each other.

''Did you notice?'' S'Armuna asked.

''Yes. Do you know what it means?'' Ayla said.

''I have an idea, but I think we'll just have to wait and see.''

Jondalar had been trying to stay out of the way, and he

approached the two women slowly. Something about their expressions made him sense that they felt some concern, which caused him to worry as well. He sat down on a sleeping platform and absently stroked the wolf's head.

As they waited, Jondalar paced nervously while Wolf watched him. He wished the time would pass more quickly, or that the storm would let up, or that he had something to do. He talked to the young woman a little, trying to be encouraging, and he smiled at her often, but he felt entirely useless. There was nothing he could do. Finally, as the night dragged on, he dozed a little on one of the beds, while the ghostly sound of the storm outside wailed an eerie counterpoint to the waiting scene inside, punctuated by periodic sounds of straining labor, slowly but inexorably drawing closer together.

He awoke to the sound of excited voices amidst a flurry of activity. Light was coming through the cracks around the smoke hole. He got up, stretched, and rubbed his eyes. Ignored by the three women, he went outside to pass his morning water. He was glad to see the storm had abated, though a few dry flakes were swirling in the wind.

As he started into the lodge, he heard the unmistakable squall of a newborn. He smiled but waited outside, not sure if it was an appropriate moment to go back in. Suddenly, to his surprise, he heard another squall, which caused the first one to make it a duet. Two of them! He couldn't resist. He had to go in.

Ayla, holding a swaddled infant in her arms, smiled as he came through the entrance. "A boy, Jondalar!"

S'Armuna was lifting a second baby, preparing to tie the umbilical cord. "And a girl," she said. "Twins! It's a favorable sign. So few babies were born while Attaroa was leader, but now I think that will change. I think this is the Mother's way of telling us the Camp of the Three Sisters will soon be growing and full of life again."

"Will you come back someday?" Doban asked the tall man. He was getting around much better, though he still used the crutch that Jondalar had made for him.

"I don't think so, Doban. One long Journey is enough. It's time to go home, settle down, and establish my hearth."

"I wish you lived closer, Zelandon."

"So do I. You are going to be a good flint knapper, and I would like to continue training you. And, by the way, Doban, you can call me Jondalar."

"No. You are Zelandon."

"You mean Zelandonii?"

"No, I mean Zelandon."

S'Amodun smiled. "He doesn't mean the name of your people. He has made your name Elandon, but honors you with S'Elandon."

Jondalar flushed with embarrassment and pleasure. "Thank you, Doban. Maybe I should call you S'Ardoban."

"Not yet. When I learn to work the flint like you, then they may call me S'Ardoban."

Jondalar gave the young man a warm hug, clasped the shoulders of a few others, and chatted with them. The horses, packed and ready to go, had wandered off a short distance, and Wolf had dropped to the ground, watching the man. He got up when he saw Ayla and S'Armuna coming out of the lodge. Jondalar was glad to see them, too.

". . . It is beautiful," the older woman was saying, "and I'm overwhelmed that she cared so much that she wanted to do it, but . . . you don't think it's dangerous?"

"As long as you keep the carving of your face, how can it be dangerous? It may bring you closer to the Mother, give you deeper understanding," Ayla said.

They hugged each other, then S'Armuna gave Jondalar a big hug. She stepped back when they called the horses, but she reached out and touched his arm to detain him another moment.

"Jondalar, when you see Marthona, tell her S'Armu . . . no, tell her Bodoa sends her love."

"I will. I think it will please her," he said, mounting the stallion.

They turned around and waved, but Jondalar was relieved to be going. He would never be able to think of this Camp without mixed feelings.

Snow began filtering down again as they rode away. The people of the Camp waved and wished them well. "Good Journey, S'Elandon." "Safe travels, S'Ayla."

As they disappeared into the softly obscuring white flakes, there was hardly a soul who did not believe—or want to believe—that Ayla and Jondalar had come to rid them of

Attaroa and free their men. As soon as the horse-riding couple were out of sight, they would transform themselves into the Great Earth Mother and Her Fair Celestial Mate, and they would ride the wind across the skies, trailed by their faithful protector, the Wolf Star.

34

They started back to the Great Mother River with Ayla leading the way over the same trail that she had followed to find the S'Armunai Camp, but when they reached the river crossing, they decided to ford the smaller tributary and then head southwest. They rode across country over the windy plains of the ancient lowland basin that separated the two major mountain systems, heading for the river.

Despite the scant snowfall, they often had to take cover from blizzardlike conditions. In the intense cold, the dry snowflakes were picked up and blown from place to place by the unremitting winds until they were ground into frozen grit, sometimes mixed with the pulverized particles of rock dust—loess—from the margins of the moving glaciers. When the wind blew especially hard, it blasted their skin raw. The withered grass in the most exposed places had long since been flattened, but the winds that kept snow from accumulating, except in sheltered pockets, bared the sere and yellowed fodder enough for the horses to graze.

For Ayla, the trek back was much faster—she was not

trying to follow a trail over difficult terrain—but Jondalar was surprised at the distance they had to travel before reaching the river. He hadn't realized how far north they had been. He guessed that the S'Armunai Camp was not far from the Great Ice.

His speculation was correct. If they had gone north, they could have reached the massive frontal wall of the continental ice sheet in a walk of a handful or two of days. In early summer, just before they started on their Journey, they had hunted mammoths at the frozen face of the same vast northern barrier, but far to the east. Since then, they had traveled down the full length of the eastern side of a great curved arc of mountains, around the southern base, and up the western flank of the range almost to the land-spanning glacier again.

Leaving behind the last outliers and flysch foothills of the mountains that had dominated their travels, they turned west when they reached the Great Mother River and began approaching the northern foreland of the even larger and loftier range to the west. They were retracing their steps, looking for the place where they had left their equipment and supplies, following the same route they had begun earlier in the season, when Jondalar thought they had plenty of time . . . until the night that Whinney was taken by the wild herd.

"The landmarks seem familiar—it should be around here," he said.

"I think you're right. I remember that bluff, but everything else looks so different," Ayla said, surveying the changed landscape with dismay.

More snow had accumulated and settled in this vicinity. The edge of the river was frozen, and, with the snow blown into drifts and filling every depression, it was hard to know where the bank ended and the river began. Strong winds and ice, which had formed on branches during an alternate freezing and thawing earlier in the season, had brought down several trees. Brush and brambles sagged under the weight of the frozen water clinging to them; covered with snow, they often appeared to the travelers to be hillocks or mounds of rocks until they broke through when they attempted to climb them.

The woman and man stopped near a small stand of trees and carefully scanned the area, trying to find something that would give them a hint of the site of their stashed tent and food.

"We must be close. I know this is the right area, but everything is so different," Ayla said, then paused and looked at the man. "Many things are different from what they seem, aren't they, Jondalar?"

He looked at her with a puzzled expression. "Well, yes, in winter things look different than in summer."

"I don't mean just the land," Ayla said. "It's hard to explain. It's like when we left, and S'Armuna told you to tell your mother that she sends her love, but she said Bodoa sends it. That was the name your mother called her, wasn't it?"

"Yes, I'm sure that's what she meant. When she was young she was probably called Bodoa."

"But she had to give up her own name when she became S'Armuna. Just like the Zelandoni you talk about, the one you knew as Zolena," Ayla said.

"The name is given up willingly. It's part of becoming One Who Serves the Mother," Jondalar said.

"I understand. It was the same when Creb became The Mog-ur. He didn't have to give up his birth name, but when he was conducting a ceremony as The Mog-ur, he was a different person. When he was Creb, he was like his birth totem, the Roe Deer, shy and quiet, never saying much, almost as though he were watching from a hiding place. But when he was Mog-ur, then he was powerful and command-ing, like his Cave Bear totem," Ayla said. "He was never quite what he seemed."

"You're a little like that, Ayla. Most of the time you listen a lot and don't say much, but when someone is hurting or in trouble, you almost become a different person. You take control. You tell people what to do, and they do it."

Ayla frowned. "I never thought of it that way. It's just that I want to help."

"I know that. But it's more than wanting to help. You usually know what to do, and most people recognize that. I think that's why they do what you say. I think you could be One Who Serves the Mother, if you wanted to," Jondalar said.

Ayla's frown deepened. "I don't think I would want that. I wouldn't want to give up my name. It's the only thing I have left from my real mother, from the time before I lived with the Clan," the young woman said. Then she suddenly tensed and pointed at a snow-covered mound that seemed unusually symmetrical. "Jondalar! Look over there."

The man looked where she pointed, not seeing what she saw at first; then the shape leaped into his awareness. "Could that be . . . ?" he said, urging Racer forward.

The mound was in the middle of a tangle of briars, which increased their excitement. They dismounted. Jondalar found a sturdy branch and beat their way through the thicket of canes. When he reached the middle and hit the symmetrical mound, the snow fell away, revealing their upturned bowl boat.

"That's it!" Ayla cried.

They stomped and beat down the long thorny runners until they could reach the boat and the carefully wrapped packages cached underneath.

Their storage place had not been entirely effective, though it was Wolf who gave them the first indication. He was obviously agitated by a scent still clinging to the area, and when they found wolf scat, they understood why. Wolves had vandalized their cache. Attempts to tear open carefully wrapped bundles had succeeded in some cases. Even the tent was torn, but they were surprised it wasn't worse. Wolves usually couldn't stay away from leather, and once they got hold of it, they loved to chew it up.

"The repellent! That must have been what kept them from doing more damage," Jondalar said, pleased that Ayla's mixture had kept not just their canine traveling companion away from their things, but had later kept away the other wolves as well. "And all the while I thought that Wolf was making our Journey more difficult. Instead, if it hadn't been for him, we probably wouldn't have a tent. Come here, boy," Jondalar said, patting his chest and inviting the animal to jump up and put his paws on it. "You did it again! Saved our lives, or at least our tent."

Ayla watched him grab the thick fur of the wolf's neck and smiled. She was pleased to see his change in attitude toward the animal. It wasn't that Jondalar had ever been unkind to him, or even that he disliked him. It was just that he'd never been so openly friendly and affectionate before. It was obvious that Wolf enjoyed the attention, too.

Though they would have sustained much more damage if it hadn't been for the wolf repellent, it hadn't kept the wolves

away from their emergency food stores. They suffered a devastating loss. Most of their dried meat and cakes of traveling
food were gone, and many of the packets of dried fruit, vegetables, and grain had been torn open or were missing, perhaps
taken by other animals after the wolves had left.

"Maybe we should have taken more of the food the S'Armunai offered us when we left," Ayla said, "but they had
little enough for themselves. I suppose we could go back."

"I'd rather not go back," Jondalar said. "Let's see what
we have. With hunting, we may have enough to make it as
far as the Losadunai. Thonolan and I met some of them and
stayed overnight with them. They asked us to come back and
spend some time with them."

"Would they give us food to continue our Journey?"
Ayla asked.

"I think so," Jondalar said. Then he smiled. "In fact, I
know they will. I have a future claim on them!"

"A future claim?" Ayla said, with a questioning frown.
"Are they your kin? Like the Sharamudoi?"

"No, they're not kin, but they are friendly, and they
have traded with the Zelandonii. Some of them know the
language."

"You've talked about it before, but I never have quite
understood what a 'future claim' means, Jondalar."

"A future claim is a promise to give whatever is asked
for, at some time in the future, in exchange for something
given or, more usually, won in the past. Mostly it's used to
pay a debt when someone has been gaming and lost more
than that person can pay, but it's used in other ways, too,"
the man explained.

"What other ways?" Ayla asked. She had a feeling there
was more to the idea, and that it would be important for her
to understand.

"Well, sometimes to repay someone for something he's
done, usually something special, but difficult to value," Jondalar said. "Since there is no limit placed on it, a future
claim can be a heavy obligation, but most people will not
ask for more than is appropriate. Often just accepting the
obligation of a future claim shows trust and good faith. It's
a way of offering friendship."

Ayla nodded. There was more to it.

"Laduni owes me a future claim," the man continued.
"It is not a major claim, but he is required to give me what-

ever I ask, and I could ask for anything. I think he'll be glad to fulfill his obligation with nothing more than a little food, which he would probably give us anyway."

"Is it far to the Losadunai?" Ayla asked.

"It's quite a distance. They live at the western end of these mountains, and we're at the eastern end, but it's not hard traveling if we follow the river. We will have to cross it, though. They live on the other side, but we can do that farther upstream," Jondalar said.

They decided to camp there overnight, and they carefully went through all their belongings. It was mostly food that was gone. When they put all they could salvage together, it made a meager pile, but they realized the situation could have been worse. They would have to hunt and gather extensively along the way, but most of their gear was intact and would be entirely serviceable with some mending and repairing, except for the meat-keeper, which had been chewed to shreds. The bowl boat had protected their cache from the weather, if not from the wolves. In the morning they had to make a decision about whether or not to continue dragging along the round, skin-covered boat.

"We're getting into more mountainous country. It could be more trouble taking it than leaving it behind," Jondalar said.

Ayla had been checking over the poles. Of the three poles she had used to keep their food away from animals, one was broken, but they only needed two for the travois. "Why don't we take it along for now, and if it turns out to be a real problem, we can always leave it later," she said.

Traveling west, they soon left behind the low-lying basin of windy plains. The east-west course of the Great Mother River, which they followed, marked the line of a great battle between the most powerful forces of the earth, waged in the infinitely slow motion of geologic time. To the south was the foreland of the high western mountains, whose uppermost reaches were never warmed by the gentle days of summer. The lofty prominences accumulated snow and ice year after year and, farther back, the tallest peaks of the range glistened in the clear, cold air.

The highlands on the north were the basic crystalline rock of an immense massif, rounded and smoothed vestiges of

ancient mountains worn down over eons of time. They had
risen from the land in the earliest epoch and were anchored
to the deepest bedrock. Against that immovable foundation,
the irresistible force of continents, moving slowly and inexorably from the south, had crushed and folded the earth's crust
of hard rock, uplifting the massive system of mountains that
stretched across the land.

But the ancient massif did not escape unscathed from the
great forces that created the high-peaked mountains. The tilting, faulting, and breaking of the rock, seen in the disruption
of its solidified crystal structure, told a story in stone of the
violent folding and thrusting it endured as it held firm against
the inconceivable pressures from the south. In the same
epoch, not only were the high western range on their left,
and another even farther west, uplifted by moving continents
pushing against unyielding bedrock, but so were the long
curved eastern range they had skirted, and the entire series
of ranges that continued eastward to the tallest peaks on earth.

Later, during the age of ice, when yearly temperatures
were lower, the frozen crown extended far down the sides of
the massive mountain ranges, covering even moderate elevations with a sparkling crystal crust. Filling in and enlarging
valleys and rifts as it slowly crept along, the glacial ice left
behind outwashing sheets and terraces of gravel, and it carved
sharp projecting towers of stone out of the rough-hewn
younger pinnacles. Snow and ice also covered the northern
highlands in winter. But only the highest elevation, nearest
the frosted mountains, sustained an actual glacier, an enduring layer of ice that persisted summer and winter.

With the rounded roots of the eroded mountains to the
north sprawling out in comparatively level tablelands and terraces, the upper courses of the rivers that flowed across the
ancient land had shallow valleys and gentle grades, though
they became more rugged through the middle of their courses.
Except for those that fell directly off the face of the massif,
rivers coming down the steeper slopes of the southern side
flowed faster. The demarcation between the gentle northern
highland and the mountainous south was the fertile land of
rich loess through which the Great Mother River flowed.

Ayla and Jondalar were heading almost due west as they
continued their Journey, traveling along the northern bank of
the waterway through the open plains of the river valley.
While no longer the huge voluminous Mother of rivers that

she had been downstream, the Great Mother River was still substantial, and after a few days, true to character, she separated once again into several channels.

Half a day's travel beyond, they reached another large tributary whose roiling confluence, tumbling down from higher ground, looked formidable, with icicles extended into frozen curtains and mounds of broken ice lining both banks. No longer were the rivers joining on the north coming from the uplands and foothills of the familiar mountains they were leaving behind. This water came from the unfamiliar terrain to the west. Rather than cross the perilous river, or attempt to follow it upstream, Jondalar decided to backtrack and cross the several branches of the Mother instead.

It turned out to be a good choice. Though some of the channels were wide and choked with ice along the edges, for the most part the frigid water barely reached as high as the horses' flanks. They didn't think much about it until later that evening, but Ayla and Jondalar, the two horses, and the wolf had finally crossed the Great Mother River. After their dangerous and traumatic adventures on other rivers, they accomplished it with so little incident that it seemed an anticlimax, but they were not sorry.

In the deep cold of winter, simply traveling was dangerous enough. Most people were snugly settled in warm lodges, and friends and kin would come looking if anyone was outside for too long. Ayla and Jondalar were entirely on their own. If anything happened, they had only each other, and their animal companions, to depend on.

The land gradually sloped upward, and they began to notice a subtle shift in the vegetation. Fir and larch appeared among the spruce and pine near the river. The temperature on the plains of the river valleys was extremely cold; due to atmospheric inversions, often colder than it was higher in the surrounding mountains. Although snow and ice whitened the highlands that flanked them, snow seldom fell on the river valley. The few light, dry siftings that did produced little buildup on the frozen ground, except in hollows and depressions, and sometimes not even there. When snow was lacking, the only way they could get drinking water for themselves and the animals was to use their stone axes to chop ice from the frozen river and then melt it.

It made Ayla more aware of the animals that roamed the plains along the valley of the Mother. They were the same varieties as those they had seen on the steppes all along the way, but the cold-loving creatures predominated. She knew these animals could subsist on the dry vegetation that was easily available on the subfreezing but essentially snowless plains, but she wondered how they found water.

She thought that wolves and other carnivores probably derived some of their liquid requirement from the blood of those they hunted for food, and they ranged over a large territory and could find pockets of snow or loose ice to chew. But what about horses and the other grazing and browsing animals? How did they find water in a land that in winter was a frozen desert? There was enough snow in some areas, but others were barren regions of rock and ice. Yet no matter how dry, if there was some kind of fodder, it was inhabited by animals.

Although still rare, Ayla saw more woolly rhinoceroses than she had ever seen in one place, and though they didn't herd together, whenever she saw rhinos, they often saw musk-oxen, too. Both species preferred the open, windy, dry land, but the rhinos liked grass and sedge, and musk-oxen, true to the goatlike creatures they were, browsed on woodier brush. Large reindeer and the gigantic megaceroses with massive antlers also shared the frozen land, and horses with thick winter coats, but if there was one animal that stood out among the populations in the valley of the upper course of the Great Mother River, it was mammoths.

Ayla never grew tired of watching the huge beasts. Though they were occasionally hunted, they were so unafraid that they seemed almost tame. They often allowed the woman and man to come quite close, sensing no danger from them. The danger was, if anything, to the humans. Though woolly mammoths were not the most gigantic examples of their species, they were the most gigantic animals the humans had ever seen—or that most people were ever likely to see—and with their shaggy coats even more filled out for winter, and their immense curved tusks, they looked bigger, up close, than Ayla remembered.

Their enormous tusks began, in calves, with inch-and-a-half-long tushes, enlarged upper incisors. After a year, the baby tushes were lost and replaced by permanent tusks that grew continually from then on. While the tusks of mammoths were social adornments, important in interactions with their own kind, they also had a more practical function. They were used to break up ice, and the ice-breaking abilities of mammoths were phenomenal.

The first time Ayla observed the practice, she had been watching a herd of females approach the frozen river. Several of them used their tusks, somewhat smaller and straighter than the ivory shafts of males, to tear out ice that was caught in the lee of rock crevices. It puzzled her at first, until she noticed a small one pick up a piece with her little trunk and put it in her mouth.

"Water!" Ayla said. "That's how they get water, Jondalar. I was wondering about that."

"You're right. I never thought much about it before, but now that you mention it, I think Dalanar said something about that. But there are lots of sayings about mammoths. The only one I remember is, 'Never go forth when mammoths go north,' though you could say the same for rhinos."

"I don't understand that saying," Ayla said.

"It means a snowstorm is coming," Jondalar said. "They always seem to know. Those big woollies don't like snow much. It covers up their food. They can use their tusks and their trunks to brush away some, but not when it gets really deep, and they get bogged down in it. It's especially bad when it's thawing and freezing. They lie down at night when it's still slushy from the afternoon sun, and by morning their fur is frozen to the ground. They can't move. They are easy to hunt then, but if there are no hunters around and it doesn't thaw, they can slowly starve. Some have been known to freeze to death, especially little ones."

"What does that have to do with going north?"

"The closer you get to the ice, the less snow there is. Remember how it was when we went hunting mammoths with the Mamutoi? The only water around was the stream coming from the glacier itself, and that was summer. In winter, that's all frozen."

"Is that why there's so little snow around here?"

"Yes, this region is always cold and dry, especially in winter. Everyone says it's because the glaciers are so close. They are on the mountains to the south, and the Great Ice is not very far north. Most of the land in between is flathead . . . I mean Clan country. It starts a little west of here." Jondalar noticed Ayla's expression at his slip of the tongue, and he felt embarrassed. "Anyway, there's another saying about mammoths and water, but I can't remember exactly how it goes. It's something like, 'If you can't find water, look for a mammoth.' "

"I can understand that saying," Ayla said, looking beyond him. Jondalar turned to see.

The female mammoths had moved upstream and joined forces with a few males. Several females were working on a narrow, almost vertical, bank of ice that had built up along the river's edge. The bigger males, including one dignified elder with streaks of gray hair, whose impressive, if less useful, tusks had grown so long that they were crossed in front, were scraping and gouging out huge chunks of ice from the banks. Then, lifting them high with their trunks, the mammoths threw the ice down with a loud crash to shatter into more usable pieces, all accompanied by bellowings, snortings, stompings, and trumpetings. The huge woolly creatures seemed to be making a game of it.

The noisy business of breaking ice was a practice that all mammoths learned. Even young ones only two or three years old, who had barely lost their baby tushes, showed wear on the outside edges at the ends of their tiny two-inch tusks from scraping ice, and the tips of the twenty-inch prongs of ten-year-olds were worn smooth from moving their heads up and down against the vertical surfaces. By the time the young mammoths reached twenty-five, their tusks were beginning to grow forward, upward, and inward, and the way they used them changed. The lower surfaces began to show some of the wear of scraping ice and brushing aside what snow did fall on the dry grass and plants of the steppes. Ice breaking, though, could be a dangerous business, since tusks often broke along with the ice. But even broken ends were often worn smooth again by later scraping and gouging of ice.

Ayla noticed that other animals had gathered around. The herds of woolly animals, with their powerful tusks, broke up enough ice for themselves, including their young and old, and for a community of followers as well. Many animals benefited by trailing close on the heels of migrating mammoths. The big woollies not only created piles of loose chunks of ice in winter that were chewed for moisture by animals other than themselves, in summer they sometimes used their tusks and feet to dig holes in dry riverbeds, which would fill with water. The waterholes thus created were also used by other animals to slake their thirst.

As they followed the frozen waterway, the woman and man rode, and often walked, fairly close to the banks of the Great Mother River. With so little snow, there was no soft blanket of concealing white to cover the land, and the dormant vegetation exposed its drab winter face. The tall stalks of last summer's phragmite reeds and spikes of cattails rose valiantly from their frozen bed of marshland, while dead ferns and sedges lay prostrate near the ice heaped up along the edges. Lichens clung to rocks like the scabs of healing wounds, and mosses had shriveled into brittle dry mats.

The long, skeletal fingers of leafless limbs rattled in the sharp and piercing wind, though only a practiced eye could discern whether they were willow, birch, or alder brush. The deep green conifers—spruces, firs, and pines—were easier to distinguish, and though the larches had dropped their needles, their shape was revealing. When they climbed to higher elevations to hunt, they saw recumbent dwarf birch and knee pine clinging close to the ground.

Small game provided most of their meals; big game usually required more time to stalk and hunt than they wanted to spend, although they didn't hesitate to try for a deer when they saw one. The meat froze quickly, and even Wolf didn't have to hunt for a while. Rabbit, hare, and an occasional beaver, abundant in the mountainous region, were more usual fare, but the steppe animals of drier continental climates, marmots and giant hamsters, were also prevalent, and they were always glad to see ptarmigan, the fat white birds with the feathered feet.

Ayla's sling was often put to good use; they tended to save the spear-throwers for larger game. It was easier to find stones than to make new spears to replace missiles that were lost or broken. But some days hunting took more of their time than they wished, and anything that took time made Jondalar edgy.

They often supplemented their diet, which was heavily concentrated on lean meat, with the inner bark of conifers and other trees, usually cooked into a broth with meat, and they were delighted when they found berries, frozen but still clinging to the bush. Juniper berries, which were particularly good with meat if they didn't use too many, were prevalent;

rose hips were more sporadic, but usually plentiful when
found, and always sweeter after freezing; creeping crowberry,
with a needlelike evergreen foliage, had small shiny black
berries that often persisted through the winter, as did blue
bearberries and red lingonberries.

Grains and seeds were also added to the meat soups, gathered painstakingly from dried grasses and herbs that still bore
seed heads, though it took time to find them. Most of the
foliage of seed-bearing herbs had long since disintegrated,
the plants lying dormant until spring thaws would awaken
them to new life. Ayla wished for the dried vegetables and
fruits that had been destroyed by the wolves, though she
didn't begrudge the supplies she had given to the S'Armunai.

Though Whinney and Racer were grass eaters almost
exclusively in summer, Ayla noticed that their diet had
extended to browsing on twig tips, chewing through to the
inner bark of trees, and included a particular variety of lichen,
the kind reindeer preferred. She collected some and tested
small amounts on herself, then made some for both of them.
They found the taste strong but tolerable, and she was experimenting with ways to cook it.

Another source of winter food was small rodents such as
voles, mice, and lemmings; not the animals themselves—
Ayla usually let Wolf have those as a reward for helping to
sniff them out—but their nests. She looked for the subtle
features that hinted at a burrow, then broke through the frozen
ground with a digging stick to find the small animals surrounded by the seeds, nuts, and bulbs they had laid by.

And Ayla also had her medicine bag. When she thought
of all the damage that had been done to the things they had
cached, she shuddered to think about what would have happened if she had left her medicine bag. Not that she would
have, but the thought of losing it made her stomach churn.
It was so much a part of her that she would have felt lost
without it. But even more, the materials in the otter-skin bag,
and the long history of lore accumulated by trial and error
that had been passed down to her, kept the travelers healthier
than either of them fully realized.

For example, Ayla knew that various herbs, barks, and
roots could be used to treat, and avoid getting, certain diseases. Though she didn't call them deficiency diseases, or
have a name for the vitamins and trace minerals the herbs
contained, or even know exactly how they worked, she car-

ried many of them with her in her medicine bag, and she regularly made them into the teas they drank.

She also used the vegetation that was readily available even in winter, such as the needles of evergreens, particularly the newest growth from the tips of branches, which were rich in the vitamins that prevented scurvy. She regularly added them to their daily teas, mostly because they liked the tangy, citruslike flavor, though she did know they were beneficial and had a good idea of when and how to use them. She had often made needle tea for people with soft bloody gums whose teeth became loose during long winters of subsisting essentially on dried meats, either by choice or necessity.

They developed a pattern of opportunistic foraging as they moved west that allowed them as much time as possible for traveling. Though an occasional meal was skimpy, they seldom missed one entirely, but with so little fat in their diet and the constant exercise every day, they did lose weight. They didn't talk about it often, but they were both getting weary of the traveling and longed to reach their destination. During the day, they didn't talk much at all.

Riding the horses, or walking and leading them, Ayla and Jondalar often went single-file, close enough to hear a comment if it was spoken in a loud voice, but not close enough for casual conversation. As a result, they both had long stretches of quiet time to think their own thoughts, which they sometimes talked about in the evening when they were eating or lying together side by side in their sleeping furs.

Ayla often thought about their recent experiences. She had been thinking about the Camp of the Three Sisters, comparing the S'Armunai and their cruel leaders, like Attaroa and Brugar, with their relatives, the Mamutoi, and their cooperative and friendly sister-brother coleaders. And she wondered about the Zelandonii, the people of the man she loved. Jondalar had so many good qualities, she felt sure they had to be basically good people, but considering their feelings toward the Clan, she still wondered how they would accept her. Even S'Armuna had made oblique references to their strong aversion to the ones they called flatheads, but she felt sure no Zelandonii would ever be as cruel as the woman who had been the leader of the S'Armunai.

"I don't know how Attaroa could do the things she did, Jondalar," Ayla remarked as they were finishing an evening meal. "It makes me wonder."

"What do you wonder about?"

"My kind of people, the Others. When I first met you, I was so grateful just to finally find someone like me. It was a relief to know I wasn't the only one in the world. Then, when you turned out to be so wonderful, so good and caring and loving, I thought all of my kind of people would be like you," she said, "and it made me feel good." She was going to add, until he reacted with such disgust when she told him about her life with the Clan, but she changed her mind when she saw Jondalar smiling, flushed with embarrassed delight, obviously pleased.

He had felt a rush of warmth at her words, thinking that she was pretty wonderful, too.

"Then, when we met the Mamutoi, Talut and the Lion Camp," Ayla continued, "I was sure the Others were all good people. They helped each other, and everyone had a voice in the decisions. They were friendly and laughed a lot, and they didn't reject an idea just because they hadn't heard about it before. There was Frebec, of course, but he turned out not to be so bad, either. Even those at the Summer Meeting who sided against me for a while because of the Clan, and even some of the Sharamudoi, did it out of misplaced fear, not evil intentions. But Attaroa was as vicious as a hyena."

"Attaroa was only one person," Jondalar reminded her.

"Yes, but look how many she influenced. S'Armuna used her sacred knowledge to help Attaroa kill and hurt people, even if she did feel sorry about it later, and Epadoa was willing to do anything Attaroa said," Ayla said.

"They had reasons for it. The women had been badly treated," Jondalar said.

"I know the reasons. S'Armuna thought she was doing the right thing, and I think Epadoa loved to hunt and loved Attaroa for letting her do it. I know that feeling. I love to hunt, too, and I went against the Clan and did things I wasn't supposed to so I could hunt."

"Well, Epadoa can hunt for the whole Camp now, and I don't think she was so bad," Jondalar said. "She seemed to be discovering the kind of love a mother feels. Doban told me she promised him she would never hurt him again and would never let anyone else hurt him," Jondalar said. "Her feelings for him may be even stronger because she hurt him so much and now she has a chance to make up for it."

"Epadoa didn't want to hurt those boys. She told S'Armuna that she was afraid if she didn't do what Attaroa wanted, she would kill them. Those were her reasons. Even Attaroa had reasons. There was so much in her life that was bad, she became an evil thing. She wasn't human anymore, but no reasons are good enough to excuse her. How could she do the things she did? Even Broud, as bad as he was, was not as bad, and he hated me. He never purposely hurt children. I used to think my kind of people were so good, but I'm not so sure anymore," she said, looking sad and distressed.

"There are good people and bad people, Ayla, and everyone has some good and some bad in them," Jondalar said, his wrinkled forehead showing his concern. He sensed that she was trying to fit the new sensibilities she had gathered from her latest unpleasant experience into her personal scheme of things, and he knew it was important. "But most people are decent and try to help each other. They know it's necessary—after all, you never know when you may need help—and most people would rather be friendly."

"But there are some who are twisted, like Attaroa," Ayla said.

"That's true." The man nodded, having to agree. "And there are some who only give what they must and would rather not give at all, but that doesn't make them bad."

"But one bad person can bring out the worst in good people, like Attaroa did to S'Armuna and Epadoa."

"I suppose the best we can do is try to keep the evil and cruel ones from causing too much harm. Maybe we should count ourselves lucky there aren't more like her. But, Ayla, don't let one bad person spoil the way you feel about people."

"Attaroa can't make me feel any different about the people I know, and I'm sure you are right about most people, Jondalar, but she has made me more wary, and more cautious."

"It doesn't hurt to be a little cautious, at first, but give people a chance to show their good side before you judge them bad."

The highland on the north side of the river paced along with them as they continued their westward trek. Wind-sculp-

tured evergreens on the rounded tops and level plateaus of
the massif were silhouetted against the sky. The river split
out again into several channels across a lowland basin that
formed an embayment. The southern and northern boundaries
of the valley maintained their characteristic differences, but
the base rock was cracked and down-faulted to great depths
between the river and the limestone foreland of the high
southern mountain. Toward the west was the steep limestone
edge of a fault line. The course of the river turned northwest.

The east end of the lowland basin was also bordered by
a fault ridge, caused not so much by uplifting of the limestone
as by the depression of the land of the embayment. Toward
the south, the land spread out on a level grade for some
distance before it rose up toward the mountains, but the granite plateau in the north drew closer to the river, until it was
rising steeply just across the water.

They camped within the low embayment. In the valley
near the river, the smooth gray bark and the bare branches
of beech made an appearance among the spruce, fir, pine,
and larch; the area was protected enough to shelter the growth
of a few large-leafed deciduous trees. Milling around near
the trees in seeming confusion was a small herd of mammoths, both females and males. Ayla edged closer to see
what was going on.

One mammoth was down, a giant of an elder with enormous tusks that crossed in front. She wondered if it was the
same group they had seen earlier breaking ice. Could there
be two mammoths who were so old in the same region?
Jondalar walked up beside her.

"I'm afraid he's dying. I wish there was something I
could do for him," Ayla said.

"His teeth are probably gone. Once that happens, there
is nothing anyone can do, except what they are doing. Staying
with him, keeping him company," Jondalar said.

"Perhaps none of us can ask for more," Ayla said.

In spite of their relatively compact size, each adult mammoth consumed large quantities of food every day, primarily
woody-stemmed tall grass and occasional small trees. With
such a rough diet, their teeth were essential. They were so
important that a mammoth's lifespan was determined by its
teeth.

A woolly mammoth developed several sets of large grinding molars throughout its span of some seventy years, usually

six to a side both upper and lower. Each tooth weighed about
eight pounds and was especially adapted to grinding coarse
grasses. The surface was made up of many extremely hard,
thin, parallel ridges—plates of dentine covered with enamel—
and had higher crowns and more ridges than the teeth of any
other of its species, before or since. Mammoths were primarily grass eaters. The shreds of bark that they tore from trees,
particularly in winter, the spring forbs, and the occasional
leaves, branches, and small trees, were only incidental to
their main diet of tough fibrous grass.

The earliest and smallest grinders were formed near the
front of each jaw, and the rest grew in behind and moved
forward in a steady progression during the animal's life, with
only one or two teeth in use at any one time. As hard as it
was, the important grinding surface wore down as it moved
toward the front, and the roots dissolved. Finally the last thin
useless fragments of tooth were dropped as the new ones
moved into place.

The final teeth were in use by age fifty, and when they
were nearly gone, the old gray-hair could not chew the tough
grass anymore. Softer leaves and plants could still be eaten,
spring plants, but in other seasons they were not available.
In desperation, the undernourished elder often left the herd,
searching for greener pastures, but found only death. The
herd knew when the end was close, and it wasn't uncommon
to see them sharing the elder's last days.

The other mammoths were as protective of the dying as
they were of newborns, and they gathered around trying to
make the fallen one get up. When all was over, they buried
the dead ancestor under piles of dirt, grass, leaves, or snow.
Mammoths were even known to bury other dead animals,
including humans.

Ayla and Jondalar and their four-legged traveling companions found their way getting steeper and more difficult when
they left behind the lowland and the mammoths. They were
approaching a gorge. A foot of the ancient massif of the north
had stretched too far south and was split by the dividing
waters of the river. They climbed higher as the river rushed
through the narrow defile, moving too fast to freeze but carrying with it ice flocs from quieter sections farther west. It
was strange to see moving water after so much ice. In front

of the high-peaked ramparts to the south were mesas, massiflike hills topped with extensive plateaus, carrying thick stands of conifers, their branches sprinkled with snow. The thin limbs of deciduous trees and brush were etched in white from a coating of freezing rain, which accentuated each twig and branch, captivating Ayla with their winter beauty.

The altitude continued to increase, the lowlands between the ridges never dipping quite as low as the preceding ones. The air was cold, crisp, and clear, and even when it was cloudy, no snow fell. Precipitation decreased as winter deepened. The only moisture in the air was the warm breath expelled by humans and animals.

The river of ice became smaller each time they passed a frozen tributary valley. At the west end of the lowland was another gorge. They climbed the rocky ridge, and when they reached the highest place, they looked ahead and stopped, awed by the sight. Ahead the river had split again. The travelers didn't know it was the last time that it would divide into the branches and channels that had characterized its progress across the flat plains over which it had flowed for so much of its length. The gorge just before the lowlands curved sharply as it gathered the separate channels into one, causing a furious whirlpool that carried ice and floating debris into its depths, before disgorging it in a gush farther downstream, where it rapidly refroze.

They stopped at the highest place, looked down, and watched a small log whirling around and around, going deeper and deeper with each spiraling turn.

"I would not want to fall into that," Ayla said, shuddering at the thought.

"Nor would I," Jondalar responded.

Ayla's gaze was drawn to another site in the distance. "Where are those clouds of steam coming from, Jondalar?" she asked. "It's freezing, and the hills are covered with snow."

"There are pools of hot water over there, water warmed by the hot breath of Doni Herself. Some people are afraid to go near such places, but the people I want to visit live near such a deep hot well, or so they told me. The hot wells are sacred to them, even though some smell very bad. It's said they use the water to cure illness."

"How long before we reach those people you know? The ones who use water to cure illness," she asked. Anything that might add to her wealth of medical knowledge always piqued her interest. Besides, food was getting scarcer, or they didn't want to take the time to look for it—but they had gone to bed hungry a couple of days.

The slope of the land increased noticeably beyond the last flat basin. They were hemmed in by highlands on both sides as the mountains pressed in. The mantel of ice to the south was increasing in height as they continued west. Far to the south and still somewhat west, two peaks soared far above all the other rugged mountaintops, one higher than the other, like a mated pair watching over their brood of children.

Where the highland leveled out near a shallower place in the river, Jondalar turned south, away from the river, toward a cloud of rising steam in the distance. They climbed a low ridge and looked down from the top across a snow-covered meadow at a steaming pool of water near a cave.

Several people had noticed their approach and stared in consternation, too shocked to move. One man, however, was aiming a spear at them.

35

I think we'd better get off the horses and approach them on foot," Jondalar said, watching several more spear-carrying men and women warily coming forward. "You'd think by now I would remember that people are scared and suspicious of riding on horses. We probably should have left them out of sight and walked in, then gone back for them after we had time to explain about the animals."

They both dismounted, and Jondalar had a sudden and poignant memory of his "little brother," Thonolan, smiling his big, friendly grin and walking confidently up to a Cave or Camp of strangers. Taking it as a sign, the tall blond man smiled broadly, waved in friendliness, pushed back the hood of his parka so he could be more easily seen, then stepped forward with both hands outstretched, showing he was coming to them openly, with nothing to hide.

"I'm looking for Laduni of the Losadunai. I am Jondalar of the Zelandonii," he said. "My brother and I were traveling east on a Journey a few years ago, and Laduni asked us to stop and visit on the way back."

"I am Laduni," said a man, speaking a slightly accented Zelandonii. He walked toward them, holding his spear in readiness, looking closely to make sure the strange man was who he said he was. "Jondalar? Of the Zelandonii? You do look like the man I met."

Jondalar sensed the cautious tone. "That's because I am! It's good to see you, Laduni," he said with warmth. "I wasn't sure if I turned off at the right place. I've been all the way to the end of the Great Mother River, and beyond, and then, closer to home, I had trouble finding your Cave, but the steam from your hot wells helped. I brought someone I'd like you to meet."

The older man eyed Jondalar, trying to detect any hint that he was something other than what he seemed: a man he knew who happened to arrive in a most peculiar fashion. He looked a little older, which was reasonable, and even more like Dalanar. He had seen the old flint knapper again a few years before when he came on a trading mission and, Laduni suspected, to find out whether the son of his hearth and his brother had passed that way. Dalanar will be very glad to see him, Laduni thought. He walked toward Jondalar, holding his spear more easily, but still in a position from which it could be thrown quickly. He glanced toward the two unusually docile horses, and he saw for the first time that it was a woman who was standing near them.

"Those horses are not anything like the ones around here. Are eastern horses more docile? They must be much easier to hunt," Laduni said.

Suddenly the man tensed, brought his spear into position to throw, and had it aimed toward Ayla. "Don't move, Jondalar!" he said.

It happened so fast, Jondalar didn't have time to react. "Laduni! What are you doing?"

"A wolf has been trailing you. One fearless enough to come in plain sight."

"No!" Ayla shouted, throwing herself between the wolf and the man with the spear.

"This wolf travels with us. Don't kill him!" Jondalar said, rushing to interpose himself between Laduni and Ayla.

She dropped down and wrapped her arms around the wolf, holding him firmly, partly to protect him, and partly to protect the man with the spear. Wolf's hair was bristling, his

lips were pulled back to show his fangs, and a savage snarl
issued from his throat.

Laduni was taken aback. He had moved to protect the
visitors, but they were acting as if he meant to harm them.
He gave Jondalar a questioning look.

"Put down your spear, Laduni. Please," Jondalar said.
"The wolf is our companion, just as the horses are. He saved
our lives. I promise, he won't hurt anyone as long as no one
threatens him, or the woman. I know it must seem strange,
but if you'll give me a chance, I'll explain."

Laduni slowly lowered his spear, eying the large wolf
warily. Once the threat was removed, Ayla calmed the animal, then stood up and walked toward Jondalar and Laduni,
signaling Wolf to stay close to her side.

"Please excuse Wolf for raising his hackles," Ayla said.
"He really likes people, once he gets to know them, but we
had a bad experience with some people east of here. It has
made him more nervous around strangers, and he has become
more protective."

Laduni noticed that she spoke Zelandonii quite well, but
her strange accent branded her as a foreigner immediately.
He also noticed . . . something else . . . he wasn't sure. It
was nothing he could specifically define. He'd seen many
blond, blue-eyed women before, but the set of her cheekbones, the shape of her features or face, something gave her
a foreign look as well. Whatever it was, it did not detract in
the least from the fact that she was a strikingly beautiful
woman. If anything, it added an element of mystery.

He looked at Jondalar and smiled. Remembering his last
visit, it didn't surprise him that the tall, handsome Zelandonii
would return from a long Journey with an exotic beauty, but
no one could have expected living, breathing souvenirs of his
adventures, like horses and a wolf. He could hardly wait to
hear the stories they had to tell.

Jondalar had seen the look of appreciation in Laduni's
eyes when he saw Ayla, and, when the man smiled, he began
to relax.

"This is the person I wanted you to meet," Jondalar said.
"Laduni, hunter of the Losadunai, this is Ayla of the Lion
Camp of the Mamutoi, Chosen by the Cave Lion, Protected
by the Cave Bear, and Daughter of the Mammoth Hearth."

Ayla had raised both hands, palms up, in the greeting
of openness and friendship, when Jondalar began the formal

introduction. "I greet you, Laduni, Master Hunter of the Losadunai," Ayla said.

Laduni wondered how she knew he was the hunt leader of his people. Jondalar hadn't said it. Perhaps he'd said something to her before, but she was astute for mentioning it. But then, she would understand those kinds of things. With so many titles and affiliations, she must be a woman of high standing among her people, he thought. I might have guessed that any woman he brought back would be, considering that both his mother and the man of his hearth have known the responsibilities of leadership. The child will tell the blood of the mother and the spirit of the man.

Laduni took both her hands. "In the name of Duna, the Great Earth Mother, you are welcome, Ayla of the Lion Camp of the Mamutoi, Chosen of the Lion, Protected by the Great Bear, and Daughter of the Mammoth Hearth," Laduni said.

"I thank you for your welcome," Ayla said, still in a formal mode. "And if I may, I would like to introduce you to Wolf, so that he will know you are a friend."

Laduni frowned, not sure if he really wanted to meet a wolf, but under the circumstances he felt he had no choice.

"Wolf, this is Laduni of the Losadunai," she said, taking the man's hand and bringing it to the wolf's nose. "He is a friend." After he smelled the hand of the strange man, mixed with the smell of Ayla's hand, Wolf seemed to understand that this was someone to accept. He sniffed the man's male parts, much to Laduni's consternation.

"That's enough, Wolf," Ayla said, signaling him back. Then to Laduni, she added, "He has now learned that you are a friend, and that you are a man. If you would like to welcome him, he likes to be petted on the head and scratched behind the ears."

Though still wary, the idea of touching a living wolf intrigued him. Gingerly he reached out and felt the rough fur, and seeing that his touch was accepted, he stroked the animal's head, then rubbed a little behind his ears, pleased about the whole thing. It wasn't that he hadn't touched wolf fur before, just not on a living animal.

"I am sorry I threatened your companion," he said. "But I have never seen a wolf accompany people of his own free will before, or horses either, for that matter."

"It is understandable," Ayla said. "I will take you to

meet the horses later. They tend to be shy of strangers, and they need some time to get used to new people."

"Are all the eastern animals this friendly?" Laduni asked, pressing for an answer to a question that would be of interest to any hunter.

Jondalar smiled. "No, animals are the same everywhere. These are special because of Ayla."

Laduni nodded, fighting his impulse to ask them further questions, knowing the whole Cave would want to hear their stories. "I have welcomed you, and I invite you to come inside to share warmth and food, and a place to rest, but I think I should go first and explain about you to the rest of the Cave."

Laduni walked back toward the group gathered in front of a large opening in the side of a rock wall. He explained about meeting Jondalar a few years before, when he was starting on his Journey, and inviting him to visit on his way back. He mentioned that Jondalar was related to Dalanar, and emphasized that they were people, not some kind of threatening spirits, and that they would tell them about the horses and the wolf. "They should have some interesting stories to tell," he concluded, knowing what an enticement that would be to a group of people who had been essentially cavebound since the beginning of winter and were getting bored.

The language he spoke was not the Zelandonii he had spoken to the travelers, but after listening for a while, Ayla was sure she heard similarities. She realized that although they had a different stress and pronunciation, Losadunai was related to Zelandonii in the same way that S'Armunai, and Sharamudoi, for that matter, were related to Mamutoi. This language even had a link with S'Armunai. She had understood some of the words and had picked up the gist of some of his comments. She would be speaking with these people in a few days.

Ayla's gift for languages did not seem unusual to her. She didn't consciously try to learn them, but her sharp ear for nuance and inflection and her ability to see the connections made it easy for her. Losing her own language in the trauma of losing her people when she was very young, and having to learn a different way of communicating, but one that utilized the same areas of the brain as spoken language, enhanced her inherent language skills. Her need to learn to communicate again when she discovered that she could not, gave her an unconscious but profound incentive to learn any unfamiliar language. It was the combination of natural ability and circumstances that made her so adept.

"Losaduna says you are most welcome to stay at the visitors' hearth," Laduna said to them after his explanation.

"We need to unpack the horses and get them settled first," Jondalar said. "This field right outside your cave seems to have some good winter graze. Will anyone mind if we leave them here?"

"You are welcome to use the field," Laduni said. "I think everyone will be intrigued to see horses so close." He couldn't help glancing at Ayla, wondering what she had done to the animals. It seemed obvious that she commanded very powerful spirits.

"I must ask something else," Ayla said. "Wolf is accustomed to sleeping near us. He would be quite unhappy anywhere else. If having the wolf inside would make your Losaduna, or your Cave, uncomfortable, we will set up our tent and sleep outside."

Laduni spoke again to the people, and after some conversation he turned back to the visitors. "They want you to come in, but some of the mothers fear for their children," he said.

"I understand their fear. I can promise that Wolf will not harm anyone, but if that is not enough, we will stay outside."

There was more conversation, then Laduni said, "They say you should come in."

Laduni went with them when Ayla and Jondalar went to unpack the horses, and he was just as thrilled to meet Whinney and Racer as he had been to meet Wolf. He had done his share of horse hunting, but he had never touched one, except by chance when he managed to get close enough during the chase. Ayla recognized his enjoyment, and she thought that later she might offer him a ride on Whinney's back.

As they walked back toward the cave, dragging their things in the bowl boat, Laduni asked Jondalar about his brother. When he saw pain flash across the tall man's face, he knew there had been a tragedy before Jondalar answered.

"Thonolan died. He was killed by a cave lion."

"I'm sorry to hear that. I liked him," Laduni said.

"Everyone liked him."

"He was so eager to follow the Great Mother River all the way to the end. Did he get there?"

"Yes, he did reach the end of Donau before he died, but he had no heart for it by then. He had fallen in love with a woman, and mated her, but she died in childbirth," Jondalar said. "It changed him, took the heart out of him. He didn't want to live after that."

Laduni shook his head. "What a shame. He was so full of life. Filonia thought about him for a long time after you left. She kept hoping he would come back."

"How is Filonia?" Jondalar asked, remembering the pretty young daughter of Laduni's hearth.

The older man grinned. "She's mated now, and Duna smiles on her. She has two children. Shortly after you and Thonolan left, she discovered she had been blessed. When the word got around that she was pregnant, I think every eligible Losadunai man found a reason to visit our Cave."

"I can imagine. As I recall, she was a lovely young woman. She made a Journey, didn't she?"

"Yes, with an older cousin."

"And she has two children?" Jondalar said.

Laduni's eyes sparkled with pleasure. "A daughter from the first blessing, Thonolia—Filonia was sure she was a child of your brother's spirit—and not long ago, she had a son. She is living with her mate's Cave. They had more room, but it's not too far away and we see her, and the children, regularly." There was satisfaction and joy in Laduni's voice.

"I hope Thonolia is a child of Thonolan's spirit. I'd like to think that there is still a piece of his spirit in this world," Jondalar said.

Could it happen so fast? Jondalar wondered. He only spent one night with her. Was his spirit so potent? Or, if Ayla is right, could Thonolan have started a baby growing inside Filonia with the essence of his manhood that night we stayed with them? He remembered the woman he had been with.

"How is Lanalia?" he asked.

"She is fine. She is visiting kin at another Cave. They are trying to arrange a mating for her. A man lost his mate and is left with three young children at his hearth. Lanalia never had any children, though she always wanted some. If she finds him compatible, they will mate, and she will adopt the children. It could be a very happy arrangement, and she is very excited about it.''

"I'm pleased for her, and wish her much happiness," Jondalar said, covering up his disappointment. He was hoping that she might have become pregnant after sharing Pleasures with him. Whatever it is, a man's spirit or the essence of his manhood, Thonolan has proved the strength of his, but what about me? Is my essence or spirit potent enough? Jondalar wondered.

As they entered the cave, Ayla looked around with interest. She had seen many dwellings of the Others: lightweight or portable shelters that were used in summer, and sturdier permanent structures able to withstand the rigors of winter. Some were constructed out of mammoth bones and covered with sod and clay, some out of wood and tucked away under an overhang or on a floating platform, but she had not seen a cave like this since she left the Clan. It had a large mouth that faced southeast, and it was nice and roomy inside. Brun would have liked this cave, she thought.

Once her eyes became accustomed to the dim light and she saw the interior, she was surprised. She had expected to see several fireplaces in various locations, the hearths of each family. There were family fireplaces within the cave, but they were inside or near the openings of structures made of hides fastened to poles. They were similar to tents, but not conical in shape, and open at the top—they needed no protection from the weather inside the cave. As far as she could tell, they were used as panels to screen the interior space from casual sight. Ayla recalled the Clan's prohibition against looking directly into the living space, as defined by boundary stones, of another man's hearth. It was a matter of tradition and self-control, but the purpose, she realized, was the same: privacy.

Laduni was leading them toward one of the screened-off dwelling spaces. "Your bad experience didn't involve a band of rowdies, did it?" he asked.

"No, has there been trouble?" Jondalar asked. "When we met before, you spoke about some young man who had gathered together several followers. They were making sport of the Cl . . . flatheads." He glanced at Ayla, but he knew Laduni would never understand "Clan." "They were baiting the men, then taking their Pleasures with the women. Something about high spirits leading to trouble for everyone."

When Ayla heard "flatheads," she listened closely, curious to know if there were many Clan people nearby.

"Yes, those are the ones. Charoli and his band," Laduni said. "It may have started with high spirits, but it has gone much beyond that."

"I would have thought by now that those young men would have given up that kind of behavior," Jondalar said.

"It's Charoli. Individually, I suppose, they are not bad young men, but he encourages them. Losaduna says he wants to show how brave he is, to show he is a man, because he grew up without a man at his hearth."

"Many women have raised boys alone, who have turned out to be fine men," Jondalar said. They had become so involved in the conversation that they had stopped walking and were standing in the middle of the cave. People were gathering around.

"Yes, of course. But his mother's mate disappeared when he was just a baby, and she never took another. Instead she lavished all her attention on him, indulging him long beyond his early years, when he should have been learning a craft and the duties of an adult. Now it's up to everyone to put a stop to him."

"What happened?" Jondalar asked.

"A girl of our Cave was near the river setting snares. She had just become a young woman a few moons before, and she hadn't yet had her Rites of First Pleasures. She was looking forward to the ceremony at the next gathering. Charoli and his band happened to see her alone, and they all took her . . ."

"All of them? Took her? By force?" Jondalar said, appalled. "A girl, not yet a woman. I can't believe it!"

"All of them," Laduni said, with a cold anger that was worse than any heat of the moment. "And we will not put up with it! I don't know if they got tired of flathead females, or what excuse they gave themselves, but that was too much. They caused her pain, and bleeding. She says she wants nothing more to do with men, ever again. She has refused to go through with her womanhood rites."

"That's terrible, but it's hard to blame her. It is not the way for a young woman to learn of Doni's Gift," Jondalar said.

"Her mother is afraid that if she forgoes honoring the Mother with the ceremony, she will never have children."

"She could be right, but what can be done?" Jondalar asked.

"Her mother wants Charoli dead, and she wants us to declare a blood feud against his Cave," Laduni said. "Revenge is her right, but a blood feud can destroy everyone. Besides, it's not Charoli's Cave that has caused the trouble. It's that band of his, and some of them aren't even from the Cave of Charoli's birth. I've sent a message to Tomasi, the hunt leader there, and put an idea to him."

"An idea? What's your plan?"

"I think it's up to all of the Losadunai to stop Charoli and his band. I'm hoping that Tomasi will join with me in trying to convince everyone to bring those young men back under the supervision of the Caves. I've even suggested that he allow Madenia's mother her revenge, rather than suffer the bloodshed of a feud over them. But Tomasi is related to Charoli's mother."

"That would be a hard decision," Jondalar said. He noticed that Ayla had been listening closely. "Does anyone know where Charoli's band stays? They can't be with any of your people. I can't believe any Cave of Losadunai would shelter such ruffians in their midst."

"South of here is a barren area, with underground rivers and many caves. It is rumored that they are hiding in one of the caves near the edge of that region."

"They could be hard to find if there are many caves."

"But they can't stay there all the time. They have to get food, and they can be trailed and followed. A good tracker could trail them easier than he could an animal, but we need all the Caves to cooperate. Then it wouldn't take long to find them."

"What will you do with them after you find them?" This time it was Ayla who asked the question.

"I think that once all those young ruffians are separated, it wouldn't take long to break their ties to each other. Each Cave can handle one or two of their own in their own way. I doubt if most of them really want to live outside the Losadunai, and not be a part of a Cave. They will want mates, someday, and not many women would choose to live the way they do."

"I think you are right," Jondalar said.

"I'm very sorry to hear about this young woman," Ayla

said. "What was her name? Madenia?" Her expression showed how troubled she was.

"I am, too," Jondalar added. "I wish we could stay and help, but if we don't cross the glacier soon, we may have to stay until next winter."

"It may already be too late to make it across this winter," Laduni said.

"Too late?" Jondalar said. "But it's cold, winter. Everything is frozen solid. All the crevasses should be filled with snow."

"Yes. It is winter now, but this late in the season, you never know. You could still make it, but if the foehn winds come early—and they could—then all the snow will melt fast. The glacier can be treacherous during the first spring melt, and under the circumstances, I don't think it's safe to go around through the flathead country to the north. They are not too friendly these days. Charoli's band has antagonized them. Even animals have some feeling of protection for their females and will fight to protect their own."

"They are not animals," Ayla said, springing to their defense. "They are people, just a different kind of people."

Laduni held his tongue; he did not want to offend a visitor and a guest. With her closeness to animals, she might think of all animals as people. If a wolf protects her, and she treats it like a human, is it any wonder that she thinks of flatheads as people, too? he thought. I know they can be clever, but they are not human.

Several people had gathered around while they were talking. One of them, a small, thin, rather rumpled middle-aged man with a shy smile, spoke up. "Don't you think you should let them get settled, Laduni?"

"I'm beginning to wonder if you are going to keep them here talking all day," the woman standing beside him added. She was a plump woman, just a shade shorter than the man, with a friendly face.

"I'm sorry, you are right, of course. Let me introduce you," Laduni said. He looked at Ayla first, then turned toward the man. "Losaduna, the One Who Serves the Mother for Hot Well Cave of the Losadunai, this is Ayla of the Lion Camp of the Mamutoi, Chosen of the Lion, Protected by the Great Bear, and Daughter of the Mammoth Hearth."

"The Mammoth Hearth! Then you are One Who Serves

the Mother, too," the man said with a surprised smile, before he even greeted her.

"No, I am a Daughter of the Mammoth Hearth. Mamut was training me, but I have never been initiated," Ayla explained.

"But born to it! You must be chosen of the Mother, too, along with all the rest," the man said, obviously delighted.

"Losaduna, you have not greeted her yet," the plump woman chided.

The man looked befuddled for a moment. "Oh, I guess not. Always these formalities. In the name of Duna, the Great Earth Mother, may I welcome you, Ayla of the Mamutoi, Chosen by the Lion Camp, and Daughter of the Mammoth Hearth."

The woman beside him sighed and shook her head. "He got it mixed up, but if it was some little-known ceremony, or legend about the Mother, he wouldn't forget a bit of it," she said.

Ayla couldn't help smiling. She had never met One Who Served the Mother who seemed more unlikely to function in that capacity. Those she had met before were each self-possessed, easily recognized individuals, with a powerful presence, not at all like this absentminded, diffident man, unmindful of his appearance, with a pleasant, rather shy demeanor. But the woman seemed to know where his strengths were, and Laduni showed no lack of respect. Losaduna was obviously more than he seemed.

"That's all right," Ayla said to the woman. "He didn't really get it wrong." She was, after all, chosen by the Lion Camp, too; adopted, not born to them, Ayla thought. Then she addressed the man, who had taken both her hands and was still holding them. "I greet the One Who Serves the Great Mother of All, and thank you for your welcome, Losaduna."

He smiled at Ayla's use of another of the names of the Duna, as Laduni began to speak. "Solandia of the Losadunai, born to the Hill River Cave, Mate of the Losaduna, this is Ayla of the Lion Camp of the Mamutoi, Chosen of the Lion, Protected by the Great Bear, and Daughter of the Mammoth Hearth."

"I greet you, Ayla of the Mamutoi, and invite you to our lodgings," Solandia said. The full titles and affiliations had been said enough times. She didn't think they needed to be repeated again.

"Thank you, Solandia," she said.

Laduni then looked at Jondalar. "Losaduna, One Who Serves the Mother for the Hot Well Cave of the Losadunai, this is Jondalar, Master Flint Knapper of the Ninth Cave of the Zelandonii, son of Marthona, former leader of the Ninth Cave, brother of Joharran, leader of the Ninth Cave, born to the Hearth of Dalanar, leader and founder of the Lanzadonii."

Ayla had never heard all of Jondalar's titles and ties before, and she was surprised. Though she didn't fully understand the significance, it sounded impressive. After Jondalar repeated the litany and was formally introduced, they were finally led to the large living and ceremonial space allocated to Losaduna.

Wolf, who had been sitting quietly close to Ayla's leg, gave a little yip when they reached the entrance to the dwelling space. He had seen a child inside, but his reaction frightened Solandia. She ran in and snatched the baby up off the floor. "I have four children; I don't know if that wolf should be in here," she said, fear raising the pitch of her voice. "Micheri can't even walk. How can I be sure he won't go after my little boy?"

"Wolf will not harm the little one," Ayla said. "He grew up with children and loves them. He is more gentle with them than with adults. He wasn't going after the baby, he was just so happy to see him."

Ayla had signaled Wolf to stay down, but he couldn't hide his eager anticipation in seeing the children. Solandia eyed the carnivore warily. She couldn't tell if he was showing eagerness out of happiness or hunger, but she was also curious about the visitors. One of the best parts of being the mate of Losaduna was that she had the advantage of being the first to talk with the infrequent visitors, and she could spend more time with them because they usually stayed at the ceremonial hearth.

"Well, I did say he could stay," she said.

Ayla walked Wolf inside, led him to an out-of-the-way corner, and signaled him to stay. She stayed with him for a while, knowing it would be particularly difficult for him, but just having children to watch seemed to satisfy him for the moment.

His behavior calmed Solandia, and after serving her

guests a warming hot tea, she introduced her children, then went back to preparing the meal she had started. The presence of the animal slipped to the back of her mind, but the children were fascinated. Ayla studied them, trying to be unobtrusive. The oldest of the four youngsters, Larogi, was a boy of about ten years, she guessed. There was a girl of perhaps seven years, Dosalia, and another of four or so, Neladia. Though the baby was not yet walking, that did not limit his mobility. He was at the crawling stage and was fast and efficient on all fours.

The older children were wary of Wolf, and the elder of the girls picked up the baby and held him while they watched the animal, but after a while when nothing happened, she put him down. While Jondalar spoke with Losaduna, Ayla began to set out their things. There was spare bedding for guests and she hoped she would have time to clean their sleeping furs while they were here.

Suddenly there was a peal of babyish laughter. Ayla caught her breath and looked in the corner where she had left Wolf. There was absolute silence in the rest of the dwelling space as everyone stared in wonder and awe at the baby, who had crawled to the corner and was sitting beside the large wolf, pulling on his fur. Ayla glanced at Solandia and saw her staring transfixed as her precious baby boy proceeded to poke and prod and pull at the wolf, who simply wagged his tail and looked pleased.

Finally Ayla walked over, picked up the child, and brought him to his mother.

"You're right," Solandia said with amazement, "that wolf loves children! If I hadn't seen it myself, I would never have believed it."

It wasn't long before the rest of Solandia's children approached the wolf who liked to play. After a small problem with some teasing by the oldest boy, which Wolf responded to by taking the child's hand in his teeth and growling, but not biting down, Ayla explained that they had to treat him with respect. Wolf's reaction frightened the boy just enough to make him pay attention. When they went outside, all the children of the community watched Solandia's four and the wolf with fascination. Solandia's children were envied for their special privilege of living with the animal.

Before it got dark, Ayla went out to check on the horses. When she stepped outside the cave, she heard Whinney nicker

in greeting, and she felt that her friend had been a little
worried. When she nickered back, causing several heads to
turn in her direction and stare in surprise, Racer responded
with a somewhat louder neigh. She walked across the field,
heavy with snow nearer the cave, to give the horses some
attention and make sure they were both all right. Whinney
watched her coming with her tail raised, looking alert and
responsive. As the woman neared, she dropped her head,
then flipped it high and described a circle in the air with her
nose. Racer, just as happy to see her, pranced and reared up
on his hind legs.

It was a new situation for them to be around so many
people again, and the familiar woman brought reassurance.
Racer arched his neck and pricked his ears forward when
Jondalar appeared at the mouth of the cave, and he met the
man halfway across the field. After hugging and petting and
talking to the mare, Ayla decided she would comb Whinney
the next day, for the relaxation it would give them both.

Led by Solandia's four, all the children had clustered
together and were edging toward them and the horses. The
fascinating visitors allowed the children to touch or pet one
or the other of the horses, and Ayla let a few ride on Whinney's back, which many of the adults watched with a little
envy. Ayla planned to let any adults ride who wanted to try
it, but she felt that it was too soon for that. The horses needed
rest, and she did not want to put too much strain on them.

With shovels made from large antlers, she and Jondalar
began to clear heavy snow away from some of the pasturage
nearer the cave, to make it easier for the horses to forage.
Several others joined in, making it fast work, but shoveling
snow reminded Jondalar of a concern he had been trying to
resolve for some time. How were they going to find food
and forage, and, more important, enough drinkable water for
themselves, a wolf, and two horses while crossing a frozen
expanse of glacial ice?

Later in the evening everyone gathered in the large ceremonial space to listen to Jondalar and Ayla tell about their
travels and adventures. The Losadunai were particularly interested in the animals. Solandia had already begun to rely on
Wolf to keep her children distracted, and watching the wolf

playing with them even distracted the adults. It was hard to believe. Ayla didn't go into detail about the Clan, or the death curse that had forced her to leave, though she did hint at differences that had arisen.

The Losadunai thought the Clan were just a group of people who lived far to the east, and though she tried to explain that the process of making animals accustomed to people was not anything supernatural, no one quite believed her. The idea that just anyone could tame a wild horse or wolf was too hard to accept. Most people assumed that her time of living alone in a valley was a period of trial and abstinence that many who felt called to Serve the Mother endured, and to them her way with animals verified the appropriateness of her Calling. If she wasn't One Who Served yet, it was only a matter of time.

But the Losadunai were distressed to learn of their visitors' difficulties with Attaroa and the Sarmunai.

"No wonder we've had so few visitors from the east during the past several years. And you say one of the men who was held there was a Losadunai?" Laduni asked.

"Yes. I don't know what his name was here, but there he was called Ardemun," Jondalar said. "He had hurt himself and was crippled. He couldn't walk very well, and he certainly couldn't run away, so Attaroa let him move around the Camp freely. He's the one who set the men free."

"I remember a young man who went on a Journey," an older woman said. "I did know his name once, but I can't recall . . . let me think—he had a nickname . . . Ardemun . . . Ardi . . . no, Mardi. He used to call himself Mardi!"

"You mean Menardi?" a man said. "I remember him from Summer Meetings. He was called Mardi, and he did go on a Journey. So that's what happened to him. He has a brother who would be glad to know he's alive."

"It's good to know that it's safe to travel that way again. You were lucky you missed them on your way east," Laduni said.

"Thonolan was in a hurry to get as far along the Great Mother River as we could. He didn't want to stop," Jondalar explained, "and we stayed on this side of the river. We were lucky." When the gathering broke up, Ayla was glad to go to bed in a warm, dry place with no wind, and she fell asleep quickly.

•   •   •

Ayla smiled at Solandia, who was sitting beside the fireplace nursing Micheri. She had awakened early and decided to make the morning tea for herself and Jondalar. She looked for the pile of wood or dried dung, whatever fuel they used, that was usually kept nearby, but all she saw was a pile of brown stones.

"I want to make some tea," she said. "What do you burn? If you tell me where it is, I'll go get it."

"Don't have to. Plenty here," Solandia said.

Ayla looked around and, still not seeing the fireplace burning material, wondered if she had been understood.

Solandia saw her puzzled look and smiled. She reached over and picked up one of the brown stones. "We use this, burning stone," she said.

Ayla took the stone from her hand and examined it closely. She saw a distinctive wood grain, yet it was definitely stone, not wood. She had never seen anything quite like it before; it was lignite, brown coal, a material between peat and bituminous coal. Jondalar had awakened, and he walked up behind her. She smiled at him, then gave the stone to him. "Solandia says this is what they burn in the fireplace," she said, noticing the smudge it left on her hand.

It was Jondalar's turn to examine it and look puzzled. "It does look something like wood, but it's stone. Not a hard stone like flint, though. This must break up easily."

"Yes," Solandia said. "Burning stone breaks easy."

"Where does it come from?" Jondalar asked.

"South, toward the mountains, are fields of it. Still use some wood, start fires, but this burns hotter, longer than wood," the woman said.

Ayla and Jondalar looked at each other, and a knowing expression passed between them. "I'll get one," Jondalar said. By the time he returned, Losaduna and the eldest boy, Larogi, were awake. "You have burning stones, we have a firestone, a stone that will start a fire."

"And it was Ayla who discovered it?" Losaduna said, more a statement than a question.

"How did you know?" Jondalar said.

"Maybe because he discovered the stones that burn," Solandia said.

"It looked enough like wood that I thought I would try burning it. It worked," Losaduna said.

Jondalar nodded. "Ayla, why don't you show them," he said, giving her the iron pyrite and flint along with the tinder.

Ayla arranged the tinder, then turned the metallic yellow stone around in her hand until it felt comfortable and the groove worn into the iron pyrite from continued use faced the right way. Then she picked up the piece of flint. Her motion was so practiced that it almost never took more than one strike to draw off a spark. It was caught by the tinder, and, with just a few blows of air, a little flame burst forth. There was a collective sigh from the watchers, who had been holding their breaths.

"That is amazing," Losaduna said.

"No more amazing than your stones that burn," Ayla said. "We have a few extra. I'd like to give you one, for the Cave. Perhaps we can demonstrate it during the Ceremony."

"Yes! That would be a perfect time, and I will be happy to accept your gift for the Cave," Losaduna said. "But we must give you something in return."

"Laduni has already promised to give us whatever we need to get over the glacier and continue our Journey. He owes me a future claim, though he would have done as much anyway. Wolves broke into our cache and got our traveling food," Jondalar said.

"You plan to cross the glacier with the horses?" Losaduna asked.

"Yes, of course," Ayla said.

"What will you do for food for them? And two horses must drink much more than two people—what will you do for water when everything is frozen solid?" the One Who Serves asked.

Ayla looked at Jondalar. "I've been thinking about that," he said. "I thought we could take some dry grass in the bowl boat."

"And perhaps burning stones? If you can find a place to start a fire on top of the ice. You don't have to worry about getting them wet, and it would be much less to carry," Losaduna said.

Jondalar looked thoughtful, and then a big happy grin warmed his face. "That would do it! We can put them in the bowl boat—it will slide across the ice even with a heavy load—and add a few other stones to use as a base for a fireplace. I've been worrying about that for so long . . . I can't thank you enough, Losaduna.''

Ayla discovered by accident, when she happened to overhear some of the people talking about her, that they considered her unusual speech mannerism to be a Mamutoi accent, although Solandia thought it was a minor speech impediment. No matter how hard she tried, she could not overcome the difficulty she had with certain sounds, but she was glad that no one else seemed very concerned about it.

Over the next few days, Ayla became better acquainted with the group of Losadunai who lived near the hot well— the group was called a "Cave" whether they lived in one or not. She particularly enjoyed the people whose dwelling space they shared, Solandia, Losaduna, and the children, and she realized how much she had missed the company of friendly people who behaved in a normal way. The woman spoke the language of Jondalar's people reasonably well, with some Losadunai words mixed in, but she and Ayla had no trouble understanding each other.

She was even more drawn to the mate of the One Who Served when she discovered they had a common interest. Although Losaduna was the one who was supposed to have learned about plants, herbs, and medicines, it was actually Solandia who had picked up most of the lore. The arrangement reminded Ayla of Iza and Creb, with Solandia treating the Cave's illnesses with practical herbal medicine, leaving the exorcism of spirits and other unknown harmful emanations to her mate. Ayla was also intrigued by Losaduna with his interest in histories, legends, myths, and the spirit world—the intellectual aspects she was forbidden to know when she lived with the Clan—and she was coming to appreciate the wealth of knowledge he possessed.

As soon as he discovered her genuine interest in the Great Earth Mother and the nonmaterial world of the spirits, and her quick intelligence and amazing ability to memorize, he was eager to pass on the lore. Without even understanding them completely, Ayla was soon reciting long verses of legends and histories and the precise content and order of rituals and ceremonies. He was fluent in Zelandonii, though he spoke it with a strong Losadunai flavor in the expression and phrasing, making the languages so close that most of the rhythm and meter of the verses were retained although some of the rhyme was lost. Even more fascinating to both of them were the minor differences, and many similarities, between his interpretation and the received wisdom of the Mamutoi. Losaduna wanted to know the variations and divergences, and Ayla found herself being not only an acolyte, as she had been with Mamut, but a teacher of sorts, explaining the eastern ways, at least those she knew.

Jondalar was also enjoying the Cave of people, and becoming aware of how much he had missed having a variety of individuals around. He spent quite a lot of time with Laduni and several of the hunters, but Solandia was surprised at the interest he showed in her children. He did like children, but it wasn't so much her offspring that interested him, as watching her with her youngsters. Especially when she nursed the baby, it made him long for Ayla to have a baby, a child of his spirit, he hoped, but at least a son or daughter of his hearth.

Solandia's youngest, Micheri, aroused similar feelings in Ayla, but she continued to make her special contraceptive tea each morning. The descriptions of the glacier they had yet to cross were so intimidating that she would not even consider trying to make a baby with Jondalar yet.

Though he was grateful it hadn't happened while they were traveling, Jondalar was filled with mixed emotions. He was getting worried about the failure of the Great Earth Mother to bless Ayla with pregnancy, feeling that in some way it was his fault. One afternoon he brought up his misgivings to Losaduna.

"The Mother will decide when the time is right," the man said. "Perhaps She understood how difficult your travels would be. However, this may be the time for a ceremony to honor Her. Then you could ask Her to give Ayla a baby."

"Maybe you're right," Jondalar said. "It certainly couldn't hurt." He laughed disparagingly. "Somebody once told me that I was a favorite of the Mother, and that She would never refuse anything I asked." Then his brow wrinkled. "But Thonolan still died."

"Did you actually ask Her not to let him die?" Losaduni said.

"Well, no. It happened too fast," Jondalar admitted. "That lion mauled me, too."

"Think about it sometime. Try to remember if you have ever directly asked Her for anything, and if She complied or refused your request. Anyway, I will talk to Laduni and the council about a ceremony to honor the Mother," Losaduna said. "I want to do something to try to help Madenia, and an Honoring Ceremony might be exactly the right thing. She won't get out of bed. She wouldn't even get up to hear your stories, and Madenia used to love stories about traveling."

"What a terrible ordeal it must have been for her," Jondalar said, shuddering at the thought.

"Yes. I was hoping she would be recovering from it by now. I wonder if a cleansing ritual at the Hot Well would help," he said, but it was obvious he didn't expect an answer from Jondalar. His mind was already lost in thought as he began to consider the ritual. Suddenly, he looked up. "Do you know where Ayla is? I think I'll ask her to join us. She could be a help."

"Losaduna has been explaining it, and I'm very interested in this ritual we are planning," Ayla said. "But I'm not so sure about the Ceremony to Honor the Mother."

"It's an important one," Jondalar said, frowning. "Most people look forward to it." If she were not happy about it, he wondered whether it would work.

"Perhaps if I knew more about it, I would, too. I have so much to learn, and Losaduna is willing to teach me. I'd like to stay a while."

"We have to leave soon. If we wait much longer, it will be spring. We'll stay for the Ceremony to Honor the Mother, and then we have to go," Jondalar said.

"I almost wish we could stay here until next winter. I'm so tired of traveling," Ayla said. She didn't voice her next thought, though it had been bothering her. These people are willing to accept me; I don't know if your people will.

"I'm tired of traveling, too, but once we get across the glacier, it won't be far. We'll stop off to visit with Dalanar and let him know I'm back, and then the rest of the way will be easy."

Ayla nodded in agreement, but she had the feeling they still had a long way to go, and the saying would be easier than the going.

36

"W ill you want me to do anything?" Ayla asked.

"I don't know yet," Losaduna said. "I feel, under the circumstances, that a woman should be with us. Madenia knows I am the One Who Serves the Mother, but I am a man, and she has a fear of men right now. I believe it would be very helpful if she would talk about it, and sometimes it's easier to talk to a sympathetic stranger. People fear that someone they know will always remember the deep secrets that they reveal, and every time they see that person again, it may remind them of their pain and anger."

"Is there anything I should not say or do?"

"You have a natural sensitivity and will know that yourself. You have a rare, natural ability for new language, too. I am genuinely amazed at how quickly you have learned to speak Losadunai, and grateful, too, for Madenia's sake," Losaduna said.

Ayla felt uncomfortable with his praise and glanced away. It didn't seem especially amazing to her. "It is quite similar to Zelandonii," she said.

He could see her discomfort and didn't make any further issue of it. They both looked up when Solandia came in.

"Everything's ready," she said. "I'll take the children and have this place prepared for you when you are through. Oh, and that reminds me, Ayla, do you mind if I take Wolf? The baby has grown so attached to him, and he keeps them all occupied." The woman chuckled. "Who would have thought that I'd ever be asking for a wolf to come and watch my children?"

"I think it would be better if he went with you," Ayla said. "Madenia doesn't know Wolf."

"Shall we go and get her, then?" Losaduna said.

As they walked together toward the dwelling space of Madenia and her mother, Ayla noticed she was taller than the man, and she recalled that her first impression of him had been that he was small and shy. She was surprised at how much her perception of him had changed. Although he was short in height, and reserved in demeanor, his sure intellect lent stature, and his quiet dignity cloaked a deep sensitivity and a strong presence.

Losaduna scratched at the stiff rawhide leather stretched between a rectangle of slender poles. The entry door was pushed outward and they were admitted by an older woman. She frowned when she saw Ayla and gave her a sour look, obviously unhappy that the stranger was there.

The woman started right in, full of bitterness and anger. "Has that man been found yet? The one who stole my grandchildren from me, before they ever had a chance to be born."

"Finding Charoli won't return your grandchildren, Verdegia, and he is not my concern right now. Madenia is. How is she?" Losaduna said.

"She won't get out of bed, and she hardly eats a thing. She won't even talk to me. She was such a pretty child, and she was growing into a beautiful woman. She would have had no trouble finding a mate, until Charoli and his men ruined her."

"Why do you think she is ruined?" Ayla asked.

The older woman looked at Ayla as if she were stupid. "Doesn't this woman know anything?" Verdegia said to Losaduna, then turned to Ayla. "Madenia didn't even have her First Rites. She is fouled, ruined. The Mother will never bless her now."

"Don't be too sure of that. The Mother is not so unforgiv-

ing,'' the man said. "She knows the ways of Her children
and has provided means, other ways to help them. Madenia
can be cleansed and purified, renewed, so that she can still
have her Rites of First Pleasures.''

"It won't do any good. She refuses to have anything to
do with men, not even for First Rites,'' Verdegia said. "All
my sons have gone to live with their mates; everyone said
we didn't have room in our cave for so many new families.
Madenia is my last child, my only daughter. Ever since my
man died, I have been looking forward to her bringing a mate
here, having a man around to help provide for the children
she would bear, my grandchildren. Now I won't have any
grandchildren living here. All because of that . . . that man,''
she sputtered, "and no one is doing anything about it.''

"You know that Laduni is waiting to hear from Tomasi,''
Losaduna said.

"Tomasi!'' Verdegia spat out the name. "What good is
he? It was his cave that spawned that . . . that man.''

"You have to give them a chance. But we don't have to
wait for them in order to help Madenia. After she is cleansed
and renewed, she may change her mind about her First Rites.
At least we need to try.''

"You can try, but she won't get up,'' the woman said.

"Perhaps we can encourage her,'' Losaduna said. "Where
is she?''

"Over there, behind the drape,'' Verdegia said, pointing
to an enclosed space near the stone wall.

Losaduna went to the place and pulled the drape back,
admitting light into the darkened alcove. The girl on the bed
put up her hand to ward off the brightness.

"Madenia, get up now,'' he said. His tone was firm but
gentle. She turned her face away. "Help me with her, Ayla.''

The two of them pulled her to a sitting position, then
helped her to her feet. Madenia didn't resist, but she didn't
cooperate. With one on each side, they led her out of the
enclosed space, and then out of the cave. The girl didn't
seem to notice the freezing, snow-covered ground, even with
bare feet. They guided her toward a large conical tent that
Ayla hadn't noticed before. It was tucked away around the
side of the cave, screened by rocks and brush, and steam
came from the smoke hole at the top. A strong smell of sulfur
permeated the air.

After they entered, Losaduna pulled a leather covering

across the opening and fastened it. They were in a small
entrance space that was partitioned from the rest of the interior by heavy leather drapes, mammoth hide, Ayla thought.
Although the temperature was freezing cold, it was warm
inside. A double-walled tent had been erected over a hot
spring, which provided the heating; but for all the steam, the
walls were reasonably dry. Though some moisture collected,
beading up and running down the sloping sides to the edge
of the ground cloth, most of the condensation occurred on
the inside of the outer wall, where the cold outside met the
steamy warmth inside. The insulating air space in between
was warmer, keeping the inner liner nearly dry.

Losaduna directed them to undress, and when Madenia
did nothing, he told Ayla to do it for her. The young woman
clutched at her clothes when Ayla attempted to remove them,
staring with wide eyes at the One Who Served the Mother.

"Try to get her clothes off, but if she won't let you,
bring her in with them on," Losaduna said, then slipped
behind the heavy drape, allowing a wisp of steam to escape.
Once the man left, Ayla managed to ease the girl's clothing
off, then quickly undressed herself and led Madenia to the
room beyond the drape.

Clouds of steam obscured the space inside with a warm
fog that blurred outlines and concealed details, but Ayla could
make out a pool lined with stones beside a steaming natural
hot spring. A hole connecting the two was plugged with a
carved wooden stopper. On the other side of the pool, a
hollowed-out log, which brought in cold water from a nearby
stream, had been lifted and made to slope the wrong way,
stopping the flow from entering the pool. When the billowing
steam cleared for a moment, she saw that the inside of the
tent was painted with animals, many of them pregnant, most
of them faded from water condensation, along with enigmatic
triangles, circles, trapezoids, and other geometric shapes.

Around the pools, extending not quite all the way to the
wall of the tent, thick pads of felted mouflon wool had been
placed on top of the ground cloth, wonderfully soft and warm
under bare feet. They were marked with shapes and lines that
led to the more shallow left side of the pool. Stone benches
could be seen under the water, against the wall of the deeper
right side. Near the back was a raised dais of earth supporting
three flickering stone lamps—saucer-shaped bowls filled with

melted fat with a wick of something aromatic floating in the center—that surrounded a small statue of an amply endowed woman. Ayla recognized it as a figure representing the Great Earth Mother.

A carefully laid hearth within a nearly perfect circle of round stones, almost identical in shape and size, was in front of the earthen altar. Losaduna appeared out of the steaming mist and picked up a small stick beside one of the lamps. It had a blob of dark material at one end, which he held to the flame. It caught quickly, and from the smell, Ayla knew it had been dipped in pitch. Losaduna carried the small brand, cupping the flame with his hand, to the prepared fireplace, and by lighting the tinder, started the fire. It gave off a strongly aromatic but pleasant smell that masked the odor of sulfur.

"Follow me," he said. Then, placing his left foot on one of the wool pads between the two parallel lines, he started walking around the pool along a precisely laid-out path. Madenia shuffled along behind him, neither knowing nor caring where she put her feet, but Ayla, watching him, followed in his footsteps. They made a complete circuit of the pool and the hot spring, stepping over the cold water inlet and across a deep outlet trench. As he started around a second time, Losaduna began chanting in a singsong voice, invoking the Mother with names and titles.

"O Duna, Great Earth Mother, Great and Beneficent Provider, Great Mother of All, Original One, First Mother, She Who blesses all women, Most Compassionate Mother, hear our plea." The man repeated the invocation over and over as they circled the water for the second time.

As he placed his left foot between the parallel lines of the starting mat to begin the third circle, he had reached "Most Compassionate Mother, hear our plea," but instead of repeating, he continued with, "O Duna, Great Earth Mother, one of Your own has been harmed. One of Your own has been violated. One of Your own must be cleansed and purified to receive Your blessing. Great and Beneficent Provider, one of Your own needs Your help. She must be healed. She must be mended. Renew her, Great Mother of All, and help her to know the joy of Your Gifts. Help her, Original One, to know Your Rites of First Pleasures. Help her, First Mother, to receive Your Blessing. Most Compas-

sionate Mother, help Madenia, daughter of Verdegia, child
of the Losadunai, the Earth's Children who live near the high
mountains.''

Ayla was moved and fascinated by the words and the
ceremony and she thought she noticed signs of interest in
Madenia, which pleased her. After completing the third circuit, Losaduna led them, again with carefully placed steps as
he continued his plea, to the earthen altar where the three
lamps burned around the small Mother figure, the dunai.
Beside another lamp was a knifelike object, carved out of
bone. It was fairly wide, double edged, with a somewhat
rounded tip. He picked it up, then led them to the fireplace.

They sat down around the fire facing the pool, close
together, with Madenia in the middle. The man added brown
burning stones to the flames from a nearby pile. Then, from
an alcove at the side of the raised platform of earth, Losaduna
took a bowl. It was made of stone and probably originally had
a natural bowl shape, but it had been deepened by pecking at
it with a hard hammerstone. The bottom of it was blackened.
He filled the bowl with water from a small waterbag that was
also in the niche, added dried leaves from a small basket,
and put the stone bowl directly on top of the hot coals.

Then, in a flat area of fine dry soil surrounded by wool
pads, he made a mark with the bone knife. Suddenly, Ayla
understood what the bone implement was. The Mamutoi had
used a similar tool to make marks in the dirt, to keep track
of scores and gambling counts, to plan hunting strategies,
and as a storytelling knife, drawing pictures as illustrations.
As Losaduna continued making marks, Ayla realized he was
using the knife to help tell a story, but not one meant simply
to entertain. He told it in the chanting singsong that he had
used to make his plea, drawing birds to emphasize and reinforce the points he wanted to stress. Ayla soon realized that
the story was an allegorical retelling of the attack on Madenia, using birds as the characters.

The young woman was definitely responding now, identifying with the young female bird he was telling about, and
suddenly, with a loud sob, she began to cry. With the flat
side of the drawing knife, the One Who Served the Mother
wiped out the whole scene.

''It is gone! It never happened,'' he said, then drew only
a picture of the young bird. ''She is whole again, just as she
was in the beginning. With the help of the Mother, that's

what will happen to you, Madenia. It will be gone, as though it never happened.''

A minty aroma with a familiar pungency that Ayla couldn't quite place began to fill the steamy tent. Losaduna checked the steaming water on the coal, then dipped out a cupful. ''Drink this,'' he said.

Madenia was caught off guard, and before she could think, or object, she downed the liquid. He scooped out another cup for Ayla and took one for himself. Then he got up and led them to the pool.

Losaduna moved into the steaming water slowly, but without hesitation. Madenia followed him and, without thinking, Ayla followed her. But when she put her foot in the water, she yanked it out again. It was hot! This water is nearly hot enough to cook with, she thought. Only by great concentration of will did she force herself to put her foot back in the water, but she stood there for some time before she could make herself take another step. Ayla had often bathed or swum in the cold waters of rivers, streams, and pools, even water so cold she broke through a film of ice, and she had washed with water warmed by a fire, but she had never stepped into hot water before.

Though Losaduna led them into the pool slowly, to allow them to get used to the heat, it took Ayla much longer to reach the stone seats. But as she went in deeper, she felt a soothing warmth penetrate. When she sat down, and the water reached her chin, she began to relax. It wasn't so bad, once you got used to it, she thought. The heat felt good, in fact.

Once they were settled and accustomed to the water, Losaduna instructed Ayla to hold her breath and dip her head under the water. When she came up, smiling, he told Madenia to do the same. Then he submerged himself and led them out of the pool.

He walked to the draped entrance and picked up a wooden bowl that was just inside. Mounded in the bowl was a thick, pale yellowish material that resembled heavy foam. Losaduna put the bowl down in an area that was paved with close-fitting flat stones. He dipped in, took a handful of the foam, and smoothed it over his body, telling Ayla to do the same to Madenia and then herself, and not to forget their hair.

The man chanted without words while he rubbed himself with the soft slippery stuff, but Ayla had the feeling that his

chanting was not so much ritual as an expression of enjoyment. She was feeling a little light-headed, and she wondered
if it might be from the decoction they had drunk.

When they were through, and had used all of the sudsy
foam, Losaduna picked up the wooden bowl, walked to the
pool and filled it with water, then walked back to the stone-
paved area and poured it over himself, rinsing the foam away.
He poured two more bowlfuls of water on himself, then
brought more and poured it over Madenia, and then Ayla.
The water ran off away from the pool and between the cracks
of the paving stones. Then the One Who Served the Mother
led them back to the hot pool, chanting wordlessly again.

As they sat and soaked, almost floating in the mineralized
water, Ayla felt completely relaxed. The hot pool reminded
her of the Mamutoi sweat baths, but was, perhaps, even better. When Losaduna decided they had had enough, he reached
down into the deep end of the pool and removed a wooden
stopper. As the water began to run out of the deep outlet
trench, the man began to shout, which shocked her for a
moment.

"Evil spirits, go! Cleansing waters of the Mother, take
away all traces of the touch of Charoli and all of his men.
Impurities, run out with the water, leave this place. When
this water is gone, Madenia will be cleansed, purified. The
powers of the Mother have made her as she was before!"
They walked out of the water.

Not stopping for their clothes, Losaduna led them out.
They were so warm from the hot water that the cold wind
and the freezing ground on their bare skin felt refreshing.
The few people who were out ignored them or turned their
heads aside as they passed. With an unpleasant feeling, Ayla
was suddenly reminded of another time when people looked
directly at her but refused to see her. But this wasn't like
being cursed by the Clan. She could tell that the people really
did see them. They just affected not to, more as a courtesy
than a curse. The walk cooled them down quickly, and by
the time they reached the ceremonial shelter, they were happy
to find soft dry blankets to wrap themselves in and hot mint
tea.

Ayla looked at her hands curved around the cup. They
were wrinkled, but absolutely clean! When she began to comb
her hair with an implement with several teeth made of bone,

she noticed that her hair squeaked when she pulled it through her fingers.

"What was that soft, slippery foam?" she asked. "It cleans like soaproot, but much more thoroughly."

"Solandia makes it," Losaduna said. "It has something to do with wood ashes and fat, but you'll have to ask her."

When she finished her own, Ayla began to comb Madenia's hair. "How do you make the water so hot?"

The man smiled. "That's a Gift of the Mother to the Losadunai. There are several hot springs in this region. Some are used by anyone, any time, but some are more sacred. We consider this one to be the center, the one from which the others come, so it is the most sacred of all. It makes this Cave especially honored. That's why it's so hard for anyone to leave, but our cave is getting so crowded that a group of young people are thinking of founding a new Cave. There is a place downstream and across the river they would like, but that's flathead territory, or very close to it, so they haven't decided what they will do."

Ayla nodded, feeling so warm and relaxed that she didn't want to move. She noticed that Madenia was more relaxed, too, not as stiff and withdrawn. "What a wonderful Gift that heated water is!" Ayla said.

"It's important that we learn to appreciate all the Mother's Gifts," the man said, "but especially her Gift of Pleasure."

Madenia stiffened. "Her Gift is a lie! It is no pleasure, only pain!" It was the first time she had actually spoken. "No matter how I begged them, they wouldn't stop. They just laughed, and when one got through, another started! I wanted to die," she said, then heaved a sob.

Ayla got up, went over to the girl, and held her. "It was my first time, and they wouldn't stop! They wouldn't stop," Madenia cried over and over. "No man will ever touch me again!"

"You have a right to be angry. You have a right to cry. It was a terrible thing they did to you. I know how you feel," Ayla said.

The young woman pulled away. "How do you know how I feel?" she said, full of bitterness and anger.

"Once it was pain and humiliation for me, too," Ayla said.

The young woman looked surprised, but Losaduna nodded, as though he suddenly understood something.

"Madenia," Ayla said gently, "when I was near your age, a little younger I think, but not long after I started my moon time, I was forced, too. It was my first time. I didn't know it was meant for Pleasure. For me it was only pain."

"But only one man?" Madenia said.

"Only one man, but he demanded it of me many times after that, and I hated it!" Ayla said, surprised herself at the anger she still felt.

"Many times? Even after being forced the first time? Why didn't someone stop him?" Madenia said.

"They believed it was his right. They thought I was wrong for feeling such anger and hatred, and they didn't understand why I should feel pain. I began to wonder if there was something wrong with me. After a while, I felt no pain, but no Pleasure either. It was not done for Pleasure. It was done to humiliate me, and I never stopped hating it. But . . . I stopped caring. Something wonderful happened, and no matter what he did, I thought about something else, something happy, and I ignored him. When he couldn't make me feel anything, not even anger, I think he felt humiliated, and he finally stopped. But I didn't ever want a man to touch me again."

"No man will ever touch me again!" Madenia said.

"All men are not like Charoli and his band, Madenia. Some are like Jondalar. He was the one who taught me the joy and the Pleasure of the Mother's Gift, and I promise you, it is a wonderful Gift. Give yourself a chance to meet a man like Jondalar, and you will learn the joy, too."

Madenia shook her head. "No! No! It is terrible!"   •

"I know it was terrible. Even the best Gifts can be misused, and the good turned to evil. But someday you will want to be a mother, and you will never be a mother, Madenia, if you don't share the Mother's Gift with a man," Ayla said.

Madenia was crying, her face wet with tears. "Don't say that. I don't want to hear that."

"I know you don't, but it's true. Don't let Charoli spoil the good for you. Don't let him take away your chance to be a mother. Have your First Rites so you can learn that it doesn't have to be terrible. I finally learned, though there was no gathering and no ceremony to celebrate it. The Mother found a way to give me that joy. She sent me Jondalar. The

Gift is more than Pleasures, Madenia, much more, if it is shared with caring, and love. If the pain I had the first time was the price I had to pay, I would gladly pay it many times for the love I have known. You have suffered so much, maybe the Mother will give you someone special, too, if you give Her a chance. Just think about it, Madenia Don't say no until you think about it.''

Ayla woke up feeling more rested and refreshed than she could ever remember. She smiled lazily to herself and reached for Jondalar, but he was up and gone already. She felt a moment of disappointment, then remembered that he had awakened her to remind her that he was going hunting with Laduni and some of the hunters, and to ask her again if she wanted to join them. She had declined the same offer made the evening before because she had other plans for the day, and she had stayed in bed enjoying the rare luxury of snuggling back into the warm furs.

This time she decided to get up. She stretched and ran her hands through her hair, delighting in the silky softness of it. Solandia had promised to tell her how to make the foamy lather that made her feel so clean and her hair so soft.

Breakfast was the same food they'd eaten ever since they arrived, a broth with reconstituted pieces of a dried freshwater fish, netted earlier in the year from the Great Mother River.

Jondalar had told her that the Cave was low on supplies, which was why they were going hunting, though it wasn't meat or fish that most people craved. They weren't starving, or even lacking food—they had enough to eat—but it was so close to the end of winter that the variety was limited. Everyone was tired of dried meat and dried fish. Even fresh meat would be a change, though it wouldn't satisfy completely. They were hungry for the greens and shoots of vegetables, and new fruits, the first products of spring. Ayla had made a foray into the area around the cave, but the Losadunai had been out all season and it was picked clean. They still had a reasonable supply of fat left, which kept them from protein starvation and supplied enough calories to keep them healthy, though it was usually added to the soups that were made for later meals.

The feast that was to be part of the Mother Ceremony the next day would be a limited one. Ayla had already decided to contribute the last of her salt, and some other herbs to season and add flavor as well as valuable nutrients; the vitamins and minerals their bodies needed, which was the primary cause of the cravings. Solandia had shown her the small supply of fermented beverages, mostly birch beer, that she said would make the occasion festive.

The woman would also be using some of her stored fat to make a new batch of soap. When Ayla voiced her concern that they would be using necessary food, Solandia said Losaduna liked to use it for ceremonies, and she claimed their soap supply was almost exhausted. While the older woman tended to her children and got everything ready, Ayla went out with Wolf to check on Whinney and Racer and spend some time with them.

Solandia went to the large opening of the cave to tell Ayla she was ready, but she stood at the mouth for a while and watched the visitor. Ayla had just returned from a gallop across the field and was laughing and playing with the animals. It occurred to the older woman, from the way Ayla behaved toward them, that the animals were like her children.

Some of the youngsters of the Cave were watching, too, including a couple of her own. They were shouting and calling to Wolf, who looked back at Ayla, obviously eager to join them but waiting for her approval. Ayla saw the woman standing at the mouth of the cave and hurried to her.

"I was hoping Wolf could keep the baby entertained," Solandia said. "Verdegia and Madenia are coming over to help, but the process takes concentration."

"Oh, Mother!" the eldest girl, Dosalia, said. She was one who had been trying to entice the wolf to come. "The baby always gets to play with him."

"Well, if you want to watch the baby instead . . ."

The girl frowned; then she smiled. "Can we take him outside? It's not blowing, and I'll dress him warm."

"I guess you can," Solandia said.

Ayla looked down at the wolf who was looking up at her expectantly. "Watch the baby, Wolf," she said. He yipped, seemingly in response.

"I've got some good mammoth fat that I rendered out last fall," Solandia said as they walked to the area of her enclosed dwelling space. "We had good luck hunting mammoth last year. That's why we still have so much fat, and a good thing, too. It would have been a hard winter without it.

I've started the fat melting." They reached the entranceway just as the children were running out, carrying the youngest. "Don't lose Micheri's mitts," Solandia called out after them.

Verdegia and Madenia were already inside. "I brought some ashes," Verdegia said. Madenia just smiled, a bit hesitantly.

Solandia was pleased to see her willing to get up out of bed and be around people again. Whatever they did at the hot spring, it seemed to have helped. "I put some cooking stones in the fire for tea. Madenia, would you make some for us?" she asked. "Then I'll use the rest to reheat the water melting the fat."

"Where do you want these ashes?" Verdegia asked.

"You can mix them with mine. I started them leaching, but not long ago."

"Losaduna said you use fat and ashes," Ayla commented.

"And water," Solandia added.

"That seems to be a strange combination."

"Yes, it is."

"What made you decide to mix those things together? I mean, how did you come to make it? The first time?"

Solandia smiled. "It was really an accident. We had been hunting. I had a fire going outside in a fireplace with a deep pit, and some fat mammoth meat roasting over it. It started to rain, hard. I grabbed the meat, spit and all, and ran for cover. As soon as it let up, we headed back here to the cave, but I forgot a good wooden cooking bowl, and went back for it the next day. The fireplace was full of water, with something that looked like thick foamy scum floating on it. I would never have bothered with it, except I dropped a ladle in it and had to reach in and fish it out. I went to the stream to rinse it off. It felt smooth and slippery, like good soaproot, but more, and my hands got so clean! The ladle, too. All the grease washed off. I went back and put the foam in the bowl, and brought it back."

"Is it that easy to make?" Ayla asked.

"No. It really isn't. Not that it's hard to make, but it does take some practice," Solandia said. "The first time I was lucky. Everything must have been just right. I've been working with it ever since, but it still fails sometimes."

"How do you make it? You must have developed some ways that work most of the time."

"It's not hard to explain. I melt clean rendered fat —any

kind will work, but each one makes it a little different. I like mammoth fat best. Then I take wood ashes, mix them with warm water and let them soak for a little while. Then strain it through a mesh, or a basket with holes in the bottom. The mixture that leaches out is strong. It can sting or burn your skin, I found out. You need to rinse it off right away. Anyway, you stir the strong mixture into the fat. If you are lucky, you get a soft foam, that will clean anything, even leather.''

"But you're not always lucky," Verdegia said.

"No. Lots of things can go wrong. Sometimes you can stir and stir and stir, and it won't mix. If that happens, heating it a little will sometimes help. Sometimes it separates and you get a layer that's too strong and a layer that's too greasy. Sometimes it curdles into lumps that are not quite mixed. Sometimes it comes out harder than others, but that's not bad. It tends to harden as it ages, anyway."

"But sometimes it does work, like the first time," Ayla said.

"One thing I've learned is that both the fat and the liquid from the ashes have to be about the same warmth as the skin of your wrist," Solandia said. "When you sprinkle a little on, it shouldn't feel either cool or warm. The ash liquid is harder to tell because it's strong and can burn a little, then you have to wash it off right away with cool water. If it burns too much, you know you need to add more water. It doesn't burn too bad, usually, but I wouldn't want to get it in my eyes. It can sting if you just get too close to the fumes."

"And it can stink!" Madenia said.

"That's true," Solandia said. "It can stink. That's why I usually go out into the middle of the cave to mix it, even though I get everything ready to mix here."

"Mother! Mother! Come quick!" Solandia's second daughter Neladia came dashing in, then ran out.

"What's wrong? Did something happen to the baby?" the woman said, rushing out after her. Everyone else followed behind and ran to the mouth of the cave.

"Look!" Dosalia said. They all looked outside. "The baby is walking!"

There was Micheri, standing up beside the wolf, hanging on to his fur, with a big self-satisfied smile, taking unsteady steps as Wolf carefully and slowly moved forward. Everyone smiled with relief and then delight.

"Is that wolf smiling?" Solandia asked. "It looks to me as though he is. He seems to be so pleased with himself that he's smiling."

"I think he is, too," Ayla said. "I have often thought he could smile."

"It's not only for ceremony, Ayla," Losaduna was saying. "We often use the hot waters just to soak. If you want to take Jondalar in just to relax, we have no objections. The Sacred Waters of the Mother are like Her other Gifts to Her children. They are meant to be used and enjoyed, and appreciated. Just as this tea you made should be appreciated," he added, holding up the cup.

Nearly the whole Cave, those that had not gone hunting, were sitting around a fireplace in the open central area of the cave. Most meals were very unstructured, except for special occasions. The people sometimes ate separately, in family groups, and sometimes with others. This time, those who had stayed at the cave had stopped for a midday meal and eaten together, largely because they were all interested in the visitors. The meal consisted of a hearty meat soup of lean, dried deer, made rich with the addition of some mammoth fat, which made it filling and satisfying enough. They were finishing off with tea that Ayla had made, and all had remarked on how good it was.

"When they come back, maybe we will use the pool. I think he'd enjoy a hot soak, and I'd like to share it with him," Ayla said.

"You'd better warn her, Losaduna," a woman said, with a knowing smile. She had been introduced as Laduni's mate.

"Warn me of what, Laronia?" Ayla said.

"Sometimes you have to choose between the Mother's Gifts."

"What do you mean?"

"She means the Sacred Waters can be too relaxing," Solandia said.

"I still don't understand," Ayla said, frowning. She knew everyone was talking about the subject, and there was an element of humor involved.

"If you take Jondalar for a hot soak, it will relax the strength right out of his manhood," Verdegia said, more direct than the others, "and it may take a couple of hours before it can stand up again. So don't expect too much of him, after a soak. Not right away. Some men won't soak in the Mother's Sacred Waters for that reason. They are afraid their manhood will drain out in the Sacred Waters and never come back.''

"Can that happen?'' Ayla asked, looking at Losaduna.

"Not that I've ever seen, or heard about,'' the man said. "If anything, the opposite seems to be true. A man is more eager, after a while, but I think that's because he's relaxed and feels good.''

"I did feel wonderful after the hot soak, and I slept very well, but I think there was more than water to it,'' Ayla said. "Perhaps the tea?''

The man smiled. "That was an important ritual. There is always more to a ceremony.''

"Well, I'm ready to go back to the Sacred Waters, but I think I'll wait for Jondalar. Do you think the hunters will be back soon?''

"I'm sure they will,'' Laronia said. "Laduni knows there are things to do before the Mother Festival tomorrow. I don't think they would have gone today, except that he wanted to see how Jondalar's long-range hunting weapon works. What does he call it?''

"A spear-thrower, and it works very well,'' Ayla said, "but like anything, it takes practice. We've had lots of practice on this Journey.''

"Do you use his spear-thrower?'' Madenia asked.

"I have my own,'' Ayla said. "I've always liked to hunt.''

"Why didn't you go with them today?'' the girl asked.

"Because I wanted to learn how to make that cleansing material. And I have some clothes I want to clean and mend,'' Ayla said, getting up and heading toward the ceremonial tent. Then she stopped. "I have something I'd like to show everyone, too,'' she said. "Has anyone ever seen a thread-puller?'' She saw puzzled looks and shaking heads. "If you wait here a moment, I'll get mine and show you.''

Ayla returned from the dwelling space with her sewing kit and some clothing she wanted to repair. With everyone crowded around to see yet another amazing thing brought by the travelers, she took a small cylinder out of her kit—it had come from the lightweight, hollow leg of a bird—and shook two ivory needles out of it. She handed one to Solandia. The woman examined the highly polished miniature shaft closely. It was brought to a sharp point at one end, somewhat like an awl. The other end was a bit thicker and, surprisingly, had a very small hole that went all the way through. She thought about it, and suddenly got an inkling of what it was for. "Did you say this was a thread-puller?" she said, handing it to Laronia.

"Yes. I'll show you how I use it," Ayla said, separating a thin piece of sinew from a fibrous thicker strand. She wet the end and smoothed it to a point, then waited for it to dry. The thread of tendon hardened slightly and held its shape. She threaded it through the hole at the back end of the tiny ivory shaft, then put it aside for the moment. Next she picked up a small flint tool with a sharp point and used it to poke holes near the edges of a garment whose stitches along a side seam had pulled out, a few of them tearing through the leather in the process. The new holes were back slightly from the previous ones.

Once she had made the holes for a new seam, Ayla settled down to demonstrate the new implement. She put the point of the ivory needle through the holes in the leather and, grasping the small shaft, pulled the thread through, ending with a flourish.

"Oooh!" The people seated nearby, especially the women, breathed out a collective sigh. "Look at that!" "She didn't have to pick the thread out, she pulled it right through." "Can I try that?"

Ayla passed the garment around and let them experiment, explaining and showing, and telling them how the idea had come to her, and how everyone at Lion Camp had helped her to develop and make it.

"This is a very well-made awl," Solandia commented, examining it closely.

"Wymez, of the Lion Camp, made it. He also made the borer that was used to make the hole that the thread goes through," Ayla said.

"That would be a very difficult tool to make," Losaduna said.

"Jondalar says Wymez is the only flint knapper he's ever met who is as good as Dalanar and, possibly, a little better."

"That's high praise from him," Losaduna said. "Everyone acknowledges Dalanar as the master stoneworker. His skill is known even on this side of the glacier, among the Losadunai."

"But Wymez is also a master."

They all turned in surprise at the sound of the voice that had just spoken, and saw Jondalar, Laduni, and several others coming into the cave, bringing with them an ibex they had killed.

"You had luck!" Verdegia said. "And if no one minds, I'd like to have the skin. I've been wanting some ibex wool to make bedding for Madenia's Matrimonial." She wanted to get her bid in before anyone else.

"Mother!" Madenia said, embarrassed. "How can you talk about a Matrimonial?"

"Madenia must have First Rites before any Matrimonial can be considered," Losaduna said.

"As far as I'm concerned, she can have the hide," Laronia said, "whatever she wants to use it for." She knew there was a touch of avarice in Verdegia's request. They didn't often hunt the elusive wild goat, and its wool was rare and therefore valuable, particularly in late winter after a whole season of growing thick and dense, but before the shedding of spring gave it a tattered look.

"I don't care either. Verdegia can have it," Solandia said. "Fresh ibex meat will be a welcome change no matter who gets the hide, and especially nice for the Mother Festival."

Several others acquiesced, and no one objected. Verdegia smiled and tried not to look smug. By laying claim first, she had secured the valuable hide, just as she had hoped.

"Fresh ibex will be good with the dried onion I brought, and I have blueberries, too."

Again everyone looked toward the mouth of the cave. Ayla saw a young woman she hadn't met before, carrying a baby and leading a little girl by the hand, followed by a young man.

"Filonia!" several people chorused.

Laronia and Laduni rushed toward her, joined by all the rest of the Cave. The young woman was obviously not a stranger here. After happy hugs of greeting, Laronia took the baby, and Laduni picked up the little girl, who had run toward him, and put her up on his shoulders. She looked down at everyone with a pleased grin.

Jondalar was standing beside Ayla, smiling at the happy scene. "That girl could be my sister!" he said.

"Filonia, look who's here," Laduni said, leading the young woman toward them.

"Jondalar? Is it you?" she said, looking at him with shocked surprise. "I didn't think you'd ever come back. Where's Thonolan? There is someone I want him to meet!"

"I'm sorry, Filonia. He walks the next world now," Jondalar said.

"Oh. I'm sorry to hear that. I wanted him to meet Thonolia. I'm sure she's the child of his spirit."

"I am sure, too. She looks just like my sister, and they were both born to the same hearth. I wish my mother could see her, but I think it will please her to know that there is something left of him in this world, a child of his spirit," Jondalar said.

The young woman noticed Ayla. "But you didn't return alone," she said.

"No, he didn't," Laduni said, "and wait until you see some of his other traveling companions. You won't believe it."

"And you came at just the right time. We're having a Mother Festival tomorrow," Laronia said.

37

The people of the Cave of the Sacred Hot Springs were anticipating the Festival to Honor the Mother with great enthusiasm. In the deep of winter, when life was usually most dull and boring, Ayla and Jondalar had arrived and provoked enough excitement to keep the Cave stimulated for a long time, and with the inevitable storytelling that would result, the interest would last for years. From the moment they rode up, sitting on the backs of horses and followed by the Wolf Who Liked Children, everyone had been buzzing with speculation. They had enthralling stories to tell about their travels, arresting new ideas to share, and fascinating devices like spear-throwers and thread-pullers to demonstrate.

Now everyone was talking about something magical that the woman would show them during the ceremony, something having to do with fire, like their burning stones. Losaduna had mentioned it while they were eating their evening meal. The visitors had also promised to give a demonstration of the spear-thrower in the field outside the cave so everyone could see its possibilities, and Ayla was going to show what could be done with a sling. But even the promised demonstrations did not pique their curiosity as much as the mystery involving fire.

Ayla discovered that constantly being the center of attention could be as exhausting, in a different kind of way, as constantly traveling. All evening people had plied her with eager questions and sought her opinion and ideas on subjects about which she had no knowledge. By the time the sun was setting, she was tired and didn't feel like talking anymore. Soon after dark she left the gathering around the fire in the central part of the cave to go to bed. Wolf went with her and Jondalar followed shortly afterward, leaving the Cave free to gossip and speculate in their absence.

In the sleeping area allocated to them within the ceremonial and dwelling space of Losaduna, they puttered around with preparations for the next day, then crawled into their furs. Jondalar held her and considered making the initial overtures that Ayla considered his "signal" to couple, but she seemed nervous and distracted, and he wanted to save himself. One never knew what to expect at a Mother Festival, and Losaduna had hinted that it might be a good idea to hold back and wait to honor the Mother until after the special ritual they had planned.

He had spoken with the One Who Served the Mother about his concerns regarding his ability to have children born to his hearth, whether the Great Mother would find his spirit acceptable for a new life. They had decided on a private ritual before the festival to appeal directly to the Mother for Her help.

Ayla lay awake long after she heard the heavier breathing of sleep from the man beside her, tired but unable to fall asleep herself. She shifted position frequently, trying not to disturb Jondalar with her restless turnings. Though she dozed off, sound sleep was slow in coming, and her thoughts drifted in strange patterns as she wavered between wakeful imaginings and fitful dreams.

The meadow was freshly green with the lush new growth of spring, brightened by the varied hues of colorful flowers. In the distance, the ivory-white scarp face of a rock wall, pocked with caves and textured with black streaks sweeping up and around into roomy cliff overhangs, almost gleamed

*in the light blazing down from high in the clear azure sky.
Reflected sunlight glinted from the river that flowed along its
base, hugging close one moment, then veering away, generally tracing the contours of the wall without following it
exactly.*

*About halfway down the field that spread out across level
ground away from the river, a man stood watching her, a
man of the Clan. Then he turned and headed toward the cliff
leaning on a staff and dragging a foot, yet walking at a good
pace. Though he didn't say or signal a word, she knew he
wanted her to follow him. She hurried toward him, and when
they came abreast, he glanced at her with his one good eye.
It was a deep liquid brown, full of compassion and power.
She knew his bearskin cloak covered the stump of an arm
that had been amputated at the elbow when he was a boy.
His grandmother, a medicine woman of renowned reputation,
had cut off the useless, paralyzed limb when it became gan-
grenous after he was mangled by a cave bear. Creb had lost
his eye during the same encounter.*

*As they neared the rock wall, she noticed a strange for-
mation near the top of an overhanging cliff. A longish, somewhat flat, column-shaped boulder, darker than the creamy
matrix of limestone that held it, leaned over the edge as if
frozen in place just as it started to tumble down. The stone
not only gave the feeling that it would fall any moment, making her uneasy, but she knew something about it was important; something she should remember, something she had
done, or was supposed to do—or wasn't supposed to do.*

*She closed her eyes trying to recall. She saw darkness,
thick, velvet, palpable darkness, as utterly lacking in light as
only a cave deep in a mountain could be. A tiny flickering
of light appeared in the distance and she groped her way
along a narrow passage toward it. As she neared, she saw
Creb with other mog-urs, and she suddenly felt great fear.
She didn't want that memory and quickly opened her eyes.*

*And found herself on the bank of the small river that
wound its way along the base of the wall. She looked across
the water and saw Creb trudging up a path toward the falling
stone formation. She had gotten behind him and now didn't
know how to cross the river to catch up. She called after
him, "Creb, I'm sorry. I didn't mean to follow you into the
cave."*

He turned around and beckoned to her again, signaling

*great urgeney. "Hurry," he signed from across the river,
which had become wider and deeper, and full of ice. "Don't
wait any longer! Hurry!"*

*The ice was expanding, taking him farther away. "Wait
for me! Creb, don't leave me here!" she cried.*

"Ayla! Ayla, wake up! You're dreaming again," Jondalar said, shaking her gently.

She opened her eyes and felt a great sense of loss and a
strangely intense fear. She noticed the hide-covered walls of
the dwelling space and a reddish glow from the fireplace as
she looked at the shadowed silhouette of the man beside her.
She reached out and clung to him. "We have to hurry, Jondalar! We have to leave here right away," she said.

"We will," he said. "As soon as we can. But tomorrow
is the Mother Festival, and then we have to decide what we
need to take to cross the ice."

"Ice!" she said. "We have to cross a river of ice!"

"Yes, I know," he said, holding her and trying to calm
her. "But we have to plan how we're going to do it with the
horses and Wolf. We'll need food, and a way to get water
for all of us. The ice is frozen solid up there."

"Creb said to hurry. We have to leave!"

"As soon as we can, Ayla. I promise, as soon as we
can," Jondalar said, feeling a nagging edge of worry. They
did need to leave and get across the glacier as soon as possible, but they couldn't go before the Mother Festival, could
they?

Though it did little to warm the freezing air, the late
afternoon sun streamed through the branches of trees, which
broke up the coruscating rays but did not block the blinding
western light. To the east, the glaciered mountain peaks,
reflecting the brilliant orb that was descending into fiery
clouds, were suffused with a soft rosy glow that seemed to
emanate from within the ice. The light would soon be failing,
but Jondalar and Ayla were still in the field outside the cave,
although he was watching along with everyone else.

Ayla took a deep breath, then held it, not wanting to
obstruct her view with the steamy fog of her breath while
she took careful aim. She shifted the two stones in her hand,

then placed one in the pocket of the sling, whirled it around and flung it, letting go of one end. Then, starting at the end she still held, she quickly ran it through her hand to retrieve the loose end, dropped the second stone in the cup, whirled and cast it. She could cast two stones faster than anyone had ever imagined.

"Oooh!" "Look at that!" People who had been standing at the large mouth of the cave during the demonstrations of spear-throwing and rock-slinging let out the breaths they, too, had been holding and made comments of surprise and appreciation. "She broke up both snowballs from all the way across the field." "I thought she was good with the spear-thrower, but she's even better with that sling."

"She said it would take practice to learn to throw spears with accuracy, but how much practice did it take to throw rocks like that?" Larogi said. "I think it would be easier to learn to use the spear-thrower."

The demonstration was over, and as night was closing in, Laduni stepped in front of the people and announced that the feast was almost ready. "It will be served at the central hearth, but first, Losaduna will dedicate the Festival to the Mother at the Ceremonial Hearth, and Ayla is going to give another demonstration. What she is going to show you is remarkable."

As the people excitedly began making their way back into the cave away from the large open mouth, Ayla noticed Madenia talking with some friends and was glad to see that she was smiling. Many had commented on how pleased they were to see her joining in the group's activities, though she was still shy and withdrawn. Ayla could not help thinking what a difference it made when people cared. Unlike her experience, where everyone felt Broud had the right to force her any time he wanted, and thought she was odd for resisting and hating him, Madenia had the support of her people. They took her side. They were angry at those who had forced her, understood what an ordeal it had been, and wanted to correct the wrong that had been done to her.

Once everyone was settled inside the enclosed space of the Ceremonial Hearth, the One Who Served the Mother came out of the shadows and stood behind a lighted fireplace surrounded by a circle of almost perfectly matched round stones. He picked up a small stick with a pitch-dipped end, held it to the fire until it caught, then turned around and walked to the stone wall of the cave.

With his body blocking the view, Ayla could not see what he was doing, but when a glowing light spread out around him, she knew he had lit a fire of some kind, probably a lamp. He made some motions and began chanting a familiar litany, the same repetition of the various names of the Mother that he had chanted during Madenia's cleansing ritual. He was invoking the spirit of the Mother.

When he backed away and turned to face the gathering, Ayla saw that the glow came from a stone lamp he had lit in a niche in the cave wall. The fire cast dancing shadows, larger than life, of a small dunai and highlighted the exquisitely carved figure of a woman with substantial motherly attributes—large breasts and rounded stomach, not pregnant but well endowed with reserves of stored fat.

"Great Earth Mother, Original Ancestor and Creator of All Life, Your children have come to show appreciation, to thank You for all Your Gifts, great and small, to honor You," Losaduna intoned, and the people of the Cave joined in. "For the rocks and stones, the bones of the land that give of their spirit to nourish the soil, we have come to honor You. For the soil that gives of its spirit to nourish the plants that grow, we have come to honor You. For the plants that grow and give of their spirit to nourish the animals, we have come to honor You. For the animals that give of their spirit to nourish the meat-eaters, we have come to honor You. And for all of them that give of their spirit to feed and clothe and protect Your children, we have come to honor You."

Everyone knew all the words. Even Jondalar, Ayla noticed, had joined in, though he said the words in Zelandonii. She soon began repeating the "honor" part, and though she didn't know the rest, she knew they were important, and once she heard them, she knew she would never forget them.

"For Your great glowing son who lights the day, and Your fair shining mate who guards the night, we have come to honor You. For Your life-giving birth waters that fill the rivers and seas and rain down from the skies, we have come to honor You. For Your Gift of Life and Your blessing of women to bring forth life as You do, we have come to honor You. For the men, who were made to help women to provide for the new life, and whose spirit You take to help women create it, we come to honor You. And for Your Gift of Pleasures that both men and women take in each other, and that opens a woman so she can give birth, we have come to honor You. Great Earth Mother, Your children come together on this night to honor You.''

The silence that filled the cave after the communal invocation ended was profound. Then a baby cried, and it seemed entirely appropriate.

Losaduna stepped back and seemed to fade into the shadows. Then Solandia got up, picked up a basket that was near the Ceremonial Hearth, and poured ashes and dirt on the flames in the round fireplace, killing the ceremonial fire and plunging them into near darkness. There were a few surprised *oohhs* and *aahhs* from the crowd, as people sat forward expectantly. The only light came from the small oil lamp that was burning in the niche, which made the dancing shadows of the Mother figure seem to grow, until they seemed to fill the entire space. Though the fire had never been put out like that before, the effect was not lost on Losaduna.

The two visitors and the people who lived at the Ceremonial Hearth had practiced earlier, and each knew what to do. When everyone had quieted down, Ayla walked into the darkened area toward a different fireplace. It had been decided that the capabilities of the firestone would be shown to the best advantage, and with the most dramatic effect, if Ayla started a new fire at a cold hearth as quickly as possible after the Ceremonial fire was out. A quick-starting tinder of dried moss had been placed in the second fireplace, kindling beside it, and some larger sticks of wood for burning. Brown coal would then be added to keep the fire going.

When they were practicing, it had been discovered that wind helped to blow up the spark, particularly the draft that whipped in when the hide door of the Ceremonial space was opened, and Jondalar was standing beside it. Ayla knelt down and, holding the iron pyrite in one hand and a piece of flint in the other, struck them together, creating a spark that could be clearly seen in the darkened area. She struck the two together again, holding them at a slightly different angle, which caused the spark she drew off to fall on the tinder.

That was the signal to Jondalar, who opened the entry door. As the cold draft blew in, Ayla, bending close to the bare spark smoldering in the dried moss, blew gently. Suddenly the moss flared up and enveloped the tinder, bringing on a chorus of surprised and excited remarks. Kindling was then added. In the darkened shelter, the flame cast a reddish glow illuminating everyone's face and seemed larger than it actually was.

The people began talking, rapidly and excitedly, full of wonder, and it relieved the tension Ayla had built with the suspense. Within moments—to the Cave it seemed almost instantaneous—a fire had been kindled. Ayla heard a few of the comments. "How did she do it?" "How could anyone start a fire so fast?" A second fire was kindled from the first in the Ceremonial Hearth; then the One Who Served the Mother stood between the two areas of glowing flames and spoke.

"Most people who have not seen it do not believe that stones will burn, unless we have one to show, but burning stones are the Great Earth Mother's gift to the Losadunai. Our visitors have also been given a gift, a firestone; a stone that will make a fire-starting spark when it is struck with a piece of flint. Ayla and Jondalar are willing to give us a piece of firestone, not only to use, but also so that we will recognize it if we find any. In return, they want enough food and other supplies to get them over the glacier," Losaduna said.

"I've already promised that," Laduni said. "Jondalar has a Future Claim on me, and that's what he asked for—not that it's much of a claim. We'd give them food and supplies anyway." There was a refrain of agreement from the gathering.

Jondalar knew that the Losadunai would have given them food, just as Ayla and he would have given the Cave a firestone, but he didn't want them to feel sorry later about giving up food supplies that could leave them stretched thin if spring and the new growing season came late. He wanted them to feel they were getting the best of a good bargain, and he wanted something else. He stood up then.

"We have given Losaduna a firestone for everyone's use," he said, "but there is more to my claim than it seems. We need more than food and supplies for ourselves. We don't travel alone. Our companions are two horses and a wolf, and we need help to get them across the ice. We will need food for ourselves, and for them, but even more important, we will need water. If it were just Ayla and me, we could wear a waterbag full of snow or ice under our tunics next to our

skin to melt enough water for us, and maybe for Wolf, but
horses drink a lot of water. We can't melt enough for them
that way. I will tell you the truth; we need to find a way to
carry or melt enough water to get us all across the glacier."

There was a chorus of voices full of suggestions and
ideas, but Laduni quieted them. "Let's think about it and
meet tomorrow with suggestions. Tonight is Festival."

Jondalar and Ayla had already brought delicious excitement and mystery to enliven the usually quiet winter months
of the Cave, and to give them stories to tell at Summer Meetings. Now there was the gift of the firestone and, as a bonus,
the challenge of solving a unique problem, a fascinating practical and intellectual puzzle that would give them all a chance
to stretch their mental muscles. The travelers would have
willing and eager assistance.

Madenia had come to the Ceremonial Hearth to see the
firestone demonstration, and Jondalar could hardly help noticing that she had been watching him closely. He had smiled
at her several times, to which she had responded by blushing
and looking away. He walked over to her as the gathering
was breaking up and leaving the Ceremonial Hearth.

"Hello, Madenia," he said. "What did you think of the
firestone?"

He felt the attraction he often had for shy young women
before their First Rites, who didn't know what to expect and
were a little afraid, especially those he had been called upon
to introduce to the Mother's Gift of Pleasures. He had always
enjoyed showing them Her Gift during their First Rites, and
he had a special feeling for it, which was why he was called
upon so often. Madenia's fear was well grounded, not the
amorphous worries of most young women, and he would
have considered it an even greater challenge to bring her
around to knowing the joy rather than the pain.

Jondalar looked at her with his amazingly vivid blue eyes,
and he wished they were staying long enough to participate
in the Losadunai summer rituals. He genuinely wanted to
help her to overcome her fears, and was truly attracted to
her, which brought out the full power of his charm, his sheer
male magnetism. The handsome and sensitive man smiled at
her then and left her nearly breathless.

Madenia had never experienced a feeling like it before.

Her whole being felt warm, almost on fire, and she had an overwhelming urge to touch him, and to have him touch her, but the young woman had no idea what to do with such feelings. She tried to smile; then, embarrassed, she opened her eyes wide and gasped at her audacity. She backed away and almost ran to her dwelling space. Her mother saw her leaving and followed after her. Jondalar had seen Madenia's reaction before. It was not unusual for shy young women to respond to him that way, and it only made her more endearing.

"What did you do to that poor child, Jondalar?"

He looked at the woman who had spoken, and turned his smile on her.

"Or need I ask? I remember a time when that look very nearly overpowered me. But your brother had his charm, too."

"And left you blessed," Jondalar said. "You are looking well, Filonia. Happy."

"Yes, Thonolan did leave a piece of his spirit with me, and I am happy. You seem happy, too. Where did you meet this Ayla?"

"It's a long story, but she saved my life. It was too late for Thonolan."

"I heard a cave lion got him. I'm sorry."

Jondalar nodded, and closed his eyes with the inevitable frown of pain.

"Mother?" a girl said. It was Thonolia, holding hands with Solandia's eldest daughter. "Can I eat at 'Salia's hearth and play with the wolf? He likes children, you know."

Filonia looked at Jondalar with an apprehensive frown.

"Wolf won't hurt her. He does like children. Ask Solandia. She uses him to entertain her baby," Jondalar said. "Wolf was raised with children and Ayla has trained him, and you're right. She is a remarkable woman, particularly with animals."

"I guess it's all right, Thonolia. I don't think this man would let you do anything that might harm you. He is the brother of the man you're named after."

There was a loud commotion. They looked to see what the trouble was, as the girls ran off together.

"When is someone going to do something about that . . . that Charoli? How long does a mother have to wait?" Verdegia complained to Laduni. "Maybe we need to call a Council of Mothers, if the men can't handle it. I'm sure they would understand the feelings in a mother's heart, and pass judgment fast enough.''

Losaduna had joined Laduni, to lend him support. Calling a Council of Mothers was usually a last resort. It could have serious repercussions and was used only when no other way could be found to solve a problem. "Let's not be hasty, Verdegia. The messenger we sent to talk to Tomasi should be back any time. Certainly you can wait a little longer. And Madenia is much better. Don't you think so?''

"I'm not so sure. She ran away to our hearth and won't tell me what's wrong. She says it's nothing, and tells me not to worry about it, but how can I help it?'' Verdegia said.

"I could tell her what's wrong,'' Filonia said under her breath, "but I'm not sure Verdegia would understand. She's right, though. Something does have to be done about Charoli. All the Caves are talking about him.''

"What can be done?'' Ayla asked, joining the two.

"I don't know,'' Filonia said, smiling at the woman. Ayla had come to see her baby and had obviously enjoyed holding him. "But I think Laduni's plan is a good one. He thinks all the Caves should work together to find and bring the young men back. He would like to see the members of that band separated from each other, and away from Charoli's influence.''

"It does seem like a good idea,'' Jondalar said.

"The problem is Charoli's Cave, and whether Tomasi, who is related to Charoli's mother, would be willing to go along with it,'' Filonia said. "We'll know better when the messenger gets back, but I can understand how Verdegia feels. If anything like that ever happened to Thonolia . . .'' She shook her head, unable to go on.

"I think most people understand how Madenia and her mother feel,'' Jondalar said. "People are mostly decent, but a bad one can make a lot of trouble for everyone else.''

Ayla was remembering Attaroa and thinking the same thing.

"Someone's coming! Someone's coming!'' Larogi and several of his friends came running into the cave shouting the news, making Ayla wonder what they had been doing outside in the cold and dark. A few moments later they were followed in by a middle-aged man.

"Rendoli! You couldn't have come at a better time,''

Laduni said, his relief obvious. "Here, let me take your pack and get you something hot to drink. You made it back in time for a Mother Festival."

"That's the messenger Laduni sent to Tomasi," Filonia said, surprised to see him.

"Well, what did he say?" Verdegia demanded.

"Verdegia," Losaduna said. "Let the man rest and catch his breath. He just got here!"

"It's all right," Rendoli said, shrugging off his pack and accepting a cup of hot tea from Solandia. "Charoli's band raided the Cave that lives near the barrens where they've been hiding. They stole food and weapons and almost killed someone who tried to stop them. The woman is still badly hurt, and she may not recover. All the Caves are angry. When they heard about Madenia, it was the final blow. In spite of his kinship with Charoli's mother, Tomasi is ready to join with the other Caves to go after them and put a stop to them. Tomasi called for a meeting with as many Caves as possible—that's what took me so long getting back. I waited for the meeting. Most of the nearby Caves sent several people. I had to make some decisions for us."

"I'm sure they were good ones," Laduni said. "I'm glad you were there. What did they think of my suggestion?"

"They have already taken it, Laduni. Each Cave is going to send out scouts to track them—some have already left. Once Charoli's band is found, most of the hunters of each Cave will go after them and bring them back. No one wants to put up with them anymore. Tomasi wants to have them before the Summer Meeting." The man turned to look at Verdegia. "And they would like you to be there to make a charge and a claim," he said.

Verdegia was almost appeased, but still not happy about Madenia's reluctance to participate in the ceremony that would officially make her a woman, and, with luck, able to bear children—her potential grandchildren.

"I'll be glad to charge and claim," Verdegia said, "and if she won't agree to First Rites, you can be certain I won't forget it."

"I am hopeful that by next summer, she will change her mind. I do see progress since the cleansing ritual. She is out mingling with people more. I think Ayla helped," Losaduna said.

After Rendoli went to his dwelling space, Losaduna

caught Jondalar's eye and nodded to him. The tall man excused himself and followed Losaduna into the Ceremonial Hearth. Ayla would have liked to follow them, but she sensed from their manner that they wanted to be alone.

"I wonder what they are going to do," Ayla said.

"I would guess it's some kind of personal ritual," Filonia said, which made Ayla even more curious.

"Have you brought something you made?" Losaduna asked.

"I made a blade. I didn't have time to haft it, but it is as perfect as I could make it," Jondalar said, taking a small leather-wrapped package from inside his tunic. He opened it to reveal a small stone point with an unretouched edge that was sharp enough to shave with. One end was worked to a point. The other end had a tang that could be fitted into a knife handle.

Losaduna looked it over carefully. "This is excellent workmanship," he commented. "I feel certain it will be acceptable."

Jondalar breathed a sigh of relief, though he hadn't realized he was so concerned.

"And something of hers?"

"That was harder. We have been traveling with only the bare essentials, for the most part, and she knows where she puts everything she has. She has a few things packed away, gifts from people, mostly, and I didn't want to disturb them. Then I remembered that you said it didn't matter how small it was, so long as it was very personal," Jondalar said, picking up a tiny object that was also in the leather package, then went on to explain. "She wears an amulet, a small decorated pouch with objects from her childhood inside. It's very important to her, and the only time she takes it off is when she's swimming or bathing, and not always then. She left it behind when she went to the sacred hot springs, and I cut away one of the beads that decorate it."

Losaduna smiled. "Good! That's perfect! And very clever. I've seen that amulet, and it is very personal to her. Wrap them back up together and give me the package."

Jondalar did as he was told, but Losaduna noticed a questioning look when he handed it to him.

"I cannot tell you where I will put it, but She will know.

Now, there are some things I must explain to you, and some questions I must ask," Losaduna said.

Jondalar nodded. "I will try to answer."

"You want a child to be born to your hearth, to the woman, Ayla, is that right?"

"Yes."

"You do understand that a child born to your hearth may not be of your spirit?"

"Yes."

"How do you feel about that? Does it matter to you whose spirit is used?"

"I would like it to be of my spirit, but . . . my spirit may not be right. Maybe it isn't strong enough or the Mother can't use it, or maybe She doesn't want to. No one is ever sure whose spirit it is, anyway, but if a child was born to Ayla, and born to my hearth, that would be enough. I think I would almost feel like a mother myself," Jondalar said, and his conviction was obvious.

Losaduna nodded. "Good. Tonight we honor the Mother, so this is a very propitious time. You know that those women who honor Her most are the ones who are most often blessed. Ayla is a beautiful woman, and she will have no trouble finding a man or men to share Pleasures with."

When the One Who Served the Mother saw the tall man's frown, he realized that Jondalar was one of those who found it difficult to see the woman he chose choose someone else, even though it was only for ceremony. "You must encourage her, Jondalar. It honors the Mother and is most important if you are sincere in wanting Ayla to have a child born to your hearth. I have seen it work before. Many women become pregnant almost immediately. The Mother may be so pleased with you. She might even use your spirit, especially if you also honor Her well."

Jondalar closed his eyes and nodded, but Losaduna saw his jaw clench and grind. It was not going to be easy for the man.

"She has never taken part in a Festival to Honor the Mother. What if she . . . doesn't want anyone else?" Jondalar asked. "Should I refuse her?"

"You must encourage her to share with others, but the choice is, of course, hers. You must never refuse any woman, if you can help it, at Her Festival, but especially not the one you have chosen to be your mate. I wouldn't worry about it,

Jondalar. Most women get into the spirit of it and have no trouble enjoying the Mother Festival,'' Losaduna said. ''But it is strange that Ayla wasn't raised to know the Mother. I didn't know there were any people who don't acknowledge Her.''

''The people who raised her were . . . unusual in many ways,'' Jondalar said.

''I'm sure that's true,'' Losaduna said. ''Now, let's go ask the Mother.''

Ask the Mother. Ask the Mother. The phrase went through Jondalar's thoughts as they walked toward the back of the ceremonial space. He suddenly remembered being told that he was favored by the Mother, so favored that no woman could refuse him, not even Doni Herself; so favored that if he ever asked the Mother for anything, She would grant his request. He had also been warned to be wary of such favor; he might get what he asked for. At that moment, he fervently hoped it was true.

They stopped at the niche where the lamp still burned. ''Pick the dunai up and hold her in your hands,'' the One Who Served the Mother instructed.

Jondalar reached into the niche and gently picked up the Mother figure. It was one of the most beautifully made carvings he had ever seen. Her body was perfectly shaped. The figure in his hand looked as if the sculptor had carved it from a living model of a well-proportioned woman who was quite substantial in size. He had seen naked women often enough, in the normal course of living in close quarters, to know how one looked. The arms, resting on top of the ample breasts of the figure, were only suggested, but even so, fingers were defined, as well as the bracelets on her forearms. Her two legs came together into a kind of peg that went into the ground.

The head was most surprising. Most of the donii he had seen had hardly more than a knob for the head, sometimes with a face defined by the hairline but no features. This one had an elaborate hairstyle of rows of tight knobby curls that went all the way around the head and face. Except for the difference in shape, there was no difference between the back and the front of the head.

When he looked closely, he was surprised to see that it had been carved out of limestone. Ivory or bone or wood were much easier to work, and the figure was so perfectly detailed and beautifully made that it was hard to believe someone had made her out of stone. Many flint tools must have been dulled to make this, he thought.

The One Who Served the Mother had been chanting, Jondalar realized. He had been so involved in studying the donii that he hadn't noticed it at first, but he had learned enough Losadunai that when he listened carefully, he understood some of the names of the Mother, and he knew that Losaduna had started the ritual. He waited, hoping his appreciation of the material aesthetic qualities of the carving would not distract from the greater spiritual essence of the ceremony. Although the donii was a symbol for the Mother and, it was thought, offered a resting place for one of Her many spirit forms, he knew the carved figure was not the Great Earth Mother.

"Now, think about it clearly, and in your own words, from your heart, ask the Mother for what you want," Losaduna said. "Holding the dunai will help you to concentrate all your thoughts and feelings into your request. Don't hesitate to say anything that comes to you. Remember, what you are asking for is pleasing to the Mother of All."

Jondalar closed his eyes to think about it, to help himself concentrate. "O Doni, Great Earth Mother," he began. "There have been times in my life when I thought . . . some things I did may have displeased You. I did not mean to displease You, but . . . things happened. There was a time when I thought I would never find a woman I could really love, and I wondered if it was because You were angry about . . . those things."

Something very bad must have happened in this man's life. He is such a good man, and he seems so confident; it is hard to believe that he could suffer from so much shame and worry, Losaduna thought.

"Then, after traveling beyond the end of Your river, and losing . . . my brother, whom I loved more than anyone, You brought Ayla into my life, and finally I knew what it meant to fall in love. I am grateful for Ayla. If there was no one else in my life, no family, no friends, I would be content as long as Ayla was there. But, if it would please You, Great Mother, I would like . . . I would wish for . . . one thing more. I would ask for . . . a child. A child, born to Ayla, born to my hearth, and, if it is possible, born of my spirit, or born of my own essence as Ayla believes. If it is not possible, if my spirit is not . . . enough, then let Ayla have the baby she wants, and let it be born to my hearth, so it can be mine in my heart.''

Jondalar started to put the donii back, but he wasn't quite through. He stopped and held the figure in both hands. ''One more thing. If Ayla should ever become pregnant with a child of my spirit, I would like to know that it is the child of my spirit.''

Interesting request, Losaduna thought. Most men might like to know, but it doesn't really matter that much. I wonder why it's so important to him? And what did he mean by a child of his essence . . . as Ayla believes? I'd like to ask her, but this is a private ritual. I can't tell her what he has said here. Maybe we can discuss it from a philosophical point of view sometime.

Ayla watched the two men leave the Ceremonial Hearth. She felt sure they both had accomplished what they meant to do, but the shorter man had a questioning expression and an unsatisfied set to his shoulders, and the tall one had stiffened and looked rather unhappy, but determined. The strange undercurrent made her even more curious about what went on inside.

''I hope she will change her mind,'' Losaduna was saying as they drew near. ''I think the best way for her to overcome her terrible experience is to go ahead with her First Rites. We will have to be very careful who we choose for her, though. I wish you were staying, Jondalar. She seems to have developed an interest in you. I think it's good to see her warming toward a man.''

''I would like to help, but we just can't stay. We have to leave as soon as we can, tomorrow or the next day, if possible.''

''You're right, of course. The season could turn any time. Be wary if you notice either one of you getting irritable,'' Losaduna said.

''The Malaise,'' Jondalar said.

''What is Malaise?'' Ayla asked.

''It comes with the foehn, the snow-melter, the spring wind,'' Losaduna said. ''The wind comes out of the south-west, warm and dry, and hard enough to uproot trees. It melts snow so fast that high drifts can be gone in a day, and if it hits when you are on the glacier, you may not make it across. The ice could melt beneath your feet and drop you into a crevasse, or it could send a river across your path, or open a crack in front of you. It comes so fast that the evil spirits that like the cold can't get out of its way. It cleans them out, sweeps them out of hidden places, pushes them on ahead. That's why the evil spirits ride the head winds of the snow-melter and usually arrive just before it. They bring the Malaise. If you know what to expect and can control them, they can be a warning, but they're subtle, and it's not easy to turn the evil spirits to your advantage.''

"How do you know when the evil spirits have come?" Ayla asked.

"As I mentioned, watch out if you start feeling irritable. They can make you sick, and if you are already sick, they can make it worse, but more often they just make you want to argue or fight. Some people go into a rage, but everyone knows that it's caused by the Malaise, and people are not held to blame—unless they do serious damage or injury, and even then much is excused. Afterward, people are glad for the snow-melter because it brings new growth, new life, but no one looks forward to the Malaise.''

"Come and eat!" It was Solandia who spoke; they hadn't seen her coming. "People are already going back for second portions. If you don't hurry, there won't be any left."

They walked toward the central hearth where a large fire was burning, whipped up by drafts coming in the mouth of the cave. Though not fully dressed for the intense cold out-side, most people wore warm clothes in the unscreened areas of the cave that were open to the cold and winds. The roast haunch of ibex was rare in the middle, though keeping it hot was cooking it a bit more; fresh meat was welcome. There was also a rich meaty soup, made with dried meat, mammoth fat, a few bits of dried roots, and mountain bilberries; nearly the last of their stored vegetables and fruits. Everyone could hardly wait for the fresh greens of spring.

But the hard cold winter was still upon them, and as much as he wished for spring, Jondalar wished even more for the winter to last a little longer, just until they got across the glacier that still lay beyond them.

38

After the meal Losaduna announced that something was being offered at the Ceremonial Hearth. Ayla and Jondalar didn't understand the word, but they soon learned it was a drink that was served warm. The taste was pleasant and vaguely familiar. Ayla thought it might be some kind of mildly fermented fruit juice flavored with herbs. She was surprised to learn from Solandia that birch sap was a primary ingredient, though fruit juice was only part of the recipe.

It turned out that the taste was deceiving. The drink was stronger than Ayla had thought, and when she asked, Solandia confided that the herbs contributed a large measure of its potency. Then Ayla realized that the vaguely familiar taste came from wormwood artemisia, a very powerful herb that could be dangerous if too much was taken, or if it was used too frequently. It had been difficult to detect because of the pleasant-tasting but highly perfumed woodruff and other aromatic flavors. It made her wonder what else was in it, which led her to taste and analyze the drink more seriously.

She asked Solandia about the powerful herb, mentioning

its possible dangers. The woman explained that the plant, which she called absinthe, was seldom used except in that drink, reserved only for Mother Festivals. Because of its sacred nature, Solandia was usually reluctant to reveal the specific ingredients in the drink, but Ayla's questions were so precise and knowledgeable that she couldn't help but answer. Ayla discovered that the beverage was not at all what it seemed. What she had first thought to be a simple, pleasant-tasting, mild drink was in fact a potent, complex mixture made especially to encourage the relaxation, spontaneity, and warm interaction that were desirable during the Festival to Honor the Mother.

As the people of the Cave began coming into the Ceremonial Hearth, Ayla first noticed a heightened awareness as a result of all her tasting, but it soon gave way to a pleasant, languorous, warm feeling that made her forget about analyzing. She noticed Jondalar and several others talking to Madenia, and, abruptly leaving Solandia, she headed toward them. Every man there saw her coming and liked what he saw. She smiled as she approached the group, and Jondalar felt the powerful love her smile always evoked. It was not going to be easy to follow Losaduna's instructions and encourage her to experience the Mother Festival fully, even with the relaxing drink that the One Who Served the Mother had urged on him. He took a deep breath, then downed the balance of the liquid in his cup.

Filonia, and especially her mate, Daraldi, whom she had met earlier, were among those who greeted Ayla warmly.

"Your cup is empty," he said, dipping out a ladleful from a wooden bowl and filling Ayla's cup.

"You can pour a little more for me, too," Jondalar said in an overly hearty voice. Losaduna noticed the man's forced friendliness, but he didn't think the others would pay much attention. There was one who did, however. Ayla glanced at him, saw his jaw working, and knew something was bothering him. She caught Losaduna's quick observation, too. Something was going on between them, she realized, but the drink was having its effect on her, and she put it in the back of her mind to think about later. Suddenly drumbeats filled the enclosed space.

"The dancing is starting!" Filonia said. "Come on, Jondalar. Let me show you the steps." She took his hand and led him toward the middle of the area.

"Madenia, you go along, too," Losaduna urged.

"Yes," Jondalar said. "You come too. Do you know the steps?" He smiled at her, and Ayla thought he seemed to relax.

Jondalar had been talking and paying attention to Madenia throughout the day, and though she had felt shy and tongue-tied, she had been acutely conscious of the tall man's presence. Every time he looked at her with his compelling eyes, she had felt her heart race. When he took her hand to lead her to the dancing area, she felt a tingling of chills and heat at the same time, and she could not have resisted even if she had tried.

Filonia frowned for a moment, but then smiled at the girl. "We can both teach him the steps," she said, leading them to the dancing area.

"May I show . . ." Daraldi started to say to Ayla, just as Laduni said, "I would be happy . . ." They smiled at each other, trying to give each other a chance to speak.

Ayla's smile took them both in. "Perhaps both of you could show me the steps," she said.

Daraldi bobbed his head in agreement, and Laduni gave her a happy grin as they each took one of her hands and led her toward the area where the dancers were gathering. While they were arranging themselves in a circle, the visitors were shown some basic steps; then they all joined hands as a flute sounded. Ayla was startled by the sound. She hadn't heard a flute since Manen's playing at the Summer Meeting of the Mamutoi. Had it been less than a year since they left the Meeting? It seemed so long ago, and she would never see them again.

She blinked away tears at the thought, but as the dancing began, she had little time to dwell on poignant reminiscences. The rhythm was easy to follow in the beginning, but became faster and more complex as the evening progressed. Ayla was unquestionably the center of attention. Every man found her irresistible. They crowded around her, vying for her attention, making innuendos and even blatant invitations thinly veiled as jokes. Jondalar flirted gently with Madenia and more obviously with Filonia, but he was aware of every man circling around Ayla.

The dancing became more complicated, with intricate steps and changing of places, and Ayla danced with them all.

She laughed at their jokes and bawdy remarks as people broke away to refill their cups, or couples retreated to secluded corners. Laduni jumped into the middle and did an energetic solo performance. Toward the end, his mate joined him.

Ayla was feeling thirsty, and several people went with her to get another drink. She found Daraldi walking beside her.

"I would like some, too," Madenia said.

"I'm sorry," Losaduna said, putting his hand over her cup. "You have not had your Rites of First Pleasures yet, my dear. You will have to settle for tea." Madenia frowned and started to object; then she went to get a cup of the innocuous beverage she had been drinking.

He did not intend to allow her any of the privileges of womanhood until she went through the ceremony that bestowed womanhood, and he was doing everything he could to encourage her to agree to the important ritual. At the same time, he was letting everyone know that in spite of her terrible experience, she had been purified, restored to her former state, and was to be subject to the same restrictions and treated with the same special care and attention given to any other girl on the verge of becoming a woman. He felt it was the only way she would ever fully recover from the unconscionable attack and multiple rape she had suffered.

Ayla and Daraldi were the last to drink, and as everyone else wandered away in one direction or the other, they were left alone. He turned to her.

"Ayla, you are such a beautiful woman," he said.

When she was growing up she had always been the tall, ugly one, and as many times as Jondalar had told her she was beautiful, she always thought it was because he loved her. She didn't think of herself as beautiful, and his comment surprised her.

"No," she said, laughing. "I'm not beautiful!"

Her remark took him aback. It wasn't what he had expected to hear.

"But . . . but, you are," he said.

Daraldi had been trying to interest her all evening, and though her conversation was friendly and warm, and she obviously enjoyed the dancing, moving with a natural sensuality that encouraged his efforts, he hadn't been able to strike the spark that would lead to further advances. He knew he was not an unattractive man, and this was a Mother Festival, but he couldn't seem to make his desires known. Finally he decided on a more direct approach.

"Ayla," he said, putting his arm around her waist. He felt her stiffen for a moment, but he persisted, leaning over to nuzzle her ear. "You *are* a beautiful woman," he whispered.

She turned to face him, but instead of leaning toward him in a willing response, she pulled back. He put his other arm around her waist to bring her closer. She leaned back and put her hands on his shoulders and looked him full in the face.

Ayla hadn't quite understood the real meaning of the Mother Festival. She had thought it was just a warm and friendly gathering, even though they had talked about "honoring" the Mother and she knew what that usually meant. As she had noticed couples, and sometimes three or more, retiring to the darker areas around the hide partitions, she was getting more of an idea, but it wasn't until she looked at Daraldi and saw his desire that she finally knew what he expected.

He pulled her toward him and leaned forward to kiss her. Ayla felt a warmth for him, and she responded with some feeling. His hand found her breast, and then he tried to reach under her tunic. He was attractive, the feeling wasn't unpleasant, she was relaxed and in the mood to be willing, but she wanted time to think. It was hard to resist, her mind was not clear; then she heard rhythmic sounds.

"Let's go back to the dancers," she said.

"Why? There aren't many left dancing anyway."

"I want to do a Mamutoi dance," she said. He acquiesced. She had responded; he could wait a little longer.

When they reached the central area, Ayla noticed that Jondalar was still there. He was dancing with Madenia, holding both her hands and showing her a step he had learned from the Sharamudoi. Filonia, Losaduna, Solandia, and a few others were clapping their hands nearby; the flute player and the one beating the rhythms had found partners.

Ayla and Daraldi joined in clapping their hands together. She caught Jondalar's eye and changed from slapping both hands together to slapping her thighs, in the Mamutoi style. Madenia stopped to look, then backed away as Jondalar joined Ayla in a complicated thigh-slapping rhythm. Soon they were moving together, then backing away and around each other, looking at each other over their shoulders. When they came face-to-face, they reached for each other's hands. From the moment she caught his eye, Ayla saw no one but Jondalar. The generalized warmth and friendliness she had felt for Daraldi was lost in her overpowering response to the desire, the need, and the love in the blue, blue eyes looking at her at that moment.

The intensity between them was apparent to everyone. Losaduna watched them closely for a while, then nodded imperceptibly. It was clear that the Mother was making Her wishes known. Daraldi shrugged his shoulders, then smiled at Filonia. Madenia's eyes opened wide. She knew she was seeing something rare and beautiful.

When Ayla and Jondalar stopped dancing, they were in each other's arms oblivious to everyone around them. Solandia started clapping and soon all of those who were left joined in the applause. The sound finally reached them. They backed away from each other, feeling a bit self-conscious.

"I think there is still a drink or two left," Solandia said. "Shall we finish it off?"

"That's a good idea!" Jondalar said, his arm around Ayla. He wasn't about to let her go now.

Daraldi picked up the large wooden bowl to pour out the last of the special drink, then looked at Filonia. I'm really very lucky, he thought. She is a beautiful woman, and she has brought two children to my hearth. Just because it was Mother Festival didn't mean he had to honor Her with someone other than his mate.

Jondalar finished his drink in one swallow, put his cup down, then suddenly picked Ayla up and carried her to their bed. She felt strangely giddy, full of joy, almost as though she had escaped some unpleasant fate, but her joy was nothing to Jondalar's. He had watched her all night, seen the way all the men wanted her, tried to give her every opportunity as Losaduna had advised, and was sure she would end up choosing someone else.

He could have gone with someone else many times himself, but he wouldn't leave until he was sure she was gone. Instead, he stayed with Madenia, knowing she was not available to any man yet. He enjoyed paying attention to her, seeing her relax around him, appreciating the beginnings of the woman she was going to be. Although he wouldn't have blamed Filonia if she had gone with someone else, and she had many opportunities, he was glad she'd stayed near him. He would have hated being left alone if Ayla had chosen someone else. They talked about many things. Thonolan and their travels together, her children, especially Thonolia, and Daraldi and how much she cared for him, but Jondalar couldn't bring himself to speak very much about Ayla.

Then, in the end, when she came to him, he could hardly believe it. He laid her down carefully on their sleeping platform, looked at her and saw the love in her eyes, and felt an aching soreness in his throat as he held back tears. He had done everything Losaduna had said, given her every chance, even tried to encourage her, but she had come to him. He wondered if that was a sign from the Mother telling him that if Ayla became pregnant, it would be a child of his spirit?

He changed the position of the movable privacy screens, and when she started to get up and remove her clothes, he gently pushed her back down. "Tonight is mine," he said. "I want to do it all."

She lay back down and nodded with a little smile, feeling a thrill of anticipation. He went outside the screens, brought back a lighted stick, lit a small lamp, and set it in a niche. It didn't shed much light, just enough to barely see. He started to remove her clothes, then stopped.

"Do you think we could find our way to the hot springs with this?" he asked, indicating the lamp.

"They say it drains a man, makes his manhood soften," Ayla said.

"Believe me, that won't happen tonight," he said, with a grin.

"Then I think it might be fun," she said.

They put on their parkas, picked up the lamp, and quietly headed outside. Losaduna wondered if they were going to relieve themselves, then thought again, and he smiled. The hot springs had never slowed him down for very long. It just gave him a little extra measure of control sometimes. But Losaduna was not the only one watching them go.

Children were never excluded from Mother Festivals. They learned the skills and activities they were expected to know as adults by watching adults. When they played games, they often mimicked their elders, and before they were actually capable of any serious sexual acts, boys bounced on girls in imitation of their fathers, and girls pretended to give birth to dolls in imitation of their mothers. Soon after they were capable, they passed into adulthood with rituals that not only brought them adult status but adult responsibilities, although they didn't necessarily choose a mate for several years. Babies were born in their own time, when the Mother chose to bless a woman, but surprisingly were seldom born to very young women. All babies were welcomed, supported, and cared for by the extended family and close friends that made up a Cave.

Madenia had observed Mother Festivals as long as she could remember, but this time it took on new meaning. She had watched several of the couples—it did not seem to hurt anyone, not the way she had been hurt, even when some of the women chose several men—but she was particularly interested in Ayla and Jondalar. As soon as they left the cave, she put on her parka and followed them.

They found their way to the double-walled tent and went into the second enclosure, welcoming the steamy warmth. They stood just inside, looked around, then put the lamp down on the raised earth altar. They took off their outer parkas and sat down on the felted wool pads that covered the ground.

Jondalar began by taking off Ayla's boots; then he removed his own. He kissed her long and lovingly, while he undid the fastenings on her tunic and undergarment, and pulled them up over her head, then bent down to kiss each nipple. He untied her fur-lined leggings and breechcloutlike underwear and pulled them off, stopping to caress her mound covered with soft hair—they hadn't bothered to put on their outer leggings with the fur facing out. Then he undressed himself and took her in his arms, delighting in the feel of her skin next to his, and wanted her that instant.

He led her into the steaming pool, they immersed once, then went to the washing area. Jondalar scooped out a handful of soft soap from the bowl and began rubbing it over Ayla's back and her twin mounds, avoiding her enticingly warm, moist places for the moment. It was smooth and slippery, and he loved the way it felt on her skin. Ayla closed her eyes, felt his hands caress her in the way he knew best to please her, and gave herself over to his wonderfully smooth touch, feeling every tingling sensation.

He took another handful and smoothed it on her legs, lifting each foot and feeling her slight spasm at the tickling

of the bottom of her feet. Then he turned her around and
faced her front, but took time to kiss her, gently and slowly
exploring her lips and her tongue, feeling her response. His
own response had swelled, and his manhood seemed to move
of its own volition, striving to reach her.

With another small handful of soap, he started under her
arms, caressing with the delightful slippery foam down to her
full firm breasts, feeling her nipples harden under his palms.
Shivers, like lightning, raced through her body when he
touched her amazingly sensitive nipples, and found the place
deep inside her that wanted him. When he moved down to
her stomach and her thighs, she moaned with anticipation.
With hands still soapy, he caressed her folds and found her
place of Pleasures, rubbing just lightly. Then he picked up
the rinsing bowl, filled it with water from the hot pool, and
began pouring it over her. He poured several more bowlfuls
over her before he led her back into the hot water.

They sat on the stone seats and held each other close,
pressing warm skin against warm skin, and dunking under
until only their heads were above the water. Then, taking her
hand, Jondalar led Ayla out of the water once more. He laid
her down on the soft mats, and just looked at her for a while,
glowing and wet, and waiting for him.

To her surprise, he spread her thighs first and ran his
tongue the full length of her folds. He tasted no salt, and
her special taste was gone; it was a new experience, to taste
her without tasting her, but as he reveled in the novelty of
it, he heard her begin to moan and cry out. It had seemed
so sudden, but she realized she was so ready. She felt her
excitement build, and reach a peak, then spasms of delight
washed over her again and again, and suddenly he tasted her.

She reached for him, and as he mounted and penetrated,
she guided him inside. She pressed up as he plunged down,
and they sighed with deep satisfaction. As he pulled out, she
ached to have him back. He felt her full warm caress enclose
his member completely, and he nearly reached his pulsing
burst. When he pulled back again, he knew he was ready, as
a high-pitched moan escaped his lips. She pulled up to him
and he was ready as the bursting momentum escaped and
filled her deep well and mixed with her own warm wetness
and he cried out the fullness of her joy.

He rested on her for a time, because he knew she loved
his weight on her then. When he finally rolled over, he looked

down at her and saw her languid smile and had to kiss it.
Their tongues explored, softly, gently, without prodding, and
she began to feel a touch of excitement again. He noticed
her heightened response and responded in kind. Without the
great urgency this time, he kissed her mouth, then each of
her eyes, and found her ears, and the tender, ticklish places
of her throat. He moved lower and found her nipple. In no
hurry, he suckled and nibbled on one while he fondled and
squeezed the other, then traded off, until she was pressing
herself to him, wanting more and more as the sensation grew.

And his own as well. His spent manhood was swelling
again, and when she felt it, she abruptly sat up and bent
down to take it into her mouth and help it along. He lay back
to enjoy the sensations she sent coursing through him, as she
took in as much as she could, sucking hard, then releasing
and letting it slide back. She found the hard ridge on the
underside and rubbed her tongue across it rapidly; then, pulling back the foreskin a little, she circled the smooth head
with her tongue faster and faster. He moaned with the fiery
waves coursing through him, then pulled her around until she
straddled him, and he reached up to taste the warm petal of
her flower.

At almost the same moment, they felt themselves and
each other mount and mount, and when he tasted her again,
he pulled himself back, turned her around so that she was
on her knees, guided himself in, and felt her full, deep
well again. She pushed back with each stroke, rocking,
moving, plunging in and pulling back, feeling every push,
every pull, and then, it came again, first she and, at the
next stroke, he felt the marvelous surge of the Mother's
great Gift of Pleasure.

They both collapsed, exhausted, pleasurably, wonderfully, languorously exhausted. They felt a draft for a moment,
but didn't move, and they even dozed off for a time. When
they woke, they got up and washed again, then soaked in the
hot waters. To their surprise, when they got out, they found
clean, dry, velvety soft leather blankets to dry themselves
with beside the entrance.

Madenia walked back to the cave, experiencing feelings
she had never known before. She had been moved by Jondalar's intense but controlled passion and his caring tenderness,

and by Ayla's eager response and unreserved willingness to abandon herself to him, to trust him completely. Their experience was not at all like the one she had endured. Their Pleasures had been fiery and physical but not brutal; it was not taking from one to serve the other's lust, but giving and sharing to please and gratify each other. Ayla had told her the truth; the Mother's Pleasures could be an exciting, sensual delight, a joyful and pleasurable celebration of their love.

And though she didn't quite know what to do about it, she was aroused, physically and emotionally. She had tears in her eyes. At that moment, she wanted Jondalar. She wished he could be the one to share her womanhood rites, though she knew that wasn't possible. But she decided, at that moment, that if she could have someone like him, she would agree to go through with the ceremony and have her Rites of First Pleasures at the next Summer Meeting.

No one was feeling particularly lively the next morning. Ayla made the "morning-after" drink she had developed for the after-celebration headaches at the Lion Camp, though she only had enough ingredients for the people of the Ceremonial Hearth. She carefully checked her supply of the contraceptive tea she took each morning, and decided it should last until the growing season when she could collect more. Fortunately it wasn't necessary to take much.

Madenia came to see the visitors before noon. Smiling shyly at Jondalar, she announced that she had decided to have her First Rites.

"That's wonderful, Madenia. You won't be sorry," the tall, handsome, wonderfully gentle man said. She looked up at him with such adoring eyes that he bent down and kissed her cheek, then nuzzled her neck and breathed in her ear. He stood up and smiled at her, and she was lost in his remarkable blue eyes. Her heart was beating so fast that she could hardly breathe. At that moment, more than anything, Madenia wished that Jondalar could be the one who would be chosen for her Rites of First Pleasures. Then she felt embarrassed, afraid, that somehow he knew what she was thinking. Suddenly she ran out of the hearth area.

"Too bad we don't live closer to the Losadunai," he said, watching her go. "I would like to help that young woman, but I'm sure they'll find someone."

"Yes, I'm sure they will, but I hope she hasn't built up her expectations too high. I told her that someday she might find someone like you, Jondalar, that she had suffered enough and deserved it. I hope so, for her sake," Ayla said. "But there aren't many like you."

"All young women have high hopes and expectations," Jondalar said, "but it's all imagination before the first time."

"But she has something to base her imagination on."

"Of course, they all know more or less what to expect. It's not like they haven't been around men and women," he said.

"It's more than that, Jondalar. Who do you think left us those dry blankets last night?"

"I thought it was Losaduna, or maybe Solandia."

"They went to their bed before we did; they had their own honoring to do. I asked them. They didn't even know we had gone to the sacred waters—although Losaduna seemed particularly pleased about it."

"If they didn't, then who . . . Madenia?"

"I'm almost certain it was."

Jondalar frowned with concentration. "We've been traveling alone together for so long that . . . I've never really said it before, but . . . I feel a little . . . I don't know . . . reluctant, I guess, to be as impetuous, as free when we're around people. I thought we were alone last night. If I'd known she was there, I might not have been as . . . unrestrained," he said.

Ayla smiled. "I know," she said. She was becoming more and more aware that he didn't like to reveal the deeply sensitive side of his nature, and she was pleased that he would express himself to her, in words and actions. "I'm glad you didn't know she was there, both for me, and for her."

"Why for her?" he asked.

"I think that's what convinced her to go ahead with her womanhood ceremony. She had been around men and women sharing Pleasures often enough that she didn't think about it, until those men forced her. Afterward she could only think about the pain, and the horror of being used as a thing, with no thought for her as a woman. It's hard to explain, Jondalar. Something like that makes you feel so . . . terrible."

"I'm sure that's true, but I think there was more to it," the man said. "After a girl has her first moon time, but before she has had her First Rites, a woman is most vulnerable—and most desirable. Every man is drawn to her, perhaps because she may not be touched. At any other time, a woman is free to choose any man, or none, but at that time, it is dangerous for her.''

"Like Latie wasn't even supposed to look at her brothers," Ayla said. "Mamut explained about that."

"Maybe not entirely," Jondalar said. "It is up to the girl-woman to show restraint then, and it's not always easy. She is the center of attention; every man wants her, particularly the younger ones, and it can be hard for her to resist. They follow her around, trying every way they can to get her to give in to them. Some girls do, especially those who have a long wait before the Summer Meeting. But if she allows herself to be opened without the proper rituals, she is . . . not well thought of. If it's found out, and sometimes the Mother blesses her before she is a woman, making sure everyone knows that she was opened—people can be cruel. They blame her and make fun of her.''

"But why should they blame her? They should blame the men who won't let her alone," Ayla said, irked at the unfairness.

"People say if she can't show restraint, she lacks the qualities to assume the responsibilities of Motherhood and Leadership. She will never be chosen to sit on the Council of Mothers, or Sisters, or whatever name her people give to their council of highest authority, so she loses status, which makes her less desirable as a mate. Not that she loses the status of her mother or her hearth—nothing she is born with is taken away—but she will never be chosen by a man of high status, or even one who has the potential for it. I think Madenia feared that as much as anything," Jondalar said.

"No wonder Verdegia said she was ruined." Ayla's brow creased with concern. "Jondalar, will her people accept Losaduna's cleansing ritual? You know that once she is open, she can never really go back to the way she was."

"I think so. It wasn't that she didn't show restraint. She was forced, and people are angry enough about Charoli to use that against him. There may be a few who will have reservations, but she will have a lot of defenders, too.''

Ayla was silent for a while. "People are complicated, aren't they? Sometimes I wonder if anything is really what it seems.''

• • •

"I think it will work, Laduni," Jondalar said. "I do think it will work! Let me go through it again. We'll use the bowl boat to carry dried grass, and enough burning stones to melt ice for water, plus extra rocks to build a fire on, and the heavy mammoth hide to put the rocks on so they won't sink into the ice when they get hot. We can carry food for us, and probably Wolf, in pack baskets and our backframes."

"It will be a heavy load," Laduni said, "but you don't have to boil the water—that will save on burning stones. You just have to melt it enough so the horses can drink it; both of you and the wolf, too. It doesn't have to be hot, but make sure it's not icy. And make sure you drink enough; don't try to be sparing. If you have warm clothes, get enough rest, and drink enough water, you can resist the cold."

"I think they should try it out in advance, to see how much they will need," Laronia said.

Ayla saw that Laduni's mate had made the suggestion. "That's a good idea," she said.

"But Laduni's right, it will be a heavy load," Laronia added.

"Then we'll have to go through our things and get rid of everything we can," Jondalar said. "We won't need much. Once we get across, we'll be close to Dalanar's Camp."

They were already down to bare necessities. How much more could they get rid of? Ayla thought as the meeting broke up. Madenia fell in beside her as she walked back to their sleeping place. The girl-woman had not only developed a strong crush on Jondalar, but a bit of hero-worship toward Ayla, which made Ayla a little uncomfortable. But she liked Madenia and asked her if she would like to sit with her while she sorted through her things.

As Ayla began unpacking and spreading out her belongings, she tried to remember how many times she had done this before on this Journey. It would be difficult to make choices. Everything had some meaning to her, but if they were going to get across this formidable glacier that Jondalar had been worrying about from the beginning, with Whinney and Racer, and Wolf, she had to eliminate as much as possible.

The first package she opened contained the beautiful outfit

made of soft chamois that Roshario had given to her. She held it up, then spread it out in front of her.

"Oooh! How beautiful! The patterns that are sewn on, and the way it's cut, I've never seen anything like it," Madenia said, unable to resist reaching out to touch it. "And so soft! I have never felt anything so soft."

"It was given to me by a woman of the Sharamudoi, people who live far away from here, near the end of the Great Mother River, where she is truly a great river. You wouldn't believe how big the Mother River gets. The Sharamudoi are really two people. The Shamudoi live on the land and hunt chamois. Do you know that animal?" Ayla asked. Madenia shook her head. "It is a mountain animal, something like an ibex, but smaller."

"Yes, I do know that, but we call it by a different name," Madenia said.

"The Ramudoi are River People and hunt the great sturgeon—that's a huge fish. Together, they have a special way of curing the hides of the chamois to make them soft and supple like this."

Ayla picked up the embroidered tunic and thought about the Sharamudoi people she had met. It seemed so long ago. She could have lived with them; she still felt the same way, and she knew she would never see them again. She hated the thought of leaving the gift from Roshario behind. Then she looked into Madenia's shining eyes as she admired it, and Ayla made a decision.

"Would you like to have this, Madenia?"

Madenia jerked her hands back as though she had touched something hot. "I couldn't! It was a gift to you," she said.

"We have to lighten our load. I think Roshario would be pleased if you would accept it, since you love it so. It was meant to be a matrimonial outfit, but I already have one."

"Are you sure?" Madenia said.

Ayla could see her eyes glistening, incredulous at the thought of such a beautiful, exotic outfit. "Yes, I'm sure. You might consider it for your Matrimonial, if it is appropriate. Think of it as a gift to remember me."

"I don't need a gift to remember you," Madenia said, her eyes brimming with tears. "I will never forget you. Because of you, maybe, someday, I will have a Matrimonial, and if I do, I will wear it then." She couldn't wait to show it to her mother, and to all her friends and age-mates at the Summer Meeting.

Ayla was glad she had decided to give it to her. "Would you like to see my Matrimonial outfit?"

"Oh, yes," Madenia said.

Ayla unwrapped the tunic Nezzie had made for her when she had planned to mate with Ranec. It was an ochre yellow, the color of her hair. A carving of a horse had been wrapped inside it, and two almost perfectly matched pieces of honey-colored amber. Madenia couldn't believe Ayla could have two outfits that were so exotically beautiful, yet so different from each other, but she was afraid to say too much, for fear Ayla might feel required to give her this one, too.

Ayla studied it, trying to decide what to do with it. Then she shook her head. No, she could not part with it, it was her Matrimonial tunic. She would wear it when she mated with Jondalar. In a way, it had a part of Ranec in it, too. She picked up the small horse carved out of mammoth ivory and fondled it absentmindedly. This, too, she would keep. She thought about Ranec, wondered how he was. No one had ever loved her more, and she would never forget him. She could have mated him and been happy with him, if she hadn't loved Jondalar so much.

Madenia had tried to restrain her curiosity, but finally she had to ask. "What are those stones?"

"They're called amber. They were given to me by the headwoman of the Lion Camp."

"Is that a carving of your horse?"

Ayla smiled at her. "Yes, it's a carving of Whinney. It was made for me by a man with laughing eyes and skin the color of Racer's coat. Even Jondalar said he had never known a better carver."

"A man with brown skin?" Madenia asked, incredulous.

Ayla smiled wryly. She couldn't blame her for doubting. "Yes. He was a Mamutoi, and his name was Ranec. The first time I saw him, I couldn't help staring at him. I'm afraid I was very impolite. I was told that his mother was as dark as . . . a piece of that burning stone. She lived far to the south, across a great sea. A Mamutoi man named Wymez made a long Journey. He mated her, and her son was born to his hearth. She died on their way back, so he returned with only the boy. The man's sister raised him."

Madenia gave a little shiver of excitement. She thought the only thing south was the mountains, and that they went on forever. Ayla had traveled so far and knew so much. Maybe someday she would make a Journey like Ayla, and meet a brown man who would carve a beautiful horse for her, and people who would give her beautiful clothes, and find horses that would let her ride them, and a wolf that loved children, and a man like Jondalar, who would ride the horses and make the long Journey with her. Madenia was lost in daydreams of great adventure.

She had never met anyone like Ayla. She idolized the beautiful woman who led such an exciting life, and she hoped she might be like her in some way. Ayla spoke with a strange accent, but that only added to her mystery, and hadn't she suffered a forced attack by a man when she was a girl, too? Ayla had gotten over it but understood how someone else felt. In the warmth, love, and understanding of the people around her, Madenia was beginning to recover from the horror of the incident. She began to imagine herself, mature and wise, telling some young girl, who had suffered such an attack, about her experience, to help her overcome it.

While Madenia daydreamed, she watched Ayla pick up a neatly tied package. The woman held it but didn't open it; she knew exactly what was inside it, and she had no intention of leaving it behind.

"What's that?" the girl asked, as Ayla put it aside.

Ayla picked it up again; she hadn't seen it herself for some time. She looked around to make sure Jondalar was not in sight, then untied the knots. Inside was a pure white tunic decorated with ermine tails. Madenia's eyes became big and round.

"That's as white as snow! I've never seen any leather colored white like that," she said.

"Making white leather is a secret of the Crane Hearth. I learned how to make it from an old woman, who learned it from her mother," Ayla explained. "She had no one to pass the knowledge down to, so when I asked her to teach me, she agreed."

"You made that?" Madenia said.

"Yes. For Jondalar, but he doesn't know it. I'm going to give it to him when we reach his home, I think for our Matrimonial," Ayla said.

When she held it up, a package fell out if it, too. Madenia

could see it was a man's tunic. Except for the ermine tails, there were no decorations; no embroidered patterns or designs, no shells or beads, but it needed none. Decorations would have detracted. In its simplicity, the pure whiteness of the color made it stunning.

Ayla opened the smaller package. Inside was the strange figure of a woman with a carved face. If she hadn't just seen wonder after wonder, it would have frightened the girl; dunai never had faces. But somehow it was all right for Ayla to have one.

"Jondalar made this for me," Ayla said. "He told me he made it to capture my spirit, and for my womanhood ceremony, the first time he taught me the Mother's Gift of Pleasure. There was no one else to share in it, but we didn't need it. Jondalar made it a ceremony. Later he gave this to me to keep because it has great power, he says."

"I believe it," Madenia said. She had no desire to touch it, but she didn't doubt that Ayla could control any power it held.

Ayla sensed her uneasiness and wrapped the figure back up again. She tucked it inside the carefully folded white tunic and wrapped that in the fine, thin sewn-together rabbit hides that protected it, then tied it with the cords.

Another wrapped package held some of the gifts she had received at her adoption ceremony, when she was accepted into the Mamutoi. She would keep them. Her medicine bag would go with her, of course, firestones and fire-making kit, her sewing kit, one change of inner clothes, and felt boot liners, sleeping rolls, and hunting weapons. She looked over her bowls and cooking implements and eliminated all but the absolute essentials. She would have to wait for Jondalar to decide about the tents, ropes, and other gear.

Just as she and Madenia were about to go out, Jondalar came into the dwelling space. He and several others had just returned with a load of brown coal, and he had come in to sort through his things. Several other people came in then, too, including Solandia and her children with Wolf.

"I've really come to depend on this animal, and I'm going to miss him. I don't suppose you'd like to leave him," she said.

Ayla signaled Wolf. For all his love of the children, he came to her immediately and stood at her feet looking at her expectantly. "No, Solandia. I don't think I could."

"I didn't think so, but I had to ask. I'm going to miss you, too, you know," she added.

"And I will miss you. The hardest part of this Journey has been making friends, then leaving and knowing that I would probably never see them again," Ayla said.

"Laduni," Jondalar said, carrying a piece of mammoth ivory with strange markings incised on it. "Talut, the headman of the Lion Camp, made this map of the country far to the east, showing the first part of our Journey. I had hoped to keep it as a remembrance of him. It's not essential, but I would hate to throw it away. Would you keep it for me? Who knows, someday I may come back for it."

"Yes, I'll keep it for you," Laduni said, taking the ivory map and looking it over. "It looks interesting. Perhaps you can explain it to me before you go. I hope you do come back, but if not, perhaps someone going that way may have room for it and I can send it to you."

"I'm also leaving some tools behind. You can keep them or not. I always hate to give up a hammerstone I'm used to, but I'm sure I'll be able to replace it once we reach the Lanzadonii. Dalanar always has good supplies around. I'll leave my bone hammers and some blades, too. I'll keep an adze and an axe to chop ice, though."

After they had walked over to their sleeping area, Jondalar asked, "What are you taking, Ayla?"

"It's all here, on the bed platform."

Jondalar saw the mysterious package among her other things. "Whatever is in that must be very valuable," he said.

"I will carry it," she said.

Madenia smiled slyly, pleased to know the secret. It made her feel very special.

"What about this?" he asked, pointing to another package.

"These are gifts from the Lion Camp," she said, opening it up to show him. He spied the beautiful spear point Wymez had given her, and he picked it up to show Laduni.

"Look at this," he said.

It was a large blade, longer than his hand, and as wide as his palm, but less than the size of the tip of his small finger in thickness, tapering to a fine sharpness at the edges.

"It's bifacially worked," Laduni said, turning it over. "But how did he get it so thin? I thought working both sides of a stone was a crude technique used for simple axes and

such, but this is not crude. This is as fine a piece of workmanship as I've ever seen."

"Wymez made it," Jondalar said. "I told you he was
good. He heats the flint before he works it. It changes the
quality of the stone, makes it easier to detach fine flakes,
that's how he gets it so thin. I can hardly wait to show this
to Dalanar."

"I'm sure he will appreciate it," Laduni said.

Jondalar gave it back to Ayla, and she rewrapped it carefully. "I think we'll just take a single tent, more as a wind-
break," he remarked.

"What about a ground cloth?" Ayla said.

"We have such a heavy load of rocks and stones, I hate
to take any more than we need to."

"A glacier is ice. We might be glad for a ground cover."

"I suppose you're right," he said.

"What about these ropes?"

"Do you really think we need them?"

"I'd suggest you take them," Laduni said. "Ropes can
be very useful on a glacier."

"If you think so, I'll take your advice," Jondalar said.

They had packed as much as possible the night before
and spent the evening saying their farewells to the people
they had come to care for so much in the short time they
were there. Verdegia made a point of coming to talk to Ayla.

"I want to thank you, Ayla."

"It's not necessary to thank me. We need to thank everyone here."

"I mean for what you did for Madenia. To be honest,
I'm not sure what you did, or what you said to her, but I
know that you made the difference. Before you came, she
was hiding in a dark corner, wishing she were dead. She
wouldn't even talk to me, and she wanted nothing to do with
becoming a woman. I thought all was lost. Now, she's almost
like her old self, and looking forward to her First Rites. I
just hope nothing happens to make her change her mind again
before summer."

"I think she will be all right, as long as everyone contin-
ues to support her," Ayla said. "That has been the biggest
help, you know."

"I still want to see Charoli punished," Verdegia said.

"I think everyone does. Now that everyone has agreed to

go after him, I think he will be. Madenia will be vindicated, and she will have her First Rites and become a woman. You will have grandchildren yet, Verdegia.''

In the morning they got up early, did their final packing, and came back into the cave for a last morning meal with the Losadunai. Everyone was there to bid them farewell. Losaduna had Ayla memorize a few more verses of lore, and then almost became emotional when she hugged him good-bye. Then he quickly went to talk to Jondalar. Solandia made no qualms about how she felt, and she told them how sorry she was to see them go. Even Wolf seemed to know he would not see the children again, and so did they. He licked the baby's face and for the first time Micheri cried.

But as they walked out of the cave, it was Madenia who surprised them. She had put on the magnificent outfit Ayla had given her, and she clung to Ayla and tried not to cry. Jondalar told her how beautiful she was, and he meant it. The clothes lent her an air of uncommon beauty and maturity and hinted at the real woman she would someday become.

As they mounted the horses, rested now and eager to go, they looked back at the people standing around the mouth of the cave, and it was Madenia who stood out. But she was still young and, as they waved, tears streamed down her face.

''I will never forget you, either of you,'' she called out, then ran into the cave.

As they rode away, back toward the Great Mother River, which was hardly more than a stream, Ayla thought she would never forget Madenia, or her people either. Jondalar was sorry to say goodbye, too, but his thoughts were on the difficulties they had yet to face. He knew the toughest part of their Journey still lay ahead.

39

Jondalar and Ayla headed north, back toward Donau, the Great Mother River that had guided their steps for so much of their Journey. When they reached her, they turned west again and continued to follow the stream back toward her beginnings, but the great waterway had changed character. She was no longer a huge meandering surge rolling with ponderous dignity across the flat plains, taking in countless tributaries and volumes of silt, then breaking into channels and forming oxbow lakes.

Near her source, she was fresher, sprightlier, a leaner, shallower stream that tumbled over her wide rocky bed as she raced down the steep mountainside. But the westward route of the travelers along the swiftly flowing river had become a continuous uphill climb, one that took them ever closer to their inevitable rendezvous with the thick layer of unmelting ice that capped the broad high plateau of the rugged highland ahead.

The shapes of glaciers followed the contours of the land. Those on mountaintops were craggy tors of ice, those on level ground spread out like pancakes, with a nearly uniform thickness, rising slightly higher in the middle, leaving behind gravel banks and gouging out depressions that became lakes and ponds. At its farthest advance, the southernmost lobe of the vast continental cake of ice, whose nearly level top was as high as the mountains around them, missed by less than five degrees of latitude a meeting with the northern reaches of the mountain glaciers. The land between the two was the coldest anywhere on earth.

Unlike mountain glaciers, frozen rivers creeping slowly down the sides of mountains, the unmelting ice on the rounded, nearly flat highland—the glacier Jondalar was so concerned about still to the west of them—was a plateau glacier, a miniature version of the great thick layer of ice that spread across the plains of the continent to the north.

As Ayla and Jondalar continued along the river, they gained altitude with each step. They made the ascent with an eye toward sparing the heavily laden horses, most often leading them instead of riding. Ayla was particularly concerned for Whinney, who was hauling the major portion of the burning stones that they hoped would ensure the survival of their traveling companions when they crossed the icy surface, a terrain that horses would never attempt on their own.

In addition to Whinney's pole drag, both horses carried heavy packs, though the load on the mare's back was lighter, to compensate for the travois she pulled. Racer's load was piled so high that it was somewhat unwieldy, but even the backpacks of the woman and man were substantial. Only the wolf was free of additional burdens, and Ayla had begun to eye his unfettered movements, thinking that he, too, could carry a share.

"All this effort to carry rocks," Ayla remarked one morning as she shrugged on her backpack. "Some people would think we were strange to be hauling this heavy load of stones up these mountains."

"Many more think we're strange for traveling with two horses and a wolf," Jondalar countered, "but if we're going to get them across the ice, we're going to have to get these stones up there. And there is one thing to be glad for."

"What is that?"

"How easy it will be once we reach the other side."

The upper course of the river traversed the northern foreland of the range of mountains to the south, which was so huge that the travelers had little real sense of its immense scale. The Losadunai lived in a region, just south of the river, of more rounded, massiflike limestone mountains with extensive areas of relatively level plateaus. Though worn down by eons of wind and water, the eroded eminences were lofty enough to bear glistening crowns of ice throughout the year. Between the river and the mountains was a landscape of dormant vegetation overlaying a flysch zone of sandstone. This in turn was covered by a light mantle of winter snow that blurred the lower boundary of the unmelting ice, but the shimmer of glacial blue revealed its nature.

Farther south, gleaming in the sun like giant shards of broken alabaster, the exalted crags of the central zone, almost a separate range within the great mass of uplifted earth, soared high above the nearer heights. As the travelers continued their climb toward the higher western chain within the complex range, the silent march of the central mountains followed their progression, watched over by a brooding pair of jagged peaks towering far above the rest.

To the north, across the river, the ancient crystalline massif rose steeply, its undulating surface occasionally overtopped by rocky crags and covered by block fields with raised meadows in between. Looking ahead, westward, higher rounded hills, some topped with small icy crowns of their own, reached across the frozen river, no boundary to frost, to join the ice of the younger folded ridges of the southern range.

Dry, powdery snow drifted down less frequently as their Journey took them closer to the coldest part of the continent, the region between the farthest northern extension of the mountain glacier and the southernmost reaches of the vast, continent-spanning ice sheets. Not even the windy loess steppes of the eastern plains could match the severity of its bitter cold. The land was saved from the desolation of frozen ice sheets only by the moderating maritime influence of the western ocean.

The highland glacier they planned to go over, without the air warmed by the unfrozen ocean keeping the encroaching ice at bay, could have expanded and become impossible to cross. The maritime influences that allowed passage to the western steppes and tundras also kept the glaciers away from the land of the Zelandonii, sparing it the heavy layer of ice that covered other lands at the same latitude.

• • •

Jondalar and Ayla fell easily back into their traveling routine, although it seemed to Ayla that they had been traveling forever. She longed to reach the end of their Journey. Memories of the quiet winter in the earthlodge of the Lion Camp flashed into her mind as they plodded forward through the monotony of the winter landscape. She recalled small incidents with pleasure, forgetting the misery that had overshadowed her days the whole time when she'd thought that Jondalar had stopped loving her.

Although all their water had to be melted, usually from river ice rather than snow—the land was bleak and barren with few snowdrifts—Ayla decided there were some benefits to the freezing cold. The tributaries to the Great Mother River were smaller, and frozen solid, making them easier to cross. But they invariably hurried across the right-bank openings because of the fierce winds that roared through valleys of the rivers and streams. These blasts funneled frigid air from the high-pressure areas of the southern mountains, adding wind chill to the already freezing air.

Shivering even in her heavy furs, Ayla felt relieved when they finally made it across a wide valley to the protective barrier of nearby higher ground. "I'm so cold!" she said through chattering teeth. "I wish it would warm up a little."

Jondalar looked alarmed. "Don't wish that, Ayla!"

"Why not?"

"We have to be across the glacier before the weather turns. A warm wind means the foehn, the snow-melter, that will break the season. Then we'll have to go around to the north, through Clan country. It will take much longer, and with all the trouble Charoli has been causing them, I don't think they will be very welcoming," Jondalar said.

She nodded with understanding, looking across to the north side of the river. After studying it for some distance, Ayla said, "They have the better side."

"What makes you say that?"

"Even from here you can see that there are plains that have good grass, and that would bring more animals to hunt. On this side are mostly scrub pines—that means sandy earth and poor grass, except for a few places. This side must be just enough closer to the ice to be colder, and less rich," she explained.

"You may be right," Jondalar said, thinking her evaluation was astute. "I don't know what it's like in summer; I've only been here in winter."

Ayla had judged accurately. The soils of the northern plains of the valley of the great river were primarily loess over a limestone bedrock, and more fertile than the southern side. In addition, the mountain glaciers of the south crowded closer, making the winters more harsh and the summers cooler, barely warm enough to melt the accumulated snows and ground frost of winter back to the previous summer's snow line—almost. Most of the glaciers were growing again, slowly, but enough to signal a shift from the current milieu, the slightly warmer interval, back to colder times, and one last glacial advance before the long melt that would leave ice only in polar regions.

The dormant state of the trees often left Ayla unsure of their variety, until she tasted a twig tip or bud or bit of inner bark. Where alder dominated near the river, and along the lower valleys of its tributaries, she knew they would be in peaty fen woods if it were summer; where it was mixed with willow and poplar would be the wettest parts, and the occasional ash, elm, or hornbeam, hardly more than woody brush, indicated drier ground. The rare dwarfed oak, struggling to survive in more protected niches, barely hinted at the massive oak forests that would one day cover a more temperate land. Trees were absent entirely from the sandy soils of the raised heath land, able to nourish only heather, whins, sparse grasses, mosses, and lichens.

Even in the frigid climate, some birds and animals thrived; cold-adapted animals of the steppes and mountains abounded, and hunting was easy. Only rarely did they use the supplies given to them by the Losadunai, which they wanted to save for the crossing anyway. Not until they reached the frozen wasteland would they need to rely entirely on the resources they carried.

Ayla saw an uncommon pygmy snow owl and pointed it out to Jondalar. He became adept at finding willow grouse, which tasted like the white-feathered ptarmigan that he had grown so fond of, particularly the way that Ayla cooked them. Its mixed coloration gave it better camouflage in a landscape not entirely covered by snow. Jondalar seemed to recall that there had been more snow the last time he had come that way.

The region was influenced by both the continental east and the maritime west, revealed by the unusual mixture of plants and animals that seldom lived near each other. The small furry creatures were an example that Ayla noticed, although during the freezing season, the mice, dormice, voles, susliks, and hamsters were seldom seen, except when she broke through a nest for the vegetable foods they had stored. Though she sometimes took the animals too, for Wolf or, particularly if she found giant hamsters, for themselves, the little animals more commonly gave sustenance to martens, foxes, and the small wildcats.

On the high plains and along river valleys, they often sighted woolly mammoths, usually in herds of related females, with an occasional male traveling along for company, though in the cold season groups of males often banded together. Rhinoceroses were invariably loners, except for females with one or two immature young. In the warmer seasons, bison, aurochs, and every variety of deer, from the giant megaceros to small shy roe deer, were numerous, but only reindeer stayed on in winter. Instead mouflon, chamois, and ibex had migrated down from their high summer habitat, and Jondalar had never seen so many musk-oxen.

It seemed to be a year when the musk-ox population was at a high point in its cycle. Next year they would probably crash down to minimum numbers, but in the meantime, Ayla and Jondalar found the spear-thrower proving its worth. When threatened, musk-oxen, particularly the belligerent males, formed a tight phalanx of lowered horns facing outward from a circle in order to protect the calves and certain females. This behavior was effective against most predators, but not against a spear-thrower.

Without having to get close enough to put themselves in danger from a swift, break-away charge, Ayla and Jondalar could take their pick of the animals standing their ground and aim from a safe distance. It was almost too easy, although they had to be accurate and throw hard to make sure the spear would penetrate the dense undercoat.

With several varieties of animals to choose from, they didn't often lack for food, and they frequently left the less choice pieces of meat for other carnivores and scavengers. It wasn't a matter of waste but of need. Their high-protein diet of lean meat often left them less than satisfied, even when they had eaten their fill. Inner barks, and teas made from the needles and twig tips of trees offered only limited relief.

Omnivorous humans could subsist on a variety of foods, and proteins were essential, but not adequate alone. People had been known to die of protein starvation without, at least, one or the other of vegetable produce or fats. Traveling at the end of winter with very little in the way of plant food, they needed fat to survive, but it was so late in the season that the animals they hunted had used most of their own reserves. The travelers selectively took the meat and inner organs that contained the most fat, and left the lean, or gave it to Wolf. He found ample nourishment on his own from the woods and plains along the way.

Another animal did inhabit the region, and though they always noticed them, neither Jondalar nor Ayla could bring themselves to hunt horses. Their fellow travelers fared well enough on the rough dry grass, mosses, lichens, and even small twigs and thin bark.

Ayla and Jondalar traveled west, following the course of the river and angling slightly north, with the massif across the river pacing them. When the river turned somewhat southwest, Jondalar knew they were getting close. The depression between the ancient northern highland and the southern mountains climbed upward toward a wild landscape that outcropped in rugged crags. They passed the place where three streams joined to form the recognizable beginning of the Great Mother River, then crossed over and followed the left bank of the middle course, the Middle Mother. It was the one that Jondalar had been told was considered the true Mother River, though any one of the three could have been.

Reaching what was essentially the beginning of the great river was not the profound experience that Ayla had thought it might be. The Great Mother River didn't spring forth from some clearly defined place, like the great inland sea where she ended. There was no clear beginning, and even the boundary of the northern territory, considered flathead country, was uncertain, but Jondalar had a familiar feeling about the area they were in. He thought they were close to the edge of the actual glacier, though they had been traveling over snow for some time and it was hard to tell.

Although it was only afternoon, they decided to start looking for a place to set up camp, and they cut across the land to the right bank of the upper feeder. They decided to stop ahead, just beyond the valley of a fairly large stream that joined from the north side.

When Ayla saw an exposed gravel bar beside the river, she stopped to pick out several smooth round stones that would be perfect for her sling, and she put them in her pouch. She thought she might go hunting for ptarmigan or white hare later in the afternoon, or perhaps the next morning.

Memories of their short stay with the Losadunai were already fading, replaced by concerns about the glacier ahead, particularly for Jondalar. On foot and heavily loaded, they had been traveling more slowly than he had planned and he feared the end of the long winter would come too soon. The arrival of spring was always unpredictable, but this was one year that he hoped it would be late.

They unloaded the horses and set up their camp. Since it was early, they decided to hunt fresh meat. They entered a lightly wooded area and came across deer tracks, which surprised them both and worried Jondalar. He hoped that returning deer were not a sign that spring would soon follow. Ayla signaled Wolf, and they continued through the woods single file, with Jondalar in front. Ayla followed close behind, with Wolf at her heel. She did not want him dashing off and scaring away their prey.

They followed the trail through the open woods toward a high jutting outcrop that blocked their view ahead. Ayla saw Jondalar's shoulders slump and the tension of his stalking relax, and she understood why when the tracks of the deer showed that it had bounded away. Something had obviously scared it off.

They both froze at the sound of Wolf's low growl. He sensed something and they had come to respect his warnings. Ayla was sure she heard scuffling noises from the other side of the large rock projecting out of the earth and blocking their path. She and Jondalar looked at each other; the man had heard it too. They crept ahead slowly, edging around the outcrop. Then there were shouts, the sound of something landing heavily, and, almost simultaneously, a scream of agony.

There was a quality to the scream that sent a chill down Ayla's back, a chill of recognition. "Jondalar! Someone's in trouble!" she said, dashing around the stone.

"Wait, Ayla! It could be dangerous!" he called in warning, but it was already too late. Clutching his spear, he raced to catch up.

Around the outcrop, several young men were struggling with someone on the ground who was trying to fight them off without much success. Others were making crude remarks to a man who was on his knees and stretched out on top of a person that two others were trying to hold down.

"Hurry up, Danasi! How much more help do you need? This one's struggling."

"Maybe he needs help finding it."

"He just doesn't know what to do with it."

"Then give someone else a chance."

Ayla caught a glimpse of blond hair and, with an angry feeling of disgust, she realized that they were holding down a woman and she knew what they were trying to do. As she ran toward them, she had another insight. Perhaps it was the shape of a leg or an arm, or the sound of a voice, but suddenly she knew it was a Clan woman—a blond Clan woman! She was stunned, but only for a moment.

Wolf was growling, eager, but watching Ayla and holding back.

"It must be Charoli's band!" Jondalar said, coming up behind her.

He dropped off his hunting pack with his spear holder, and in a few long strides he reached the three men who were molesting the woman. He grabbed the one on top by the back of his parka at the scruff of his neck and yanked him off the woman. Then he stepped around and, doubling up his fist, slammed it into the man's face. The man dropped to the ground. The other two gaped in shock, then let go of the woman and turned to attack the stranger. One jumped on his back, while the other threw punches at his face and chest. The big man flung off the one on his back, took a hard blow to his shoulder, and countered with a powerful belt to the stomach of the man in front of him.

The woman rolled over and backed off to get away when the two men went after Jondalar, and she ran toward the other group of struggling men. While one man was doubled over in pain, Jondalar turned to the other. Ayla saw the first one struggling to get up.

"Wolf! Help Jondalar! Get those men!" she said, signaling to the animal.

The big wolf raced eagerly into the fray, while she dropped her pack, loosened the sling from around her head, and reached into her pouch for stones. One man of the three was down again, and she watched another, with terror in his eyes, fling up an arm to fend off the huge wolf that was coming for him. The animal jumped up on his hind legs, sank his teeth into the arm of a heavy winter coat, and ripped off the sleeve, while Jondalar landed a solid punch on the jaw of the third.

Putting a stone in the pocket of her sling, Ayla turned her attention toward the other group of struggling men. One had raised a heavy bone club with two hands and was ready to smash it down. She quickly hurled the stone and watched the man with the club fall to the ground. Another man, who was holding a spear in a threatening stance over someone on the ground, watched his friend fall with a look of incredulity. He shook his head and didn't see the second stone coming but yelled in pain when it hit. The spear dropped to the ground as he grabbed for his injured arm.

Six men had been struggling with the one on the ground, yet having a hard time of it. Her sling had brought two down, and the woman who had been attacked was pummeling a third, to good effect. The man was holding up his arms in defense. Another, who had gotten too close to the man they had been trying to restrain, was jarred by a powerful blow. He staggered back. Ayla had two more stones ready to go. She let fly with one, aimed at a nonvital muscular thigh, giving the downed man—a man of the Clan, as Ayla had guessed—an opening. Though he was sitting, he grabbed the man closest to him, lifted him off the ground, and threw him at another man.

The Clan woman renewed her frenzied attack, finally driving away the man she had been struggling with. Though not accustomed to fighting, women of the Clan were as strong as their men, in proportion to their size. And though she would have preferred to acquiesce rather than fight to defend herself against a man who wanted to use her to relieve his needs, this woman had been moved to fight in defense of her injured mate.

But there was no fight left in any of the young men. One lay unconscious near the leg of the Clan man, a wound on his head oozing blood that matted his dirty blond hair and was swelling into a discolored bruise. Another was rubbing his arm, glowering at the woman who held her sling ready. The others were bruised and battered, one with an eye that was puffing up and closing. The three who had been after the woman were cowering in a huddle on the ground, their clothes in tatters, in fear of a wolf who was standing watch over them with fangs bared and a mean snarl in his throat.

Jondalar, who had also taken a share of punishment but didn't seem to notice, walked over to make sure Ayla was unharmed, then looked closely at the man on the ground and was suddenly struck by the fact that it was a man of the Clan. He had known it when they first came upon the scene, but it hadn't made an impression until that moment. He wondered why the man was still down. He pulled the unconscious man away from him, and rolled him over; he was breathing. And then he saw why the man of the Clan did not get up.

The reason was immediately apparent. The thigh of his right leg, just above the knee, was bent at an unnatural angle. Jondalar looked at the man with awe. With a broken leg, he had been holding off six men! He knew flatheads were strong, but he hadn't realized how strong, or how determined. The man had to be in great pain, but he was not showing it.

Suddenly another man, who had not been involved in any of the struggles, swaggered into view. He looked around at the battered band and raised an eyebrow. All the young men seemed to squirm with discomfort under his disdain. They didn't know how to explain what had happened. One moment they were in the midst of roughing up and making sport with the two flatheads unfortunate enough to have crossed their path, and the next they were at the mercy of a woman who could sling rocks, hard, a big man with fists as hard as rocks, and the biggest wolf they had ever seen! Not to mention the two flatheads.

"What happened?" he asked.

"Your men have finally gotten a little back," Ayla said. "It will be your turn next."

The woman was a total stranger. How did she know this was his band, or anything else about them? She spoke in his language, but with a strange accent, and he wondered who she was. The woman of the Clan turned her head at the sound of Ayla's voice and studied her closely, though it was not apparent to anyone else. The man with the bump on his head was waking up, and Ayla went to see how badly he was hurt.

"Get away from him," the man said, but the bravado was belied by the fear she detected in his voice.

Ayla paused, frankly appraised the man, and realized his objection was for the benefit of the band of men, not because he particularly cared about the one who was wounded.

She continued her examination. "He'll have a headache for a few days, but he'll be fine. If I had seriously meant to harm him, I would not have held back. He would be dead, Charoli."

"How do you know my name?" the young man blurted out, frightened but trying not to show it. How did this stranger know who he was?

Ayla shrugged. "We know more than your name."

She glanced in the direction of the man and woman of the Clan. To most of the people there, they seemed impassive, but Ayla could see their shock and uneasiness in the subtle shadings of expression and posture. They were warily watching the people of the Others, trying to make sense out of the strange turn of events.

For the time being, the man thought, they seemed to be in no danger of further attack, but that big man, why had he helped them . . . or seemed to help them. Why would a man of the Others fight men of his kind to help them? And what about the woman? If she was a woman. She used a weapon, one he understood, better than most men he knew. What kind of woman used a weapon? Against men of her own kind? Even more disquieting was the wolf, an animal that seemed to be threatening those men that had been hurting his woman . . . his own very special new woman. Perhaps the tall man had a Wolf Totem, but totems were spirits, and that was a real wolf. All he could do was wait. Hold the pain inside himself and wait.

Seeing his subtle glance at Wolf, and guessing his fears, Ayla decided to get all the shocks over with at once. She whistled, a distinctive, imperative sound that resembled the call of a bird, but no bird anyone had ever heard. Everyone stared at her, apprehensively, but when nothing happened immediately, they relaxed. Too soon. Before long, they heard hoofbeats, and then two docile horses, a mare and an unusual brown stallion, appeared and went straight to the woman.

What kind of strangeness was this? Was he dead, and in the world of the spirits? the man of the Clan wondered.

The horses seemed to frighten the young men even more

than the people of the Clan. Though they buried it under sarcasm and bravado, prodding each other into more and more daring and degrading activities, each of them carried a tight knot of guilt and fear deep inside. Someday, each man was sure, he would be discovered and held accountable. Some of them actually wished for it, to get it over with before things got even worse, if it wasn't too late already.

Danasi, the one who had been subject to derision because he was having trouble subduing the woman, had talked about it to a couple of the others that he thought he could trust. Flathead women were one thing, but that girl, not even a woman yet, who cried and fought. Granted, it was exciting at the time—women at that stage were always exciting— but afterward he had been ashamed, and fearful of Duna's retribution. What would She do to them?

And now, suddenly here was a woman, a stranger, with a big fair-haired man—wasn't Her lover supposed to be bigger and more fair than other men?—and a wolf! And horses that came at her call. No one had ever seen her before, yet she knew who they were. She had a strange way of speaking, she must have come from far away, but she knew their language. Did they speak where she came from? Was she a dunai? A Mother spirit in human form? Danasi shuddered.

"What do you want with us?" Charoli said. "We weren't bothering you. We were just having a little fun with some flatheads. What's wrong with having a little sport with some animals?"

Jondalar watched Ayla struggle to restrain herself. "And Madenia?" he asked. "Was she animal, too?"

They knew! The young men looked at each other, and then to Charoli for guidance. The man's accent was not the same as hers. He was Zelandonii. If the Zelandonii knew, they wouldn't be able to go there and hide if they needed to, pretending to be on a Journey, the way they'd planned. Who else knew? Was there any place they could go?

"These people are not animals," Ayla said, with a cold rage that made Jondalar look twice. He had never seen her quite so angry, but she was so controlled that he wasn't sure if the young men knew it. "If they were animals, would you even try to force them? Do you force wolves? Do you force horses? No, you are looking for a woman, and no woman wants you. These are the only women you can find," she said. "But these people are not animals." She glanced at the

Clan couple. "You are the animals! You are hyenas! Snuffling around the middens and smelling rotten, smelling of your evil. Hurting people, forcing women, stealing what is not yours. I will tell you, if you don't return now, you will lose everything. You will have no family, no Cave, no people, and you will never have a woman at your hearth. You will spend your life as a hyena, always taking the leavings of others, and having to steal from your own people."

"They know about that, too!" one of the men said.

"Don't say anything!" Charoli said. "They don't know, they're only guessing."

"We know," Jondalar said. "Every people know." His command of their language was not perfect, but perfectly understandable.

"That's what you say, but we don't even know you," Charoli said. "You're a stranger, not even Losadunai. We're not going back. We don't need anyone. We have our own Cave."

"Is that why you need to steal food and force women?" Ayla said. "A Cave without women at your hearths is no Cave."

Charoli tried to assume a casual tone. "We don't need to listen to this. We'll take what we want, when we want— food, women. No one has stopped us before, and no one is going to now. Come on, let's get away from here," he said, turning to leave.

"Charoli!" Jondalar said, calling after the young man and catching up in a few strides.

"What do you want?"

"I have something to give you," the big man said.

Then, without warning, Jondalar doubled up his fist and rammed it into Charoli's face. Charoli's head jerked back and he was lifted off his feet by the stunning blow.

"That's for Madenia!" Jondalar said, looking down at the man sprawled out on the ground. Then he turned on his heel and walked away.

Ayla looked at the dazed young man. A trickle of blood flowed from the corner of his mouth, but she made no move to offer assistance. Two of his friends helped him up. Then she turned her attention to the band of young men, eying each one individually. They were a sorry-looking lot, unkempt and dirty, their clothes tattered and grimy. Their gaunt faces spoke of hunger, too. No wonder they had stolen food. They were in need of the help and support from the family and friends of a Cave. Perhaps the unrestricted life of roaming freely with Charoli's band had begun to lose its appeal and they were ready to return.

"They are looking for you," she said. "Everyone has agreed that you have gone too far, even Tomasi, who is kin to Charoli. If you return to your Caves and take what's coming to you, you may have a chance to join your families again. If you wait until they find you, it will go worse for you."

Is that why She was here? Had She come to warn them, Danasi wondered, before it was too late? If they returned before they were found, and tried to make amends, would their Caves take them back?

After Charoli's band left, Ayla approached the Clan couple. They had watched with amazement both Ayla's direct confrontation of the men and Jondalar's final punch that had knocked the other man down. Men of the Clan never hit other men of the Clan, but all the men of the Others were strange. They looked something like men, but they didn't act much like men, especially the man that had been struck. All the clans knew about him, and the man on the ground had to admit that he felt a certain satisfaction in seeing that one downed. He was even more pleased to see them all go.

Now he wished the other two would go. Their actions had been so unexpected that they made him uncomfortable. He just wanted to get back to his clan, although he didn't know how he was going to do it with a broken leg. Ayla's next gesture took both the man and woman completely by surprise. Even Jondalar could see their stunned confusion. She gracefully lowered herself to a cross-legged position in front of the man and looked demurely down at the ground.

Jondalar was surprised himself. She had done that to him on occasion, usually when she had something important to say to him and was frustrated because she couldn't find the words to express herself, but this was the first time he had ever seen her use that posture in its proper context. It was a gesture of respect. She was requesting permission to address him, but it astonished the tall man to see Ayla, who was so capable and independent, approach this flathead, this man of the Clan, with such deference. She had tried to explain to him once that it was courtesy, tradition, their manner of speaking, and not necessarily denigrating, but Jondalar knew that no Zelandonii woman, or any other woman he knew, would ever approach anyone, man or woman, in that way.

As Ayla sat patiently waiting for the man to tap her shoulder, she wasn't even sure if the sign language of these Clan people was the same as the language of the clan that had raised her. The distance between them was great, and these people had a different look. But she had noticed similarities of spoken languages, although the farther apart people lived, the less alike the language was. She could only hope that the sign language of these people would also be similar.

She thought their gestural language, like much of their knowledge and patterns of activities, came from their memories; the racial memories, akin to instinct, that each child was born with. If these people of the Clan came from the same ancient beginnings as the ones she had known, their language should be, at least, similar.

As she waited nervously, she began to wonder if the man had any idea what she was trying to do. Then she felt a tap on her shoulder and took a deep breath. It had been a long time since she had spoken with people of the Clan, not since she had been cursed. . . . She had to forget about that. She couldn't let these people know that she was dead as far as the Clan was concerned or they would cease to see her, just as though she didn't exist. She looked up at the man, and they studied each other.

He could see no hint of Clan in her. She was a woman of the Others. She was not like one of those that seemed oddly deformed by a mixture of spirits, the way so many were born these days. But where had this woman of the Others learned the correct way to address a man?

Ayla had not seen a Clan face for many years, and his was a true Clan face, but it was not quite like the faces of the people she had known. His hair and beard were a lighter brown and appeared soft, and not quite as curly. His eyes were lighter, too, brown, but not the deep, liquid, almost black eyes of her people. His features were stronger, more accentuated: his brow ridges were heavier, his nose sharper, his face jutted out farther, his forehead even seemed to sweep back more abruptly, and his head was longer. He seemed somehow more Clan than her Clan.

Ayla started speaking with the gestures and words of the

everyday language of Brun's clan, the language of the Clan she had learned as a child. It was immediately apparent that he did not understand. Then the man made some sounds. They had the tone and quality of voice of the Clan, rather guttural with the vowels almost swallowed, and she strained to understand.

The man had a broken leg and she wanted to help him, but she also wanted to know more about these Clan people. In a certain way, she felt more comfortable around them than the people of the Others. But to help him, she needed to communicate with him, to make him understand. He spoke again and made signs. The gestures seemed as though they ought to be familiar, but she couldn't make sense of them, and his word sounds were not familiar to her at all. Was the language of her Clan so different that she wouldn't be able to communicate with the clans in this region?

40

Ayla thought about how to make herself understood to the man of the Clan, glancing at the young woman sitting nearby, who looked nervous and upset. Then, remembering the Clan Gathering, she tried the ancient, formal, and primarily silent language that was used to address the world of the spirits, and to communicate with other clans that had a different common language.

The man nodded and made a gesture. Ayla felt a great wash of relief when she found that she understood him, and a rush of excitement. These people did come from the same beginnings as her Clan! Sometime, in some far distant past, this man had the same ancestors as Creb and Iza. With a sudden insight, she recalled a strange vision, and knew that she, too, shared roots, even more ancient, with him, but her line had diverged, taken a different path.

Jondalar watched, fascinated, as they began to talk with signs. It was hard to follow the quick flowing movements they made, which gave him a sense of much greater complexity and subtlety to the language than he had supposed. When

Ayla had taught people of the Lion Camp some of the Clan sign language so that Rydag could communicate with them for the first time in his life—the formal language because it was easier for the youngster to learn—she had taught them only the basic rudiments. The boy had always enjoyed talking with her more than anyone. Jondalar had guessed that Rydag could communicate with her more fully, but he was beginning to understand the range and depth of the language.

Ayla was surprised when the man skipped over some of the formalities of introduction. He didn't establish names, places, or kinship lines. "Woman of the Others, this man would know where you learned to speak."

"When this woman was a young child, family and people were lost to an earthquake. This woman was raised by a clan," she explained.

"This man knows of no clan that took in a child of the Others," the man signed.

"The clan of this woman lives far away. Does the man know of the river known to the Others as Great Mother?"

"It is the boundary," he motioned impatiently.

"The river goes on for a greater distance than many know, to a great sea, far to the east. The clan of this woman lives beyond the end of Great Mother," Ayla signed.

He looked incredulous, then studied her. He knew that, unlike the people of the Clan whose language included the understanding of unconscious body movements and gestures, which made it almost impossible to say one thing and mean something else, the people of the Others, who spoke with sounds, were different. He couldn't be sure about her. He could see no signs of dissimulation, but her story seemed so farfetched.

"This woman has been traveling since the beginning of last warm season," she added.

He became impatient again, and Ayla realized he was in great pain. "What does the woman want? Others are gone, why does the woman not go?" He knew that she had probably saved his life and had helped his mate, which meant he owed her an obligation; that would make them the next thing to kin. The thought was unsettling.

"This woman is a medicine woman. This woman would look at the man's leg," Ayla explained.

He snorted with disdain. "The woman cannot be a medicine woman. The woman is not Clan."

Ayla did not argue. She thought a moment, then decided to try another approach. "This woman would speak to the man of the Others," she requested. He nodded approval. She stood up, then backed away before she turned around and went to talk to Jondalar.

"Are you able to communicate with him very well?" he asked her. "I know you are making a good attempt, but the Clan you lived with is so far away, I can't help but wonder how successful you are."

"I started out using the everyday language of my clan, and we couldn't understand each other. I should have known their ordinary signs and words would not be the same, but when I used ancient formal language, we had no trouble communicating," Ayla explained.

"Did I understand you right? Are you saying that the Clan can communicate in a way that is understood by all of them? No matter where they live? That's hard to believe."

"I suppose it is," she said, "but their ancient way is in their memories."

"You mean they are born knowing how to speak in that way? Any baby can do it?"

"Not exactly. They are born with their memories, but they have to be 'taught' how to use them. I'm not sure how it works, I don't have the memories, but it seems to be more like 'reminding' them of what they know. Usually they only have to be reminded once, and then it's set. That's why some of them thought I wasn't very smart. I was so slow to learn, until I taught myself to memorize fast, and even then it wasn't easy. Rydag had the memories, but he didn't have anyone to teach him . . . to remind him. That's why he didn't know the sign language until I came."

"You, slow to learn! I've never seen anyone learn languages so fast," Jondalar said.

She shrugged off the comment. "That's different. I think the Others have a kind of memory for word language, but we learn to speak the sounds of those around us. To learn a different language, you just have to memorize another set of sounds, and sometimes another way of putting them together," she said. "Even if you aren't perfect, you can understand each other. His language is more difficult, for us, but communication isn't the problem I'm having with him. Obligation is the problem."

"Obligation? I don't understand," Jondalar said.

"He's in terrible pain, though he'll never let you know it. I want to help him, I want to set that leg. I don't know how they're going to get back to their clan, but we can worry about that later. First I need to fix his leg. But he is already in our debt, and he knows that if I can understand his language, I understand the obligation. If he believes we saved his life, it's a kinship debt. He doesn't want to owe us more," Ayla said, trying to explain a very complex relationship in a simple way.

"What's a kinship debt?"

"It's an obligation . . . ." Ayla tried to think of a way to put it that would make it clear. "It's usually between hunters of a clan. If one man saves another man's life, he 'owns' a piece of the other's spirit. The man that would have died gives up a piece to be restored to life. Since a man doesn't want any pieces of his spirit to die—to walk the next world before he does—if another man owns a piece of his spirit, he will do anything to save that man's life. That makes them kin, closer than brothers."

"That makes sense," Jondalar said, nodding.

"When men hunt together," Ayla continued, "they have to help each other, and they often save each other's lives, so a piece of each one's spirit usually belongs to each of the others. It makes them kin in a way that goes beyond family. Hunters in a clan may be related, but the kinship of family cannot be stronger than the bond between the hunters, because they cannot favor one over the other. They all have to depend on each other."

"There is wisdom in that," Jondalar said thoughtfully.

"That's called a kinship debt. This man doesn't know the customs of the Others, and he doesn't think much of what he does know."

"After Charoli and his band, who can blame him?"

"It goes much beyond that, Jondalar. But he's not happy about being in our debt."

"He told you all this?"

"No, of course not, but the language of the Clan is more than signs made with the hands. It's the way a person sits, or stands, expressions on the face, small things, but they all have meaning. I grew up with a clan. Those things are as much a part of me as they are of him. I know what's bothering him. If he could accept me as a medicine woman of the Clan, it would help."

"What difference would that make?" Jondalar said.

"It means I already own a piece of his spirit," Ayla said.

"But you don't even know him! How can you own a piece of his spirit?"

"A medicine woman saves lives. She could claim a piece of the spirit of everyone she saves, could 'own' pieces of everyone before many years have gone by. So when she is made a medicine woman, she gives a piece of her spirit to the Clan, and receives a piece of every Clan person in return. That way, no matter who she saves, the debt is already paid. That's why a medicine woman has status in her own right." Ayla looked thoughtful, then said, "This is the first time I'm glad the Clan spirits were not taken back . . ." She paused.

Jondalar started to speak. Then he noticed that she was staring into the empty air, and he realized she was looking inside herself.

". . . When I was cursed with death," she continued. "I've worried about that for a long time. After Iza died, Creb took all the spirit pieces back, so they would not go with her to the next world. But when Broud had me cursed, no one took them back from me, even though to the Clan I am dead."

"What would happen if they knew that?" Jondalar asked, indicating with a discreet twist of his head the two Clan people who were watching them.

"I would not exist to them anymore. They would not see me; they would not let themselves see me. I could stand right in front of them and scream, and they would not hear it. They would think I was a bad spirit trying to trap them into the next world," Ayla said, closing her eyes and shuddering with the memory.

"But why did you say you were glad that you still had the spirit pieces?" Jondalar asked.

"Because I can't say one thing and mean something else. I can't lie to him. He would know it. But I can refrain from mentioning. That's allowed, out of courtesy, for the sake of privacy. I don't have to say anything about the curse, even though he would probably know I was holding something back, but I can talk about being a medicine woman of the Clan, because it's true. I still am. I still own the spirit pieces." She frowned then, with worry. "But someday I will really die, Jondalar. If I go to the next world with the spirit pieces of everyone in the Clan, what will happen to them?"

"I don't know, Ayla," he said.

She shrugged, putting the thought aside. "Well, it's this world I need to worry about now. If he will accept me as a medicine woman of the Clan, then he won't have to be so concerned about owing a debt to me. It's bad enough for him to owe a kinship debt to one of the Others, but worse if it's a woman, especially one who used a weapon."

"But you hunted when you lived with the Clan," Jondalar reminded her.

"That was a special exception, and only because I survived a moon-cycle curse of death for hunting and using a sling. Brun allowed it because my Cave Lion totem protected me. He thought of it as a testing, and I think it finally gave him a reason to accept a woman with such a strong totem. He's the one who gave me my hunting talisman and called me the Woman Who Hunts."

Ayla touched the leather bag she always wore around her neck, and thought of her first one, the simple drawstring pouch that Iza had made for her. As her mother, Iza had put the piece of red ochre inside it when Ayla was accepted by the Clan. That amulet was nothing like the finely decorated one she wore now, which had been given to her at her Mamutoi adoption ceremony, but it still held her special tokens, including that original piece of red ochre. All the signs her totem had given to her were in it, as well as the red-stained oval from the tip of a mammoth tusk that was her hunting talisman, and the black stone, the small chunk of black manganese dioxide that held the spirit pieces of the Clan, which had been given to her when she became the medicine woman of Brun's clan.

"Jondalar, I think it would help if you would talk to him. He's unsure. His ways are very traditional, and too many unusual things have been going on. If he had a man to talk to, even one of the Others, rather than a woman, it might ease his mind. Do you remember the sign for a man to greet a man?"

Jondalar made a motion, and Ayla nodded. She knew it lacked finesse, but the meaning was clear. "Don't attempt to greet the woman yet. It would be in bad taste, and he might consider it an insult. It is not customary or appropriate for men to talk to women without a good reason, especially strangers, and you will need his permission even then. With kin, there are fewer formalities, and a close friend could even relieve his needs—share Pleasures—with her, though it's considered polite to ask his permission first."

"Ask his permission, but not hers? Why do the women allow themselves to be treated as though they are less important than men?" Jondalar asked.

"They don't think of it that way. They know, within themselves, that women and men are just as important, but men and women of the Clan are very different from each other," Ayla tried to explain.

"Of course they are different. All men and women are different . . . I'm glad to say."

"I don't just mean different in the way you can see. You can do anything a woman can do, Jondalar, except have a baby, and although you are stronger, I can do almost everything you can do. But men of the Clan cannot do many things that women do, just as women cannot do the things that men do. They don't have the memories for it. When I taught myself to hunt, many people were more surprised that I had the ability to learn, or even the desire, than that I had gone against the way of the Clan. It wouldn't have astounded them any more if you had given birth to a baby. I think the women were more surprised than the men. The idea would never occur to a Clan woman."

"I thought you said the people of the Clan and the Others are very much alike," Jondalar said.

"They are. But in some ways, they are more different than you can imagine. Even I can't imagine it, and I was one of them, for a while," Ayla said. "Are you ready to talk to him now?"

"I think so," he said.

The tall, blond man walked toward the powerful, stocky man who was still sitting on the ground, with his thigh bent at an unnatural angle. Ayla followed. Jondalar lowered himself to sit in front of the man, glancing at Ayla, who nodded approval.

He had never been so close to an adult flathead male before, and his first thought was a memory of Rydag. Looking at this man, it was even more obvious that the boy had not been full Clan. As Jondalar recalled the strange, bright, sickly child, he realized that Rydag's features had been greatly modified in comparison—*softened* was the word that came to him. This man's face was large, both long and wide, and jutted out somewhat, led by a sizable, protruding, sharp nose. His fine-haired beard, which showed signs of having been recently trimmed to a uniform length, did not entirely succeed in hiding a rather receding jaw, with no chin.

His facial hair blended into a mass of thick, softly curled, light brown hair covering a huge, long head, that was full and rounded at the back. But the man's heavy brow ridges took up most of his forehead, which sloped back into a hairline that started low. Jondalar had to restrain an urge to reach up and touch his own sharply rising high forehead and domed head. He could understand why they were called flatheads. It was as if someone had taken a head that was shaped like his, but somewhat larger, and made of material as malleable as wet clay, then reshaped it by pushing down and flattening his forehead, forcing the bulk of the size toward the back.

The man's heavy brows were accentuated by bushy eyebrows, and his gold-flecked, almost hazel eyes showed curiosity, intelligence, and an undercurrent of pain. Jondalar could understand why Ayla wanted to help him.

Jondalar felt clumsy making the gesture for greeting; but he was heartened by the look of surprise on the face of the man of the Clan, who returned the gesture. Jondalar wasn't sure what to do next. He thought about what he would do if he were meeting any stranger from another Cave or Camp, and he tried to remember the signs he had learned to make with Rydag.

He gestured, "This man is called . . ." then spoke his name and primary affiliation, "Jondalar of the Zelandonii."

It was too melodic, too full of syllables, too much for the man of the Clan to hear all at once. He shook his head, as if trying to unplug his ear, inclined his head, as though it would help him to listen better, then tapped Jondalar's chest.

It wasn't hard to understand what he meant, Jondalar thought. He made the signs again for "This man is called . . ." then spoke his name, but only his given name, and more slowly, "Jondalar."

The man closed his eyes, concentrating, then opened them and, taking a breath, spoke out loud, "Dyondar."

Jondalar smiled, and nodded yes. There was a deep-voiced, not fully articulated quality to the word, and a sense of swallowing the vowels, but it was close enough. And strangely familiar. Then it came to him! Of course! Ayla! Her words still had that same quality, though not nearly as strong. That was her unusual accent. No wonder no one could identify it. She had a Clan accent, and no one knew they could talk!

Ayla was surprised at how well the man had said Jondalar's name. She doubted if she had said it that well the first time she tried, and she wondered if this man had had contact with Others before. If he had been chosen to represent his people, or make some form of contact with the ones known as the Others, it would be an indication of high status. All the more reason, she understood, for him to be wary of kinship bonds with Others, especially Others of unknown status. He would not want to devalue his own status, but an obligation was an obligation, and whether he or his mate was ready to admit it, they still needed help. Somehow she had to convince him that they were Others who understood the significance and were worthy of the association.

The man facing Jondalar slapped his chest once, then leaned forward slightly. "Guban," he said.

Jondalar had as much trouble repeating his name as Guban had had with "Jondalar," and Guban was as generous in accepting the tall man's mispronunciation as Jondalar had been of his.

Ayla felt relieved. An exchange of names wasn't much, but it was a start. She glanced at the woman, still startled to see hair coloring lighter than her own on a woman of the Clan. Her head was covered with a fluff of soft curls, so light that it was almost white, but she was young and very attractive. Probably a second woman at his hearth. Guban was a man in his prime, and this woman was probably from a different clan, and quite a prize.

The woman looked at Ayla, then away quickly. Ayla wondered. She had seen worry and fear in the woman's eyes and looked more closely, but with as much subtlety as the young Clan woman had used. Was there a thickening at the waist? Did her wrap fit a little tight across her breasts? She's pregnant! No wonder she's worried. A man with a badly healed broken leg would no longer be in his prime. And while this man might have high status, he no doubt had heavy responsibilities as well. Somehow, Ayla thought, she had to convince Guban to let her help him.

The two men had been sitting watching each other. Jondalar was not sure what to do next, and Guban was waiting to see what he would do. Finally, in desperation, he turned to her.

"This woman is Ayla," he said, using his simple signs and then speaking her name.

At first Ayla thought he might have committed a social blunder, but seeing Guban's reaction, decided perhaps not. Introducing her so quickly was an indication of the high esteem in which she was held, appropriate for a medicine woman. Then, as he continued, she wondered if he had seen into her thoughts.

"Ayla is healer. Very good healer. Good medicine. Want help Guban."

To the man of the Clan, Jondalar's signs were hardly more than baby talk. There were no nuances to his meaning, no suggestive shadings, no degrees of complexity, but his sincerity was clear. It was a surprise in itself to discover a man of the Others who could speak properly at all. Most of them chattered, or muttered, or growled like animals. They were like children in their excessive use of sound, but then, the Others weren't considered very bright.

The woman, on the other hand, had a surprising depth of understanding with a fine grasp of nuance; and a clear and expressive ability to communicate. With inconspicuous finesse, she had translated some of Dyondar's subtler meanings, easing their communication without embarrassment to anyone. As difficult as it was to believe that she had been raised by a clan and had traveled such a great distance, she was so adept at speaking that one could almost believe she was Clan.

Guban had never heard of the clan of whom the woman spoke, and he knew many, but the common language she had used was quite unfamiliar. Even the language of the clan of his yellow-hair was not as strange, yet this woman of the Others knew the ancient sacred signs and could use them with great skill and precision. Rare for a woman. There was a suggestion that she might be withholding something, though he couldn't be certain. She was, after all, a woman of the Others, and he wouldn't ask in any case. Women, especially medicine women, liked to keep a few things to themselves.

The pain of his broken leg throbbed and threatened to escape his control, and he had to focus on holding it in for a time.

But how could she be a medicine woman? She wasn't Clan. She had no memories for it. Dyondar claimed she was a healer, and he spoke of her skill with great conviction . . . and his leg was broken—Guban flinched inwardly, then grit-

ted his teeth. Perhaps she was a healer; the Others had to
have them, too, but that didn't make her a medicine woman
of the Clan. His obligation was already so great. A kinship
debt to this man would be bad enough, but to a woman, and
a woman who used a weapon?

Yet where would he and his yellow-hair be without their
help? His yellow-hair . . . and expecting a young one
already. The thought of her made him feel soft inside. He
had felt anger beyond anything he had ever known when
those men went after her, hurting her, trying to take her.
That was why he had jumped down from the top of the rock.
It had taken him a long time to climb to the top, and he
couldn't wait that long to get back down.

He had seen deer tracks and had climbed up to look
around, to see what he might hunt, while she collected inner
bark and set taps for the juice that would soon be rising. She
had said it would warm soon, though some of the others hadn't
believed her. She was still a stranger, but she said she had
the memories for it and knew. He wanted to let her prove it
to the others, so he had agreed to take her out, though he
knew the dangers . . . from those men.

But it was cold, and he thought they'd avoid them if they
stayed close to the icetop. The top of the rock seemed like
a good place to scout the area. The agonizing pain when
he landed hard and felt his leg snap made him dizzy, but he
could not succumb. The men were on top of him, and he
had to fight them, pain or no. He felt warmed remembering
how she had rushed to him. He had been surprised to see her
hitting at those men. He had never known a woman to do
that, and he would never tell anyone, but it had pleased him
that she had tried so hard to help him.

He shifted his weight, controlling the sharp stab of pain.
But it wasn't so much the pain. He had learned long ago to
resist pain. Other fears were harder to control. What would
happen if he could never walk again? A broken leg or arm
could take a long time to heal, and if the bones mended
wrong, twisted, or misshapen, or too short . . . what if he
couldn't hunt?

If he couldn't hunt, he would lose status. He would no
longer be leader. He had promised the leader of her clan to
take care of her. She had been a favorite, but his status was
great, and she wanted to go with him. She even told him, in
the privacy of their own furs, that she had wished for him.

His first woman had not been too happy when he came home with a young and beautiful second woman, but she was a good Clan woman. She had taken good care of his hearth, and she would keep the status of First Woman. He promised to take care of her and her two daughters. He hadn't minded that. Though he had always wished she would have a son, the daughters of his mate were a delight to have around the hearth, though they would soon be grown and gone.

But if he couldn't hunt, he wouldn't be able to take care of anyone. Like an old man, the clan would have to take care of him instead. And his beautiful yellow-hair, who might give birth to a son, how could he take care of her? She would have no trouble finding a man willing to take her, but he would lose her.

He could not even get back to the clan if he couldn't walk. She would have to go for help, and they would have to come and get him. If he couldn't make it back on his own, he would be less in the eyes of his clan, but it would be so much worse if the broken leg slowed him down and he lost his skill at hunting, or could never hunt again.

Perhaps I should talk to this healer of the Others, he thought, even if she is a woman who uses a weapon. Her status must be high, Dyondar holds her in high regard, and his must be high, or he would not be mated to a medicine woman. She had made those other men leave as much as the man . . . she and the wolf. Why would a wolf help them? He had seen her talking to the animal. The signal was simple and direct, she told him to wait over there, by the tree near the horses, but the wolf understood her and did it. He was still there, waiting.

Guban looked away. It was difficult even to think about those animals without feeling a deep, underlying fear of spirits. What else would draw the wolf or the horses to them? What else would make animals behave so . . . unlike animals?

He could tell his yellow-hair was worried; how could he blame her? Since Dyondar had seen fit to acknowledge his woman, perhaps it would be appropriate to mention his. He would not want them to think the status she gained from him was any less than Dyondar's. Guban made a very subtle motion to the woman who had watched and seen everything, but, like a good Clan woman, had managed to make herself very inconspicuous.

"This woman is . . ." he motioned, then tapped her shoulder and said, "Yorga."

Jondalar had the impression of two swallows separated by a rolled R. He could not even begin to reproduce the sound. Ayla saw his struggle, and she had to think of a way to gracefully handle the situation. She repeated her name in a way Jondalar could say it, but addressed her as a woman.

"Yorga," adding with signs, "this woman greets you. This woman is called . . ." and very slowly and carefully said, "Ayla." Then in both signs and words, so Jondalar could understand, "The man named Dyondar would also greet the woman of Guban."

It was not the way it would have been done in the Clan, Guban thought, but then these people were Others, and it was not offensive. He was curious to see what Yorga would do.

She flicked her eyes in Jondalar's direction, very briefly, then looked back down at the ground. Guban shifted position just enough to let her know he was pleased. She had acknowledged Dyondar's existence, but no more.

Jondalar was less subtle. He had never been so close to Clan people . . . and he was fascinated. His look took much longer. Her features were similar to Guban's, with feminine modifications, and he had noticed before that she was sturdy but short, the height of a girl. She was far from beautiful, at least in his opinion, except for her pale yellow, downy-soft fluff of curls, but he could understand why Guban might think so. Suddenly mindful of Guban watching him, he nodded perfunctorily, then looked away. The Clan man was glowering; he would have to be careful.

Guban hadn't liked the attention Jondalar had paid to his woman, but he did sense there was no lack of respect intended, and he was having more difficulty controlling his pain. He needed to know more about this healer.

"I would speak to your . . . healer, Dyondar," Guban signed.

Jondalar got the sense of his meaning and nodded. Ayla had been watching, quickly came forward, and sat in respectful posture in front of the man.

"Dyondar has said the woman is a healer. The woman says medicine woman. Guban would know how a woman of the Others can be a medicine woman of the Clan."

Ayla spoke as she made the signs, so that Jondalar would

understand exactly what she was telling Guban. "The woman who took me in, who raised me, was a medicine woman of highest rank. Iza came from most ancient line of medicine woman. Iza was like mother to this woman, trained this woman with the daughter born to the line," Ayla explained. She could see he was skeptical but interested in knowing more. "Iza knew this woman did not have the memories as her true daughter did."

Guban nodded, of course not.

"Iza made this woman remember, made this woman tell Iza over and over, show over and over, until the medicine woman knew this woman would not lose the memories. This woman was happy to practice, to repeat many times to learn the ways of a medicine woman."

Although her gestures remained stylized and formal, her words became less so as she continued her explanation.

"Iza told me she thought this woman came from a long line of medicine women, too, medicine women of the Others. Iza said I thought like a medicine woman, but she taught me how to think about medicine like a woman of the Clan. This woman was not born with the memories of a medicine woman, but Iza's memories are my memories now."

Ayla had everyone's attention. "Iza got sick, a coughing sickness that not even she could heal, and I began to do more. Even the leader was pleased when I treated a burn, but Iza gave status to the clan. When she was too sick to make the trip to the Clan Gathering, and her true daughter was still too young, the leader and the Mog-ur decided to make me medicine woman. They said that since I had her memories, I was a medicine woman of her line. The other mog-urs and leaders at the Clan Gathering didn't like the idea at first, but they finally accepted me, too."

Ayla could see Guban was interested, and she sensed he wanted to believe her, but he still had doubts. She took off the decorated bag from around her neck, untied the cords, and spilled out some of the contents into her palm, then picked out a small black stone and held it out to him.

Guban knew what it was, the black stone that would leave a mark was a mystery. Even the smallest piece could hold a tiny fraction of the spirits of all the people of the Clan, and was given to a medicine woman when a piece of hers was taken. The amulet she wore was strange, he thought, typical of the way the Others made things, but he hadn't known they wore amulets at all. Maybe the Others weren't all ignorant and brutish.

Guban noticed another of the objects from her amulet and pointed to it. "What is that?"

Ayla put the rest of her objects back in her amulet and put it down so she could answer. "It is my hunting talisman," she said.

That could not be true, Guban thought. This would prove her wrong. "Women of the Clan do not hunt."

"I know, but I was not born to the Clan. I was chosen by a Clan totem who protected me and led me to the clan that became mine, and my totem wanted me to hunt. Our mog-ur reached back and found the old spirits who told him. They made a special ceremony. I was called the Woman Who Hunts."

"What is this Clan totem that chose you?"

Much to Guban's surprise, Ayla lifted her tunic, unloosened the drawstring ties from around the waist of her leggings, and lowered the side enough to show her left thigh. Four parallel lines, the scars left by the claws that had raked her thigh when she was a girl, showed clearly. "My totem is the Cave Lion."

The Clan woman caught her breath. The totem was too strong for a woman. It would be difficult for her to have children.

Guban grunted acknowledgment. The Cave Lion was the strongest hunting totem, a man's totem. He had never known a woman to have it, yet those were the marks that were cut into the right thigh of a boy whose totem was the Cave Lion, after he'd made his first major kill and become a man. "It is on the left leg. The mark is put on a man's right leg."

"I am a woman, not a man. The woman's side is the left side."

"Your mog-ur marked you there?"

"The Cave Lion himself marked me, when I was a girl, just before my clan found me."

"That would explain using the weapon," Guban signed, "but what about children? Does this man with hair the color of Yorga's have a totem strong enough to overcome such a totem?"

Jondalar looked uncomfortable. He had wondered something like that himself.

"The Cave Lion also chose him, and left his mark. I

know because The Mog-ur told me the Cave Lion chose me, and put the marks on my leg to show it, just as the Cave Bear chose him, and took his eye . . ."

Guban sat up, visibly shaken. He slipped out of the formal language, but Ayla understood him.

"Mogor One-Eye! You know Mogor One-Eye?"

"I lived at his hearth. He raised me. He and Iza were siblings, and after her mate died, he took her and her children in. At the Clan Gathering, he was called the Mog-ur, but to those who lived at his hearth, he was Creb."

"Even at our Clan Gatherings, there is talk of Mogor One-Eye, and his powerful . . ." He was going to say more, but thought better of it. Men were not supposed to talk about the private esoteric male ceremonies around women. That would explain her skill with the ancient signs, too, if she was taught by Mogor One-Eye. And Guban did recall that the great Mogor One-Eye had a sibling who was a respected medicine woman from an ancient line. Suddenly Guban seemed to relax, and he allowed a fleeting look of pain to cloud his face. He took a deep breath, then looked at Ayla, who was sitting cross-legged, looking down, in the position of a proper Clan woman. He tapped her shoulder.

"Respected medicine woman, this man has a . . . small problem," Guban signaled in the ancient silent language of the Clan of the Cave Bear. "This man would ask the medicine woman to look at leg. The leg may be broken."

Ayla closed her eyes and let out her breath. She had managed to convince him. He would allow her to treat his leg. She signaled to Yorga, telling her to prepare a sleeping place for him. The broken bone had not pierced the skin, and she thought there was a good chance that he would have full use of it again, but for the leg to heal properly, she would have to straighten it, set it back in place, and then she would make a birchbark cast to hold it stiff, so he could not move it.

"It will be painful to straighten it, but I have something that will relax the leg, and make him sleep." Then she turned to Jondalar. "Will you move our camp here? I know it's a chore with all those burning stones, but I want to set up the tent for him. They didn't plan to be gone overnight, and he needs to be out of the cold, especially when I give him something to sleep. We'll need some firewood, too, I don't want to use the burning stones, and we'll need to cut some wood for splints. I'll get birchbark when he's asleep, and maybe I can make some crutches for him. He'll want to move around later.''

Jondalar watched her take charge, and he smiled to himself. He hated the delay, even one more day seemed too much, but he wanted to help, too. Besides, Ayla wouldn't leave now. He just hoped they wouldn't be there too long.

Jondalar took the horses to their first camp, repacked, moved, and unpacked again, then led Whinney and Racer to a clearing where they could search out dried grass. There was some standing hay, but more flat against the ground under old snow. It was a little distance from their new location, but out of sight so the animals would trouble the Clan people less. They seemed to think that the tame animals were another manifestation of the strange behavior of Others, but Ayla noticed that both Guban and Yorga seemed relieved when the unnaturally complaisant horses were out of sight, and she was pleased that Jondalar had thought of it.

As soon as he returned, Ayla got her medicine bag out of a pack basket. For all that he had decided to accept her help as a medicine woman, Guban was relieved to see her old Clan-style otter-skin medicine bag, functional and not decorated. She made a point of keeping Wolf out of the way as well, and strangely, the animal, though usually curious and approachable by people whom Ayla and Jondalar had made friends with, showed no inclination to befriend the people of the Clan. He seemed content to stay in the background, watchful, though in no way menacing, and Ayla wondered if he sensed their uneasiness about him.

Jondalar helped Yorga and Ayla move Guban into the tent. He was surprised at how much the man weighed, but the sheer volume of muscle in a body so strong that six men could barely hold it down, was bound to add weight. Jondalar also realized that the move was very painful, though Guban's impassive face showed no sign of it. The man's refusal to admit pain made Jondalar wonder if he felt it as much, until Ayla explained that such stoic denial was ingrained in Clan men from boyhood. Jondalar's respect for the man increased. His was not a race of weaklings.

The woman was amazingly strong, too, smaller than the man but not greatly so. She could lift as much as Jondalar could, and when she chose to exert force, the grip of her hand was unbelievably powerful; yet he'd seen her use her hands with fine precision and control. He was becoming intrigued with discovering the similarities between people of the Clan and his own kind, as well as the differences. He wasn't sure exactly when it happened, but at some point he realized that he no longer questioned in any way the fact that they were human. They were different, certainly, but most definitely the people of the Clan were people, not animals.

Ayla ended up using a few of the burning stones after all to make a hotter fire to prepare the datura more quickly, adding hot cooking stones directly to the water to make it boil. But Guban resisted drinking all that she felt he should, claiming that he didn't like the idea of waiting too long for its effects to wear off, but she wondered if part of the problem was his doubt whether she could prepare the datura properly. With help from both Yorga and Jondalar, Ayla set the leg, and then made a sturdy splint. When it was all over, Guban finally slept.

Yorga insisted on making the meal, although Jondalar's interest in the processes and tastes embarrassed her. At night, by the fire, he began whittling out a pair of crutches for Guban, while Ayla enjoyed getting acquainted with Yorga and explained to her how to make medicine for pain. Ayla described the use of crutches and the need for padding under the arms. Yorga was constantly surprised at Ayla's knowledge of the Clan and Clan ways, but she had noticed her Clan "accent" earlier. Eventually she told Ayla about herself, and Ayla translated for Jondalar.

Yorga wanted to get inner bark and tap certain trees. Guban had come along to protect her because so many women had been attacked by Charoli's band that no women were allowed to go out alone anymore, which was a hardship on the clan. Men had less time to hunt since they had to spend time accompanying women. That was why Guban decided to climb the big rock, to look for animals to hunt while Yorga collected inner bark. Charoli's men probably thought she was alone, and they might not have attacked if they had seen Guban, but when he saw them attack her, he jumped off the wall to her defense.

"I'm surprised all he broke was one leg," Jondalar said, looking up at the top of the wall.

"Clan bones are very heavy," Ayla said, "and thick. They don't break very easily."

"Those men didn't have to be so rough with me," Yorga commented, with signs. "I would have assumed the position if they had given me the signal, and if I hadn't heard his scream. I knew something was very wrong then."

She continued with the story. Several men attacked Guban, while three tried to force Yorga. From his scream of pain, she knew something was wrong with Guban, so she tried to get away from the men. That's when the other two held her down. Then suddenly Jondalar was there, hitting the men of the Others, and the wolf jumped at them and was biting them.

She looked at Ayla slyly. "Your man is very tall, and his nose is very small, but when I saw him there fighting the other men, this woman could think of him as a child."

Ayla looked puzzled, and then she smiled.

"I didn't quite understand what she said, or what she meant," Jondalar said.

"She made a little joke."

"A joke?" he said. He didn't think they were capable of making jokes.

"What she said, more or less, is that even though you are an ugly man, when you came to her rescue, she could have kissed you," Ayla said, then explained to Yorga.

The woman looked embarrassed, but glanced toward Jondalar, then looked again at Ayla. "I am grateful to your tall man. Perhaps, if the child I carry is a boy, and if Guban will allow me to suggest a name, I will say to him, Dyondar is not such a bad name."

"That wasn't a joke, was it, Ayla?" Jondalar said, surprised at the sudden rush of feeling.

"No, I don't think that was a joke, but she can only suggest, and it could be a difficult name for a boy of the Clan to grow up with because it's unusual. Guban might be willing, though. He's exceptionally open to new ideas, for a man of the Clan. Yorga told me about their mating, and I think they fell in love, which is quite rare. Most matings are planned and arranged."

"What makes you think they fell in love?" Jondalar asked. He was interested in hearing a Clan love story.

"Yorga is Guban's second woman. Her clan lives quite far from here, but he went there to bring word of a large Clan Gathering, and plans to discuss us, the Others. Charoli bothering their women, for one thing—I told her about the

Losadunai plans to put a stop to them—but if I understand it right, some group of Others have approached a couple of clans about some trading."

"That's a surprise!"

"Yes. Communication is the biggest problem, but men of the Clan, including Guban, don't trust the Others. While Guban was visiting the distant clan, he saw Yorga, and she saw him. Guban wanted her, but the reason he gave was to establish closer ties with some of the distant clans, so they could share news, particularly about all these new ideas. He brought her back with him! Men of the Clan don't do that. Most of them would have made an intention known to the leader, returned and discussed it with his own clan, and given his first woman a chance to get used to the idea of sharing her hearth with another woman," Ayla said.

"The first woman at his hearth didn't know? That's a brave man," Jondalar said.

"His first woman had two daughters; he wants a woman who will make a son. Men of the Clan put great store in the sons of their mates, and, of course, Yorga hopes the baby she is carrying will be the boy he wants. She has had some trouble getting used to the new clan—they've been slow to accept her—and if Guban's leg doesn't heal properly, and he loses status, she's afraid they will blame her."

"No wonder she seemed so upset."

Ayla refrained from mentioning to Jondalar that she had told Yorga she was on her way to her man's home, away from her people, too. She didn't see any reason to add to his worries, but she was still concerned about how his people would accept her.

Ayla and Yorga both wished it was possible to visit with each other and share their experiences. They felt they were almost kin, since there was probably a kinship debt between Guban and Jondalar, and Yorga felt closer to Ayla, in the brief time they had known each other, than to any of the other women she had met. But Clan and Others didn't visit.

Guban woke up in the middle of the night, but he was still groggy. By morning he was alert, but reaction to the stresses of the previous day left him exhausted. When Jondalar ducked his head in the tent in the afternoon, Guban was surprised at how glad he was to see the tall man, but he didn't know what to make of the crutches he held.

"I use same thing after lion attack me," Jondalar explained. "Help me walk."

Guban was suddenly interested and wanted to try them, but Ayla would not allow it. It was too soon. Guban finally acquiesced, but only after announcing that he would try them the next day. In the evening, Yorga let Ayla know that Guban wanted to talk to Jondalar about some very important matters and was requesting her help with translation. She knew it was serious, guessed what it was about, and talked to Jondalar in advance so she could help him to understand what the difficulties might be.

Guban was still concerned about owing a kinship debt to Ayla, beyond the acceptable medicine woman spirit exchange, since she helped save his life using a weapon.

"We need to convince him that the debt is owed to you, Jondalar. If you tell him that you are my mate, you could tell him that since you have responsibility for me, any debts owed to me are actually owed to you."

Jondalar agreed, and after some preliminaries to establish procedures, they began the more serious discussion. "Ayla is my mate, she beløngs to me," he said, while Ayla translated with the full range of subtleties. "I am responsible for her, debts owed to her are owed to me." Then, to her surprise, Jondalar added, "I, too, have an obligation that weighs on my spirit. I owe a kinship debt to the Clan."

Guban was curious.

"The debt has weighed heavily on my spirit because I haven't known how to repay it."

"Tell me about it," Guban signed. "Perhaps I can help."

"I was attacked by a cave lion, as Ayla mentioned. Marked, chosen by the Cave Lion, which is now my totem. It was Ayla who found me. I was near death, and my brother, who was with me, already walked the spirit world."

"I am sorry to hear that. It is hard to lose a brother."

Jondalar only nodded. "If Ayla had not found me, I, too, would be dead, but when Ayla was a child, and near death, the Clan took her in and raised her. If the Clan had not taken Ayla in when she was a child, she would not have lived. If Ayla had not lived and been taught to heal by a Clan medicine woman, I would not be alive. I would be walking in the next world now. I owe my life to the Clan, but I don't know how to pay that debt, or to whom."

Guban nodded with great sympathy. It was a serious problem and a large debt.

"I would make a request of Guban," Jondalar continued. "Since Guban owes a kinship debt to me, I ask him to accept my kinship debt to the Clan in exchange."

The man of the Clan considered the request gravely, but he was grateful to learn of the problem. Exchanging a kinship debt was far more acceptable than simply owing his life to a man of the Others, and giving him a piece of his spirit. Finally he nodded. "Guban will accept the exchange," he said, feeling great relief.

Guban took his amulet from around his neck and opened it. He shook the contents into his hand and picked out one of the objects, a tooth, one of his own first molars. Though he had no cavities, his teeth were worn down in a peculiar way, mainly because he used them as a tool. The tooth in his hand was worn, but not nearly so badly as his permanent teeth.

"Please accept this as a token of kinship," Guban said.

Jondalar was embarrassed. He hadn't realized there would be an exchange of some personal token to mark the exchange of debts, and he didn't know what to give to the man of the Clan that would be as meaningful. They were traveling very light, and he had very little to give. Suddenly it came to him.

He took a pouch from a loop of his belt and poured its contents into his hand. Guban looked surprised. In Jondalar's hand were several claws and two canine teeth of a cave bear, the cave bear he had killed the previous summer shortly after they had started on their long Journey. He held out one of the teeth. "Please accept this as a token of kinship."

Guban restrained his eagerness. A cave bear tooth was a powerful token, it bestowed high status, and the giving of one showed great honor. It pleased him to think that this man of the Others had acknowledged his position, and the debt he owed the entire Clan so appropriately. It would make the proper impression when he told the rest about this exchange. He accepted the token of kinship, closed it inside his fist, and gripped it firmly.

"Good!" Guban said with finality, as though completing a trade. Then he made a request. "Since we are now kin, perhaps we should know the location of each other's clan, and the territory they use."

Jondalar described the general location of his homeland.
Most of the territory across the glacier was Zelandonii or
related, and then he described specifically the Ninth Cave of
the Zelandonii. Guban described his homeland, and Ayla got
the impression they were not as far from each other as she
had supposed.

Charoli's name came up before they were through. Jondalar talked about the problems the young man had been creating for everyone, and he explained in some detail what they
planned to do to stop him. Guban thought the information
was important enough to tell other clans, and he wondered
to himself if his broken leg might not turn out to be a great
asset.

Guban would have much to tell to his clan. Not only that
the Others themselves had problems with the man, and
planned to do something about it, but that some of the Others
were willing to fight their own kind to help people of the
Clan. There were also some who could speak properly! A
woman who could communicate very well, and a man with
limited but useful ability, which in some ways could be more
valuable because he was a male, and he was now kin. Such
contact with Others, and the insights and knowledge about
them, could bring him even more status, especially if he had
full use of his leg again.

Ayla applied the birchbark cast in the evening. Guban
went to bed feeling very good. And his leg hardly pained
him at all.

Ayla woke up in the morning feeling very uneasy. She
had a strange dream again, very vivid, with caves and Creb
in it. She mentioned it to Jondalar; then they talked about
how they were going to get Guban back to his people. Jondalar suggested the horses, but he was very worried about
delaying any longer. Ayla felt that Guban would never consent. The tame horses upset him.

When they got up, they helped Guban out of the tent,
and while Ayla and Yorga prepared a morning meal, Jondalar
demonstrated the crutches. Guban insisted on trying, over
Ayla's objections, and after a little practicing, was surprised
at how effective they were. He could actually walk without
putting any weight on his leg.

"Yorga," Guban called to his woman, after he put the
crutches down, "make ready to leave. After the morning
meal, we will go. It is time to return to the clan."

"It's too soon," Ayla said, using the Clan gestures at the same time. "You need to rest your leg, or it will not heal properly."

"My leg will rest while I walk with these." He motioned toward the crutches.

"If you must go now, you can ride one of the horses," Jondalar said.

Guban looked startled. "No! Guban walks on own legs. With the help of these walking sticks. We will share one more meal with new kin, and then we go."

41

After sharing their morning meal, both couples prepared to go their separate ways. When Guban and Yorga were ready, they simply looked at Jondalar and Ayla for a moment, avoiding the wolf and two horses packed with gear. Then, leaning on his crutches, Guban began hobbling away. Yorga fell in behind him.

There were no goodbyes, no thank-yous; such concepts were foreign to the people of the Clan. It wasn't customary to comment on one's departure, it was obvious, and acts of assistance or kindness, especially from kin, were expected. Understood obligations required no thanks, only reciprocity, should it ever be necessary. Ayla knew how difficult it could be if Guban ever had to reciprocate. In his mind, he owed them more than he might ever be able to repay. He had been given more than his life; he had been given a chance to retain his position, his status, which meant more to him than simply being alive—especially if that meant living as a cripple.

"I hope they don't have far to go. Traveling any distance

on those walking sticks is not easy," Jondalar said. "I hope he makes it."

"He'll make it," Ayla said, "no matter how far it is. Even without the walking sticks, he would get back, if he had to crawl the whole way. Don't worry, Jondalar. Guban is a man of the Clan. He will make it . . . or die in the trying."

Jondalar's brow wrinkled into a thoughtful frown. He watched Ayla take Whinney's lead rope; then he shook his head and found Racer's. In spite of the difficulty for Guban, he had to admit he was glad they had refused his offer of riding back to their clan on the horses. There had been too many delays already.

From their campsite, they continued riding through open woods until they reached a high point; then they stopped and looked out over the way they had come. Tall pines, standing straight as sentinels, guarded the banks of the Mother River for a long distance back; a winding column of trees leading away from the legion of conifers they could see below, spreading out over the flanks of the mountains that crowded close from the south.

Ahead their uphill climb temporarily leveled off, and an extension of the pine forest, starting at the river, marched across a small valley. They dismounted to lead the horses into the dense woodland and entered a twilight space of profound and eerie silence. Straight dark boles supported a low canopy of spreading long-needled boughs that blocked sunlight and inhibited undergrowth. A layer of brown needles, accumulating for centuries, muffled both footsteps and hoofbeats.

Ayla noticed a collection of mushrooms at the base of a tree, and she knelt to examine them. They were frozen solid, caught by a sudden frost of the previous autumn that had never let up. But no snow had filtered in to betray the season. It was as though the time of harvest had been captured and held in suspension, preserved in the still cold forest. Wolf appeared beside her and pushed his muzzle into her ungloved hand. She rubbed the top of his head, noticed his steamy breath and then her own, and had a fleeting impression that their small company of travelers were the only things alive.

On the far side of the valley, the climb became precipitous and shimmery silver fir appeared, accented by stately deep green spruce. The long-needled pines became stunted with increasing elevation and finally disappeared, leaving the spruce and fir to march beside the Middle Mother.

As he rode, Jondalar's thoughts kept returning to the Clan people they had met—he would never again be able to think about them as anything other than people. I need to convince my brother. Perhaps he could try to make contact with them—if he is still leader. When they stopped to rest and make some hot tea, Jondalar spoke his thoughts out loud.

"When we get home, I'm going to talk to Joharran about the Clan people, Ayla. If other people can trade with them, we could, too, and he should know that they are meeting with distant clans to discuss the troubles they are having with us," Jondalar said. "It could mean trouble and I would not want to fight the likes of Guban."

"I don't think there is any hurry. It will take a long time for them to reach any decisions. Change is difficult for them," Ayla said.

"What about trading—do you think they would be willing?"

"I think Guban would be more willing than most. He's interested in knowing more about us, and he was willing to try the walking sticks, even if he wouldn't ride the horses. Bringing home such an unusual woman from a faraway clan shows something about him, too. He was taking a chance, even if she is beautiful."

"Do you think she is beautiful?"

"Don't you?"

"I can see why Guban would think so," Jondalar said.

"I guess what a man considers beautiful depends on who he is," she said.

"Yes, and I think you are beautiful."

Ayla smiled, making him all the more convinced of her beauty. "I'm glad you think so."

"It is true, you know. Remember all the attention you got at the Mother Ceremony? Did I ever tell you how glad I was that you picked me?" he said, smiling at the memory.

She recalled something he had said to Guban. "Well, I belong to you, don't I?" she said, then grinned. "It's good that you don't know Clan language too well. Guban would have seen that you were not speaking true when you said I was your mate."

"No, he wouldn't. We may not have had a Matrimonial yet, but in my heart, we are mated. It wasn't a lie," Jondalar said.

Ayla was moved. "I, too, feel that way," she said softly, looking down because she wanted to show deference to the emotions that filled her. "I have since the valley."

Jondalar felt such a fierce surge of love fill him that he thought he would burst. He reached for her and took her in his arms, feeling at that moment, with those few words, that he had experienced a Mating Ceremonial. It didn't matter if he ever had one that would be recognized by his people. He would go through with it, to please Ayla, but he didn't need it. He only needed to get her home safely.

A sudden gust of wind chilled Jondalar, driving away the flush of warmth he had felt and leaving him with a strange ambivalence. He got up and, walking away from the warmth of the small fire, took a deep breath. It left him gasping as the desiccating, freezing air seared his lungs. He ducked behind his fur hood and pulled it tight around his face to allow his body heat to warm the air he breathed. Though the last thing he wanted to feel was a warm wind, he knew such bitter cold was extremely dangerous.

To the north of them the great continental glacier had dipped southward, as though straining to encompass the beautiful icy mountains within its overwhelming frozen embrace. They were in the most frigid land on earth, between the glistening mountain tors and the immense northern ice, and it was the depths of winter. The air itself was sucked dry by the moisture-stealing glaciers greedily usurping every drop to increase their bloated, bedrock-crushing mass, building up reserves to withstand the onslaught of summer heat.

The battle between glacial cold and melting warmth for control of the Great Mother Earth was almost at a standstill, but the tide was turning; the glacier was gaining. It would make one more advance, and reach its farthest southward point, before it was beaten back to polar lands. But even there, it would only bide its time.

As they continued to mount the highland, each moment seemed colder than the one before. Their increasing altitude was bringing them inexorably closer to their rendezvous with ice. Fodder was getting harder for the horses to find. The sere withered grass near the stream of solid ice was flat against the frozen ground. The only snow was made up of hard dry stinging grains, whipped by driving wind.

They rode silently, but after they made camp and were cuddled together warmly within their tent, they talked.

"Yorga's hair is beautiful," Ayla said, snuggling into their furs.

"Yes, it is," Jondalar said, with honest conviction.

"I wish Iza could have seen it, or anyone from Brun's clan. They always thought my hair was so unusual, though Iza always said it was my best feature. It used to be light like hers, but it's darker now."

"I love the color of your hair, Ayla, and the way it falls in waves when you wear it loose," Jondalar commented, touching a strand next to her face.

"I didn't know people of the Clan lived so far away from the peninsula."

Jondalar could tell her mind was not on hair, or on anything close and personal. She was thinking about the Clan people, as he had been earlier.

"Guban looks different, though. He seems . . . I don't know, it's hard to explain. His brows are heavier, his nose is bigger, his face is more . . . out. Everything about him seems more . . . pronounced, more Clan, in a way. I think he is even more muscular than Brun was. He didn't seem to notice the cold as much, either. His skin was warm to the touch even when he was lying on the frozen ground. And his heart beat faster."

"Maybe they've gotten used to cold. Laduni said a lot of them live north of here, and it hardly gets warm at all up there, even in summer," Jondalar said.

"You may be right. They think alike, though. What made you tell Guban you were repaying a kinship debt to the Clan? It was the best argument you could have made."

"I'm not sure. It's true, though. I do owe my life to the Clan. If they hadn't taken you in, you wouldn't be alive, and then neither would I."

"And by giving him that cave bear tooth, you could not have given him a better token. You were quick to understand their ways, Jondalar."

"Their ways are not so different. The Zelandonii are careful about obligations, too. Any obligations left unpaid when you go to the next world can give the one you owe control over your spirit. I've heard that a few of Those Who Serve the Mother try to keep people in their debt, so they can control their spirits, but it's probably just talk. Just because people say things doesn't mean they're true," the man said.

"Guban believes that his spirit and yours are now intertwined, in this life and the next. A piece of your spirit will always be with him, just as a piece of his will always be with you. That's why he was so concerned. He lost his piece when you saved his life, but you gave him one back, so there is no hole, no emptiness."

"I wasn't the only one who saved his life. You did as much as I did, and more."

"But I am a woman, and a woman of the Clan is not the same as a man of the Clan. It is not an even exchange because one cannot do what the other does. They don't have the memories for it."

"But you set his leg and fixed it so he could get back."

"He would have gotten back; I wasn't worried about that. I was afraid his leg wouldn't heal right. Then he wouldn't be able to hunt."

"Is it so bad not to hunt? Couldn't he do something else? Like those S'Armunai boys?"

"The status of a Clan man depends on his ability to hunt, and his status means more to him than his life. Guban has responsibilities. He has two women at his hearth. His first woman has two daughters, and Yorga is pregnant. He promised to care for all of them."

"What if he can't?" Jondalar asked. "What will happen to them?"

"They wouldn't starve, his clan would take care of them, but their status—the way they live, their food and clothes, the respect they are shown—depends on his status. And he would lose Yorga. She's young and beautiful, another man would be glad to take her, but if she has the son Guban has always wanted, she would take him with her."

"What happens when he gets too old to hunt?"

"An old man can give up hunting slowly, gracefully. He would go to live with the sons of his mate, or the daughters if they were still living with the same clan, and he wouldn't be a burden on the whole clan. Zoug developed his skill with a sling so he could still contribute, and even Dorv's advice was still valued, though he could hardly see. But Guban is a man in his prime, and a leader. To lose it all at once would take the heart out of him.''

Jondalar nodded. "I think I understand. Not hunting wouldn't bother me so much. I would hate it, though, if something happened to me so that I couldn't work the flint anymore." He paused to reflect, then said, "You did a lot for him, Ayla. Even if Clan women are different, shouldn't that count for something? Couldn't he at least acknowledge it?''

"Guban expressed his gratitude to me, Jondalar, but it was subtle, as it had to be.''

"It must have been subtle. I didn't see it," Jondalar said, looking surprised.

"He communicated directly to me, not through you, and he paid attention to my opinions. He allowed his woman to speak to you, which acknowledged me as her equal, and since he has a very high status, so was hers. He thought very highly of you, you know. Paid you a compliment.''

"He did?''

"He thought your tools were well made and he admired your workmanship. If he hadn't, he would not have accepted the walking sticks, or your token," Ayla explained.

"What would he have done? I accepted his tooth. I thought it was a strange gift, but I understood his meaning. I would have accepted his token, no matter what it was.''

"If he had felt it was not appropriate, he would have refused it, but that token was more than a gift. He accepted a serious obligation. If he did not respect you, he would not have accepted your spirit piece in exchange for his; he values his too much. He would rather have an emptiness, a hole, than accept a piece of an unworthy spirit.''

"You're right. There are many subtleties to those Clan people, shades of meaning within shades of meaning. I don't know if I'd ever be able to sort it all out," Jondalar said.

"Do you think the Others are any different? I still have trouble understanding all the shades within shades," Ayla said, "but your people are more tolerant. Your people do more visiting, more traveling than the Clan, and they are more used to strangers. I'm sure I've made mistakes, but I think your people have overlooked them because I'm a visitor and they realize the customs of my people may be different.''

"Ayla, my people are your people, too," Jondalar said, gently.

She looked at him as if she didn't quite understand him at first. Then she said, "I hope so, Jondalar. I hope so."

The spruce and fir trees were thinning out and becoming stunted as the travelers climbed, but even though they could see past the vegetation, their route along the river took them beside outcrops and through deep valleys that blocked their view of the heights around them. At a bend in the river, an upland stream fell into the Middle Mother, which itself came from higher ground. The marrow-chilling air had caught and stilled the waters in the act of falling, and the strong dry winds had sculpted them into strange and grotesque shapes. Caricatures of living creatures captured by frost, poised to begin a headlong flight down the course of the long river, seemed to be waiting impatiently, as if knowing the turning of the season, and their release, was not far off.

The man and woman led the horses carefully over the jumbled broken ice, and around to the higher ground of the frozen waterfall, then stopped, spellbound, as the massive plateau glacier loomed into view. They had caught glimpses of it before; now it seemed close enough to touch, but the stunning effect was misleading. The majestic, brooding ice with its nearly level top was farther away than it seemed.

The frozen stream beside them was unmoving, but their eyes followed its tortuous route as it twisted and turned, then ducked out of sight. It reappeared higher up, along with several other narrow channels spaced at irregular intervals that leaked off the glacier like a handful of silvery ribbons trimming the massive cap of ice. Far mountains and nearer ridges framed the plateau with their rugged, sharp-edged, frozen tops, so starkly white their undertones of glacial blue seemed only to reflect the clear deep hue of the sky.

The twin high peaks to the south, which for a while had accompanied their recent travels, had long since passed from view. A new high pinnacle that had appeared farther west was receding to the east, and the summits of the southern range that had traced their path still showed their glistening crowns.

To the north were dual ridges of more ancient rock, but

the massif that had formed the northern edge of the river valley had been left behind at the bend where the river turned back from its most northern point, before the place where they had met the people of the Clan. The river was closer to the new highland of limestone that had taken over as the northern boundary as they climbed southwest, toward the river's source.

The vegetation continued to change as they ascended. Spruce and silver fir gave ground to larch and pine on the acid soils that thinly covered the impervious bedrock, but these were not the stately sentinels of lower elevations. They had reached a patch of mountainous taiga, stunted evergreens whose crowns held a covering of hard-packed snow and ice that was cemented to the branches for most of the year. Though quite dense in places, any shoot brave enough to project above the others was quickly pruned by wind and frost, which reduced the tops of all the trees to a common level.

Small animals moved freely along beaten tracks they had made beneath the trees, but large game forged trails by main force. Jondalar decided to veer away from the unnamed small stream they had been following, one of many that would eventually form the beginning of a great river, and take a game trail through the thick fringe of dwarfed conifers.

As they approached the timberline, the trees thinned out and they could see the region beyond that was completely bereft of upright woody growths. But life is tenacious. Low-growing shrubs and herbs, and extensive fields of grassy turf, partly buried under a blanket of snow, still flourished.

Though much more expansive, similar regions existed in the low elevations of the northern continents. Relict areas of temperate deciduous trees were maintained in certain protected areas and at the lower latitudes, with hardier needled evergreens appearing in the boreal regions to the north of them. Farther north, where they existed at all, trees were usually dwarfed and stunted. Because of the extensive glaciers, the counterparts of the high meadows that surrounded the perpetual ice of the mountains were the vast steppes and tundras, where only those plants that could complete their life cycles quickly survived.

Above the timberline many hardy plants adapted to the harshness of the environment. Ayla, leading her mare, noticed the changes with interest, and she wished she had more time to examine the differences. The mountains in the region where she had grown up were much farther south, and because of the warming influence of the inland sea, the vegetation was primarily of the cold temperate variety. The plants that existed in the higher elevations of the bitterly cold arid regions were fascinating to her.

Stately willows, which graced nearly every river, stream, or brook that sustained even a trace of moisture, grew as low shrubs, and tall sturdy birches and pines became prostrate woody growths that crawled along the ground. Blueberries and bilberries spread out as thick carpets, only four inches high. She wondered if, like the berries that grew near the northern glacier, they bore full-size but sweeter and wilder fruits. Though the bare skeletons of withered branches gave evidence of many plants, she didn't always know what variety they were, or how familiar plants might be different, and she wondered how the high meadows would look in warmer seasons.

Traveling in the dead of winter, Ayla and Jondalar did not see the spring and summer beauty of the highlands. No wild roses or rhododendrons colored the landscape with blooms of pink; no crocuses or anemones, or beautiful blue gentians, or yellow narcissus were tempted to brave the harsh wind; and no primroses or violets would burst with polychrome splendor until the first warmth of spring. There were no bellflowers, rampions, worts, groundsels, daisies, lilies, saxifrages, pinks, monkshoods, or beautiful little edelweiss to ease the bitter cold monotony of the freezing fields of winter.

But another, more awesome sight filled their view. A dazzling fortress of gleaming ice lay athwart their path. It blazed in the sun like a magnificent, many-faceted diamond. Its sheer crystalline white glowed with luminous blue shadows that hid its flaws: the crevasses, tunnels, caves, and pockets that riddled the gigantic gem.

They had reached the glacier.

As the travelers neared the crest of the worn stump of the primordial mountain that bore the flat-topped crown of ice, they weren't even sure if the narrow mountain stream beside them was still the same river that had been their companion for so long. The diminutive trail of ice was indistinguishable from the many frozen little waterways waiting for spring to release their cascading flows to race down the crystalline rocks of the high plateau.

The Great Mother River they had followed all the way from her broad delta where she had emptied into the inland sea, the great waterway that had guided their steps over so much of their arduous Journey, was gone. Even the ice-locked hint of a wild little stream would soon be left behind. The travelers would no longer have the comforting security of the river to show them the way. They would have to continue their Journey west by dead reckoning, with only the sun and stars to act as guides, and landmarks that Jondalar hoped he would remember.

Above the high meadow, the vegetation was more inter-mittent. Only algae, lichens, and mosses that were typical of rocks and scree could derive a struggling existence beyond the cushion plants and a few other rare species. Ayla had begun to feed the horses some of the grass they carried for them. Without their heavy, shaggy coats and thick undercoat, neither horses nor wolf would have survived, but nature had adapted them to the cold. Lacking fur of their own, the humans had made their own adaptations. They took the furs of the animals they hunted; without them they would not have survived. But then, without the protection of furs and fire, their ancestors would never have come north in the first place.

Ibex, chamois, and mouflon were at home in mountain meadows, including those in more precipitous rugged regions, and frequented higher ground, though usually not so late in the season, but horses were an anomaly at this high elevation. Even the gentler slopes of the massif did not usually encour-age their kind to climb so high, but Whinney and Racer were sure-footed.

The horses, with their heads bent low, plodded up the incline at the base of the ice hauling supplies and brownish-black burning stones that would mean the difference between life and death for all of them. The humans, who led the horses to places they would not ordinarily go, were looking for a level spot to set up a tent and make camp.

They were all weary of fighting the intense cold and sharp wind, of climbing the steep terrain. It was exhausting work. Even the wolf was content to stay close rather than to run off and explore.

"I'm so tired," Ayla said as they were trying to set up camp with gusty winds blowing. "Tired of the wind, and tired of the cold. I don't think it'll ever get warm again. I didn't know it could be so cold."

Jondalar nodded, acknowledging the cold, but he knew the cold they had yet to face would be worse. He saw her glance at the great mass of ice, then look away as though she didn't want to see it, and he suspected she was concerned with more than cold.

"Are we really going to go across all that ice?" she asked, finally acknowledging her fears. "Is it possible? I don't even know how we're going to get up to the top."

"It's not easy, but it's possible," Jondalar said. "Thonolan and I did it. While there is still light, I'd like to look for the best way to get the horses up there."

"It feels like we've been traveling forever. How much farther do we have to go, Jondalar?"

"It's still a ways to the Ninth Cave, but not too far, not near as far as we have come, and once we get across the ice, it's only a short distance to Dalanar's Cave. We'll stop there for a while; it will give you a chance to meet him, and Jerika and everyone—I can hardly wait to show Dalanar and Joplaya some of the flint-knapping techniques I learned from Wymez— but even if we stay and visit, we should be home before summer."

Ayla felt distressed. Summer! But this is winter, she thought. If she had really understood how long the Journey would be, she wondered if she would have been so eager to go with Jondalar all the way back to his home. She might have tried harder to persuade him to stay with the Mamutoi.

"Let's go take a closer look at that glacier," Jondalar said, "and plan the best way to get up on it. Then we should make sure we have everything and are ready to cross the ice."

"We'll have to use some of the burning stones to make a fire tonight," Ayla said. "There's nothing to burn around here. And we'll have to melt ice for water . . . we shouldn't have any trouble finding enough of that."

Except for a few shaded pockets of negligible accumulation, there was no snow in the area where they camped, and there had been very little for most of their trek up the slope. Jondalar had only been that way once before, but the whole area seemed much drier than he remembered. He was right. They were in the rain shadow of the highland, the back side; the sparse snows that did fall in the region usually arrived a little later, after the season had begun to turn. He and Thonolan had run into a snowstorm on their way down.

During the winter, the warmer, water-laden air, riding the

prevailing winds coming from the western ocean, rose up the
slopes until it reached the large level area of cold ice with
high pressure centered over it. Having the effect of a giant
funnel that was aimed at the high massif, the moist air cooled,
condensed, and turned to snow, which fell only on the ice
below, feeding the hungry maw of the demanding glacier.

The ice covering the entire worn and rounded top of the
ancient massif spread the precipitation over the whole area,
creating a nearly level surface, except at the periphery. The
cooled air, milked dry of liquid, dropped low and raced down
the sides, bringing no snow beyond the edges of the ice.

As Jondalar and Ayla hiked around the base of the ice
looking for the easiest way up, they noticed areas that seemed
newly disturbed, with dirt and rocks gouged up by prongs of
advancing ice. The glacier was growing.

In many areas, the ancient rock of the highland was
exposed at the foot of the glacier. The massif, folded and
uplifted by the immense pressures that had created the mountains to the south, had once been a solid block of crystalline
granite that incorporated a similar highland to the west. The
forces that pushed against the immovable old mountain, the
most ancient rock on earth, left evidence in the form of a
great rift, a fault that had cleaved the block asunder.

Directly across toward the west, on the opposite side of
the glacier, the massif's western slope was steep, and
matched by an east-facing parallel edge across the rift valley.
A river flowed along the middle of the broad valley floor of
the fault trough protected by the high parallel sides of the
cracked massif. But Jondalar planned to head southwest, to
cross the glacier diagonally and come down a more gradual
grade. He wanted to cross the river nearer its source high in
the southern mountains, before it flowed around the glaciered
massif and through the rift valley.

"Where did this come from?" Ayla asked, holding up
the object in question. It consisted of two oval wooden disks
mounted in a frame that held them rigid and fastened fairly
close together, with leather thongs attached to the outside
edges. A thin slit was cut the long way down the middle of
the wooden ovals for almost the full length, nearly dividing
them in half.

"I made it before we left. I have one for you, too. It's

for your eyes. Sometimes the glare of the ice on the glacier is so bright that you can't see anything but white—people call it snow-blind. The blindness usually goes away after a while, but your eyes can get awfully red and sore. This will protect your eyes. Go ahead, put it on," Jondalar said. Then, seeing her fumble with them, he added, "Here, I'll show you." He put the unusual sunshields on and tied the thongs behind his head.

"How can you see?" Ayla asked. She could just barely make out his eyes behind the long horizontal slits, but she put on the pair he gave her. "You can see almost everything! You just have to turn your head to see to the side." She was surprised; then she smiled. "You look so funny with your big blank eyes, like some kind of strange spirit . . . or a bug. Maybe the spirit of a bug."

"You look funny, too," he said, smiling back, "but those bug eyes could save your life. You need to see where you are going up on the ice."

"These mouflon-wool boot liners from Madenia's mother have been so nice to have," Ayla commented as she put them in a handy place, to get at them easily. "Even when they're wet, they keep your feet warm."

"We may be grateful to have the extra pair when we're on the ice, too," Jondalar said.

"I used to stuff my foot-coverings with sedge grass, when I lived with the Clan."

"Sedge grass?"

"Yes. It keeps your feet warm and dries fast."

"That's useful to know," Jondalar said, then picked up a boot. "Wear the boots with the mammoth-hide soles. They're almost waterproof and they're tough. Sometimes ice can be sharp, and they're rough enough so you won't slip, especially on the way up. Let's see, we'll need the adze to chop up ice." He put the tool on top of a pile he was making. "And rope. Good strong cord, too. We'll need the tent, sleeping furs, food, of course. Can we leave some of the cooking equipment? We won't need much on the ice, and we can get more from the Lanzadonii."

"We'll be using traveling food. I won't be cooking, and I decided to use the big skin pot attached to the frame that we got from Solandia to melt the ice for water, and put it directly over the fire. It's faster that way, and we don't have to boil the water. Just melt it," Ayla said.

"Be sure to keep a spear with you."

"Why? There are no animals on the ice, are there?"

"No, but you can use it to prod ahead of you to make sure the ice is solid. What about this mammoth hide?" Jondalar asked. "We've carried this with us ever since we started out, but do we need it? It's heavy."

"It's a good hide, nice and pliable now, and a good waterproof cover for the bowl boat. You said it snows on the ice." She really hated to throw it away.

"But we can use the tent as a cover."

"That's true . . . but," Ayla said, pursing her lips, considering . . . Then she noticed something else. "Where did you get those torches?"

"From Laduni. We'll be up before sunrise and will need light to pack. I want to reach the top of the plateau before the sun is very high, while everything is still frozen solid," Jondalar said. "Even when it's this cold, the sun can melt the ice a little and it will be difficult enough to reach the top."

They went to bed early, but Ayla couldn't fall asleep. She was nervous and excited. This was the glacier that Jondalar had talked about from the beginning.

"Wha . . . What's wrong?" Ayla said, startled wide awake.

"Nothing's wrong. It's time to get up," Jondalar said, holding up the torch. He pushed the handle into the gravel to support it, then handed her a cup of steaming tea. "I started a fire. Here's some tea."

She smiled, and he looked pleased. She had made his morning tea nearly every single day of their Journey, and he was delighted that he'd gotten up first, for once, and made tea for her. Actually, he'd never gone to sleep. He hadn't been able to. He'd been too nervous, too excited, and too worried.

Wolf watched his humans, his eyes reflecting the light. Sensing something unusual, he capered and pranced back and forth. The horses were frisky, too, full of snorting, nickering, and vibrato blowing with clouds of steam. Using the burning stones, Ayla melted ice for water and fed them grain. She gave Wolf a cake of Losadunai traveling food along with one for her and Jondalar. By the light of the torch, they packed

the tent, the sleeping furs, and a few implements. They left
a few odds and ends behind, an empty container of grain, a
few stone tools, but at the last moment Ayla threw the mammoth hide over the brown coal in the bowl boat.

Jondalar picked up the torch to light the way. Taking
Racer's lead rope, he started out, but the firelight was dis
tracting. He could see a small lighted circle in the immediate
vicinity, but not much beyond, even when he held it up high.
The moon was nearly full, and he began to feel he could find
their way better without the fire. The man finally threw it
down and walked ahead in the dark. Ayla followed, and in
a few moments their eyes adjusted. Behind them the torch
still burned on the graveled ground as they moved away.

In the light of a moon that lacked only a sliver from
being full, the monstrous bastion of ice glowed with an eerie,
evanescent light. The black sky was hazy with stars, the air
brittle and crackling with cold; an amorphous ether charged
with a life of its own.

As cold as it was, the freezing air had a deeper intensity
as they neared the great wall of ice, but Ayla's shiver was
caused by the thrill of awe and anticipation. Jondalar watched
her glowing eyes, her slightly open mouth as she took deeper,
faster breaths. He was always aroused by her excitement, and
he felt a stirring in his loins. But he shook his head. There
was no time now. The glacier was waiting.

Jondalar took a long rope out of his pack. "We need to
tie ourselves together," he said.

"The horses, too?"

"No. We might be able to support each other, but if the
horses slip, they'll take us with them." As much as he would
hate to lose either Racer or Whinney, it was Ayla he was
most concerned about.

Ayla frowned, but she nodded her agreement.

They spoke in hushed whispers, the silent brooding ice
quieting their voices. They didn't want to disturb its hulking
splendor or warn it of their impending assault.

Jondalar tied one end of the rope around his waist and
the other end around Ayla, coiling up the slack and putting
his arm through to carry it on his shoulder. Then each of
them picked up the lead rope of a horse. Wolf would have
to make his own way.

Jondalar felt a moment of panic before he started. What
could he have been thinking of? What ever made him think

he could bring Ayla and the horses across the glacier? They
should have gone the long way around. Even if it took longer,
it was safer. At least they would have made it. Then he
stepped on the ice.

At the foot of a glacier there was often a separation
between the ice and the land, which created a cavelike space
beneath the ice, or an overhanging ice shelf that extended out
over the accumulated gravels of glacial till. At the place Jondalar chose to start, the overhang had collapsed, providing a
gradual ascent. It was also mixed with gravel, giving them
better footing. Starting from the collapsed edge a heavy accumulation of gravel—a moraine—led up the side of the ice
like a well-defined trail and, except near the top, it did not
appear too steep for them or the sure-footed horses. Getting
over the top edge could be a problem, but he wouldn't know
how much of one until he got there.

With Jondalar leading the way, they started up the slope.
Racer balked for a moment. Although they had trimmed it
down, his large load was still unwieldy and the shift in elevation from a moderate to a steeper grade unsettled him. A
hoof slipped, then caught hold, and with some hesitation the
young stallion started up. Then it was Ayla's turn, and Whinney dragging the travois. But the mare had hauled the pole
drag for so long, across such varied terrain, that she was
accustomed to it, and, unlike the large load Racer carried on
his back, the wide-spaced poles helped to steady the mare.

Wolf brought up the rear. It was easier for him. He was
lower to the ground and his callused paws provided friction
against slipping. But he sensed the danger to his companions
and followed behind as though guarding the rear, watchful
for some unseen menace.

In the bright moonlight, reflections from jagged outcrops
of bare ice shimmered, and the mirrorlike surfaces of sheer
planes had a deep liquid quality, like still black pools. It was
not difficult to see the moraine that was spilling down, like
a river of sand and stones in slow motion, but the night
lighting obscured the size and perspective of objects and hid
small details.

Jondalar set a slow and cautious pace, carefully leading
his horse around obstructions. Ayla was more concerned with
finding the best path for the horse she was leading than she
was for her own safety. As the slope became steeper, the

horses, unbalanced by the sharper incline and their heavy loads, struggled for footing. When a hoof slipped as Jondalar tried to lead Racer up a precipitous rise near the top, the horse neighed and tried to rear.

"Come on, Racer," Jondalar urged, pulling his lead rope taut, as if he could pull him up by sheer brute strength. "We're almost there, you can do it."

The stallion made an effort, but his hooves slipped on treacherous ice below a thin layer of snow, and Jondalar felt himself pulled back by the lead rope. He eased up on the rope, giving Racer his head, and finally let go altogether. There were things in the pack he would hate to lose, and even more, it would pain him to lose the animal, but he feared the stallion could not make it.

But when his hooves found gravel, Racer's slide stopped, and with no restraint on him, he lifted his head and plunged forward. Suddenly the stallion was over the edge, adroitly stepping over a narrow crack at the end of a crevasse as the way leveled out. Jondalar noticed that the color of the sky had shifted from black to deep indigo blue, with a faint lightening of the shade on the eastern horizon, as he stroked the horse and praised him warmly.

Then he felt a tug on the rope over his shoulder. Ayla must have slipped back, he thought, as he gave her more slack. She must have reached the steep rise. Suddenly the rope was slipping through his hand, until he felt a strong tug at his waist. She must be holding on to Whinney's lead rope, he thought. She's got to let go.

He grabbed the rope with both hands and shouted, "Let go, Ayla! She'll pull you down with her!"

But Ayla didn't hear, or if she did, she didn't comprehend. Whinney had started up the incline, but her hooves could find no purchase and she kept slipping back. Ayla was holding on to the lead rope, as though she could keep the mare from falling, but she was sliding back, too. Jondalar felt himself being pulled dangerously close to the edge. Looking for something to hold on to, he grabbed Racer's lead rope. The stallion neighed.

But it was the travois that checked Whinney's descent. One of the poles caught in a crack and held long enough for the mare to get her balance. Then her hooves plunged through a snowdrift that held her steady, and she found gravel. As

he felt the pull ease, he let go of Racer's lead. Bracing his
foot against the crack in the ice, Jondalar pulled up on the
rope around his waist.

"Give me a little slack," Ayla called out, as she held on
to the lead rope while Whinney pushed forward.

Suddenly, miraculously, he saw Ayla over the edge, and
he pulled her the rest of the way. Then Whinney appeared.
With a forward vault, she scrambled up past the crack and
her feet were on the level ice, the poles of the travois jutting
out into the air and the bowl boat resting on the edge they
had surmounted. A streak of pink appeared across the early
morning sky, defining the edge of the earth, as Jondalar
heaved a great sigh.

Wolf suddenly bounded up over the edge and raced over
to Ayla. He started to jump up on her, but, feeling none too
steady, she signaled him down. He backed off, looked at
Jondalar and then the horses. Lifting his head and starting
with a few preliminary yips, he howled his wolf song loud
and long.

Although they had climbed up a steep incline and the ice
had leveled out, they were not quite on the top surface of the
glacier. There were cracks near the edge, and broken blocks
of expanded ice that had surged up. Jondalar crossed a mound
of snow that covered a jagged, splintered pile behind the
edge, and finally he set his feet on a level surface of the ice
plateau. Racer followed him, sending broken chunks bouncing and rolling in a clattering fall over the edge. The man
kept the rope attached to his waist taut as Ayla traced over
his last steps. Wolf raced ahead while Whinney followed
behind.

The sky had become a fleeting and unique shade of dawn
blue, while coruscating rays of light radiated from just behind
the edge of the earth. Ayla looked back over the steep incline
and wondered how they had made it up the slope. From their
vantage point at the top, it didn't look possible. Then she
turned to go on, and she caught her breath.

The rising sun had peeked over the eastern edge with a
blinding burst of light that illuminated an incredible scene.
To the west, a flat, utterly featureless, dazzling white plain
stretched out before them. Above it the sky was a shade of
blue she had never seen in her life. It had somehow absorbed
the reflection of the red dawn, and the blue-green undertone
of glacial ice, and yet remained blue. But it was a blue so

stunningly brilliant that it seemed to glow with its own light
in a color beyond description. It shaded to a hazy blue-black
on the distant horizon in the southwest.

As the sun rose in the east, the faded image of a slightly
less than perfect circle that had glowed with such brilliant
reflection in the black sky of their predawn awakening hovered over the far western edge; a dim memory of its earlier
glory. But nothing interrupted the unearthly splendor of the
vast desert of frozen water; no tree, no rock, no movement
of any kind marred the majesty of the seemingly unbroken
surface.

Ayla expelled her breath explosively. She hadn't known
she was holding it. "Jondalar! It's magnificent! Why didn't
you tell me? I would have journeyed twice the distance just
to see this," she said in an awed voice.

"It is spectacular," he said, smiling at her reaction, but
just as overwhelmed. "But I couldn't tell you. I've never
seen it like this before. It's not often this still. The blizzards
up here can be spectacular, too. Let's move while we can
see the way. It's not as solid as it seems, and with this
clear sky and the bright sun, a crevasse could open up or an
overhanging cornice give way."

They started across the plain of ice, preceded by their
long shadows. Before the sun was very high, they were
sweating in their heavy clothes. Ayla started to remove her
hooded outer fur parka.

"Take it off, if you want," Jondalar said, "but keep
yourself covered. You can get a bad sunburn up here, and
not just from above. When the sun shines on it, the ice can
burn you, too."

Small cumulus clouds began to form during the morning.
By noon they had drawn together into large cumulus clouds.
The wind started picking up in the afternoon. About the time
Ayla and Jondalar decided to stop to melt snow and ice for
water, she was more than happy to put her warm outer fur
back on. The sun was hidden by moisture-laden cumulonim-
bus that sprinkled a light dusting of dry powder snow on the
travelers. The glacier was growing.

The plateau glacier they were crossing had been spawned
in the peaks of the craggy mountains far to the south. Moist
air, rising as it swept up the tall barriers, condensed into

misty droplets, but temperature decided whether it would fall as cold rain or, with just a slight drop, as snow. It was not perpetual freezing that made glaciers; rather, an accumulation of snow from one year to the next gave rise to glaciers that, in time, became sheets of ice that eventually spanned continents. In spite of a few hot days, solid cold winters in combination with cool cloudy summers that don't quite melt the leftover snow and ice at winter's end—a lower yearly average temperature—will swing the balance toward a glacial epoch.

Just below the soaring spires of the southern mountains, too steep themselves for snow to rest upon, small basins formed, cirques that nestled against the sides of the pinnacles; and these cirques were the birthplaces of glaciers. As the light, dry, lacy snowflakes drifted into the depressions high in the mountains, created by minute amounts of water freezing in cracks and then expanding to loosen tons of rock, they piled up. Eventually the weight of the mass of frozen water broke the delicate flakes into pieces that coalesced into small round balls of ice: firn, corn snow.

Firn did not form at the surface, but deep in the cirque, and when more snow fell, the heavier compact spheres were pushed up and over the edge of the nest. As more of them accumulated, the nearly circular balls of ice were pressed together so hard by the sheer weight above that a fraction of the energy was released as heat. For just an instant, they melted at the many points of contact and immediately refroze, welding the balls together. As the layers of ice deepened, the greater pressure rearranged the structure of the molecules into solid, crystalline ice, but with a subtle difference: the ice flowed.

Glacier ice, formed under tremendous pressure, was more dense; yet at the lower levels the great mass of solid ice flowed as smoothly as any liquid. Separating around obstructions, such as the soaring tops of mountains, and rejoining on the other side—often taking a large part of the rock with it and leaving behind sharp-peaked islands—a glacier followed the contours of the land, grinding and reshaping it as it went.

The river of solid ice had currents and eddies, stagnant pools and rushing centers, but it moved to a different time, as ponderously slow as it was massively huge. It could take years to move inches. But time didn't matter. It had all the time in the world. As long as the average temperature stayed below the critical line, the glacier fed and grew.

Mountain cirques were not the only birthplaces. Glaciers formed on level ground, too, and once they covered a large enough area, the chilling effect spread the precipitation out of the anticyclone funnel, centered in the middle, to the extreme margins; the thickness of the ice remained nearly the same throughout.

Glaciers were never entirely dry. Some water was always seeping down from the melting caused by pressure. It filled in small cracks and crannies, and when it chilled and refroze, it expanded in all directions. The motion of a glacier was outward in all directions from its origin, and the speed of its motion depended on the slope of its surface, not on the slope of the ground underneath. If the surface slope was great, the water within the glacier flowed downhill faster through the chinks in the ice and spread out the ice as it refroze. They grew faster when they were young, near large oceans or seas, or in mountains where the high peaks assured heavy snowfall. They slowed down after they spread out, their broad surface reflecting the sunlight away and the air above the center turning colder and drier with less snow.

The glaciers in the mountains to the south had spread out from their high peaks, filled the valleys to the level of high mountain passes, and spilled through them. During an earlier advancing period, the mountain glaciers filled the deep trench of a fault line separating the mountain foreland and the ancient massif. It covered the highland, then spread across to the old eroded mountains on the northern fringe. The ice receded during the temporary warming—which was coming to an end—and melted in the lowland fault valley, creating a large river and a long, moraine-dammed lake, but the plateau glacier on the highland they were crossing stayed frozen.

They could not build a fire directly on the ice and had planned to use the bowl boat as a base for the river stones they had brought to build the fire on. But first they had to empty all the burning stones out of the round craft. As Ayla picked up the heavy mammoth hide, it occurred to her that they could just as well use it as a base upon which to build a fire. Even if it scorched a little, it wouldn't matter. It pleased her that she had thought to bring it. Everyone, including the horses, had water and a little food.

While they were stopped, the sun disappeared entirely behind heavy clouds, and before they started on their way again, thick snow began falling with grim determination. The north wind howled across the icy expanse; there was nothing on the whole vast sheet covering the massif to stand in its way. A blizzard was in the making.

42

As the snowfall thickened, the force of the wind from the northwest suddenly increased. It slammed into them with a blast of cold air that shoved them along as though they were no more than an insignificant piece of the horizontal curtain of white that surrounded them.

"I think we'd better wait this out," Jondalar shouted to be heard above the howl.

They fought to set up their tent while the icy blasts seized the small shelter, tore the stakes out of the ice, and left the tent billowing and flapping. The violent, sinewy wind threatened to rip the sheet of leather from the grasp of the two puny living souls trying to make their way across the ice, daring to present an obstacle to the furious, snow-choked blizzard raging across the flat surface.

"How are we going to keep the tent down?" Ayla asked. "Is it always this bad up here?"

"I don't remember it blowing this hard before, but I'm not surprised."

The horses were standing mutely, their heads down, stoically enduring the storm. Wolf was close beside them, digging out a hole for himself. "Maybe we could get one of the horses to stand on the loose end and hold it down until we get it staked," Ayla suggested.

With one thing leading to another, they came up with a makeshift solution, using the horses as both stakes and tent supports. They draped the leather tent over the backs of both horses, then Ayla coaxed Whinney to stand on one of the edges, turned under, hoping the mare wouldn't shift too much and let it up. Ayla and Jondalar huddled together, with the wolf under their bent knees, sitting, almost under the bellies of the horses, on the other end of the tent that was wrapped around underneath them.

It was dark before the squall blew itself out, and they had to camp for the night at the same place, but they set the tent up properly first. In the morning, Ayla was puzzled by some dark stains near the edge of the tent that Whinney had stood on. She wondered about them as they hurried to break camp early the next morning.

They made more progress the second day, in spite of climbing over pressure mounds of broken ice and working their way around an area of several yawning cracks, all oriented in the same direction. A storm blew up in the afternoon again, though the wind was not as strong, and it blew over more quickly, allowing them to continue their Journey during the late afternoon.

Toward evening, Ayla noticed that Whinney was limping. She felt her heart beat faster and a rush of fear when she looked closer and saw red smudges on the ice. She picked up Whinney's foot and examined her hoof. It was cut to the quick and bleeding.

"Jondalar, look at this. Her feet are all cut up. What did that to her?" Ayla said.

He looked, and then he examined Racer's hooves while Ayla was looking at the rest of Whinney's. He found the same kind of injuries, then frowned. "It must be the ice," he said. "You'd better check Wolf, too."

The pads of the wolf's paws showed damage, though not quite as bad as the horses' hooves. "What are we going to do?" Ayla said. "They're crippled, or will be soon."

"It never occurred to me that the ice could be so sharp it could cut up their hooves," Jondalar said, very upset. "I

tried to think of everything, but I didn't think about that."
He was stricken with remorse.

"Hooves are hard, but they're not like stone. More like
fingernails. They can be damaged. Jondalar, they can't go
on. They'll be so crippled in another day that they won't be
able to walk at all," Ayla said. "We've got to help them."

"But what can we do?" Jondalar said.

"Well, I still have my medicine bag. I can treat their
injuries."

"But we can't stay here until they're healed. And as soon
as they start walking again, it will be just as bad." The man
stopped and closed his eyes. He didn't even want to think
what he was thinking, much less say it, but he could see only
one way out of their dilemma. "Ayla, we're going to have
to leave them," the man said, as gently as he could.

"Leave them? What do you mean, 'leave them'? We
can't leave Whinney, or Racer. Where would they find water?
Or food? There's nothing to graze on the ice, not even twig
tips. They'd starve, or freeze. We can't do that!" Ayla said,
her face showing her distress. "We can't leave them here
like that! We can't, Jondalar!"

"You're right, we can't leave them here like that. It
wouldn't be fair. They would suffer too much . . . but . . .
we do have spears and the spear-throwers . . ." Jondalar
said.

"No! No!" Ayla screamed. "I won't let you!"

"It would be better than leaving them here to die slowly,
to suffer. It's not like horses haven't been . . . hunted before.
That's what most people do."

"But these aren't like other horses. Whinney and Racer
are friends. We've been through so much together. They've
helped us. Whinney saved my life. I can't leave her."

"I don't want to leave them any more than you do,"
Jondalar said, "but what else can we do?" The idea of killing
the stallion after traveling so far together was almost more
than he could bear, and he knew how Ayla felt about
Whinney.

"We'll go back. We'll just have to turn back. You said
there was another way around!"

"We've already traveled two days on this ice, and the
horses are almost crippled. We can try to go back, Ayla, but
I don't think they will make it," Jondalar said. He wasn't

even sure if Wolf would be able to make it. Guilt and remorse filled him. "I'm sorry, Ayla. It's my fault. It was stupid of me to think we could cross this glacier with the horses. We should have gone the long way around, but I'm afraid it's too late now."

Ayla saw tears in his eyes. She had not often seen him in tears. Though it was not so unusual for men of the Others to cry, it was his nature to hide those emotions. In a way, it made his love for her more intense. He had given of himself, almost completely, only to her, and she loved him for it, but she could not give up Whinney. The horse was her friend; the only friend she had had in the valley, until Jondalar came.

"We've got to do something, Jondalar!" she sobbed.

"But what?" He had never felt so desolate, so totally frustrated at his inability to find some solution.

"Well, for now," Ayla said, wiping her eyes, her tears freezing on her face, "I'm going to treat their injuries. I can do that much, anyway." She got out her otter-skin medicine bag. "We'll have to make a good fire, hot enough to boil water, not just melt ice."

She took the mammoth hide off the brown burning stones and spread it out on the ice. She noticed some scorch marks on the supple leather, but they hadn't damaged the tough old hide. She put the river rocks on a different spot, but near the middle, as a base upon which to build a fire. At least they didn't have to worry about conserving fuel anymore. They could leave most of it behind.

She didn't talk, she couldn't, and Jondalar had nothing to say either. It seemed impossible. All the thought, planning, and preparation that had gone into the trek across this glacier, only to be stopped by something they hadn't even considered. Ayla stared at the small fire. Wolf crawled up to her and whined, not in pain, but because he knew something was wrong. Ayla checked his paws again. They weren't as bad. He had more control over where he put his feet, and he carefully licked off snow and ice when they stopped to rest. She didn't want to think about losing him, either.

She hadn't consciously thought of Durc for some time, though he was always there, a memory, a cold pain that she would never forget. She found herself musing about him. Has he started to hunt with the clan yet? Has he learned to use a sling? Uba would be a good mother to him, she would take care of him, make his food, make him warm winter clothes.

Ayla shivered, thinking about the cold, then thought about the first winter clothes Iza had made for her. She had loved the rabbit skin hat with the fur worn on the inside. The winter foot-coverings had fur inside too. She recalled stomping around in a pair of new ones, and she remembered how the simple foot-coverings were made. It was just a piece of hide, gathered up and tied at the ankle. They conformed to the shape of the foot after a while, though at first they were rather clumsy, but that was part of the fun of new ones.

Ayla kept staring at the fire, watching the water start to simmer. Something was nagging her. Something important, she was sure. Something about . . .

Suddenly she drew in her breath. "Jondalar! Oh, Jondalar!"

She seemed agitated to him. "What's the matter, Ayla?"

"It's not what's wrong, it's what's right," she cried. "I just remembered something!"

He thought she was acting strangely. "I don't understand," he said. He wondered if the thought of losing her two horses was too much for her. She pulled at the heavy tarp of mammoth hide under the fire, knocking a hot coal directly onto the leather.

"Give me a knife, Jondalar. Your sharpest knife."

"My knife?" he said.

"Yes, your knife," she said. "I'm going to make boots for the horses!"

"You're going to do what?"

"I'm going to make boots for the horses, and Wolf, too. Out of this mammoth hide!"

"How do you make horse boots?"

"I'll cut circles out of the mammoth leather, then cut holes around the edges, thread some cord through, and tie it around the horses' ankles. If mammoth hide can keep our feet from getting cut up by the ice, it's bound to protect theirs," Ayla explained.

Jondalar thought for a moment, visualizing what she described; then he smiled. "Ayla! I think it will work. By the Great Mother, I think it will work! What a wonderful idea! Whatever made you think of it?"

"That's the way Iza made boots for me. That's how the

people of the Clan make foot-coverings. Hand-coverings, too. I'm trying to remember if that's the kind Guban and Yorga wore. It's hard to tell, because after a while they shape to your feet.''

"Will that hide be enough?''

"It should be. While I've got the fire going, I'll finish preparing this remedy for the cuts, and maybe some hot tea for us. We haven't had any for a couple of days, and we probably won't again until we get down off this ice. We're going to have to conserve fuel, but I think a cup of hot tea would taste very good right now.''

"I think you're right!'' Jondalar agreed, smiling again and feeling good.

Ayla very carefully examined each hoof on both horses, trimmed away the rough places, applied her medication, then tied the mammoth-hide horse boots on them. They tried to shake off the strange foot-coverings at first, but they were tied on securely, and the horses quickly got used to them. Then she took the set she had made for Wolf and tied them on. He chewed and gnawed at them, trying to get rid of the unfamiliar encumbrances, but after a while he stopped fighting them, too. His oversize wolf feet were in much better shape.

The next morning they loaded a slightly lighter pack on the horses; they had burned some of the brown coal, and the heavy mammoth hide was now on their feet. Ayla unloaded them when they stopped for a rest, and she took on a little more of the load herself. But she couldn't begin to carry what the sturdy horses could. In spite of traveling, their hooves and feet seemed much improved by that night. Wolf's seemed perfectly normal, which was a great relief for both Ayla and Jondalar. The boots provided an unexpected benefit: they acted as a kind of snowshoe when there was deep snow, and the large, heavy animals didn't sink in as far.

The pattern of the first day held, with some variation. They made their best time in the morning; the afternoons brought snow and wind of varying intensity. Sometimes they were able to travel a little farther after the storm, other times they had to stay where they stopped in the afternoon through the night, and on one occasion for two days, but none of the blizzards were as fierce as the one they had encountered the first day.

The surface of the glacier wasn't quite as flat and smooth

as it had appeared on that first glistening day in the sun. They floundered through deep drifts of soft powdered snow piled high from localized snowstorms. Other times, where driving winds cleared the surface, they crunched over sharp projections and slid into shallow ditches, their feet catching in narrow spaces and their ankles twisting under them on the uneven surface. Instant squalls blew down without warning, the fierce winds almost never let up, and they felt constant anxiety about unseen crevasses covered over with flimsy bridges or overhanging cornices of snow.

They detoured around open cracks, especially near the center, where the dry air held so little moisture that the snows were not heavy enough to fill the crevasses. And the cold, the deep, bitter, bone-chilling cold, never let up. Their breath froze on the fur of their hoods around their mouths; a drop of water spilling from a cup was frozen before it touched the ground. Their faces, exposed to raw winds and bright sun, cracked, peeled, and blackened. Frostbite was a constant threat.

The strain was beginning to tell. Their responses were beginning to deteriorate, and so was their judgment. A furious afternoon storm had held on into the night. In the morning, Jondalar was anxious to get under way. They had lost much more time than he had planned. In the bitter cold, it took longer for the water to heat, and their supply of burning stones was dwindling.

Ayla was going through her backpack; then she began searching around her sleeping fur. She couldn't remember how many days they had been on the ice, but as far as she was concerned, it was too many, she thought as she searched.

"Hurry up, Ayla! What's taking you so long?" Jondalar snapped.

"I can't find my eye protectors," she said.

"I told you not to lose them. Do you want to go blind?" he exploded.

"No, I don't want to go blind. Why do you think I'm looking for them?" Ayla retorted. Jondalar snatched her fur up and shook it vigorously. The wooden goggles fell to the ground.

"Be careful where you put them next time," he said. "Now let's get moving."

They quickly packed up their camp, but Ayla sulked and refused to talk to Jondalar. He came over and double-checked her lashings, as he usually did. Ayla grabbed Whinney's rope and started out taking the lead, moving the horse away before Jondalar could examine her pack.

"Don't you think I know how to pack a horse myself? You said you wanted to get moving. Why are you wasting time?" she flung back over her shoulder.

He had just been trying to be careful, Jondalar thought angrily. She doesn't even know the way. Wait until she wanders around in circles for a while. Then she will come asking me to lead, he thought, falling in behind her.

Ayla was cold and fatigued from the grueling march. She plunged ahead, careless of her surroundings. If he wants to hurry so much, then we'll hurry, she thought. If we ever get to the end of this ice, I hope I never see a glacier again.

Wolf was nervously racing between Ayla in the lead and Jondalar following behind. He didn't like the sudden change in their positions. The tall man had always started out ahead before. The wolf struck out ahead of the woman, who was trudging blindly on, oblivious to everything except the miserable cold and her injured feelings. Suddenly he stopped directly in front of her, blocking her way.

Ayla, leading the mare, went around him. He ran back around and stopped in front of her again. She ignored him. He nudged at her legs; she shoved him aside. He ran ahead a short distance, then sat down whining to get her attention. She plodded past him. He raced back toward Jondalar, pranced and whined in front of him, then bounded a few steps toward Ayla, whining, then advanced toward the man once more.

"Is something wrong, Wolf?" Jondalar said, finally noticing the animal's agitation.

Suddenly he heard a terrifying sound, a muffled boom. His head shot up as fountains of light snow filled the air ahead.

"No! Oh no!" Jondalar cried out in anguish, running forward. When the snow settled, a lone animal stood on the brink of a yawning crack. Wolf pointed his nose straight up and wailed a long, desolate howl.

Jondalar threw himself flat on the ice at the edge of the crevasse and looked over the edge. "Ayla!" he cried in desperation. "Ayla!" His stomach was a hard knot. He knew it was useless. She would never hear him. She was dead, at the bottom of the deep crack in the ice.

"Jondalar?"

He heard a small frightened voice coming from far away.

"Ayla?" He felt a rush of hope and looked down. Far below him, standing on a narrow ice ledge that hugged the wall of the deep trench, was the terrified woman. "Ayla, don't move!" he commanded. "Stand perfectly still. That ledge could go, too."

She's alive, he thought. I can't believe it. It's a miracle. But how am I going to get her out?

Inside the icy chasm, Ayla leaned in toward the wall, clinging desperately to a crack and a projecting piece, petrified with fear. She had been plodding through snow halfway to her knees, lost in her own thoughts. She was tired, so tired of it all: tired of the cold, tired of fighting her way through deep snow, tired of the glacier. The trek across the ice had drained her energy, and she was bone-weary with exhaustion. Though she struggled on, her only thought was to reach the end of the massive glacier.

Then she was startled out of her brooding thoughts by a loud crack. She felt the sickening sensation of the solid ice giving way beneath her feet, and she was suddenly reminded of an earthquake many years before. Instinctively she tried to reach for something to hold on to, but the falling ice and snow offered nothing. She felt herself dropping, nearly suffocating in the midst of the avalanching snow bridge that had collapsed beneath her feet, and she had no idea how she had ended up on the narrow ledge.

She looked up, afraid to move even that much, for fear the slightest shift in weight would jar her precarious support loose. Above, the sky looked almost black, and she thought she saw the faint glimmerings of stars. An occasional sliver of ice or puff of snow dropped belatedly from the edge, finally letting go of its precarious hold and showering the woman with fragments on the way down.

Her ledge was a narrow jutting extension of an older surface long buried by new snows. It rested on a large jagged boulder that had been torn from solid rock as the ice slowly filled a valley and overflowed down the sides of an adjacent one. The majestically flowing river of ice accumulated great quantities of dust, sand, gravel, and boulders that it gouged out of hard rock, which were slowly carried toward the faster-moving current at the center. These moraines formed long ribbons of rubble on the surface as they moved along the current. When the temperature eventually rose enough to melt the massive glaciers, they would leave evidence of their passage in ridges and hills of unsorted rock.

While she was waiting, afraid to move and holding herself very still, she heard faint mutterings and muted rumblings in the deep icy cavern. She thought at first that she imagined them. But the mass of ice was not as solid as it seemed on the hard surface above. It was constantly readjusting, expanding, shifting, sliding. The explosive boom of a new crack opening or closing at some distant point, on the surface or deep within the glacier, sent vibrations through the strangely viscous solid. The great mountain of ice was riddled with catacombs: passages that came to an abrupt halt, long galleries that turned and twisted, dropped off or soared upward; pockets and caves that opened invitingly, then sealed shut.

Ayla began to look around her. The sheer walls of ice glowed with a luminous, unbelievably rich blue light that had a deep undertone of green. With a sudden jolt, she realized she had seen that color before, but in only one other place. Jondalar's eyes were the same rich, stunning blue! She longed to see them again. The fractured planes of the huge ice crystal gave her the sensation of mysterious flitting movement just beyond her peripheral vision. She felt that if she turned her head quickly enough she would see some ephemeral shape disappearing into the mirrored walls.

But it was all illusion, a magician's trick of angles and light. The crystal ice filtered out most of the red spectrum of the light from the burning orb in the sky, leaving the deep blue-green, and the edges and planes of the tinted, mirrored surfaces played games of refraction and reflection with each other.

Ayla glanced up when she felt a shower of snow. She saw Jondalar's head extending beyond the rim of the crevasse, then a length of rope came snaking down toward her.

"Tie the rope around your waist, Ayla," he called, "and make sure you tie it well. Let me know when you're ready."

He was doing it again, Jondalar said to himself. Why did he always recheck what she did when he knew she was more than capable of doing it herself? Why did he tell her to do something that was perfectly obvious? She knew the rope had to be tied securely. That was why she had gotten angry and stomped off ahead and was now in this dangerous predicament . . . but she should have known better.

"I'm ready, Jondalar," she called, after wrapping it around her and fastening it with many knots. "These knots won't slip."

"All right. Now hang on to the rope. We're going to pull you up," he said.

Ayla felt the rope grow taut, then lift her from the ledge. Her feet were dangling in air as she felt herself slowly rising toward the edge of the crevasse. She saw Jondalar's face, and his beautiful, worried blue eyes, and she gripped the hand he held out to her to help her over the rim. Then she was on the surface again, and Jondalar was crushing her in his arms. She clung to him as tightly.

"I thought you were gone for sure," he said, kissing and holding her. "I'm sorry I yelled at you, Ayla. I know you can load your own packs. I just worry so much."

"No, it's my fault. I shouldn't have been so careless with my eye protectors, and I should never have rushed ahead of you like that. I'm still not familiar with ice."

"But I let you, and I should have known better."

"I should have known better," Ayla said at the same time. They smiled at each other at the inadvertent matching of words.

Ayla felt a tug at her waist and saw that the other end of the rope was fastened to the brown stallion. Racer had pulled her out of the crevasse. She fumbled to untie the knots around her waist while Jondalar held the sturdy horse close by. She finally had to use a knife to cut the rope. She had made so many knots and had pulled them so tight—and they'd grown even tighter as she was lifted out—that they were impossible to untie.

Detouring around the crack that had so nearly proved disastrous, they continued their southwesterly course across the ice. They were growing seriously concerned as their supply of burning stones was becoming depleted.

"How much longer before we reach the other side, Jondalar?" Ayla asked in the morning after melting water for them all. "We don't have many burning stones left."

"I know. I had hoped that we would be there by now. The storms have caused more delay than I planned on, and I'm getting worried that the weather will turn while we are on the ice. It can happen so fast," Jondalar said, scanning the sky carefully as he spoke. "I'm afraid it may be coming soon."

"Why?"

"I got to thinking about that silly argument we had before you fell into the crevasse. Remember how everyone was warning us about the evil spirits that ride ahead of the snow-melter?"

"Yes!" Ayla said. "Solandia and Verdegia said they make you feel irritable, and I was feeling very irritable. I still do. I am so sick and tired of this ice, I have to force myself to keep going. Could that be what it is?"

"That's what I was wondering. Ayla, if it's true, we have to hurry. If the foehn comes while we're up on this glacier, we may all fall into the cracks," Jondalar said.

They tried to ration the peaty brown stones more carefully, drinking their water barely melted. Ayla and Jondalar started carrying their waterbags full of snow underneath their fur parkas so their body heat would melt enough for them and Wolf. But the conservation wasn't enough. Their bodies couldn't melt enough for the horses that way, and when the last of the burning stones were gone, there was no water for the horses. She had run out of feed for them, too, but water was more important. Ayla noticed them chewing ice, but it worried her. Both dehydration and eating ice could chill them so that they wouldn't be able to maintain sufficient body heat to keep warm on the freezing cold glacier.

Both horses had come to her looking for water, after they had set up their tent, but all Ayla could do was give them a few sips of her own water and break up some ice for them. There had been no afternoon storm that day, and they had kept going until it was almost too dark to see. They had traveled a good distance, and should have been glad, but she felt strangely uncomfortable. She had trouble getting to sleep that night. She tried to shrug it off, telling herself she was just worried about the horses.

Jondalar lay awake for a long time, too. He thought the horizon was looking closer, but he was afraid it was wishful thinking and didn't want to mention it. When he finally dozed off, he awoke in the middle of the night to find Ayla wide awake, too. They got up at the first faint shift from black to blue, and they started out with stars still in the sky.

By midmorning the wind had shifted, and Jondalar was sure his worst fears were about to materialize. The wind wasn't so much warm as less cold, but it was coming from the south

"Hurry, Ayla! We've got to hurry," he said, almost breaking into a run. She nodded and kept up with him.

By noon the sky was clear, and the brisk breeze blowing in their faces was so warm that it was almost balmy. The force of the wind increased, enough to slow them down as they leaned into it. And its warmth blowing across the cold surface of the ice was a deadly caress. The drifts of dry powdery snow became wet and compact, then turned to slush. Little puddles of water began to form in small depressions on the surface. They became deeper and took on a vivid blue color that seemed to glow out of the center of the ice, but the woman and man had no time, or heart, to appreciate the beauty. The horses' need for water was easily satisfied, but it gave them little comfort now.

A soft mist began to rise, clinging close to the surface; the driving, warm south wind carried it away before it could get too high. Jondalar was using a long spear to feel the way ahead, but he was still almost running, and Ayla was hard-pressed to keep up. She wished she could jump on Whinney's back and let the horse carry her away, but more and more cracks were opening in the ice. He was almost certain the horizon was closer, but the low-lying fog made distances deceptive.

Little rivulets began streaming over the surface of the ice, connecting the puddles and making footing treacherous. They splashed through the water, feeling its icy chill penetrate, then squish through their boots. Suddenly, a few feet in front of them, a large section of what had seemed to be solid ice fell away, exposing a yawning gulf. Wolf yipped and whined, and the horses shied away, squealing with fear. Jondalar turned and followed the edge of the crack, looking for a way around.

"Jondalar, I can't keep going. I'm exhausted. I've got to stop," Ayla said with a sob, then started crying. "We'll never make it."

He stopped, then went back and comforted her. "We're almost there, Ayla. Look. You can see how close the edge is."

"But we almost walked into a crevasse, and some of those puddles have become deep blue holes with streams falling into them."

"Do you want to stay here?" he said.

Ayla took a deep breath. "No, of course not," she said.
"I don't know why I'm crying like this. If we stay here,
we'll die for sure."

Jondalar worked his way around the large crack, but as
they turned south again, the winds were as strong as any
from the north had been, and they could feel the temperature
rising. Rivulets turned into streams crisscrossing the ice and
grew into rivers. They worked their way around two more
large cracks and could see beyond the ice. They ran the last
short distance, and then they stood looking down over the
edge.

They had reached the other side of the glacier.

A waterfall of milky clouded water, glacier milk, was just
below them, gushing out of the bottom of the ice. In the
distance, below the snowline, was a thin cover of light green.

"Do you want to stop here and rest a while?" Jondalar
asked, but he looked worried.

"I just want to get off this ice. We can rest when we
reach that meadow," Ayla said.

"It's farther than it looks. This is not the place to rush
or be careless. We'll rope ourselves together, and I think you
should go first. If you slip, I can support your weight. Pick
a way down carefully. We can lead the horses."

"No, I don't think we should. I think we should take off
their halters and packs, and the pole drag, and let them find
their own way down," Ayla said.

"Maybe you're right, but then we'll have to leave the
packs here . . . unless . . ."

Ayla saw where he was looking. "Let's put everything
in the bowl boat and let it slide down!" she said.

"Except a small pack with some necessities that we can
take with us," he said, smiling.

"If we tie it all down well, and watch which way it goes,
we should be able to find it."

"What if it breaks up?"

"What would break?"

"The frame could crack," Jondalar said, "but even if it
did, the hide would probably hold it together."

"And whatever was inside would still be all right,
wouldn't it?"

"It should be." Jondalar smiled. "I think that's a good
idea."

After the round boat was repacked, Jondalar picked up the small pack of essentials while Ayla led Whinney. Although somewhat fearful of slipping, they walked along the edge looking for a way down. As if to make up for the delays and dangers they had endured in the crossing, they soon found the gradual slope of a moraine, with all its gravel, that appeared possible, just beyond a somewhat steeper grade of slick ice. They dragged the boat to the icy slope; then Ayla unfastened the travois. They removed all the halters and ropes from both animals, but not the mammoth-hide horse boots. Ayla checked them to make sure they were securely tied; they had conformed to the shape of the horses' hooves and now fit snugly. Then they led the horses to the top of the moraine.

Whinney nickered, and Ayla calmed her, calling her by the whinny name she was most familiar with, and she spoke in their language of signals and sounds and made-up words. "Whinney, you need to make your own way down," the woman said. "No one else can find your footing on this ice better than you can."

Jondalar reassured the young stallion. The descent would be dangerous, anything could happen, but at least they had gotten the horses across. They would have to get themselves down. Wolf was pacing nervously back and forth along the edge of the ice, the way he did when he was afraid to jump into a river.

With Ayla's urgings, Whinney was the first to go over the edge, picking her way carefully. Racer was close on her heels and soon outdistanced her. They came to a slick spot, slipped and slid, gained momentum, and moved down faster to keep up. They would be down safely—or not—by the time Ayla and Jondalar reached the bottom.

Wolf was whining at the top, his tail tucked between his legs, not ashamed to show the fear he felt as he watched the horses go.

"Let's push the boat over and get started. It's a long way down, and it won't be easy," Jondalar said.

As they pushed the boat near the steeper icy edge, Wolf suddenly jumped in it. "He must think we're getting ready to ride across a river," Ayla said. "I wish we could float down this ice."

They both looked at each other and started to smile.

"What do you think?" Jondalar said.

"Why not? You said it should hold together."

"But will we?"

"Let's find out!

They shifted a few things around to make room, then climbed into the bowl-shaped boat with Wolf. Jondalar sent a hopeful thought to the Mother, and, using one of the travois poles, they pushed off.

"Hold on!" Jondalar said as they started over the edge.

They gained speed quickly, but headed straight ahead at first. Then they hit a bump and the boat bounced and spun around. They swerved sideward, then rode up a slight incline and found themselves in midair. They both screamed with the fearful excitement. They landed with a jolt that lifted them all up, the wolf included, then spun around again while they clutched the edge. The wolf was trying to crouch down and poke his nose over the side at the same time.

Ayla and Jondalar held on for all they were worth; it was all they could do. They had absolutely no control over the round boat that was racing down the side of the glacier. It zigged and zagged, bounced and spun around as though leaping with joy, but it was heavily loaded, bottom heavy enough to resist tipping over. Though the man and woman screamed involuntarily, they couldn't help smiling. It was the fastest, most thrilling ride either of them had ever taken, but it was not over.

They didn't think about how the ride would end, and, as they neared the bottom, Jondalar remembered the usual crevasse at the foot separating the ice from the ground below. A hard landing on gravel could throw them out and cause injury, or worse, but the sound didn't make an impression on him when he first heard it. It wasn't until they landed with a hard bump and a huge splash into the middle of a roaring waterfall of cloudy water that he realized their descent down the wet slippery ice had taken them back toward the river of meltwater that was gushing out of the bottom of the glacier.

They landed at the bottom of the falls with another splash, and soon they were floating calmly in the middle of a small lake of cloudy green glacier melt. Wolf was so happy that he was all over both of them, licking their faces. He finally sat down and lifted his head in a howl of greeting.

Jondalar looked at the woman, "Ayla, we made it! We made it! We're over the glacier!"

"We did, didn't we?" she said, smiling broadly.

"That was a dangerous thing to do, though," he said. "We could have been hurt, or even killed."

"It may have been dangerous, but it was fun," Ayla said, her eyes still sparkling with excitement.

Her enthusiasm was contagious, and for all his concern about getting her home safely, he had to smile. "You're right. It was fun, and fitting, somehow. I don't think I'll ever try to cross a glacier again. Twice in one lifetime is enough, but I'm glad I can say I did it, and I'll never forget that ride."

"Now, all we have to do is reach that land over there," Ayla said, pointing toward the shore, "and then find Whinney and Racer."

The sun was setting, and, between the blinding brightness at the horizon and twilight's deceptive shadows, it was difficult to see. The evening chill had brought the temperature to below freezing again. They could see the comforting security of the black loam of solid ground, intermixed with patches of snow, around the perimeter of the lake, but they didn't know how to get there. They had no paddle, and they had left the pole on top of the glacier.

But although the lake seemed calm, the fast-flowing glacial melt gave it an undercurrent that was slowly taking them toward the shore. When they were close, they both jumped out of the boat, followed by the wolf, and pulled it up on the land. Wolf shook himself, spraying water, but neither Ayla nor Jondalar noticed. They were in each other's arms, expressing their love and their relief at having actually reached solid ground.

"We did make it. We're almost home, Ayla. We're almost home," Jondalar said, holding her, grateful that she was there to be held.

The snow around the lake was beginning to refreeze, turning soft slush into hard-crusted ice. They walked across the gravel in the near dark holding hands, until they reached a field. There was no wood for a fire, but they didn't care. They ate the dry concentrated traveling food that had been their sustenance on the ice, and they drank water from bags filled on the glacier. Then they set up their tent and spread out their sleeping furs, but before they settled in, Ayla looked across the darkened landscape and wondered where the horses were.

She whistled for Whinney and waited to hear the sound of hooves, but no horses came. She looked up at the swirling clouds above and wondered where they were, then whistled again. It was too dark to look for them now; it would have to wait until morning. Ayla crawled into her sleeping furs beside the tall man and reached for the wolf who was curled up beside her place. She thought about the horses as she sank into an exhausted sleep.

The man looked at the tousled blond hair of the woman beside him, her head resting comfortably in the hollow beneath his shoulder, and he changed his mind about getting up. There was no longer a need to keep moving, but the absence of worry left him at loose ends. He had to keep reminding himself they were over the glacier; they didn't have to hurry anymore. They could lie around in their sleeping furs all day if they wanted to.

The glacier was behind them now, and Ayla was safe. He shivered at the thought of her close call, and he tightened his hold on her. The woman raised herself up on her elbow and looked at him. She loved looking at him. The dim light inside the hide tent softened the vivid blue of his eyes, and his forehead, so often knotted in concentration or concern, was relaxed now. She ran a finger lightly across the worry lines, then traced his features.

"Do you know, before I saw you I tried to imagine how a man would look. Not a man of the Clan, one like me. I never could. You are beautiful, Jondalar," she said.

Jondalar laughed. "Ayla, women are beautiful. Not men."

"What is a man, then?"

"You might say he's strong, or brave."

"You are strong and brave, but that's not the same as beautiful. What would you call a man who is beautiful?"

"Handsome, I suppose." He felt a little embarrassed. He had been called handsome too often.

"Handsome. Handsome," she repeated to herself. "I like beautiful better. Beautiful I understand."

Jondalar laughed again, his rich, surprisingly lusty laugh.

The uninhibited warmth of it was unexpected, and Ayla caught herself staring at him. He had been so serious on this trip. Though he had smiled, he'd seldom laughed out loud.

"If you want to call me beautiful, go ahead," he said, pulling her closer to him. "How can I object to a beautiful woman calling me beautiful?"

Ayla felt the spasms of his laughter, and she started giggling. "I love it when you laugh, Jondalar."

"And I love you, funny woman."

He held her after they stopped laughing. Feeling her warmth and soft full breasts, he reached for one and pulled her down so he could kiss her. She slipped her tongue into his mouth and felt herself respond with a surprising hunger for him. It had been some time, she realized. All the time they were on the glacier, they both had been so anxious and so exhausted that they hadn't been in the mood, or able to relax enough to get there.

He sensed her eager willingness and felt his own sudden need. He rolled her over as they kissed; then, moving the furs out of the way, he kissed her throat and neck on the way to finding her breast. He enclosed her hard nipple with his mouth and suckled.

She moaned as a sharp shiver of unbelievable Pleasure charged through her with an intensity that left her gasping. She was stunned by her own reaction. He had barely touched her, and she was ready, and she felt so eager. It hadn't been that long, had it? She pushed herself toward him.

Jondalar reached down to touch her place of Pleasures between her thighs, felt her hard knob and massaged it. With a few cries, she reached a sudden peak, and was there, ready for him, wanting him.

He felt her sudden moist warmth, and understood her readiness. His need had risen to match hers. Pushing at the furs to get them out of the way, she opened to him. He reached for her deep well with his proud manhood and entered.

She pulled him to her as he thrust forward, penetrating deeply. He felt her full embrace, and she cried out with her joy. She had needed him, and he felt so right, it was beyond delight, more than Pleasure.

He was as ready as she. He pulled back, then thrust again, and only once more, and suddenly, there was no holding back. He felt the surge rise, reach, and overflow. With a last few motions, he drained himself, then pushed in, and relaxed on top of her.

She lay still with her eyes closed, feeling his weight on her, and feeling wonderful. She didn't want to move. When he finally got up and looked down at her, he had to kiss her. She opened her eyes and looked up at him.

"That was wonderful, Jondalar," she said, feeling languid and satisfied.

"It was fast. You were ready; we were both ready. And you had the strangest smile on your face just now."

"That's because I'm so happy."

"I am, too," he said, kissing her again, then rolling onto his side.

They lay together quietly and dozed off again. Jondalar woke before Ayla did, and he watched her while she slept. The strange little smile appeared again and made him wonder what she was dreaming of. He couldn't resist. He kissed her softly and caressed her breast. She opened her eyes. They were dilated, dark and liquid, and full of deep secrets.

He kissed each eyelid, then nibbled playfully at an earlobe and then a nipple. She smiled at him when he reached for her mound and felt her soft hair, receptive, if not quite ready again, making him wish they were just beginning instead of just through. Suddenly he held her tight, kissed her fiercely, stroked her body, her breasts and hips and thighs. He could hardly keep his hands away from her, as though coming so close to losing her had created a need as deep as the crevasse that almost took her. He couldn't touch her enough, hold her enough, love her enough.

"I never thought I'd fall in love," he said, relaxing again and idly caressing the dip at the small of her back and the smooth mound beyond. "Why did I have to travel beyond the end of the Great Mother River to find a woman I could love?"

He had been thinking about that ever since he woke up and realized they were almost home. It was good to be on this side of the glacier, but he was full of anticipation, wondering about everyone, and eager to see them.

"Because my totem meant you for me. The Cave Lion guided you."

"Then why did the Mother cause us to be born so far apart?"

Ayla lifted her head and looked at him. "I've been learning, but I still know very little about the ways of the Great Earth Mother, and not much more about the protective spirits of the Clan totems, but I know this: you found me.''

"And then I almost lost you." A sudden rush of cold fear clutched at him. "Ayla, what would I do if I lost you?" he said, his voice hoarse with the emotion he seldom showed openly. He rolled over, covering her body with his, and buried his head in her neck, holding her so tightly she could hardly breathe. "What would I do?"

She clung to him, wishing there was some way she could become a part of him, and she gratefully opened herself to him when she felt his need swell again. With an urgency as demanding as his love, he took her as she came to him with a need as driving.

It was over even more quickly, and with the release, the tension of their fierce emotion melted into a warm afterglow. When he started to move aside, she held him, wanting to cling to the intensity of the moment.

"I wouldn't want to live without you, Jondalar," Ayla said, picking up the conversation begun before their lovemaking. "A piece of me would go with you to the spirit world, I'd never be whole again. But we're lucky. Think of all the people who never find love, and those who love someone who cannot love them back."

"Like Ranec?"

"Yes, like Ranec. I still hurt inside when I think of him."

Jondalar rolled over and sat up. "I feel sorry for him. I liked Ranec—or I could have." Suddenly he was eager to be moving. "We'll never get to Dalanar's this way," he said, starting to roll up sleeping furs. "I can't wait to see him again."

"But first, we have to find the horses," Ayla said.

43

Ayla got up and went outside the tent. A mist hovered close to the ground and the air felt cold and damp on her bare skin. She could hear the roar of the waterfall in the distance, but the vapor thickened into a dense fog near the back end of the lake, a long narrow body of greenish water, so cloudy it was nearly opaque.

No fish lived in such a place, she was sure, just as no vegetation grew along the edge; it was too new for life, too raw. There was only water and stone, and a quality of time before time, of ancient beginnings before life began. Ayla shivered and felt a stark taste of Her terrible loneliness before the Great Mother Earth gave birth to all living things.

She stopped to pass her water, then hurried across the sharp-edged gravel shore, waded in, then ducked down. It was icy cold and gritty with silt. She wanted to bathe—it hadn't been possible while they were crossing the ice—but not in this water. She didn't mind the cold so much, but she wanted clear, fresh water.

She started back to the tent to dress and help Jondalar

pack up. On the way, she looked through the mist across the lifeless landscape to a hint of trees below. Suddenly she smiled.

"There you are!" she said, sounding a loud whistle.

Jondalar was out of the tent in an instant. He smiled as broadly as Ayla to see the two horses galloping toward them. Wolf followed along behind, and Ayla thought he looked pleased with himself. He hadn't been around that morning, and she wondered if he had played any part in the horses' return. She shook her head, realizing she would probably never know.

They greeted each horse with hugs, caressing strokes, friendly scratches, and words of affection. Ayla checked them over carefully at the same time, wanting to be sure they had not injured themselves. The horse boot on Whinney's right rear foot was missing and the mare seemed to flinch when Ayla examined her leg. Could she have broken through the ice at the edge of the glacier and, in pulling free, torn off the boot and bruised her leg? It was the only thing she could think of.

Ayla removed the rest of the mare's boots, lifting each leg to untie them while Jondalar stood close to steady the animal. Racer still had all his horse boots, although Jondalar noticed they were wearing thin over the sharp hooves; even mammoth hide would not last long worn over hooves.

When they had gathered all their things together and gone to drag the bowl boat closer, they discovered the bottom was wet and soggy. It had developed a leak.

"I don't think I'd want to try getting across a river in this anymore," Jondalar said. "Do you think we should leave it?"

"We have to, unless we want to drag it ourselves. We don't have the poles for the travois. We left them behind when we came flying down that ice, and there are no trees around here for new ones," Ayla said.

"Well, that settles it!" Jondalar said. "It's a good thing we don't need to haul rocks anymore, and we've lightened our load so much that I think we could carry everything ourselves, even without the horses."

"If they hadn't come back, that's what we'd be doing while we were looking for them," Ayla said, "but I am so glad they found us."

"I was worried about them, too," Jondalar said.

• • •

As they descended the steep southwestern face of the ancient massif that supported the harrowing ice field on its worn summit, a light rain fell, flushing out pockets of dirty snow that filled shaded hollows in the open spruce forest they passed through. But a watercolor wash of green tinged the brown earth of a sloping meadow and brushed the tips of shrubs nearby. Below, through openings in the misty fog, they caught glimpses of a river curling from west to north, forced by the surrounding highlands to follow a deep rift valley. Across the river to the south, the rugged alpine foreland faded into a purple haze, but rising wraithlike out of the haze was the high mountain range with ice halfway down its slopes.

"You're going to like Dalanar," Jondalar was saying as they rode comfortably side by side. "You'll like all the Lanzadonii. Most of them used to be Zelandonii, like me."

"What made him decide to start a new Cave?"

"I'm not sure. I was so young when he and my mother parted, I didn't really get to know him until I went to live with him, and he taught Joplaya and me how to work the stone. I don't think he decided to settle and start a new Cave until he met Jerika, but he chose this place because he found the flint mine. People were already talking about Lanzadonii stone when I was a boy," Jondalar explained.

"Jerika is his mate, and . . . Joplaya . . . is your cousin, right?"

"Yes. Close-cousin. Jerika's daughter, born to Dalanar's hearth. She's a good flint knapper, too, but don't ever tell her I said so. She's a great tease, always joking. I wonder if she's found a mate. Great Mother! It's been so long. They are going to be so surprised to see us!"

"Jondalar!" Ayla said in a loud, urgent whisper. He pulled up short. "Look over there, near those trees. There's a deer!"

The man smiled. "Let's get it!" he said, reaching for a spear as he pulled out his spear-thrower and signaled Racer with his knees. Although his method of guiding his mount was not quite the same as hers, after nearly a year of traveling, he was as good a rider as Ayla.

She turned Whinney almost in tandem—she enjoyed being free and unencumbered by the travois for a change—

and set her spear in her spear-thrower. Startled by the quick movement, the deer bounded off with high leaps, but they raced after it, coming up on either side and, with the help of the spear-throwers, dispatched the young, inexperienced buck easily. They butchered out their favorite parts and selected other choice cuts to bring as a gift to Dalanar's people, then let Wolf have his pick of what was left.

Toward evening, they found a racing, bubbling, healthy-looking stream and followed it until they came to a large open field with a few trees and some brush beside the water. They decided to make camp early and cook some of their deer meat. The rain had let up and there wasn't any hurry anymore, though they had to keep reminding themselves of that.

The following morning, when Ayla stepped out of the tent, she stopped and gaped in amazement, stunned by the sight. The landscape seemed unreal, with the quality of an especially vivid dream. It seemed impossible that they could have endured the most harshly bitter intensity of extreme winter conditions only days ago and, suddenly, it was spring!

"Jondalar! Oh, Jondalar. Come and see!"

The man put his sleepy head out of the opening, and she watched his smile grow.

They were at a lower elevation, and the rainy drizzle and fog of the day before had given way to a bright new sun. The sky was a rich azure blue decorated with mounds of white. Trees and brush were flocked with the fresh bright green of new leaves and the grass in the field looked good enough to eat. Flowers—jonquils, lilies, columbines, irises, and more—bloomed in profusion. Birds of every color and many varieties darted and wheeled through the air, chirping and singing.

Ayla recognized most of them—thrushes, nightingales, bluethroats, nutcrackers, black-headed woodpeckers, and river warblers—and whistled their song back to them. Jondalar got up and came out of the tent in time to watch with admiration while she patiently coaxed a gray shrike to her hand.

"I don't know how you do that," he said, as the bird flew away.

Ayla smiled. "I'm going to look for something fresh and delicious to eat this morning," she said.

Wolf was gone again, and Ayla was sure he was exploring

or hunting; spring brought adventures for him, too. She headed toward the horses, who were in the middle of the spring meadow grazing on the fine short blades of sweet grass. It was the rich season, the time of growth throughout the land.

For most of the year the broad plains surrounding the miles-thick sheets of ice, and the high mountain meadows, were dry and cold. Only scant rain or snow managed to fall on the land; the glaciers usually captured most of the moisture circulating in the air for themselves. Though permafrost was as pervasive on the ancient steppes as in the wetter northern tundras of later times, the glacier-driven winds kept the summers arid, and the land dry and firm, with few bogs. In winter, the winds kept the light snows blown into drifts, leaving large sections of the frozen ground bare of snow, but covered with grass that had dried into hay; feed that maintained the uncountable numbers of huge grazing animals.

But not all grasslands are the same. To create the rich abundance of the Ice Age plains, it wasn't so much the amount of precipitation—so long as it was sufficient—as when it fell; a combination of moisture and drying winds in the right proportions and at the right times made the difference.

Because of the angle of incoming sunlight, in lower latitudes the sun begins to warm the earth not long after the winter solstice. Where snow or ice have accumulated, most of the early spring sunlight is reflected back into space, and the little that is absorbed and converted to heat must be used to melt the snow cover before plants can grow.

But on the ancient grasslands, where winds had laid the plains bare, the sun poured its energy onto the dark soil, and received a warm welcome. The dry, frozen top layers of permafrost began to warm and thaw, and though it was still cold, the wealth of solar energy impelled seeds and extensive roots to prepare to send up shoots. But water in usable form was necessary if they were to flourish.

The glistening ice resisted the warming rays of spring, reflecting back the sunlight. But with so much moisture stored in the mountain-high icy sheets, it could not entirely reject the sun's advances or its caress of warming winds. The tops of the glaciers began to melt, and some water trickled down through the fissures and slowly began to fill streams, and then rivers, which would bring the precious liquid to the parched land later in summer. But even more important were the fogs and the mists evaporating off the glacial masses of frozen water, because they filled the skies with rain clouds.

In spring, the warm sunlight caused the great mass of ice to give off moisture rather than to take it. For almost the only time during the entire year, rain fell, not on the glacier, but on the thirsty and fertile land that bounded it. An Ice Age summer could be hot, but it was brief; the primeval spring was long and wet, and plant growth was explosive and profuse.

Ice Age animals also did their growing in spring when everything was fresh and green, and rich in the nutrients they needed, at just the time they needed them. By nature, whether the season is lush or dry, spring is the time of the year when animals add size to young bones or to old tusks and horns, or grow new and bigger antlers, or shed thick winter coats and begin new ones. Because spring started early and lasted long, the growing season for animals was long as well, which encouraged their lavish size, and the impressive horny adornments.

During the long spring, all the species partook of the herbaceous green bounty indiscriminately, but with the end of the growing season they faced fierce competition from each other for the maturing and less nutritious or less digestible grasses and herbs. The competition did not express itself in squabbling over who would eat first or most, or in guarding boundaries. Herding animals of the plains were not territorial. They migrated over great distances and were highly social, seeking the company of their own kind as they traveled, and sharing their ranges with others that were adapted to open grasslands.

But whenever more than one species of animal had nearly identical eating and living habits, invariably only one would prevail. The others would evolve new ways to exploit another niche, utilize some other element of the available food, migrate to a new area, or die off. None of the many different grazing and browsing animals were in direct competition with each other for exactly the same food.

Fighting was always between males of the same kind, and was saved for rutting season, when often the mere display of a particularly imposing rack of antlers or pair of horns or tusks was enough to establish dominance and the right to breed—genetically compelling reasons for the magnificent embellishments that the rich spring growth encouraged.

But once the surfeit of spring was over, life for the itinerant dwellers of the steppes settled into established patterns, and it was never as easy. In summer they had to maintain the spectacular growth spring had wrought and fill out and put on fat for the harsh season ahead. Autumn brought the demanding rutting season for some; for others the growth of heavy fur and other protective measures. But hardest of all was winter; in winter they had to survive.

Winter determined the carrying capacity of the land; winter decided who would live and who would die. Winter was hard on males, with a larger body size and heavy social adornments to maintain or regrow. Winter was hard on females, who were smaller in size because they had not only to sustain themselves with essentially the same amount of available food, but also the next generation either developing inside them, or nursing, or both. But winter was particularly hard on the young, who lacked the size of adults to store reserves, and spent what they had accumulated on growth. If they could survive their first year, their chances were much better.

On the dry, cold, ancient grasslands near the glaciers, the great diversity of animals shared the complex and productive land and were maintained because eating and living habits of one species fit in between or around those of another. Even the carnivores had preferred prey. But an inventive, creative new species, one that didn't so much adapt to the environment as alter the environment to suit itself, was beginning to make its presence felt.

Ayla was strangely quiet when they stopped for a rest near another gurgling mountain stream, to finish the venison and fresh greens they had cooked that morning.

"It's not very far now. Thonolan and I stopped near here when we left," Jondalar said.

"It's breathtaking," she answered, but only part of her mind appreciated the breathtaking view.

"Why so quiet, Ayla?"

"I've been thinking about your kin. It makes me realize, I don't have any kin."

"You have kin! What about the Mamutoi? Aren't you Ayla of the Mamutoi?"

"It's not the same. I miss them, and I'll always love

them, but it wasn't so hard to leave. It was harder the other time, when I had to leave Durc behind." A look of pain filled her eyes.

"Ayla, I know it must have been difficult to leave a son." He took her in his arms. "It wouldn't bring him back, but the Mother may give you other children . . . someday . . . perhaps even children of my spirit."

She didn't seem to hear him. "They said Durc was deformed, but he wasn't. He was Clan, but he was mine, too. He was part of both. They didn't think I was deformed, just ugly, and I was taller than any man of the Clan . . . big and ugly . . ."

"Ayla, you are not big and ugly. You are beautiful, and remember, my kin are your kin."

She looked up at him. "Until you came, I had no one, Jondalar. Now I have you to love and maybe, someday, a child of yours. That would make me happy," she said, smiling.

Her smile relieved him, and her mention of a child even more. He looked up at the sun's position in the sky. "We won't make it to Dalanar's cave today if we don't hurry. Come on, Ayla, the horses need a good run. I'll race you across the meadow. I don't think I could stand another night in the tent when we're so close."

Wolf bounded out of the woods, full of energy and playfulness. He jumped up, put his paws on her chest, and licked her jaw. This was her family, she thought, as she grabbed his neck fur. This magnificent wolf, the faithful and patient mare, the spirited stallion, and the man, the wonderful caring man. Soon she would be meeting his family.

She fell silent while she packed the few things; then suddenly she started digging things out of a different pack. "Jondalar, I'm going to take a bath in this stream and put on a clean tunic and leggings," she said, taking off the leather tunic she had been wearing.

"Why don't you wait until we get there. You'll freeze, Ayla. That water is probably straight off the glacier."

"I don't care, I don't want to meet your kin all dirty and travel stained."

They came to a river, cloudy green with glacial runoff, and running high, though the rushing water would be much higher when it reached its full volume later in the season. They turned east, upstream, until they found a place shallow enough to ford, then climbed in a southeasterly direction. It was late afternoon when they reached a gradual slope that leveled out near a rock wall. The dark hole of a cave was tucked under an overhanging ledge.

A young woman was seated on the ground, her back to them, surrounded by broken chips and nodules of flint. She held a punch, a pointed wooden stick, to a core of the dark gray stone with one hand, concentrating on the exact placement, and preparing to hit the punch with a heavy bone hammer held in the other. She was so absorbed in her task that she didn't notice Jondalar slipping up silently behind her.

"Keep practicing, Joplaya. Someday you'll be as good as I am," he said with a grin.

The bone mallet came down wrong, shattering the blade she was about to flake off as she whirled around, a look of stunned disbelief on her face.

"Jondalar! Oh, Jondalar! Is it really you?" she cried, throwing herself into his arms. With his arms around her waist, he picked her up and spun her around. She clung to him as though she never wanted to let him go. "Mother! Dalanar! Jondalar's back! Jondalar came back!" she shouted.

People came running out of the cave, and an older man, as tall as Jondalar, raced toward him. They grabbed each other, stood back and looked, then hugged again.

Ayla signaled Wolf, who crowded close to her as she stood back and watched, holding the lead ropes of both horses.

"So, you came back! You were gone so long, I didn't think you would," the man said.

Then, over Jondalar's shoulder, the older man spied a most astounding sight. Two horses, with baskets and bundles fastened to them, and hides draped across their backs, and a large wolf, were hovering close to a tall woman, dressed in a fur parka and leggings cut in an unusual style and decorated with unfamiliar patterns. Her hood was thrown back, and the woman's deep golden hair cascaded around her face in waves. There was a decidedly foreign cast to her features, rather like the unfamiliar cut of her clothing, but it only added to her outstanding beauty.

"I don't see your brother, but you did not return alone," the man said.

"Thonolan is dead," Jondalar said, closing his eyes involuntarily. "I would be, too, if it wasn't for Ayla."

"I'm sorry to hear that. I liked the boy. Willomar and your mother will be grief-stricken. But I notice your taste in women has not changed. You always did have a liking for beautiful Zelandonia."

Jondalar wondered why he thought Ayla was One Who Served the Mother. Then he looked at her, surrounded by the animals, and suddenly saw her as the older man would, and he smiled. He strode to the edge of the clearing, took Racer's lead, and started walking back, followed by Ayla, Whinney, and Wolf.

"Dalanar of the Lanzadonii, please welcome Ayla of the Mamutoi," he said.

Dalanar held out both hands, palms up, in the greeting of openness and friendship. Ayla grasped them with both of hers.

"In the name of Doni, the Great Earth Mother, I welcome you, Ayla of the Mamutoi," Dalanar said.

"I greet you, Dalanar of the Lanzadonii," Ayla replied, with the proper formality.

"You speak our language well for someone from so far away. It is my pleasure to meet you." His formality was belied by his smile. He had noticed her manner of speaking and thought it most intriguing.

"Jondalar taught me to speak," she said, hardly able to keep from staring. She glanced at Jondalar, then back at Dalanar, stunned by their resemblance.

Dalanar's long blond hair was a little thinner on top and his waist a little thicker, but he had the same intensely blue eyes—a few creases at the corners—and the same high forehead, his worry lines etched a little deeper. His voice had the same quality, too, the same pitch, the same tone. He even stressed the word *pleasure* the same way, giving it the hint of a double meaning. It was uncanny. The warmth of his hands started a tingling response in her. His similarity even confused her body for a moment.

Dalanar felt her response and smiled Jondalar's smile, understanding the reason and liking her for it. With that strange accent, he thought, she must come from someplace quite far away. When he dropped her hands, the wolf suddenly approached him, quite fearlessly, although he couldn't say he felt the same way himself. Wolf insinuated his head under Dalanar's hand, looking for attention, as though he knew the man. To his own surprise, Dalanar found himself stroking the handsome animal, as though it were perfectly natural to pet a large living wolf.

Jondalar was grinning. "Wolf thinks you're me. Everyone always said we looked alike. Next you'll be on Racer's back." He held the lead rope toward the man.

"Did you say 'Racer's back'?" Dalanar said.

"Yes. Most of the way here, we rode on the backs of those horses; Racer is the name I gave the stallion," Jondalar explained. "Ayla's horse is Whinney, and this big beast that's taken such a liking to you is called 'Wolf.' That's the Mamutoi word for a wolf."

"How did you ever get a wolf, and horses . . . ." Dalanar began.

"Dalanar, where are your manners? Don't you think other people want to meet her and hear their stories?"

Ayla, still slightly flustered by Dalanar's amazing resemblance to Jondalar, turned to the one who spoke—and found herself staring again. The woman resembled no one Ayla had ever seen before. Her hair, pulled back from her face into a roll at the back of her head, was glossy black, streaked with gray at the temples. But it was her face that held Ayla's attention. It was round and flat with high cheekbones, a tiny nose, and dark slanting eyes. The woman's smile contradicted her stern voice and Dalanar beamed as he looked down at her.

"Jerika!" Jondalar said, smiling with delight.

"Jondalar! It's so good to have you back!" They hugged with obvious affection. "Since this great bear of a man of mine has no manners, why don't you introduce me to your companion? And then you can tell me why those animals stand there and don't run away," the woman said.

She moved between the two men and was dwarfed by them. They were exactly the same height, and the top of her head barely reached midway up their chests. Her walk was quick and energetic. She reminded Ayla of a bird, an impression reinforced by her diminutive size.

"Jerika of the Lanzadonii, please greet Ayla of the Mamutoi. She is the one responsible for the behavior of the animals," Jondalar said, beaming at the small woman with Dalanar's expression. "She can tell you better than I why they don't run away."

"You are welcome here, Ayla of the Mamutoi," Jerika

said, with hands outstretched. "And the animals as well, if you can promise they will continue such uncommon ways." She was eying Wolf as she spoke.

"I greet you, Jerika of the Lanzadonii." Ayla returned her smile. The small woman's grip had a strength that was surprising and, Ayla sensed, a character to match. "The wolf will not harm anyone, unless someone threatens one of us. He is friendly, but very protective. The horses are nervous around strangers and may rear if they are crowded, which could be dangerous. It would be better if people would stay away from them in the beginning, until they get to know everyone better."

"That's sensible, but I am glad you told us," she replied, then looked at Ayla with disconcerting directness. "You have come a long way. The Mamutoi live beyond the end of Donau."

"Do you know the land of the Mammoth Hunters?" Ayla asked, surprised.

"Yes, and even farther east, though I don't remember as much of that. Hochaman will be glad to tell you about it. Nothing would please him more than a new ear to listen to his stories. My mother and he came from a land near the Endless Sea, as far east as the land goes. I was born on the way. We lived with many people, sometimes for several years. I remember the Mamutoi. Good people. Fine hunters. They wanted us to stay with them," Jerika related.

"Why didn't you?"

"Hochaman wasn't ready to settle down. His dream was to travel to the ends of the world, to see how far the land would go. We met Dalanar not long after my mother died and decided to stay and help him get the flint mine started. But Hochaman has lived to see his dream," Jerika said, glancing at her tall mate. "He has traveled all the way from the Endless Sea of the east to the Great Waters of the west. Dalanar helped him finish his Journey, some years ago, carried him on his back most of the way. Hochaman shed tears when he saw the great western sea, and he washed them away with salt water. He can't walk much now, but no one has made so long a Journey as Hochaman."

"Or you, Jerika," Dalanar added proudly. "You've traveled nearly as far."

"Hmmmf." She shrugged. "It's not as though I made the choice. But here I scold Dalanar, and then I talk too much."

Jondalar had his arm around the waist of the woman he had surprised. "I'd like to meet your traveling companion," she said.

"I'm sorry, of course," Jondalar said. "Ayla of the Mamutoi, this is my cousin, Joplaya of the Lanzadonii."

"I welcome you, Ayla of the Mamutoi," she said, holding out her hands.

"I greet you, Joplaya of the Lanzadonii," Ayla said, suddenly conscious of her accent and glad she had a clean tunic under her parka. Joplaya was as tall as she, perhaps a shade taller. She had her mother's high cheekbones, but her face was not as flat and her nose was like Jondalar's, only more delicate and finely chiseled. Smooth dark eyebrows matched long black hair, and thick black lashes framed eyes with a hint of her mother's slant, but a dazzling green!

Joplaya was a stunningly beautiful woman.

"I am pleased to greet you," Ayla said. "Jondalar has spoken of you so often."

"I'm pleased he didn't forget me altogether," Joplaya replied. She stepped back and Jondalar's arm found her waist again.

Others had crowded around, and Ayla went through a formal greeting with each member of the Cave. They were all curious about the woman Jondalar had brought back, but their scrutiny and questions made her uncomfortable, and she was glad when Jerika intervened.

"I think we should save some questions for later. I'm sure they both have many stories to tell, but they must be tired. Come, Ayla, I will show you where you can stay. Do the animals require anything special?"

"I just need to remove their loads and find a place for them to graze. Wolf will stay inside with us, if you don't object," Ayla said.

She saw that Jondalar was deep in conversation with Joplaya, and she unloaded the packs from both horses herself, but he hurried over to help her take their things into the cave.

"I think I know just the place for the horses," he said. "I'll take them there. Do you want to keep the lead on Whinney? I'm going to tie Racer down with a long rope."

"No, I don't think so. She'll stay near Racer." Ayla noticed that he was feeling so entirely comfortable, he didn't even have to ask. But why not? These people were his kin. "I'll go with you, though. To settle her in."

They walked to a small grassy dell with a creek running through it that was off around the side. Wolf came with them. After he tied Racer's lead securely, Jondalar started back. "Are you coming?" he asked.

"I'll stay with Whinney a little longer," she said.

"Why don't I go carry our things in, then?"

"Yes, go ahead." He seemed eager to get back, not that she blamed him. She signaled the wolf to stay with her. Everything was new to him, too. They all needed some time to settle in, except for Jondalar. When she returned she looked for him and found him deep in conversation with Joplaya. She hesitated to interrupt.

"Ayla," he said, when he noticed her. "I was telling Joplaya about Wymez. Later, will you show her the spear point he gave you?"

She nodded. Jondalar turned back to Joplaya. "Wait until you see it. The Mamutoi are excellent mammoth hunters, they tip their spears with flint instead of bone. It pierces thick hides better, especially if the blades are thin. Wymez developed a new technique. The point is bifacially knapped, but not like a crude axehead. He heats the stone—that makes the difference. Finer, thinner flakes sheer off. He can make a point that is longer than my hand with a cross-section so thin and an edge so sharp, you won't believe it."

They were standing so close together their bodies were touching as Jondalar excitedly explained the details of the new technique, and their casual intimacy made Ayla uneasy. They had lived together during their adolescent years. What secrets had he told her? What joys and sorrows had they known together? What frustrations and triumphs had they shared as they both learned the difficult art of knapping flint? How much better did Joplaya know him than she did?

Before, they had both been strangers to the people they met on their Journey. Now, only she was a stranger.

He turned back to Ayla. "Why don't I go and get that point? What basket was it in?" he asked, already on his way.

She told him and smiled nervously at the dark-haired woman after he left, but neither of them spoke. Jondalar was back almost instantly.

"Joplaya, I told Dalanar to come—I've been wanting to show him this point. Wait until you see it."

He carefully opened the wrapped package and uncovered a beautifully made flint point just as Dalanar came up. At the sight of the fine spear point, Dalanar took it from Jondalar and examined it closely.

"It's a masterwork! I have never seen such fine craftsmanship," Dalanar exclaimed. "Look at this, Joplaya. It's bifacially worked, but very thin, small flakes are removed. Think of the control, the concentration it must have taken. The feel of this flint is different, and the sheen. It seems almost . . . oily. Where did you get this? Do they have a different kind of flint in the east?"

"No, it's a new process, developed by a Mamutoi man named Wymez. He's the only knapper I've ever met who compares with you, Dalanar. He heats the stone. That's what gives it the sheen, and the feel, but even better, after it's heated, you can remove those fine flakes," Jondalar was explaining with great animation.

Ayla found herself watching him.

"They almost chip off by themselves—that's what gives you the control. I'll show you how he does it. I'm not as good as he is—I need to work on perfecting my technique—but you'll see what I mean. I want to get some good flint while we're here. With the horses, we can carry more weight, and I'd like to bring some Lanzadonii stone home with me."

"This is your home, too, Jondalar," Dalanar said quietly. "But, yes, we can go to the mine tomorrow and quarry some fresh stone. I'd like to see how this is done, but is this really a spear point? It looks so thin, and graceful, it almost seems too fragile to hunt with."

"They use these spear points for hunting mammoth. It does break more easily, but the sharp flint pierces the thick hide better than a bone point and will slide in between ribs," Jondalar said. "I have something else to show you, too. I developed it when I was recovering from the cave lion mauling, in Ayla's valley. It's a spear-thrower. With it, a spear will fly twice as far. Wait until you see how it works!"

"I think they want us to come and eat, Jondalar," Dalanar said, noticing people at the mouth of the cave, beckoning. "Everyone will want to hear your stories. Come inside where you can be comfortable and all can hear. You tease us with these animals that obey your wishes, and comments about cave lion maulings, spear-throwers, new stone-knapping techniques. What other adventures and marvels do you have to share?"

Jondalar laughed. "We haven't even begun. Would you

believe we have seen stones that make fire and stones that burn? Dwellings made out of the bones of mammoths, ivory points that pull thread, and huge rivercraft used to hunt fish so big, it would take five men your size, one on top of the other, to reach tip to tail.''

Ayla had never seen Jondalar so happy and relaxed, so free and unrestrained, and she realized how glad he was to be with his people.

He put an arm around both Ayla and Joplaya as they walked toward the cave. "Have you chosen a mate yet, Joplaya?'' Jondalar asked. "I didn't see anyone who seemed to have a claim on you.''

Joplaya laughed. "No, I've been waiting for you, Jondalar.''

"There you go, making a joke again,'' Jondalar said, chuckling. He turned to explain to Ayla. "Close-cousins can't mate, you know.''

"I have it all planned,'' Joplaya continued, "I thought we'd run off together and start our own Cave, like Dalanar did. But, of course, we'd only allow flint knappers.'' Her laugh seemed forced, and she looked only at Jondalar.

"See what I mean, Ayla?'' Jondalar said, turning to her but giving Joplaya a squeeze. "Always joking. Joplaya is the worst tease.'' Ayla wasn't sure she understood the joke.

"Seriously, Joplaya, you must be promised anyway.''

"Echozar has asked, but I haven't decided yet.''

"Echozar? I don't think I know him. Is he Zelandonii?''

"He's Lanzadonii. He joined us a few years ago. Dalanar saved his life, found him almost drowned. I think he's still in the cave. He's shy; you'll understand why when you meet him. He looks . . . well, different. He doesn't like meeting strangers, he says he doesn't want to come with us to the Zelandonii Summer Meeting. But he's sweet when you get to know him, and he'd do anything for Dalanar.''

"Are you going to the Summer Meeting this year? I hope so, at least for the Matrimonial. Ayla and I are going to be mated.'' This time he gave Ayla a squeeze.

"I don't know,'' Joplaya said, looking at the ground. Then she looked at him. "I always knew you would never mate that Marona woman who was waiting for you the year you left but I didn't think you'd bring a woman back with you.''

Jondalar flushed at the mention of the woman he had

promised to mate and left behind, and he didn't notice Ayla stiffen as Joplaya hurried toward a man just coming out of the cave.

"Jondalar! That man!" He caught the startled tone in her voice and turned to look at her. She was ashen.

"What's wrong, Ayla?"

"He looks like Durc! Or maybe the way my son will look when he grows up. Jondalar, that man is part Clan!"

Jondalar looked closer. It was true. The man Joplaya was urging toward them had the look of the Clan. But as they approached, Ayla noticed one striking difference between this man and the men of the Clan she knew. He was almost as tall as she.

When he neared, she made a motion with her hand. It was subtle, hardly noticeable to anyone else, but the man's large brown eyes opened wide with surprise.

"Where did you learn that?" he asked, making the same gesture. His voice was deep, but clear and distinct. He had no problem speaking; a sure sign he was a mixture.

"I was raised by a clan. They found me when I was a little girl. I don't remember any family before that."

"A clan raised you? They cursed my mother because she gave birth to me," he said bitterly. "What clan would raise you?"

"I didn't think her accent was Mamutoi," Jerika interjected. Several people were standing around them.

Jondalar took a deep breath and squared his shoulders. He had known from the beginning Ayla's background would come out sooner or later. "When I met her, she couldn't even talk, Jerika, at least not with words. But she saved my life after I was attacked by a cave lion. She was adopted by the Mamutoi into the Mammoth Hearth because she is so skilled in healing."

"She is Mamut? One Who Serves the Mother? Where is her mark? I don't see any tattoo on her cheek," Jerika said.

"Ayla learned to heal from the woman who raised her, a medicine woman of the people she calls Clan—flatheads—but she's as good as any zelandoni. The Mamut was only starting to train her t Serve the Mother before we left; she was never initiated. ' hat's why she has no mark," Jondalar explained.

"I knew she was zelandoni. She has to be to control animals like that, but how could she learn healing from a flathead woman?'' Dalanar exclaimed. ''Before I met Echozar, I thought they were little more than animals. I understand from him that they can talk, in a way, and now you say they have healers. You should have told me, Echozar.''

''How would I know? I'm not a *flathead*!'' Echozar spat the word out. ''I only knew my mother, and Andovan.''

Ayla was surprised at the venom in his voice. ''You said your mother was cursed? And yet she survived to raise you? She must have been a remarkable woman.''

Echozar looked directly into the gray-blue eyes of the tall blond woman. There was no hesitation, no drawing back to avoid staring at him. He felt strangely drawn to this woman he had never seen before, comfortable with her.

''She didn't talk about it much,'' Echozar said. ''She was attacked by some men, who killed her mate when he tried to protect her. He was the brother of the leader of her clan, and she was blamed for his death. The leader said she brought bad luck. But later, when she learned she was expecting a child, he took her as a second woman. When I was born, he said it proved she was a bad-luck woman. She had not only killed her mate, she gave birth to a deformed baby. Then he cursed her, a death curse.'' He was talking more openly to this woman than he normally did, and he was surprised at himself.

''I'm not sure what that means—a death curse,'' Echozar continued. ''She only told me once, and then she couldn't finish. She said everyone turned away from her, as though they could not see her. They said she was dead, and even though she tried to make them look at her, it was like she wasn't there, like she was dead. It must have been terrible.''

''It was,'' Ayla said softly. ''It's hard to go on living if you don't exist to the ones you love.'' Her eyes misted with memory.

''My mother took me and left them to go and die, like she was supposed to, but Andovan found her. He was old even then, and living alone. He never did tell me why he left his Cave, it was something about a cruel leader . . .''

''Andovan . . .'' Ayla interrupted. ''Was he S'Armunai?''

''Yes, I think so,'' Echozar said. ''He didn't talk about his people much.''

''We know about their cruel leader,'' Jondalar said, grimly.

''Andovan took care of us,'' Echozar continued. ''He

taught me to hunt. He learned to speak the sign language of the Clan from my mother, but she never could say more than a few words. I learned both, though it surprised her that I could make his word sounds. Andovan died a few years ago, and with him my mother's will to live. The death curse finally took her.''

"What did you do then?" Jondalar asked.

"I lived alone."

"That is not easy," Ayla said.

"No, it's not easy. I tried to find someone to live with. No clan would let me near them. They threw stones at me and said I was deformed and unlucky. No Cave would have anything to do with me, either. They said I was an abomination of mixed spirits, half-man and half-animal. After a while I got tired of trying. I didn't want to be alone anymore. One day I jumped off a cliff into the river. The next thing I knew, Dalanar was looking at me. He took me to his Cave. Now I am Echozar of the Lanzadonii," he finished proudly, glancing at the tall man he idolized.

Ayla thought of her son, grateful he had been accepted as a baby, and grateful there were people who loved him and wanted him when she had to leave him behind.

"Echozar, don't hate your mother's people," she said. "It is not that they are bad, they are just so ancient that it's hard for them to change. Their traditions go back so far, and they don't understand new ways."

"And they are people," Jondalar said to Dalanar. "That's one thing I've learned on this Journey. We met a couple just before we started over the glacier—that's another story—but they're planning meetings about the problems they've been having with some of us, especially some young Losadunai men. Someone has even approached them about trading."

"Flatheads having meetings? Trading? This world is changing faster than I can understand," Dalanar said. "Until I met Echozar, I wouldn't have believed it."

"People may call them flatheads, and animals, but you know your mother was a brave woman, Echozar," Ayla said, then held out her hands to him. "I know how it feels to have no people. Now I am Ayla of the Mamutoi. Will you welcome me, Echozar of the Lanzadonii?"

He took her hands and she felt them tremble. "You are welcome here, Ayla of the Mamutoi," he said.

Jondalar stepped forward with his hands outstretched. "I greet you, Echozar of the Lanzadonii," he said.

"I welcome you, Jondalar of the Zelandonii," Echozar said, "but you don't need to be welcomed here. I've heard about the son of Dalanar's hearth. There's no doubt you were born of his spirit. You are much like him."

Jondalar grinned. "Everyone says so, but don't you think his nose is a little bigger than mine?"

"I don't. I think yours is bigger than mine," Dalanar laughed, clapping the younger man's shoulder. "Come inside. The food is getting cold."

Ayla lingered a moment to talk to Echozar, and when she turned to go in, Joplaya detained her.

"I want to talk to Ayla, Echozar, but don't go in yet. I want to talk to you, too," she said. He walked away quickly to leave the two women alone, but not before Ayla saw the adoration in his eyes when he looked at Joplaya.

"Ayla, I . . ." Joplaya began. "I . . . think I know why Jondalar loves you. I want to say . . . I want to wish you both happiness."

Ayla studied the dark-haired woman. She sensed a change in her, a drawing in, a feeling of grim finality. Suddenly Ayla knew why she had been so uneasy about the woman.

"Thank you, Joplaya. I love him very much; it would be hard to live without him. It would leave me with a great emptiness inside that would be very hard to bear."

"Yes, very hard to bear," Joplaya said, closing her eyes for a moment.

"Aren't you going to come in and eat?" Jondalar said, coming back out of the cave.

"You go ahead, Ayla. There's something I have to do first."

44

Echozar glanced at the large piece of obsidian, then looked away. The ripples in the shiny black glass distorted his reflection, but nothing could change it, and he didn't want to see himself today. He was dressed in a deerskin tunic, fringed with tufts of fur and decorated with beads made of hollow bird bones, dyed quills, and sharp animal teeth. He had never owned anything so fine. Joplaya had made it for him, for the ceremony that officially adopted him into the First Cave of the Lanzadonii.

As he walked into the main area of the cave, he felt the soft leather, smoothing it with reverence knowing her hands had made it. It almost hurt just to think about her. He had loved her from the first. It was she who had talked to him, listened to him, tried to draw him out. He would never have faced all those Zelandonii at the Summer Meeting that year if it hadn't been for her, and when he saw how the men flocked around her, he wanted to die. It had taken months to work up the courage to ask her: How could anyone who looked like him dare to dream of a woman like her? When she didn't refuse, he nourished his hope. But she had put off giving him an answer for so long, he was sure it was her way of saying no.

Then, on the day Ayla and Jondalar arrived, when she asked him if he still wanted her, he couldn't believe it. Wanted her! He had never wanted anything so much in his life. He waited for a time when he could talk to Dalanar alone. But the visitors were always with him. He didn't want to bother them. And he was afraid to ask. Only the thought of losing his one chance for more happiness than he ever dreamed possible gave him the courage.

Then Dalanar said she was Jerika's daughter and he'd have to talk it over with her, but all he had asked was did Joplaya agree, and did he love her. Did he love her? Did he love her? O Mother, did he love her!

Echozar took his place among the people waiting expectantly, and he felt his heart beat faster when he saw Dalanar get up and walk toward a hearth in the middle of the cave. A small wood sculpture of a well-rounded female was stuck in the ground in front of the hearth. The ample breasts, full stomach, and broad buttocks of the donii were accurately portrayed, but the head was little more than a knob with no features and the arms and legs were only suggested. Dalanar stood beside the hearth and faced the assembled group.

"First I want to announce that we are going to the Zelandonii Summer Meeting again this year," Dalanar began, "and we invite any who want to join us to come. It's a long trip for us, but I hope to persuade one of the younger Zelandoni to return and make a home with us. We have no Lanzadoni, and we need One Who Serves the Mother. We are growing, soon there will be a Second Cave, and someday the Lanzadonii will have their own Summer Meetings.

"There is another reason for going. Not only will the mating of Jondalar and Ayla be sanctified at the Matrimonial, we will have another reason to celebrate it this year, too."

Dalanar picked up the wooden representation of the Great Earth Mother and nodded. Echozar was nervous, even though he knew this was only an announcement ceremony and much more casual than the elaborate Matrimonial would be, with its purifying rituals and taboos. When they both stood before him, Dalanar began.

"Echozar, Son of Woman blessed of Doni, of the First Cave of the Lanzadonii, you have asked Joplaya, Daughter of Jerika mated to Dalanar, to be your mate. This is true?"

"It is true," Echozar said in a voice so weak it could hardly be heard.

"Joplaya, Daughter of Jerika mated to Dalanar . . ."

The words were not the same, but the meaning was, and Ayla shook with sobs as she recalled a similar ceremony when she stood beside a dusky man who looked at her the way Echozar looked at Joplaya.

"Ayla, don't cry, this is a happy occasion," Jondalar said, holding her tenderly.

She could hardly speak; she knew how it felt to stand beside the wrong man. But there was no hope for Joplaya, not even dreams that someday the man she loved would flout custom for her. He didn't even know she loved him, and she couldn't speak of it. He was a cousin, a close-cousin, more sibling than cousin, an unmatable man—and he loved another. Ayla felt Joplaya's pain as her own as she sobbed beside the man they both loved.

"I was thinking of the time I stood beside Ranec like that," she finally said.

Jondalar remembered only too well. He felt a constriction in his chest, a pain in his throat, and he held her fiercely. "Hey, woman, you're going to have me crying soon."

He glanced at Jerika, who sat with stiff dignity while tears rolled down her face. "Why do women always cry at these things?" he said.

Jerika looked at Jondalar with an unfathomable expression, then at Ayla sobbing quietly in his arms. "It's time she mated, time she put away impossible dreams. We can't all have the perfect man," she whispered softly, then turned back to the ceremony.

" . . . Does the First Cave of the Lanzadonii accept this mating?" Dalanar asked, looking up.

"We accept," they all replied in unison.

"Echozar, Joplaya, you have promised to mate. May Doni, the Great Earth Mother, bless your mating," the leader concluded, touching the wooden carving to the top of Echozar's head and Joplaya's stomach. He put the donii back in front of the hearth, pushing the peglike legs into the ground so it would stand unsupported.

The couple turned to face the assembled Cave, then began to walk slowly around the central hearth. In the solemn silence, the ineffable air of melancholy surrounding the compellingly beautiful woman added a quality that made her seem even more exquisitely lovely.

The man beside her was a fraction shorter. His large beaky nose protruded beyond a heavy chinless jaw that jutted forward. His overhanging brow ridges, joined at the center, were accented by thick, unruly eyebrows that crossed his forehead in a single hairy line. His arms were heavily muscled, and his huge barrel chest and long body were supported by short, hairy, bowed legs. Those were the features that marked him as Clan. But he could not be called flathead. Unlike them, he lacked the low sloping forehead that swept back into a large long head—the squashed-flat look that prompted the name. Instead, Echozar's forehead rose as straight and high above his bony brow ridges as that of any other member of the Cave.

But Echozar was incredibly ugly. The antithesis of the woman beside him. Only his eyes belied the comparison, but they overwhelmed. His large, liquid, brown eyes were so full of tender adoration for the woman he loved, they even overwhelmed the unspeakable sadness that hung in the atmosphere through which Joplaya moved.

But not even that evidence of Echozar's love could overcome the pain Ayla felt for Joplaya. She buried her head in Jondalar's chest because it hurt too much to look, though she fought to overcome the desolation of her empathy.

When the couple completed the third circuit, the silence was broken as people got up to offer good wishes. Ayla held back, trying to compose herself. Finally, urged by Jondalar, they went to extend their wishes of happiness.

"Joplaya, I'm so glad you'll be celebrating your Matrimonial with us," Jondalar said, giving her a hug. She clung to him. He was surprised at the intensity of her embrace. He had the disconcerting feeling she was saying goodbye, as though she would never see him again.

"I don't have to wish you happiness, Echozar," Ayla said. "I will wish instead that you are always as happy as you are now."

"With Joplaya, how can it be any other way?" he said. Spontaneously, she hugged him. He wasn't ugly to her, he had a comfortable, familiar look. It took him a moment to respond; beautiful women didn't hug him often, and he felt a warm affection for the golden-haired woman.

Then she turned to Joplaya. As she looked into eyes as green as Jondalar's were blue, the words she meant to say stuck in her throat. With an aching cry she reached for Joplaya, overcome by her hopeless acceptance. Joplaya held her, patting her back as though it were Ayla who needed consolation.

"It's all right, Ayla," Joplaya said, in a voice that sounded hollow, empty. Her eyes were dry. "What else could I do? I'll never find a man who loves me as much as Echozar does. I've known for a long time I would mate him. There just wasn't any reason to wait anymore."

Ayla stood back, fighting to control tears she shed for the woman who could not, and she saw Echozar move closer. He put a tentative arm around Joplaya's waist, still not quite able to believe it. He was afraid he would wake up and find it was all a dream. He didn't know he had only the shell of the woman he loved. It didn't matter. The shell was enough.

"Well, no. I didn't see it with my own eyes," Hochaman said, "and I can't say that I believed it then. But if you can ride horses and teach a wolf to follow you around, then why couldn't someone ride the back of a mammoth?"

"Where did you say this happened?" Dalanar asked.

"It was not long after we started out, far to the east. It must have been a four-toed mammoth," Hochaman said.

"A four-toed mammoth? I've never heard of such a thing," Jondalar said, "not even from the Mamutoi."

"They are not the only ones who hunt mammoths, you know," Hochaman said, "and they don't live far enough to the east. Believe me, they are close neighbors, in comparison. When you really go east, and get close to the Endless Sea, mammoths have four toes on their hind feet. They tend to be darker, too. A lot of them are almost black."

"Well, if Ayla could ride on the back of a cave lion, I don't doubt that someone could learn to ride a mammoth. What do you think?" Jondalar asked, looking at Ayla.

"If you got one young enough," she said. "I think if you raised almost any animal around people from the time it was a baby, you could teach it something. At least not to be afraid of people. Mammoths are smart; they could learn a lot. We watched the way they broke up ice for water. Many other animals used it, too.''

"They can smell it from a long distance away, too," Hochaman said. "It's a lot drier in the east, and the people there always say, 'If you run out of water, look for a mammoth.' They can go for quite a while without it, if they have to, but eventually they will lead you to it.''

"That's good to know,'' Echozar said.

"Yes, especially if you travel much,'' Joplaya said.

"I don't plan to travel much,'' he said.

"But you will be coming to the Zelandonii Summer Meeting,'' Jondalar said.

"For our Matrimonial, of course,'' Echozar said. "And I'd like to see you again.'' He smiled tentatively. "It would be nice if you and Ayla lived here.''

"Yes. I hope you will both consider our offer,'' Dalanar said. "You know this is always your home, Jondalar, and we don't have a healer, except for Jerika, who is not really trained. We need a lanzadoni and we both think Ayla would be perfect. You could visit with your mother, and return with us after the Summer Meeting.''

"Believe me, we appreciate your offer, Dalanar,'' Jondalar said, "and we will consider it.''

Ayla glanced at Joplaya. She had withdrawn, closed in on herself. She liked the woman, but they talked mostly of superficial things. Ayla could not overcome her sorrow at Joplaya's plight—she had come too close to a similar circumstance—and her own happiness was a constant reminder of Joplaya's pain. As much as she had grown to like everyone, she was glad they would be leaving in the morning.

She would particularly miss Jerika and Dalanar, and listening to their heated "discussions.'' The woman was tiny; when Dalanar held his arm out, she could walk under it with room to spare, but she had an indomitable will. She was as much a leader of the Cave as he was and argued vociferously when her opinion differed from his. Dalanar listened to her seriously, but by no means did he always yield. The welfare of his people was his main concern, and he often took the question at issue to them, but he made most decisions himself as matter-of-factly as any natural leader. He never made demands, he simply commanded respect.

After the first few times, when she misunderstood, Ayla

loved to listen to them argue, hardly bothering to hide a smile at the sight of the child-size woman in heated debate with the giant of a man. What amazed her most was the way they could interrupt a violent discussion with a tender word of affection, or to talk of something else, just as though they had not been at each other's throats, and then resume the verbal combat as though they were the bitterest of enemies. Once the arguments were resolved, they were promptly forgotten. But they seemed to enjoy the intellectual duels, and for all their difference in size, it was a battle of equals. They not only loved each other, they had great respect for each other.

The weather was warming and spring was in full bloom when Ayla and Jondalar started out again. Dalanar passed on good wishes to the Ninth Cave of the Zelandonii, and he reminded them again of his offer. They had both felt welcome, but Ayla's sensitivity to Joplaya made it difficult for her to think about living with the Lanzadonii. It would be too hard on both of them, but it was not something she could explain to Jondalar.

He did sense a peculiar strain in the relationship between the two women, though they seemed to like each other. Joplaya behaved differently toward him, too. She was more distant, didn't joke and tease the way she always had. But he had been surprised at the vehemence of her last embrace. Tears had filled her eyes. He had reminded her that he was not going on a long Journey, he had just come back, and they would see each other soon, at the Summer Meeting.

He had been relieved that they had both been so warmly welcomed, and he would definitely consider Dalanar's offer, particularly if the Zelandonii were not as accepting of Ayla. It was good to know they would have a place, but in his heart, as much as he loved Dalanar and the Lanzadonii, the Zelandonii were his people. If possible, that was where he wanted to live with Ayla.

When they finally left, Ayla felt as though a burden had lifted. In spite of the rains, she was happy to feel the weather warming, and on sunny days it was too beautiful to be sad for long. She was a woman in love traveling with her man, and going to meet his people, going to her new home. She could not help feeling ambivalent about it, though, full of hope and worry.

It was country Jondalar knew, and he greeted every familiar landmark with excitement, and often a comment or story about it. They rode through a pass between two mountain ridges, then picked up a river that twisted and turned in the right general direction. They left it at its source, and crossed several large rivers flowing from north to south across a low valley, then climbed a large massif overtopped with volcanoes, one still smoking, others quiescent. Crossing over a plateau, near the source of a river, they passed by some hot springs.

"I'm sure this is the beginning of the river that flows right in front of the Ninth Cave," Jondalar said, full of enthusiasm. "We're almost there, Ayla! We can be home by nightfall."

"Are these the hot healing waters you told me about?" Ayla asked.

"Yes. We call them Doni's Healing Waters," he said.

"Let's stay here tonight," she said.

"But we're almost there," Jondalar said, "almost at the end of our Journey, and I've been away for so long."

"That's why I want to spend the night here. It's the end of our Journey. I want to bathe in the hot water, and I want to spend one last night alone with just you, before we meet all your kin."

Jondalar looked at her and smiled. "You're right. After all this time, what's one more night? And it is the last time we'll be alone together for a long time. Besides"—his smile warmed—"I like being with you around hot springs."

They put up their tent at a site that had obviously been used before. Ayla thought the horses seemed agitated when they were let free to graze on the fresh grass of the plateau, but she had seen some young coltsfoot and sorrel leaves. When she went to pick them, she saw some spring mushrooms and then crab apple blossoms and elder shoots. She returned to their campsite holding the front of her tunic out like a basket, full of fresh greens and other delicacies.

"I think you are planning a feast," Jondalar said.

"It's not a bad idea. I saw a nest that I want to go back and check for eggs," Ayla said.

"Then what do you think of this?" he said, holding up a trout. Ayla smiled with delight. "I thought I saw it in the stream, sharpened a green stick into a gorge, and dug up a worm to thread around it. This fish bit so fast, it was almost like it was waiting for me."

"Definitely the makings for a feast!"

"But it can wait, can't it?" Jondalar said. "I think I'd rather see a hot bath right now." His blue eyes filled with his thoughts of her and aroused her response.

"A wonderful idea," she said, emptying her tunic beside the firepit, then walking into his arms.

They sat side by side, a little back from the fire, feeling replete, satisfied, and entirely relaxed, watching sparks dance an arabesque and disappear into the night. Wolf was dozing nearby. Suddenly he raised his head and cocked his ears toward the dark plateau. They heard a loud, full-throated neigh, but it was not familiar. Then the mare squealed, and Racer whinnied.

"There's a strange horse in the field," Ayla said, jumping up. It was a moonless night and hard to see.

"You'll never find your way out there tonight. Let me try to find something to make a torch."

Whinney squealed again, the strange horse neighed, and they heard hoofbeats racing off into the night.

"That does it," Jondalar said. "It's too late tonight. I think she's gone. A horse has captured her again."

"This time, I think she left because she wanted to. I thought she seemed nervous; I should have paid closer attention," Ayla said. "It's her season, Jondalar. I'm sure that was a stallion, and I think Racer went with them. He's too young yet, but I'm sure other mares are in season, too, and he would be drawn to them."

"It's too dark to look for them now, but I do know this region. We can track them in the morning."

"The last time, I took her out, and the brown stallion came for her. She came back to me on her own, and later, she had Racer. I think she's out starting a baby again," Ayla said, sitting down by the fire. She looked at Jondalar and grinned. "It seems right, both of us pregnant at the same time."

It took a moment for her statement to register. "Both of you . . . pregnant . . . at the same time? Ayla! Are you saying you are pregnant? Are you going to have a baby?"

"Yes," she said, nodding. "I am going to have your baby, Jondalar."

"My baby? You're going to have my baby? Ayla! Ayla."

He picked her up, spun her around, and then kissed her. "Are you sure? I mean, are you sure you are going to have a baby? The spirit could have come from one of the men at Dalanar's Cave, or even the Losadunai. . . . That's all right, if that's what the Mother wants."

"I passed my moon time without bleeding, and I feel pregnant. I've even been getting a little sick in the morning. Not bad, though. I think we started it when we got down off the glacier," Ayla said. "And it is your baby, Jondalar, I'm sure of it. It can't be anyone else's. Started with your essence. The essence of your manhood."

"My baby?" he said, a look of soft wonder in his eyes. He put his hand on her stomach. "You have my baby in there? I've wanted that so much," he said, looking away and blinking his eyes. "Do you know, I even asked the Mother for it."

"Didn't you tell me the Mother always gives you what you ask for, Jondalar?" She smiled with his happiness, and her own. "Tell me, did you ask for a boy or a girl?"

"Just a baby, Ayla. It doesn't matter which."

"Then you won't mind if I hope for a girl this time?"

He shook his head. "Just your baby, and maybe, mine."

"The trouble with tracking horses on foot is that they can travel so much faster than we can," Ayla said.

"But I think I know where they might be going," Jondalar said, "and I know a shorter way, up over the top of that ridge."

"What if they aren't where you think?"

"Then we'll have to come back and pick up their trail again, but their tracks are heading in the right direction," he said. "Don't worry, Ayla. We'll find them."

"We have to, Jondalar. We've been through too much. I can't let her go back to a herd now."

Jondalar led the way to a sheltered field where he had often seen horses before. They found many horses there. It did not take Ayla long to identify her friend. They clambered down to the edge of the grassy bottomland, although Jondalar watched Ayla closely, a little worried that she might be doing more than she should. She whistled the familiar call.

Whinney lifted her head and galloped toward the woman, followed by a large pale stallion and a young brown one.

The pale stallion detoured to challenge the young one, who quickly backed away. Although he was excited by the presence of females in heat, he was not ready to challenge the experienced herd stallion for his own dam. Jondalar ran toward Racer, spear-thrower in hand, ready to protect him from the powerful dominant animal, but the young stallion's own actions had protected him. The pale horse veered back toward the receptive mare.

Ayla was standing with her arms around Whinney's neck when the stallion arrived, reared, and displayed his full potential. Whinney backed away from the woman and answered. Jondalar approached, leading Racer with a sturdy rope attached to his halter, looking worried.

"You can try putting her halter on her," Jondalar said.

"No. We'll have to camp here tonight. She's not ready to come yet. They are making a baby, and Whinney wants one. I want to let her," Ayla said.

Jondalar shrugged his acquiescence. "Why not? There's no hurry. We can camp here for a while." He watched Racer strain toward the herd. "He wants to join the others, too. Do you think it would be safe to let him go?"

"I don't think they'll go anyplace. This is a big field, and if they do go away, we can climb up and see where they're heading. It might be good for him to be with other horses for a while. Maybe he can learn from them," Ayla said.

"I think you're right," he said, slipping off the halter, and watching Racer gallop down the field. "I wonder if Racer will ever be a herd stallion? And share Pleasures with all of the females." And, maybe, start young horses growing inside them, he thought.

"We might as well find a place to make camp and make ourselves comfortable," Ayla said. "And think about hunting something to eat. There may be willow grouse in those trees by that stream."

"Too bad there are no hot springs here," Jondalar said. "It's amazing how relaxing a hot bath is."

Ayla looked down from a great height at an unending expanse of water. In the opposite direction, the broad grassy plains stretched out as far as she could see. Nearby was a familiar mountain meadow, with a small cave in a rock wall at the edge. Hazelnut brush grew against the wall, hiding the entrance.

She was afraid. It was snowing outside the cave, blocking the entrance, but when she pushed the brush aside and stepped out, it was spring. Flowers were blooming and birds singing. New life was everywhere. The lusty cry of a newborn came from the cave.

She was following someone down the mountain, carrying a baby on her hip with the help of a carrying cloak. He limped and walked with a staff and carried something in a cloak on his back that bulged out. It was Creb, and he was protecting her newborn. They walked, it seemed forever, but traveled a great distance across mountains and vast plains, until they came to a valley with a grassy sheltered field. Horses went there frequently.

Creb stopped, took off his bulging cloak and laid it on the ground. She thought she saw the white of bone inside, but a young brown horse stepped away from the cloak, and ran to a dun yellow mare. She whistled to the horse, but she galloped away with a pale stallion.

Creb turned and beckoned to her, but she couldn't quite understand his sign. It was an everyday language she didn't know. He made a new signal. "Come, we can be there before dark."

She was in a long tunnel deep in a cave. Ahead a light flickered. It was an opening to the outside. She was walking up a steep path along a wall of creamy white rock, following a man taking long, eager strides. She knew the place, and she hurried to catch up.

"Wait! Wait for me. I'm coming," she called out.

"Ayla! Ayla!" Jondalar was shaking her. "Were you having a bad dream?"

"A strange dream, but not a bad dream," she said. She got up, felt a wave of nausea, and lay back down, hoping it would go away.

Jondalar flapped the leather ground cloth at the pale stallion, and Wolf yipped and harried him, while Ayla slipped a halter over Whinney's head. She had only a small pack. Racer, tied securely to a tree, carried most of the burden.

Ayla leaped to the mare's back and urged her to a gallop, guiding her along the edge of the long field. The stallion chased them, but he slowed as they gained distance from the rest of the mares. Finally he pulled to a halt, reared, and neighed, calling to Whinney. He reared again and raced back toward the herd. Several stallions had already tried to take advantage of his absence. He closed in and reared again, screaming a challenge.

Ayla on Whinney kept going, but she slowed down from the fast gallop. When she heard hoofbeats behind, she stopped and waited for Jondalar and Racer, with Wolf on their heels.

"If we hurry, we can be there before dark," Jondalar said.

Ayla and Whinney fell in beside them. She had the strange feeling that she had done this before.

They rode at a comfortable pace. "I think we are both going to have babies, now," Ayla said, "our second ones, and we both had sons before. I think that's good. We can share this time together."

"You'll have many people to share your pregnancy with," Jondalar said.

"I'm sure you are right, but it will be nice to share it with Whinney, too, since we both got pregnant on this Journey." They rode in silence for a while. "She's a lot younger than I am, though. I'm old to be having a baby."

"You're not so old, Ayla. I'm the old man."

"I am nineteen years this spring. That's old to have a baby."

"I am much older. I am past twenty and three years, by now. That is old for a man to be settling down to his own hearth for the first time. Do you realize I've been gone five years? I wonder if anyone will even remember me," Jondalar said.

"Of course they will remember you. Dalanar didn't have any trouble, and neither did Joplaya," Ayla said. Everyone will know him, she thought, but no one will know me.

"Look! See that rock over there? Just beyond the turn in the river? That's where I made my first kill!" Jondalar said, urging Racer on a little faster. "It was a big deer. I don't know what I was most afraid of—those big antlers, or missing and going home empty-handed."

Ayla smiled, pleased at his remembrances, but there was nothing for her to remember. She would be a stranger again. They would all stare at her, and they would ask about her strange accent and where she came from.

"We had a Summer Meeting here once," Jondalar said. "There were hearths set up all over this place. It was my first after I became a man. Oh, how I strutted, trying to act so old, but so afraid that no young woman would invite me to her First Rites. I guess I didn't have to worry. I was invited to three, and that scared me even more!"

"There are some people over there, watching us, Jondalar," Ayla said.

"That's the Fourteenth Cave!" he said, and waved. No one waved back. Instead they disappeared under a deep overhang.

"It must be the horses," Ayla said.

He frowned, then shook his head. "They'll get used to them."

I hope so, Ayla thought, and me, too. The only thing familiar around here will be Jondalar.

"Ayla! There it is!" Jondalar said. "The Ninth Cave of the Zelandonii."

She looked in the direction he was pointing, and she felt herself blanch.

"It's always easy to find because of that outcrop on top. See, where it looks like a stone is ready to fall? It won't though, unless the whole thing does." Jondalar turned to look at her. "Ayla, are you ill? You're so pale."

She stopped. "I've seen that place before, Jondalar!"

"How could you? You've never been here before."

Suddenly it all came together. It was the cave in my dreams! The one that came from Creb's memories, she thought. Now I know what he was trying to tell me in my dreams.

"I told you my totem meant you for me and sent you to come and get me. He wanted you to take me home, the place where my Cave Lion spirit will be happy. This is it. I have come home, too, Jondalar. Your home is my home," Ayla said.

He smiled; but before he could answer, they heard a voice shouting his name. "Jondalar! Jondalar!"

They looked up along a path to a cliff overhang, and saw a young woman.

"Mother! Come quick," she said. "Jondalar is back. Jondalar is home!"

And so am I, Ayla thought.

ACKNOWLEDGMENTS

Each of the books in this Earth's Children™ series has posed its own unique challenges, but from the beginning, when the sometime novel/six-book outline was first conceived, the fourth book, the "travel book," has been both the most difficult and the most interesting to research and write. *The Plains of Passage* required some additional travel for the author as well, including a return visit to Czechoslovakia, and trips to Hungary, Austria, and Germany to follow a portion of the Danube (the Great Mother River). But to put the setting into the Ice Age, even more time was needed for library research.

I am again indebted to Dr. Jan Jelinek, Director Emeritus, Anthropos Institute, Brno, Czechoslovakia, for his unfailing kindness, assistance, and astute observations and interpretations of the rich Upper Paleolithic artifacts of the region.

I am also grateful to Dr. Bohuslav Klima, Archeologicky Ustav CSAV, for the wonderful wine tasting in his own cellar from his vineyards near Dolni Věstonice, but more for giving so generously of his lifetime of knowledge and information about that most important early site.

I would also like to thank Dr. Jiri Svoboda, Archeologicky Ustav CSAV, for information on his startling new discoveries that add greatly to our knowledge about our Early Modern Human ancestors who lived more than two hundred fifty centuries ago when ice covered a quarter of the globe.

To Dr. Olga Soffer, the leading American expert on the Upper Paleolithic people of Central and Eastern Europe, I extend thanks and gratitude beyond measure for keeping me informed about the most recent developments, and supplied with the latest papers, including the results of a new study on the earliest ceramic art in human history.

I want to thank Dr. Milford Wolpoff, University of Michigan, for his insights during our discussion about population distributions on the northern continents during the last Ice Age, when our modern human forebears clustered in concentrations in certain favorable areas and left most of the land, though rich in animal life, without people.

Finding the pieces of the puzzle that were necessary to create this fictional world of the prehistoric past was a challenge; putting them together was another. After studying the material available about glaciers and the environment that surrounded them, I still could not get a completely clear picture of all the northern lands, so that I could move my characters through their world. There were questions, theories at odds with each other—some of which did not seem very well thought out—pieces that did not fit.

Finally, with great relief and growing enthusiasm, I found the one clearly explained and thoughtfully constructed study that brought the Ice Age world into sharp focus. It answered the questions that had risen in my mind, and enabled me to fit in the rest of the pieces from other sources and my own speculations so that I could make a logical setting. I will be eternally grateful to R. Dale Guthrie for his article "Mammals of the Mammoth Steppe as Paleoenvironmental Indicators," pages 307–326, from *Paleoecology of Beringia* (Ed. by David M. Hopkins, John V. Matthews, Jr., Charles E. Schweger, and Steven B. Young, Academic Press, 1982). More than any other single work, that paper helped this book come together as a cohesive, comprehensive, and comprehensible whole.

Since woolly mammoths symbolize the Ice Age, considerable effort was devoted to bringing those prehistoric pachyderms to life. My research included searching out everything I could find on mammoths and, since they were so closely related, modern elephants. Among these sources, *Elephant Memories: Thirteen Years in the Life of an Elephant Family* by Dr. Cynthia Moss (William Morrow & Co., Inc., 1988), stands out as a definitive work. I am indebted to Dr. Moss for her many years of study and her intelligent and highly readable book.

In addition to research, a writer is concerned about the way her words come together and the quality of the finished work. I am forever grateful to Laurie Stark, Executive Managing Editor of the Crown Publishing Group, who makes sure the finished manuscript becomes the printed pages of a well-made book. She has been responsible for all four books, and, in a changing world, I appreciate the continuity and consistently high quality she has given them.

I am also thankful for Betty A. Prashker, Editor-in-Chief, Vice President, and more important, outstanding editor, who marshals—or mothers—the manuscript I turn in to its finished form.

My thanks go in full measure to Jean V. Naggar; in the Literary Olympics, a world-class, first-place, gold-medal-winning agent!

And finally to Ray Auel, love and appreciation beyond words.

ABOUT THE AUTHOR

Jean M. Auel lives in Oregon, where she is currently engaged in researching and writing the fifth novel in the Earth's Children™ series.

AN UNFORGETTABLE ODYSSEY
INTO A WORLD OF AWESOME MYSTERY

Jean M. Auel's
EARTH'S CHILDREN™ SERIES

The Clan of the Cave Bear
Through Jean Auel's magnificent storytelling, we are
taken back to the dawn of mankind and swept up in
the wonderful world of a very special heroine, Ayla.
In her blood flows the future of humanity.

❑ 25042-6 $6.99

The Valley of Horses
Cruelly cast out by the clan, Ayla finds a hidden
valley where she learns the secrets of fire and raw
survival. Fate brings her Jondalar, a handsome
stranger, who carries Ayla to an awakening of desire
that would shape the future of mankind.

❑ 25053-1 $6.99

The Mammoth Hunters
Ayla's epic journey takes her to the hearth of the
Mamutoi. Soon comes the great spring mammoth
hunt, when Ayla must choose her mate and her
destiny--to remain in the hearth with Ranec, the ivory
carver she is drawn to, or to follow Jondalar into a
far-off place and an unknown future.

❑ 28094-5 $6.99

Available at your local bookstore or use this page to order.

DON'T MISS
THESE CURRENT
Bantam Bestsellers